TORTURED SOULS

AVONLEYA SERIES
BOOK ONE

MELISSA K. ROEHRICH

Also by Melissa K. Roehrich

LADY OF DARKNESS SERIES (COMPLETE)

Lady of Darkness

Lady of Shadows

Lady of Ashes

Lady of Embers

The Reaper (A Lady of Darkness Novella)

Lady of Starfire

Unrelenting Winds (A Lady of Darkness Novella)

Treasures of Darkness (A Lady of Darkness Compilation)

THE LEGACY SERIES (COMPLETE)

Rain of Shadows and Endings

Storm of Secrets and Sorrow

Tempest of Wrath and Vengeance

Dawn of Chaos and Fury

THE AVONLEYA SERIES

Tortured Souls

Book 2- Coming Soon!

Tortured Souls- 1st Ed.

Editing Services: Megan Visger; Jasmine McKie, @faye_reads

Cover Design: MerryBookRound Designs

Hard Case Design: Melissa Roehrich

MKR Exclusive Hard Case Design and Edges: Fen Inkwright

2026 Signing Exclusive Design: Marialuna Grassi

Interior Page Designs: Melissa K. Roehrich

Map Design: Virginia Allyn

Subsidiary Rights and Representation by Katie Shea Boutillier: ksboutillier@maassagency.com at Donald Maas Literary Agency.

ISBN:

978-1-960923-17-2 *(Standard Hardcover)*

978-1-960923-18-9 *(Standard Paperback)*

A COUPLE THINGS &
CONTENT INFORMATION

-⟩⟩ ☾ ⊙ ☽ ⟨⟨-

Hello, Dearest Lover of Chaos-

If you're new to my worlds, welcome. If you've been a part of the Chaosverse for a while now, welcome home. Before we dive into things, let's answer the most prominent question first: do I need to read any other series before this one?

The answer is forever a resounding no. You can read my series in whatever order you choose. We make our own fate here. While the series within the Chaosverse are interconnected, the series themselves stand on their own. I wrote them that way on purpose. I never wanted someone to find me and then panic thinking they need to read nine other books before they can dive into this one. Each series has its own conclusion to its story and main couples. If you're still not sure, I highly encourage you to check out the "Where to Start" page on my website (www.melissakroehrich.com) to choose the path that's best for you.

If you choose to start here, be aware that there will be some spoilers for the Lady of Darkness series in the same way there is set up for the Avonleya series in Darkness. Those who read Darkness first are simply coming in with different knowledge in the same way

v

you'd be going into Darkness with knowledge they didn't have at the start. Again, we make our fate and choose our own paths.

While the main story and couple itself will have its own wrapped-up conclusion at the end of the Avonleya series, be aware there are a few things that won't be entirely resolved until later books in the Lady of Darkness series. Avonleya is a "prequel" series of sorts, despite it being its own story in and of itself.

Finally, keep in mind that I write dark fantasy romance. While the romance itself in this series isn't as dark as other series I've written, the darkness is there along with darker themes. You can always find up-to-date Content Information (including tropes, tags, and potential triggers) on my website. You can also find the Content Information in the back of this book that is current as of January 2026 when this book was printed. I'm doing my part, and it's up to you to do yours.

Alright! I think we've covered all our bases. Reading order? ✔ Spoiler potential? ✔ Content information? ✔ All that's left is to dive in, so welcome home to the kingdom that loves the night. I'll see you on the other side-

Melissa

-))·☽☾·((-

PLAYLIST

I adore when books come with playlists that follow along with the story. You feel everything more. It immerses you more. It brings everything to life. If you find this to be true for you too, here you go! I spend a good chunk of time meticulously picking a song for each chapter (usually when I'm avoiding writing, haha!) Enjoy!

If you don't have Spotify, the full playlist can also be found on my website: https://www.melissakroehrich.com under Book Extras!

For my fellow neurodivergents afraid to be seen, this one is for you.

AVONLEYA SERIES REFERENCE GUIDE

I know. There's a lot to keep track of in the kingdom that loves the night.
So here's a little reference guide to help you out!
See the next page for a Kingdom Breakdown.

OUR MAIN PLAYERS

Cethin Sutara:
See-thin Soo-tār-uh
King of Avonleya

Kailia:
Kī-lee-uh
Ash Rider

Razik Greybane:
Raz-ic Grā-bān
Dragon Shifter, Cadre Member

OTHERS OF NOTE

Wren: Ren
Fae, Razik's Source

Tybalt Greybane: Tib-ult Grā-bān
Dragon Shifter, Commander of the
Avonleyan Forces

Niara: Nee-ar-uh
Healer, High Witch of Avonleya

Bram: Bram
Cadre Member

Jarek: Jār-ic
Cadre Member

Fallon: Fal-un
Cadre Member

Ariadne: Ar-ee-ahd-nā
Cadre Member

Draven: Drā-vun
Cadre Member

Valric: Val-ric
Cadre Member

Zayan: Zā-in
Hand of the King

Tethys: Teth-is
Former King of Avonleya,
Cethin's father

Selinya: Sel-in-yuh
Former Queen of Avonleya,
Cethin's mother

AVONLEYA SERIES REFERENCE GUIDE

OTHERS OF NOTE

Magdalena: Mag-duh-lān-uh
Head Housekeeper at the Greybane
Estate

Lady Mariel: Lā-dee
Advisory Council Member

Lady Carlin: Lā-dee Cār-lin
Advisory Council Member

Shirina: Shuh-ree-nuh
Spirit Animal

Lord Tovan: Lōrd Tō-vin
Advisory Council Member

Lord Harlin: Lōrd Hār-lin
Advisory Council Member

Lord Corveth Astor:
Lōrd Cōr-vith As-tōr
Advisory Council Member

Altaria: Al-tār-ee-uh
Spirit Animal

PLACES

Aimonway: Am-un-way
Edria Sea: Ed-ree-uh See
Lake Noctus: Lāk Nok-tus
Elshira: El-sheer-uh
Korra Forest: Kōr-uh Fōr-est

Avonleya: Av-un-lā-uh
Lunae Falls: Loon-ā Falls
Shadowfen: Shad-ō-fen
Shira Forest: Sheer-uh Fōr-est
Olwen Mountains: Ōl-win Mownt-ins

CREATURES OF OLD

nagasky: nah-guh-skį
stryx: str-iks

nagasea: nah-guh-see
felidae: fel-ee-dā

AVONLEYA SERIES REFERENCE GUIDE

THE GODS

THE FIRSTS

Achaz (Ā-kaz)
God of light and beginnings

Serafina (Sār-uh-fee-nuh)
Goddess of dreams and stars

Anala (Uh-nall-uh)
Goddess of sun, day, and fire

Arius (Ar-ee-us)
God of death and endings

Falein (Fā-leen)
Goddess of wisdom/cleverness

Celeste (Sel-est)
Goddess of moon and sky

THE LESSERS

Zinta (Zēn-tuh)
Sister Goddess of
magic and sorcery

Sargon (Sar-gon)
God of war and courage

Silas (Sī-lus)
God of earth and land

Saylah (Say-luh)
Goddess of shadows and night

Temural (Tem-oo-rul)
God of the wild and untamed

Taika (Tah-kuh)
Sister Goddess of
magic and sorcery

Anahita (On-uh-hee-tuh)
God of sea, water, and ice

Reselda (Rez-el-duh)
Goddess of healing

Sefarina (Sef-uh-ree-nuh)
Goddess of winds and air

FULL
WANING
AVO
OLWEN MOUNTAINS
GORRA F
EVERFALL
SHIRA FOREST
ELSHIRA
NORTH
SUTARA FAMILY
COUNTRY ESTATE

...evа
Lunae Falls
Razik's Cave
Lake Noctus
Avonleya Castle
Greybane Estate
Aimonway
Edria Sea
Nightmist Mountains
Shadowfen
Harrow's Bay
Half
Waxing

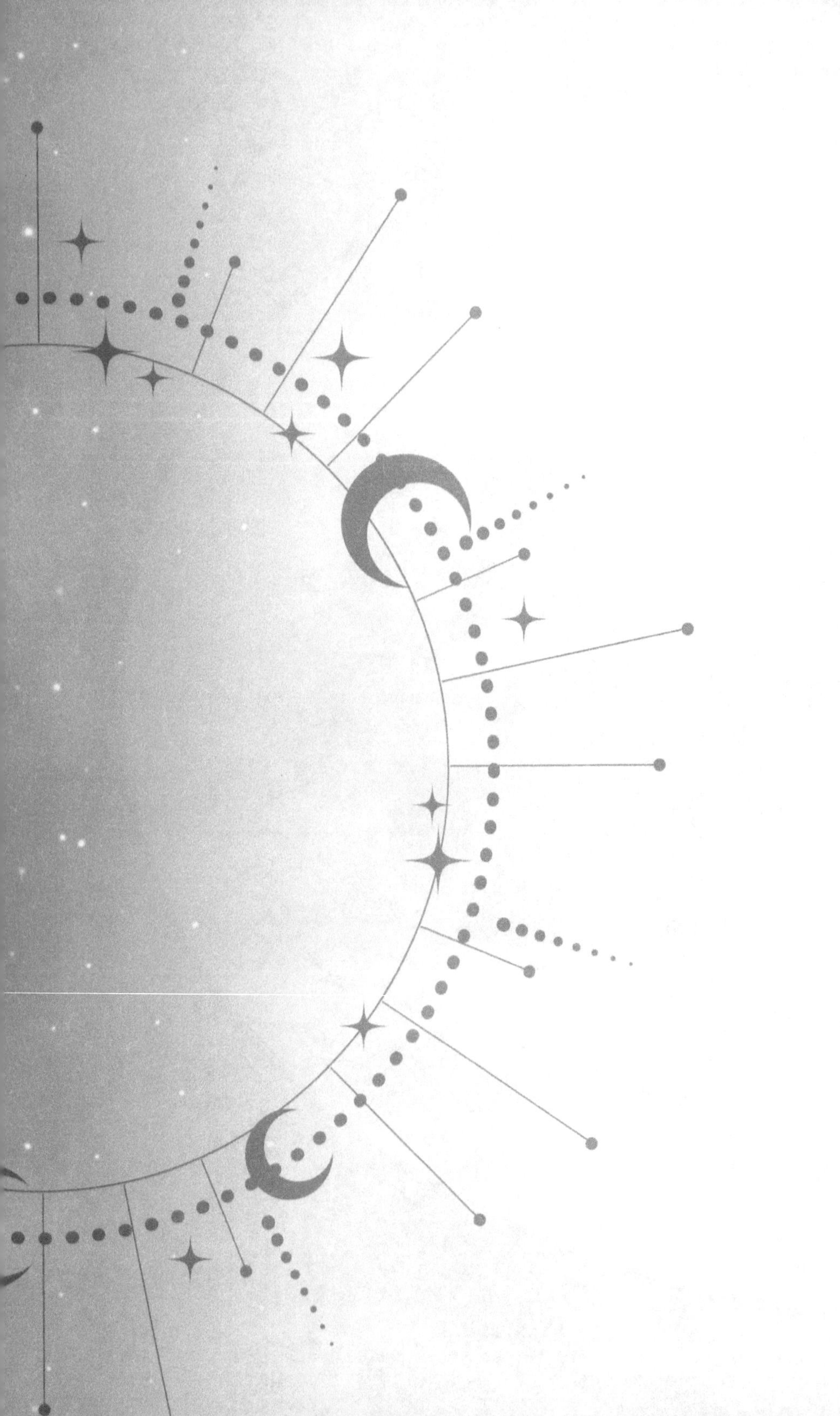

THE NEW KING

The frantic knocking on his door woke him well before the voice carried into the room.

"Prince— I mean, your Majesty," a sentinel spluttered, bursting into his bedchamber.

He arched a brow at the lack of propriety. Or he tried to. Judging by the way the male paled, he must have been scowling at him.

"My apologies, Prin— King Cethin," the male said, stumbling over the words again. Cethin couldn't blame him. He'd been the king for only a handful of weeks. He'd been the prince for centuries.

Swiping a hand down his face, he sighed. "What is it?"

"There's a ship on the horizon!" the male blurted, eyes wide.

Cethin blinked in response before he said, "Are you saying you woke me to tell me a ship is arriving? Ships arrive every godsdamn day, Nevin."

"This ship is coming from the east, Prince. Er— your Majesty," the sentinel replied, fidgeting where he stood. Whether from excitement or nerves, Cethin wasn't sure.

But the words had him flying out of his bed, any lingering drowsiness immediately vanishing.

Within moments, he'd pulled on a tunic and pants, shoved his feet into boots, and Traveled through a rip in the air to the docks of the main port.

Among those waiting on the docks was Razik Greybane, a member of the Avonleya Cadre. The male sneered, only deigning to look at him at all because there were others around. He had to show some sort of acknowledgment to the presence of the king. He was shirtless, his dark wings out and arms crossed over his broad chest. But Cethin was far more focused on the black dragon approaching quickly from the east than he was on the male he'd had a rivalry with since the time they could walk.

The beast dove straight for them, shifting midair so his boots hit the wood of the docks several feet away, the pier shuddering under the force. He closed the distance quickly, offering a small bow when he reached them.

"King Cethin," the male greeted.

"Please don't, Tybalt," Cethin muttered, gaze still fixed on the incoming ship that shouldn't be there. Couldn't be there.

It should be impossible.

There hadn't been ships from across the Edria Sea in over half a millennium.

But as the sun broke over the horizon, a ship sailed closer. It wasn't a large vessel by any means, but it was a ship nonetheless. A ship that had managed to make it past the islands and through the black fog that marked the boundaries of their curse.

"How many passengers does it carry?" Razik asked gruffly.

"Not many from what I can tell. A couple dozen. Maybe a few more below deck," Tybalt answered. Then he paused before adding, "There are a few Fae and some mortals among the passengers. Saylah must have found a way to allow them through."

Cethin kept his features impassive.

The goddess of night and shadows had nothing to do with people entering the Wards, despite having everything to do with being the reason their people were confined behind those Wards to begin with.

No, *he* was the reason that ship was making its way to their docks. After years of failing over and over, it appeared he'd finally been successful. Of course, if anyone knew what he'd been doing these last decades to make this happen, they'd all feel very differently about the new arrivals.

But no one needed to know. It was the king's business.

And as of a month ago, he was the king.

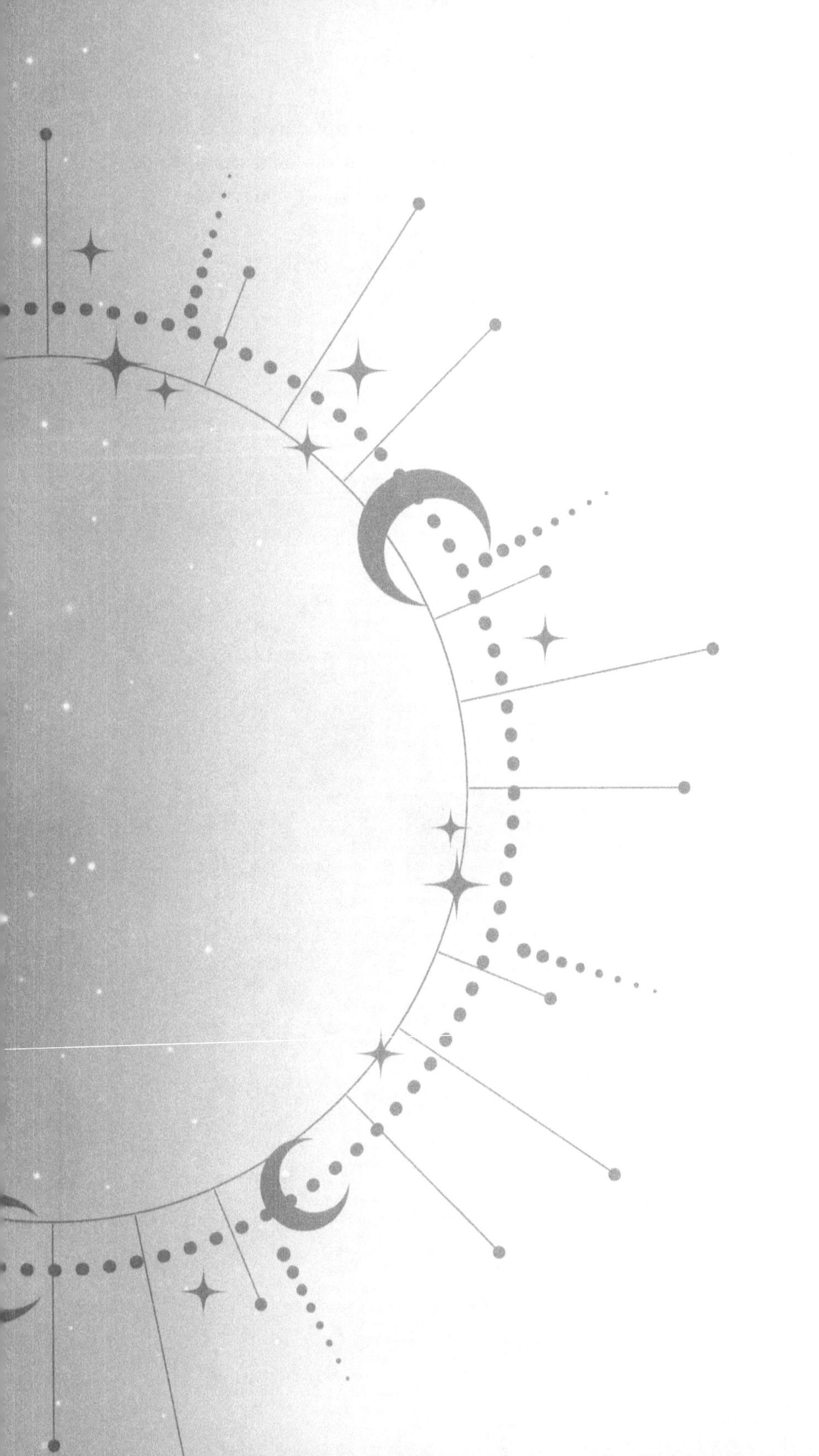

PART ONE
OF QUEENS
AND BARGAINS

RAZIK

THREE SEASONS LATER

A roar pierced the night, and thank fuck for that. He'd used more than half of his magic reserves in a very short amount of time. Dragon fire seemed to be the only thing that worked against these phantoms.

And phantoms they were.

They weren't Avonleyan or Fae. Razik wasn't even sure if he could call them people.

There were around a dozen of them left of the twenty or so that had appeared, and they shimmered in the moonlight. Their bodies were translucent, more phantom than flesh, and they glided rather than walked. Their legs moved, but they hovered a few inches off the ground. Yet none of that was the most disturbing part.

They all looked exactly alike.

Pale skin. Short hair as white as freshly fallen snow. White eyes with no pupils. Sharp, angular features.

Razik Greybane watched as Valric shoved a barbed ice sword into one of them. Or rather, as it went right through the thing and the sword dissipated into nothing. As if the being had snuffed the magic right out.

He supposed *that* was the most disturbing part.

But then Razik was running through the open field, trying to reach the warrior as a gold sword appeared in the being's hand and went through Valric's chest. The thing had pulled it straight out of the air. There had been no swirl of magic. No warning.

"No!" Razik bellowed, his boots slipping on the grass. He could summon his wings to get there faster, but with dragon fire being the only thing that had done any damage to the creatures, he was trying to conserve his power.

As he neared the being, he lifted a palm. Black flames flared, spearing for the thing, and when they collided, a high-pitched keen sounded. Razik fought the urge to slap his hands over his ears, continuing to feed his flames to the creature. The scream felt like it was trying to claw its way into his bones until finally it ceased when the being dissolved into black ashes.

"Valric, get up!" he barked, skidding to a halt beside the male. Razik dropped to a knee, pressing a palm over the wound in an attempt to staunch the bleeding while taking in the battle still raging around them. Thankfully, the beings hadn't infiltrated the forest behind them. If that happened, they were fucked. The trees were too thick to move properly, and with the way the things glided, their forces would be at an even greater disadvantage.

"I feel…" Valric rasped, blinking rapidly as though his vision was going in and out of focus. Those couple words were sluggish and slurred, as if merely speaking was taxing.

"You'll be fine. We'll get you back to Aimonway," Razik said, preparing to Travel. He'd take him to the castle and come right back. He'd only be gone for a few seconds.

Traveling was the way all Avonleyans moved throughout the kingdom. At its core, Traveling was stepping through a rip in the air between time and space from one location to another.

Except he didn't move through a rip in the air. They stayed on that battlefield near the edge of Shira Forest, a thousand miles away from the capital city on the opposite side of the continent. The sounds of fighting continued to ring out. He tried to Travel again, but it was as if he were stuck, unable to step through that rip in the air like he'd done countless times.

"Can't…move," Valric murmured.

"Give me a minute," Razik snapped, trying to figure out what he was going to do while keeping an eye on the being that was drifting closer. Its white eyes were flaring faintly, and if the thing had pupils, he was sure they would be trained on him.

Tybalt roared again, and Razik was trying to figure out why his uncle had Traveled in so far away when the being that was making its way to him suddenly stilled. The figure tipped its head back, inhaling deeply, and then its head slowly turned to the left, as if looking off into the distance.

"Blood of death," the creature hissed, and the voice was unearthly. Raspy and icy, it was a whisper that latched on to his marrow. Razik's dragon lifted its head within his soul, lip curling back and baring its teeth. The voice reminded him of the entrancing abilities the Night Children possessed that enabled them to control the weak-minded.

Trying to figure out what had distracted the being from coming for him, he tried to follow its line of…sight? Could it even be called that?

Pressing down on Valric's wound more, Razik shifted his eyes, the pupils becoming the vertical slits of his dragon. He could see farther distances this way, everything sharp and crisp. It also allowed him to see better in the dark and shadows.

But when he finally saw what the being had locked on to, he was fighting a full shift as rage coursed through him.

What in the ever-loving fuck was Cethin doing here? Why was the godsdamn king on a battlefield with beings that weren't even fucking corporeal?

He already knew the answer to that. Cethin Sutara was an arrogant ass who believed nothing could touch him. Of course he would show up on a battlefield and distract everyone from doing their godsdamn jobs. Egotistical didn't even begin to describe the male.

Razik turned away from the king. Someone else could deal with him while he figured out how to get Valric back to the castle. They'd need Niara, the best healer in the kingdom, for this because—

He looked down at the male. A comrade he'd known for over a century. Valric was one of the most skilled in the Cadre. Or he had been. Because the male's chest was no longer moving. His dark green eyes were glassy, staring vacantly at nothing. Killing an Avonleyan was not an easy task, yet these beings made it appear easier than breathing.

"Razik," Tybalt snarled in the way only a dragon could. He'd shifted at some point, coming to a halt and standing over him. "Go to Cethin. He's your responsibility until we can figure this shitstorm out."

"No," Razik retorted, standing so he was eye-to-eye with the male. "Send Jarek. I'm more useful out here. Dragon fire is the only thing that seems to be—"

"Exactly," Tybalt interrupted. "Dragon fire will keep our *king* safe."

"I'm not his fucking Guardian, Tybalt," Razik snapped.

"At this moment, you are. It's not a request. It's an order from your Commander."

Razik straightened, smoke furling on his exhale. These so-called *orders* had been coming more and more lately. Tybalt knew how he felt about this. Even if his uncle didn't agree, he'd never forced him to do something he didn't want to. But as of late, he was starting to wonder if his uncle was having a change of heart on the matter.

As if knowing what he was thinking, Tybalt ground out, "This has nothing to do with that right now, Razik. This is our king. If something happens to him, I have no idea what will befall Avonleya. The Sutara bloodline has ruled for over a millennium."

"I know that," Razik bit out.

"We can discuss this more later—"

But Razik was already striding away. They didn't have time to sit around and chat like Cethin did in those fucking council meetings every twenty days. He was sure Tybalt would indeed come find him later, they would discuss this, and like every other time, nothing would change.

"You! Stay by Valric! Do not leave his side until this is over," he barked at another warrior. He was young, maybe three decades past his Staying. The Staying was something most magical beings went through in their mid-twenties. It kept them from aging further, and thus they remained perpetually frozen in time physically.

"Understood," the male said, already running.

Razik increased his pace to a jog, then to a sprint as he realized every single being had stilled and was homed in on Cethin now. None of them moved. They just stood there, watching him. Warriors did everything they could. Nothing disturbed them. Not blades or magic. In fact, everyone was slowly falling still, waiting to see what would happen next. Waiting for orders.

He arrived at Cethin's side, not bothering to look at the male. He only turned to face the…phantoms? Spirits?

"What the fuck are you doing here?" he growled, letting black flames slowly wreath his forearms.

"Tybalt told me we were under attack. I came to help," Cethin retorted.

"Help?" Razik said doubtfully. "You came to see the Fae death site, even after all the warnings to stay away for now. Your curiosity is a distraction to everyone here."

"I can help," Cethin snarled, and Razik almost smirked at the irritation.

It was at that point that Tybalt must have attacked because a being let out that gods-awful keening wail that only Razik had been able to evoke. Suddenly, the battle resumed, but this time, all the beings were focused solely on Cethin.

"Do not let them near the king!" he heard Jarek order from somewhere in the melee.

Gods, did their forces try, but without dragon fire, they were useless. Weapons went through the beings as if slicing through air. Magic was snuffed out, and gold blades spilled blood.

"What are they?" Cethin asked, his dark magic pooling around him. It writhed and coiled. Inky pools that called to all the magic around them.

Razik ground his teeth, keeping his own power in check. "We don't know. We've never encountered them before."

"Are they what's killing the Fae?"

"Do you really think now is the time to discuss this?"

Cethin didn't answer, but he went rigid at the reprimand. Three of the beings were nearing, and as if he had something to prove, that dark power struck. With the speed of asps, those coils of pure death and darkness wound around the beings.

And then they disappeared when the beings simply waved them away as if they were brushing off an annoying insect.

Which, fair. He felt the same way about Cethin.

"For the record, that didn't help," Razik said flatly.

"Fuck off, you prick," Cethin retorted, already rallying his magic, apparently to try again.

"You're not helping. You've assuaged your curiosity. Now leave so the rest of us can do our godsdamn jobs and not have to worry about your pampered ass," he shot back.

"I'm as trained as you are," Cethin sneered, pulling daggers from swirls of black. The silver blades glinted until his magic slithered up the weapons. He cocked his arm back and threw one, his aim dead on, but like every other weapon, it went right through the things.

The beings drew closer, four more having joined the three. They were all failing.

"Leave, Cethin!" Razik growled out again, sending his dragon fire to intercept the closest one. Its head tipped back, and it wailed like its soul was being ripped from its body.

"You are not in a position to tell your king what to do," he snarled, pulling up more of that dark power and letting it swell around both of them.

"I can't do my job with you here."

"You're not my fucking Guardian, Razik," Cethin bit out, pulling two more daggers from the inky pools.

"Thank me for that," Razik muttered, because he wasn't about to thank the Fates. If the Fates or Sargon—or most of the gods for that matter—had their way, things would be very different.

Cethin threw his daggers again, and again they did absolutely nothing, useless, much like him.

"Still not helpful," Razik said, pointedly sending more dragon fire at another being as it drifted closer, brandishing twin golden short swords.

"And what's the plan when your power wells run dry? I don't see Wren nearby," Cethin said, gripping a sword now. He stood ready for a fight, as if he hadn't been watching how utterly ineffective weapons were against them.

"Wren is none of your concern," he spat, finally able to pull his flames back as the being disintegrated into ashes.

But Cethin wasn't wrong. It took *a lot* of power to kill these creatures, and the jackass would know exactly how much his power was waning. Tybalt was handling some of the beings, but there were still three to take out. No one else could do anything, and the ones that were left were drifting dangerously closer. Close enough that when Razik sent another up in black flames, the wind blew the ashes back at them. It coated their clothing and skin, drifting through their hair.

"Enough with the righteous act. You need to fucking go," he ordered Cethin again, dragging up the last of his reserves. If Cethin was killed on his watch… He wouldn't really care, but the rest of the kingdom would. They all loved him. He was fairly certain it was more that the kingdom had adored King Tethys than it was actual loyalty to Cethin. At least it was for him.

"I can't leave," Cethin gritted out.

"What do you mean, you can't leave?"

"I can't Travel. It's not— Clearly my power isn't working right. You should Travel both of us away. You're tapped out of power the way it is. You have enough to take out maybe one more, if that."

Gods, Razik hated Cethin knew that. Hated that the male knew anything about him.

The fact that neither of them could Travel was an issue. It appeared *no one* could Travel for some reason. That must be why

Tybalt had Traveled in so far away. Cethin had also Traveled in a good distance from the beings when he'd first arrived. The only explanation was the beings themselves. Razik had never heard of any creatures that could prevent one from Traveling. He'd read thousands and thousands of books and never come across them. Various stones, Marks, and curses that could keep a person from stepping through the air, yes. But beings? Nothing in all his tomes and books, scrolls and research.

It appeared the only way anyone was leaving was if they killed the last two beings, and Cethin was right. He could maybe take down one, and that was a big hypothetical. He hadn't heard the deathly wail in a few minutes, which led him to believe Tybalt's power was also lagging or completely depleted.

As if he'd heard his thoughts, Tybalt was racing across the field, the rest of the Cadre with him, attempting to clear a path among all the bodies, both breathing and fallen. If anything, they distracted the beings long enough for Razik and his uncle to pull up the last of their magic from the depths of their souls.

"Now!" his uncle bellowed, and Razik released the last of his flames. They merged with Tybalt's, engulfing one of the things. Its wail filled the air, and Razik gritted his teeth. If this didn't work, they were fucked. The dragon in his soul thrashed as the final remnants of his power were expended. He wouldn't be able to shift or summon his wings. Not having access to his magic would slowly drive him mad. He needed to get back to Aimonway. He needed Wren.

He'd trained himself to fight with low reserves. Numerous times he'd let his power levels fall until they were nearly nonexistent, learning to fight without magic and to push on through the agony. It didn't mean he fucking *liked* it. It didn't mean there wasn't a buzzing in his ears, and it didn't mean there wasn't an emptiness and desperation at not being able to feel the other part of him that was always there.

Finally, the creature disintegrated into ashes. Flecks of black floated in the breeze and drifted to the ground, mixing with all the spilled blood.

Avonleyan blood.

His kingdom.

His fellow warriors.

People he'd known for decades.

His vision was a little blurred at the edges, and his heart was beating far too fast. Even his godsdamn legs were shaking like a newborn foal. He was about to be as useless as Cethin.

"No!"

Fallon's cry had him jerking upright. He hadn't even realized he was bent over, hands braced on his knees. He spun, following where everyone was racing. Where Cethin was engaged with a being, his silver blade stark against a gold one as strikes were parried and countered. As the being brushed aside darkness and death with a swipe of its hand, gliding and circling and biding its time. No one would make it to them, but Razik was running with the rest of the warriors, unsure of when or how Cethin had moved from his side.

They were all shouting. Some were panicked cries; others were defiant bellows. Razik didn't make a sound. He was too focused, too concentrated on not falling to the ground in exhaustion.

Cethin lifted his sword, blocking another strike. The sound of metal on metal mixed with battle cries. Then the being feinted so quickly, even Razik missed the move. The being's hand shot out, and the translucent creature somehow gripped Cethin's forearm, twisting sharply and forcing him to drop his weapon. None of it seemed possible. How could a transparent being grip something corporeal? It didn't make any sense.

The one thing that became clear was that none of them were going to be able to stop the death of the king.

"Blood of death," the creature hissed again, and Razik could swear its mouth tipped into a smile.

A swirl of smoke and ashes appeared in the midst of everything, and before Razik could comprehend what he was seeing, two arrows were flying through the air. Whoever had shot them was gone in the next blink. Cethin's back was to the newcomer, but he somehow knew to move, lurching to the side the moment before an arrow would have embedded in his back. His hand snapped up, catching the second arrow, while the first one struck the being.

And stuck.

The shaft protruded from the being's chest. He released Cethin, stumbling back. Its perfect features were twisted into rage as his eyes flared brightly.

"Your kind is not supposed to be here," he hissed, yanking the arrow free. It drifted away, becoming the same wispy light that he was. Except for the arrowhead. That fell to the ground, and the being scrambled away from it.

It tipped its head back, releasing a final wail of rage as white wisps poured out of its mouth before the entire being faded into the darkness, leaving black ashes and what appeared to be faint embers behind.

Cethin still held the other arrow, spinning and searching for the one who'd nearly injured him but also saved him.

There was another swirl of smoke, and a female stood among the destruction. Her bow still held in one hand, she stooped and swiped up the arrowhead. Razik had seconds to take her in. Hair as black as night. She was on the shorter side, and her black dress had deep slits up both sides that reached to her hips and revealed the brown skin of her thighs.

Another swirl of smoke and ashes, and she was gone.

Razik stalked forward. Or he tried to. It was probably more akin to a limp, but he didn't want to think about that. The others followed, Cethin and Tybalt stopping on either side of him, all of them staring at the same thing.

A single pair of ashy footprints.

The female had been barefoot.

"An Ash Rider?" Cethin asked, twirling the other arrow between his fingers.

Razik didn't have it in him to answer. Or to care, for that matter.

"Jarek?" he rasped out.

He heard the Cadre member move before he felt him behind him. "What do you need, Razik?"

"Take me to Wren. And someone grab Valric's body."

A hand landed on his shoulder. His duty was done. Cethin was out of harm's way, and one of the others would see that he made it back to the castle. He thanked the Fates when he felt the familiar tug at his navel before he was pulled through a rip in the air. Jarek landed them outside his quarters, and Razik pushed the door to his rooms open.

Then he was thanking whatever god was responsible for Wren being there and not in a hundred other places she could have been.

Her navy blue eyes went wide, and she lurched to her feet. Tea spilled all over the floor as she rushed to him.

"By the gods, Razik. What happened?" she cried.

Razik didn't answer. He grabbed her arm and forced himself to pull a dagger from where it was sheathed at his hip, rather than simply sink his canine teeth into her flesh. When his reserves were completely empty, knowing he could simply take her blood and have instant relief was so godsdamn tempting…

"I've got it," Wren said gently, taking the dagger from his hand. Her movements were slow, as if trying not to startle or provoke him.

He hadn't realized he'd stilled. The struggle must have been evident in his features. Wren had been his Source for years now. They knew one another's tells.

She slid the blade across the back of her right hand, directly over the black Source Mark. Then she turned his hand over, gliding the blade through the flesh of his palm. The scent of her blood hit him a second later, and he lost any control. He grabbed her hand while shoving her back and back and back until she was against the wall. His next inhale was stuttered as he reached for her power, yanking and taking. He heard her gasp, but he couldn't register it. All he could comprehend was that she could give him back his power, his dragon, all that he was, and he was going to take it.

"You'll be okay, Razik," she murmured, the words sounding pained as he pulled more and more magic from her.

Of course he'd be okay. He was always okay. He'd learned long ago how to be *okay*.

Several minutes passed before the power-depletion craze started to lift. It was then he realized he was holding Wren up where she'd sagged against him.

"Godsdammit," he muttered, scooping her into his arms.

Because that was where the power lay. It was in her blood, and it was how Avonleyans originally restored their powers. They drank blood from the Fae. The problem was Avonleyans became greedy fools. They abused the gift from the gods, forcing Fae to be their sources of power rather than the give-and-take that it was meant to be. It had upset a balance, and Arius, the god of endings and death, had cursed them for it. If an Avonleyan took too much, became addicted and abused the Fae, they became enslaved to the bloodlust themselves. Their power was taken from them, and they became a Night Child. The mortals referred to them as vampyres.

Instead, an Avonleyan could take a Source, forming an unbreakable bond between them and a Fae. Only death could sever the bond, and it restored what was always meant to be. The Fae gave their own power to restore the Avonleyan's, and in return, they were offered protection.

Razik forced himself to pull his hand from Wren's, breaking their connection. His reserves weren't even half full, but he'd taken nearly everything she had already. He was one of the most powerful Avonleyans in the realm, and while Wren wasn't weak by any means, there were far more powerful Fae out there. Normally, an Avonleyan and a Fae would be a match of some kind in terms of power, but seeing as there weren't many Fae left in Avonleya, they'd had little choice.

But he'd taken enough to be able to Travel. His dragon was once more stirring in his soul, waking back up from its forced slumber. He would never stay in the castle when he was so vulnerable. It wasn't even a question.

So he stepped through the air to the one place that felt like home. The one place that was his and his alone. A place only two other people knew about. The only place he ever felt safe.

Wren had passed out the moment he'd lifted her off her feet, exhausted from giving him everything she had. He lowered her to the bed, a mess of blankets and pillows atop a plush mattress on the floor. Pulling his tunic over his head, he toed off his boots before removing his pants as well. He burned it all, and then burned the ashes, not wanting to remember a single moment of today's events.

When he was done, he pulled on a pair of loose linen pants and crawled onto the bed beside Wren. She slept, and he propped a hand behind his head. He may not want to remember today, but he did want to know what they'd fought against. There had to be a book with the information somewhere. He'd find it.

Tomorrow.

He'd find it tomorrow.

CHAPTER 2

CETHIN

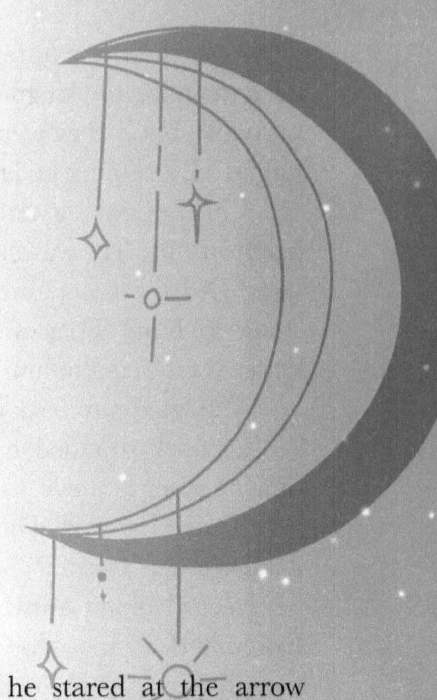

Finger steepled along his temple, he stared at the arrow sitting on the low table before him.

It'd been two days since the attack with the translucent beings. Two days of recovering and trying to figure out what they were. Two days of attending Farewells for the fallen who had given their lives protecting their kingdom and their sovereign.

They'd held the final Farewell when the moon was at its highest tonight, burning Valric's body. The Fae released the ashes of the deceased back to whichever one of the four elements they could wield. Avonleyans scattered the ashes beneath the stars so the body could rest eternally in the night while the soul went to the After.

All the deaths haunted him. People who were his responsibility, now dead because he couldn't figure out what was harming his kingdom. But Valric…

He'd known the male for over a century. Cethin had sat at a table with him, drinking and feasting, more times than he could count. It was rare for a Cadre member to meet death so early, and while they were immortal in terms of aging and lifespan, it was a reminder that death still claimed whatever he wanted, whenever he wanted.

Were those creatures responsible for the Fae deaths that had been plaguing the kingdom for generations now? It certainly seemed probable, but if they were, this went deeper. Why the sudden shift in targets? Everything he knew thus far pointed to all this being a plan years in the making. And when he'd shown up? All attention had been on him. He was clearly the target. Had that always been the case? Did those creatures somehow think the Fae were a stepping stone to him? That was preposterous. There were hundreds of better ways to get to him than through the Fae.

Which led him back to the belief that this was all calculated.

A knock sounded on the main door to the floor, but Cethin didn't bother to move.

"Your Majesty?" Then, when he didn't respond, Tybalt said in a gentler tone, "Cethin?"

He still didn't answer, and after another minute, he heard the Commander's footsteps as he left, letting him be. Only then did Cethin stand, grabbing the bottle of wine that sat next to the arrow. He emptied it into his chalice before moving to a balcony. There were several of them on his floor, allowing him to see in any direction, but this one faced the Nightmist Mountains. His mind was back on the outskirts of Shira Forest. He could see Valric slumping to the ground. See warriors bleeding from wounds given by golden swords. Magic and weapons powerless against a threat they hadn't even known existed.

Even his own darkness had been useless. Something he'd never experienced before. His darkness had always been unpredictable. Uncontrollable. Chaotic. He'd worked his entire life to master that dark power, and yet it was a struggle. Just when he'd think he had finally gained the upper hand, his magic would prove otherwise. It was why others were leery when it appeared and were grateful for it amidst threats.

Until two days ago.

When he'd been useless and one of the only things that had succeeded in killing the beings was dragon fire from Tybalt and Razik.

Of course it had been Razik Greybane that could end the creatures while he'd stood helplessly by. He hadn't seen the male since that night. Cethin assumed he was holed up in his study at Tybalt's Estate.

Tybalt had remodeled an entire floor for Razik, and while Cethin had been to the Greybane Manor more times than he could count, he'd only been in that particular space once. Razik had glowered the entire time, eyes narrowed and never leaving Cethin as if he'd expected him to steal something, but the study was nothing but bookshelves filled to the brim. There were a few small sitting areas near hearths with overstuffed leather furniture, and a desk that had been organized and tidy. It was accessible by a main set of doors that were always locked, but also via a winding staircase in Razik's bedchamber. That was where he was certain the male was. Probably researching in one of his precious books while slowly refilling his power from Wren. He'd been completely drained after that battle. It would take a few days at minimum to fully replenish his reserves. He'd take from Wren, wait for her power to refill, then do it all over again.

Except dragon fire wasn't the only thing that had killed the creatures.

The thought had him wandering back inside and picking up the arrow as he drank his wine. He twirled the shaft between his fingers. It was as inky black as his magic with small glyphs on the shaft. And the arrowhead? That was a material he'd never come across.

He'd also never seen the female who'd shot the damn thing and nearly struck him either. Sure, she'd saved him in the process, but it wouldn't have mattered if she'd killed the creature if he'd also died in the process. Then again, a simple arrow likely wouldn't kill him. Even shirastone and ashwood arrows didn't kill Avonleyans like they did the Fae.

He'd scarcely caught a glimpse of her. Her hair, dark as the night sky. Her warm brown skin. Those amber eyes that had swirled with smoke as she glared at him before disappearing among ashes. The only plausible conclusion was that she was an Ash Rider.

It'd been quite some time since an Ash Rider had been known in Avonleya. Believed to be descendants of Anala, the goddess of the sun and fire, Ash Riders didn't have the typical fire magic that most Fire Fae and Anala descendants possessed. Ash Riders, instead, could move through smoke and ashes. Not only that, they could hide in them, observing everything unnoticed. They were invaluable to kingdoms and often served as spies with their obvious stealth abilities. He'd only met two other Ash Riders in his life, and they'd both disappeared centuries ago. His father had told him stories of a few others from when he was a child, but they'd long since disappeared too.

Which made it all the more interesting that one had suddenly emerged. Had she been in hiding? For how long? And why? More than that, what did she know about the creatures she could so easily slaughter?

He needed more wine for this.

With a sigh, he left his rooms, not wanting to disturb anyone at this hour to bring him another bottle. Or rather, he didn't really want to speak with anyone right now. He didn't have it in him at the moment to fake pleasantries. Solitude was a luxury he was rarely afforded these days.

He was halfway to the wine cellars when he realized he still had the arrow in his hand. Distracted with thoughts of the mystery female, he'd forgotten he was holding the thing. Maybe one of the weapons-makers in the castle armory would know what it was.

Reaching for the door that would lead down to the wine cellars, he stilled at what sounded like a...scream? Was somebody screaming?

It sounded again, and that was definitely someone screaming.

Cethin took off, sprinting down the hall toward the terrified sound. Skidding around a corner, he saw the female pressed against the wall. Her hand was covering her mouth, eyes wide as she stared at the floor. A member of the castle staff, the basket of linens she'd been carrying was spilled at her feet. The white fabrics among the blacks and greys were slowly turning pink.

A body lay there, blood pooling beneath another female. A female he knew.

Lady Nessira. A member of his advisory council who was in town for the meeting that was set to begin tomorrow.

And hovering between him and the body was one of the phantom creatures from the battle two days ago.

It looked identical to the others. Pale, translucent skin. Sharp features. White, pupil-less eyes.

Eyes that were somehow pinned on him. The thing tipped its head back, and with nostrils flaring, it inhaled deeply. Those haunting eyes flashed brighter, and it hissed, "Blood of death."

The female staff member had fallen to her knees in terror, hands clutched at her chest as she whispered prayers to the gods.

"What are you?" Cethin demanded, taking a single step forward and stilling. His darkness writhed around him, but only to offer a source of comfort to the female. She didn't know it wouldn't work against the thing.

"I hunt those that defy him," the creature crooned, gliding closer with two steps of its own.

That was good. It moved him farther from the female, and Cethin was clearly who it was after anyway.

"Who is 'him?'"

The being smiled, and it was haunting, eliciting a chill he felt to the depths of his soul.

"Who do you work for?" Cethin demanded again, taking the next step in this dance they were performing.

"You shall see when you meet him, blood of the traitorous ones," the creature said with a sneer. "Their betrayal is the sin of all their blood."

Then the thing lunged, and Cethin scarcely had time to process the attack. He lurched to the side as the being glided past him. He spun to face it once more, and the being's cold, dark smile grew. But now it was Cethin who stood between him and the female.

Finally recalling her name, he didn't dare look back at her as he said, "Paesha, go find Commander Greybane or Razik." When a few seconds passed and he didn't hear her footfalls, he said sternly, "Paesha, now!"

He heard her scramble up then, her feet pounding as she ran in the other direction.

"How did you get here?" Cethin asked the being, hovering no more than ten feet away.

"I go where I am summoned. Where the traitors dwell," the creature answered.

"Do you always speak with such dramatics?" he drawled, gaze roving over the thing, trying to find any sort of weaknesses, but there were none. It was so still, not even the air rippled around it. He couldn't track his eyes because of the lack of pupils. There was no gait or movement to give away a vulnerability.

There was no warning of its attack.

In a flash, the thing flew towards him. It had clearly been studying him too. Because this time when he tried to dodge to the side, its incorporeal hand shot out, gripping his throat. Stronger than he should have been, the being slammed him against the wall. His head snapped back, spots appearing at the edges of his vision.

With a flourish, the being pulled a dagger from the air. The hilt and blade were as gold as the swords had been two nights ago, but before the creature could bring it to Cethin's flesh, he thrust his hand forward.

The arrow he still held went deep into the being's side, and the creature stumbled back with an outraged hiss, releasing Cethin's throat.

"They aren't supposed to be here," it snarled, the words broken and raspy. Then its head tipped back too far, and its mouth fell open, wisps of light spewing from it. Moments later, it dissipated into ashes and…faint embers?

The arrow clattered to the floor, everything turning to the same wispy light except for the arrowhead.

When Razik had killed the beings, they'd turned to ash, but this had been different somehow. He hadn't realized it before—in the heat of everything—but now that he had a moment to think, the same thing had happened when the female had killed one.

The sound of boots running had him swiping up the arrowhead and shoving it into his pocket as Tybalt rounded the corner with

Razik behind him. The younger Greybane still looked exhausted, with dark circles under his eyes and disheveled hair. He glared at Cethin as if this attack was his fault.

"What happened?" Tybalt demanded. If his features didn't betray how furious he was, the shifted reptilian pupils and glowing sapphire irises did.

"I heard screaming and found them," Cethin answered, making his way back to Lady Nessira's body.

"You ran *to* the screaming?" Razik drawled, crossing his arms over his chest. "How noble of you."

"Razik," Tybalt growled, but then he turned back to Cethin. "But I'm going to have to repeat that question, Cethin. You ran *towards* the screaming?"

"Of course I did," he replied, crouching beside the body. "Where is Paesha? We need to talk to her. Find out what she saw."

When no one answered, he glanced up to find Razik still glaring at him and Tybalt rubbing his brow with his thumb and forefinger. "Cethin, I don't know why I need to keep reminding you that you are the king. You can't—" He stopped himself, sighing deeply.

"If you get yourself killed, the kingdom has no one," Razik said flatly.

"You don't care if I'm killed," Cethin grumbled under his breath, but with their enhanced hearing, of course Razik heard him.

"You're right. I don't. But even I recognize how disastrous that would be. That's why *I* haven't killed you yet. You're the one person who doesn't seem to understand the effects that would have." He paused before adding with a shrug, "Or maybe you simply don't care."

"I swear to all the gods, Greybane—" Cethin started, but Tybalt interrupted.

"Tell us what happened. Then we'll find Paesha and take care of..." He trailed off, gesturing vaguely at Lady Nessira's lifeless body.

"One of those spirit beings was here," Cethin said flatly, gaze now fixed on the pool of red beneath the lady.

The lords and ladies of the advising council didn't usually stay at the castle. They all had their own homes in the territories they governed, Traveling to the castle every twenty days for council meetings. However, with the recent and escalating attacks, an urgent meeting had been called to discuss what to do. But how do you prepare for more attacks when you don't know what you're fighting against?

Clearly any preparation would be meaningless anyway, because how the fuck had that being even gotten inside? There were wards covering a wide radius around the castle. There were a handful of people who could Travel directly into the building or even onto the grounds for that matter. Everyone and everything else had to physically enter through doors, passing numerous sentinels that patrolled the entrances, grounds, and halls.

Several seconds of silence ticked by before Razik said, a trace of doubt in his tone, "And where is the creature now?"

"Dead," Cethin answered, pushing back to his feet.

"How? Only dragon fire can kill them. Your parlor tricks were useless."

Cethin gritted his teeth, those *parlor tricks* churning in his soul, the darkness writhing beneath his skin. With a sneer, he replied, "You wouldn't have been much help anyway. Your reserves aren't even half refilled."

Smoke furled with Razik's next exhale, and Cethin felt his lips twitch at his success in getting under the male's skin.

"Razik's question is important," Tybalt interjected again with another audible sigh. He had bent, retrieving some of the laundry that had been spilled from the basket and using it to cover the body. It was then Cethin realized it was *his* laundry. His own various tunics and pants.

Gently laying a black tunic over Lady Nessira's face and chest, Tybalt continued, "If you've found another way to defeat them, it needs to be shared."

"I didn't really," Cethin answered, slipping his hand into his pocket and fingering the arrowhead. "Not another way, I mean. I had an arrow."

Razik's gaze whipped to him. "One of hers?"

Cethin nodded, his hand wrapping around the arrowhead possessively, feeling it cut into his flesh and causing blood to well. Something inside him twisted at the idea that Razik seemed interested in her. Which was ridiculous. They were all interested in her. Aside from dragon fire, she was the only other person who'd effectively defeated the things. There were only two Sargon descendants in the realm, but how many of *her* were there?

"Where is this arrow?" Tybalt asked, straightening once more.

"Disappeared with the creature," Cethin answered.

Razik was rubbing his jaw. "That happened with the other one too. Other than the arrowhead." He looked around as if expecting to see it on the floor somewhere.

And for a reason he couldn't explain, Cethin said, "There was nothing left behind."

Razik made a grunt of acknowledgment, clearly mulling over something.

"We need to find her," Tybalt said, as they all started down the hall. They'd locate Paesha and send someone to collect Lady Nessira's body. "In the meantime, there is now a vacancy on the advisory council that will need to be filled, and..." Another heavy sigh sounded. "More concrete plans need to be put in place if something should happen to you until you have a partner or heir."

Cethin's lips thinned, but he said nothing.

He wasn't stupid or naïve. He understood that if he were killed somehow, the kingdom would be in distress. They could have all kinds of plans in place. He could make a decree naming someone his heir if he died without one, but the truth was, there would be power grabs. All manner of beings would come out to challenge for the throne. Most of them wouldn't have the best for Avonleya at heart.

They found Paesha, and Cethin listened while Tybalt coaxed information from her. She didn't know why Lady Nessira had been down on that level of the castle. Paesha had heard the lady scream and went to help, only to witness the being slide a gold knife across her throat.

She kept apologizing profusely to Cethin about his laundry, as if that was of any importance. It didn't matter how many times he told her the same, but she was clearly in shock. Niara was summoned to give her an elixir to help her sleep, while a couple of sentinels were sent to retrieve the lady's body. They'd have to hold yet another Farewell tomorrow.

It was hours later, the first rays of dawn already breaking the horizon, when he found himself back in his chambers. He didn't sleep. No, he sat in the same chair, finger once again steepled along his temple, toying with the arrowhead in his other hand.

Tybalt wasn't wrong. They needed to find her.

He flipped the arrowhead again, feeling the edges scrape against his palm and draw blood. The wound would heal as quickly as the others had, nothing but small cuts and scrapes.

They needed to find her.

The morning hours slowly crept by, dawn becoming full daylight. Rays of sunshine streamed into the room, and still he hadn't moved. All he could think about was the way those amber eyes had glared at him.

They needed to find her.

But he'd felt her before. Knowing what she was, it all made sense. He hadn't realized it was a person and not a feeling. Something powerful. Something predatory. Something that had been watching him.

He needed to find her.

The thing was, he wasn't entirely sure what he was going to do with her when he did.

CHAPTER 3
CETHIN

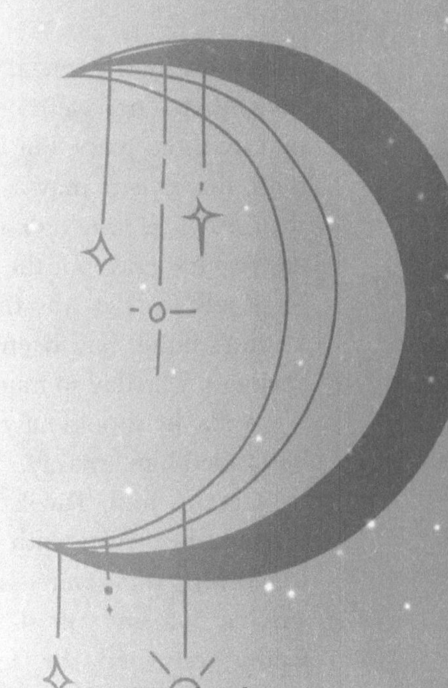

"**M**otherfucker!" Cethin growled under his breath when a black, leathery wing hit the back of his head so hard he spilled a glass of pomegranate juice down the front of his light grey tunic. Now he was going to have to change. He had meetings with his advising council later this morning, and while no one would say anything to their king, it was the principle of the matter. His father was always walking perfection, easily commanding an entire room. One would think the centuries of training to eventually take the throne would have prepared him to be the same. Turned out nothing prepared you for your parents suddenly leaving you to run an entire kingdom.

Razik didn't look at him as he rounded the table, making his way to his usual chair at the other end of the long table. It'd been nearly two weeks since the attacks, and he'd clearly refilled his reserves completely. The fucker never walked around with his wings out, but apparently today was a special occasion, and he was doing just that.

Wren, a Fae female, took the seat beside Razik, avoiding Cethin's eye. She was nice enough, but her closeness to the male kept them from being anything more than formal acquaintances.

Cethin had been at odds with Razik for as long as he could remember. They were nearly the same age, Razik being older than him by three years, but in terms of the centuries they'd been alive, those three years may as well be three hours. They'd gone through their Stayings long ago, both of them appearing as mortals in their late twenties, save for the slightly pointed ears.

Razik's uncle was the Avonleyan Commander of Forces, and Cethin's father had been the Avonleyan King until slightly under a year ago. The day so much had changed.

A day he should have seen coming, but a day that had somehow blindsided him anyway.

Cethin and Razik had been forced together for several reasons, but even with all the encouragement to form a close friendship, they were rivals. Except they weren't competing or striving for any of the same things. Razik loathed him, and Cethin returned the sentiment. This feud between them had always been a part of who they were. Nothing could change centuries of animosity.

He went back to his plate of eggs and sausages, pointedly ignoring Razik at the other end of the table, and when the sound of several pairs of boots sounded down the hall, he held back his sigh of irritation. Those footsteps belonged to members of the Cadre, which Razik was part of. Technically, so was Cethin, but seeing as he was now their king, he wasn't included in much of their antics or debauchery. Not that he had been as their prince either. Nobody wanted to be responsible for getting the prince in trouble, or worse, injured. Nobody wanted to be responsible for the prince, period. Then the whole king thing had happened, and the dynamics had shifted even more.

A group of mostly males entered the dining hall, voices loud and boisterous echoing around them, although a bit more subdued than usual with the loss of Valric. The two females who were part of the Cadre held their own. Cethin had sparred with them on more than one occasion, and on more than one occasion, he'd gotten his ass handed to him.

"Where'd you go last night, broody fucker?" Jarek asked,

yanking out the chair on Razik's other side and taking a seat. "Thought we had a rematch to handle?"

Razik shrugged, not bothering to look up as he loaded eggs onto a piece of toast and took a bite. Truthfully, the male was a prick to everyone; it was just magnified when it came to Cethin.

When Razik continued to stay silent, Jarek turned to the Fae female. "Where'd you sneak off to, Wren?"

She shot him a flat look as she popped a piece of melon into her mouth. Her navy blue eyes narrowed, and her dark brown, nearly black, hair slid over a shoulder as she tipped her head. "Some of us were out working all night, Jarek. The last thing we wanted to do was deal with your drunken asses as the sun rose."

Another male a few chairs down snorted a huff of laughter. "Tell me more about this *work*, Wren. I'm sure it was difficult for both of you— Fucking Fates!" he suddenly cursed, diving for the ground when his chair went up in black flames.

The other members of the Cadre snickered as the male glared at Razik. Getting to his feet, he grumbled, "I didn't mean anything by it."

"You should know better than to insinuate anything about Wren," Fallon quipped, her long blonde hair in a plait that hung over her shoulder. "She's off limits in every way, Bram."

The youngest member of the Cadre grumbled under his breath as he slid into another seat a few chairs down, his light green eyes now fixed on his breakfast with a glare.

"What are the plans for today? The usual training, or do we get to do something different?" Jarek asked, tying back his dark blond hair before digging into his food.

"Glad you asked," came another voice moments before Tybalt entered the room. All the Cadre straightened as their Commander appeared, and no, it didn't escape Cethin that they showed him more respect than they did their king. He didn't really care. They were the closest thing he had to friends, and even at that, he didn't think he could classify them as such. He'd told them long ago they didn't need to bother with decorum when no one else was around. He'd been told countless times by his advising council that should have changed, especially when he was crowned king, but there were too many other changes happening for him to care about that one.

But things had changed anyway.

Cethin held in his sigh as a stack of reports was placed atop the ones he was already going through. His life had become nothing more than endless reports and meetings.

He rubbed his brow with his forefinger, skimming the first page before glancing up to find Tybalt already staring at him. The male's warm brown eyes were hard, his jaw tight.

More Fae had been found dead last night.

The Fae numbers in Avonleya had been dismal for centuries. Until recently, they couldn't figure out what was killing them, and Cethin still wasn't sold on the idea that it had been these phantom creatures the entire time. Either way, the Fae numbers were nearly nonexistent now, which for Avonleyans was disastrous.

Avonleyans were the descendants of the gods. They originally descended from a god or goddess who had a child with a demigod— half god, half mortal. The bit of mortal blood from the demigod weakened their magic, making them less than the gods they descended from. Along the way, those Avonleyans had children with other mortals, but some had children with other magical beings: Fae, Legacy, Shifters, Witches. Most of those living in Avonleya were those descendants. More powerful than an average Legacy, a descendant of a demigod and a mortal, but not as powerful as the gods. Not even as powerful as a deity, a child of a god and another magical being. Centuries later, the terms Avonleyan and Legacy were nearly interchangeable, even if Avonleyans were more powerful.

None of that would have mattered if it weren't for the fact that the gods were fearful of their Legacy, and thus Avonleyans, becoming too powerful. To assuage those fears, they made both dependent on the Fae to refill their power rapidly. A gift it had been called. Cethin had always thought it to be more of a curse.

Their magic reserves could refill over time, but the process was excruciatingly slow. And living with low power reserves was an agony in and of itself. It kept most Avonleyans from even using their magic unless forced to. Without a Fae counterpart, it was their only option. It was forbidden in their kingdom to force a Fae to become their sources of power though. The Fae had to be willing, the choice consensual between the two parties.

Which is why Razik had a Source bond with Wren, while Cethin, the ruler of the kingdom, didn't have a Source at all.

It was also why the dwindling number of Fae was a problem. One he'd thought he'd found a solution to three seasons ago when a ship from across the sea had found its way here. Since then, two more ships had arrived. All of them brought a small number of Fae among the passengers, fleeing a continent where the Fae were feared by mortals, only to find a worse fate here. He'd promised safety, and instead they were meeting death.

"Where were they found? Was it the same beings?" Cethin demanded, the question more of a low growl that had the entire room falling silent.

"Same area. In the southwest part of Shira Forest, on the edge of the trees," Tybalt replied just as tightly. "We have no way of knowing for sure if they were the same beings. Wounds didn't match those of the recent attack, but they were the same as previous attacks over the last years. Something needs to be done, Cethin, especially with another ship being spotted coming from the east."

"Have they crossed the Wards yet?" Cethin asked.

Tybalt shook his head. "It remains to be seen whether they'll make it."

Because not all the ships did, and for the life of him, Cethin couldn't figure out why some were able to cross the Wards and others weren't. Far more failed than made it, likely returning to spread tales of how the rumors were false and that the Wards still stood.

Which they did.

For now.

"Night Children?" Jarek asked, and Cethin clenched his jaw.

Night Children hadn't been an issue in Avonleya his entire life. If they were suddenly going to become a problem, of course Fate would make that happen during his first year as king. But while

Night Children were a possibility, it didn't seem likely. The Fae numbers had been declining for years, long before a few ships had managed to traverse the Wards.

"We'll go investigate the area where the Fae were found," Razik cut in, getting to his feet, the Fae female following suit.

"You won't," Cethin retorted. "Not with Wren."

The female froze under Cethin's stare, and Razik's lip curled back, baring his teeth. "You think I won't keep her safe?" the male demanded.

"I think there are others who can go so we don't need to risk it. Jarek, Fallon, and Bram can go. If anything, *I* should be going with them."

"With all due respect, Cethin, until we figure this out, you shouldn't be anywhere near the scenes of discovery. Especially considering the events of two weeks ago," Tybalt cut in.

"I'm the king. I should be part of uncovering what is harming my people," he argued, hands flat on the wood table. Inky darkness seeped from his palms, and he inhaled sharply, working to keep his power from overtaking him. The same godsdamn magic for centuries, and he still felt like he could scarcely control it at times. He much preferred his other gifts.

"You are the king," Tybalt agreed. "Which means you have responsibilities—"

"To ensure this kingdom is safe for my people," Cethin interrupted.

Tybalt's gaze darted away, eyeing the rest of the room where the Cadre were all eating, looking anywhere but at them and trying to appear otherwise occupied. Except for Razik. He was glaring at both of them, his arms crossed and features telling exactly how irritated he was with all of this.

"Jarek, Fallon, and Bram go search the area where the Fae were found," Tybalt said after a tense moment of silence. "The rest of you can go lead drills with the sentinels."

Everyone else filed out, but Razik stayed put, feet planted where he stood. Jerking his chin, Wren followed the Cadre from the dining room. Razik waited until the heavy doors thudded closed before his arms dropped to his sides, hands curling into fists.

"This is bullshit, and you know it," Razik spat, his sapphire eyes flickering with black flames.

"Razik," Tybalt said sternly, but before he could go on, Cethin interjected.

"It's not bullshit. Whatever this is, it's targeting Fae. You think it a wise idea to willingly bring Wren to the last place of attack? It's your job to protect her—"

"Do not lecture me on my responsibilities, Cethin," Razik snarled, leaning towards him and bracing his hands on the table.

"Someone has to because you sure seem to shirk a lot of them."

"Fuck off," Razik snapped, his pupils shifting to vertical slits and glowing bright blue.

"Both of you, enough!" the Commander cut in. "You both have responsibilities. Things could be different if—"

"Don't you dare say it, Tybalt," Razik snarled.

Tybalt straightened, all his features tightening as he looked at his adopted son. "Then fall in line and go do your job, Razik."

Razik said nothing else, stalking from the room. The doors banged behind him, and Cethin heard him bark something to the other Cadre members before the sound of boots echoed.

Cethin stared at Tybalt. The male who could best be described as an uncle to him. Cethin had known him his entire life. He'd served as the Commander of the Avonleyan Forces for as long as Cethin could remember, and he'd been close to both his parents. Even when the Commander had been trapped on the other side of the Wards for far too long, he'd returned and gone right back to his duties.

"I'll talk to him," Tybalt said. "He shouldn't speak to you like that."

"Don't bother," Cethin muttered, grabbing the stacks of papers and straightening them. Nothing ever changed with the male, and he was fine with that. He had bigger things to worry about, and he avoided speaking with Razik unless necessary.

"You're not as different as you think," Tybalt tried. "If the two of you could just—"

"I have meetings to get to," Cethin interrupted. "Thank you for the reports this morning. Let me know what the Cadre learns upon their return."

"Of course, your Majesty," Tybalt said with a small bow of his head.

The title irked him coming from someone he was so close to, but he understood. At the moment, he was pulling rank. He was the king, and Tybalt was the Commander.

Nothing was as it should be.

But he would fix all of this, even if it killed him in the end.

Just like it'd killed his father.

CHAPTER 4

CETHIN

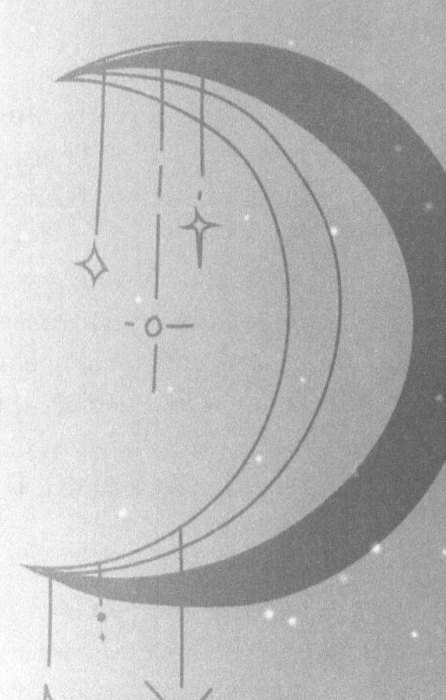

H e drummed his fingers on the marble tabletop as dinner plates were cleared. Staring out the window, he could almost glimpse the sea beyond. The sound of waves rolling to the shore was just out of reach, and he was wishing he could be feeling the ocean spray rather than the slight breeze drifting through the open balcony doors.

He'd been in this room all godsdamn day with the advisory council. Meetings didn't typically take up an entire day, but every twentieth day they did.

Every twenty days he sat in this room at a table of twelve advisors discussing anything and everything. Lunch and dinner were served here, and he'd likely still be sitting here well into the night. The sun was already setting, which wasn't the problem. His kingdom loved the night. They favored the dark and the shadows so much, their days didn't begin at dawn. No, the kingdom came to life mid-morning, well after the sun had risen. That's when the streets started bustling and businesses opened their doors, and they stayed that way long after the sun had set, when the stars and the moon lit their paths home. It was the early morning hours before most people found their beds, the sun rising a few hours later.

"Your grace?"

Cethin turned from the window, finding the eyes of everyone on him. A glass of liquor had been placed before him, along with a piece of dessert. Some kind of spiced cake that he wasn't going to eat.

The male who'd spoken was Zayan, Hand of the King, and he sat to his right. He'd been his father's Hand, and with all the turmoil of a sovereign change, Cethin had kept him in that role. He didn't know who'd replace him anyway, but Zayan had served at his father's side for most of the last century. Before that, he'd served on the advisory council as the lord of a city on the west side of the continent.

"What's next on the agenda?" Cethin asked, swiping up his liquor as they got back to business.

"The matter concerning the Fae," another male said from down the table, looking up from a piece of parchment.

He swiped a hand down his face.

The Fae.

As if he hadn't been thinking about that issue for months. As if they hadn't had this very discussion every twenty days since he'd taken the throne. Fuck, this conversation had been occurring regularly since *before* he took the throne, and nothing was ever resolved. The debate was always the same because everyone came to the same conclusion: until the Wards were gone, there was nothing they could do.

The Wards had been in place for centuries, cutting them off from the rest of the realm. No one could leave, and no one could enter. They had been intended for protection, meant to exist for a short period of time until the danger had passed. Instead, they'd become a curse that the kingdom had paid dearly for. Sure, there'd been a glimmer of hope when a ship had made it past the Wards three seasons ago, but then the deaths had increased too, and they were back at the beginning. Words without actions.

He'd rejected that inaction decades ago, willing to do what others wouldn't. Willing to risk things his parents refused to entertain. Doing what needed to be done to bring their kingdom the freedoms they once knew.

"Is it true there were more discovered this morning?" a female with short, wispy black hair asked.

"It is," Cethin answered, eyeing the empty seat to his left where Tybalt usually sat. He'd excused himself nearly two hours ago and hadn't returned. "Tybalt and I have already discussed it and sent three Cadre members to search the area for any information."

A male scoffed. "We never find anything with their searches."

Cethin slid his gaze to the male, eyes narrowing. "While not entirely factual, what is found often leads to dead ends. I would like to go search some of the more recent sites myself—"

"You can't go out there and play detective," another male interrupted. "You're the king. More than that, you were nearly killed the last time you were on a battlefield."

Cethin arched a brow, his fingers drumming once more on the table. "Am I understanding correctly that you are instructing your king as to what he can and cannot do?"

The male's brown eyes widened slightly, his brows pinching. Hayes was another advisor who'd been on this council as long as Cethin could remember. "No, your grace," he answered slowly. "I am simply stating that as the sovereign of the kingdom, it would be unwise for you to put yourself in harm's way. Especially since you… are not in the same position as your father was."

"Not in the same position? He was the king. I am now the king. What is the difference?" Cethin demanded, his hand falling to the arm of his chair. His fingers curled around the armrest, and he willed his darkness to remain hidden, but it churned in his soul.

Everyone at the table glanced at each other, clearly debating who was going to be the one to answer him. Finally, Zayan said, "Your father had an heir, Cethin, but more than that he had a wife who was very involved in the running of the kingdom until her passing."

His mother.

Queen Selinya.

His father had come from a long line of rulers before them, but his mother had been the more powerful of the two. It was his mother's bloodline that mattered here. Why the council was so adamant about preserving him. Why he was already well aware of the next argument before it had even had the chance to pass anyone's lips.

"Perhaps it is time for you to take a partner," Zayan ventured.

One would think they'd be nervous to hold his stare after past discussions of this nature, but every member of the advisory council was watching him. Waiting to see what his response would be this time. He supposed he could give them some credit. They hadn't brought it up in nearly a year.

His hands flexed around the armrests once more, threads of inky power seeping from his fingertips as he worked to maintain control of his magic.

"That is not a priority right now," Cethin replied tightly, snatching up his liquor glass and draining it.

"While it is certainly not *your* priority, it should be one of the king's," a female down the table said. "You wish to investigate death scenes without a partner or an heir? If you cross the Veil to the After, what then, your grace?"

He sat back, pinching the bridge of his nose at the same old arguments.

"Your father—" someone else started.

Cethin didn't even know who was speaking when he interrupted. "My father ruled for centuries without a wife, and they were together for decades more before I was born."

"Be that as it may, we have a proposal that may satisfy several urgent matters," Zayan cut in as a staff member refilled Cethin's glass. "If I may present this proposal to you, your grace?"

He didn't dare reach for that liquor glass, knowing the dark power he possessed was thickening beneath his palms. With a sharp jerk of his chin, Zayan continued.

"It has long been the tradition of the Sutara kings that their partners be Fae, with the recent exception of your father. With the continued decline in the Fae population as of late, we agree this is even more urgent now. It would show the kingdom that you have a personal interest in the matter."

"I *do* have a personal interest in the matter," Cethin gritted out. He was only half-listening anyway, too focused on keeping his power in check. "They are part of my kingdom. That is all that is needed for me to have a personal interest."

"And that is noble. No one is discrediting that, but taking a Fae as a wife would reiterate long-standing alliances," Hayes piped in. "It would provide reassurance that you are taking the threat against their kind seriously, especially after the last few decades of history and the need to strengthen the laws around taking Sources."

His jaw clenched. He'd sat in on countless meetings when his father had sat at the head of this table. Nobody had questioned him or spoken down to him. Truth be told, he felt like he had more respect and freedoms as their prince than as their king.

"Beyond all that, it would be beneficial to you as the king and leader of the kingdom to have a wife that could potentially provide a Source of your own. The fact you don't have one after centuries is, quite frankly, troublesome," another female contributed.

"You are growing rather bold, Lady Odessa," Cethin ground out, his voice as dark as the power he was working hard to contain.

Everyone straightened, recognizing the edge in his tone. His father had been known to be levelheaded. Strong-willed and uncompromising, yes, but he rarely lost his composure. Cethin was known to be just as strong-willed, but he was also said to have a temper that came with an unfavorable recklessness when he lost control.

It didn't happen often. He was the epitome of discipline; his mother had ensured it once his power had emerged. Everyone had assumed he'd control the water element like his father—who was a descendant of Anahita, the god of the seas, water, and ice—but his parents had known that wouldn't be the case, even if they hadn't known which gifts would emerge.

All of Avonleya knew of his darkness. They all assumed it was the same magic his mother's shadows had been, except more powerful because of his father's bloodline. When two Avonleyan bloodlines crossed, the offspring emerged with one side's power—

whichever side was stronger. The other bloodline simply strengthened or weakened that power.

His mother's shadows were more powerful than his father's water magic, but his father had been one of the most powerful water-wielders of the realm. All that power merged in Cethin's soul, and the entire kingdom knew it. Knew his power was vast and mighty. Their kingdom was relatively safe, tucked behind the Wards and locked away from the rest of the realm. But that didn't mean there hadn't been threats. That there hadn't been instances when he'd had to stand beside his father and wield that darkness to assert dominance or answer a threat. It kept him on the throne now and prevented anyone from ever entertaining the idea of challenging him. No one would take the throne from him and the legacy his bloodline had left to him.

"So your proposal is that I take a Fae wife? That is not a new revelation, Zayan," Cethin said flatly.

"That is not the entirety of the proposal," Zayan answered. "The Spring Esbat Festival will commence in a few weeks. We suggest extending a special invitation to all the Fae in the kingdom. You can address them at the Festival, reassure them you are working to ensure their safety. And with all the Fae here, you could perhaps...get to know some of them better."

An entire minute ticked by, the advisors shifting uncomfortably in their seats as they waited for Cethin to respond to their *proposal*.

"You want me to use the Esbat Festival to find a partner," Cethin said slowly.

"No," Zayan said quickly, nervously running a hand through his dark blond hair. "We are suggesting you use the festival to reassure the Fae, and if you happen to connect with one on a deeper level, then we would thank the Fates."

"Perhaps the lot of you should simply narrow it down and present me with a pool of potential partners to choose from," he replied coolly.

Zayan's eyes widened, recognizing the dangerous tone, but apparently not everyone at the table picked up on the warning. Not as Lady Odessa muttered under her breath, "As if we haven't discussed doing that."

His control slipped, darkness snapping out like whips and dragging down the marble table, leaving long scratches across the smooth surface. The council members lurched to their feet, magic appearing and shields forming to protect themselves.

Cethin leisurely stood, that heavy darkness drifting around him like a dense fog. "I believe we are done here for today."

"But, your grace, we still have the matter of the vacant advisory seat, and—"

His gaze slid to Zayan, and he said nothing. He didn't need to. He knew his face said it all as he stared down the male. Zayan bowed his head as he murmured, "Of course, your grace."

Cethin didn't bother saying anything to the others. He left the room with his dark magic trailing him. A reminder to everyone of who he was.

He climbed to the top floor of the castle, the entire level serving as the king's private quarters. But he was merely there to discard the crown that sat on his brow. Tybalt and Zayan insisted he wear it for council meetings. It was ridiculous.

He unceremoniously tossed the silver thing inlaid with rubies into a velvet-lined box on his dresser before he Traveled from the room. A moment later, he was on the shore he'd been longing for earlier. The waves called to him, the same way they'd called to his father. He could think here with nothing but the sea breeze and the stars overhead.

The moon was waning leading up to the Spring Esbat Festival. Esbat itself was a celebration of the new moon, when the sky was dark and the shadows reigned. It was said to be a time of introspection. When things hidden in the shadows might reveal themselves. New beginnings and new intentions were set on Esbat, and while each new moon brought the sacred day with it, the ones that fell closest to the Spring and Autumnal Equinoxes were celebrated with festivals.

And apparently his council wanted him to use the coming sacred day to scout for a godsdamn partner. He wasn't a fool.

They'd accept a husband, but they were all hoping for a wife. A wife could produce an heir and keep his bloodline—and power—alive.

Cethin sighed, slipping his boots and socks off and leaving them in the sand as he walked to the water's edge. It was so cold it nearly burned as the surf rolled over his bare toes, but he didn't mind. The bite made him feel…

It just made him feel.

Not much seemed to do that these days. Paperwork and meetings made for dull days, and his title made for faux friends and suspicious motives.

He slipped his hands into his pockets as he stared out at the Edria Sea. Perhaps he should go to his study in the catacombs of the castle and work there for the rest of the evening. It would keep him busy and distract from thoughts of an impending marriage.

Before he turned to leave, he paused. Something stirred in the air. Something he couldn't see, but that he could feel. Something powerful. Something predatory. Something watching him. A feeling he'd had more and more of as of late.

A feeling he'd recently discovered wasn't a feeling at all but a person.

He debated calling her out, but in the end decided against it. She could simply leave, and he wasn't quite ready for her to know he could sense her presence. Not yet.

So he let her be, and he lingered longer, a plan taking shape as he stood listening to the song of the waves. He'd sacrificed much to keep his people safe, and he refused to believe those sacrifices were for nothing.

Because sometimes you had to be the villain in one story to be the savior in another.

CHAPTER 5
KAILIA

Why were pants so godsdamn constricting? That was all Kailia could think as she tugged her cloak tighter around herself, navigating through the streets and trying to avoid as much of the Esbat crowd as she could. She missed her usual dress. It was much easier to move in and gave her more range of motion.

That, and she liked the feel of daggers strapped to her bare thighs rather than atop fabric.

Everything about being dressed in these fitted pants and tunic felt off and foreign, but the worst part was the boots. Her toes curled at the thought, missing the feel of the dirt and earth beneath them. She couldn't feel any vibration of movement, and that was unsettling.

It was fine. She could do this for a few hours. Get through this night, with all these people around her…

Hoping she blended in well enough, she kept moving. It seemed like the best time to venture beyond her smoke and ashes. Everyone was hidden in cloaks and shadows, most with hoods up to conceal their features, as part of the Esbat festivities. Despite all that, she hadn't felt this exposed in ages. Her fingers itched for her bow, and she felt too bare without a quiver at her back. She understood the irony of more clothing making her feel so…naked.

With a new moon, only the stars shimmered above them. Lamps along the streets were lit by fire Fae and the Avonleyans descended from Anala, but even those flames were low, just enough to allow people to see as they meandered. The smell of food filled the air, and her stomach took notice. She hadn't eaten since yesterday when she'd stolen bread and apples from a cart beyond Aimonway. She'd feel bad about it if she knew how to feel regret, but that was a trivial emotion that served no purpose. Nevertheless, the aroma of roasting meat made her mouth water, and she wondered if she could swipe some of that before the night was over.

No.

Blend in.

She needed to blend in if she wanted to have any chance of getting close to him, and getting caught stealing would definitely hinder her plans. Not that she'd get caught, but it was an unnecessary risk.

Keeping to the outskirts, she paused to observe the crowd and figure out what she should be doing. Surely he would be recognizable in the masses, right?

Children giggled and ran, playing games with one another. Some had sugary treats in their hands, while others had toys that twinkled like stars. Adults wandered too, conversing with one another, drinks in hand. Most of them appeared to know each other, even with their faces hidden by the night and shadows. They ambled among the various vendors, exchanging coin for wares. The atmosphere felt a little lighter as the city shook off the last of the winter season and stepped fully into spring. As if this Esbat was a new beginning for nature too.

Steeling herself, Kailia stepped farther into the throngs of people, avoiding any physical contact as much as she could. She still kept to the edges. She was fairly small, and she used her size to her advantage as she slipped among the bodies. Making her way to a section of vendors, she took in the merchandise. Luxurious fabrics. Perfumes and tonics. Trinkets and jewelry.

She meandered, trying to look interested as she did. Touching silk and studying small statues. It wasn't until she paused at a crystal jeweler that she finally overheard anything useful.

"What time is the address with the king?" a female was asking another.

"At the top of the hour," her companion answered. "We've been assured members of the Avonleyan Guard will mind our stands while the Fae attend his address. They should be here any moment."

The first female nodded, and her hood slipped back, revealing some of her features. She worried her bottom lip, sky-blue eyes alight with emotions—a mixture of curiosity, anxiety, and excitement if Kailia was interpreting them correctly.

"That one is beautiful, isn't it?" the second female said, and it took Kailia a moment to realize the Fae was speaking to her. It also took her a moment to understand what she was referring to.

Looking down, she found her fingers hovering over a necklace. It was simple enough. A black leather cord with a single blue crystal. It was rather lovely, but she'd never had use for such things.

"It's blue kyanite," the female offered, pulling her hood back and giving her a bright smile. "It helps channel your self-worth and opens your mind to more lucid dreams."

Kailia nodded but didn't speak as she ran a fingertip over the crystal. Her dreams were lucid enough, and self-worth? She knew where her value lay. The necklace was beautiful in its simplicity though. Trivial, but beautiful.

She hissed as an arm brushed hers, the physical contact jarring. Her hand already halfway to her dagger, she forced herself to stop.

"I have noted this business requires a stand-in so you may attend the address," a guard said. He didn't wear the cloak of the festivities. Instead, his black and silver uniform was on display to clearly mark who he was.

"Yes, please," the females answered in unison, quickly gathering small satchels and pulling their hoods back into place before setting off without a backward glance.

The guard glanced down at Kailia, his brow creasing slightly, and she pulled her hood up more.

"Are you Fae as well?" he asked. He didn't give her time to respond, not that she would have anyway. "If you are, your presence is requested in the city center."

He gestured to the north, and when she still didn't respond, she watched him shift on his feet. It was subtle, but she could tell he was uncomfortable. Silence did that to most people.

Clearing his throat, he stepped into the merchant space. "If, uh, you're not, you'll have to wait until the females return to make a purchase."

Nodding, she continued on, heading north anyway. She wanted to hear what the king had to say.

The closer she got to the city center, the harder it was to avoid being touched. Bodies brushed against her, and she ground her teeth, her skin crawling with every bump.

The street opened into a central square, and she sucked in a deep breath as the people spread out. There were still too many, but at least she could breathe here, not to mention keep her distance.

There was a platform in the middle, but it was empty. She'd expected to see the king sitting there on a grand throne of sorts. People milled about, most of them Fae she presumed. It was hard to tell the difference between the Fae and the Avonleyans. They all had slightly pointed ears along with enhanced speed and senses. They all had their magic, and some Fae were more powerful than others, depending on bloodlines. The fact that they were so similar was something she planned to use to her advantage.

She stumbled suddenly when someone ran into her, and she couldn't help but think she wouldn't have stumbled in her bare feet. It was these godsdamn boots. And all these people. She'd been prepared for it on the streets, but not here, at this moment. She certainly wasn't prepared for the hand that caught her upper arm to keep her on her feet, not as the feel of fingers wrapping around her flesh made her want to scream.

A haze fell over her vision, and everything in her zeroed in on the touch that felt like a searing brand, just like any other time someone touched her. It wasn't real. She knew that. It felt the same no matter who or what was touching her. It was the touch itself that made her want to crawl out of her skin and scream and *die*. It made her want to be someone else completely.

Purely on instinct, she grabbed a dagger at her thigh and spun, breaking his hold on her. Her hand came down, the blade sinking into a male forearm. It wasn't until after the male yanked his arm back, her dagger slicing a wide gash before coming free, that she realized what she'd done.

In front of far too many people.

But no one else had seemed to notice the small female at the back of the crowd. They were all facing the platform, anxiously awaiting the king.

A drop of blood slid from the blade, hitting the ground at her feet, and she lifted her chin defiantly as she stared into the depths of the dark hood. She couldn't see his features, but her hood had slipped back in her near fall, revealing her face and the braid that hung over her shoulder.

A stupid, careless mistake.

The male took a step forward, lifting a hand as if to reach for her, and she raised her dagger between them, the warning clear. She wasn't sorry she'd stabbed him, and she'd do it again.

He stilled, his hand frozen between them for a moment, before he dropped it to his side. Without a word, he turned away from her, striding into the crowd.

Kailia tracked him, absentmindedly wiping her dagger on her pants before placing it back in the sheath at her thigh. They weren't her usual daggers, so she didn't really care if it was clean or not. She rarely had use for them.

Reaching behind her, she pulled her hood back up, tucking her braid out of sight and mentally calculating how much longer until she could undo the plait. The male was still making his way through the throng of bodies, and others were keeping pace with him on the edges of the crowd. It was almost as if they were—

Fucking Temural.

She silently cursed the god of the wild and untamed as the male she'd stabbed climbed the wooden steps to the platform, pulling back his hood before unclasping the cloak and handing it to a waiting guard. His shoulder-length silver hair seemed to shimmer in the light of the torches that stood at the four corners. Tall and broad, white skin, and wearing all black, silver irises locked onto her across the crowd as he rolled back the sleeve of his tunic. First the left arm, then the right, a stream of red steadily sliding across his flesh.

The godsdamn king of Avonleya.

What had he been doing out in the crowd of people anyway? Without guards at his sides? Out here blending in with everyone else?

There were audible gasps and murmurs broke out as a guard rushed to him with a cloth. Kailia tsked under her breath. It would heal fine, and it wouldn't even take long. Fae healed fairly quickly, and Avonleyans were even faster. A big deal was being made out of nothing.

But the fuss over a little blood had pulled the king's attention from her, and she used the distraction to slip farther back away from the crowd until she was near one of the lampposts dimly illuminating the space. With a sigh of relief, she slipped into the faintly wafting smoke, relishing the feeling of being weightless.

Of not having to worry about anyone touching her.

She couldn't stay hidden here for long. It drained her power reserves, and she wasn't entirely sure where the night would lead. She just needed to escape the king's notice for a little bit. Maybe he'd forget about the random female who'd stabbed him…

Silver eyes flicked back up, going right back to where she'd been standing. She saw the slight crease on his brow as he scanned the crowd, and then the way he pressed his lips into a thin line.

Okay, so he probably wasn't going to forget about the stabbing.

The king cleared his throat, the crowd going silent at the sound.

"Let's address the obvious, shall we?" he started with a smile as he raised his wounded arm. "This is nothing but a scratch. My own fault really. There was an area of particularly dense *smoke* that made it hard to see much of anything else." He paused, and Kailia could swear he looked directly where she was hidden in her power. But then his gaze skipped over the crowd again as he added with a wink, "Or maybe it was Harrison Reyes's excellent mead."

The crowd chortled, some raising tankards and cheering.

"Now that that's out of the way," the king continued, the Fae once again falling quiet as they clung to his every word. "I know there are concerns, especially among the Fae in our kingdom."

Kailia listened as he offered placating words to try to soothe the anxious crowd. Everyone was well aware of the increasing attacks on the Fae, and the king assured them he was doing everything in his power to figure out who and why. She watched him as he casually moved back and forth across the platform while he spoke, his grace and poise as effortless as the words falling from his lips.

Growing restless, she flitted to another post, drawing closer to the platform as he moved on to offering lodgings for the Fae who wished to remain closer to Aimonway for their safety. As if staying on this side of the Nightmist Mountains would be any more secure. That was ridiculous. There had been nearly as many casualties found on this side as the west of the black mountain range.

She'd stopped listening at some point, only becoming aware the king had finished his speech when the crowd began clapping and cheering.

Daring to move closer still, now hovering in the smoke of one of the stage torches, she watched the king leave the platform. The way he moved was more like a prowl, a predator who'd honed in on prey.

"Rumor is the king is seeking a partner."

Her attention slid to a small group of females nearby. They'd all pushed their hoods back, running fingers through their hair. The one who'd spoken was bouncing on her toes, face flush with excitement.

"It's part of the reason all the Fae were summoned," she went on. "He wants to return to tradition by taking a Fae to his side."

"Do you think it's true?" another asked, biting her lip as she pushed onto her tiptoes, trying to see over the crowd.

A third female shrugged, smoothing her hands down her cloak.

"Gathering all the Fae together certainly makes it seem true. What better way to survey the options?"

They all giggled as if something they'd said was funny.

But over the next few hours, those rumors appeared to gain more and more traction. The king didn't leave the city center, making his way through the crowd. He visited with everyone, and as others seemed to realize this as well, more Fae seemed to appear and clamor for his attention.

Kailia had to leave her sanctuary after the second hour, feeling her reserves draining too quickly. It'd become harder to blend in now. Males and females alike had pulled their hoods back, trying to ensnare the king's notice. Keeping her hood in place would draw attention to her, so she begrudgingly pulled it back and stayed on the fringes yet again. She kept to the darkened corners and shadowed doorways, biding her time.

When it was closer to dawn than dusk and people had more mead than food in their bellies, the king finally took a seat. Not on a throne atop the platform, but on a common wood chair off to the side. The crowd was thinning, people stumbling as they began to make their ways home, and it was then that Kailia slipped from the darkness.

There were guards nearby, of course, but they were keeping their distance, clearly trying to create the illusion of a casual air around the king. The king himself was waving off an offering of food and drink as he smiled at two females he was speaking with, one of them blushing at whatever he'd said.

She waited even longer, until there were a handful of people left milling about, clearly hoping for some more…intimate time with the king. But it wasn't until those silver irises landed on her again that she finally approached. She didn't really have much of a choice. He'd seen her, clearly still recognized her, and his stare didn't leave her this time.

Lifting her chin, she skirted around a male who'd fallen asleep on the ground and closed the distance between them. The king said something, and the nearby guards left. Well, they didn't *leave*, but they moved far enough away to give some privacy. She couldn't decide if that made the king stupid or his supposed guards who would now be too far away to actually protect him from anything.

As she came to a stop in front of him, she planted her feet, and her fingers curled into her palms. He sat casually in his seat, elbow planted on the armrest and a finger steepled along his temple. Neither of them spoke, and when the silence stretched on, the king simply arched a brow. Clearly he was not bothered by the quiet.

That was disappointing.

It was the easiest way to extract information. People revealed much when trying to fill awkward silences.

Her eyes narrowed. "You have my arrow."

The male said nothing.

"I want it back," she continued.

He blinked once, studying her in a way that made her want to stab him.

Again.

"No," he finally said.

The word was so…simple. Spoken from a male who was used to being obeyed.

"No," she repeated, her head tilting to the side.

His lips twitched in the smallest of smirks as he waited for her to make the next move.

"The arrow is mine. You have it. I demand you return it," she insisted, feeling her ashes vibrate around her.

"An arrow that you tried to kill me with."

Tried to…

"You'd know if I was trying to kill you," she scoffed.

A perfect brow arched again in clear amusement at her, the little female speaking to a king.

That made her want to stab him even more.

"And how, pray tell, would I know? I assumed having an arrow shot at me was a pretty telling sign," he drawled.

"If I were trying to kill you, you'd be dead," she retorted just as simply as he'd dismissed her request.

"Is that why you stabbed me?"

"That was an accident."

"You accidentally stabbed me?"

"Yes. It's rare. Usually when I stab someone, it's on purpose."

A huff of laughter came from him, his hand dropping to the armrest. "What is your name?"

She clenched her fists tighter as she held his stare, fingers itching to reach for her blade.

His fingers drummed once on the chair. "I didn't realize that was such a difficult question."

"I *did* stab you," she snapped. "Providing my name doesn't seem like a wise idea at the moment."

"I think the actual stabbing was the poor idea," he replied, getting to his feet.

Kailia lurched back. "What are you doing?"

He paused, both brows rising this time as he slowly extended a hand. "I was going to take you back to my castle."

"Why?"

"Because that's where your arrow is. If you want it back, you'll need to come collect it."

Pushing her braid back over her shoulder, she pursed her lips and eyed his outstretched hand. She didn't realize her fingers were tracing the hilt of her dagger until his eyes dipped to the movement. She froze because normal people didn't constantly feel the need to be caressing pointy objects, and she was supposed to be blending in.

Then again, she'd already stabbed him, so...

He was still staring at her, and she couldn't read his expression. His hand was also still outstretched, far too close for comfort. Taking another step back from him, she said, "Go get the arrow and meet me back here."

"No," he answered. Again. But as she opened her mouth to argue with him, he continued, "You stabbed me on top of trying to kill me with said arrow—"

"I wasn't trying to—"

"I could have you arrested and held for questioning," he continued, raising his voice to speak over her.

"You could try," she muttered.

He'd dropped his hand at some point, but now he once again

extended it to her. "Let me escort you to the castle to retrieve your arrow, and then we can move on."

"Forget this happened?" she said doubtfully.

The corner of his lips turned into some kind of a wry smile. "Something like that."

She eyed his hand again. "Fine. But we'll walk."

His features twisted into something unimpressed. "It would take hours. Even on horseback it would take at least two."

She shrugged. "Either go get the arrow and return it to me here, or fetch some horses, king."

"Your Majesty."

"What?"

His hand dropping back to his side yet again, he clarified, "Most people address me as your Majesty."

"I'll address you however I please."

He went quiet, once more studying her too closely. She was becoming too brazen. This was *not* the way things were supposed to go, and there was no way this was furthering her plans—

"Fair enough, tiny fiend."

She bristled, her face scrunching in disgust. "Don't call me that."

"I'll address you however I please. Part of the king title and all that," he returned. "More than that, you haven't provided your name."

"Go get the horses," she gritted out.

"*Horse*," he replied, emphasizing the lack of plurality. "Only one."

"No."

There was absolutely no way in all the realm she was riding on a horse with him. That would involve far too much touching. A small shudder rolled down her spine at the thought.

"We are once again at an impasse, tiny fiend," he drawled, crossing his arms over his chest and staring down at her.

"You not getting your way does not classify as an impasse," she retorted, not caring that she was once again fingering her dagger. He noticed too, and she could swear he was fighting a smile. "I will meet you at the castle," she finally conceded. Then added, "Mid-morning."

"We go now," he all but growled, stepping closer to her.

She went rigid as he reached for her hand again, but this time it wasn't slow and tentative. His hand snapped out, clearly done with debates as his long fingers closed around her wrist.

In the next breath, there was a pull at her navel as she was tugged through a rip in the air. She'd been Traveled before, and she hated it. It was nothing like moving through ashes and smoke. That was fluid and graceful. Calming. Traveling was jarring and unsettling.

When they reappeared, she sucked in a breath and yanked her arm from his grasp. Taking in the new space, she tried to get her heart rate to slow and the phantom burning at her wrist to fade. Light grey marble floors were offset by dark walls that matched the outside of the castle she'd observed from afar. Sconces every few feet cast a soft glow along with the windows that would let in the natural light during the day. There were soft white window curtains tied back with silver cords. Somehow the space was warm and inviting despite the cool tones of the decor.

The king was watching her with smug satisfaction, letting her put space between them.

"I'm here. Where's my arrow?" she snarled, reminding herself over and over again that she could not stab him right now. In his home. Where surely there were guards around every corner.

"Ah," he replied, that knowing smile returning. "That part can wait until mid-morning."

"I'm not staying here," she argued.

But he strode to a nearby door and threw it open. "We have quite a bit to discuss later today, tiny fiend. I suggest getting some rest."

"I don't need to discuss anything with you."

"If you'd rather discuss the stabbing with my Commander of Forces, you're more than welcome to," he said with faux innocence.

"And if I simply leave?" she countered.

"You are not one of the few people who can Travel in and out of the castle. Even your intriguing smoke and ashes won't serve you here. So you'll be left to walk out on your own two feet, and that won't happen either."

He waited expectantly, and what was she supposed to say? Of course he knew about her smoke and ashes. He'd seen her with those creatures, and she knew she couldn't move among them here. She also knew all about the wards surrounding the castle. It was why she'd had to watch him from afar when he ventured out to the shores or beyond the Nightmist Mountains.

"You are holding me against my will?" she finally said, every part of her vibrating with the words.

"No, tiny fiend," he replied condescendingly. "I'm graciously hosting you for the night before we enter negotiations tomorrow."

She couldn't keep the surprise off her face. "Negotiations for what?"

"I need a wife and more of those arrows," he answered. "I think you're the answer to both."

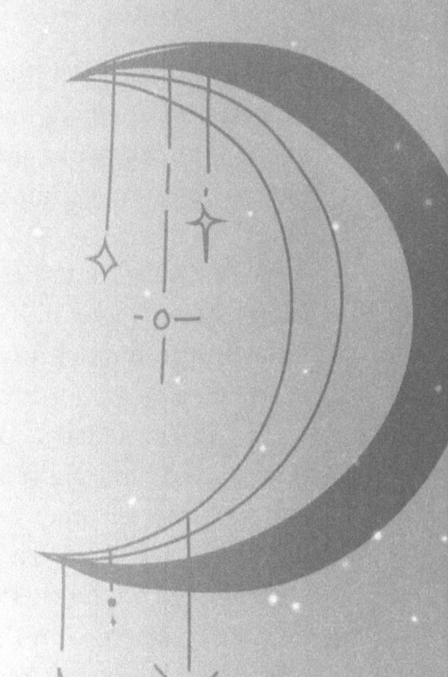

CHAPTER 6
RAZIK

"Do you ever sleep?" Wren grumbled as she languidly stretched beside him in bed.

Sitting against the headboard, he glanced down at her as she pulled the pillow over her head to hide from the sunlight. He didn't bother responding. She already knew the answer to that. The sheets slid down with her movement, revealing bare skin. They'd fucked last night, which wasn't uncommon. They'd simply both needed to relieve some tension, and the Source bond between them allowed them a deeper connection. Sometimes it was just more convenient to take care of each other's needs, and that had been the case last night after the Esbat Festival.

But fucking was all it was. Nothing more. There was nothing exclusive about their arrangement, and they each took other partners when they wanted. Except for the other Cadre members. He drew a line there, but that was at Wren's request because they spent so much time with them. She didn't want the others to know she'd requested the boundary, afraid of offending them, and Razik was fine with that. It was the least he could do when she'd willingly bound herself to him as his Source. Besides, he didn't particularly care who he offended.

Snapping closed the book he'd been combing through, he slipped from the bed, making his way to the bathing chamber. "It's about time you woke up," he called, looking back over his shoulder. "I've been wanting to go down for breakfast for the last hour."

Wren rolled onto her back, propping herself up on her elbows. Long brown locks slid over her shoulder as her navy blue eyes locked on to him, clearly unimpressed. "Last I checked, you didn't need me to escort you around the castle."

Razik ignored her, pushing the door to the bathing chamber shut behind him. He splashed water on his face, cleaned his teeth, and took care of other needs before going to the dressing room. He dressed in his usual black pants and black tunic, the Cadre crest embroidered on the chest. Boots and weapons were next, and by the time he re-emerged in the bedchamber, Wren was out of bed and slipping on her own tunic.

"Put this in the laundry," she said, tossing her Esbat cloak at him as she made her way to the bathing chamber. While he'd been in uniform last night, she'd been in the festival garb, enjoying the celebrations.

He waited impatiently for her to get ready, taking the ridiculous time females needed to do whatever they did in the mornings.

He'd been put on the team in charge of Cethin's security last night, and as much as it had irked him, he couldn't argue with the logic. There hadn't been any more attacks—phantom beings or otherwise—since the one at the castle a few weeks ago. A large celebration was the perfect opportunity to strike, especially with so many Fae gathered in one place. More than that, if the phantom beings *had* appeared, he'd be needed with his dragon fire, which is why Wren had stayed at his side the entire night as well.

Of course, nothing dire had happened, and it had put him in a sour mood that he'd had to spend his evening watching the arrogant king rather than doing...anything else. And somehow, the bastard had still managed to get himself sliced up. Cethin had played it off, but Razik was trained well enough to recognize a stab wound when he saw one. How none of his guards had seen what had happened was still a mystery to him, but everyone had been on high alert the rest of the evening.

For no reason.

It'd been hours of watching females and males alike swoon over him. Watching him give smiles and polite conversation in return. Watching everyone get drunk.

It hadn't been all bad, he supposed. After the king had fucked off back to the castle with a random female, they'd been relieved of their duties. He'd met up with Jarek, Fallon, and the rest of the Cadre at a pub, where they'd toasted Valric and drank in his memory. They'd done so a few times since his death, but today Tybalt was supposed to be appointing a warrior to fill the vacancy. Today it would feel more final as they all moved on without a trusted member of their family.

The bathing room door flung open, and before Razik could say a word, Wren sighed dramatically. "Yes, yes, I know. I take too long, but I'd like to remind you once again that I do not need an escort through this castle."

Razik sent her an unimpressed look, and she only smiled brighter before she pushed past him. He followed her through the sitting room and out to the hall. Everyone in the castle appeared to be moving slower this morning. Despite the tired faces, the staff all had smiles, clearly having enjoyed themselves at the festival.

Normally, he'd go back to Tybalt's estate house for breakfast. Magdalena made the best pastries he'd ever had, but with the Cadre meeting later this morning, it made more sense to simply stay here.

"Are you staying for the meeting today?" he asked Wren as they descended a set of stairs.

She scoffed. "No. Your meetings are boring," she replied airily. He huffed at her response and glanced down to find her smirking up at him in amusement. Then she elbowed him in the side. "Someday you're going to realize it's okay to smile every once in a while."

He did smile. When it was warranted. Which was rare.

"Then what are you going to do today?" he inquired, turning the last corner that would take them to the dining room.

She shrugged beside him, keeping pace. "Go help assist the Fae who are choosing to relocate into the city for a while. There's so few of us left, that..." She shrugged again, trailing off. "I feel like I could offer reassurance or something. Maybe—"

Wren cut off abruptly as they entered the dining room, both of them pausing mid-step.

The table was laden with the usual breakfast offerings, but it was still fairly early for Avonleya. He preferred to be the first one down here so he could be finished when everyone else showed up, and usually he was. Granted, he was later than usual, but he'd thought he'd still be fine considering everyone had been at the festival last night.

Which is why neither of them had expected to find a female sitting at the table.

Her midnight hair flowed around her shoulders, and she wore a black long-sleeved top. Amber eyes swirling with smoke narrowed on them, marking her as an Ash Rider, but what was she doing here by herself?

Recovering from the momentary surprise, he said nothing as he made his way down the table to his usual chair. He'd seen Cethin leave with her last night, but he hadn't realized she was the Ash Rider. Had Cethin actually done something useful for once in his life?

"Hello," Wren ventured with a tentative smile because that was who she was. Kind-hearted to a fault. She didn't see it, but people took advantage of that. Or they had before she'd become his Source. He'd put a stop to that shit real quick.

"I'm Wren," she continued, reaching for the bowl of fruit and waiting.

Apparently she was going to wait forever because the female didn't say a godsdamn word. Only continued to watch them.

"That's Razik," Wren went on because she also babbled when she was nervous, which was clearly the female's intention. "Are you one of the Fae who are relocating here?"

Of course she wasn't. Ash Riders had Avonleyan blood in their line somewhere that gave them their gifts. Wren knew this too, but she was trying to make some kind of conversation for whatever reason.

Razik slid a hotcake onto her plate along with two sausage links, and when she peered up at him helplessly, he poured some syrup on the hotcake too. Then he said, "I believe Orson and Riggs were tending to the Fae today. If you're still planning to accompany them, you'd best take that plate to go."

Her shoulders sagged with relief as she pushed to her feet. "Yes, I had better do that." She gathered the plate and a fork, Razik adding a hard-boiled egg to the other food. He'd been taking a lot of power from her lately. "Send a message if you need me?"

He nodded and returned to filling his own plate as she quickly left the room. Feeling the other female's eyes on him the entire time, he didn't even glance at her. Not until his plate was full and he'd shoved a piece of ham into his mouth did he settle back in his chair and make eye contact.

She was still staring, her plate clean and empty. She hadn't touched any of the spread. Those swirling eyes narrowed again at his attention. He took a bite of his orange scone. If she thought silence was going to unnerve him, she was sitting with the wrong male. He relished the silence. Fuck, he wished every meal was like this.

And that was how the next fifteen minutes passed in blessed silence. Maybe the gods had finally stopped punishing him.

Or not.

Cethin appeared a moment later, looking a little flustered. His silver hair wasn't tied back like it usually was, and his clothing was wrinkled.

"My apologies for being late. I lost track of time," he said to the female. Silver eyes flicked to Razik in a glare before going back to her. "Have you been waiting long?"

She stayed silent, and Razik smirked. See? He could smile when things were actually amusing.

Cethin sighed, taking the seat across from her. "We both know how the not speaking thing works out, tiny fiend."

"Don't call me that," she ground out from between her teeth.

Cethin wasn't fazed. "As discussed last night, until you grace me with your name, I'll call you whatever I please." He glanced at Razik once more. "You didn't offer our guest any food?"

"Your guests aren't my responsibility," he said simply before taking a bite of his eggs. "But beyond that, she was waiting here before I got to the hall, so the rude one in this situation is you, *your Majesty.*"

The king tensed, eyes darting back to the female. "Why aren't you eating?"

"I'm not here to eat. You have my arrow. I'm here to retrieve it," she retorted.

Razik stood, having finished his own breakfast. He needed to get down to the training arenas for the Cadre meeting.

But before he left, he grabbed a raspberry muffin from the tray and made his way down the table. Stopping beside her, he set the baked good on her plate and leaned in. She leaned away, her stare hard.

"He's easier to deal with when you have food in your stomach," Razik said in a low voice. He saw Cethin stiffen in his periphery, and it made him move in even closer. "If you need company after you deal with him, let me know."

Then he straightened, swiping up another muffin for himself as he left the dining room without a backward glance. But he knew Cethin was glaring at him as he went, and it was the perfect way to start his day.

⇾⟩⊙⟨⇽

"Valric's death was noble and honorable," Tybalt said, looking each of the Cadre members in the eye as he spoke. "But death still hurts, even when met with honor."

Everyone's expressions were somber. Bram was the last member they'd welcomed into the Cadre, and not because of a death. Xavier had served in the Cadre for nearly three centuries, but his wife had been with child. With a growing family, he'd asked to be relieved of the duty. They'd all agreed without question, and a festival had been held in his honor.

"You are elite and the best this kingdom has to offer," Tybalt went on. "The best this *realm* has to offer, and when we lose one to the After, a piece of our souls goes with them because we serve as one. We live as one."

"And we die as one," they all echoed in melancholy.

Usually that chant was bellowed during training or when they entered a battle. Usually that call rang with pride and conviction, stirring up confidence and adrenaline.

Today, it only stirred memories.

"It will be hard to welcome a new member into the fold," Tybalt continued. "But this unit operates best with six members, and Valric's vacancy must be filled. Beyond that, Valric's death leaves an additional opening. As you are all aware, Valric was the second-in-command of the Cadre."

Everyone tried to hide it, but they all sat up straighter at the words. Because yes, they were mourning a lost brethren, but Valric had held the Second-in-Command position for decades. This is what Razik wanted. Everyone assumed it would be him when they'd discussed it over ale in the taverns various nights, the alcohol consumed in remembrance of Valric loosening tongues.

"I won't make a decision on the new second-in-command for a few weeks," Tybalt said, gaze once again sweeping over them. "But we do have a new Cadre member to welcome. Get him in shape and teach him how we do things. You are only as strong as your weakest member. Remember that. Draven!"

Tybalt summoned the male with a growl only a dragon could make, and the newest member of the Cadre entered the room. Shoulders back and chin high, he put on a good performance, but they could all sense his trepidation. None of them smiled. None of them greeted him.

Razik sat back and crossed his arms, surveying their newest member. Black hair cropped close to his skull. Light green eyes. Golden skin. The muscles and build expected of someone who'd served in the Avonleyan forces for the last several decades of his life.

They all knew who he was. All knew he'd been in the running for the vacancy.

He just wasn't Valric, and they'd all need a little time to get past that fact.

Jarek was the first to get up and shake the male's hand, followed by Fallon and the rest of them. These next weeks would be long and grueling for everyone. Draven would need to learn their tells and signals. When you'd worked as a team for so long, that was all natural and came easily. Adding someone new fucked it up, and they all knew it would take time to get back to that place.

But time was a luxury they didn't have with the uptick in attacks this last year.

As they filed out, Tybalt called out for Razik to wait a moment, and he sighed because he already knew where this was going to go.

Or he thought he did.

Which is why he was caught off guard when his uncle said, "It was reported to me there was someone new in the castle this morning."

Razik's brow creased. "The female Cethin brought back from the Esbat Festival? Since when does who he's fucking concern any of us?"

Tybalt sent him a flat look, and Razik stared back.

"It should concern *you*," Tybalt finally said.

And there it was. This is where he'd assumed this conversation was going.

"No," Razik countered. "It should concern his personal guards. Maybe the advisory council. It should concern the castle sentinels, and maybe her family, depending on whether he plucked her off the streets willingly—"

"Razik, he is still your sovereign," Tybalt interjected in warning. "You yourself have made comments about what would befall this kingdom if something happens to him. This isn't about Cethin—"

"It's always about Cethin," Razik interrupted. "Cethin and his godsdamn bloodline that's trying to decide my fate. That I've paid the price for my entire fucking life."

He watched Tybalt take a deep breath, clearly calming his own dragon, before he said, "It was different before. When Tethys was alive. When Selinya—"

He paused when Razik gave a snort of disgust at the mention of the queen.

Rubbing his brow for several seconds, Tybalt sighed, then swiped his hand down his face. "I know I was gone for a long time, Razik. Too long. I know those years were…trying for you. Alone here with the royal family. I understand nothing has been fair for you from the moment you stepped foot into this realm."

That was an understatement, but Razik said nothing. Life wasn't fair. He'd learned that when he'd watched his parents leave him in a realm with only his uncle when he was scarcely seven years.

No, life wasn't fair. Being immortal simply made the misery last longer.

"Do you want to leave?" Tybalt asked, his tone a touch softer.

"If we're done speaking, yes. I'd like to go train," Razik replied, suddenly feeling the need to do just that. Work his body into a state of exhaustion. Go through stances and movements that made sense. Follow routines that made him feel in control of something—anything—in his life.

Tybalt shook his head. "No. I mean do you want to *leave?* Avonleya. This realm." When Razik didn't answer, he said, "Because Cethin is our sole way to do that."

"Our?" Razik repeated, eyeing his uncle.

"I think you forget this is not my home world either, Razik," he replied, side-stepping him and making his way to the door. "You think I've grown complacent, but you forget I've had centuries longer than you to learn patience and strategy. It's in our blood. Moves and countermoves." He paused in the doorway, looking back at Razik once more as he repeated, "And Cethin is our only way out."

He stared at the empty doorway for several minutes after Tybalt left, leaving him with those words and his thoughts. Razik had spent his entire life reading every book he could find. Devouring knowledge. Preparing himself to fight against a destiny being pushed on him.

It had never occurred to him that maybe his uncle was doing the same in his own way.

As he made his way to the arena to join the Cadre, he let himself recall his earliest years. What he could remember of them anyway. A time that was merely glimpses of memory. Parents who'd cared for him in those brief years. Cousins. Flying. Lands in the sky.

They'd left the world he was born in to come here when he was four years. But while he remembered little of his homeland, Tybalt refused to talk about it. He'd stopped asking his uncle questions about the world now known as The Requiem decades ago. Partly because his uncle had been gone for ages. More than that, there was hardly any mention of it in the thousands upon thousands of books he'd combed through in his centuries of life.

It was as if that world had never really existed at all.

"About time the favorite joins us," Jarek called as he entered the arena, the others snickering.

Razik didn't bother replying. He simply flipped them the middle finger over his shoulder before pulling off his tunic and picking up a sword.

He wasn't the favorite. He was only wanted for his bloodline. That was where his value was. Had always been. They only wanted to use him for it.

But maybe he could use Cethin in the same way. Maybe his uncle was right.

And maybe Cethin's new female was the perfect way to get to him.

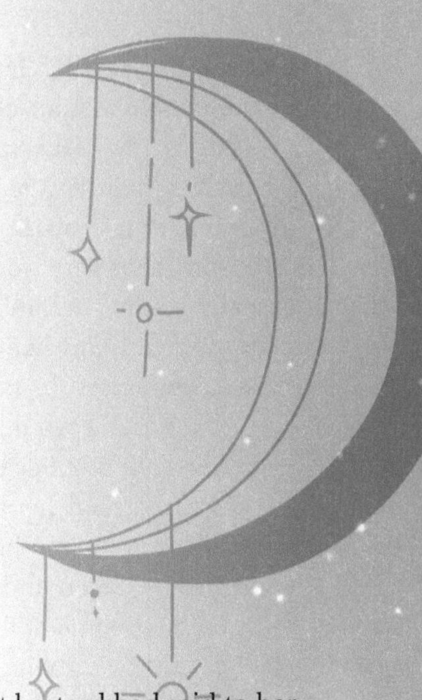

CHAPTER 7

CETHIN

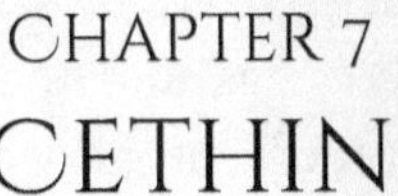

By Arius, he needed to know what that bastard had said to her. How long had they been alone in this dining room? Long enough for Razik to plant lies and rumors if she'd been here before him and he'd already finished his godsdamn breakfast.

Cethin hadn't been able to sleep after leaving the female in her rooms with strict orders to the castle guards to alert him immediately if she tried to leave. Apparently, he should have been more specific, because while he'd meant if she tried to leave her rooms, they'd interpreted his orders as if she tried to leave the castle. When sleep had evaded him, he'd slipped down to his personal study and workroom in the castle catacombs. No one knew of it, but he could still receive messages there.

Which is why he'd been more than a little perturbed when he'd emerged mid-morning and gone to her rooms to find her not there.

He'd rushed down here, finding the dragon with her, and then the male had leaned in and spoken low to her and—

She was staring at him.

Or rather, she was glaring at him.

He cleared his throat, reaching for the bowl of fried potatoes.

79

"So you met Razik," he said, trying to keep his voice even and void of the vitriol the male elicited.

"My arrow," she said tightly, her fingers flexing on the table where her palms were pressed flat to the surface. Ashes fluttered around her fingertips.

"You seem very concerned about a single arrow," he went on casually, adding scrambled eggs and toast with marmalade to his plate. "Would you like some?" he added, holding out the tray of toast to her across the table.

"No. What I would like is my arrow," she snapped. "And I'm concerned about it because it's mine."

Cethin clicked his tongue as he stood and reached across the table. Moving the muffin to the side, he replaced it with toast before adding some bacon and eggs as well. "You have to eat. Or does your magic refill in some other way?"

"It refills by stabbing people," she shot back.

He smirked, settling back into his chair. "Your reserves must be full after last night then."

Those amber eyes narrowed even more as she pointedly shoved her plate away.

Stabbing a few potatoes with his fork, he didn't react. Instead, he said, "We have some negotiating to do, tiny fiend."

"I'm not negotiating anything."

"Then I'm not returning your arrow."

Fury sparked, her warm skin seeming to darken even more with it. "What is it, exactly, that you want from me?"

He took his time with his bite, slowly sliding the fork from his lips as he made a show of debating his next words. "Your name to start."

"And if I share my name, you will return my arrow?"

"No."

"Is that your favorite word?"

He flashed a feral grin. "No."

She scoffed, sitting back in her seat and crossing her arms.

"I'll start," he said. "My name is Cethin."

"You're the king," she all but drawled. "Everyone knows who you are."

"Did you know when you stabbed me?"

"If I had, I would have aimed for somewhere far more painful than your arm," she replied with faux sweetness.

He hummed in response, scooping up some eggs. "I'm still confused as to what I did to deserve a stabbing."

"I'm still confused as to why I don't have my arrow back."

Continuing as if she hadn't spoken, he added, "All I did was save your face from meeting the ground."

"Save my…" She trailed off, as if perplexed by his wording, before her resolve snapped back into place. "I wouldn't have nearly fallen if you hadn't run into me."

"Something I tried to rectify by saving you."

"You are what I need saving from," she muttered under her breath.

He didn't know why, but her words rubbed him the wrong way. The darkness in his soul writhed in his chest, and he straightened with indignation. "I would never hurt you," he said, his voice low.

"Merely hold me hostage?"

"That's not what I'm doing." When she stared back at him in silence, he sighed, pushing his plate aside. "I need your help."

"No," she said simply.

He held back his smile. "Those arrows of yours can kill beings that are threatening my people. Aside from dragon fire, it's the only other weapon we've found that can kill them."

"Then give it back so I can continue to do so."

"I'd like to partner with you to create more for my forces to use."

"No."

His brows flew up. "I just told you it's one of two ways to kill threats to Avonleya, and you decline?"

"You use the word often enough. I assumed you knew what it meant."

By the Fates.

"Okay," he said through gritted teeth, his patience waning, as he pulled his plate back in front of him. "Let's forgo the negotiations for a little longer. Did you enjoy the Esbat Festival?"

Her brow creased in confusion. "What?"

"The festivities last night. Did you enjoy the evening?"

She studied him for another long moment, as if trying to figure out an underlying meaning in his words. Finally, she said, "Until the hostage part, I suppose the evening was…fine."

"Fine?" he pushed, polishing off his eggs.

"There were a lot of people there."

"Were you planning on stabbing anyone else then? Or only me?"

She threw her hands up, shaking them out a little as she muttered, "By Temural."

Temural?

That was an interesting god to invoke.

Temural and his sister, Saylah, were the children of Arius, the god of death and endings, and Serafina, the goddess of dreams and stars. Arius and Serafina were two of the six original First Gods. The four of them were often only whispered of by the beings of this realm. It was believed that even speaking their names could anger them and summon unfavorable outcomes.

"Are you going to eat?" he asked, eyes dipping to her still untouched plate.

She followed his gaze before looking back up at him.

Then she reached over and picked up the muffin, taking a bite.

He went still, watching her as she chewed that bite of the food *Razik* had given her. Surely that wasn't the reason. She simply liked baked goods more than eggs. And bacon. And toast.

Except then she *was* eating everything else, as if she'd needed to prove some point by starting with that godsdamn muffin.

Or maybe that bite of muffin had made her realize precisely how hungry she was.

The eggs. The bacon. The toast. Fruit and cheeses. She ate as though she hadn't had a decent meal in weeks.

"Which part of the kingdom did you say you were from?" Cethin asked, watching her warily because clearly he needed to visit the town and ensure the people there weren't godsdamn starving.

As if suddenly realizing what she was doing, she froze, a piece of bacon halfway to her lips. Amber eyes snapped to his as she said, "I didn't."

"I'm aware," he drawled. "That was me asking."

Her brow furrowed. "Then why not simply state the question?"

"Because direct questions seem to get me nowhere with you."

She huffed, dropping the bacon back onto her plate. Then she went rigid when the sound of footfalls echoed. She really was an anxious thing around…well, anyone.

Cethin already knew who was about to enter the dining room though, and despite the majority of his days starting this way, he was more than a little irritated at his time with her being interrupted.

Zayan appeared moments later, pausing briefly when he spotted her. His chin-length dark blond hair was tied back in a barely there ponytail, and his dark brown eyes skipped from her to Cethin.

"Good morning, your grace," he said tentatively. "Am I inter-rupting?"

"No," he sighed, because despite the irritation, it was the truth. The conversation with her was going nowhere other than in circles, but if she wanted to continue down this path, that was fine. He'd continue with her games. Gesturing to the male, he continued, "This is Zayan, Hand of the King. Zayan, this is tiny—"

"Kailia," she interjected quickly.

Fucking finally.

He almost muttered the words out loud.

"This is Kailia," he finished, watching her lips purse slightly as her name left his.

"It is a pleasure, Kailia," Zayan said with a nod of his head, studying her. "Did you two meet at the Esbat Festival?"

"We did," Cethin answered. "After the address to the Fae."

Zayan's smile was tight. Cethin had expected him to be over-joyed at his having a female at the breakfast table. This is what he and the advisory council had been pushing for, after all.

"And will we be seeing Kailia around the castle more often?" the Hand asked.

By Arius. He didn't need to be *that* painfully obvious. Then again, it did work in Cethin's favor with his current predicament.

"You will," he said simply, holding Kailia's stare the entire time. "We were finishing our meals before I showed her around the castle and grounds."

"Well, don't let me interfere," Zayan said quickly, taking a step back. "The matters I have can wait."

Gods, this female needed to stick around forever if this was all it was going to take to get Zayan to leave him the fuck alone for a few hours a day.

The male's steps were hurried as he left the room, and Kailia's features twisted into a glare while Cethin smirked back in satisfaction.

"Do you always lie to your advisors?" she asked sharply.

"Which part of what I said was a lie? You offered your name, and I confirmed we met last night at the festival."

"The part about seeing me around the castle more often."

Each word was slow and deliberate.

His chair scraped softly as he stood. "I believe after our coming negotiations this morning that will be the case."

"That's absurd."

"That's confidence," he corrected. "Now, I'm assuming you don't plan to eat any more so we can go on a walk?"

"I'm not walking around your castle with you."

"If you want that arrow back, you are."

He could swear the smoke swirled faster in those amber depths.

With a huff, she got to her feet. "Do you always manipulate people to get your way, king?"

He tilted his head in mock confusion. "My apologies. I thought you *wanted* the arrow back."

He was suddenly thankful she didn't have the fire gifts others from the Anala bloodline possessed. If she did, he was certain he'd be burning right now based on the look she was giving him.

"Shall we?" he asked when she said nothing. He gestured to the door at the other end of the hall. It would be a shorter path to the back gardens. Still within the wards, the gardens would leave her unable to move among her smoke and ashes. She wasn't leaving unless he allowed it.

Kailia stalked past him, and he fell into step beside her. Neither of them spoke for a minute as they made their way down a long corridor. Not until he said, "Tell me again why this *one* arrow is so important to you?"

"It's mine. That's all that matters," she retorted.

"But you can create more?"

"That's not the point."

"It most certainly is the point," he countered. "As previously discussed, those weapons are one of only two ways we've found to defeat an enemy."

"Then use the other way."

"You cannot—"

He didn't get to finish the thought. Not as he brought a hand to her lower back to guide her to the left since she didn't know where they were going. But the moment his fingertips grazed her back, she lurched away from him, her back against the opposite wall in the next blink. Her eyes were wide, one hand was wrapped around the hilt of a dagger at her thigh. She hadn't drawn it fully, but it was partially out of the sheath.

A castle guard had advanced, his hand on his weapon as well. The guard was halfway to them, but Cethin quickly waved him off as he continued to watch her.

"Nothing will hurt you here," he said carefully, watching for anything that would clue him in as to what had triggered such a response. When she remained silent, he pushed, "Kailia?"

"I…" Taking a shuddering breath, she straightened, shoving the blade back into the sheath before smoothing down her tunic. "I hate that you know my name."

He barked a laugh. "You prefer I continue calling you tiny fiend?"

"No," she retorted, stepping away from the wall. She jerked her chin to the left. "This way?"

He nodded slowly, still not entirely sure what had just happened, but she started down the hall, and he found himself following.

After several seconds of silence, he cleared his throat. "Back to the topic at hand, are you suggesting that I not use any means possible to protect the people in my care?"

"That is not what I said," she replied tightly, glancing at him as they came to another crossroads.

He gestured left once more, leaving plenty of space between them, and she nodded before continuing on.

"That is exactly what you said," he argued. "'Use the other method.' Why should I not use every method available to me?"

"Because my arrows are *not* available to you, nor am I."

He nearly tripped at the simplicity of her statement. She couldn't be serious. The lives of not just the Fae but hundreds of thousands in the kingdom could be at stake.

"What if they were *your* people?" he proposed, working to keep his tone casual as he pushed open a door to the back gardens.

Her brow creased in confusion. "I don't understand."

"I told you last night that I am in need of a wife. If you were queen and these people were also your people, what would you do to protect them? Would you care then?"

Her features smoothed out, slipping back into impassivity. "I'm not going to be your wife."

"You're not very good at negotiating."

"I'm excellent at negotiating. I see no benefit in this for me, whereas you seem to benefit greatly. Negotiations are usually mutually beneficial," she replied, following a path through the various plants and flowers.

"Then tell me what would make this beneficial for you, tiny fiend," he said, clasping his hands behind his back while they walked. "I assure you I could fulfill any manner of desires."

She huffed, and he wasn't sure if it was in amusement or annoyance.

Probably the latter.

"All I want is my arrow. That hardly seems enough to agree to a *marriage* over," she mused, stopping to finger a closed flower bud.

"It depends on how badly you want the arrow back, I suppose. You need to be here at night to see those," he added.

"What?" she asked, her fingers stilling as she looked up at him. Her hair was out of its plait, and midnight strands slipped over her shoulder with the movement.

He nodded at the closed buds. "They are star dahlias. They bloom in the evening, and stay open all night before closing to hide their secrets from the sun."

Her head tilted as she resumed studying them. "That makes sense for a kingdom that loves the night," she murmured, more to herself than to him.

She spoke as if she were new to the kingdom and were still learning all their intricacies and customs. Either she'd been incredibly sheltered her entire life, or…

Or she'd come over on one of the ships that had managed to pass through the Wards.

Son of a bitch.

It all fit.

Her sudden appearance. The uncertainty of their customs. Why she wouldn't say which town she was from.

He opened his mouth to ask her which ship she'd arrived on, then snapped it shut. She didn't notice. She was still enthralled with the star dahlias. It wouldn't do any good to ask her anyway. He'd had to coerce her into giving up her godsdamn name. She wasn't going to simply answer a question about where she'd come from.

But that was fine.

If anything, he was even more intrigued than he had been before. He had other ways to learn more about who she was and what secrets she was harboring. If she didn't want to give them over willingly, he'd take them from her.

He'd get what he wanted from her one way or another.

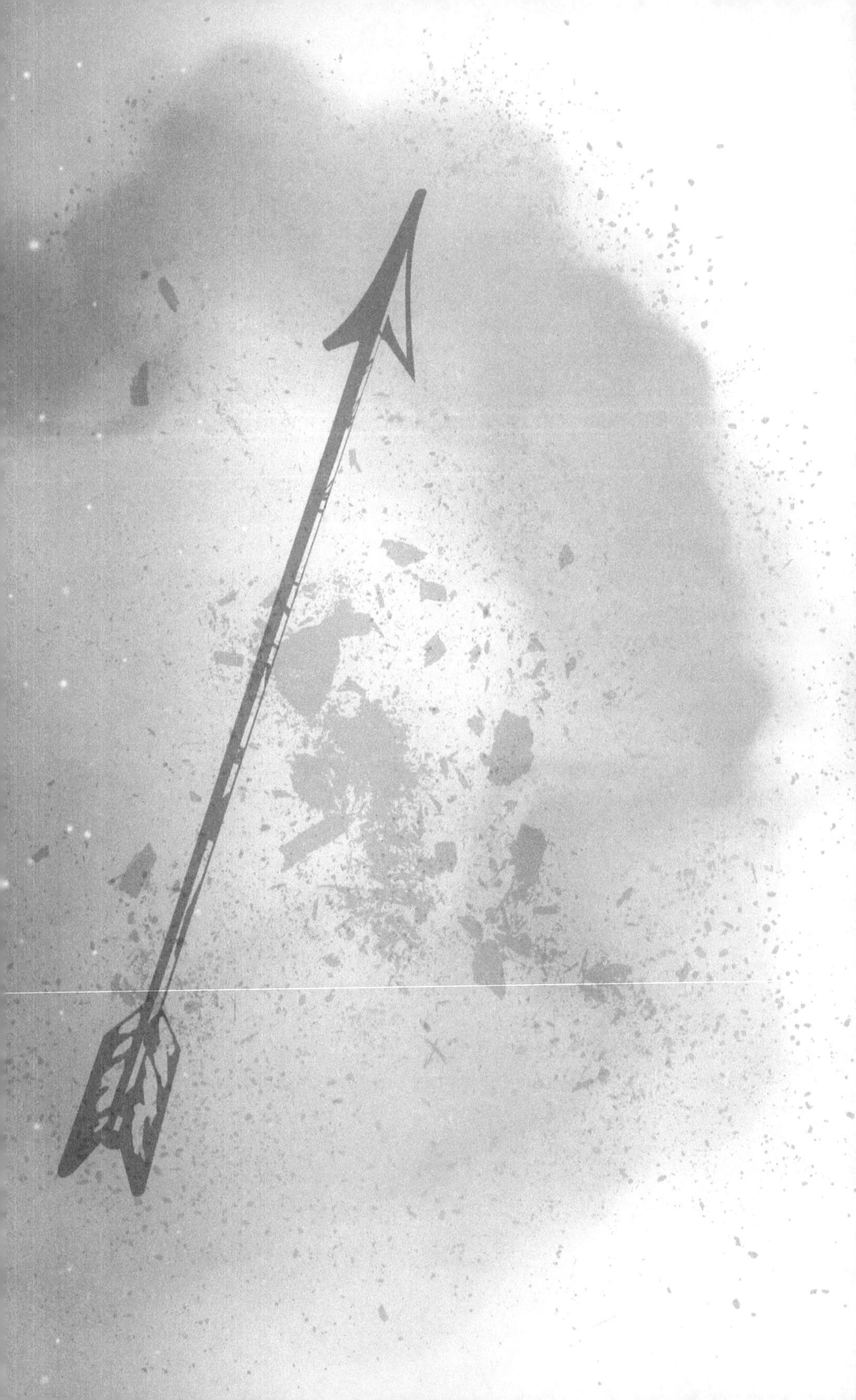

CHAPTER 8
KAILIA

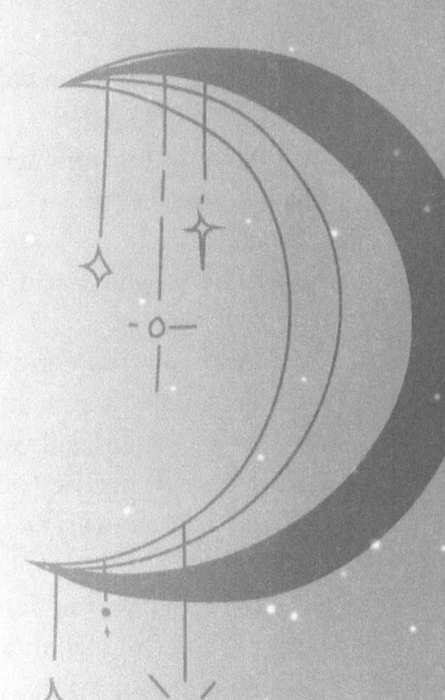

"**S**o how badly do you want it?" Cethin asked, pulling her from her thoughts.

Her hand dropped to her side, and she turned to face him fully. His hands were clasped behind his back, and his silver eyes were alight with something new. Something she didn't quite understand.

"How badly do I want what?" she asked.

"Your arrow returned," he clarified. "What is it going to take to convince you of my proposal?"

He couldn't be serious. What kind of king made a random female he'd met the night before his queen?

An arrogant one who was used to getting what he wanted by any means necessary, she supposed. Maybe she shouldn't be surprised at all. She was well aware of what the male was capable of.

Kailia turned to face him fully, looking him up and down. He didn't shift under the scrutiny. Instead, he was still. Too still. And looking at her with far too much…something she couldn't place. Social interactions and cues had never been her strength, but even with that weakness, she could swear his demeanor had shifted to something akin to predatory. And that she had plenty of experience with.

After several moments of silence that the king appeared unaffected by, she finally said, "You want me to be the queen of Avonleya?"

"That is what I said," he all but drawled.

Asshole.

"And you don't find that irresponsible or problematic? To ask a female you met last night to rule over your kingdom with you? What if I were trying to kill you?" she pushed, her irritation continuing to grow despite her best efforts to keep it tamped down. She knew better than to let her emotions gain so much control. She was trained better than this.

His lips tipped up into an arrogant smirk that only infuriated her more. "You can't kill me, tiny fiend."

That fucking name.

It was ridiculous, and she certainly didn't want it to spread, which is why she'd finally given up her name when he'd been about to introduce her as such to his Hand.

"Stabbing you wasn't all that difficult," she quipped dryly, turning away from him. Her fingers curled into the hem of her tunic. She needed to get out of here so she could get out of these clothes and change into her dress.

He hummed in response. "Stabbing is vastly different from killing, wouldn't you agree?"

She tsked in annoyance. As if she didn't know the difference between the two.

"Something to say?" he pushed, and then she felt his fingers brush through her hair. It was barely a touch, but it was enough to make her tense. At least she didn't reach for her dagger this time. That had almost been a disaster inside the castle. Thankfully Cethin had waved off the sentinels, or she would have surely ended up in the castle cells.

Pushing down every urge to do something violent, she took a measured step back from him. He said nothing as he observed the move. Thankfully, he let her set that boundary and didn't close the distance she put between them. She'd picked up on the fact he was intentionally pushing her to react, but at least he appeared to have some kind of awareness when someone was on an edge.

The king once again clasped his hands behind his back, his head tilting slightly while he continued to watch her. Waiting. Studying.

She hated being on this side of things, but she should have expected the sovereign to be well-trained. Not like she was, and certainly not in the same manner as she had been. He clearly had no issues with physical touch or reading social cues.

And he was still waiting for her response.

"You didn't answer my question," she finally said, her toes curling in her boots. Those needed to go too. "What kind of king brings a female he's known less than a day to his side to rule his kingdom?"

"Plenty of royalty do the same, Kailia," he said, and the use of her name was a little jarring. His features had darkened with the words, and she was pretty sure she'd struck some kind of sore spot with her last words. She just didn't understand why.

"Many a prince and princess are betrothed upon birth. Some even before conception. Many never meet until it is time to wed and produce an heir," he continued. He paused, those silver irises once again sweeping over her. "I suppose the same concerns could be said for them. Would you agree?"

"That doesn't assuage the concerns," she countered.

"Fair point," he said, the new tension in his shoulders easing some. "Either way, that is not an issue in this case. Our…arrangement would make you the queen in title only. You would have no say in rulings or how the kingdom is run."

"Yet I am to protect the people as my own? Use my magic to keep people safe that are not actually my people?"

His brow arched. "Do you want them to be your people? You are sending mixed signals here, tiny fiend."

"No," she snapped. "I do not wish for that. All I wish for is my arrow, followed by the freedom to leave this place."

He moved then, taking long strides as he brushed past her, which forced her to take two steps to his one in order to keep up. As though he suddenly realized just that, he slowed his pace, leading her along the garden path.

"I answered your question. I think it only fair you answer one of mine," Cethin said thoughtfully, gesturing to the right to guide her deeper into the gardens. They'd taken so many turns and he'd distracted her enough, she wasn't entirely sure she could find her way back easily. "That arrow must have more significance than just belonging to you. Simply create more."

"It is not that simple," she retorted, immediately stilling as the words left her lips.

Cethin paused a few steps ahead when he realized she was no longer at his side. He turned to face her, a hand coming to his jaw. Rubbing at it, he was clearly trying to hide his smile with his thumb, but she saw it. He was obviously pleased with what he'd learned.

"Tell me more about that, tiny fiend," he said.

He was entirely focused on her, everything about him intent. She wasn't sure she'd ever had someone look at her like that. Like she held the answers to something he was desperate to know. All because of her arrows?

She cleared her throat, continuing to walk and striding past him. He followed her this time, no longer guiding and letting her choose her own path. He said nothing for the next several minutes, waiting until she was good and truly lost among the fucking plants and flowers. Waited until she turned to him in annoyance.

Her hands clenching into fists at her sides, she spun on him. "Tell me the way out of here."

He didn't bother to hide his smirk this time. "The way out is to agree to my proposal, Kailia."

"I'm not going to wed you, king."

"No?"

"No."

"Then tell me more about your arrows and magic."

"If I do so, do you agree to tell me the way out?"

"If you tell me why it is not so simple to create new arrows, I will tell you a way out of the gardens," he agreed.

She didn't miss his wording, but if he got her out of this maze of plants, she'd take the offering. She felt far too exposed out here.

"Fine," she agreed, and then eyed the hand he extended to her. He'd already sliced his palm, blood dripping and waiting for her to make the proposed bargain binding. "I don't need a bargain with you on this."

He blinked in surprise. "You are simply going to take my word?"

"If you go back on your word, that damages your character more than mine. You're the one attempting to convince me to marry you," she replied, bending down to unlace her boots. She'd had it with the cumbersome things.

"That's fair," he said after a moment, watching her slide her feet from the footwear that reached nearly to her knees.

Stuffing the socks inside the boots, her eyes fell closed at the cool stone path beneath her bare feet. Her toes flexed, feeling exponentially more grounded.

She gave herself a few seconds to relish the feeling before she opened her eyes and continued on her way. If he wanted her answer, he'd have to follow, and a glance over her shoulder found him doing just that. He'd also swiped up the boots she'd left behind, carrying them in one of his large hands as he caught up to her.

"My magic is tied to the arrows," she said, not looking at him. "Without the full set, I cannot create more. It's why I collected the arrowheads that night. I've never had an arrow disintegrate like that. But since that night, my magic hasn't worked properly."

"You were moving through your smoke and ashes fine last night," the king replied skeptically.

"Just because you can't perceive a weakness doesn't mean it's not there," she said sharply. "My power is not refilling like it should. I cannot linger in my ashes as long as I once could. I can't travel as great a distance. It took me far longer than it should have to get from Shira Forest to Aimonway. It will only get worse without that arrow. Does that explanation satisfy your curiosity, king?"

"Yes, but it also raises more questions," Cethin mused.

"I agreed to answer one. Now fulfill your end of the deal."

He nodded, extending a hand to her once more. With his palm

now healed, there was only a smear of blood there. She looked from his hand to his face, her expression flat while he smiled a satisfied thing that said he'd achieved something.

"I can Travel us out," Cethin coaxed.

"We can walk," she countered.

"The agreement was I'd tell you a way out of the gardens."

"And you're doing a terrible job at convincing me to marry you by tricking me."

"There are no tricks, tiny fiend," he said, his eyes once more bright with something she didn't understand.

"Unfortunately, I do not have the entire day to guide you through these gardens," he said. "I have other matters to attend to."

Her mouth dropped open. "You are the one who insisted on this walk."

"I did," he agreed. "And I got part of what I wanted. You are obviously not going to agree to my other proposal at this time—"

"Ever," Kailia corrected. "I will not agree to that proposal ever."

He made a show of tipping his head from side to side as if debating her words. "We shall have to agree to disagree on that matter. For now, I will escort you from the gardens by Traveling, or I can leave you here to find your own way back. However, know that the castle guard will not like an unknown female wandering the premises alone."

"You… I—" She spluttered, trying to collect her thoughts, and his godsdamn smile only widened. "You are as arrogant and heartless as the rumors claim, king," she finally managed to get out, each word laced with venom.

That smile of his vanished, replaced with something far more menacing. She'd seen death enough to know that was what lingered behind the look suddenly pinned on her. His hand snapped out, gripping hers and tugging her closer. Everything in her screamed at the contact, and she went rigid. If he noticed—and she was sure he did—he didn't appear to care. Instead, he bent down so his words brushed along her cheek as he whispered low and dark, "Believe the rumors, tiny fiend. Every single one is true."

Then she was being pulled through the air before he unexpectedly released her hand. She stumbled away from him, looking up into eyes where darkness now drifted among the silver. Briefly, she wondered when he'd dropped her boots. His gaze dipped to her other hand, and she had no idea when she'd pulled the dagger from its sheath, but she held the blade in the space between them.

His smile was all predator as his eyes darted to something over her shoulder. "The guards approach, Kailia. You have a choice to make. Make a new bargain with me or spend time in accommodations not nearly as comfortable as those provided last night."

"You cannot be serious," she said, panic creeping in. She couldn't be trapped here. The wards kept her from her magic, and being separated from her smoke and ashes was already taking its toll.

He clicked his tongue in admonishment. "Come now. I just told you all the rumors were true."

"Cethin, I—"

Something new flashed across his features. Something feral and wanton. Something she again didn't understand.

Whatever it was, he recovered quickly. His face twisted back into the harshness of seconds ago, and he took a single step towards her. She took one back, and the answering smirk was cruel.

"Agree to a bargain with me, and you can leave here," he proposed. "But decide quickly. Your fate hangs in the balance."

"I will not marry you."

"The bargain is that the next time our paths cross, these negotiations will go very differently."

She took the step towards him this time, the dagger still poised between them. "The next time our paths cross, I will stab you somewhere far more painful."

"Do we have an accord then?" he asked, his demeanor nothing but arrogance personified.

Her brow scrunched. "An accord for what? That I will stab you the next time I see you?"

"The bargain is that the next time our paths cross, you shall either agree to my proposal or stab me."

"Fine, we have an accord," she scoffed, slicing her dagger along her palm before throwing it at him. It flipped, blade over hilt, and Cethin caught it by the steel. Blood immediately seeped between his fingers, and he let it drop to the ground with a clatter, never once breaking her stare.

She braced herself for the touch, biting down on her grimace when he closed his fingers around hers. Their blood met, and she felt the telltale tingle of a Bargain Mark marring the flesh along the back of her shoulder.

He lifted his other hand, presumably to halt his advancing guard, but he still gripped her fingers, keeping their connection. He leaned in closer, forcing her to tip her head back to hold his stare. "See you soon, tiny fiend."

Her answering smile was pure vitriol. "You should pray to the gods that doesn't happen."

"No need. Either way, you'll end up back here. In a cell or at my side, it doesn't matter to me," he replied simply. So sure of how this was going to end. So certain he'd get what he wanted.

She'd make sure he regretted every moment of their time together.

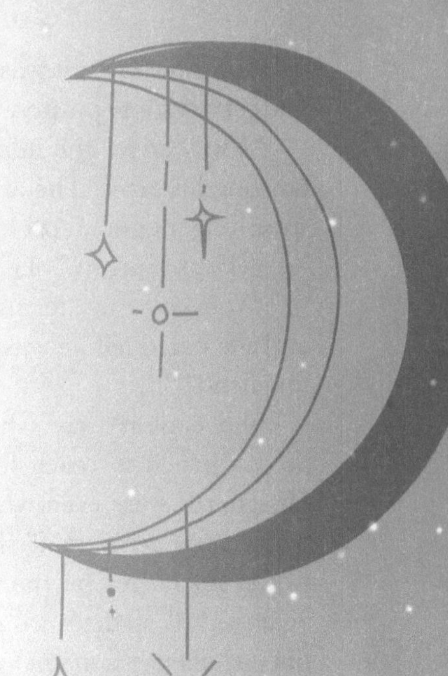

CHAPTER 9
KAILIA

"Y ou're going to leave me here?" she demanded.
True to his word, Cethin had Traveled them out of the gardens where they'd proceeded to make this stupid bargain. It was only now that she realized where exactly he'd Traveled them too.

They were at the front gates of the castle. A long bridge of steep steps stretched out before them, obscured by a wall of misty, dark fog. Looking over her shoulder, the castle towered above them. It was such a dark shade of grey, it was nearly black, but it shimmered slightly in the sunlight. It was nestled into the black Nightmist Mountains. Since Cethin had Traveled them directly inside after the Esbat Festival, she was just now taking in the structure up close.

The front of the castle had three separate archways, side by side, with various towers rising behind them and reaching towards the clear sky. More towers flanked the main ones, various buildings visible, but more than that were the winding stairs that led up to the building. They cascaded down, continuing to the stepped bridge before them. It spanned a ravine so deep, she was certain she wouldn't be able to see the bottom if she looked.

And now Cethin was depositing her at the front gates as if she had served some purpose for him and he was done with her.

"I was under the impression you wanted to leave," he drawled, crossing his arms. The action pulled at the fabric of his black tunic, stretching it tight across his arms and chest.

"*With* my arrow," she retorted, mirroring his stance.

"You know my terms for that to happen." Her eyes narrowed, and she could tell he was fighting another smirk. "Something to say, tiny fiend?"

She couldn't say what she wanted to, and even though her fingers itched to reach for her dagger, she couldn't do that either. His guards were everywhere, and despite his promises that nothing would hurt her here, if she harmed their king, she was certain that would no longer be the case. Her skills were well-honed, but one against…all of them would still be a challenge. Probably enjoyable, but a challenge nonetheless.

When she remained silent, his features flickered in irritation. "Then, yes. I'm going to leave you here. I'm a busy male, and I've given you as much of my time as I can today."

"Given me— I… *You* brought me here," she gritted out, trying to keep from losing control completely, while simultaneously trying to figure out what he was playing at.

"For a purpose. Which you declined. Now I have other things to tend to."

She could feel all the sentinels' eyes on them, but the only thing she could focus on was Cethin. The harsh mask of indifference. Cold and unreadable. All because he didn't get what he wanted from her.

"Fine," she finally retorted, squaring her shoulders. "But one would think the least you could do after forcing me to your home is escort me back to town."

"Once you cross the wards, you can use your smoke and ashes to go wherever you please," he said dryly. "I already stated I do not have any more time to give you today."

"And *I* already stated that my magic is not working properly without my fucking arrow," she spat. His brow arched at the cursing, and she could swear amusement flashed across his silver irises before they became obscured by his dark magic once more. "You said last night it would take hours to walk here from the city center."

"It will," he affirmed. "If your power is as weakened as you claim, once you cross the bridge, you'll find stables. The horses don't like the trek along the steps, so they are kept on the other side of the ravine. I'll send word to have one waiting for you." He paused, then added. "Along with an escort."

"I don't need an escort," she snapped.

"Yet you just requested that *I* escort you moments ago. Again with the mixed messages, tiny fiend."

Kailia was more than done with the king for the day. Without another word, she turned her back on him and stalked past the guards.

"Careful on the bridge, Kailia," Cethin called after her. "The steps are rather steep, and you don't want to meet what lives in the ravine."

She ignored him, carefully navigating the steps of the bridge. It was wide enough for three or four people to walk side by side. Then again, four might be pushing it.

Kailia stayed in the center, fighting the urge to look over the side and see how deep the canyon went. And maybe spot what Cethin had referred to. He'd likely been running his mouth in an attempt to scare her. Keep her there longer. Coerce her into doing what he wanted.

Little did he know she'd faced far bigger monsters than whatever pets he kept in his chasm.

When she reached the other side, there was a horse and an escort waiting for her as promised. She waved them off in refusal, silently cursing Cethin. Surprisingly, they let her go without a fuss, telling her that if she followed the main road, it would eventually lead right into the city.

The walk did indeed take the hours Cethin claimed it would. She didn't really mind though. She enjoyed the quiet moments to herself. Time to think. Time to evaluate. Time to plan.

It was well past high noon when she reached the city center

where all this had started the night before. Grateful she'd eaten as much of the king's food as she did this morning, Kailia slowed, trying to avoid being touched. It was busier than she'd expected it to be. It appeared most had spent the entire night celebrating Esbat and then sleeping off the festivities. From what she could tell, most of the bustle was people taking down their merchant stands from the night before.

She'd paused on the outskirts, observing and trying to decide where to go next, when her gaze landed on a familiar face. Not familiar in that she knew her, but familiar in that she'd seen the female before. That morning, in fact.

The female's dark brown hair was half up, half down, and she was deep in conversation with some males that Kailia vaguely recognized. She'd seen them around Cethin at times during her scouting. Members of the Cadre. She wasn't really interested in them though. Not right now anyway.

As if the female could feel her eyes on her, she turned, looking right at Kailia where she stood on the corner. The female—Wren, that was what she'd said her name was—gave her a tentative smile, lifting her hand in a small wave. Kailia didn't return the gesture, and she took a step back when the two males lifted their heads to see what had drawn Wren's attention.

They asked Wren a question, and she shook her head, saying something in return. The one with long blond hair laughed while the one with shorter black hair and tattoos up his neck whipped his head back to Kailia. A moment later, all three were making their way over to her.

She briefly debated trying to lose them in the crowd, or even disappearing into her power, but she *was* trying to conserve it. It didn't refill as quickly as the Fae, and she always had to be mindful of that. So she stayed put, trying to decide what this type of social situation was going to call for.

"Hello again," Wren said as the trio reached her.

The words were kind but hesitant, likely because Kailia hadn't said a single word to her at the breakfast table. So she definitely should say something now, but when she didn't, Wren filled the silence.

"Anyway, did you need help finding something? Or some place? You're new to Aimonway, right?"

"She is definitely new. We've never seen her before," the blond male cut in. "Wren here tells us you were at the castle this morning. Cethin usually keeps his bedmates sequestered to his floor."

He arched a brow, letting the words hang there as if waiting for an explanation. But she didn't owe anyone anything, especially not a male she'd only observed from afar until now.

"Don't be a dick, Jarek," the other male cut in. "She wasn't his bedmate. She had a room of her own last night. The guards were under orders to report immediately to Cethin if she attempted to leave the castle grounds."

Kailia held back her scoff. And he'd tried to argue he wasn't holding her hostage.

Arrogant ass.

"Her own room *and* a seat at the breakfast table?" the first male —Jarek—said, intrigue sparking across his face. "Tell us more, Bram."

The male rolled his eyes. "There's nothing more to tell."

Jarek's gaze went back to Kailia. "Oh, I'm sure that's not the case at all, is it?"

The way those dark eyes bored into her told Kailia all she needed to know. This male knew she'd stabbed their king last night, but for whatever reason, he wasn't calling her out. He'd likely try to use the information against her in some way. That was what she would do.

"Jarek, stop," Wren cut in, elbowing the male in the side. "Go be useful somewhere else. You too, Bram."

Jarek chuckled under his breath as Bram grabbed his arm, tugging him along. "I'm sure we'll see you again soon," Jarek called with a wink, walking backward as he went.

Kailia stared after him, pulling her gaze from them when Wren started talking again. "Sorry about them. They mean well," she said, shifting on her feet. "But did you need help with something? I can try—"

"A dress," Kailia blurted out, wincing internally because that is not how she meant to enter this conversation. But the pants. And the tunic. And the morning in general. It was all wearing on her. She wanted a dress she could move in, and then she wanted to find her own bed.

She smiled, hoping it was kind and welcoming, as she said more calmly, "I was hoping to find a new dress before I take my leave."

Wren nodded slowly, clearly caught off guard by the random first words Kailia had blurted out. Because who wouldn't be? This is precisely why social situations were not for her.

"There are a few places nearby. I can show you where they are. I can't stay long, but—"

"I don't want to inconvenience you," Kailia cut in. "You can simply point me in the right direction."

"It's not an inconvenience," Wren said. "They're just a few streets over." Kailia nodded, falling into step beside her. She didn't miss the glance down, so she wasn't surprised when the female asked, "Do you need footwear as well?"

"No," Kailia said simply.

Wren only lasted a few seconds before she was filling the silence. "Sorry about Jarek and Bram. They are good males despite... Well, their manners."

Kailia hummed. She didn't care about the males or their manners. She never had high expectations of males to begin with.

They were turning a corner, and suddenly there were fingers at her elbow. In the next breath, Kailia spun, shoving the person up against the window of a small pastry shop, her lip curled back in a snarl.

The female's eyes were wide, and she held her hands up, trying to placate her. "I'm sorry!" she cried. "I didn't mean to startle you. I was only trying to get your attention."

"It's okay," Wren said gently, as if she had experience talking someone down. "That's Marissa. She owns a crystal and jewelry shop with her sister."

Kailia looked back at the female, recognition dawning. She'd spoken to her last night.

Suddenly realizing she was still holding the female against the wall, Kailia dropped her hands, taking several steps back. Patrons of the pastry shop were all watching, sugary treats and steaming cups of tea forgotten.

"My apologies," Kailia murmured. "I don't… I apologize."

Marissa's tight smile betrayed her nerves, but she said, "It's okay. I wanted to give you this."

She slowly reached into her pocket, pulling out a necklace. Black leather cord. Blue crystal dangling from it.

"I remember you admiring it last night at the festival," Marissa went on, her confidence growing with each word. "I wanted to give it to you."

"Why?" Kailia asked. She might not understand social situations, but she did understand that nothing was free. There were always strings attached.

"It's just a gift," Marissa insisted, holding it out to her. When Kailia didn't reach for it, her smile faltered. "I truly mean no ill-will. I was packing up my stall and saw you across the way at the same moment I was placing this necklace into a pouch. I trust the signs the Fates send my way and believe you're meant to have it."

Unsure what to do, Kailia glanced at Wren, who gave her a small shrug. Which was not helpful in the slightest.

Marissa was still holding the necklace out to her, and Kailia just wanted this interaction to be over. Reminding herself to move slowly, she took the necklace and offered a tight smile. "Thank you."

Marissa's face lit up. "You're welcome," she cooed brightly. "I just know it's meant for you."

Then she practically skipped off back to her stall, and Kailia was left holding the necklace awkwardly.

"They really are kind females," Wren offered, stepping closer. "Want me to help you put it on?"

"Have they ever gifted you jewelry?" Kailia countered.

Wren laughed. "No, but that doesn't mean they aren't genuine. May I?"

She reached for the necklace, and not wanting this to get any more uncomfortable, Kailia nodded, handing it over. She pulled her hair over her shoulder while Wren secured the necklace, clearly taking care not to touch her. The blue crystal sat on her chest above her breasts. It was cool against her skin, and she could swear it was pulsing faintly.

But she didn't dabble in the ways of Witches and their gifts with plants, crystals, and the stars. They were too close to the Fates, and she wasn't about to question their ways. The only fates she cared about were hers and her enemies.

Wren started walking once more, and Kailia followed. It wasn't even a few seconds before Wren said, "You know, I never did get your name?"

It was kind and subtle enough, and what did she have to lose at this point? The king already knew her name.

"Kailia," she answered.

"It's nice to meet you, Kailia," Wren replied. "I'm helping with the Fae that are relocating to Aimonway, so if you need anything— Wait, Razik said you're not Fae, but you *are* new in town. So if you're staying and need anything, just let me know."

Kailia could hardly keep up with the female as she prattled on, but she'd homed in on the subject she was interested in.

Razik.

"How does Razik know I'm not Fae?" Kailia asked, knowing that the swirling in her eyes should make it more than obvious. Either Wren was oblivious, or Kailia made her that nervous.

Wren huffed a laugh and rolled her eyes. "He spends hours in books researching everything and anything. I truly don't know how he remembers half the things he's read over the centuries."

"And you've been with him that long?"

Her eyes went wide, and she glanced over at Kailia. "By Anahita, no. I've known Razik for a little over a decade, and I've been his Source for nearly as long."

"His Source? By choice?"

She nodded. "He'd never force a bond. Not with his past."

"His past?" Kailia asked, those two words sparking her interest.

Wren's brow creased. "Is not mine to tell."

"Understandable. So you are his Source and his partner?"

Her features smoothed out, mirth entering her eyes. "We share a bed from time to time, but we are not bound to each other in that way. We do not share a Union Mark or a bond outside of the Source bond."

"My apologies. I just assumed…"

"Most do," she reassured, clearly not taking any offense. "Razik lets them assume because he doesn't care."

"But you do?"

She paused then, and Kailia immediately wondered if she'd said the wrong thing. This whole time she'd been mentally congratulating herself on carrying on a normal conversation. She was pretty sure this was the first time Wren had let silence extend longer than a few seconds.

"He's very protective," she finally said, flashing her another bright smile.

Kailia wasn't sure how that answered her question.

"So you are Razik's Source, and he is…what to Cethin?" Kailia ventured, hoping that was an okay thing to ask.

"Nothing," Wren said with a shrug. "Just the way he likes it. He's part of the Cadre, and his uncle is the Commander of all the Avonleyan forces."

"But he was in the castle at the breakfast table. Surely he's more than that?" Kailia pushed.

Wren stopped, turning to face her fully. "You were also in the castle at the breakfast table. Was Jarek right? There is more to it?"

Kailia stared back, familiar irritation creeping up her spine. This female was… Well, she was very good at making someone feel at ease to get information. Kailia used manipulation all the time. Apparently, so did Wren. If it weren't so fucking clever, she'd be impressed. Instead, she was annoyed at having missed something so obvious.

Wren didn't push for an answer though. Instead, she flashed another warm smile before turning and pulling open the door to a shop. She didn't wait for Kailia, and it wasn't until she peered at the shop window that she realized they'd come to a dress shop of sorts. Judging by what was on display though, Kailia knew this was *not* the kind of shop she was going to find anything in. It was all lace and frills and corsets. Nothing she could move freely in.

Sighing, she pulled the door open once more, a bell jingling faintly as she stepped inside. It smelled inviting—vanilla and spices—and Wren was already talking to a female at the counter.

She didn't really *need* a dress. She had plenty at the flat where she was staying. The entire purpose of this was to get information about Razik. Instead, it had become a fiasco of sorts.

But she needed to know about the male. It had taken everything in her to hide her utter shock when he'd strode into the dining room that morning.

Because she'd seen him before, and not just since she'd stepped foot in Avonleya.

Well, not *him* exactly.

Before she'd come to Avonleya, she'd been stuck on the continent across the Edria Sea. There were far worse places to be confined. She would know. She'd been trapped in such a place for two decades. But while she was on the continent, she'd found her way to an Oracle.

Each continent had an Oracle. They were bound to their continent as part of their role, and they were regarded as highly as the gods were. Maybe even more so, considering you could at least try to see an Oracle. It was excessively difficult to summon a god or goddess to this realm. Kailia wasn't even sure it was possible.

The Oracles of the realms were often sought when one was desperate for answers or guidance. Or she sought you out when you were running from truths and destinies. Either way, if you encountered an Oracle, you were going to be given information that left you with a choice to make.

But to even get to the Oracle across the sea, she had to come to you, or you had to try your luck in the Witch Kingdoms. The High Witch was vicious and formidable, and with her various covens throughout the kingdoms, most never made it past the borders of their territory. More than that, Kailia assumed the Oracle was female because most Witches were. But that was where the conundrum came in. Not many knew what their true identity was. In fact, so few had seen an Oracle, that some considered them to be myths of old. If you found yourself in the Oracle's presence, they appeared to you as something other. A person from your past. A creature that would greatly impact your future. Someone or something that would play a crucial role in your life—for better or worse.

She knew the Oracles were real because she'd dared to venture into the Witch Kingdoms. Dared to square off with the High Witch. Dared to request an audience. And when she'd finally wandered into the dark passages of the Oracle's home, she'd been met by a tall male with piercing sapphire eyes, unruly brown hair, and a muscular build. She hadn't known who he was—had never met or seen him before—and until recently, had never seen him again. Even then, he was scarce, and learning information had been difficult. Beyond his position in the Cadre and his name being Razik Greybane, she didn't know much. She'd been here half a year, and she'd only seen him from afar a handful of times. She certainly had not expected to find him strolling into the dining room this morning.

The Oracle had appeared to her as Razik, and now she was desperately trying to understand how a member of the Avonleyan king's forces was going to have such a profound impact on her future and the outcome of her plans. Was he going to help her? Hinder her? Did he have information she needed?

"Kailia?"

She blinked, finding both Wren and the shop owner staring at her. "Yes?"

"Fiona asked if you were looking for something in particular," Wren said, her smile pointed.

"No. I mean, yes. Black, but I just remembered I need to be somewhere," Kailia said, backing towards the entry door. "I appreciate your time. Both of you."

"Kailia, wait—" Wren started, but she didn't get to finish.

Kailia was gone, wrapped up in smoke and ashes. The scent of her power was like coming home, and she relished the freedom.

She'd go to the flat she was staying in, put on her usual attire, and plan—

Except something was wrong.

The ashes yanked on her, wrapping around her wrists and ankles as if they were manacles. Her power thrashed and bucked against a force that was pulling them elsewhere. She'd never experienced anything like this. Never had her magic take over. Control her.

But she was being pulled through the air, spinning so quickly she couldn't get her bearings. Not as she was deposited beside a lake in a heap of limbs. She quickly straightened, brushing at her pants and tunic as she took in the sunny sky. The sparkling blue waters. The phantom figures floating above the ground, gold swords in hand. Numerous warriors with weapons drawn.

And across the way stood Razik Greybane with the Avonleyan king at his side.

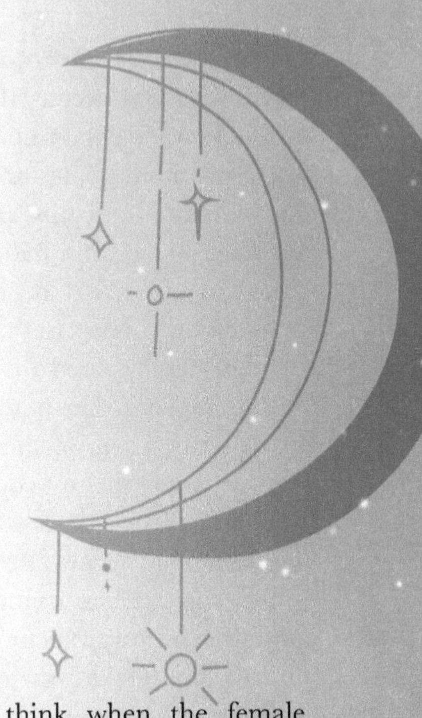

CHAPTER 10
RAZIK

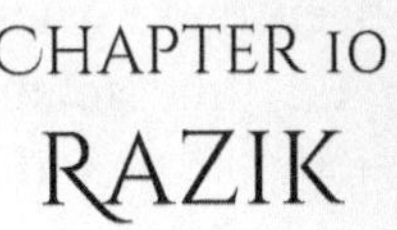

hank the gods.

That was all Razik could think when the female appeared across from them, right on the shores of Lake Noctus. And that was saying something because the gods didn't deserve his gratitude.

The gods didn't deserve shit.

She seemed confused about being there though. She hadn't landed gracefully on her feet. Instead, it looked like she'd fallen out of a plume of smoke and ashes. It wasn't until she'd gotten back to her feet, dusting off her pants, that she'd realized she stood among danger. It wasn't until her gaze landed on Cethin that her eyes narrowed, features twisting into something filled with fury and loathing. *That* he understood completely.

Her bow appeared in her hand, two arrows a moment later. She stared at the two of them the entire time as she nocked the arrows, lifted her weapon, and released them. They found their targets, and Razik would be lying if he said he wasn't impressed. Because how in the fuck? Who had trained her?

They'd been battling the phantom creatures for the last hour, Cethin once again drawing their entire attention and forcing the rest of them to keep his royal ass safe. The only reason he was here to begin with was because he'd shown up at the Greybane Estate and insisted on speaking to him. Asking questions about Ash Riders and these phantom beings and something else that, quite frankly, Razik had forgotten because he tried not to listen to Cethin whenever possible. But Cethin had been there when word had arrived of the attack, and there'd been no time to argue with him about the stupidity of coming to the fight, so here they were.

The female fired off another set of arrows, the phantoms all taking notice of her now. Irritated hisses echoed among the sounds of battle. A group of them split from the horde, half a dozen going her way while the rest continued to make their way to Cethin.

"Shit. Everyone needs to protect Kailia," Cethin said, his eyes on the female, who was currently firing off another arrow.

"I know you're trying to impress her and all, but she's not the one who needs protecting here," Razik retorted, drawing up more dragon fire. He'd been conserving his power as much as possible, which was a pain in the ass. Having to concentrate so hard on *not* using too much of his power was distracting.

"She does need protection, you ass," Cethin growled back, holding his sword as though he was going to accomplish anything with it. "She told me her power isn't working properly right now, which is affecting her ability to conjure arrows."

"Why isn't her magic working properly?"

"Does now really seem like the time for this conversation?" he replied, parroting words similar to what Razik had thrown at him the last time they were in this same situation.

Rather than punching the king in the godsdamn face, Razik released a flare of his power on two advancing phantoms, feeding his flames and feeling his power drain with every passing second. Their keening wails sounded, the ashes that remained in the wake swirling around them and settling onto their clothing like peppered snow.

"Fallon and Ariadne!" Cethin bellowed, the two females looking to their king from where they were stationed on the right flank closest to the female. The female Cethin was suddenly very protective over. "Cover her," he ordered, pointing in Kailia's direction.

They didn't question the orders, immediately sprinting to the other female as they dodged and parried gold swords. The moment they reached her side, Kailia tossed them each something small and dark.

"What is she—" Razik started, but the question died on his tongue as the female Cadre members struck out, whatever they were holding sinking deep into two of the phantom creatures. Their heads tipped back, white wisps pouring from their mouths.

"She gave them the arrowheads," Cethin said, his shock evident in the words.

The creatures also seemed to realize what was happening, more of them breaking away to converge on the females. They ducked and spun, throwing the arrowheads like daggers as Kailia fired off more arrows. Ariadne swiped up two more arrowheads from the ground, tossing them to Fallon before retrieving two more, phantom spirits being decimated one after another.

"Do we…help them?" Cethin asked, his sword arm having lowered to his side.

"Does it look like they need help?" Razik grumbled. "We help everyone else."

There were still warriors in the midst of battle. There was still brethren blood being spilled. Death was still taking and devouring good males and females who were fighting against beings they could never beat.

"We need her weapons," Razik said, sending a wave of dragon fire to a group of overwhelmed warriors.

"I'm working on it," Cethin grunted back, sending his own magic to try and create a shield between their forces and the beings. The beings simply brushed it aside, but it did slow them down, if only for a moment. "We need to call a retreat for the forces. Get as many of them to us as possible, then a shield of dragon fire so we can move as one towards Kailia until this is handled."

That wasn't a terrible idea. Razik hated that Cethin was the one who'd come up with it, but it would save as many of their people as possible. The issue was that it put the entire burden of victory on the females.

"Or," Razik gritted out, "you shield our forces, and I shift, taking out these fuckers from the sky."

His dragon fire couldn't penetrate the dark magic Cethin possessed, and it would take less of his power to rain down targeted attacks from the sky rather than a massive wave of power. But the problem was the phantoms being able to break through, which would leave Cethin vulnerable.

"We don't have time for that," Cethin argued. "Call a retreat, Greybane!"

They were wasting valuable time arguing about this, which was costing more warriors their lives.

Razik surveyed the battlefield before them, making a choice that he might regret later.

Sounding the retreat signal, he then shifted. Not just summoning his wings, but transforming into his full dragon form. With scales as dark as Cethin's magic, he flapped his black wings, the talons on the ends glinting in the sun. With his vertical pupils, everything was sharper. Even the edges of the phantom beings seemed more solid.

He stretched his neck, releasing another roar to tell the warriors to move their asses before he twisted in the air, circling tightly above Cethin. Seeing some phantoms rushing for him, Razik loosed a stream of black flames, keeping the fire as tight and as controlled as he could. Warriors gave them a wide berth, Cethin's power arching over them in an attempt to give them more time. Still some fell as they made their retreat. Still the females fought near the lake. Still Razik rained down black fire, feeling his magic drain more and more with each onslaught.

Knowing he couldn't keep this up forever, he widened the radius of the circle he was keeping, soaring as low as he could. A ring of fire followed, encircling Cethin and the forces and keeping the phantoms on the other side. As warriors neared, Razik parted the fire enough for them to pass.

Fallon had caught on to what he was doing, and she left Ariadne to keep up with Kailia while she ran to the warriors who were struggling. There were a handful of the phantoms left, their dying wails seeming to echo around them until finally there was silence as the last one fell. The final kill went to Kailia, not that Razik had been keeping track or anything.

The moment the last creature drifted away in white wisps and ashes, Razik let the ring of black flames extinguish. He immediately shifted, dropping to the ground halfway between Cethin and the females.

Relief was palpable among the forces, and many collapsed to the ground, weapons clattering, as they fought to catch their breath and keep their composure. They hadn't lost as many as last time, but even one loss was too many. They were friends. They had families and loved ones. Some children would now know life with one less person to care about them; some children only had one of those people to begin with and now they had no one.

Razik barked orders to start Traveling the wounded back to the castle. Turning to the females, he found Ariadne and Fallon handing what he assumed were the arrowheads back to Kailia. They were speaking, but Kailia didn't seem to be paying any attention. Her stare was aimed across the way, and when Razik followed it, he found it on Cethin once again. His gaze was just as fixed on hers, a smirk as arrogant as he was tilted on his lips. Razik didn't know what the fuck was going on between the two of them, but he did know this was not the place for… Well, whatever the fuck that was.

Planning to simply ignore the king like he usually did, he turned and began making his way to his Cadre family. He offered words of encouragement to warriors as he passed them, moving slowly. Fallon and Ariadne met him, Kailia still several feet away.

"Did you keep any of them?" Razik asked, his voice low, but they knew what he meant.

Fallon shook her head, her blonde hair half out of her plait from the fight. "She demanded every single one back. We tried to ask her about them, but she didn't say anything. Only made them disappear within her power. She's…"

She trailed off, ending with a shrug.

"An excellent fighter though," Ariadne offered, pushing back the longer portion of her hair. There were splatters of gold on her brown skin and across both females' leathers. "If she's sticking around, she should be watched for the Cadre."

"If she's sticking around, I don't think it's to join our forces," Razik said flatly as Cethin stalked past them, still homed in on Kailia.

The females both turned, watching the king cut a path to her. Kailia didn't move an inch. Her feet were planted, shoulders squared, and hands loose at her sides. Razik swallowed his amusement at making the king come to her.

Cethin stopped directly in front of her, and the way they were standing, Razik had a perfect view of both of their features. The king's gaze raked over her from head to toe before he leaned in and reached for a pendant of some sort hanging from her neck. Even in the bustle of the battle aftermath, Razik could hear them perfectly with his enhanced hearing.

"Pretty necklace," Cethin drawled. "Where'd you get it, tiny fiend?"

This time, Razik didn't hide his huff of laughter because even he could hear the hint of jealousy in his words.

Kailia finally moved then, and so did Razik and the females. They were running as Kailia struck, the movement a blur that happened too fast. One moment she was still, glaring up at Cethin; the next, she had her hand wrapped around the hilt of the king's own dagger, and the blade shoved into Cethin's thigh.

"Fucking Sargon!" Razik barked, reaching them within seconds. He looped his arm around Kailia's waist, lifting her off the ground and pulling her away from the king.

If he thought she was violent on the battlefield, it was nothing compared to what happened next.

An ear-piercing shriek of what he could only describe as panicked madness pierced the air.

Kailia was flailing in his hold. A hold he tightened as her limbs kicked and struck out at all angles. Her body swirled, as if she was trying to leave in her smoke, but she didn't go anywhere, as though her magic indeed wasn't working properly.

"Kailia!" Cethin yelled, his eyes wide. He tried to take a step towards them, but Fallon and Ariadne stopped him, the former pressing a hand to his leg where blood was dripping in a steady stream to the ground.

Kailia tried to move in her power again, and when it still didn't work, she switched tactics, still screaming as if she was the one who had been stabbed. Scratch that. She was carrying on as if she were dying. Those ashes she wielded became something much more solid, dragging along his body like claws. He was already bare from the waist up from his shift, and now he was bleeding too. Not only that, she was tearing her own clothing to shreds in the process.

"By Arius and Serafina, calm down," he grunted, jostling her as he tried to get a better grip while simultaneously trying to keep her from going for the daggers strapped to her thighs. She only twisted and flailed and screamed more.

"Put her down!" Cethin demanded, breaking free of Fallon and Ariadne and stalking over to him as though he wasn't bleeding all over the place.

But Razik twisted away from him, holding Kailia out of reach. His other hand shot out, fisting into the front of Cethin's tunic. "She stabbed you in front of your forces. People who would die for you. Some who *did* die today. I'm not going to put her down and release her. Get your head out of your ass and be a godsdamn king," he growled, the words low so they stayed between them.

Still holding Cethin's tunic, he glanced over at the females. "Fallon, go find Wren, Jarek, and Bram. Meet us at the castle in the Healers' wing. Ariadne, send a message to Niara that we're on our way. Then stay here and take over command until the area is cleared. I'll send Jarek and Bram to help."

The females nodded, and that was all Razik waited for before he Traveled to the castle, Cethin and Kailia in tow. He took them straight to the Healers' wing, all the Witches jolting when he appeared with a tiny screaming thing and their king bleeding steadily. The Healers scrambled, jumping into motion, but also clearly not sure what to do.

"Where is Niara?" Razik barked, scanning the large circular

room for the best Healer on the continent, despite being far younger than most of the Witches in this room.

"Here," came a voice that was both soft and stern, somehow carrying over the chaos.

The other Healers parted, leaving a path as Niara strode calmly forward. Earthy brown eyes darted from Cethin to Razik to Kailia. Her tight black curls were piled atop her head, and when she reached them, she lifted a hand. Her dark ebony skin was stark against Kailia's brown complexion when Niara cupped her cheek.

Faint green light pulsed as the Healer whispered, "*Somnia*," and then Kailia was limp in his arms, falling into a deep sleep.

He slipped an arm beneath her knees, adjusting his other arm at her back so he cradled her against him. Turning to Cethin, his lip curled back. "Either clear this room or find us somewhere else."

"This way," Niara said simply, guiding them through the others tending to the wounded.

There were four passages off the circular room, and Niara led them to the north one. While the Witches weren't Fae with elemental powers, they were intricately attuned to nature and energy. It made sense that Niara's personal apothecary space was to the north, aligning with the earth element and the grounding properties.

The passage itself was warm and smelled of spices and sage. She pushed open a wood door. It groaned on its hinges, and she stepped to the side, allowing them to pass before she closed it.

"Place her on the bed, Razik. There's a basin and cloth to clean up with next to it. Your Majesty, the exam table, please," she said, gesturing to the wood table in the center of the room.

While Cethin limped his way there, he said, "It's not a big deal, Niara. I'll heal."

"And you'll heal faster with my help," she replied, brushing past him to a long workstation on the back wall. It was laden with herbs and plants, crystals and salts. Witch things that Razik wouldn't dare touch, and certainly not in Niara's sacred space.

He placed Kailia onto the bed, covering her with a wool blanket. Her clothing was so shredded from her own magic, there was more of her uncovered than there was covered. When she was situated, he turned to clean the blood from his skin to find Cethin glaring at him.

"Your face is portraying nothing of the gratitude you should be expressing," Razik said flatly, dipping the cloth into the basin, spelled to keep the water warm.

"None of this was necessary."

"None of this was necessary?" Razik repeated. "I'd say you can't be this dense, but you continue to prove otherwise."

"Still your king," Cethin retorted.

"Still don't give a fuck when it's just us."

Niara didn't count. They'd known her for centuries. She was one of the few who knew the nature of what they were. What Cethin was. What Razik was. When her mother, Sidora, had Faded, Niara had become the High Witch of not just the coven in Aimonway but on the entire continent. She just didn't like what came with that title. Preferring to be in this room perfecting her craft and dealing in healing, she delegated most tasks to others. Despite that, there were still times she was required to step into her full role.

But this was not one of those times, and she ignored their bickering as she mixed up some kind of paste for Cethin's wound.

"What did you want me to do?" Razik clipped when Cethin didn't respond. "Let her continue to stab you? With your own blade, I might add. Let her go, knowing other *loyal* warriors would go after her. You saw her firing those godsdamn arrows. She'd probably kill those same warriors who would only be trying to avenge their king, not knowing their king has become infatuated with the very female who sank a blade into his thigh for no apparent reason."

"There was a reason," Cethin muttered. Then louder, he added, "But that's not the point."

"I can't wait to hear what it is," Razik said, sounding as apathetic as he felt.

"I don't need to explain myself to you," Cethin snapped. "Despite what you think, I do understand how that appeared to everyone."

"Somehow I doubt that."

"Fuck off, Greybane. I—"

But he was interrupted by a knock on the door. "Razik?"

That was Fallon's voice, which meant Wren and the others were with her.

Crossing the room to let them in, Niara called after him, "This is not a room to congregate in, Razik Greybane."

"I know, Niara. My apologies. We won't stay long."

Pulling the door open, the two females and two males filed into the room. All of them were quiet and tentative. They all knew better than to piss off the Witch.

"Ariadne is getting the field cleared. Someone needs to go help her," Razik said, swiping the cloth over his chest while he spoke.

"I'll get Draven, and we can head over there," Bram said, glancing from the king to the female on the bed before sending a knowing look to Jarek.

"I'll go back too," Fallon added. "Unless I'm needed for something else?"

Razik shook his head. The two left, and Jarek waited until the door closed once more before he said, "The Commander is looking for you. Wants a full report."

"Fuck," Razik muttered, tossing the cloth to a pile of soiled rags and pushing a hand through his hair. His uncle was going to be livid.

"I shouldn't have let her go," Jarek said, his gaze fixed on Kailia.

"What does that mean?" Cethin demanded.

Razik had forgotten about him.

"We ran into her in the city," Jarek explained. "Wren, Bram, and I were getting supplies for the relocating Fae. I recognized her from the Esbat Festival, but Cethin said he had things under control last night."

"Did he now?" Razik growled, leveling the king with another glowering glare. "Who was with her?"

"No one."

"What was she doing?"

Jarek shrugged. "Ask Wren."

Razik glanced down at the Fae, and she shifted under his stare. "She was looking for somewhere to buy a dress."

"Razik!" Niara snapped in irritation.

"Sorry, Niara," he said again. "We just need to figure out what to do with her."

"The cells," Cethin cut in. "Put her in the cells. Away from any other prisoners."

Razik turned to face him fully, and the king held his stare, impassive and revealing nothing. First, he didn't want her apprehended at all; now he wanted her placed in their cells? None of this made sense, and despite his earlier statement, Cethin wasn't stupid. He was actually quite clever and cunning. It was annoying.

"Fine," Razik finally said. "Jarek, can you take care of that? I need to talk to Wren. And Tybalt, apparently."

Jarek nodded, easily lifting Kailia into his arms, blanket and all, and leaving the room. Without a word, Razik followed, Wren at his side. The moment they were outside Niara's apothecary room, he grabbed Wren's hand and Traveled them to his study in Tybalt's estate home. He got himself a glass of liquor before taking a seat on one of the overstuffed sofas, his head tipping back and eyes falling closed. The scratches from Kailia's magic still burned faintly. He needed to bathe and clean them properly before they healed over and trapped an infection.

"Can I draw from you?" he asked, unsure of how full Wren's magic reserves were.

"Of course," Wren answered, and he felt the sofa dip beside him a moment later.

"You have enough magic right now?"

"I'll be fine, Razik. But seriously? Again?"

He opened his eyes, setting his liquor aside to take the dagger she was holding out, already having sliced the Mark on her hand. He did the same to his palm before taking her hand in his to merge their blood. With her feet tucked under her, she propped her head on her other fist and waited for him to say something as power flowed between them.

Sighing, he said, "Dragon fire is one of two defenses we seem to have against these new threats. And we don't have control over the second way. You didn't tell me you spent time with her today."

"I haven't seen you to be able to tell you," Wren said pointedly. "We ran into her in the city. She said she was looking to buy a dress. I took her to Elenor's, but she left shortly after we entered the shop. By the time I went back to find Jarek and Bram, they were just getting word of the attack. A minute later, Fallon appeared, telling us to come to the castle."

That about summed it up, he supposed.

"Did she say anything? About where she's from? Any indication of what she's doing here or what she wants?"

Wren shook her head, but the way she was worrying her bottom lip told him she was hiding something.

"Wren," he said flatly.

"It's nothing, Razik."

"I'm pretty sure everything is something with her."

"Kailia. She said her name was Kailia."

"And?"

She sighed. "She asked a lot of questions about you. And us together, but mostly you."

"Me?" he repeated, failing to hide the surprise.

She nodded. "Asked if we were together. If I was forced to be your Source. Things like that. But I know she was here with Cethin this morning, and I don't know what any of it means."

He didn't either. But he'd figure it out, and in the meantime, he'd use any knowledge to his advantage.

The sound of boots on the iron staircase told him his uncle had found him, and Wren stiffened at his side.

"It's okay," he reassured her, pulling his hand back. He'd drawn enough for now. Wren didn't need to be here for this conversation. "Go wait downstairs. I'll take you back to the castle after I speak with him."

She nodded, standing and plucking a wide leaf off a plant near the window. Using her power, she soaked it with water and wound it around her hand. The cut would heal within an hour, but the leaf would keep the blood from dripping everywhere for now.

"I'll send word to have Magdalena get you some food," he added.

"No need. I'll find her," she said, her smile weak as Tybalt entered the room.

The Commander didn't say a single word as she ducked her head and scurried past him.

Razik stared back at the male with features so similar to his own yet different. One could easily guess they were related, and many assumed Tybalt was his father. He didn't correct them. Despite the argument they were about to have, Razik still considered Tybalt his father, even if the male hadn't sired him. He was the one who'd cared enough to raise him. Who'd tried to convince the people who'd birthed him to take him with them.

Instead, he'd been left here when he was seven years to fulfill a duty he didn't understand and hated now that he knew exactly what he'd been abandoned for.

Lifting his glass to his lips, he asked, "Want one?" before he took a drink, ice clinking.

"No, Razik. I don't want a fucking drink," Tybalt growled, a faint trace of smoke wafting into the air on his exhale. Yep, he was definitely irate.

Razik shrugged, taking another swallow.

"What in the realms happened today?" Tybalt demanded.

"Cethin went and got himself stabbed. Again," Razik answered.

"Under your watch."

It was a statement, not a question, and it made something beneath his skin itch and his dragon bristle.

When he remained silent, Tybalt continued, "I know you don't like Cethin, but I thought you understood that being a member of the Cadre means protecting him anyway."

"I do know that," Razik snapped.

"Then explain what the fuck happened today!" Tybalt repeated, the words ringing with rage.

"It didn't even happen during the battle," Razik retorted, his own voice rising in defensiveness. Restless and agitated, he got to his feet so he wouldn't feel like he was being looked down upon by the one person whose opinion actually mattered to him. "It happened afterwards. None of us were expecting it."

"No one was expecting it? That's your excuse?"

"It's not an excuse. It's—"

"Your job—all of your godsdamn jobs—is to be ready for the unexpected. You failed today, Razik."

Then he was gone, Traveling out of the room and leaving Razik standing there.

Alone.

It hadn't been an excuse. Merely an explanation as he tried to break down exactly how fast everything had happened. No one had expected the tiny violent ally to turn on Cethin, grabbing his own dagger from where it had been sheathed on his belt.

He paused, thinking it over for a second.

Because now that he'd had a moment to really evaluate it all, that wasn't true. Cethin hadn't seemed surprised at all. In fact, he *had* almost seemed to expect it. Had let it happen.

And Razik was getting his ass handed to him for it.

Glass met the wall as Razik hurled the crystal tumbler. Ice dropped to the floor while liquid dripped down the flat surface.

Kailia should have aimed higher.

CHAPTER 11
CETHIN

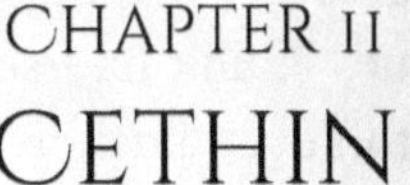

The paste was cool against his thigh as Niara smoothed the pale green mixture onto his skin with a flat stick. It smelled terrible, but she was right. He'd heal far faster with whatever she'd concocted.

"Thank you," Cethin said quietly as she worked.

She hummed an acknowledgment, but she said nothing else.

His gaze wandered to the now empty bed. Jarek had stopped back by moments ago, letting him know exactly which cell he'd put Kailia in and asking if he needed anything else before he went to help at the battle site. Cethin had sent him off, and he hadn't heard a word from Razik since he'd left earlier.

"How long will she sleep?" he asked Niara after another few silent minutes.

"Until her soul decides she's ready to wake," the Healer answered flatly.

That wasn't comforting or in any way informative.

Yet another knock on the door had the Witch straightening, her lips pursing as the door creaked open.

"My deepest apologies, Niara," Tybalt said when he entered the room. "I know this is your space, and I regret having to intrude."

"We are finished here anyway," Niara said, setting the small bowl aside and wiping her hands on the folds of her dress. "Take your discussions elsewhere."

"Of course," Tybalt said with a small nod of his head. "Cethin?"

He slid to the floor, gingerly placing weight on his leg. Despite knowing he'd heal just fine, Kailia had sunk that blade in nice and deep, then she'd twisted it in even farther.

"Thank you again, Niara," he said. "I'll have your blanket returned."

She waved him off. "No need. I'll find another. She requires it."

He didn't want to think about how she'd shredded through her pants and tunic. How she'd been pressed against Razik's bare chest. How she'd screamed frantically, the sound still echoing in his mind.

"Ready?" Tybalt asked, placing a hand on Cethin's shoulder.

He nodded, and a moment later they were outside the king's personal study. He was the only one who could Travel directly inside his rooms. Even entering through the main doors required his magical signature unless he granted entry from inside.

Placing a palm on the door, a faint trace of black drifted from beneath it, the doors swinging open a second later.

He immediately rounded the large onyx desk, sinking into a plush chair while Tybalt took a seat on the other side. It wasn't nearly as comfortable as Cethin's, but it was padded and fine enough.

"Are you all right?" Tybalt asked. "Do you need anything?"

"I'll be fine. There's a reason I went to Niara," Cethin answered, resting an elbow on the armrest and steepling a finger along his temple. His other hand was on the desktop, fingers drumming in succession.

"She's as gifted as her mother was," Tybalt agreed, settling deeper into his chair. "Despite that, this could have been prevented. You shouldn't have been at that battle."

His fingers drummed again. "It does not matter how many times you lecture me, Tybalt. I will continue to choose to fight alongside those who defend this kingdom."

"I'm not discounting the nobility of that sentiment."

"Then what is your purpose?"

"The same purpose I have had in our previous discussions on this topic. I need you to think about what will befall this kingdom if you cross the Veil, Cethin."

His fingers paused mid-drum, and he sat back in his chair, stretching his injured leg out beneath the desk.

"Your parents worked tirelessly to ensure this kingdom survived. If you go to the After without a partner or heir, you risk it all." Cethin started to argue, but Tybalt held up a hand to stop him. "I know you've heard these arguments time and again. I know you have plans in place should something happen to you without a partner or heir, but we both know those plans will be challenged. You've lived hundreds of years, but you've only been a king for one. Until a year ago, there was an heir upon the king's death. Until a year ago, you could be reckless. Tethys's death changed all of that."

"You think I don't know that?" Cethin demanded.

His father's death had changed everything. He'd lost more than a father. He'd lost a freedom he'd taken for granted. Lost those he'd once considered friends. Lost being able to adventure, replaced by daily monotony.

The silence grew heavy between them, weighted by a shared grief that affected them both differently. Tybalt, for all his kindness and concern, remained loyal to his parents, not to him. Always pushing for him to follow their example rather than forge his own path as the world and circumstances changed around them.

Tybalt cleared his throat, the sound jarring in the quiet. "The female in the cells. Tell me about her."

Of course he knew about that already.

Cethin sighed, getting to his feet and crossing to the window. It faced the east. Faced the sea. Even if he couldn't quite see it from here, he could picture it. He'd go there later tonight. After he dealt with this. The sun was setting. Then he could listen to the waves beneath the stars and figure out what his next moves were going to be.

"There's not much to tell," he said, finally answering Tybalt.

"She stabbed you. Twice, according to Jarek," Tybalt countered.

"It's more complicated than that."

"It doesn't appear to be complicated at all. She stabbed the king."

"And she's the only one who can create the weapons that kill the creatures threatening my people," Cethin ground out.

"That only started appearing around the time she did. You don't find that at all coincidental?"

Had he truly been so wrapped up with everything—with *her*—that he'd missed that?

No.

She was fighting them. Killing them. She didn't bring them here.

But she *was* unwilling to help him fight against them…

If she were responsible, that was all the more reason to bring her to their side.

Bring her to *his* side.

"I'm handling it," he finally replied, turning to face the male who was like a second father to him.

"She is a danger to you and to this kingdom, Cethin," Tybalt said sharply.

"I said I'll handle it," he ground out. "Is that all?"

"No, it is not all," the Commander said, his words tight and pointed. "You need to stop putting yourself in harm's way until all of this is sorted."

"There will always be another threat. I'm the king. It comes with the job," he replied, dropping back into his chair. "So if we're simply going to repeat past conversations, you're dismissed."

"Cethin—"

"It wasn't a request, Commander."

Tybalt stared back at him, and he could see the conflict play out across his face: follow the orders of his king or try to talk to the male he considered family.

"Be careful, Cethin," he finally said before he stood and left the room. Duty had won out; it always did for the male.

The door thudding closed echoed in the enormous study, and he stared at nothing for the longest time.

Being careful had never served him. His parents had ruled with caution, all their actions being reactions to something else. He preferred to be proactive, willing to push boundaries and take risks.

Pricking his finger, he swiped a smear of blood along the bottom desk drawer to his right. The magic keeping it sealed tight lifted, and he pulled it open, retrieving a leather-bound journal. Worn with time and use, the dark brown cover was soft and pliable.

Flipping it open, he read through the copious notes he'd taken over the decades.

If others only knew the risks he'd taken for his people.

The laws of old he'd broken.

But in all his research and experimenting, in searching across the lands of a kingdom that was now his, he'd yet to find a rumored land. He was certain it held answers he needed, but the city itself was said to be a myth.

He'd even gone to the Greybane Estate to casually bring it up to Razik, but before he'd gotten the chance, the attack had happened.

In the end, he was running out of options, and still, the female in the cells seemed to be the one thing that would fix everything. So he'd find a way to force her hand. He was, after all, the king, but more than that, he'd been bending fate to his will for a while now. She would be no different.

❂

Spending the entire night and dawn hours sitting on the shore, he'd gone over his options. Weighing possible outcomes. Pros and cons. Costs and risks. But he knew better than anyone that you can only plan for so much. Eventually, you have to make a move and figure the rest out as you go.

So that was what he was doing as he exited a shop in the city, a bundle of female clothing under his arm. He was having more delivered to the castle later in the day, but he needed one set of items now. A dress. Undergarments. Socks and shoes.

He also stopped at a bakery and picked up a small order of rolls baked with cinnamon and topped with swirls of sweet frosting. More so for himself than anything.

Traveling back to the castle, he bathed quickly and put on fresh clothing before grabbing his purchases and making his way to the cells. He took his time, descending several sets of stairs and taking the path to the west wing.

There were two ways into the cells. One way was inside the castle, the entrance he would use. It was guarded by no fewer than three sentinels at all times, and a minimum of six if there were people being held in the cells. The other entrance led outside, emerging onto a path. There were stone walls on either side, the walls patrolled at all times, and the path led straight into the Night-mist Mountains. There were no side paths. Your options were facing the terrors of the mountains or going back inside the castle.

The current rotation of guards straightened at his approach, and he nodded at them. "No escort is needed."

They all glanced at each other because protocol mandated that no one went down to the cells alone. Even the guards went in pairs, and two always escorted visitors.

But not everyone else was the king.

He arched a brow, waiting for someone to challenge him, but they all bowed their heads.

The lead guard opened the door for him, and as he passed, Cethin said, "I'll send word if I need anything."

"We'll be ready, your Majesty."

Descending another set of stairs that took him beneath the castle, he heard the door snick shut behind him. His boots echoed in the stairwell, everything cooler down here. Despite routine cleaning, traces of moss clung to the stone walls. Moisture in the air made everything a little musty, and the smell mixed with that of those being held within the bars.

Jarek had ensured she was at the end with no one around her, and Cethin didn't look at the other few prisoners. His focus was singular, and he was determined to leave here with the outcome he wanted.

He knew she was awake. He'd given orders to send word as soon as she stirred, and that message had come as the sun was rising.

That message had set everything in motion.

Finally, he reached her cell, stopping directly in front of it and facing her fully. She was seated on a pallet of straw, her knees pulled up to her chest and the blanket wrapped around herself. He could see the tattered remains of her pants, her bare toes curling into the straw. Her hair was a wild tangle of knots. He could have brought her a brush. Then again, she could have ten of them once she agreed to his proposal.

With her chin resting on her knees, her amber eyes flickered up to his, smoke and ashes swirling slowly within their depths. He didn't know what that meant. Was she tired? Weakened? Still under the effects of Niara's enchantment?

"Tiny fiend," he said after an extended silence.

"King," she rasped, her voice scratchy and raw, he assumed from the violent screaming. He was amazed she could speak at all, and he should have thought to bring her tea. Again, something to remedy after this conversation.

"I didn't expect to see you again so soon," he said, stepping closer to the bars.

She lifted her head, brow furrowing slightly. "Did you not choose to walk down here? Seems you controlled how soon you saw me considering I cannot go anywhere."

"That's not… I meant so soon after you left the castle yesterday. Our bargain came to fruition sooner than expected."

Her lips pursed, and she shifted where she sat, the blanket slipping down her shoulder.

"I brought you fresh clothing," he offered, holding up the package.

She glanced at the parchment-wrapped bundle and then back at him. "Why?"

"Because your clothing is torn to nothing."

Kailia looked down as though she were just realizing that was a true statement. Then she pulled the blanket tighter around herself.

"And what must I do to have that clothing?" she asked, the words dripping with derision.

"I'm glad you asked. We do have some negotiations to tend to," he replied, dropping the clothing bundle at his feet. Keeping hold of the other bag, he reached inside and pulled out a roll with cinnamon and frosting. "Want one?"

"No," she snapped, and he shrugged, bringing the sweet treat to his mouth. She watched the movement, gaze glued to the food.

Swallowing his bite, he said, "We have a lot to talk about, Kailia. Do you really want to do so with a set of bars between us?"

"I didn't make these arrangements."

"You didn't?"

"No," she scoffed, shifting on the pallet of straw once more.

"Did I not tell you if you stabbed me again, you'd end up in these cells? And did you not stab me again?" he asked, taking another bite of the roll.

"Which has fulfilled our bargain," she retorted.

"Exactly. So we need to make a new one."

"No."

He shrugged again. "Then you remain behind these bars."

"It's comfortable enough. I've stayed in much worse," she said airily.

His lips turned up into something sinister. "I can ensure that is no longer the case."

"That's not the threat you think it is," she muttered.

Not sure what to make of that, he took his time finishing the cinnamon roll while he watched her. Her eyes stayed trained on him, features giving nothing away. She had no tells as she sat there. No, she only reacted when she was touched unexpectedly.

He'd had suspicions as they'd walked the gardens a few days ago. Watching her lose complete control when Razik had picked her up though? It was all the confirmation he needed; now he wanted to know *why*. But that was a conversation for another time. Once he'd gained her trust. Right now, he needed her to agree to his proposal. The rest could come later.

Stepping closer still, his voice was low as he said, "I have a warm bath being drawn for you as we speak. We agree to a new bargain, and I can take you to it."

"I made that mistake once. I won't make it again," she replied.

"You would rather stay in there? Unable to access your magic? I know you're not in manacles, but the bars themselves will slowly drain your reserves. In the meantime, innocent people will continue to die because you refuse to help us," Cethin said. "We come to an agreement, or you face a trial for attempting to murder the king."

"You set this all up," she seethed, suddenly shooting to her feet. "This was your plan all along!" When he didn't offer a denial and simply stared back at her, she scoffed. Coming to the bars, she stuck her arm through, the blanket dropping to the floor. "Give me the clothes. I won't walk through your castle on display. Or is that what you wish as well?"

"I don't want anyone seeing you like this," Cethin growled.

Because there was far too much skin showing. Her entire midriff was exposed. One sleeve of her tunic was completely gone. One leg of her pants had so many rips it may as well not even be there. The other was torn completely up the side clear to her hip. If she turned to the side a fraction, he was definitely seeing the curves of her ass.

But he couldn't give her the clothing until she agreed to his terms.

"I'll give you the clothing, and you will agree to negotiate terms on becoming my wife," he said, pulling a dagger from his belt. The same dagger she'd shoved into his thigh.

"Do we have an accord?" he asked, the blade poised over his palm.

"I hate you," she replied. The words were flat, but the loathing swirling in her eyes echoed the sentiment. "With every piece of my soul, I hate you and what you've done."

"What I've done?" he asked, tilting his head. "We've only known one another for a handful of days, tiny fiend."

"And in that time, you've managed to coerce me into marriage or face a public trial that will result in my death," she replied, rotating her wrist, so her palm faced up. "Is that what you want? A wife who loathes you?"

"My kingdom doesn't seem to care who is at my side so long as I have a wife," he deadpanned. "If anything, I live to serve. It's all I do these days."

Kailia clicked her tongue before muttering a foul name under her breath.

"Do we have an accord?" he asked again.

"Not willingly," she sneered.

"But agreed nonetheless," he said simply, slicing his palm.

She held his stare as he drew the tip of the blade across her flesh, red immediately welling. Clasping her hand in his, he felt the Bargain Mark prickle along his skin, right above the place where she'd stabbed his thigh.

How fitting.

Yanking her hand back, she crouched, reaching for the bundle of clothing. Cethin merely moved it closer with his foot, letting her pull it through the bars.

"I suppose you went back to the same shop Wren took me to," she muttered, pulling on the twine that was wound around the paper.

"I did," he agreed. "But the offerings there didn't seem like something you'd wear."

"As if you know anything about me and what I'd wear. Turn around or move out of sight. I'm not changing in front of you."

He gave a mocking bow of his head, but stepped to the side, just out of view.

"And how do you find the clothing, tiny fiend?"

"Dreadful," she retorted.

He smirked to himself, and after a few minutes, she let him know she was finished.

His gaze swept over her in a black dress with deep slits up the sides. It gathered slightly at her waist, two panels covering her breasts and tying at her nape. Cut low in the front, the back scooped just as low, stopping right above her ass. The fabric had a faint pattern of stars and moons with the barest hint of silver thread.

"It seems to fit well enough," he rasped, his throat suddenly dry and the words a little hoarse.

"Better than pants," she grumbled.

Placing his palm on the cell door, his power flared faintly before it clicked, and he slid the door to the side. "Ready?"

"To step from one prison into another?" she said. The words didn't carry any emotion, as though she was simply stating a fact. He supposed that was one way to look at it.

Stepping to the side, she moved past him, the low light of the sconces catching on the blue crystal still hanging around her neck. Sliding in front of her, she lurched back, just like he'd wanted her to. Her back bumped into the stone wall, and he braced his forearms on either side of her, caging her in.

"What are you doing?" she demanded, her chest rising and falling a little too fast and betraying her panic.

With one hand, he reached for the necklace, twisting the crystal between his fingers. "Trying to figure out who gave my future wife jewelry."

"Does it matter where I got it?"

"It most certainly does. How is it going to look to announce my wife while she's wearing jewelry from another male?"

"Who said I got it from a male? Maybe I purchased it myself," she countered.

"Did you?"

Her smile was all sarcastic derision. "I suppose you'll never know."

He hummed. This close to her, he wanted to touch her, even if it was simply brushing his fingers down her arm. She'd need to get used to his touch eventually, but for now, he didn't need a repeat of yesterday.

"This way," he said, bending to retrieve the bag of dropped pastries and gesturing down the passage. "Once we're beyond the door, I can Travel us somewhere else to discuss matters."

"Can't we walk there?" she asked tightly, keeping pace at his side.

"We could, but we will inevitably be stopped by someone along the way who will likely have questions," he answered, motioning for her to ascend the steps in front of him, only to realize her feet were still bare. "You forgot your socks and shoes."

"I didn't forget them. You can't feel people coming when wearing shoes," she said simply, climbing the stairs.

By the Fates. She said the most bizarre things sometimes, and while it was somewhat annoying, he was far more intrigued by her odd mannerisms and unusual statements.

Reaching the top of the stairs, he rapped his knuckles twice as he called out, "Tobias, it's me. We're ready."

A moment later the door opened, the six sentinels standing at attention. Two even managed to hide their surprise at Kailia's presence. The other four, not so much.

"Your Majesty…" Tobias started, trailing off. He was the lead guard on the shift, and he would report today's happenings to the Captain of the Guard, who would in turn report them to Tybalt.

Something to handle once this deal with Kailia was finalized.

"Did you need something?" Cethin asked, his tone making it clear the answer to that question had better be no.

"It is nothing, your Majesty," he conceded, taking a step back. "Just making sure all is well?"

"We are fine. Thank you," Cethin replied, his hand dropping to Kailia's lower back. He didn't touch her, but his hand hovered close enough that he could feel her body heat. Looking down at her, he asked, "Are you ready?"

Her answering smile was pure poisoned sweetness, and he returned the sentiment as he pressed his fingers to her bare back, pulling them through the air and to his private floor. As soon as their feet landed in the main receiving room, she moved away from him, putting a good amount of distance between them.

While she took in the space, he moved to set the pastry bag on a side table, pulling out another roll and taking a bite.

After chewing and swallowing, he said, "Those are the main doors to our suite."

"Our," she quipped.

His answer was a mocking smile. "If anyone calls on us, they will use those doors."

Two large double doors marked the entrance. Black stars and glistening waves were etched into the wood. While there were other entrances, they were for the private use of the royal family, which for the last year had only consisted of him. Even the staff used the main doors.

"This entire floor is the king and queen's private home," he went on. "The receiving room is precisely that, but through that door is a much more informal living space. Are you sure you don't want a roll?"

She scowled, but snatched the roll out of his hand when he held his other half out to her. She took it and shoved the whole thing into her mouth as if to prove something, and then her eyes went wide.

"What is this?" she managed to get out around the food.

He huffed a laugh. "A speciality from one of my favorite bakeries in town. I always get them there. The kitchen staff has tried, but they can never get it quite right."

She nodded while she finished chewing. Cethin merely held out the bag, and she took the whole thing, pulling out another roll.

"Anyway," he said, not wanting her to see his satisfaction at her enjoying something from him. "Through here is the sitting room," he repeated, pushing past the door that separated the receiving room from the rest of the space.

He'd changed several things after his father's passing, not wanting to live in a space where pieces of his parents' spirits might linger, but there were still a few things he'd let be for nostalgia's sake.

Everything was dark greys and light creams with silver and black accents throughout. The sitting room was his favorite with three sofas arranged around the hearth. There were a set of armchairs near the window with a low table between them. A set of doors led to a balcony that faced to the east, with a set of furniture out there as well. Bookcases lined the walls, some filled with books, others with various trinkets and framed art. A room off to the right housed a small washroom, so one didn't need to go far when needed.

"There is a dining room through the door on the left," he continued to explain. "Through the door on the right is a hall leading to various rooms. A study. Washrooms. A small den. Library. Extra bedrooms. The king and queen's bedchamber is at the end of the hall with its own large bathing room, where that bath is being prepared for you."

"I can take a bath in my own bathing chamber," she spouted, wandering around the sitting room.

"And you will."

She paused, looking over her shoulder. "You just said it was the king and queen's shared bathing chamber." When he remained silent, she said, "We are not sharing a bathing room or a bedchamber for that matter."

"Part of the negotiations, I suppose," he said, slipping his hands into his pockets.

She crossed her arms, the two of them once again facing off across the room from each other.

"Do you not like the space?" he asked. "We can have it redesigned however you wish."

"Then I *wish* for separate bedchambers for the king and queen."

His features fell flat. "I meant the decor. Not the layout of the entire floor." When she continued to stare back at him, irritation prickled his skin. "Are we negotiating before or after you bathe?"

"What, exactly, is the proposal here?"

Now it was then.

"Sit," he said, motioning to the sofas. She moved stiffly, and he took a seat on the one across from her. "I require a wife, and you need to avoid a public trial and likely execution for trying to kill the king."

"I wasn't trying to kill you," she argued. "A dagger to the thigh will not take you to the After."

"Yes, but I'm afraid the people of Avonleya won't see it that way," he said with faux sincerity. "Pity if rumors started spreading that would confirm those suspicions."

Her jaw clenched, and he could see her grinding her molars.

"But if that same person were *betrothed* to the king, I'm sure he could clear it all up as a misunderstanding," he went on. "Ensure the protection of her that he's been offering her the entire time."

Her chin lifted. "And my arrow?"

"Once the union is binding, it shall be my marriage gift to you," he answered, settling back on his sofa and draping an arm along the back.

"Gifting me something that is rightfully mine," she scoffed, rolling her eyes and sinking deeper into her seat.

His head tilted. "What other gifts would you like from me, tiny fiend?"

"My own rooms."

"No. The staff will gossip if we are found to be sleeping in separate rooms."

"How in the realms would they discover that?" she asked, her exasperation creeping into her tone.

"When they clean," he said simply.

"I'll clean myself."

"We are not cleaning our own floor," he said dismissively.

"Did you never learn how? You've simply been catered to and pampered your entire life?" she threw back.

"For fuck's sake. They'd gossip even more if we started cleaning our own space. They'd think we are running out of funds and can't afford to pay them," he ground out.

He watched her think that over, and by the gods, he wanted to know what she was thinking. What arguments was she internally having with herself?

After two full minutes of silence ticked by, he cleared his throat. "Let's lay out the negotiations as they stand now. You will agree to be my wife and queen, in title only. After the union is finalized, I will give back your arrow. In return, you will be granted a full pardon for the *two* times you stabbed me and will be under my protection. Nothing will harm you."

"For how long?" Kailia asked.

His brows knitted. "For how long, what?"

"Do I have to remain your wife? How long will the protection last?"

"The marriage will be binding," he said darkly. "And my protection will last as long as the marriage does."

She uncrossed her arms, hands falling to her lap where she smoothed them along the fabric of the dress. Once. Twice. A few more times before she seemed to suddenly realize what she was doing. She was looking anywhere but at him, and he stayed silent, giving her time to process.

"And an heir?" she finally asked.

"That can be discussed at a later time."

"But it shall be expected of me?"

"Something we can decide together, years from now," he repeated.

Her bare feet tapped a chaotic rhythm as she went silent once more.

"But we will need to be convincing, Kailia. I want to make that clear," he added.

That had her gaze swinging back to his. "How can I possibly convince people I'm in love with you when I hate the fact you exist at all?"

Cethin stood then, crossing to where she still sat. He leaned over her, one hand bracing on the back of the sofa. She looked up at him, determination and loathing staring back.

With his other hand, he picked up a lock of hair, twirling it between his fingers. "The veil between love and hate is thin, tiny fiend. Both are fueled by passion, and I think I'll be fine with either one from you."

Her features scrunched. "That makes no sense."

He sighed dramatically. "Alas, love rarely does, but that is neither here nor there at the moment," he added when she opened her mouth to protest his statement. "Have we reached the end of our negotiations? Are we in agreement?"

"A forced agreement," she muttered.

"An agreement nonetheless," he said, straightening and pulling his dagger from his belt for the second time that day.

For the first time since he'd met her, something akin to fear entered her eyes. "This agreement comes with a promise of protection?" she clarified. "I agree to this arrangement, and you will return my arrow and grant me your protection?"

"A promise I swear on my crown, tiny fiend," he answered, his heart beating faster in anticipation of finally sealing this deal.

"Fine," she finally said, taking the dagger from him.

She dragged it across her own palm before doing the same to Cethin's, digging the blade in far deeper than necessary. He hissed at the discomfort, glaring at her.

"It's an accord," she said, clasping his hand.

And this bargain felt different as their blood merged. There was the normal prickling of a Bargain Mark along the left side of his chest, but there was also something more. Faint flares of silver and dark green light that Kailia clearly saw too, because she gasped, yanking her hand away.

"What was that?" she demanded, shooting to her feet and forcing him to take several steps back.

"I don't know," he answered truthfully, but her eyes narrowed, telling him she didn't believe him in the slightest.

Without another word, she turned and headed down the hall, presumably going to bathe. He swiped a hand down his face as he watched her go.

He was betrothed.

But there was no doubt in his mind that the negotiations had been the easiest part of this arrangement.

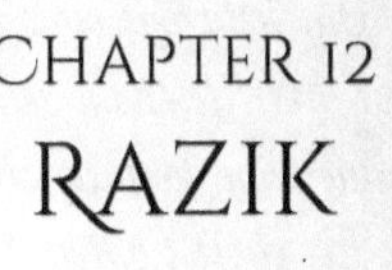
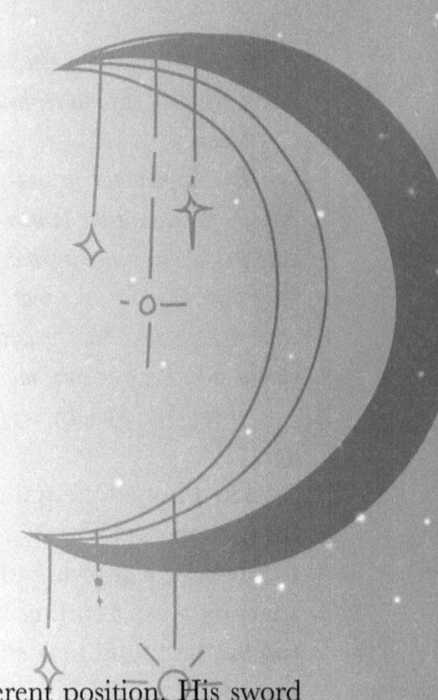

CHAPTER 12

RAZIK

Inhaling deeply, he moved into a different position. His sword arm rotated out while his right foot slid forward on the exhale. He stilled, holding the pose, focusing on breathing.

It was an ancient art form known as *serena sabre*, and it was one only a few knew of. Tybalt had taught it to him when he was younger, a few years after his parents had left him here.

His uncle had been a saint about it all, while Razik had been a little shit. He could admit that. Being abandoned led to an array of emotions, and the only one he cared to express during his adolescence was anger. After a particularly rough day, Tybalt had Traveled them to the southern part of the continent and told Razik to remove his socks and boots. He'd sunk into cool sand as the waves lapped at the shore, and then his uncle had handed him a sword and talked him through the most basic poses.

"Control your breathing," Tybalt ordered, *circling him as his arm shook with the weight of the sword. It was heavier than the one he used in training.*

"I am," Razik bit out, *but with the words, he lost his balance. "The sand is too slippery,"* he grumbled, *kicking at it and sending grains of white flying. "Why can't we spar?"*

"You spent hours sparring today, and you still lost your temper after dinner.

147

So now try something else. Something created by our bloodline. Something from home, Razik," Tybalt replied.

Home.

By Sargon did he miss Nordrir. Or at least what he remembered of it. Mostly he missed the family he'd once had. Not just his parents. No, he couldn't care less about them anymore. But he'd left cousins behind. Friends. Even if it'd only been the first four years of his life, he'd felt like he at least belonged there. And the idea of having a connection to that time of his life, even if through stupid sword movements, made his chest tighten.

"Fine," he'd finally said, planting his feet once more. "Tell me again how to do it."

He'd honed the practice to perfection, mastering every pose and movement over the years, and now it was still something he turned to when he was trying to work through…well, anything really. When sparring wasn't cutting it and flying allowed his thoughts to wander too far, he found himself on the same beach he'd been on centuries ago.

With his eyes still closed, he changed poses again with precise and controlled movements, but he felt the slight shift in the air. Someone else was here, and the dragon in his soul recognized the dragon in the newcomer.

His uncle was silent, letting Razik complete his routine, and when he finally sent his sword away in a swirl of dragon fire, he found Tybalt sitting on the shore. His knees were bent, arms resting loosely atop them as he stared out at the sea. Saying nothing, Razik dropped down beside him, mirroring his position.

Neither spoke for a long time. They only listened to the waves rolling up the shore beneath a the waxing moon. Razik was still nursing his pride from the words they'd exchanged earlier. The idea of disappointing Tybalt made him feel things he didn't like—guilt, shame, failure. Rarely did his uncle provoke such feelings, but he was also one of few who could. It was his words that had driven Razik to the southern shore tonight.

"I argued with your father. About leaving you here," Tybalt said, breaking the tension swirling between them. "Told him to bring you back when you were of age to choose the Guardian Bond. He insisted it would be better if you and Cethin grew up together, but more than that, he insisted it would be safer. Our kind were being hunted, and this world was one of the safer ones we'd come across in our quest for sanctuary. I could have made other arguments, but I…"

Tybalt pushed out a harsh breath. "None of that matters now. What matters is that it's our nature to protect whatever we view as ours. It gives the beasts in our souls purpose. Gives them an outlet to be what we are meant to be at our very core."

"I know all of this," Razik said flatly at the mention of the reason he'd been left here. The fucking Guardian Bond everyone wanted him to take with Cethin. A bond only a descendant of Sargon, the god of war and courage, could be part of. A bond that would require him to guard his Ward at any cost, including his life.

"I know you already know all this," Tybalt replied. "I ensured you knew the pillars of our homeland and our bloodline. You were left in my care, and I refused to fail you, despite doing so in other ways."

"You didn't—"

"I did," Tybalt interrupted. "You don't need to spare my feelings. I was away from you for centuries because of the Wards, not once, but twice. But again, that's not the point." He finally turned his head to meet Razik's eyes. "We are unsettled, off balance if you will, without a purpose. Our dragons become restless, and it affects every facet of our lives. You need a purpose, Razik."

"I have purpose," he said defensively. "I am devoted to the Cadre."

Tybalt shook his head. "It's not the same. It needs to be something you view as solely yours. It is why our kind are so drawn to Guardian Bonds and why they work so well. And before you get upset, I am not here to discuss that potential yet again."

Good thing he'd clarified that so quickly, because Razik's muscles had already tensed, preparing to leave. All the calmness he'd found while practicing *serena sabre* was gone, replaced by wariness about where this conversation was going. Unless…

Was he about to appoint him leader of the Cadre? Give him that purpose? Make that something that was *his?*

The thought had him straightening, anticipation thrumming through his veins. His dragon lifted his head too, because his uncle was right. His dragon had been restless. Not for days or weeks, but for years.

"There is a threat to this kingdom, and I need you to handle it," Tybalt said, his tone shifting to that of the Commander of the Forces.

"A new threat or one of old?" Razik asked, more than a little intrigued.

"New," Tybalt said. "One our king refuses to see."

Razik huffed a humorless laugh. That didn't surprise him in the least.

"It was reported to me that the female who stabbed him is already released from the cells. Cethin himself retrieved her," Tybalt continued. "He took her to his floor, and neither of them was heard from the rest of the day. However, Cethin has sent word that he has an announcement to make at the advisory council meeting today."

"And you believe it involves her?" Razik asked.

"I do. I believe he is about to do something incredibly reckless. The council has been pushing him to find a partner."

Razik twisted toward him. "Kailia? He hardly knows her."

"Not to mention she showed up at the same time these new enemies did," Tybalt replied, his feelings on this evident in his tone. "I tried to talk to him about all of this, but he refuses to listen to reason."

"And you think he'll listen to me?" Razik asked dryly.

"Not at all," Tybalt replied. "While I will always encourage you to get along with your king, it's beyond clear neither of you will ever choose a Guardian Bond."

Well, that was…not what he'd been expecting.

"I'll be honest here," Razik said. "I feel as though you've been pushing me towards the bond more and more lately. Especially since your recent return from across the Edria."

Tybalt nodded. "Admittedly, I find it hard to understand your disinterest. I understand why you do not want it, but I cannot understand the ability to fight against the instinct of your dragon. I kept thinking you would…" He paused, clearly searching for the right words. "Because of my own life experiences, I believe you would find more fulfillment in your immortal years if you accepted a Guardian Bond, but that is not my choice to make for you. So instead, I'm offering a different path."

"A different path," Razik repeated dubiously.

"If Cethin makes the announcement I believe he is going to make today, our new queen-to-be will need a personal guard," Tybalt said, and those were the last words he'd expected his uncle to say.

"You want me to be… What of my role in the Cadre?"

His uncle pushed to his feet then, brushing sand from his pants, and Razik did the same.

"I suppose that is another choice for you to make," Tybalt said, turning to face him. "And unfortunately, you do not have much time to do so. You'll need to decide by the time the council convenes." His hand landed on Razik's shoulder, and he squeezed it. "I know you wanted to lead the Cadre, Razik, but I want you to look back on these last years. Last decades. Truly evaluate all of it and then decide if maybe a new purpose isn't precisely what you've been searching for."

With one more squeeze of his shoulder, Tybalt was gone, Traveling through the air and leaving Razik alone with his thoughts.

Doing *serena sabre* these last hours had cleared his mind, but the conversation with Tybalt had erased all of that. He could go through the practice again, but that wasn't what he needed right now. No, what he needed was to fly.

So he pulled his tunic over his head before summoning his wings and launching into the dawn-filled sky.

⤛⤜ ☾ ☉ ☽ ⤙⤚

151

Later that morning, he was scooping jam onto his toast when he heard the footfalls. One set heavy. One lighter.

Razik had flown all morning, watching the sun rise from the sky. Normally, he ate breakfast before everyone else. Today, he waited until everyone else was done. Apparently Cethin had chosen to do the same, likely to avoid the others if Kailia was indeed with him.

A moment later the pair stepped into the room, Kailia first and Cethin a step behind. She faltered when she found Razik at the table, and Cethin came to a halt, glaring at him.

"Razik," Cethin greeted tightly. "It's a little late for breakfast, isn't it?"

"Evidently not too late if the king is only now getting here," Razik replied apathetically, setting his toast down and reaching for the plate of sausages. He glanced up, still finding them staring at him. "Good to see you not shrieking like a crazed spirit, Lia."

"That's not my name," she said, finally moving again.

Razik shrugged, taking a bite of his food.

The pair rounded the table. Cethin wore his usual attire, black tunic and pants, while Kailia was in a black dress that brushed the floor. There were thigh-high slits up the sides though, and the sheer sleeves stopped below her shoulders, leaving her collarbones exposed. The same necklace hung at her throat, and he found himself wondering about the significance of it. Had she been wearing it when he'd first met her with Wren?

"Kailia, this is Razik Greybane, a member of the Cadre. It is my understanding you have not been formally introduced," Cethin said tightly, taking the chair next to her.

"We've met a few times," Razik drawled. "Most recently after she stabbed you, she then proceeded to attack me with her magic. I'm surprised you let her near the cutlery at this point."

"A butter knife isn't worth it," Kailia said, several pieces of bacon already on her plate.

"A butter knife can do plenty of damage if you know where to aim," Razik countered.

"I never said it couldn't do damage. I said it wasn't worth it," she replied factually. "If I'm going to send someone to the After, I'm going to use a weapon worthy of such a thing."

That was…disturbing.

Cethin cleared his throat as he passed Kailia a platter of fruit pastries. "That was all a misunderstanding."

"I don't know how you interpret stabbing you with your own dagger any other way," Razik said flatly.

"Good thing it's not your business, and I don't owe you an explanation."

Razik's smirk was tight, barely a tilt of his lips. "Of course not, *your Majesty*. Why in the realms would I think the king would need to explain why the person who stabbed him is suddenly sharing the breakfast table with us?"

Kailia turned to Cethin, her eyes narrowed in accusation. "You said you were taking care of all of that."

"I am," Cethin ground out, his knuckles turning white where they were wrapped around his butter knife.

"You are doing a terrible job," she said simply, returning to her meal.

Razik snorted a soft laugh. If he didn't have his suspicions about her, he'd almost like her. Unfortunately for her, he was at maximum capacity for people he cared about.

"What are you even doing here, Greybane?" Cethin demanded.

Razik stared at him for a long second before he said, "Eating. I thought that was obvious."

"It is," Kailia agreed.

"By the Fates," Cethin muttered, a smattering of his dark power drifting around him before he got control over it. "Don't you have training or something else to be doing?"

"If I did, I'd be there," Razik retorted. "But instead, I was informed you have a super special announcement to make, and Tybalt asked that I be there for that."

"Why?"

"You tell me," Razik replied before biting into his toast.

"How long have you known each other?" Kailia asked suddenly, drawing both their attention to her.

"Too long," Cethin muttered, stabbing harshly at some fruit on his plate.

"There are only four years of my life that I didn't know him," Razik answered.

"How old are you?" Kailia pushed.

"How old are *you*?" Razik countered, and he didn't miss how Cethin honed in on the question too.

She hummed before saying, "Old enough to know immortality is not the blessing the mortals believe it to be."

Razik paused. "That's…cryptic."

"Is it?" she asked, picking up another strip of bacon.

For the first time in a long time, Razik wasn't entirely sure what to say. He picked up his cup of juice, watching her as she went about her meal, seemingly without a care.

"You never attend advisory meetings," Cethin said, breaking the silence.

"I tend to spend as little time in your presence as possible," Razik retorted, giving his full attention to the male.

"Yet here you are."

"I don't understand," Kailia announced.

"Don't understand what, tiny fiend?" Cethin asked, sounding slightly exasperated as he rubbed at his temple.

"The dynamic here. With you two. You don't speak as a king and a warrior. That's what Wren said you were," she added, glancing at Razik.

"It is."

"But you speak as if you are more."

"More what?"

She went quiet, thinking it over for a moment. Then she shrugged. "Familial maybe? Scorned lovers?"

Razik spat out his juice while Cethin choked on the bite of food he'd taken. She didn't seem to realize her words were the reason for both. That or she didn't care. She just continued eating her breakfast, having moved on to the fruit pastries.

"We are not and have never been lovers," Cethin said tightly after a large gulp of water.

She hummed.

"We aren't," he insisted. "We do not get along."

"You're eating breakfast together," she countered.

"Yes, but not by choice. He was already here when we arrived."

"Because he was waiting for you."

"Doubtful," Cethin said dryly.

But Razik had resumed studying her. For as quirky as she was, she was incredibly perceptive. Probably from all the time spent spying from her ashes. Perceptiveness led to cleverness, and if his uncle was right, clever enemies were far more dangerous than ones who could swing a sword.

Kailia could do both, it appeared. Or at the very least, wield a bow with deadly precision.

He didn't want to think about the fact that by taking on the role of Kailia's personal guard under the guise of keeping her safe, he was actually providing that service to Cethin. A guardian by proxy was not his intention, but becoming close to Kailia was the only way to figure out what her motives were—good or bad.

The atmosphere in the dining room thickened with tension. Kailia ate her meal as if she didn't notice. Cethin was aiming subtle glares at Razik, and Razik wasn't giving two fucks.

"Where is Wren?" Kailia asked suddenly.

Why was everything she said seemingly random? Was it a distraction tactic?

"She is helping with the Fae who are relocating," Razik answered. "Why?"

"She said she is your Source."

"She is," he replied, eyes narrowing slightly at the topic. He didn't like discussing his Source bond with anyone.

"I assumed she would always be with you," she said simply. Then added, "But I suppose she was with other males in the city, and you weren't there."

"She is free to do as she pleases," Razik said.

"Is that normal for a Source bond relationship?"

"Why so many questions, Kailia?" Cethin cut in, clearly not liking that her attention was on Razik and not him.

He was going to be furious when he learned who'd been assigned as her personal guard.

Approaching footsteps had them all turning to the sound, and a moment later, Zayan appeared. He halted upon finding the three of them together, his eyes skipping over the males and lingering on Kailia.

"Good morning, your Majesty. Greybane," he greeted, his demeanor a little stiff. "Kailia, it is wonderful to see you again."

She gave him a tight smile, glancing over at Cethin as if looking for guidance. The king's features softened, and Razik fought the urge to roll his eyes. Tybalt was right. If Kailia was here for some nefarious purpose, Cethin was falling right into whatever spell she had woven.

"Kailia will be joining our advisory meeting today," Cethin said to Zayan, dragging his eyes away from Kailia.

The Hand of the King did a terrible job of hiding his reaction at that statement. A mixture of surprise and dissatisfaction. The male rocked onto his toes, clasping his hands behind his back as his dark brown eyes slid from the king to Kailia and back.

"I see. I look forward to seeing both of you shortly then," Zayan said with a small bow of his head before quickly retreating from the room.

"Everyone is going to know your business before you even get there," Razik said dryly, picking up his glass of juice and draining it.

"I'm aware," Cethin replied, pushing back his now empty plate. "Why do you think I said anything?"

"He's terrible at his job."

"How so?" Cethin asked flatly.

"What kind of Hand of the King spreads the king's business?" Razik answered, pushing his plate aside as well.

"And who do you propose should replace him? You?"

"In your dreams, Sutara," Razik retorted with a sneer.

Cethin smirked at the word choice.

Reaching over, Cethin brushed his fingers along Kailia's arm, and she nearly jumped out of her chair. A rather dramatic reaction if Razik had ever seen one. Wait, was he—

"Kailia, can you give us a moment?" Razik asked, a low growl sounding with the words.

She looked at him in confusion, then back at Cethin. "I do need to use the privy."

"There is one down the hall on the left," Cethin said. "Do you need me to show you where?"

"I'm sure I can manage," she said, sliding back her chair and getting to her feet.

Just as she reached the door, Cethin called after her, "Don't wander, tiny fiend."

She ignored him, and Razik waited until the dining room doors closed before he slid his gaze back to Cethin.

"What is it, Greybane?" Cethin asked warily.

"Are you forcing her into this?" Razik demanded.

Cethin's features remained impassive, and the king settled back in his chair, steepling a finger along his temple. "Why would you think that?"

"Because she nearly jumped out of her skin at your touch," he replied. "Considering you basically told Zayan you're about to announce a betrothal, I'll ask you again: are you forcing her into this? Or maybe I should ask if you've forced her in *any* way?"

That had Cethin straightening, his darkness making a full appearance and drifting across the table like a dense fog. Razik summoned dragon fire to his fingertips, letting it linger there while his eyes shifted to vertical slits.

"I know we do not care for one another and that your opinion of me is so low, it may as well be buried in the depths of the Pits of Torment, but if you ever accuse me of forcing myself physically on her, or anyone, again, you'll be banished from this kingdom. You can either figure out a way across the Wards or die trying. I don't give a fuck," Cethin said, his power pulsing with his rage.

But if he thought that was going to deter him, he could fuck off himself.

"Then why did she react that way to your touch?" Razik pushed, toying with his black flames.

"She does that when *anyone* touches her," Cethin spat. "Why do you think she lost her godsdamn mind when you picked her up?"

"Why? What happened to her?"

"I haven't learned that yet," Cethin answered, shoving back from the table and getting to his feet. "But *I* will. As for you, it's none of your godsdamn business."

Then he was stalking from the room, the doors banging shut behind him, but his power lingered, slowly dissipating.

Razik continued to roll the flames along his knuckles, thinking over this new information. Cethin may have answered the question about forcing himself on her physically, but it hadn't escaped him that he *hadn't* answered the question about forcing her into whatever this was about to be.

That was fine.

Nonchalantly pushing his chair back, he stood, swiping up a fruit tart to take with him as he went to piss off the king even more.

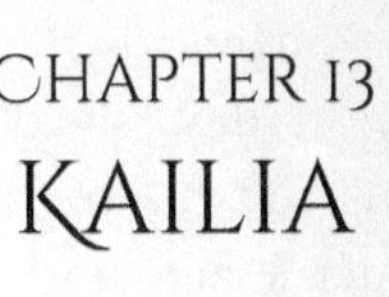
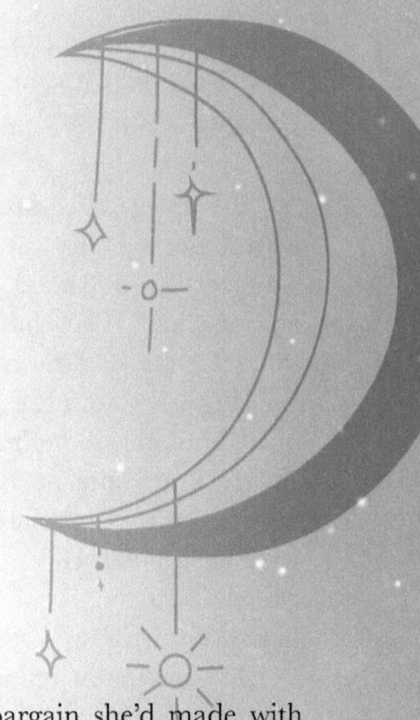

CHAPTER 13
KAILIA

She hated this.

She knew it was part of the bargain she'd made with Cethin last night, but by the gods did she hate it.

Kailia sat in a chair to Cethin's right. He, of course, sat at the head of the table, being the king and all that. He'd also donned an ornate crown before they'd made their way to the meeting room.

The other chairs around the table, save for two, were also occupied. The males and females in them were whispering to each other with a mixture of excitement and concern while also not bothering to hide their scrutinizing gazes. She could feel their eyes sliding over her. Analyzing. Speculating. Making decisions about how she measured up before Cethin had even said a word.

Razik was here too, standing next to a male who was clearly related to him. She recognized him as Tybalt Greybane, Commander of the Avonleyan Forces, but while Razik appeared apathetic and bored, the other male did not. His stare was fixed on her, and unlike everyone else in the room, he didn't bother trying to downplay how he felt about what was going to transpire. His mouth was set in a firm line, and his brown eyes told her he did not trust her in the slightest. She held his stare for several long seconds because, frankly, she preferred when people were blunt and didn't try to hide their thoughts or feelings. She liked knowing where she stood. No games. No guessing. No confusion.

Unlike Cethin.

She dragged her gaze from the male to the king, only to find his eyes on her too. She wasn't surprised. He was always watching her.

After she'd bathed yesterday, she'd spent much of the day ignoring him. They hadn't left his rooms, having meals delivered there. Cethin had given her space, and she'd welcomed the quiet. Looking back now, she probably should have asked questions and made him prepare her more for this.

He'd also already had clothing for her in the dressing room because he was a presumptuous ass who was clearly used to getting what he wanted. He'd explained how this meeting would go today and that the union would likely be finalized quickly. The actual union ceremony was quite intimate and would just be them and a Witch to anoint the union. But after that...

After that would be a celebration that would be attended by thousands from all over Avonleya.

The thought alone made her heart rate increase and her chest tighten. The attention in this room was already too much, but thousands? Yes, it was expected with the role she was suddenly finding herself in, but...

But she was already being scrutinized. It wouldn't take much to figure out she was ill-equipped to be a queen, and Cethin announcing she would be the queen only in title would feed into that belief. She was here to satisfy this council. That was all. And in return she'd be avoiding a trial and probable death sentence, get her arrow back, and find herself under the protection of the king. But she still hadn't figured out why Cethin needed to do anything for the council when he was the king.

She'd put silk slippers on when she'd come down this morning, but now seated, she toed them off, curling her bare toes on the stone floor. She felt her ashes swirl, a small comfort even if she still couldn't move among her power. Cethin had said he'd have the wards around the castle altered at some point, but never offered *when* that would be, and by Temural, she needed to have access to her magic. But she was also dreading having full access to it again because of what had transpired by that lake.

Her power hadn't had that kind of control over her since it had first manifested, and even then, it had been protecting her. What had happened a few days ago hadn't been the same. This had been…like someone *else* was controlling her magic.

Cethin shifted in his chair slightly before a faint wisp of dark power curled around her forearm, bringing her attention back to him. It lingered, an icy cold that stung a little. It was such a contrast to the usual burning of a touch.

He leaned in, and she forced herself not to flinch away because what had he said?

They need to be *convincing*.

"I'm going to start this meeting," he said, his words low so that only she could hear them. "Are you ready?"

She smiled sweetly as she said, "Do I have a choice?"

He ignored the barbed words. "Just be prepared."

He leaned back, saying something to get everyone's attention, and she straightened, trying to figure out what, exactly, she was expected to do and say here. Her gaze flicked to Razik. While the male beside him had switched his attention to the king, Razik was still watching her intently.

"I am sure there are plenty of matters on the agenda today, but I am going to request we table anything that is not of an urgent nature," Cethin was saying. "As I'm sure you have all ascertained by the present company, there is an announcement to make. One I believe you all will be very pleased by, given numerous past discussions."

He reached over, brushing his fingers down her forearm before taking her hand in his. She'd been prepared for the touch. Knew this would be required of her. After all, gentle touches and stolen moments are what people who were in love did. At least, that was what she'd observed over the years.

His power still lingered faintly, the iciness mixing with the burn of the physical touch, and the juxtaposition of the two sensations was doing things to her. Things she wasn't entirely sure what to do with. It was throwing her off balance, her stomach dipping in a way she was unfamiliar with. She couldn't decide whether she liked it or hated it. She couldn't understand it, and she definitely didn't like *that*.

"It seems the wisdom of this council has prevailed after all," Cethin went on. "I met someone at the Esbat Festival. Someone I've connected with in ways I never could have imagined. As if the Fates themselves answered your prayers."

He gave a knowing smile at the advisors, the males chuckling to themselves while the females smiled even wider at the idea of fate bringing her into all of this. Cethin was good at spinning a tale, that was for sure. With the practiced ease of someone in leadership, he'd convinced everyone at this table that their meeting had been not only destined, but that they'd had a part in it somehow.

"It is my greatest honor to introduce you to Kailia, the future queen of Avonleya," Cethin said, giving her fingers a soft squeeze. She forced herself not to look down at where he still held her hand while everyone in the room clapped, starting to chatter and ask questions at once.

Keep your chin up, she thought to herself.

Wait, should she do that? Or was the queen supposed to be demure and silent?

She didn't know. Cethin hadn't given her any direction other than to say they needed to be convincing and to follow his lead.

Glancing over at him, she saw he was smiling, and he nodded at her encouragingly. He leaned in close once more, his breath fanning across her temple as he murmured low into her ear, "Breathe, tiny fiend. Breathe and smile."

Was she not smiling?

"They will ask where you are from," he continued in a whisper. "Tell them Shadowfen."

"Why?"

"Because it doesn't have a ruling lord or lady to question you."

She nodded. That made sense.

He lifted his other hand as if he were going to touch her, but then stopped. Instead, he raised it higher, quieting the conversation instantly. "It goes without saying I will require the queen's crown."

"And when exactly is this union to take place?" asked a female from down the table. "How soon shall we be calling her Majesty?"

Cethin smiled wider, releasing Kailia's hand and settling back in his chair. "I understand the urgency, Lady Mariel. You all have made it more than clear. The union can take place as soon as arrangements can feasibly be made. However, this is all very fast. I want to give Kailia a chance to adjust. So for the immediate future, she will be the queen in title only. Until she is ready to take on the full duties and responsibility of the position."

"That doesn't solve the immediate issue at hand then, does it?" a male said, steepling his fingers together in front of him, elbows planted on the table.

"How so, Lord Harlin?" Cethin asked, and something in Kailia went on high alert at his tone. His temple was resting on his fist while his other hand was resting on the arm of his chair, finger tapping.

"How so?" the Lord repeated, and gods, did Kailia appreciate Cethin saying their names. Whether or not it was on purpose, it was useful to put names to the faces of the people she was going to be answering to.

"If she is solely going to be a queen in title, how does that help if something happens to you?" Lord Harlin continued. "And seeing as you said you just met at Esbat, we wouldn't know if there's a babe in her belly even if she's been in your bed every—"

But he didn't get a chance to finish his sentence. Not as his mouth gaped open like a fish, his features contorting in pain. A palm slammed to the table while his other hand clawed at his chest, and Kailia didn't understand what was happening. She was still, watching the male who was clearly in agony, and she slid her gaze to Cethin.

He still sat casually, finger still steepled along his temple, but his other hand was raised, closed in a fist. His features were sharp and dark, and she could swear his silver eyes were glowing faintly as he stared at the Lord. Was...*he* doing something to the Lord? His dark magic was nowhere to be seen, so that didn't seem likely. Unsure if she should be doing anything and not wanting to appear as if she weren't aware of… whatever this was, she kept her features expressionless as she slid her stare around the table. The others seated around her were tense, some with eyes wide while others had their heads bowed in submission.

Then she found the males standing along the wall. The Commander looked upset, and he was entirely focused on Cethin, but Razik was staring directly at her. He looked bored, though, with his arms crossed and shoulder leaning casually against the wall. When her gaze locked with his, his brow arched, and she had no idea what he wanted or what that meant.

The seconds that passed felt like minutes with the tension that filled the air, and she truly didn't know if she should do anything or say something. Gods, this was never going to work. Why, in all the realms, had she thought this was a wise idea?

It wasn't until she saw Cethin's arm move in her periphery that Lord Harlin slumped in his chair, chest heaving as he dragged in breath after breath.

"Should anyone ever speak so disrespectfully of the future queen again, they shall taste death. Is that clear?" Cethin asked, the words so calm they were eerie, danger dripping from each syllable.

Surely that hadn't all been because of her? That was absurd. They'd only known each other for a handful of days. He was using her to placate these very people. Why would he hurt them because of her? That didn't seem like something that would be helpful in this situation.

"I think your point has been made," the Commander said dryly.

"One would assume," Cethin all but growled, "but I'm beginning to question the intelligence of the people at this table for thinking they can be so cavalier about my future wife in my presence. Anything to say to that, Lord Harlin?"

By the gods, the male could still scarcely breathe, but he lifted his head, eyes watering and full of pain as he met the king's gaze. "My…apologies, your…Majesty," he choked out.

"It is not I who is owed the apology," Cethin snarled.

And then the lord's gaze shifted to her, and again, she didn't know what she was supposed to do or say when the lord spoke to her, each word fractured and full of the agony he was clearly still experiencing. "Apologies…your…Highness."

She was frozen, the words 'your Highness' rolling around in her head. It wasn't until the icy darkness of Cethin's magic brushed along her arm a moment before his fingers followed the same path that she glanced at him.

"Is his apology sufficient, Kailia?"

She was nearly startled at the change in his tone. There was a softness there, and she really needed to get herself together. His looks and tone and touches were far more convincing than her just…sitting here.

But not knowing what to do yet again, she nodded once more. His head tilted slightly, the barest of creases appearing at his brow as if confused. Was that not what she should have done?

A throat cleared down the table, and without looking away from her, Cethin said sharply, "What?"

"Are we allowed to ask where her Highness hails from?" a male asked.

"If done so respectfully, then yes," he answered simply, sitting back in his chair once more, his fingers slipping from her arm. He nodded at her encouragingly.

"I'm…" She cleared her throat, sitting up taller. "I'm from Shadowfen," she replied, the words a little stronger.

"Shadowfen?" the male repeated.

"You know of it, do you not, Lord Tovan?" Cethin said. "The hunting and fishing town near Harrows Bay."

"Of course," Lord Tovan replied. "I am simply surprised."

"You grew up in Shadowfen?" Lady Mariel repeated, the curiosity evident in her tone.

Why would Cethin tell her to say that town if it was going to invite surprise and questions?

"What of the sea serpents?" Lord Tovan pushed.

What of the…

Cethin scoffed under his breath. "The sea serpents slumber, Lord Tovan."

"What of your family, my dear?" the lady cut in. "What is your bloodline? You are clearly not Fae but an Ash Rider. More than many of us had hoped for. That is from your father's line, I presume?"

This was...a lot of questions being hurled at her.

"I think that's enough for now," Cethin cut in, and relief coursed through her.

She didn't know her lineage. How in the realms was she supposed to share it with strangers?

"And the union? When will that take place?" Lady Mariel pushed.

The king's smile was thin and words pointed as he replied, "After the Beltane Hunt. Is that sufficient, Lady Mariel?"

The lady quickly lowered her eyes to the table. "Of course, your Majesty. You cannot fault us for our excitement."

Cethin hummed. "If there is nothing else today—"

"There is," the Commander interrupted.

Something in Cethin shifted as his attention turned to him, and Kailia didn't understand it. He wasn't quite as...dominant as he said, "Yes, Tybalt?"

"You have a betrothed," the male continued. "The future queen needs a personal guard, just as you have."

"We can discuss that at a later time," Cethin answered.

"No need," Tybalt replied. "Razik has already been appointed."

Cethin went rigid, darkness drifting from beneath his palms that he tried to hide. "Razik has a duty to the Cadre."

"His duty to the crown supersedes those responsibilities."

"He is one of the best warriors we have," Lord Tovan agreed. "Frankly, I'm surprised he's not *your* personal guard, your Majesty."

"Is there anything else that must be handled today?" Cethin gritted out, and Kailia could swear his eyes were glowing once more, but this time with something dark.

"There is the matter of the vacant advisory seat," Lord Harlin said tentatively. But when Cethin dragged his stare to him, he added, "But that can be discussed tomorrow."

It took mere minutes for everyone to clear out of the room.

Everyone but Razik and Tybalt.

As soon as the heavy wooden doors thudded shut, Cethin was on his feet. With his hands braced on the table, he leaned towards the males. It was no longer a little darkness at his fingers, but thick, inky darkness rolling along the floor.

"No," Cethin said, the word a guttural syllable.

At least it wasn't a word he reserved just for her.

"It's already done," Tybalt said.

"Then fucking undo it," Cethin retorted.

"Lord Tovan spoke truth. He's one of our best. You can't deny that, Cethin."

Kailia's brows arched. He was familial enough to call the king by his name?

"Jarek is just as qualified. Or better yet, Fallon or Ariadne," Cethin argued.

"I'm not assigning someone else," Tybalt said. "You trust me to know who's best for positions. Let me do my job."

"Not him," Cethin ground out.

"Why don't we let Kailia have a say?" Razik cut in, the words a lazy drawl. "Or is your plan to not let her have any opinions and thoughts of her own?"

Fury darkened Cethin's features even more. "Of course not."

"Then…" Razik turned to face her fully, sapphire eyes boring into her own. "Are you comfortable with me as your personal guard, Lia?"

"That's not my name, and I don't need a personal guard," she replied simply.

The scraping of chair legs on stone sounded as Razik pulled a chair out and unceremoniously dropped into it. "That is evident from the stabbing, so I guess it's to make sure you don't do any more of that."

"Wouldn't that make you his personal guard then?" she asked, her head tilting.

Cethin and Razik both went still.

"No," Razik finally said, the word clipped. "I will be your personal guard only. The king has his own entourage that consistently fails at their jobs."

"They do not—" Cethin stopped, inhaling deeply. "My personal guard is not the topic here."

"It is fine with me," Kailia cut in. "I maintain I do not need a guard, but if it is expected, I do not wish to cause unnecessary issues during my first days at your side."

"This is not an unnecessary issue," Cethin retorted.

"Seems like it is if I'm in agreement and Razik is willing," she countered.

Cethin turned to her, once again studying her too closely, and she held his stare. This actually worked in her favor, but it was something Cethin was clearly vehemently against. If she seemed too eager, he'd become suspicious, so she'd stay the small female trying not to make waves on her first day as the future queen.

"Fine," Cethin finally acquiesced. "But only when I am not around."

"The stabbing occurs when you two are alone together," Razik said, sitting far too casually in his seat for someone who had just argued with the king.

"I'll leave the three of you to work out the details," Tybalt said. Then he added, "I assume such things will be handled like the centuries-old males you are and not like younglings who haven't gotten their way."

Kailia held in a huff of amusement at the comment. She was pretty sure she liked the male, even if the sentiment didn't appear to be mutual.

Cethin lowered back into his chair as Tybalt left, and as soon as he was gone, he turned to Razik with a sneer on his lips. "What are you playing at, Greybane?"

Unfazed, Razik propped an ankle on his knee as he said, "You flatter yourself thinking everything is about you. Tybalt heard this was coming and wanted to get things in order. He asked me, and I said yes."

"You willingly agreed to be in my presence," Cethin deadpanned.

"No. I willingly agreed to be in *her* presence."

"Why?"

"Are you sure the two of you have never been lovers?" Kailia cut in, trying to understand the animosity between the two.

"Yes," Cethin gritted out.

"Did one of you take the other's lover?"

"No."

"Anything to do with lovers?"

Finally, Cethin turned to her. "Why do you assume this has anything to do with lovers?"

"I've only seen males become this irrational when lovers are involved."

"Personal experience, Lia?" Razik cut in.

"No, simply observations."

Neither of the males said anything in response, and neither did she because this was all very confusing.

Icy black wisps flitted around her arm a moment before Cethin stood and extended a hand to her. "She doesn't need a personal guard when we're in our own rooms," he said, eyes on her until he looked over his shoulder at Razik. Then he added, "Feel free to stand outside the doors and wait until you're needed. And I expect you to be there. If you're not, I'll report you and have you replaced for failing in your responsibilities. Again."

"You motherfu—"

But Kailia never heard Razik finish the curse as she slipped her hand into Cethin's, and he immediately Traveled them to their floor.

Dropping her fingers, Cethin stalked across the room and filled a liquor glass. He downed the entire thing before refilling it. Several minutes passed as he sipped on his refilled glass of alcohol and she simply stood there, unsure of what was happening.

"You did well today," he finally said.

"No thanks to you," she retorted, lifting her chin.

"What is that supposed to mean?"

"You didn't prepare me for this."

"Of course I did. I told you what to expect today."

"And then you told me to tell them I was from Shadowfen, and they had questions, Cethin," she said, throwing her hands in the air. "How was I supposed to answer those? Was I even supposed to answer them? Was I supposed to speak? Let you do the talking?"

"You can speak whenever you wish," Cethin said, taking another sip and watching her intently. "And I stopped the questions."

She shook her head, only then realizing her ashes had appeared as they drifted from her hair to the floor. He didn't understand what she was trying to say, and she didn't know how to articulate it because she was used to solitude. Not having to rely on anyone else. She was used to watching from the shadows and—

A gasp escaped her as a dark tendril slithered along her jaw a moment before he was tipping her chin up with his hand. When had he moved in front of her? Again he said nothing, studying her features and his eyes roving over her.

A part of her wondered if this was always how their interactions were going to go. Her out of her element, and him meticulously observing her. Her feeling like she was finally gaining the upper hand only for him to prove her wrong. A push and pull that confused her and drew her attention away from what she should be focused on.

"How old are you, Kailia?" he asked, and she blinked because that question had come out of nowhere.

"Just under three centuries," she answered.

Still holding her jaw, his thumb swiped along her skin, a searing path that had her wincing. He clearly noticed based on the way his lips thinned and a muscle in his jaw ticked in irritation.

"Three centuries and you have no personal experience with lovers?"

"That's not what I said," she answered, stepping back as his touch became the burning of every other physical encounter. "I said I don't have experience with scorned or wronged lovers."

He followed, keeping the space between them minuscule, but he didn't reach for her again. "Are there any lovers I need to be aware of?"

"Isn't it a little late to be asking that?"

"Kailia," he growled, taking another step that forced her to back up again. "Are there any lovers I need to…ensure understand that you are no longer theirs?"

She studied him as he loomed over her. A slightly crazed look in his silver eyes. Silver hair that was loose around his shoulders. An aura of intensity that she didn't know what to do with.

"It is weird to me that you are jealous of people you've never met," she finally said. "But to answer your question, no."

Because she'd sworn she'd never be owned by another person the first time she saw the stars.

She'd been nineteen years.

"Is there anything else required of me today?" she asked, no longer willing to engage in casual conversation as memories swirled, reminding her of her purpose. Why she had come here to begin with.

"I thought we would spend the rest of the day together," Cethin said. "Get to know each other better."

"No," she said simply, slipping past him and making her way down the hall to the main bedchamber. She knew she was leaving footprints because she'd summoned her ashes, letting them flow around her. Letting them soothe her, comfort her.

Letting them protect and hide her like they'd always done.

⟨⟩ ☉ ⟨⟩

She blinked, taking in the space around her.

Rocky walls. A cot along the back. A bucket for personal needs in the corner. The onyx door that was shut tight.

Her heart hammering, she tugged her sleeve back, breathing a sigh of relief at the sight of the Mark on her forearm. The Mark that confirmed this was a dream. Not real. None of this was real.

She'd paid a Witch across the sea a large sum to help her find a Mark that would work. Then she'd paid an Earth Court Fae trained in bestowing Marks an equally large sum. Blood magic was not something she played around with, but desperation can turn anyone into a fool.

She didn't regret the cost of this Mark though. This Mark gave her back her sanity. It set her free from the nightmares of her past because she could only see the Mark in her dreams. It was how she knew she wasn't really trapped in a commune beneath cliffs. It was how she knew she could leave this room because in her dreams, she controlled the narrative.

Pulling the door open, she still winced at the loud squeak, wondering who would be alerted to her movements. But no one came as she stepped into the hall and peered over the railing. She was several floors above the ground. Her room had been on that floor for the entirety of the nearly twenty years she'd spent here.

It wasn't surprising she'd found herself here tonight either. Not with the memories that had surfaced after her conversation with Cethin. Still, she didn't wish to linger. Not tonight. Even knowing this was a dream, it didn't mean her nightmares couldn't torture her while here.

Not wanting to wake her demons, she padded to the stairwell, quickly descending several flights. She kept to the shadows, not wanting to risk using her magic, unsure if it would work properly in her dreams or not. Unwilling to face the possibility that she was truly fucked and broken because she didn't know how to fix it if she was. If, after all this time, after centuries of trying to put herself back together and figure out how to breathe with a tortured soul, it had all been for nothing.

The brand beneath her skin—that only appeared on those who were marked as belonging to the colony—glowed as she neared the entrance to the cliffs. It was one of three entrances. There was another one that only saw death, and there was one off the Baroness's balcony. Was she gone in this dream? Had the Reaper already bestowed his wrath, or was this dream before he'd come back for his vengeance?

Kailia didn't know, and she didn't care to find out. Sometimes she did. Sometimes she lingered in these dreams, searching for information she'd forgotten. Sometimes she stayed to bestow her own vengeance on those long gone from this world. It was dark and twisted, and she was sure it marred her soul in yet another way, but she'd never cared because the high of retribution at her own hands was as addicting as the opioids some became slaves to.

Stepping through the rocky archway that appeared, her feet sank into sand. It was night, the moon and stars bright. She breathed in the fresh air, her first full breath since she'd found herself here. Even knowing it was a dream, her heart beat at a too fast pace and sweat beaded on her brow and slid down her nape.

Taking a few steps, she came to a sudden halt when she spotted the figure that stood down the beach. Tall and broad, the moonlight made his shoulder-length silver hair seem to shimmer. His back was to her, hands in his pockets as he stared out at the sea, waves lapping at his bare feet.

She shouldn't be surprised to see him here. Not with how much he'd become a part of her life. It wasn't the first time he'd shown up in her dreams either, but it was the first time he'd been here, at the cliffs.

Like every other time he'd been in her dreams, he didn't acknowledge her. He just stared at the water, much like he did in reality when she'd watched him from her smoke and ashes for months. She couldn't get inside the castle, but he'd left often, always going to the same shore.

"You're not supposed to be out here," came a whispered voice in her ear. Before she could make a sound, a hand slipped over her mouth while an arm banded around her waist. Her heels dug into the sand as she was dragged backwards, panic filling her chest. Touch didn't burn in her dreams, but where she was being taken? She'd burn there.

The sand turned to stone, her heels scraping open, and right before the enchanted doorway took away her view of the night sky, the figure on the shore turned, and glowing silver eyes landed on her.

CHAPTER 14

CETHIN

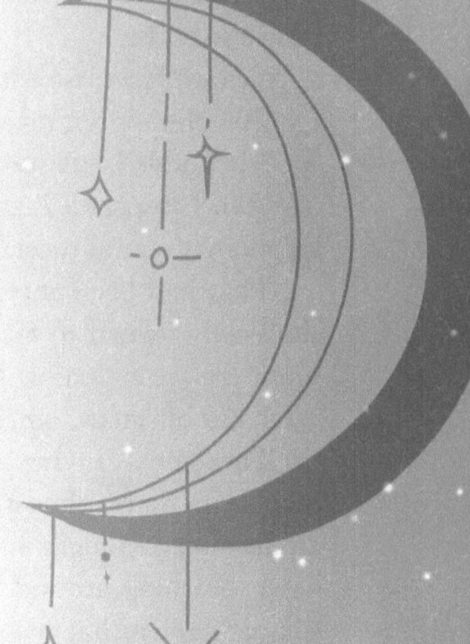

The sound of the bedchamber door opening down the hall had him glancing at the clock above the hearth. It was the early morning hours of dawn, when most people in Avonleya were only a few hours into their sleep. Despite ignoring him the rest of the day yesterday, he knew Kailia had only gone to bed a few hours ago. She might be avoiding him, but that didn't mean he wasn't aware of her every move.

Unsure if she simply didn't sleep a lot or if it was something more, he stilled and waited. He didn't hear footsteps, but he'd quickly learned she was incredibly light on her feet. Whether it was an Ash Rider thing or her own talent, there wasn't a godsdamn sound to tell him if she was nearing or if she'd stayed in the bedchamber.

It wasn't until he saw her in his periphery that he slid his piece of charcoal into the leather-bound journal in his lap and closed it. She slipped quietly into the room, leaving ashy footprints in her wake as she made her way to the windows. Pulling back a curtain, she peered out, but he didn't miss the tremble in her hand as the fabric shook where she still held it.

Clearing his throat softly, he said, "I didn't expect you to be awake so early."

"Most places rise with the sun," she murmured.

"Avonleya is not most places," he replied.

She nodded, still staring out the window.

"But I suspect it is an adjustment considering you've been in the kingdom a year at most," he added nonchalantly.

That had her entire being going still for a few moments before she slowly turned to face him, the heavy drape falling closed once more. Any satisfaction he'd briefly had at throwing this at her to catch her off guard quickly faded as he fully took her in.

The smoke in her eyes was swirling faster than normal, the amber in them almost completely obscured. Faint ashes flowed among her midnight hair that was a mess of tangles, as if she'd been thrashing around. She was still in her nightclothes—a black silk nightgown that reached the floor with thin straps at her shoulders and was more than a little revealing in the front. If it weren't for the rest of her body language, he'd be far more appreciative of the attire. It wasn't just her hand that was trembling, but her whole body shook with a faint tremor. Her breathing was a little too quick and shallow, and she kept reaching as if she was going to run her hands along her arms or torso but then stopping herself.

Haunted.

That was how she looked.

He stood, setting the journal on the side table, and she took a step back right into the drapery.

"Kailia..." he started, hesitating. He cleared his throat lightly again. "There's a robe in the bedchamber for you. Several of them, actually."

As if just realizing how she was dressed, she looked down at herself.

"I'm not cold," she replied, her brows knitting together.

He paused, as confused as she appeared. "That's not what I was suggesting." When she continued to stare back at him, he added, "That's rather revealing night clothing."

"You are the one who ordered my wardrobe. If you didn't want me to wear it, why did you provide it?" she asked, sounding exasperated. Then she lifted her arm, turning it to apparently…study her forearm?

This whole interaction was becoming rather bizarre, but by the gods, he was more than drawn in at this point. He found himself distracted, spending his time trying to come up with ways to figure her out rather than focusing on things that needed his attention. He'd already pushed off an entire council meeting, but every time he thought he was making headway, something like this conversation happened, making him realize he hadn't figured any part of her out at all. She'd become an obsession—a distraction he couldn't afford right now—and he needed to stop. He knew that.

But he also didn't want to.

Her fingers brushed over her forearm before she looked him up and down. "You are still dressed from yesterday's activities."

"I am," he agreed. He'd discarded his belt and boots, and his tunic was loose over his pants. Still far more casual than he'd ever be seen outside these rooms.

"And the other side of the bed was not slept on." It was his turn to stay silent and hold her stare. "Where did you sleep?"

"I haven't gone to bed yet."

"But you sleep?"

"Of course I sleep. At the very least to restore my magic."

She nodded, breaking their stare and her gaze darting to the side. He stepped forward, but she immediately stepped back again, pressing against the window behind the curtains.

Pushing out a frustrated breath, he ran his hands through his hair. He thought he'd made progress with the touching yesterday, but apparently not.

Slipping his hands into his pockets, he said, "While I have not been to bed yet, you didn't sleep long."

"I rarely do."

"Sleep long?"

"Sleep," she answered simply.

He nodded as he pulled a hand from his pocket and sent a

message off in a swirl of darkness. Her eyes narrowed, and before she could ask, he said, "I requested tea be brought up for us."

"I didn't ask for tea."

"Yes, but you seem…out of sorts," he ventured, settling on the phrase, but it was a lie. He didn't know her well enough to know if this was unusual. She was odd enough, it could very well be normal behavior, but that was exactly what he was trying to figure out.

Stepping to the side, he gestured to the sofa. "Come and sit, Kailia."

Surprisingly, she didn't fight him despite her tentative footsteps. Ashes still fluttered with her movement, and once she lowered to the cushions, she lifted a hand, drawing a tendril of smoke to herself from the fire burning in the hearth. It danced around her fingers as she got lost in her thoughts, and he let her be, using the time to study her until there was a knock on the door twenty minutes later.

Opening it, he found staff with the tea tray, along with Razik Greybane leaning against the wall with his arms crossed. Cethin didn't bother acknowledging him as he took the tray and thanked the staff.

Kicking the door shut behind him with his foot, he returned to the sitting room and set the tray on the low table in front of the sofa before taking a seat on the other end. Kailia seemed to have settled some. She wasn't trembling anymore, and her breathing had evened out. But she was still on edge, stiff and alert.

He took his time pouring two cups of tea and sliding hers to her. "I don't know how you take your tea," he said, adding sugar and honey to his.

She said nothing as she reached for a lemon wedge, smoke trailing her hand. More than before, it now swirled with her ashes.

Cethin waited until she took her first sip and had set her cup back down before he said, "You were upset with me earlier. Is that why you are having trouble sleeping?"

Her head tilted as she met his gaze. "Why would you affect my sleep?"

And once again, he wasn't sure how to respond to her.

"Because you were angry with me, and stewing in anger can cause restlessness," he finally ventured.

Reaching for her tea again, she said, "My thoughts do not revolve around you, king, and emotions fuel carelessness."

"Yet you were feeling many of them," he countered, ignoring the way that small hit to his ego made him bristle inside.

She rolled her lips before setting her teacup down on the saucer and pushing back to her feet. "You know nothing of my emotions."

"Which is why I'm trying to have a conversation about them," he replied, standing as well. She immediately took three steps back from him, and it only made his irritation grow. "I told you we need to be convincing, tiny fiend."

"And that requires this sort of conversation?"

"Yes," he said, not bothering to hide his exasperation now. He took a step towards her, and before she could move back, he said sharply, "Don't."

To his surprise, she actually fucking listened, whether from his warning tone or the command in it, he didn't care.

His voice was low as he caught a lock of her hair, winding it around his finger. It was the one part of her he touched as he said, "You say you have no experience with scorned or wronged lovers, but I'm beginning to suspect you have little experience with any lovers."

"It's just fucking," she retorted flatly, the smoke in her eyes swirling faster once again.

"Fucking is not what I'm speaking of, Kailia. Although, I still question your experience with that too," he said, the words fanning across her lips as he leaned in a bit more. "Lovers know each other intimately. They can predict each other's reactions and understand the other's emotions with a simple look. They share secrets that no one else knows. They steal glances and moments, appearing as if lost to their own world."

She didn't move, and he could swear his words weren't having any effect on her. There was no throat bobbing with a swallow. No hitched breath. No shifting on her feet or averting her gaze.

"But the physical is just as important," he added, releasing her hair. He let a ribbon of his darkness appear, tangling with the tendrils of smoke still lingering around her. That was when the small gasp fell from her lips. And fucking Fates, he hadn't expected to feel that sound all the way down to his cock, but there it was. Twitching behind his pants as his blood heated and something primal lifted its head in his soul.

"Lovers create excuses for small touches in public because they are craving to be behind closed doors. Because they know each other's bodies as well as they know their emotions and thoughts," he continued, the words low and sensual. Slowly, he lifted his hand, using the tip of his finger to lift her chin. The barest of touches that she still visibly winced at, clearly wanting to pull away. "That's how convincing we need to be, Kailia, and the way to become that familiar with each other is to have godsdamn conversations. *That* is why I don't believe you have any experience with lovers."

"Perhaps you should have thought of all that before you forced me into a bargain to be your wife," she retorted, shoving his hand away and breaking the small amount of contact.

"Perhaps *you* should have thought of all that before agreeing to be my wife," he bit back.

She tsked, her ashes vibrating as more smoke found its way to her, undulating around her feet and torso. "The options were a union or a death trial. That's not much of a choice."

"But a choice you made nevertheless," he said. "You were angry I didn't prepare you enough, but have you thought that maybe that's because you avoid me instead of having conversations?"

"Yes," she answered.

"Exactly, but instead—" He paused, realizing she'd actually agreed with him instead of arguing. "Wait, you *have*? If you're in agreement, then why are we having this argument?"

"I…don't have an answer for that," she admitted.

By the gods. This seemed more and more hopeless the longer this conversation went on, and it made him that much more intrigued. And yes, he recognized how fucked up that was, but this was the most engaged he'd been in something in a long time. Sure, there were the attacks and trying to figure out the Wards, but this was something that was only his. A mystery that was a break from the monotony and duty of his crown. Someone who appeared not to care about that crown or what it made him in the slightest. He didn't understand this ridiculous argument or her, but he understood it made him feel alive. More alive than he'd felt in decades, perhaps centuries. He understood he was a bastard for pulling her into this for his own entertainment, and he even understood he was a bigger dick for using his title and threats to keep her here.

Worst of all, he didn't care because she was a distraction from… well, everything really. She'd become a vice he craved as much as a drunk craved liquor to drown his sorrows.

He rubbed his brow as he studied her. Her in complete stillness aside from her power. Her with her magic and those swirling eyes that were fixed on him that suddenly made him feel a bit like prey, especially knowing she'd been watching him from her smoke for months. Her with her midnight hair and that godsdamn nightdress that clung to her curves.

Fuck.

With a sigh, he moved back to the sofa and picked up his teacup, the liquid lukewarm now. "Sit, Kailia. Tell me why you appeared apprehensive when you emerged."

"I was fine," she answered, cautiously moving closer and perching on the edge of the sofa cushion. Again, she glanced at her forearm, running her fingers over her skin.

"You were not fine. You were skittish and trembling like a youngling convinced they saw a Night Child."

"It was not that bad," she protested.

He smirked. "But you admit you were trembling?"

"I…" She paused, and he watched her think about how to respond before she said, "I simply woke up in a strange space. I'm not accustomed to the surroundings, and I've had unfavorable experiences when waking up in unfamiliar places with no one that I know around."

He nodded. That was a perfectly reasonable explanation.

"Was that so hard to share?" he asked.

"Yes," she retorted. "And you don't need to be condescending about it."

He huffed a laugh. "My apologies, your Highness."

"That was the same mocking tone, and it makes your apology insincere," she snapped. "Anyway, we don't need to do this."

"Do what?" he asked, angling his body more towards her and propping his arm on the back of the sofa, his temple resting on his fist.

"Get to know each other."

His brows crashed together. "I thought we established several reasons for why we needed to get to know each other."

"You stated decent arguments, and I agree we need to have conversations. But those conversations don't need to involve getting to know each other," she replied.

He blinked because what in the realms was he supposed to say to that?

Finally finding his voice, he said slowly, "It will be difficult to be convincing if we don't get to know each other."

"Difficult but not impossible."

Cethin straightened, his arm dropping to his side. "Why would we make this more difficult? Why are you so adamant about this?"

She shrugged, reaching to refill her teacup. "I do not wish to get to know you."

He went rigid, feeling a muscle in his jaw tick. "You understand this union isn't temporary, do you not?"

She nodded. "I do."

"And you realize we are both immortal?"

Her brow furrowed. "Of course I know that."

"So you want to spend decades, if not centuries, together and *not* get to know each other?"

"Correct."

"Kailia, that's never going to work," he said slowly, unsure of what else to say.

She stood once more, teacup in hand. "You forced me into this, Cethin. All you had to do was give me back my arrow."

He stood too, every part of him bristling and surly as he realized she was trying to punish him. Force him to do what *she* wanted. Drive him to the point of madness to release her from this bargain.

Reaching out, he gripped her elbow as she turned to walk away from him. The sound of a teacup shattering reached him a moment before she twisted out of his hold, and he felt a dagger pressing to his throat, smoke still swirling from where she'd pulled it from her magic.

And he smiled, a dark and dangerous thing.

"You're in this predicament because of your penchant for stabbing, tiny fiend," he crooned as she applied more pressure to his neck. He felt it break skin, felt the blood welling. "You're starting a dangerous game. Think about where this will lead."

Her smile was just as dark and wicked. "You started this game, *little king*. Remember that when you realize you lost before the game even began."

When she turned to walk away from him again, he let her go this time, the smile still on his face.

⋅⟩⟩ ☉ ⟨⟨⋅

Cethin drummed his fingers on the table as he waited for this godsdamn meeting to get under way. He would have rather pushed this off another day, but he also realized he would always feel this way. So instead, he'd resolved to get it over with.

All the lords and ladies were here, and after this advisory meeting, they'd all be leaving for their respective territories for the next twenty days.

Thank the Fates.

They were just waiting for Zayan to arrive. Then they could get on with this, and he could get back to Kailia.

Who was currently with Razik.

The thought alone had his power coiling beneath his skin. Because of course the fucker had stood outside their rooms all godsdamn night and day until Cethin had needed to go to this meeting. Kailia had joined him for breakfast, neither of them saying a word.

He glanced to the chair at his right where she should be sitting. She waited until it was time to head down here, waited until he'd opened the door to find Greybane standing there, until she'd finally deigned to speak. That was when she announced she hadn't slept well and wasn't feeling right.

Wasn't feeling right, his ass.

Razik immediately said he'd stay with her, sauntering into their private rooms, and when Cethin had started to object, Kailia had immediately said she didn't mind. She might be a bit odd, but she was certainly godsdamn cunning. If he'd stayed to argue any longer, he would have been late. Zayan would come looking for him, and how was he to explain any of this to anyone? No one knew this was a somewhat forced union, and if it was found out, it would fracture trust with everyone. It wasn't something he could afford after only a year on the throne. He was already struggling to prove himself with handling the mass Fae murders. They might suspect the union with Kailia was simply to appease them, but if she wasn't the queen they were hoping for, he'd be to blame for not learning more about her before putting her in the role.

He'd been reckless in this. He recognized that. But if he could convince her to get them more of those arrows, it would solve so many of the dangers facing his kingdom. A kingdom he'd do anything to protect, and if that meant playing clever games with his future wife, he was going to make damn sure he won. He'd get what he wanted out of this one way or another. Failure wasn't an option, which meant Kailia's only choice was falling in line with his plans as an equal or facing submission.

Zayan's voice drew his attention back to the room, the male coming through the door a moment later with his son at his side.

Finally.

The matter at hand shouldn't take more than a few minutes to sort out. Everyone knew who was nominated to fill the vacant advisory seat with Lady Nessira's death, and most were happy with the candidate.

"My apologies for the delay," Zayan said, genuine remorse shadowing his features.

Cethin waved a hand dismissively. "It's fine, but let's proceed. I'm sure everyone would like to get home after the extended stay in Aimonway."

There was a chorus of agreed mutterings from the others, and Cethin looked at Zayan expectantly, waiting for him to go on. But the male seemed to hesitate, sending a skeptical glance to his son.

"Zayan?" Cethin said, trying and failing to hide his impatience.

The Hand of the King cleared his throat, bringing his attention back to those seated at the table. "As we all know, there is a vacancy on this council brought about by tragedy. The mourning period has passed, and while we still carry our grief, we must also move forward for the good of Avonleya. The council has debated and put forth nominations, and it has been decided to offer the seat to Jarek Ophanim."

Zayan turned to his son, but the look on Jarek's face was not one Cethin had expected. He thought Jarek would gladly accept the honor of a seat at this table, but the male's tight features and thinned lips were not those of someone happy about an offer.

"Do you accept, Jarek?" Cethin asked, carefully watching the male he considered to be somewhat of a friend.

"Not willingly," Jarek answered.

"Jarek," Zayan hissed in a harsh whisper. "We just discussed this."

"Let him speak," Cethin cut in.

Jarek's dark eyes slid to him, gratitude staring back. The male's long blond hair had several braids at his scalp before being tied back at his nape, and he wore his Cadre uniform.

Turning to him, he addressed Cethin as he said, "I'm honored by your confidence in my ability, your grace, but this is not a position I want."

"Why in the realms would you not?" Lord Tovan asked from down the table. "It is an honor to be chosen for such a thing."

"And I just stated that I recognize that honor," Jarek replied, still looking only at Cethin. Zayan was glaring at his son, but Jarek pushed on. "I've trained my entire life for the Cadre, not to sit in on meetings. If given the choice, I will choose to serve on a battlefield and in the training rings alongside the people I've served beside my entire life."

Cethin understood the sentiment all too well. He was asking Jarek to give up everything Cethin had been forced to abandon when he took the throne. He knew what that would look like. Knew how it would slowly eat away at the male's soul. Knew the male would someday come to resent the role he was asked to step into.

But part of him had been relieved at the idea of having Jarek on this side of things with him, which is why he found himself selfishly asking, "And if I asked you to reconsider?"

Jarek hesitated, a flicker of dejection flashing in his eyes.

"Appointing Jarek to this position will create another vacancy in the Cadre," Tybalt interjected. He was the one person who hadn't voted in favor of offering the advisory seat to Jarek, so Cethin wasn't surprised the male was coming to his defense now.

"We just filled the spot left by Valric's death. Draven was appointed only days ago. Hardly enough time to learn the ways of the Cadre. Removing Jarek will leave us with three inexperienced Cadre members. It's a security risk."

"Then put Razik back on the Cadre and find another personal guard for Kailia," Cethin retorted. "I will not force Jarek to take a position he does not willingly step into."

"But Razik was willing," Tybalt countered. "You offer a choice to one but not the other?"

Godsdammit.

Refocusing on Jarek, Cethin said, "I'll ask you one last time to reconsider."

"If you demand it of me, I will obey my king," Jarek said. "But if you're offering me the choice, I will respectfully and humbly ask to remain with the Cadre."

Cethin could see the despair weighing on the male at the thought of having to sit at this table and govern. Some were made for this life; Jarek was not one of them.

"The choice is yours, Jarek, and your decision will be

honored," Cethin said, the last words forceful and directed at Zayan, who was visibly upset at his son's choice. "You are dismissed."

"Thank you, your grace," Jarek said, his relief palpable as he bowed deeply to Cethin before taking his leave.

But this left them with no one to fill the vacancy yet again.

By the Fates.

Cethin pressed his thumb and forefinger against his eyes at the realization he would be sitting at this table for the next several hours debating the merits of this person and that person. What was Kailia doing right now? Were they still in their rooms? Or was Razik escorting her around the castle? Giving her the tour that *he* should be giving her?

What if Razik took her into the city?

"What are we going to do now?" Lord Harlin demanded.

"I suppose we'll have to discuss options," Cethin said with a sigh. "Who were we choosing between when we selected Jarek?"

"There was Annalise from Oseson," Lady Mariel offered.

"But that would be two advisors from the same territory," Lord Tovan argued. "That's why we decided against her."

"The options were someone from Aimonway or someone from Lady Nessira's territory," Lord Harlin agreed.

"Corveth Astor was the option from Everfall," Zayan cut in, having taken the vacant seat for the time being. "He's younger, but very involved in the affairs of the city."

"Involved, how?" Cethin asked.

"Looks after orphans and widows, from my understanding. Volunteers his time and gives much to local businesses."

"Have I met him?"

"Once while visiting Lady Nessira, but it was very brief," Zayan replied. "He was not born noble, but he does serve on the council in Everfall and is highly respected among the citizens."

"And we all agree he is the best candidate following Jarek's rejection?"

There were several agreeable murmurs that led to Zayan sending a summons with his magic. The silence was thick as the minutes passed before the male was announced and let into the council chamber.

The male pushed a hand through his black hair, strands immediately falling back across his brow and into his grey eyes. Clearly nervous at being summoned before the king, Cethin could see the beads of sweat forming on his brown skin. He wore brown pants and a black tunic with boots that were covered in mud.

Bowing deeply, he waited until Cethin bid him to rise, then he stood silently and waited.

"Corveth Astor, welcome," Cethin said.

"Thank you, your grace," he replied. The words were strong, but his fidgeting betrayed him.

"I'm sure you're wondering why you were asked here."

He gave a nervous chuckle. "You could say that."

"As you are likely aware, there is a vacancy on this council. It is on their recommendation that I am offering you that seat," Cethin replied.

The male's eyes widened with each word, and now he stared back at Cethin in astonishment.

"Do you accept?"

"I... Me?" Corveth asked.

Cethin smiled warmly. "That is what was stated. Your reputation precedes you. Your kindness, compassion, and generosity are all traits that I find valuable in someone who helps make decisions for this kingdom. I believe your presence on this council would be a valuable asset to Avonleya."

"I am honored, your grace," Corveth replied. "But this is very sudden. Can I request some time to process?"

Forcing himself to stay pleasant, Cethin said, "Of course, but please understand this matter is urgent."

"I will have an answer for you by the time the moon rises," Corveth answered.

Cethin nodded, and everyone adjourned. They'd reconvene tonight when Corveth would give his answer. If he refused, Cethin was half inclined to leave the seat open. Fuck traditions at this point.

It took him a moment to realize Tybalt was still sitting at the table. Cethin had thought everyone had left.

He leaned back in his chair, hand back on the table and fingers drumming as he held the older male's stare.

"It was the right move, Cethin," Tybalt said.

"I am still the king, Tybalt."

"And you get to decide what kind of king you are. You can rule with an iron fist, or you can listen to the wishes of your people. That's what you did today," Tybalt replied simply.

Cethin leaned forward, pointing a finger at him. "You think I don't know what you're doing? Pushing Razik into this role? Forcing us to spend more time together?"

"This has nothing to do with you and him. Your betrothed needed a guard. I gave her the best we have."

Cethin scoffed as he stood, wooden chair legs screeching against stone. He wasn't about to sit here and argue about this again. Not when Razik was alone with Kailia at this very moment.

He didn't bother saying anything else to the Commander.

CHAPTER 15

KAILIA

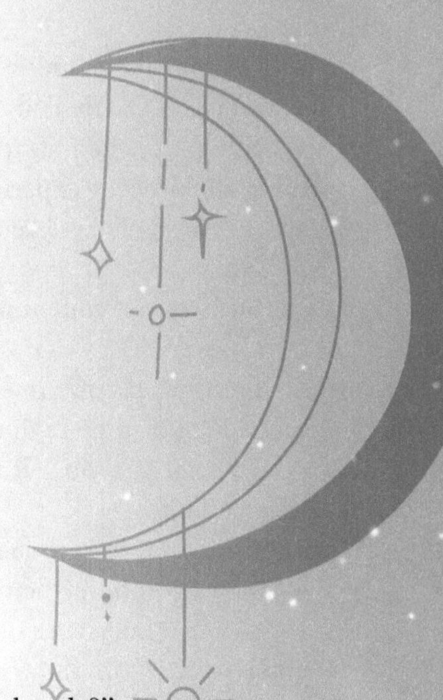

"Trouble between you and Cethin already?"

Turning away from the window she'd been staring out of, Kailia looked at her personal guard.

Razik sat lazily on the sofa, one foot on the ground while his other leg was stretched along the length of it. With an arm splayed across the back, he had a book open in his other hand. Something he'd found on one of the bookshelves. Despite being in what she'd gathered was his typical attire, he seemed comfortable enough in the king's private rooms.

And while he'd been lounging around, she'd been lost to her dream from the night before. She'd only endured a little of the torture before she'd managed to wake herself up, and she hadn't been lying when she'd told Cethin it was unnerving to wake up somewhere unfamiliar. Perhaps she'd been more disturbed with herself for being disappointed that Cethin hadn't even been in the room when she'd jolted awake. His side of the bed had not been slept on, same as the night before. For someone who insisted she stay in his chambers, he didn't appear to sleep there at all.

Still feeling phantom burns along her skin, she'd crept down the hall to find him writing in a journal of sorts. Then she'd let him draw her into a frivolous round of bickering just to distract her.

But gods, when his magic flitted along her own? That was something she'd never experienced before, but a part of her wanted to again. Was it always like that?

No.

She was not contemplating that right now.

Or ever.

Ignoring Razik's question, she asked one of her own. "Do you spend a lot of time in these rooms?"

"By Sargon, no," Razik replied, looking up from the pages he was reading.

"You appear as though you do," she went on. "You seem at ease, like you are at home here."

"I stood outside that door for hours because the king needed to prove a point to showcase his dominance," Razik replied impassively. "Then, when I was allowed in, you decided to stare out a window for the last two hours, despite telling your betrothed that you were tired and feeling under the weather. So again I'll ask you: trouble between you and Cethin already?"

She pressed her lips together, feeling outsmarted yet again. The male was similar to Cethin in some ways, but where Cethin used his title and power to get what he wanted, Razik relied on appearing constantly apathetic despite observing every minor detail in a room. Both effective methods, really. They'd simply each honed different skills, but they both used them to the same ends. However, recognizing all that also let her see the issue at hand. Razik was too observant, and she'd have to be extra convincing around him.

Clearing her throat, she curled her fingers along the fabric of her dress. She'd changed into it to make Cethin think she'd be joining him at the meeting he was currently holding.

Forcing a small smile to her lips, she said, "Cethin and I are fine. I truly did not get much rest last night, and the thought of sitting on display again today was… This is all happening very fast. It is a bit overwhelming."

She immediately went over everything she'd just said. Did it sound convincing enough? Was she proper enough for a queen? Was it too many words? Not enough?

Razik hummed, closing the book and setting it carefully on the low table. "I'm calling bullshit on the first part of that. You and Cethin are not *fine*, but that's your business."

Her brow furrowed. "Then why did you ask?"

"Because we've been sitting here in silence for two hours," he deadpanned. "And while I prefer quiet and solitude, you standing over there staring out a window like a wraith is uncouth."

Was it?

She eyed him as she said, "I'd question you speaking to your future queen in such a manner, but I've seen how you interact with Cethin."

"Cethin can fuck off, but that's not the point," Razik replied, pushing to his feet. "You say you don't want to be on display, but that's exactly the life you signed up for. You can't stand around all day staring out windows."

"You scarcely know me, yet you speak as if this is normal for me," she retorted.

"Is it?" he countered.

"No," she replied, lifting her chin.

"Practice lying more. You're terrible at it, Lia."

Her lip curled back. "Perhaps Cethin was right. Maybe a different personal guard would be best, *Raz*."

"You'd hate that," he retorted, brushing past her to head down the hallway.

"Why would you say that? And where are you going?" she demanded, following after him.

"To get you a cloak and boots," he replied over his shoulder. "And you'd hate it because any other personal guard is going to care about Cethin's opinions and demands over yours. We've already established I don't give a fuck."

"And I care about that because? And a cloak and boots for what?" she questioned as Razik pushed the doors open to the bedchamber. For someone who claimed to spend little time here, he certainly knew his way around. It only furthered her scorned lovers suspicion.

"I'm not going to ask permission from the king before taking you into the city," he called out from the dressing room.

"Into the city? For what?"

"To practice being on display. You're clearly out of your element," he answered, emerging from the dressing room with a velvet cloak and elegant black boots.

"The cloak seems a bit much," she said, eyeing the items. "And the boots are unnecessary." Then she brought her gaze to his, worrying her bottom lip. "Is it that obvious how ill-equipped I am for this?"

"Painfully."

She scowled at him. "You are an ass."

"How astute of you, but yes. Glad you figured that out now," he replied, tossing the cloak to her. She caught it with one hand, the fabric soft and plush beneath her fingers. "The cloak would be expected of a queen, and the boots are necessary because shoes are necessary among society."

"I feel as if the queen shouldn't have to conform to society," she murmured, running her finger along the elegant silver embroidery of the cloak. Stars and moons and beautiful detailing among it all ran around the edges and the hem.

Razik shrugged, dropping the boots at her feet. "You're the one concerned with being on display and not wanting to appear unsuitable for the job."

By the gods, this male was as much of a jackass as Cethin was, but…

This could work in her favor.

He clearly had some sort of vendetta against the king, and she needed to figure out why the Oracle had appeared as Razik when she'd visited. If he was willing to help her say and do the right things as the future queen, it would keep Cethin at arm's width and still accomplish her goals.

And she needed Cethin to keep his distance because his presence was unnerving. The way he'd spoken to her this morning, so close she could feel his breath stir her hair? *Gods.* He was as perceptive as Razik, and he was using it to his advantage while she was at a complete disadvantage because she didn't understand any of it. Like, why had her magic responded the way it had when his dark power had tangled with it?

No.

Still not thinking of that.

"Fine," she said, going to the dresser to retrieve stockings.

She slid them on and then the boots, hating the feel of them, but she could admit they were beautiful for shoes. They weren't riding boots or combat boots. No, these were purely for aesthetics with pointed toes and a slight lift at the heel. Silver buckles and branded designs on the leather. They were as frivolous as the necklace at her throat.

Reaching for the crystal, she twisted it between her fingers as she turned back to Razik. "What, exactly, are we going to do in town?"

"There are merchants traveling through Aimonway," he answered while she retrieved the cloak from where she'd tossed it on the bed.

Slinging it around her shoulders, she asked skeptically, "You intend to go shopping?"

"No, I intend for you to practice being among the people you are going to rule over," he said, watching her clasp the silver clip of the cloak. Then he extended a hand to her. "Are you ready?"

"You can Travel from these rooms?"

He smirked. "I'm your personal guard, Lia. The wards were altered last night in case you needed rescuing."

She rolled her eyes. "If anyone is going to need rescuing, it's Cethin."

Razik gave a low chuckle of amusement. "Believe me. I know." He motioned with his hand again with a knowing look. "It's only for a moment."

Apparently she was just as painfully obvious with what made her uncomfortable. Both Razik and Cethin had clearly deciphered how much she abhorred physical touch.

Focusing on not wincing, she placed the tips of her fingers in his palm, but it was enough. A moment later, she stood in the center of the city. The exact place she'd first spoken to Cethin.

The sun was shining, but there was still a chill in the air as the winter season desperately tried to cling to life despite spring having arrived. Instead of market stands, there were carts parked along the roads, any manner of merchandise for sale.

"Now what?" she asked, swiping strands of hair from her face as a small breeze flitted around them.

"Now you practice being among other people," Razik said simply. "Don't try to shrink to the sidelines or blend in. As soon as the betrothal is formally announced, that will never happen again unless you're in your magic."

"I don't like people," she muttered, already on edge at the crowds milling around and haggling with merchants. "These people just travel around with carts of trinkets?"

"They're traveling merchants, yes," Razik answered, walking down the road.

She hurried to keep up, her boots clicking on the stone. The sound was terrible. How would she hear anyone approaching over the sound of her own godsdamn footwear?

"Throughout the entire kingdom?" she asked, falling into step beside him. She didn't fail to notice he shortened his stride for her.

"Most of these merchants stay on this side of the Nightmist Mountains, but there are some who venture west. But the merchants on the other side of the mountains get territorial. There's an unspoken pact of sorts among them all," Razik replied, head up and eyes watching everything.

They walked in silence for a bit, and she took the opportunity to get used to the various noises and the presence of people in general. Razik subtly herded her closer and closer to the crowds until they were forced to skirt around them as they wound their way through the people.

Elbows brushed her cloak, and hips bumped into her. She gritted her teeth as every touch burned, heightened by her dream last night.

"Breathe, Kailia," Razik said, his voice low. With a jerk of his chin, he added, "Let's go that way. Take a moment."

He led the way to the edge of the crowd, parting a path for her, and she loosed a heavy breath. She'd hardly lasted a few minutes. Razik moved nearer to a cart, and she followed, sticking close. Watching everyone around her. Fingering the dagger she had strapped to her thigh beneath her dress, it offered a sick sense of comfort. She wasn't going to stab anyone.

Probably.

"Can we go back now?" she asked when the crowd began to swell around them again.

"The way to break patterns and habits is to get uncomfortable, Lia," he replied absentmindedly.

She turned to find him studying an array of gold objects. From small statues to decorative engravings to platters and bowls, he seemed to look each item over with care.

"All items are from over the mountains," came a raspy voice as a male stepped into view. Immortal as most were in Avonleya, Kailia could still tell he was a traveler. From the wool coat and thick boots, to the scruff on his face and dirt on his hands. The raspy voice, though, was from the pipe he was puffing on, tobacco smoke drifting into the air.

When Razik only hummed at his statement, the male straightened a little more, puffing out his chest. "*Over* the mountains," he repeated. Then he dropped his voice to scarcely a whisper. "From the Runic Lands."

"I already knew they were fake before you told such a blatant lie," Razik said flatly.

The male gasped, clearly affronted. "How dare you accuse me of such a thing."

"The Runic Lands have never been found," Razik replied.

"Sages and Witches of old know where they are," the male countered, lifting his chin even higher, and Kailia was mildly impressed by his gall.

"And you are neither of those things," Razik retorted. Flicking the bowl with his fingers, he added, "I don't care who you swindle if they are obtuse enough to fall for your tales, but don't continue to argue with me when I call you out on your deceit."

The male paled as he stumbled back a few steps, and Kailia didn't understand why until Razik turned and she could see his face.

See his glowing sapphire eyes where his pupils had shifted to vertical slits.

"Come, your Highness," he said with a small smirk when she glared at him.

Following, she glanced back over her shoulder to find the male scowling after them.

"You could tell they were fake by looking at them?" Kailia asked.

"They were gold, but nothing more. They were not pieces of history, and they certainly weren't from the Runic Lands," Razik answered, guiding her through the crowds. For the most part, he kept a path parted for her, but every once in a while he let someone get close enough to brush against her. Small doses of physical contact.

While he led her around the city center, he told her of important buildings and businesses. He spoke of the history of Aimonway, and how it had not always been the capital city of Avonleya. He gave her a brief overview of the territories along with the lords and ladies who oversaw them. She'd never remember all of this, but he did it all while she practiced being seen because people certainly looked at the male in the king's guard uniform escorting the female around. They all knew who he was, which drew curiosity and whispered conversations about her.

"People are going to think *you're* the one courting me," she murmured as Razik passed her a stick with roasted meat on it before handing the vendor some coin.

He shrugged, clearly not caring. "People can think what they want."

"And Cethin?"

"Already established, he can fuck off."

She took a bite of the pork, savoring the flavors that danced across her tongue. The situation wasn't ideal, but she hadn't known hunger since agreeing to this bargain with Cethin.

"So you and Wren are not married?" she asked, taking a seat beside Razik on the bench he'd commandeered.

He sighed, obviously annoyed at having this conversation again "Wren and I fuck at times, but that is all."

"Cethin said there is a difference between lovers and fucking," she mused.

"For once, he's right about something," Razik grumbled.

"So that's true?"

He paused, his stick of meat halfway to his mouth. Slowly lowering it, he studied her for a long moment. "I need to ask you something, and I need you to know your answer is between you and me, Kailia."

"All right," she agreed.

"Cethin said he hasn't forced anything on you—hasn't forced *himself* on you—but—"

She reared back, losing the grip on her food and the meat falling to the ground. "He does that?"

"I didn't think so, but the way you act, I question it."

Her entire body was heated with nerves and fury. "While demanding of my time, he is respectable with my body. I find it hard to believe he would be any other way with anyone else."

Granted, she didn't know him well, but she was well-versed in reading people. She'd spent decades studying interactions from her smoke. She'd seen more than enough despicable things committed by males and females alike. She knew he could be incredibly cruel. Her life experiences spoke to that truth, so maybe he *was* capable of such atrocities. But he'd never even indicated he *wanted* that side of this union until he spoke of lovers today, and even then, that didn't mean he wanted that from her.

She cleared her throat, unsure why she was saying anything at all. "Like anyone else, my past has shaped me and my mannerisms, not the few days I've spent with your king."

"That's fair," Razik replied, extending his food to her.

She tentatively took it from him and murmured thanks. He

nodded, stretching his legs out in front of him while she finished his food, her dropped stick already having been claimed by a stray mutt who'd scampered off.

Several silent minutes ticked by before she said, "Just to be sure, you and Cethin *aren't* past lovers? It just seems like—"

"No," he ground out. "You said Cethin explained the difference between fucking and lovers."

"So you've fucked?"

"Fucking Fates," Razik muttered under his breath. "No, Lia. Cethin and I loathe each other."

"It seems like that would make fucking more passionate," she mused.

"Kailia," he growled. "No. There will never be an interest there —fucking or lover. I don't have any interest in a lover altogether."

"Just the fucking then?"

"Just the fucking."

"And Wren," she added.

He sighed. "Wren is different because of the bond we share."

She went silent again, trying to sort through all that information, and she was about to ask him another question when there was a swirl of dark magic. Razik said nothing as he reached into the magic and retrieved the note.

"Your betrothed is looking for you," Razik said flatly, the note going up in black flames, but he didn't make any move to get up.

"We…should return to the castle then?" she asked.

Razik shrugged. "That's up to you. As your personal guard, I follow your orders, not his."

"I don't think that's how this is supposed to work."

He shrugged again, apparently channeling his 'Cethin-can-fuck-off' energy.

"I think we should go back," she said, standing and tossing the food stick into a nearby rubbish bin.

"If that's what you wish," Razik said, standing as well and extending his hand.

Seconds later, they appeared in the sitting room of their chambers to face a very irate king.

"Get out," he snarled at Razik, his dark magic clinging to him like inky rivulets on his skin.

"Calm down, Sutara," Razik drawled, crossing his arms. "We went out for some fresh air."

"Get. Out," the king said again, the words a clear warning.

"I'm not sure leaving her alone with you and your temper tantrum is a good idea."

"I swear to the Fates, Greybane—"

"I'll be fine," Kailia cut in, stepping between the two males. "Razik, please go."

He sent her a flat look, but didn't say another word as he turned and left.

The door hadn't even fully shut before Cethin was in front of her, leaning in close. "Where were you, Kailia?"

"He just told you," she retorted. "You need to step back."

"What I need is for my future wife to not be out with—"

"With my personal guard? Who else am I supposed to go out with?" she cut in.

"*Me,*" he growled, somehow stepping closer.

Until her hands landed on his chest, shoving hard. He was far stronger than her, but he was clearly so taken aback by her willingly touching him that he shuffled back a few steps.

"You had responsibilities to tend to," she said. "*You* were unavailable."

"You should have been at the meeting with me, Kailia," he retorted, beginning to pace in his fury. "You said you were feeling ill."

"I was feeling better," she bit back, lifting her chin.

He huffed a humorless laugh. "You were lying, tiny fiend. I'm no fool."

"That's debatable."

He paused mid-step, turning to face her fully. "Even if it had been true, you should have waited for me. Where did you even go?"

She rolled her eyes, moving past him. He followed as she made her way down the hall, these godsdamn boots clicking with each footfall. "He took me into the city to see the traveling merchants. Then we got some food."

"There's plenty of food here."

Perching on the edge of the bed, she unbuckled her boots as she said, "Is your plan to keep me locked in this castle unless you are at my side?"

"What if it is?" he countered.

"It will appear to your kingdom that you do not trust your wife," she said, standing and tossing the boots aside before unclasping the cloak. "That won't seem very *convincing* now, will it?"

Cethin cursed under his breath, running a hand down his face. With obvious restraint, his words were clipped and measured as he said, "Our betrothal has not even been publicly announced yet."

"You are the king. Can you not announce it whenever you wish?"

His eyes fell closed for a few seconds in obvious frustration. "Yes, Kailia. I can."

"Then I believe you are the problem here."

"Fucking Arius," he muttered.

"Besides, without that announcement, no one even knows who I am," she went on. "Your reaction to all of this is very irrational."

Cethin said nothing. He only turned and left the bedchamber. She followed, mainly because she was incredibly curious as to where he was going.

He found a liquor decanter, pouring a finger's length of the alcohol and knocking it back before doing the same again. Then he turned to face her once more.

"The Beltane Hunt is with the next full moon."

She blinked at the sudden change in subject. "I don't know what that is."

"An annual hunt in Shira Forest," he said. "I'd like you to join us."

"Who's us?"

"There are several Hunts around the kingdom, but I go on one with the Cadre every year."

"And what do we hunt?" she asked, drawing closer to him.

Because she liked to hunt. She liked that a lot. The tracking and stalking. The studying of your surroundings and listening for your prey. The instincts and the intuition. Yes, she would like to attend this hunt very much.

He offered her a small smile, the anger simmering around him fading some. "Whatever we like, usually deer and small game, but you don't have to hunt if you don't want to. You can—"

"I do want to hunt," she interrupted. "But I'll need my arrow back in order to do so."

His small smile morphed into a smirk. "You can borrow a bow and arrow set from the weaponry, tiny fiend."

"It won't be the same," she argued.

"Then you'd better start practicing."

"I'm not using another bow," she retorted, ashes swirling and her own beloved weapon appearing in her hand.

She could swear he sucked in a sharp breath as he stared at her. Looking at her like she was something exquisite and endearing, and that made no sense. He definitely should not be looking at her like that.

He stepped nearer, closing the space between them. Lifting a hand, it appeared he was going to reach for her, but he dropped it back to his side with another sigh. "I have to return to the council meeting at sundown," he said, regret and something akin to dread sounding in his tone. "Tomorrow the proclamation can be made regarding the betrothal."

She nodded.

"Things will change with the announcement," he warned.

She nodded again, because what did it matter?

Things had changed the moment she'd shot that arrow on that battlefield. And that was why he shouldn't be looking at her like she was some charming thing capable of answering his prayers and delivering salvation.

She wasn't any of those things.

Because her favorite part of a hunt was the victory of a blade sinking in deep or an arrow finding its mark.

And she'd been training to hunt Avonleyans her entire life.

CHAPTER 16

RAZIK

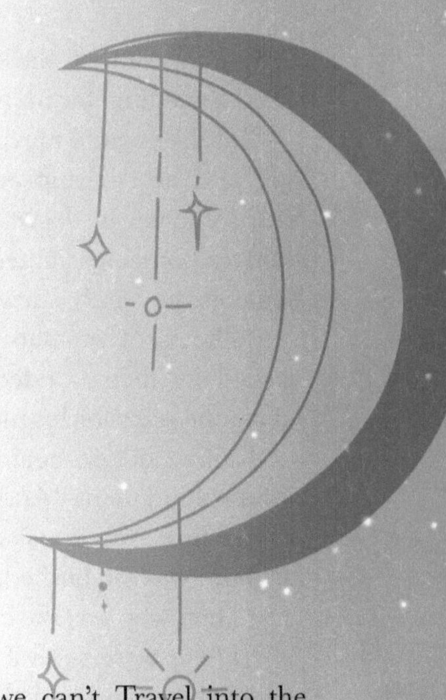

"So we can Travel to Elshira, but we can't Travel into the forest?" Kailia asked from where she stood beside Cethin while they waited for their horses.

"Few can Travel directly into Shira Forest," Cethin answered. "And those who can, don't, out of respect for the spirit animals."

She nodded, gaze fixed on the trees. "I've never seen one of the spirit animals. Have you?"

Cethin gave her a tight smile. "I have, but not lately."

Razik scoffed under his breath at the statement, Wren elbowing him lightly in the side. They'd seen plenty of spirit animals over their centuries of life, but beyond that, Cethin was bonded to one.

The spirit animals were powerful creatures bonded to the gods and goddesses. With their connection to the gods, the animals were immune from the wards and spells of the realm, but they were still beholden to this world. Razik had read a lot of history about them, but had yet to figure out how they'd become trapped here. Because they were. They used to be able to go to the gods they were connected to, and now they remained here, many of them bonded to a being in the realm at the request of their god or goddess.

Cethin was one of those beings, because why wouldn't he also be gifted something for no reason at all beyond his bloodline?

But then again, maybe Cethin was actually making a smart decision and not sharing everything about himself and the kingdom with someone he'd just met. Didn't make up for the fact he was shoving someone incredibly unqualified onto a throne though. Someone he barely knew. Someone who had fucking stabbed him.

"The spirit animals reside in Shira Forest when they are not needed by their bonded," Razik added as horses were led over, taking the reins for his mount and Wren's. "It is considered sacred."

Kailia nodded again, turning to look at the large castle that stood behind them. "And this used to be the capital of Avonleya?"

"Elshira. Yes, it was for centuries," Cethin answered. "Since the kingdom was established."

"Then why was the capital moved?" Kailia asked.

"There were several reasons," Cethin answered with a nod of thanks as he was handed the reins to his horse.

"So we cannot Travel into Shira Forest, but we can simply walk into the trees?" Kailia said doubtfully as she was handed reins as well.

"Only once a year. For the Beltane Hunt," Cethin replied. "Do you know how to ride?"

"Ride what?" she asked, attention still fixed on the trees.

Cethin glanced at Razik, and he only arched a brow. This was Cethin's bride, not his. He could figure out how to deal with her without his help. Plus, he found it comical when Cethin became irritated by her mannerisms but had to try to hide it.

Scratching his temple, Cethin said, "A horse, Kailia. Do you know how to ride a horse?"

The female slowly turned to him, and Razik swallowed his amusement at the look on her face. This side of her was just as entertaining as she stared at the king as though he were stupid for asking such a question.

"Yes, king," she replied curtly. "I know how to ride a horse."

"It was a valid question," Cethin argued. "I'm assuming you normally use your magic to travel—"

"So do you," she interjected.

"I don't know how you were raised or where," Cethin said in obvious exasperation. "I simply wanted to ensure you knew how to ride rather than find out when you cannot control your horse in the forest."

"My upbringing contained all manner of training, including riding a horse," she retorted, as she lifted her foot to the stirrup and expertly hoisted herself up.

Cethin's horse whinnied at the action, dancing back several steps and tugging its reins from his hold. Her ears flattened, and there was a wildness in her eyes anyone could see and should be wary of.

"It appears you are the one who needs to control your horse," Kailia said with an air of nonchalance.

Cethin smiled knowingly. "Thera and I will be fine. You worry about your own mount."

He turned back to his mare, the horse stilling at his approach, and he ran his palm down her neck a few times. The mare's eyes took on a soft silver glow, and Razik didn't need to see his face to know Cethin's eyes were doing the same. She lowered her head, her nose nuzzling into Cethin's shoulder.

Kailia watched with interest before she twisted to look at Razik from atop her horse. "He keeps a horse at the abandoned castle?"

"It's not abandoned," Razik answered, mounting his own mare and wondering why that was the question she asked instead of the obvious one.

"But you said the capital moved."

"It did. We didn't say this castle was no longer used."

"Who lives here then?" she asked, turning her horse to look up at the structure once more.

"It is still in the family," Cethin answered, his horse coming up alongside hers.

"Are we going to sit around and chat over tea all day, or are we going into the forest?" Bram teased, joining their company on his own horse. Then a grin curled up at one corner of his mouth as he said, "Wren, always a pleasure when you join us."

"Why aren't Fallon and Ariadne keeping you in line?" Razik growled, maneuvering his horse between Bram and Wren.

"We have better things to do than mother grown-ass males," Fallon said, passing by on her horse. "You abandoned us, so I suppose it's up to Jarek now," she added with a fake sigh of resignation.

"As if Jarek can keep anyone in line," Razik said flatly, the male coming to ride alongside Fallon.

"Says the one who left us for a cushy post in the castle," Jarek volleyed back.

"Agreed. I don't get to see Wren nearly as often now," Bram cut in.

"You're about to be eating horse shit, Bram," Razik growled.

The male chuckled under his breath before moving ahead of their company, but not before looking back over his shoulder to wink at Wren. Jarek and Fallon followed, leaving Ariadne and Draven to bring up the rear and keeping Cethin and Kailia in the center. Last year, he'd been leading at the front with Valric. Now he was stuck in the middle, getting constant shit from the rest of the Cadre. It was all in jest, but it was still annoying as fuck. And yeah, it struck a chord considering he was roped in with Cethin's company, even if it had been his choice.

"I am confused," Kailia said when they all started making their way into the forest.

Razik didn't even want to know what was about to come out of her mouth. It was bound to be something unexpected, and he was proven right when she continued.

"You and Wren have relations, but she also has relations with Bram?"

"No, she does not," Razik answered tightly.

"But..." Her brow furrowed, and she glanced at Wren where she rode beside her. "You seem overly friendly."

"I told you, Razik and I are not bound in that way," Wren replied.

The betrothal announcement had been made a few weeks ago, and the gossip mills had been abuzz. More than that, Cethin hadn't let Kailia go into the city without him since the day Razik had taken her himself. In fact, he kept Kailia at his side at nearly all times. It was ridiculous and petty, and Kailia was going along with it for whatever reason.

Except he knew the reason.

It was more comfortable for her to be in Cethin's shadow. Even if she was still being watched and was still the topic of every conversation these days, Cethin's presence was still the dominating one. She was hiding, and with Cethin's constant hovering, Razik couldn't call her out on it.

The next half hour was silent save for the sounds of twigs and stones beneath horses' hooves as they made their way south into the forest. The conversations of the others were low, barely carrying to where they were in the center. Kailia was her usual self, observing everything without an ounce of expression, while Cethin studied her.

He was actually impressed with how long it took Wren to speak. The female hated silence, something Razik had learned to live with considering his preference for quiet and solitude.

"So, Kailia," Wren started, "did I hear correctly that you are from Shadowfen?"

"Mhmm," she hummed, amber eyes focused on the trees above them.

"I've never been there. What's it like?"

Kailia slid her gaze to Cethin, who gave her a small smile. "I'd also love to hear of your life before these last weeks. Did you always live in Shadowfen?"

Kailia's eyes narrowed, and Razik was begrudgingly impressed with Cethin's manipulation of the situation. Giving her space to answer but also fishing for information that he was clearly seeking.

She cleared her throat, and Razik watched her in his periphery as she shifted the reins in her hands and pulled the sleeve of her tunic back, briefly running her fingers along her wrist and forearm. Then she straightened once more.

"No, I did not always live in Shadowfen," she answered simply.

"Where did you live before?" Wren asked.

She shrugged. "Across the Edria."

"What?" Wren gasped, the company in front of them all glancing back at the sudden outburst.

"Everything good?" Jarek called, his voice carrying as they all slowed their horses.

"Everything is fine," Cethin replied before refocusing his stare on Kailia. Lowering his voice, he said tightly, "That is not something to share so openly, tiny fiend."

"Then don't ask questions you already know the answer to."

"I was asking about your past."

"Then say that instead of asking such ambiguous questions," she retorted.

The king's lips thinned, and Razik was enjoying this far more than he'd enjoyed anything in a long time.

"I didn't mean to start something," Wren said, worrying her lip as she shot Razik a pleading look for help.

"Don't look at me," Razik said apathetically. "I was perfectly content in the quiet."

"Same," Kailia agreed. "When do we hunt?"

Cethin sighed heavily. "We can hunt whatever we find along the way."

"Then I need my arrow."

"We already discussed this. You'll need to use different arrows. That's why there's a quiver full of them attached to your saddle," Cethin answered pointedly.

"Why would Cethin have one of your arrows?" Razik asked, homing in on that bit of information.

"He stole it," Kailia answered simply.

"I did not steal it," Cethin cut in.

"You knowingly took and currently possess something that does not belong to you without permission or payment. That is the definition of stealing," she fired back.

"Perhaps you abandoned it after you shot it at me," Cethin retorted. "Consequences, tiny fiend."

"You stealing from me is certainly a consequence of saving your life."

"I was under the impression you could create more of these arrows," Razik cut in.

"She can," Cethin answered.

"When I have all my arrows," Kailia snapped. "Which I do not."

"Wait, is that why you were picking up the arrowheads that day?" Razik continued, as new pieces of that day clicked into place.

"Yes. I have them all except for one," she said, glaring at Cethin.

"For fuck's sake, Sutara. Give her back the arrow," Razik said, wondering why the fuck this was even a debate.

"I will in time," Cethin gritted out. "She knows this, but beyond that, it's none of your business, Greybane."

"It will be when— Fuck!"

Razik ducked as an arrow flew directly above his head. A moment later, a bird fell from the air, landing on the path ahead of them with a soft thud onto the forest floor.

He turned to find Kailia still with her bow raised, gaze focused on her kill. "Are we keeping score on this hunt?" she asked, slowly lowering her bow. "If so, I am ahead."

Cethin glanced at Razik, where he'd stopped his horse to dismount and collect the game. Rubbing at the nape of his neck, Cethin said, "The Cadre often makes the hunt into a friendly competition, but we don't have to—"

"Then I am ahead," Kailia cut in, her eyes seeming to brighten.

"A fan of competitions, Lia?" Razik drawled as he remounted his horse and tossed the dead bird over Wren to Kailia. She caught it, but not before blood splattered across her tunic.

Sliding her gaze to his, she held up the fallen animal. "You threw this at me."

"Your perception is truly astounding," Razik said dryly, urging his horse forward again. Those in front of them had kept going, while Draven and Ariadne had stopped behind them. "Perhaps next time, you can use that skill to not shoot a fucking arrow at my head."

"I shot the arrow at the bird," she said, lifting the animal higher in emphasis.

"And nearly took me out in the process."

"It wasn't even close to hitting you. I have better aim than that."

He stared at her for a few extra silent seconds. "Lia, if I hadn't ducked, my ear would have a new piercing along with my godsdamn skull."

She had the audacity to roll her eyes. "You are as dramatic as your king, Raz."

He felt his eyes shift to vertical slits at the insult, smoke wafting on his exhale.

"Okay, everyone take a moment," Wren interjected, always trying to diffuse situations. "Kailia was just caught up in the excitement of the hunt—"

"Which I am winning," Kailia interrupted.

"Not for long," Razik muttered under his breath, straightening his tunic as he looked straight ahead.

No one spoke for quite some time after that.

-))·⊙·((-

"She's different, isn't she?" Jarek said when he and Fallon joined Razik where he was roasting a couple of the birds they'd harvested over the open fire.

"Who?" Razik grunted, still in a sour mood from the day's festivities. Not the being shot at part, but the being compared to Cethin part. And the fact that Kailia still had the most kills today.

"You know who," Jarek said, keeping his voice low.

Cethin and Kailia were across the small clearing where everyone had decided to set up camp for the night. The couple was tending another fire with a few rabbits roasting, while Ariadne, Bram, and Draven had a third one.

"What do you think of her?" Jarek pushed, taking the bottle of liquor Fallon passed to him. "I ran into her in the city with Wren the day after the Esbat Festival, and we all know she's the one who stabbed Cethin that night and again the next day."

214

Yeah, they did all know that. Those rumors had somehow made it outside the castle walls too. Cethin had made public statements about those stabbings being misunderstandings. If it'd only happened once, he might have been able to convince people easily enough, but twice?

"Not sure what you're looking for from me," Razik said, rotating the roasting spit a quarter turn.

Jarek rolled his eyes. "No need to play dumb, Greybane. There's a reason you willingly left the Cadre to be her personal guard."

Razik glanced at him sidelong. "You had your opportunity to willingly leave too, you know."

"I never wanted the opportunity. Didn't think you had either," the male said, taking a pull from the liquor bottle and passing it back to Fallon. She had a heavy fur cloak wrapped around her shoulders, her braid loose from a day of traveling and hunting.

"Sometimes duty requires us to do things we'd rather not," Razik finally said, stoking the fire.

Jarek scoffed. "If you gave a fuck about duty, you'd have left the Cadre long ago. Something lured you, and knowing you, it has something to do with history or a way around those duties." He paused, and Razik could feel the male's eyes on him. "Or you want something you shouldn't."

"Jarek," Fallon chastised, bumping her knee against his.

"I'm just saying what everyone is thinking."

Razik turned to him, his features devoid of emotion as he asked, "Who's everyone?"

"The Cadre. The forces. The streets of the kingdom. You can't tell me you haven't heard the whisperings, Greybane. We're trained to know the rumors before they even start," Jarek said, leaning forward to turn the spit again. "And I know you don't give a fuck what people think, but in this case, you probably should."

"I'm not trying to steal Cethin's things if that's what you're suggesting," Razik said flatly, reaching around Jarek to pluck the liquor from Fallon's hand.

"As long as the king knows that…and the future queen," Jarek added pointedly.

Razik huffed humorlessly. "I'm not the one she's stabbed, Ophanim. Remember that."

"Exactly. Which would make it appear you are the one she's more beholden to."

"Not if you knew her," Razik muttered. He shifted on the log he was perched on, stretching his legs out. "Like you said, she's different, and while I find her interesting, there is nothing else from either of us. I can assure you of that. I have no interest in any sort of bond ever."

"Not even a twin flame someday?" Fallon cut in, her sky-blue eyes full of genuine curiosity.

Another humorless bark of laughter left him. "I'm denying the gods with every breath I take. They're not going to gift me a twin flame, Fallon. Even if they did, I'd still deny it. I don't want any fated bond or twist of destiny. The ones who are supposed to care never do."

Jarek and Fallon both fell quiet after those words. They knew enough of his past to know where the words came from, and more than that, they knew he would bury them in any attempt to try to rationalize away motives and actions. You don't abandon the ones you're supposed to love. He was better off simply not having those people in his life at all.

Fallon tipped her head against Jarek's shoulder, the dancing flames reflecting in her eyes while Jarek's hand held her thigh. The male's thumb stroked lazily as he took another swig of liquor. If Razik wanted to be a real ass, he'd bring up their sham of a relationship. If Kailia wanted a definition of fucking versus lovers, they were the prime example, but he didn't bring it up. He made it a point not to stick his nose in other people's godsdamn business, whereas Fallon made it a point to be a busybody.

Wren appeared then, holding a cloth full of nuts and dried fruit. Razik swiped a few up as he slid down to make room for her. Her dark hair was loose, strands peeking out of the hood she had pulled up.

"Where have you been?" he asked, pressing a hand to the small of her back so his dragon fire could warm her.

She gave him a grateful smile. "Seeking out berries for breakfast in the morning," she answered.

"You were in the trees by yourself?" he asked, glancing down disapprovingly.

Her gaze darted to the side. "No, I wasn't alone."

"Who— You didn't," he snarled.

"And that's our cue to take a walk," Fallon said, getting to her feet.

"Wait, why? I want to watch this," Jarek protested, but Fallon leaned down and grabbed his hand, pulling him to his feet and leading him to another fire.

The fire where Bram was now standing, a satisfied smirk on his smug fucking face.

Razik turned back to Wren, and she shrank back a little. "Don't look at me like that," she said, sounding more confident than she looked. "He simply accompanied me. Would you rather I had gone off alone?"

"I would rather you asked me to accompany you. What happened to wanting to be off limits to the Cadre, Wren? This was something we agreed on from the start," he said, trying to keep his voice low.

"It's nothing like that," she argued.

"The fuck it's not. I've seen the way he looks at you. You being unattainable has made it a game to him. You're not a fucking game, Wren."

"I know that, Razik," she tried. "But he didn't try anything. He walked with me in the woods, looking for berries. That's all."

He scoffed, a sneer curling on his lip. "I know you're not this stupid. He's not going to just come right out and ask to fuck. He's laying the groundwork. By the gods, Wren."

She straightened, her cheeks flushing with anger as she leaned away from his touch. "We also agreed this bond was an equal partnership. That you didn't have any claim over me when I agreed to be your Source. There was a respect there that apparently isn't anymore."

"He wants you because he can't have you. Surely you see that," Razik hissed.

Her smile was all venom. "Of course. Because he couldn't possibly want me for any other reason, right? Not a Fae who has nothing else to offer because she's already bound herself to another asshole."

"Don't twist my fucking words, Wren. I don't want you getting hurt."

"Unless you're the one doing it? Don't worry. I'm not that stupid, Razik," she retorted, getting to her feet. "I can recognize when you're projecting your own issues onto me, but I'm still going to call you a bastard for doing it."

Then she stormed off, leaving him alone.

Always alone.

⟶⟩⟩ ☉ ⟨⟨⟵

"Everyone get the fuck up! We're under attack!"

The words had him jolting awake and shooting to his feet, a sword already in his hand and dragon fire at his fingertips before he'd even fully processed the words that had been said. But the translucent beings drifting around them had him figuring it out pretty damn quickly.

"Shit," he muttered, sending his sword back to a pocket realm. It wasn't going to do any good. Instead, he pulled up more dragon fire, sending a wave of black flames to the closest phantoms, keening wails filling the air and ashes littering the forest floor.

Everyone was shuffling to the center—Kailia, Cethin, and Wren in the middle—but none of them would be effective. It was only him and—

An arrow whizzed past him so closely it ripped the sleeve of his tunic and left a scratch on his bicep deep enough to bleed. Then a tiny terror with smoke and ashes was shoving past him, bow in hand.

"For the record, that was on purpose because my aim is that good," she said airily before she was standing in front of them all.

Three arrows appeared on her string, and she pulled them back, releasing them all at once. All three found their marks, three keens of death sounding around them. Another two arrows flew before the first three beings had fully dissipated. She moved quickly, her feet leaving ashy footprints as she ran, and Razik briefly wondered why she wasn't using her smoke and ashes like she'd done the first time he'd watched her fight. This was just as impressive though, and she didn't need to be fighting them alone.

Leaving Kailia to tackle the beings to the left, Razik spun to the right, black flames writhing and consuming. He felt Cethin's dark power converge around everyone else, offering some kind of shield that wouldn't do much. It'd be as useful as the others' magic.

A creature darted closer, making it past Razik, a gold blade piercing the inky black veil. The darkness sank in on itself, shirking and convulsing, the Cadre shuffling back.

"Blood of death and dreams," the phantom hissed, his tone clawing at Razik's bones. The dragon in his soul was agitated, pushing to be let out, and he was about to shift until Cethin's hand thrust out and the being's head tipped back. That same keening howl sounded as white wisps spewed from its mouth, and that was when Razik remembered Cethin had one of Kailia's godsdamn arrowheads.

Cethin's eyes connected with his, and Razik held his stare, even when he lifted a hand and sent a wave of dragon fire to another pair of incoming spirits.

"Her arrowheads!" Razik yelled. "She'll need them back, but use them to fight now!"

The Cadre sprang into action. They didn't question anything, diving into the fray, as they'd been trained to do. It wasn't as seamless as it had been with Valric, but they'd get there in time. Despite that, the individual skill was there. That was proven with how not a single one of them suffered an injury. The phantoms were deadly because of their weapons and immunity to most magic, but they weren't quick in the ways of battle.

With a final burst of his flames, he took out the last of the beings on his side while a howling wail echoed when the last of Kailia's victims faded to nothing. Cethin rushed to her while Razik sank to the ground, resting his arms atop his knees and pressing his brow to them. That fight might have lasted less than an hour, but the amount of power it took for him to kill one of those beings was immense, let alone the total number he took out. Without Kailia's help, he had no doubt they would have lost another tonight. There was a decent chance none of them would have survived if he were being completely honest.

"Razik," Wren said, worry ringing in her tone as she dropped down beside him. Her smaller fingers took his hand, slicing a blade across his palm before he felt her power seeping into his. She scooted in closer, her other hand landing on his shoulder. "Are you hurt?"

"No, Wren," he muttered because that was all he could muster. He couldn't even lift his head to look at her. Not as adrenaline and exhaustion warred in his soul. Not as he sat there tense and rigid, unable to relax because instead of protecting the future queen, he'd been forced to fight alongside her. Something Cethin was sure to hurl at him the next time they argued.

"We can go back to Aimonway, Razik," Wren said softly.

And he finally lifted an arm and curled it around her, pulling her into his side. He'd been an ass to her, and here she was, still offering him something she didn't have to.

"After the hunt tomorrow," he answered.

He still had responsibility here, and he wasn't about to give his uncle yet another reason to lecture him about his duties.

So he stayed, Wren tucked in close as the others adjusted the watch schedule, and they slept. But he'd be having words with Cethin because if Kailia needed that arrowhead back to make more of those weapons, then he'd make sure that was what fucking happened.

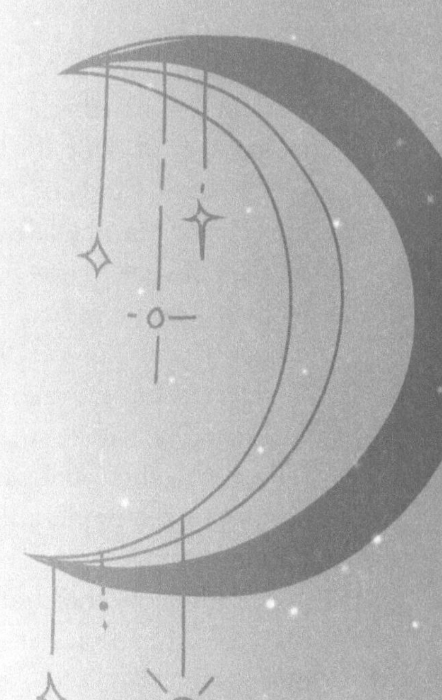

CHAPTER 17

CETHIN

"All I'm saying is that I would feel better if we shared a horse from here on out," Cethin said for what felt like the tenth time.

Kailia didn't even look at him as she finished adjusting the saddle on her horse. "I'm sure you would, but I assure you I can protect you just as well from atop my own horse."

"That's not what I meant," Cethin said dryly, but of course, Razik heard it.

"She has a point. Maybe you should stay in the middle from here on out," the dragon said, wandering by with two horses trailing him. Despite drawing from Wren, he still looked exhausted, and Cethin was sure Wren was in a similar state.

"Maybe you should stay the fuck out of things that don't concern you," Cethin retorted, but Razik hadn't even slowed, and he didn't bother acknowledging the comment.

By the gods, he needed to get his shit together. Tolerating Razik was so much easier when he was a Cadre member and not a personal guard to his future wife. The male was around all the gods-damn time now. He just needed to focus on her and nothing else.

Moving closer, he sent a whisper of his power skittering along her fingers before he placed his hand atop hers where she was working on securing a saddlebag. He gently moved her hand aside, taking over working the buckle.

"I had it handled," she said defensively, the fingers he'd touched now curled into the fabric of her cloak.

"I know you are more than capable, tiny fiend," he replied without looking at her. "But agreeing to this partnership means you do not have to do everything yourself."

Her features turned thoughtful, studying him as he turned to face her. The smoke swirling in her eyes was so much slower, drifting rather than the usual whirl of magic. She'd used a good amount of her power last night, and he still hadn't worked out how long it took for her to recover.

Sending another trace of his magic, this time along her side, he placed his hand on her hip a moment later. She stiffened but didn't pull away, even if she did take a small step back. Small touches. That was what he'd been working on. Small touches to get her used to it. Used to *him*. People would expect affection from their king and queen, especially if he was breaking the same tradition his father had by not taking a Fae as a partner.

He'd been told that was the sole reason his parents' union had been accepted. That their love and devotion to one another was so obvious and candid that no one could argue or stand in the way of it. Some even believed they were bonded in a way known only to the stars. Something similar to the twin flame bond but different, since that bond could only be forged between a Legacy and a Fae.

Despite his best efforts, they were failing. He could sense the hesitancy of the advisory council as they observed her. He knew of the rumors that were whispered—or blatantly gossiped about—in the streets. If they couldn't be convincing, she would never be fully accepted as their queen. More than that, his judgment would always be questioned, even more than it was right now.

And yeah, part of him *wanted* to touch her more. Fuck, Wren and Razik showed more affection for each other than he did with his betrothed. Kailia was living in his quarters, sleeping in his bed, wearing those fucking nightclothes…

Yeah, he wanted to touch her. Found himself getting lost to fantasies he had no business having when he knew so little about her. When she had a clear and severe aversion to touch. When he'd forced her into this partnership. But he'd thought…

He'd thought it would be easier, if he were being honest, but there was nothing easy about her.

His hand on her hip, he swiped his thumb along the band of her pants a few times, watching for any sign it had any effect on her. But there was nothing. Always nothing.

Swallowing his sigh, he said, "I need to thank you."

"Thank me?" she repeated, her head tilting and her black braid sliding over her shoulder.

"Yes, thank you," he said again, slowly reaching with his other hand to move her hair back. "For fighting for all of us last night. We have no defenses against them, save for Razik and Tybalt. But now there's you."

And gods, he couldn't read her because her features remained impassive. She didn't shift on her feet or fidget. She didn't do a godsdamn thing. Twin flames had the easier path, being able to feel each other's emotions and hear one another's thoughts. This was raw and real and godsdamn difficult.

He cleared his throat softly, letting his hand fall back to his side. "Did you retrieve all your arrowheads?"

"No," she answered.

"Aside from the one I have," he amended.

"The others collected them and returned them. Because they are mine. But you no longer have my arrow. You used it," she accused.

"I did," he confirmed. "To defend a member of the castle staff weeks ago and again tonight to defend those in my care. I will not apologize for it."

"And now you have done the noble thing twice and can return it," she insisted, a hint of pleading coming through in her words that he was surprised to hear.

"Not until the union is anointed," he said simply.

"What will that matter?" she demanded.

"Keep your voice down. We are not alone," he hissed, glancing around to where the others were busy tearing down the campsite. It didn't mean they weren't listening though.

With a flick of his wrist, darkness pooled, a hazy dome of thick black fog encircling them and keeping their words only for their ears. Her gaze slid over the magic, and for a moment, he thought she was going to lift a hand to touch it. Her arm twitched, fingers flexing, and then she stilled once more.

Returning her stare to his, she said, "What does the union matter? Truly?"

"You won't be able to leave once it's anointed."

"You think a union will keep me from disappearing? Did you forget we have a Bargain? I do not wish to be cursed as you are."

"First, let me be very clear. If you disappear, I will find you, tiny fiend," he said, his tone becoming as dark as the power surrounding them. "There is nowhere you can go in this kingdom that I would not find you."

Her smile was serpentine, and her tone just as vicious when she said, "I came from across the sea, king. You think I can't find my way back? How will you follow then?"

His mouth thinned, and he knew his power now drifted in his glowing silver irises. "You just said yourself you do not wish to be cursed."

"Perhaps that curse will be more tolerable than the one I'm currently facing."

"Outside of forcing your hand in the agreement, I have been nothing but kind to you on all accounts, Kailia," he said, his patience hanging on by its last thread. "How can you possibly have such vitriol for me when you don't even know me?"

"I know enough," she said simply, pushing past him to mount her horse. Looking down at him, she added, "Your reputation precedes you."

Then she was urging her horse forward, making her way to Wren and Razik as he pulled his power back.

How could he have any reputation across the sea? The Wards had been in place for centuries. He'd never stepped foot outside the Avonleyan borders. If she considered him cursed for that, she was going to find herself in the same torment.

Because he wasn't about to let her go back across the sea. If anything, last night had proven how much they needed her to protect the people of this kingdom.

She'd come to accept her fate, even if he had to bend fate to his will yet again.

-)) ☉ ((-

"We need to talk."

Cethin looked up from his midday meal to find Razik standing over him. Setting the tin plate of food aside, he stood, not liking that he was having to look up at the male.

"What?" Cethin asked sharply.

"Do you still have that arrowhead of hers?"

"It's not your business, Greybane," Cethin said, starting to turn away, but Razik gripped his shoulder, spinning him back.

"Do you understand she is the one real defense we have against these things?"

Razik was glaring at him as if he were stupid, and Cethin wanted to punch the male in the godsdamn face.

"Of course I know that," Cethin retorted, shoving his hand away. "Why do you think I'm working so hard to bring her to our side?"

Razik stared back at him for a few long seconds. "You're serious? You are forcing her into a union to utilize her weapons? For fuck's sake, Cethin."

"We're not talking about this here," Cethin snapped, turning and striding into the trees. He didn't give a fuck if Razik followed or not, but he did, heavy footfalls sounding.

They walked a good hundred feet until they were obscured from the others before he turned back to Razik. "It didn't start this way.

She came to me looking for her arrow, and I asked for her help. She refused."

"So this was your solution?"

"She refused to listen to any argument, and this is my fucking kingdom, Greybane," Cethin spat back. "People I am responsible for. People I am sworn to protect. Just as you are, but when you fail, the pressure on me increases. So yes, once again, I'm the one willing to do whatever it takes to ensure the safety of my kingdom. I'm not sorry about it."

"What do you mean 'once again?'"

"What?"

Razik's arms were folded across his chest, everything about him broody and apathetic, but his tone said otherwise. "You said, 'once again, I'm the one willing to do whatever it takes.' What does that mean?"

Cethin's darkness clawed at his being, begging to be let out. Begging to put Razik in his place. Begging to consume, but he shoved it down. He stepped forward, nearly toe-to-toe with him, and each word was measured and controlled as he said, "I do not care that you became Kailia's guard. I am still the fucking king, and I still do not owe you any godsdamn explanations. But apparently your workaround for that is persuading my future wife to talk."

"Kailia didn't tell me shit about whatever it is you've coerced her into," Razik replied, and while he'd slipped into his uncaring facade, his eyes had shifted to vertical pupils, betraying his own barely leashed control. "In fact, she's denied you forcing her into anything. But if you truly understand that she is needed to fight these creatures, then you'd give her back her fucking arrow. She said she can't make more without the set."

"I have it handled," Cethin gritted out.

"Do you? Because she saved all our asses last night, Sutara."

"Yes, I'm well aware that instead of you guarding her, she was defending all of us. That this is yet another responsibility you can't handle."

That was when the first fist flew.

It took a second for Cethin to register the blow to his jaw. It wasn't until he spat blood to the side that he felt the pain radiating along his face. He slowly lifted his head, dragging his eyes back to the male standing in front of him.

The two stared at each other for several seconds, and then it was Cethin lunging at him, throwing all his weight behind the hit to the fucker's face, followed immediately by another to his gut. Then he didn't know who had the upper hand. Not as they each took swings. Not as they fell to the ground, rolling and shoving.

Cethin let out a grunt as a boot connected with his side, fairly certain a rib or two had cracked with the hit, but he was scrambling, grabbing Razik's ankle and twisting. The male snarled and flipped to his stomach, and Cethin was there, raining punches to his lower back. Until Razik's wings appeared, launching him up and getting him back on his feet.

Cethin took the opportunity to push to his own feet, his breaths short gasps due to the aching ribs. Swiping a hand across his mouth, blood smeared across his flesh. The same dripped from a cut along Greybane's brow, while his other eye was already bruising. Cethin was certain he didn't look any better.

"Did you two get that out of your system?" drawled a female voice, and they both turned to find not only Ariadne, who'd spoken, but the entire Cadre standing there. Bram and Jarek were smirking like fools. Fallon had the same look of annoyed disapproval as Ariadne, and Draven looked like he wasn't sure what he should be doing.

"None of you thought you should step in?" Cethin muttered, removing crushed leaves and twigs that were stuck to his jacket.

"Not even once," Jarek replied from where he was leaning against a tree. "Out here, you're still just one of us."

"He's never been one of us," Razik sneered, stalking past them all and disappearing into the trees.

Cethin followed, the Cadre trailing him. His magic was pushing to be let loose. Even if it wasn't physical, Razik had still managed to get the final blow in with those parting words.

"Seriously, Cethin. The two of you need to figure your shit out,"

Ariadne scolded, handing him a leather strap so he could tie his hair back.

"It's been this way for centuries. I don't think it's ever going to change," he replied flatly. "Some people aren't meant to be friends."

"That doesn't mean you have to be enemies," she countered. "And either way, I don't think that's the case here, considering who he is and who you are." When Cethin said nothing, she added, "All I'm saying is he's the queen's personal guard now. You two are going to have to at least be civil with each other."

"Where is she?" Cethin asked as they stepped into the clearing where they'd stopped for their midday meal. They'd harvested a few more birds, a fox, and some other smaller game that morning, planning to stalk larger game this afternoon and evening.

"Who?" Ariadne asked, glancing up at him.

"Kailia. Where is she?" he demanded, scanning the area, the horses, all of it.

"She was with Wren."

"She's not with me," the Fae answered, looking up from where she was pressing a wet cloth to Razik's brow, the male's wings already banished.

Ariadne's brows crashed together. "But I thought—"

"Where the fuck is she?" Cethin demanded again. He turned, advancing on Wren, and she scrambled back at the same time that Razik lurched to his feet.

"Back the fuck up, Cethin," Razik growled, his eyes shifting. Cethin knew the male was moments away from shifting fully, and then they'd be having an entirely different type of brawl. One with power thrown about and likely causing massive destruction in a sacred space, but he didn't give a fuck.

"She was the last one to see her!" Cethin bellowed.

"I didn't!" Wren cried, peering around Razik, her eyes wide. "I swear it to you, Cethin. I didn't see her. The others left to see what the commotion was. I stayed to finish packing up everything. I thought Kailia went with them."

"She doesn't know, Cethin," Bram said, his tone coaxing as he stepped next to Razik to shield Wren. "Take a beat and think about this. Get yourself under control. Kailia isn't her responsibility to look after."

No, it wasn't. It was Razik's, who'd insisted on having a conversation about things that were none of his godsdamn business.

"Cethin," Bram said again, sharper and more forceful. The male looked pointedly at the ground, and Cethin looked to find pools of inky darkness at his feet, creeping along the ground.

"We'll help you find her," Fallon said gently, taking a step towards him but stilling at the magic. Jarek was tense beside her. They were all tense. All of them waiting to see what their king was going to do next. All of them waiting to see if they were going to have to intervene in some way.

Inhaling sharply, he pulled his power back. His words were jagged and raspy when he said, "Don't bother. I'll find her myself."

Then he was striding through the trees. A few called after him, and he heard others say to "let him have a minute." He knew they'd follow from afar. None of them would let the king go too far without additional protection.

As if he couldn't handle himself.

As if he hadn't trained with them for centuries.

As if he weren't just as skilled.

As if he were indeed the incompetent king that Razik claimed he was when *he* was the one who'd failed to keep tabs on her. The one person he was supposed to watch and guard with his life. It was his one fucking job.

Unable to keep his power completely contained anymore, he let some of the darkness out. It trailed him, leaving a path of dying foliage in its wake. He tried to keep it as subdued as possible, but with his attention and focus homed in on something else, it was the best he could do.

Why would she wander off? Was she testing him? Seeing just how true his words about always finding her were? Was she trying to prove a point of her own?

Because he could find her, and he would. He could sense power. It was a gift few knew he possessed, one his family had purposefully kept a secret, but he could feel someone's power and the strength of it. It was how he knew that Razik's power was only partially refilled, and it was how he knew she hadn't moved among her smoke and ashes halfway across the continent. It was how he was tracking her now. How he'd known she'd been watching him for months.

He could feel her. It was fleeting, as if her power was flickering in and out like when she moved among her magic, but he could still sense it. It was all he needed to be able to follow her path.

They'd stuck to the eastern edge of the forest, slowly making their way from the Elshira castle to his family's old estate. The home he'd lived in for so many decades with his parents. It was the same path they took every year, but she wouldn't have known that. And she was moving deeper into the trees. Deeper into sacred spaces guarded by more than the spirit animals.

Why couldn't she give just a fucking inch? He was trying. Trying to make her feel at home. Trying to acclimate her to what her new life would entail. Trying to get to know her, to make her comfortable. Trying to include her. To show her the people and lives she would save by agreeing to use her power to help them. What kind of person didn't want to save thousands and thousands of lives?

She accused him of wanting to lock her away in the castle, and now he was beginning to think that wouldn't be a bad idea. At least until they came to a new understanding.

He continued his search, a new and different kind of hunt from what these days had started out as, but a hunt nonetheless. With long strides, he moved, homed in on her power and the call of her magic. Feeling it more acutely the nearer he came. It consumed him.

Until he heard the scream.

Then he was running because he'd only known her a short time, but she never screamed. She never asked for aid. She was annoyingly self-sufficient. More than that, she was as skilled with weapons and combat as the warriors in their company. In fact, the only time he'd heard her scream like this was when Razik had been holding her in an attempt to subdue her.

Which meant someone was touching her.

Every primal piece of him snarled in fury. She may not be his wife yet, but he had still claimed her. She was still his. No one touched her.

Darkness scattered, rolling along the ground, up the trees. His veins darkened with the power, and death sang through him.

Clearing a cluster of dense trees, he found her, and the scene made him come to a halt.

Several bodies were on the ground, blood pooling, some with weapons still in hand. Some had arrows protruding from their backs, while others had met blades. A harvested deer lay nearby.

What the fuck had happened here?

Kailia was standing in the center of it all, two black daggers in her hands. Her chest was heaving, and her cloak was nowhere to be seen. With another scream of what Cethin could only describe as manic agony, Kailia dropped to the ground. Her daggers within reach, she clawed at her boots, ripping at the laces and the buckles.

"Fucking Fates," Cethin cursed under his breath, her frenzied movements enough to break him out of his shock.

He rushed to her as she pulled the first boot free, ducking to avoid yet another blow to his face as she threw it away from her as hard as she could.

"Kailia," he said sharply, dropping to his knees beside her. "Kailia, you need to— Are you hurt?"

There was blood splattered all over her skin and clothing, and her tunic was as shredded as it had been the night Razik had picked her up. Her fingernails were cracked and broken from clawing at her boots, but there was also blood that was fresh and still flowing, as if she had an actively bleeding wound somewhere.

"Kailia, let me look," he said, reaching for her tunic. She was still thrashing, trying to get her other boot off. The erratic movements made her tunic rip more, and that was definitely a stab wound in her abdomen.

"Shit. We need to get you—"

But he didn't get to finish the sentence because he'd instinctively reached for her, instinctively tried to scoop her up to Travel her to a Healer. If he'd thought she was manic before, it was nothing compared to her actions now.

Another scream sounded, this one full of agony. She twisted in his hold, falling back to the ground face first.

"Kailia!" Cethin barked, eyes wide as he reached for her again. "It's me, Kailia. It's Cethin!"

But she clearly couldn't hear him over her hysteria. She was stuck in a fight-or-flight mindset, and she was clearly going to fight.

Her magic swirled around her. Her body even flitted in and out of view, but she didn't go anywhere. She cried out again as her knees hit the blood-soaked ground once more. Once more her ashes swirled, and once more she remained in place.

He needed to get her out of here. Get her to Niara, who could make her sleep again and then heal her wound that was still gushing blood. It had undoubtedly been made worse by her renewed thrashing.

Knowing it was going to make matters worse but not having any other choice, Cethin lunged for her. His arm looped around her waist, pulling her into him. Her front pressed against his chest, and he tried to press his other hand to the stab wound, but she twisted yet again, breaking his hold.

"Godsdammit, Kailia," he growled, catching her as she tried to crawl away.

Then he was releasing her fully as searing agony ripped through his side. Curses fell from his lips, and he looked down to find a dagger shoved into his side, right next to the broken ribs.

One of *her* daggers.

She'd fucking stabbed him.

Again.

Yanking the blade free, he slid it down his boot before refocusing on his future wife. Ashes and smoke were once again swirling, and she was once again not going anywhere.

"What in the fuck?" he heard someone yell. It sounded like Bram. Then there was the sound of several pairs of boots running. The Cadre had finally found their way here, but there was nothing they could do. There was nothing any of them could do other than try to hold her down until she came out of whatever this was.

But there was something he could do.

With one hand pressed to his side to staunch his own bleeding, he lifted his other arm. Focusing on her power, he closed his fist, cutting it off from her soul.

A different cry came from her as she clutched at her chest, curling in on herself. Razik stepped forward, bending down to grab her, but Cethin growled, "Don't touch her."

Razik's lip curled back. "This isn't the time for your—"

"Go fetch Niara and meet us at the estate," Cethin interrupted. "It's an order from your king."

Razik stared back, hatred radiating off him, but Cethin didn't give a fuck. Not as he pushed to his feet and made his way to Kailia. He bent down, pulling her tightly into him again, this time prepared for all the volatile twisting and thrashing.

"Now, Greybane!" he barked before he Traveled through the air and into the home he hadn't stepped a foot inside of in over a year.

"Kailia," he said, trying to be calming, but still trying to be heard over her screams. "Kailia, you need to— *Motherfucker!*"

Because where in the fuck had she gotten a second godsdamn dagger? A blade that was now shoved right below the first stab wound.

"You've got to stop stabbing me, tiny fiend," he muttered, breathing through the pain radiating up his side.

"Don't—touch—me," she cried out in gasps, throwing herself to the side so violently, he dropped her to the stone floor. Even the ornate rug couldn't soften that fall.

She curled into a ball, hugging her knees to her chest as ashes and smoke swirled, much slower this time. Weaker. Her cries quieting.

He crouched beside her, careful not to touch her this time. "I'm not going to touch you," he said as tormented amber eyes lifted to his. "But I'm not going to leave you either. I'm staying right here. Niara is coming." He hesitated before he asked, "Can you lift your shirt? Let me see the wound?"

Her entire body was trembling, and he was forcing himself not to reach for her again.

"Please, Kailia," he coaxed.

With shaking fingers, she reached for the hem of her tunic, dragging it up. He didn't miss her wince, as if even the touch of fabric was too much in this state.

The wound came into view, and it was definitely a stab wound, deep and severe. But that wasn't what had his darkness appearing. It wasn't what had him going preternaturally still. No, that was the burns across her torso. Burns on her hands that he could see now that she wasn't a whirl of violence. Those were marks around her wrists with puncture wounds from…thorns. Someone had tried to tie her hands. Dirt mixed with red. Her shredded tunic was soaked with more than blood.

This hadn't just been an attack with weapons. Magic had been used.

"Did they identify themselves?" he ground out, his soul vibrating with a fury he'd never known before. "Can you tell me who did this to you?"

She was looking through him though, her amber eyes still. Not a hint of swirling smoke. If she heard him, she didn't show it.

So they sat in silence. Her curled into herself, and him crouched beside her, a blade still in his side.

Neither of them moved when Razik appeared with Wren and Niara. He heard Wren's sharp inhale, and Niara's breathy, "by the gods," but he didn't take his eyes off her.

"We need to take her back to the castle," Niara said, dropping down beside them. She glanced at Cethin, eyeing the dagger. "Both of you."

"We stay here," he said. "Get what you need and come back, but first, help her sleep."

"Your grace, I—"

"It's not open for debate," he snapped.

Niara nodded and turned her attention back to Kailia, pressing a hand to her cheek and murmuring the enchantment. Kailia winced at the touch, even as sleep claimed her.

Cethin waved her off to get her supplies when she tried to remove the dagger. When she'd Traveled out, he picked Kailia's now sleeping form up from the floor and made his way out to the sitting room.

"What do you need us to do?" Wren asked as he moved past them.

Cethin didn't answer, climbing the stairs to the second floor, his own pain no longer registering. He pushed open the door to the bedchambers he hadn't used in decades, taking her to the large four-poster bed. Despite the house being unoccupied, he made sure it was still cleaned weekly. They'd stay here for the time being. He didn't want anyone at the castle to see her in this state. Or seeing him, for that matter.

Only after fetching a wet cloth and pressing it to her wound did he acknowledge Razik and Wren, who had followed them up here.

"Let me, your Majesty," Wren said softly, reaching for the cloth. "Razik will help with your..."

She trailed off, but Cethin let her take the cloth for a moment. Taking a step back, he held Razik's stare as he reached for the hilt of the dagger and slid it free. He wasn't about to let the male help with a fucking thing.

He dropped the dagger and heard it clatter onto the stone floor.

Then he followed as everything went black.

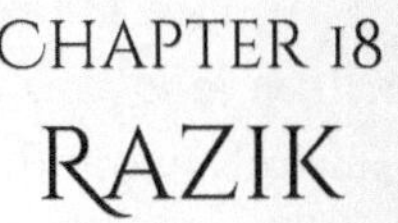

CHAPTER 18

RAZIK

The rapping of knuckles on the doorjamb had him looking up.

Jarek's face was grim when he said, "The Commander is here."

Razik waited until the male had left before he released the heavy sigh. He'd been waiting for Tybalt to show up.

Everything had been complete shit since the phantoms had attacked. The physical fight with Cethin. Kailia's attack. Coming back here only for Cethin to collapse. Yeah, it'd simply been a matter of time until his uncle showed up here. Honestly, he was surprised he hadn't returned with Niara. Tybalt was one of the few people who could Travel directly into the Sutara Family Country Estate. Instead, Fallon had waited outside for the Witch while Jarek had helped get Cethin up to the king's quarters on the third floor. Ariadne had gone with Draven and Bram to see what they could learn about Kailia's attackers, but also to gather their hunting things and the horses. At least he didn't have to deal with Bram right now.

"I'll stay with her," Wren said softly, sitting up from the sofa she'd been resting on. They'd been watching over Kailia while Jarek and Fallon had been staying with Cethin.

"Alert me if she so much as moves."

"I know, Razik," Wren said, pity in her tone.

His lips pressed in a firm line, he stood, heading downstairs to the sitting room and bracing himself for what was to come. Tybalt was the best father figure he could have asked for, but that was not who he was going to face right now. He was facing the Commander of the Avonleyan forces, whose king was once again present during an attack and had been severely wounded. On his watch. On the watch of the entire Cadre. They'd all be punished for that, but it would be different for him. It always was, and he deserved it, considering his actual charge was also unconscious in a bed.

The Sutara Family Country Estate was located on the southeast edge of Shira Forest. Far smaller than the castle and even some estates in Aimonway, it was a three-story home. And it was exactly that. A home. Instead of proper and regal, it was almost cozy and warm. More King Tethys's doing than the queen's. She didn't know how to be anything but as cold as the stars.

He'd just stepped off the last stair when Tybalt appeared, his features tight with control. That is one thing his uncle excelled at. He could be furious and still keep himself composed and in check. In other words, he wouldn't have punched the king in the face.

"Take me to Cethin," he bit out, each word clipped and harsh.

Razik nodded, turning and heading back up the stairs, climbing to the third floor. The moment they entered the room, Jarek and Fallon were on their feet and at attention, eyes down. They knew as well as he did this was going to be bad when they were all back in Aimonway. When the immediate crises had passed. And in the meantime, they knew Tybalt was meticulously planning a grueling punishment for the follies that had happened on this hunt.

"Leave us," Tybalt said sharply.

"Yes, Commander," they both said in unison, not wasting any time to head for the door.

"Check in on Wren," Razik called after them. "She's with Kailia."

Fallon glanced over her shoulder and gave him a quick nod before following Jarek from the room. Tense silence filled the space as Tybalt approached the bed where Cethin lay unconscious. His torso was wrapped in a thick bandage, but the bruises and cuts on his face from their brawl were still plenty visible. With so many injuries, it would take longer for Cethin's magic to heal him.

"Tell me everything Niara has said," Tybalt said curtly.

"She's downstairs," Razik answered, his brow creasing. Hadn't he talked to her when he got here? "I can get her for a more comprehensive report."

Glowing amber-red eyes with vertical pupils met his. "I want to hear it from *you*, Razik."

He ground his molars, a muscle twitching in his jaw and a faint trace of pain echoing it, still feeling the effects of Cethin's hits. His own magic wasn't nearly replenished after the battle with the phantoms, and it would take him longer than usual to heal too.

"Two deep stab wounds to the right side," Razik said. "One on top of the other. Normally not enough to lose consciousness, but the daggers used were not ones known to us. Niara believes the blades also caused some unexpected complications in her ability to aid the healing."

"How did he receive the stab wounds?" Tybalt pushed, focused on the king.

"Kailia," Razik ground out from between clenched teeth.

Tybalt hummed. "What else?"

"Broken ribs. Three of them. Along with the visual bruises and cuts."

"Also from the future queen?"

His tone told Razik the Commander already knew the answer. Or, at the very least, knew it hadn't been Kailia.

"No," Razik gritted out. "Those are from me."

Shame should have probably been washing through him, but it wasn't. He didn't feel an ounce of regret about having it out with Cethin. Probably shouldn't have done so in the middle of a sacred forest, but beyond that, no regrets.

Tybalt didn't seem surprised by that statement, but the obvious disappointment radiating off him still made Razik somehow even more tense. He might not regret his fist meeting Cethin's face, but

Tybalt's disapproval would always matter, even if he didn't want it to.

"What else?" Tybalt finally said.

"We were attacked in the middle of the night by more phantoms. Kailia and I defended the company, while the others helped by using her arrowheads. No one was hurt."

Tybalt finally looked at him, arching a brow.

"No one was injured in *that* battle," Razik amended begrudgingly.

"I've heard how Cethin came to this state, but not your charge?"

Your charge.

The one he was responsible for.

Point taken, uncle.

Because it was that situation that he did feel ashamed about.

"From what I've gathered, she was stalking a stag and was attacked." Razik answered.

"By the phantoms?"

Razik shook his head. "Ariadne, Bram, and Draven went to investigate the scene. We didn't get much of a chance to take it all in, but they were Avonleyan."

"You're sure?"

"As sure as I can be without seeing them closer. More than that, Kailia was covered in burns and what looked like thorn and vine imprints. Not to mention her clothing was soaking wet," Razik answered. "Leads me to believe Fae or Avonleyan."

"I'll wait for Ariadne's report before coming to that conclusion," Tybalt said tersely.

Razik once again gnashed his teeth to keep from biting back a retort.

"Niara is unsure which of them will wake first," he said when the silence stretched on. Which was ridiculous. He relished silence, but not when he was sitting here drowning in his uncle's disapproval of everything he'd done and said in the last two days. "I understand I could have handled things differently—"

"*Could* have?" His uncle finally turned to face him fully. "Everything about this should have been handled fucking differently. You are all trained better than this. I trained every godsdamn one of you, but you—"

He shook his head, turning away from him, and gods, the action shouldn't make his chest ache like this.

"It was clearly my mistake to place you in this role," he said, sounding like he was speaking more to himself.

"It wasn't," Razik cut in. "You're right. There's something off about the entire situation. About *her*."

"Clearly, based on the fact she's managed to stab our king multiple times," Tybalt said. "I obviously haven't trained any of you as thoroughly as I should have. Something I'll be taking into account for future training."

Yep, saw that coming. Brutality was in their future.

"The failings aren't yours," Razik replied.

Tybalt turned to him, a brow arching again. "Are you accepting responsibility then?"

Razik steeled his spine, holding his uncle's stare. "I am. For all of it."

A glimmer of respect flickered in Tybalt's eyes, and the relief that rushed through him eased a fraction of the tension in his limbs.

Until Tybalt said, "I'll review positions and have your replacement figured out by the time you all return to Aimonway."

"My replacement?" Razik demanded.

"How can I not assign a new personal guard to her when they are both wounded and unconscious due to situations that you just claimed full responsibility for?"

"Tybalt, I—"

"That is all. You're dismissed," the Commander said, turning back to the bed. "I'll take over guarding the future queen. Jarek and Fallon can keep watch over the king. You can return to Aimonway."

"This is bullshit," Razik growled. "I was charged with guarding her."

"And it's obviously a job you cannot fulfill due to your relationship with Cethin. They go hand in hand," Tybalt said. "Again, you're dismissed."

"He won't let me anywhere near her," Razik said, gesturing to Cethin's sleeping form. "*He* won't let me do my fucking job, Tybalt!"

"Precisely," Tybalt snapped, his eyes glowing once more as he rounded on Razik, that control slipping a fraction. "Neither one of you can put her safety above your feuds and grudges. The two of you are centuries old and still act like godsdamn younglings. I'm trying to help you find your place here, Razik. I know you don't want the life you were destined for, but everything I offer to you, you let your past and bitterness taint. I don't—"

He shook his head again, turning away from him. "For this? What this has become? I take full responsibility for that. Something I will have to answer for when the time comes."

"No," Razik said, unable to find any other words because none of this was his uncle's fault. There was definitely someone to blame, but it wasn't him.

His features were grim when he looked back at Razik. "If words could change things, the realms would look a whole lot different. You're dismissed, Razik."

"I'm not leaving," Razik said resolutely. "I can do this. I *want* to do this."

"If you wanted to, you would."

"I…" He pushed out a frustrated breath. "I'll prove myself, Tybalt. I won't disappoint you again. You entrusted me with this. I won't fail you again."

The silence was heavy, seconds ticking by, and Razik waited for his uncle to look at him. To say something. To do anything.

Finally, he shook his head, rubbing at his brow. "If she were here…"

"But she's not. Unless you know something I don't?" Razik replied.

His uncle looked up to meet his stare, something akin to resignation and defeat playing out on his face. "This is the last time I can extend you grace in this."

"It won't be needed again."

Making his way to the door, Tybalt stopped beside him, resting a hand on his shoulder and squeezing. "I need that to be true."

Then he left the room, leaving Razik alone. He glared at the sleeping king. The source of so much fucking agony and conflict. All because of *her*.

Lifting a hand, he sent a message among a swirl of black flames to Wren, checking on Kailia and asking her to let him know the moment anything changed. Then he settled into an armchair across the room. He needed to get used to being in Cethin's presence. Having him unconscious was a good way to ease into it, he supposed.

It was a start, and for now, that needed to be enough.

—⟩⟩ ⊙ ⟨⟨—

Five more fucking hours.

That was how long it took for Cethin to stir. He'd checked in on Kailia every half hour, Jarek staying with Cethin when he left. On her next round of checking wounds, Niara had said she suspected Cethin would wake first, mainly because his wounds were only physical. Whatever Kailia had faced had been more than the physical attacks, and Razik had ruminated on that for hours while sitting in the same chair. She didn't like to be touched, but what had caused such an aversion?

A groan of discomfort sounded as Cethin stirred, and he lifted an arm, swiping his hand down his face. Then he suddenly shot up, cursing at what Razik was sure was pain lancing up his side.

"What the fuck are you doing?" Razik ground out, crossing the room and easily shoving the male back down.

Confusion flitted across Cethin's face before it morphed into the hatred they reserved for each other. "Fuck off, Greybane," he growled, trying to sit up again. "Where's Kailia?" His eyes darted around wildly before going wide. "Why am I up here?"

Razik eyed him warily. "Because it's the king's quarters, and you are the king."

"No," Cethin said, once again pushing to sit up, and Razik let him this time because he might be trying to be civil, but he wasn't the male's godsdamn keeper.

"No to which part?" Razik asked, wondering if he'd hit his head harder than they'd all thought when he'd passed out. Niara had said that was the least of the worries, but now Razik wasn't so sure.

"Where is Kailia?" Cethin demanded, sucking in a sharp breath.

"She's down a floor in your old bedchambers," Razik answered. "Lie back down. You have broken ribs and were stabbed. Again. Twice." Then he sighed as Cethin pushed to his feet, using the bed to steady himself. "That's the opposite of lying back down."

"Shut up, jackass," Cethin grunted, making it to the pole of the four-poster bed before he had to stop and suck in another sharp breath.

With another audible sigh of resignation, Razik closed the distance between them, reaching for his shoulder.

Cethin jerked back, barking another curse and gripping his side gingerly as he rasped out, "What are you doing?"

"As entertaining as it would be to watch you maneuver the stairs, Niara will have my balls if I let you do that. So I figured I'd Travel you down there," he answered. It was a half truth. Niara would be livid, and she was formidable, but he wasn't about to tell Cethin that he was trying to prove himself to his uncle too.

"Yeah, all right," Cethin muttered, his body relaxing some.

"You're welcome," Razik said, gripping his shoulder and pulling them through the air before Cethin could finish the curse that he'd started to utter.

As soon as they appeared, Cethin forgot about him anyway, grimacing as he rushed to the bed. Wren had lurched to her feet, and Jarek had pushed off the wall at their arrival, both of them momentarily startled.

"Why hasn't she woken yet? Where is Niara?" Cethin demanded. He lifted a hand but stopped short, his hand hovering over her brow as though he was going to smooth her hair back.

"Niara has been monitoring both of you since our arrival here," Razik supplied, crossing his arms and leaning a shoulder along the wall. "She suspected you would wake first. I'm assuming she'll be here anytime for her rounds, and she'll be none too pleased to find you up and about."

"Here, Cethin," Wren said, tugging on the armchair to move it closer.

Razik gently moved her aside, picking the chair up to set by the bed. He'd no more than put it down before Cethin was lowering to the cushioned seat. There was a fine sheen of sweat at his brow that told him being up for those few minutes had taken its toll, and he had to agree with Niara. Those daggers of Kailia's had done something to the male and had affected his healing abilities.

Turning to Jarek, Razik said, "Notify Niara and Tybalt that Cethin's awake."

Jarek nodded, gaze bouncing between him and Cethin with a questioning look, but he said nothing as he left the room. When he turned back, Cethin was leaning forward, half out of the chair and pulling Kailia's blanket back.

"For fuck's sake, sit down, Sutara," Razik growled.

"I need to see her wound. How's it healing?"

"It's healing like the best Healer on the continent is tending to it," he snapped.

Cethin sank into the chair, tipping his head back and eyes falling closed as he pressed his hand to his side. Razik wanted to tell him it'd be better if he lay down, but the male wasn't going to listen to him, so he'd let Niara deal with that. Instead, he said, "Niara believes both of you will take longer than usual to heal for different reasons."

Cracking an eye open, Cethin met his gaze, but when he didn't say anything, Razik went on. "We believe the daggers used to stab you are having some effect on your healing speed, and the…prior injuries don't help the process."

Cethin snorted a derisive laugh, closing his eye again.

"As for Kailia," Razik continued, "her abdominal wound was substantial, but Niara believes there are mental facets that are keeping her sleeping longer."

"What does that mean?" Cethin asked, opening his eyes and

sitting up straighter. Or attempting to. He quickly slumped back against the chair again.

The door opened then, Niara and Tybalt striding through.

"It means," Niara said with a pointed glare at Cethin as she moved to the bedside, "that her mind is keeping her asleep to protect her for the time being. What happened in her past?"

"I don't know all the details," Cethin answered, watching every move the Healer made.

Niara only hummed as she worked, peeling back the wound dressing and applying more of a paste she'd made. Adding a new dressing, she replaced the blankets before turning to Cethin once more.

"You should not be up and moving so soon, your Majesty," she said, her deep brown eyes raking over the king as she assessed him. It was easy enough to do considering Cethin was shirtless, showing the bandage wrapped around his abdomen.

"I needed to see her," Cethin said, grimacing when she pressed along his torso.

"And you have, so you can return to your own chambers."

"These are my chambers."

"I believe Niara means upstairs," Tybalt said, standing next to Razik with his arms crossed and watching on.

"No," Cethin gritted out.

"You'll heal faster if you rest. In a bed," Niara said.

"I'm fine here."

The Witch threw her hands up in exasperation. "Sometimes I wonder why you call on me at all."

Cethin's features softened a fraction. "I mean no disrespect, Niara. I simply wish to remain with her."

"Then do so in the bed."

Cethin hesitated, glancing at Kailia's sleeping form before he said, "In a bit."

Niara said nothing else, but she made her disapproval known as she left the room. She didn't even do anything in particular. Witches just had that way about them.

"You're being difficult for no reason, Cethin," Tybalt said, and

Razik bit his tongue knowing if *he'd* said something like that to the king, Tybalt would have shut him down immediately. "We can summon you as soon as she wakes."

"I'm fine, Tybalt," Cethin said.

"You need to rest."

"I said I'm fine."

"You'll be more comfortable in your own chambers—"

"I'm sitting in my chambers!" Cethin snapped, and Razik almost slipped and showed his surprise at the fierceness of those words.

Tybalt had gone quiet, clearly trying to work out the same thing Razik was. Eventually, he said, "Wren, can you give us a moment please?"

"Of course," Wren replied, and Razik could hear the relief in her voice. She wasn't much for conflict. She could hold her own, but she avoided it when possible. "I'll bring up some food for everyone."

"Thank you, Wren," Cethin murmured.

She bowed her head before rushing from the room, pulling the door to the bedchamber closed behind her.

Tybalt wasted no time. "I think you should consider moving this union."

Razik waited for Cethin to immediately shut that notion down, but he stayed silent, silver gaze fixed on Kailia.

Avonleyan unions took place under full moons, and Cethin had announced that he and Kailia would be married during next month's full moon with the kingdom celebration happening a few days later.

"I know the advisory council is eager for this," Tybalt went on, "but I think we need to consider Kailia. Give her time to adjust. If we move it to the autumnal season, that gives us all time to get proper precautions in place. Perhaps we can figure out a way to handle this new threat better, as well as investigate who attacked her and why it happened."

Still staring at his betrothed, Cethin said, "I agree."

Razik nearly fell over at the simple words.

"You do?" Tybalt said, not hiding his shock.

Cethin straightened with a slight grimace as he finally shifted to face them. "I agree we need to move the union. Not back, but up. It needs to happen sooner."

"Sooner?" Tybalt repeated, sounding even more taken aback, but Razik wasn't surprised in the least. His lack of reaction from moments ago now made sense. "Cethin, the only full moon that is sooner is in four days."

"Exactly. As you said, we need to consider Kailia in all this," Cethin replied. "Her safety to be more specific. Right now, she's just my betrothed. If she carries the title of queen, it will provide more protection."

"How in the realms do you figure that?" Razik cut in. "You're the king, and you've been attacked repeatedly in these last months alone. It doesn't create less of a target; it creates a bigger one."

Cethin's silver irises leveled on him. "Then perhaps she needs a better equipped guard as well."

"You had the best we have with you out on this hunt, and both of you ended up unconscious with severe injuries," Tybalt interjected. "That's not on Razik. If anything, it's on you for even going on this hunt with the recent attacks. Like Razik said, your title puts you in more danger, not less."

"The title also carries more power," Cethin argued.

"Why are you so adamant about this?" Tybalt pushed. "Not three months ago we couldn't even get you to contemplate a marriage, and now you are wanting to rush a union? What are you not telling us?"

Razik waited to see if he'd tell Tybalt how he was all but extorting the female for the kingdom. Forcing her into a union for access to her weapons. But there was more to all this. Razik had witnessed the obsessiveness and intrigue, and the king was different around her. He had to be. Kailia's personality and mannerisms forced anyone to be different with her.

Cethin pushed slowly to his feet, determination on his face. "We need her weapons to defend this kingdom. Marriages have been arranged for less."

"Cethin," Tybalt chastised in exasperation. "It does not have to be done this way."

"Like you said, the council and citizens of the kingdom have been pushing for this for years. I've been repeatedly lectured about my disservice to the kingdom for waiting so long. My commitments and reasoning have been called into question. She's more than weapons." He paused, gaze lingering on her again. "She's so much more in ways I think we all have yet to discover."

"Maybe we should let her decide when she wakes," Razik interrupted. "She might not even be awake in four days, but are either of you really going to be ready for such a thing? And even if you are, she should have some choice in all this, even if it's as minor as when it happens."

"Take some time to get to know her more," Tybalt urged, trying to appeal to logic.

"We'll have the rest of our immortal lives for that," Cethin said, limping his way to the bathing chamber.

"And her choice in the matter?" Razik called after him, a familiar unease setting in at the idea of her not being given a choice in her own future.

Cethin paused at the doorway, turning to look at him knowingly. His words were cold and dark when he said, "It's nowhere near the same thing, but she has a choice. I'll just make sure she makes the correct one."

Then he went into the bathing chamber, closing the door.

Razik shoved a hand through his hair in frustration.

"What do you know, Razik?" Tybalt asked, his uncle's scrutinizing gaze fixed on him.

"I know she should have a fucking choice in this," Razik said, his dragon becoming restless in his soul at his own agitation.

"Cethin's right. It's not the same thing. This union and the Guardian bond are—"

"Both require a willingness," Razik snapped. "And when forced, both will lead to a resentment that can be damning."

"And if she's willing?" Tybalt asked. "Then what will your argument be?"

Razik walked to the door that led out to a small balcony, pulling it open. He needed some fresh air to cool off. He needed to shift and go flying, but he couldn't go anywhere while his charge slept.

Feeling the spring wind on his face, he stared out at Shira Forest behind the estate as he said, "If she's willing, we're inviting something in that could be just as damning. Either way, we're fucked."

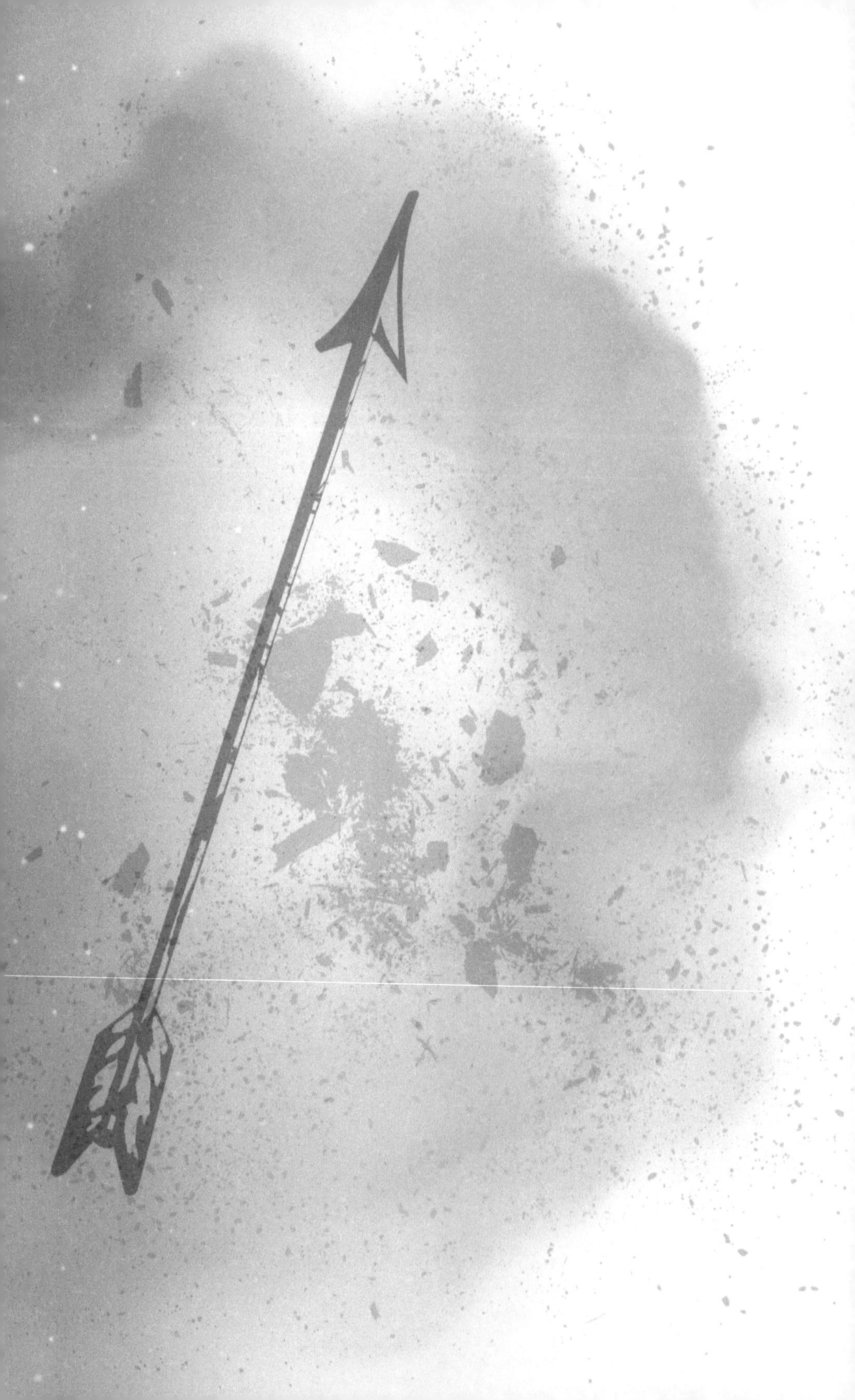

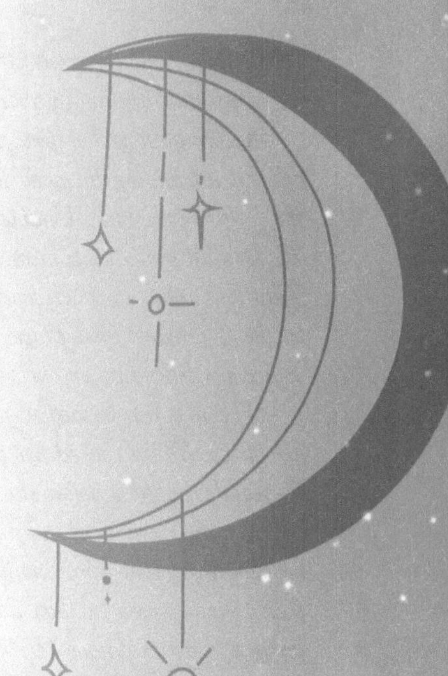

CHAPTER 19
KAILIA

*W*ith a deep breath, she released the arrow, feeling the familiar small whoosh of air on her cheek as the string snapped back into place. She watched the arrow find its mark, the stag she'd been tracking dropping instantly to the ground. If she'd been using one of Cethin's arrows, it would have likely run off into the trees, and she would have had to follow a blood trail to its final resting place. Her arrows with her magic made its death quick and merciful. At least, that was the case for animals.

This also wouldn't have taken so long if she'd been barefoot. As it were, she had boots on, and they were anything but silent as she made her way through the small clearing where the stag lay unmoving. Kneeling before it, she pulled the arrow free. Not all beings dissolved into ashes with her weapons, but all of them crossed the Veil. Placing a palm on the warm fur, she sank her fingers in, bowing her head to send a prayer of thanks to Temural. But then she saw the Mark on her forearm.

The Mark that she could only see when she was dreaming.

Her head snapped up, and she scanned the surroundings, trying to remember. But it wasn't until the figures emerged from the trees that everything came rushing back to her. These were magical beings, Fae or Avonleyan judging by their arched ears and primal grace. They wore all greens and browns, colors that would blend in with the trees, and thick leathers added another layer of defense to their attire.

While there were weapons strapped to them, her concern was the power at their fingertips and swirling in their palms.

Kailia planted her feet, conjuring two daggers from her magic. Briefly she debated attempting to move through her power, but when she'd tried last time, she'd still been stuck. Unable to drift and find the freedom she loved. Moreover, this was all a dream, a memory that could serve. She could learn something here. That was what she'd discovered over the centuries. Dreams were teachers if you let them. Dreams were places to conquer memories. Dreams could be paralyzing or freeing, depending on one's willingness to surrender to them.

The first person rushed at her, a female with bright orange hair and fire at her mercy. Kailia cocked her arm back, sending her dagger flying. It struck true, the female dropping before she could do anything more and flames winked out.

A male came next, his water winding up Kailia's legs and torso, weighing her down as vines from another twined around her wrist, thorns sinking into her flesh. She conjured another dagger in time to block a blade as the water wielder brought a sword down. Her knee came up, connecting with his groin, and as the male groaned in pain, she struck out with her blade, sinking it deep into his gut.

The other was there, and she felt the air stir behind her. She ducked a moment before a hand would have grabbed her. Touched her. The thought alone had her spinning and swiping with her daggers in one fluid motion.

But then she couldn't breathe as the air was pulled from her lungs. She gasped, trying to choke down any bit of oxygen.

A dream.

This was a dream.

Then the fire came, singeing along her flesh. And the burning. The burning she could feel because Ash Riders might descend from Anala, but they couldn't wield flames. They weren't immune to it like fire Fae were, and she couldn't scream because she couldn't breathe. Not as the flames seared across her middle.

Then came the hands.

The hands that were touching her and trying to drag her somewhere.

The hands that were as torturous as the flames.

With a violent twist, she tore through the vines, the thorns sinking deeper. Smoke and ashes swirled around her, chasing the flames, tearing at her clothing to erase the touch. Pain lanced through her stomach, but it was nothing compared to the fire and the touching.

Suddenly able to suck in a breath, she screamed. Not in pain, despite that agony still tormenting her, but in utter rage. Her ashes burst out from her in a radius, dragging anything and everything back to her. Daggers in hand, she couldn't hear them, but their mouths moved, screaming and pleading.

She didn't give a single fuck.

She dropped to a knee between the two bodies held in place by ashes. She watched them convulse and choke as her smoke swirled along their noses and mouths and eyes. And in perfect synchrony, she brought her blades down, one on either side, and sank them into their hearts.

She pushed back to her feet, everything around her muted and moving as if in slow motion. Another scream ripped from her throat. The scent of magic hung in the air, all of it assaulting her senses, but the fire.

The fire.

And the burning.

And the touching.

She dropped back to her knees, the daggers clattering beside her, and she clawed at her arm, desperate to see that Mark.

A dream.

A dream.

A—

"Easy, tiny fiend."

Her head snapped up to find Cethin slowly lowering to his knees before her. He'd been in her dreams more and more lately, which made sense, but he'd never interacted with her on a dream plane.

"I'm going to take your boots off for you, okay?" Cethin said, watching her and waiting.

This was a dream, and now that she was back in the right state of mind, she could remember that. She could take control. If she could do that, she could learn what her dreams were trying to tell her.

Nodding slowly, he reached for her foot. The leather between his skin and hers, the touch wasn't as jarring. He didn't speak as he deftly undid the laces and buckles, sliding off one and then the other.

"Would you like to handle the socks?" he asked, silver eyes meeting hers with an expression she didn't understand.

Wanting to test a theory, she shook her head, otherwise holding perfectly still.

"You're quiet today," he said conversationally, slipping his fingertips into the top of the sock and peeling it down her calf and foot. It was the barest of

touches, and a sound she'd never made before came from her throat at the cool touch to her burning skin.

He clearly noticed because his movement halted for the briefest of seconds before he continued removing the sock and then shifting to the other one.

"You were hurt," he said, his tone low and menacing. "By our own people."

"They're not my people," she said, her voice hoarse from the screaming.

He tilted his head as he watched her, hands resting on his thighs now. "They're not?"

"Why would they be?"

"Because you are their queen," he said slowly, as if this were obvious. "Are you sure you are all right? Did you hit your head?"

But she wasn't the queen. Not yet. Right?

She lifted her arm, tugging on the torn sleeve of her tunic to see her skin clearly. The Mark was there, vivid black against her warm skin tone.

"We are married?" she asked, eyeing him.

"Of course we are married, wife," he said, the corner of his lips turning up in a rogue smirk.

"I don't have a Union Mark," she countered, eyes narrowing as she studied her hand to be sure.

"We opted to do things our own way," he replied, pushing to his feet and reaching for her. "Let's go home, and we'll have Niara look you over."

She studied his outstretched hand, his fingers so close to her. Too close. But in dreams, it didn't matter, right?

So she slid her fingers into his waiting palm.

CHAPTER 20
KAILIA

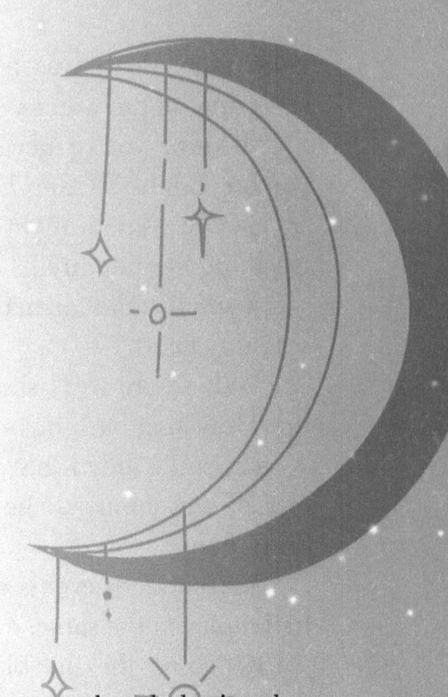

Laying perfectly still, she kept her eyes closed, letting her senses tell her about her surroundings. She was warm. A plush and soft mattress beneath her. The weight of blankets or furs atop her. The smell of fresh air. The barest brush of a breeze along her cheek. The rustle of movement told her she wasn't alone. Footfalls. A door closing.

She wanted to lay there and go unnoticed a little longer, but the pressure in her pelvis told her that would not be an option much longer. She needed a bathing chamber.

Slowly cracking her eyes open, she looked up at a ceiling with open beams running across it.

Her heart rate increased.

Gaze darting to a wall, she found a window with a view that told her she was not on the ground floor. The walls were painted a calming shade of blue the color of the sea.

Her chest squeezed as her breaths came faster.

Then silver hair and eyes filled her vision, Cethin leaning over her.

"It's okay, Kailia," he coaxed, holding her gaze. "You're safe."

She broke his stare, looking past him to another wall. The same color blue, there was a painting of a beach at night, the moon reflecting on the waters.

"I know you've never been here. That you don't know where you are, but we're safe. *You're* safe," he repeated.

Slowly, she brought her gaze back to his, finding him still watching her intently.

A small smile formed on his lips. "Staying so quiet never serves you, tiny fiend."

"Where are we?" she asked, the words raspy. Her throat was so dry. How long had she been sleeping?

His smile faded, his eyes becoming shuttered. "It's an old property of my family's," he answered. "Located to the south, outside Shira Forest."

She nodded, events and memories returning. The dream she'd had replayed the same, even with the differences.

Reaching for the blankets, she made to shove them off, but Cethin reached out, gently placing his palm atop them, right below her breasts. It was barely a touch, enough to still her, but it made every part of her tense up and *that* sent sharp agony along her torso.

"Please wait for Niara," he said, his voice tight. "Your injuries were extensive, Kailia, and you've slept for quite some time."

"How long?"

"Two days."

She nodded. That explained the urgent need.

About to express that need, she glanced over at him again, but the words stilled as she realized he was shirtless. Pale skin and toned muscles were on display, but she'd never cared about such things before. A body was a body, male or female. She could appreciate beauty, sure, but in the end, everyone had one. Some came with dicks and some came with breasts.

There was a white bandage wrapped around his abdomen, and when she dragged her gaze up farther, across a firm chest, the column of his neck, and back to his face, there were faint traces of bruising. His hair was tied back, a couple pieces having escaped the leather band and brushing along his jaw.

A small smirk kicked up on his lips as he said, "This type of silence I will take from you for as long as you'd like."

Her brow furrowed. "Silence is silence. There aren't different types."

He leaned in farther, his hand still resting atop the blankets. "That's where you're wrong," he countered, his voice low and soft. "There are several versions of silence. Meek silence, where one is trying to shrink in on themselves. Purposeful silence for hunting or thievery. Clever silence for listening and learning, both in academic and social settings. Apathetic silence when one truly doesn't care about what's happening around them. Restful silence for the obvious. Domineering silence, which you prefer, by the way, where the lack of sound exhibits a steadfast power and makes others uncomfortable."

"And which type of silence was I using?" she asked, both annoyed and intrigued by this conversation.

His smirk grew. "My favorite kind. Awe-inspired silence. When one is so stunned and enamored by what they are looking at, they can't find words."

Her features hardened. "That is *not* what that was."

He hummed, amusement dancing in his eyes.

"It wasn't," she insisted, shifting under the blankets and again attempting to uncover herself.

All humor and teasing disappeared instantly. "Wait for Niara," he warned.

"I need the bathing chamber," she retorted, wiggling her toes and rotating her ankles to get feeling back in them. Two days was a long time to not move her limbs. She felt stiff and lethargic.

He pressed his lips together in disapproval.

"You seem upset by that need," she said, trying to understand his reaction. "It is a basic one."

"I know that," he replied. "I just worry about you getting out of bed before Niara has checked you over."

"That is an unnecessary worry. I've survived worse," she said, once again moving to shove back the blankets and furs.

He let her this time, something dark in his tone when he said, "Tell me more about that."

"Not necessary. What is necessary is me using the bathing room in the next two minutes," she said sharply, and he straightened at the bite in her tone.

"Yes, all right," he relented, brushing back the strands of hair from his face. "Can I at least help you up?"

"No," she said, sucking in a sharp breath when her abdominal muscles contracted as she attempted to sit up. She could do this.

"Kailia..."

She said nothing, controlling her breathing. If he touched her, it would be worse. So much worse.

It took far too long to get her legs over the side of the bed, and she slowly slid to the floor. Her bare feet sank into a soft rug, and the hem of her tunic brushed her knees.

Her bare knees.

Her head snapped up. "I don't have pants on."

His eyes dipped as if he needed to confirm it for himself. Yet another emotion sparked in his eyes. He felt too many things for her to keep track of. Emotions were messy and confusing.

His voice was rough when he said, "You are correct, but in all fairness, you prefer not to wear pants."

"My dresses generally reach the floor," she argued.

He arched his brows. "And the slits up the sides reach your thighs, which I am not complaining about, by the way."

She didn't have time to discuss this. "Where is the bathing room?"

He gestured to the right, and she followed the motion to a doorway, immediately making her way there. She stayed close to the bed, using it as support as long as she could, and Cethin, annoyingly, stayed close to her.

"Niara is going to be pissed, and she's already upset with me," Cethin muttered.

"Yes, well, it's either this, or I piss all over the floor," she snapped in irritation.

He huffed a surprised breath of laughter. "Fair enough, tiny fiend."

Finally making it to the bathing room, she shut the door in his face. After she'd taken care of her needs, she sat on the edge of the large bathtub to catch her breath while debating getting into the thing. A hot bath sounded divine, but she could hear Cethin pacing on the other side of the door. More than that, she wasn't entirely sure how the knobs and faucet worked. She'd just gotten used to the castle tubs, and these were different.

Sighing, she pushed back to her feet and shuffled to the door, pulling it open. Sure enough, Cethin was there, waiting for her. Instead of going back to the bed, she made her way to a window, taking in the view. Judging by the sun, it was after high-noon. It looked warm out, but she'd spent the last few days in that forest. She knew how deceiving the view was.

"Did I win?" she asked, bringing her hand up and pressing her fingertips to the glass. It was cool, confirming her theory about the temperature outside.

"Win what?" Cethin asked.

She looked over her shoulder. "The hunt."

His eyes widened, a disbelieving laugh sounding. "The hunt became the least of our worries."

"Injuries don't end a competition."

"They don't…" He eyed her, grimacing a little as he shifted and pressed a hand to his side.

"What's wrong with you?" she asked, turning to face him, wincing herself when the wound on her stomach pulled.

"Can you please sit?" Cethin asked.

She should have argued, but she also desperately needed to sit down. So she made her way back to the bed, and Cethin propped up pillows so she could rest against the headboard. Once she was settled, she said, "Did you injure yourself on the hunt?"

He sent her an unimpressed look from the armchair he'd sat in that was right beside the bed. "No, Kailia. I did not injure myself. What do you remember of that day?"

"I was tracking a stag while you all went off to do the gods know what," she replied simply, hands flat in her lap. But she flexed her fingers in the soft fur that he'd spread back over her.

"You mean you went off by yourself," he said accusingly.

She stared at him. "Eight people cannot hunt a stag together. It's impossible. You are all very loud. It's amazing you're able to harvest anything."

"That's not the point."

"You are upset I went hunting without you?"

"No, I—" He pushed out a harsh breath, swiping a hand down his face. "You don't know the forest, Kailia. You went off by yourself, and you were attacked."

"Yes, I know that, but that doesn't explain how you injured yourself."

"I didn't injure myself. You stabbed me. Again. Twice."

Her entire being went utterly still. "I stabbed you."

"Twice," he repeated.

"With what?"

He gave her an incredulous look. "Daggers. What else would you stab me with?"

"*My* daggers? What color were the blades?"

Seemingly at a loss, he stared at her.

"Were they silver or black?" she pushed.

"Black," he said in curiosity. "Why does that matter?"

But she scarcely heard him. Not with the whooshing in her ears as her heart rate spiked. It wasn't possible.

"Where are they?" she demanded, shoving back the furs again.

"Kailia, what are you doing? Stay in bed."

"Where are my daggers?" she insisted. "You can't keep all my things, Cethin. I already agreed to the marriage. What else do you want from me?"

His eyes were wide as he lurched up from his chair, attempting to stop her. "Kailia, just— Calm down. The daggers are downstairs."

"Why? They are mine."

"And you've been asleep. Although Tybalt does have questions about them."

He wasn't touching her, but he was standing close enough that if she tried to get out of the bed, *she'd* touch him.

"I want them back."

"You'll get them back," he said, lifting a hand before a swirl of black appeared. "After Niara checks you over."

"I'm not a child, Cethin," she retorted. "You don't actually get to decide when I get my own belongings back."

He smirked. "Tell that to your arrow."

"Should've stabbed you three times," she muttered, sinking back into the pillows.

Cethin chuckled, and she ignored him, looking anywhere else. But without his distracting conversation, she went right back to the daggers and the stabbing and the whole fight in the forest. She couldn't have stabbed him with the same daggers. No one survived being struck with one. It didn't matter where. It could be the smallest knick to the arm; they still crossed the Veil, and she'd been *very* careful not to have them on her in his presence lately due to the way he provoked her.

A minute later, there was a soft knock before Niara came into the room, followed by Razik and Tybalt. So many people. So many hands and fingers. So much proximity.

She immediately stiffened as Niara approached, wincing at the tension and strain on her torso.

"Please tell me she hasn't been out of that bed," the Healer said tightly.

"She needed the bathing room," Cethin answered, once again watching her closely. "She will not hurt you, Kailia. You know that, right? You know Niara. And Razik and Tybalt."

She knew all of them, but it didn't assuage the growing panic. The burns and the hands from the last fight and from her dream lingered. She tried to focus on her breathing, wishing she was outside. The feel of the earth beneath her feet was grounding. A dagger to run her fingers along would be nice too, but it would invite more questions if she conjured one now.

Niara had paused at the foot of the bed, also studying her far too closely. All of them were. As if she were some foreign thing they weren't sure how to interact with. The feeling was mutual. She'd been plucked from the security of her ashes and smoke and forced to be among the masses. And that thought had her remembering that she'd tried to move among them during the attack. Or after? At one point, she'd tried, and still had been stuck. It was all so… suffocating.

"I only need to inspect the wound and apply a new dressing," Niara said after several beats of awkward silence. "However, if you'd rather Cethin do the actual touching, I am amenable to that. I only need to see it. I can instruct him."

"What?" Kailia asked, unsure of what was happening. She glanced at Cethin, who appeared as surprised as she felt, before looking back at Niara. "I don't understand."

"It is merely an offering to make you more comfortable," Niara supplied simply, seeing far too much with her keen Witch senses. "But the choice is yours."

Would that work? A touch was a touch, but…

But if she pretended it was a dream—the same dream from an hour ago—maybe it would be enough to survive these few minutes.

Her eyes fixed on the fur blanket her fingers were buried in, she said, "I would prefer Cethin do it."

She could feel his eyes on her, and she couldn't describe what she was feeling right now. It was a mixture of resentment at the situation and humiliation at her weakness, but also an odd thrill she'd never experienced before. Certainly never at the prospect of being touched.

"Lie flat," Niara instructed, and Kailia started to inch down the bed.

When Cethin reached to help, she stilled. "Not yet. Just…not until necessary."

He nodded, and she worked herself down before Niara said, "The blankets only need to go down to your waist."

Well, that was good considering the whole no pants thing. She didn't want to contemplate how she'd come to be in such a state.

As if reading her thoughts, Razik suddenly spoke from across the room.

"Wren and Fallon got you into clean clothing," he said. "Your other attire was torn, soaked, and bloody."

She nodded, meeting his sapphire gaze for a second before refocusing on Cethin and readying herself.

"Remove the bandage, Cethin," Niara instructed, passing him a small knife with a long, narrow blade.

He nodded, taking it from her and stilling again as if hesitating. Kailia closed her eyes though, trying to go anywhere but here. Thinking of the safety of her smoke. A quiet room by the sea. Frigid lands with snow and freezing temperatures.

But a small gasp fell from her lips as something icy brushed along her bare stomach, and her eyes flew open a second before Cethin's fingers followed. He was focused on his task, carefully sliding the blade beneath the bandage, but his eyes flicked to hers for the briefest of moments.

His fingertips were rough where they touched her, callused from training the way hers were. And instead of closing her eyes to suffer through all this, she studied him. The slight crease on his brow as he concentrated, trying to be cautious but also quick. The intensity in his eyes, glowing faintly as if they held starlight itself. The tense jaw. The press of his lips as he worked. The steadiness attributed to one comfortable performing under pressure.

Then he stepped back to let Niara in, the female inspecting but not touching as promised. Something eased in Kailia's chest a little.

"It's healing nicely," Niara said. Meeting Kailia's gaze, she added, "The wound was deep but done with a standard blade. The burns have all healed as well. You still need to rest. And keep applying the herbs until fully healed, which should be in a day or two."

Kailia nodded as Niara stepped back again and went to a dresser, where supplies were scattered across the surface. Picking up a small pot, she lifted the lid and brought it to Cethin along with a small, flat stick.

"Cover the wound fully," she said. Looking at Kailia, she added, "You'll need to sit up then so he can wrap the bandage around your torso."

The paste was cool on her skin as he spread it around, and it wasn't until he handed the pot back to Niara that his magic skated along her arms. He reached for her, extending a hand.

"The sooner we both get fixed up, the sooner we can go home," he said, giving her a small smile.

Tentatively, she slid her hand into his, and he gently pulled, his other hand hovering between her shoulder and lower back. Soon enough, she was sitting upright, and he wound a bandage around her torso.

"Are you doing all right?" he murmured, the words low and the moment somehow feeling intimate despite other people being in the room. It didn't make any sense.

"Yes," she answered, trying to figure out why her voice sounded odd and breathy.

He smiled again, reaching around her to take the bandage from his other hand, but he said nothing else. And did she kind of wish he would have? She knew his words were full of deceit and deception to coerce and get his way, so why were they also somewhat comforting? Or maybe it wasn't the words, but the manner in which he spoke them. Yes, that had to be it. Practiced mannerisms and inflections.

"Done," he said, stepping back a bit, but staying near as she eased back into the pillows.

"Three times a day," Niara said, striding to the dresser. She placed a few items in a satchel while organizing the remaining items. "Both of you need to rest for the next two days."

"You're leaving?" Cethin asked.

Picking up the satchel, she started for the door. "I taught you what is required. I'm no longer needed unless something drastic happens. Which it won't. Because you'll both be resting."

"Of course, Niara," Cethin replied, a smirk playing on his lips. "Thank you for all your help."

"I'll walk you out," Tybalt said, following her from the room. The male hadn't said a single word the entire time.

"Do you need anything? Something to eat?" Razik asked. His eyes begrudgingly slid to Cethin. "Either of you?"

"Kailia?" Cethin asked, all of his attention back on her.

"Water would be nice," she replied, smoothing her hands over the soft furs again before shaking them out.

"I'll bring a pitcher up and see what I can find for food," Razik said. For some reason, he sent Cethin a pointed look as he added, "I'll bring up plenty of *choices*."

Then he left, leaving the door partially open behind him.

Cethin turned back, gaze sweeping over her. "Do you need more blankets? Pillows?"

"A bath," she sighed. "I need a bath."

"I don't think that's an option for two more days," he said, lowering to the chair and fidgeting a bit as he stretched his legs out. It was then she saw the blanket on the floor beside the chair.

"Have you been sleeping in that chair this whole time?" Kailia asked, because surely not.

He nodded, shifting again. "Niara wasn't pleased."

"But why? Sleep there, I mean."

"You said you don't like waking in unfamiliar places. That it unsettles you. You've never been here, so I wanted to make sure someone you knew was here when you woke," he answered.

"But there's a bed," she said, wondering why her chest was feeling warm. Why her whole body was feeling…something.

He paused, studying her before asking, "You want me to share a bed with you, tiny fiend?"

"I *want* you to give me back my arrow," she retorted. "And my daggers. Though it doesn't seem to matter what I want."

His face fell flat at that, the small bit of humor gone. "I can get your daggers now if you'd like."

"I would," she said with a nod.

He got to his feet, pausing at the doorway to say, "Please don't get out of the bed."

Minutes later he returned, the daggers in hand. Placing them on her blanket-covered lap, he reclaimed his chair. "Am I redeemed now?"

"Still missing my arrow," she muttered, picking up a dagger and turning it over in her hand.

How was he still alive?

She held it up, the blade pointed at him. "You didn't die."

He'd gone still, looking at her as though she'd said something absurd rather than spoken a simple truth.

"I am indeed still on this side of the Veil and not in the After," he agreed, the words measured. "Were you hoping for a different outcome?"

"Not yet."

He huffed a laugh. "Sorry to disappoint," he mused, relaxing farther into the chair. "However, we do need to discuss those daggers of yours."

"Why?"

"We've never encountered ones like them. Similar to your arrows. There is a theory they delayed my healing among other things," he explained. "Do you know anything about that?"

"My daggers usually kill people," she replied, sending them away in a swirl of ashes.

He huffed another laugh. "Fair enough, tiny fiend."

She didn't know why he was amused by the statement, but she was too exhausted to try to decipher social interactions right now. So she let the silence linger, watching Cethin out of her periphery. He seemed content to sit in that chair. He'd closed his eyes, the fingers on his left hand lightly drumming on the armrest. And of all things, she found herself contemplating his earlier question.

You want me to share a bed with you, tiny fiend?

Reaching for the necklace at her throat, she toyed with the crystal as her thoughts swirled. No, she didn't want that. That was intimate. That involved touching, or at the very least, close proximity.

She glanced at him again, his eyes still closed.

No, she'd save the touching and the closeness for her dreams where she was safe.

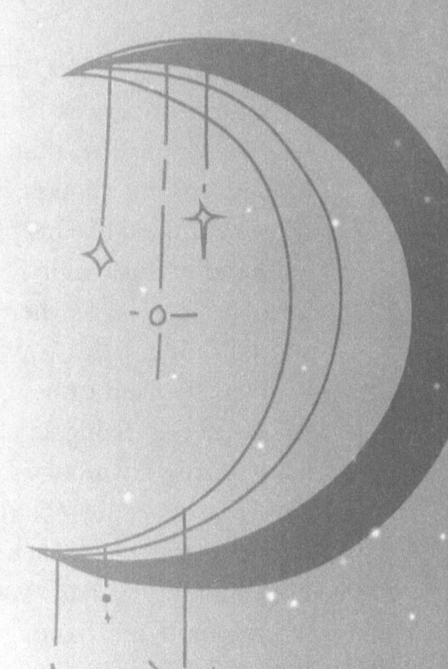

CHAPTER 21

CETHIN

He straightened from a stretch with a muffled groan. Sleeping in that godsdamn chair was getting old. There was no way to get comfortable, and he was still sore from the stabbings and the broken ribs. The external wounds had healed, not even scars left behind. Bones always took a little longer. Add in the delayed healing, and it was taking *days* longer.

Kailia emerged from the bathing chamber, her feet light as she moved, always with a predatory grace. Fallon had brought her spare clothing yesterday, which she had immediately changed into. Loose linen pants sat low enough on her hips that they didn't aggravate the wound, while the tunic was cut short, exposing her midriff.

"We need to change that," Cethin said with a nod to the bandage wrapped around her middle.

She nodded, coming closer. They'd done this three times now, and each time her hesitation appeared to lessen a fraction. She was still tense the entire time, but instead of closing her eyes tightly until it was over, she watched him. He never acknowledged it. Gods, if he did, he was certain she'd retreat right back into herself and her defenses would return. But he was also trying to be smart with their time away from Aimonway.

Here, it was just them. And Jarek, Fallon, Razik, and Wren because no one was leaving the king and future queen alone after two attacks in less than a day. He was used to people constantly milling around though, and for the most part, they were treating these chambers like his private floor at the castle.

Sending his magic first, like he always did, he dipped his fingers into the bandage where it was secured, tugging it free. They'd started doing it this way rather than cutting the bandage away like before. She liked to be up and moving around, and this allowed her to get used to being so close to someone. To *him*. And he was absolutely taking advantage of every moment.

This close, he could feel her body heat. He could smell the lavender and honey scented soap she'd just used with a cloth since a fully submerged bath wasn't an option until late tomorrow. As he maneuvered the bandage and unwrapped it from her torso, stray strands of hair, loose from her braid, fluttered against his skin, and this time, as he passed the bandage to his other hand, he let his arm brush against hers. It was feather-light, hardly a touch at all, but he still watched her stiffen. Watched her fight the urge to jolt back. Watched her fingers flex and move, searching for a dagger that wasn't strapped to her thigh. Felt her breath of relief when he stepped back, giving her space while he retrieved the pot of herbal paste.

He'd never been more aware of his movements and the space he took up until she'd snuck into his life cloaked in smoke and ashes.

Making his way back to her, she was sliding the blue crystal at her throat along the cord. Back and forth. Back and forth. She stopped when she noticed him watching the movement, letting the thing settle again, just above her breasts, and instead shaking out her hands a little.

Lowering to a crouch before her, he dipped the flat stick into the paste, smoothing it along her deeply tanned skin as he said, "I need to discuss something with you."

She was already preternaturally still as he worked, watching him, but she somehow went even more tense. Her muscles were coiled tight, and a faint trace of ashes vibrated around her, making him pause what he was doing so they didn't get caught in the paste.

His gaze flicked to hers. "We have conversations all the time, Kailia."

"Yes, but when a person starts a conversation like that, it never leads anywhere good," she said.

"Do you have a lot of experience with conversations like that?" he asked casually, tending to his task once more when her ashes faded. Her wound was also almost healed. Only a slightly raised and faint pink line remained.

There was a pause before she answered, "No, but I've observed many."

"So you are a busybody, then? Eavesdropping on other people's conversations?"

"No," she argued. "I… No, I'm not a busybody."

The way she said it, with such conviction and resoluteness, had him fighting a smile, but she was still watching him intently, so of course she saw it.

"You find this amusing?" she asked.

"I do," he agreed, setting the pot aside and reaching for the fresh dressing.

"Why?"

"Because I am teasing you, Kailia. Nothing more," he answered, pressing the dressing to the wound. "Hold this, please."

Her fingers brushed his as she took over, and that one simple point of contact had his thoughts going places they shouldn't. Wondering what those callused fingers would be like brushing along his arm. How her fingertips would feel dancing across his lips. How'd they feel other—

Fuck, he needed to get his shit together.

It'd been a long time since he'd satisfied those needs. The last time he'd fucked, his title had been prince, not king. It had become too complicated to bring anyone to his bed in the beginning, so he'd handled matters himself. Weeks had turned into months, and months into a year. Now, for reasons he'd long stopped trying to figure out, the one person he'd even consider couldn't stand to be touched.

And yes, he'd asked himself if that was the appeal. Was it some sick and twisted subconscious challenge? But that couldn't be it. He hadn't known about her aversion to touch when he'd met her at the Esbat Festival. If anything, she had some opinions of him he didn't understand, and he couldn't figure out why it mattered to him at all. Why he cared that some female from across the sea thought he was the worst the realms had to offer. And why was she going along with any of this to begin with?

Maybe in the end, it was a morbid curiosity about how far he could push her. How far could he take any of this? Maybe the challenge was to figure her out. All of it a distraction from the mundane. A way to turn this fucked up situation into something more intriguing. Perhaps that was just as dark and twisted, but he couldn't seem to stop himself.

He wrapped her torso without conscious thought, going through the motions, not realizing he was finished until he was tucking the edge of the bandage into place.

Kailia lightly cleared her throat, stepping back and putting space between them. "What did we need to discuss then?"

"I have a proposal," he said, the words lacking his usual confidence as he tried to get his thoughts back in order.

"I already agreed to that," she said, wandering to the balcony door.

He quickly moved past her, seeing where she was headed. Pulling the door open for her, he followed her out.

It wasn't a large balcony by any means. It held a small round table and two chairs, and an onyx railing ran along the edge of a raised stone wall one story off the ground. Kailia moved there, her hands gripping the rail as she looked out over Shira Forest. Cethin took a seat at the table, his fingers drumming once atop the iron surface.

It was his turn to clear his throat. "That's not the proposal I'm referring to. I mean, it is, but not—"

He stopped, frustrated with himself for fumbling over his words, and she'd turned to study him again. She did that all the time, and he understood why. She was studying him as much as he was studying her. Gathering information and tells. He'd teased her about being a busybody, knowing she watched people from her power, but they were one and the same. She just didn't realize it yet.

"Can you tell me anything about the attack?" he asked, switching tactics. "Anything that would help us figure out who they were? Or why they did this?"

Leaning against the railing now, she said, "I thought some of the others went to see if they could identify them?"

"They did," he replied. "I'm still waiting on a final report, but if they'd found anything useful, we would have heard by now. Which means I need any information that you can recall."

"This is the proposal?"

"No. This is what is leading to the proposal," he said, rubbing at his temple in an effort to assuage his irritation.

She fell quiet, and he watched as she sifted through memories and debated what to say. He wanted to encourage her to simply tell him everything. Every errant thought that was flitting through her mind, but she was too calculated. A blessing and a curse really. Something she'd need as queen, but something that was currently fucking him over greatly.

"I don't know that they said anything," she finally answered. "I was… When I—" Her lips thinned, gaze darting to the side before she turned back to the railing once more.

Cethin stood, moving to her side. Propping his forearms on the cold rail, he clasped his hands, staring out at the horizon too. Not touching her and giving her space. Her fingers gripped the railing tighter.

"You were surviving," he finally said. "Your focus was on survival, nothing else. It's okay."

She glanced at him sidelong. "What would you know of surviving, king?"

He flashed her a grim smile. "You don't live for centuries without having to simply survive at times."

"You grew up in luxury."

"I grew up with expectations and responsibilities," he countered. "Things I was forced to carry *because* of the luxury and titles."

She hummed, clearly not convinced.

"But you've known a different kind of survival," he continued. "And I… No one should have that kind of life, Kailia. Which brings me to my proposal. I'd like to move the union up. For your safety."

She turned to him, the smoke in her eyes drifting like a slow fog. "My safety?"

"If you bear the title, it will make them second-guess their intentions."

"How will it be any different? You offered your protection, and I was still attacked."

The words rankled him because they were absolutely true.

"And had any of them survived," he gritted out, "their fate would have been sealed. But you left none alive, tiny fiend."

"Exactly. I can protect myself. So I fail to see the advantage of moving the union up. A queen in title only does not offer me any more protection than I have now."

"It comes with the title itself," he pushed. "Right now, you are simply my betrothed, but with the title… It's not a lot, but it's something," he finally admitted. "We can get you an additional guard, or a different one entirely, if you wish for added protection."

"No," she said quickly. "I mean, one is more than enough, and Razik is fine."

Razik is fine.

It took everything in him not to say something about that. Or her quick response to keeping the male around. If anything, he wanted this union moved up to make a point to everyone: she was his and no one else's.

"When would it be moved to?" she asked after several beats of silence.

He winced internally, bracing himself for her reaction. "The next full moon."

He watched her brow furrow as she mentally calculated. Then her eyes slowly slid back to his. "That is tomorrow night."

"It is," he agreed.

"You want this union to happen tomorrow," she repeated.

"I do." In a rush, he added, "The celebration can wait another moon cycle as planned. We can do things our own way."

Something flickered across her features at the words. "Do things our own way," she murmured, more to herself than him.

He nodded, forcing himself not to reach for her hand. "We do the union tomorrow night under the full moon. Then we have a full moon cycle to prepare for the kingdom celebration. You have more time to acclimate, but you are still afforded all the privileges of the title."

"In title only," she clarified.

"Yes, in title only."

She rolled her lips, turning back to the horizon. "For how long?"

"It was already stated the union was eternal, Kailia," he deadpanned.

"I mean how long will it be in title only?"

His brows shot up. He hadn't been aware she wanted anything more than the title, considering he was coercing her into that to begin with.

Clearing his throat, he said, "That has to be a unanimous agreement of the advisory council and I."

She looked at him, her beautiful features almost glowing in the spring sun. "Would you agree to it? Right now? If I agreed to move the union to tomorrow?"

He'd manipulated a lot of this, but he couldn't lie to her. Not about this. "No, Kailia," he answered. "I wouldn't."

"Why?"

"Because these are my people. I took a vow to protect them, and I'm having to force you into doing that," he said. "I cannot give you the power to rule over them if I'm having to force you to protect them."

She nodded, appearing to mull that over. "So I need to be convincing in more ways than one," she said.

Unable to help himself, he reached out and took her chin between his thumb and forefinger. A single point of contact, but she still grimaced.

"No, Kailia," he replied. "In order for me to agree to you being more than queen in title only, I'd need it to be real. I'd need you to not wince at my touch or freeze in my proximity. I'd need you to truly care about the people in this kingdom, not just about getting your arrow back. I'd need you to be able to walk through the streets without worry. I'd need this—all of this—to be so much more than what it is right now. Not just a means to an end."

He released her chin, taking a measured step back and putting space between them before he did something truly stupid. That was all this was anyway. A means to an end. Something he'd orchestrated to get what he needed.

"I need to earn it then?" Kailia asked, her head tilting in question.

"This is not a competition, Kailia," he spat, the mere idea making his lip curl in a snarl. "My people are not a godsdamn prize."

She nodded, returning to staring off at the horizon.

He sighed. This was clearly going nowhere.

Leaving her to her thoughts, he went back into the room, making his way to the bathing chamber. While Kailia needed another day of healing, he did not. He filled the tub nearly to the brim. Stripping down, he lowered into the steaming water, contemplating his next moves. It wasn't the ocean, but the water was still soothing, unlike his thoughts.

Maybe he'd been wrong about this the entire time. Yes, they needed her weapons, but at the expense of her believing his kingdom was some kind of prize? That he was somehow using his people to negotiate with her? Who thought like that? How could he put someone in the position of queen who thought like that? He couldn't change that now. Not with the bargain in place. But it was clear he could never make her anything more than the queen in title. He'd have to come up with something else until there was an heir, and who knew when the fuck that would be. She couldn't stand being touched, and creating an heir definitely required some touching.

What a godsdamn mess.

When he emerged sometime later, he was no closer to an answer than before. She'd come back inside and was standing near the chair he'd been sleeping in, as if waiting for him.

"Need something?" he asked, planning to go downstairs and eat with the others tonight. He needed a bit of normalcy, and he suddenly found himself more than ready to go back to Aimonway. There was a reason he didn't stay here anymore. For the briefest of moments, she'd helped him forget. Given him something to focus on. Was the exact distraction he'd needed her to be.

"I'll do it," she said.

"Do what?"

"Agree to the union tomorrow night."

His brows shot up. "Why would you do that?"

"I thought that's what you wanted."

"Yes, but you don't. You have no reason to want that, and I already explained my people are not some competition or game," he said, turning to leave her be.

"I know that," she called after him.

He turned back to find she'd closed some of the distance between them.

"I know that," she repeated, rubbing the tips of her fingers together before shaking out her hands. "It isn't a game. I understand that. I didn't mean to imply that it was. They are real people. No one understands that better than I do."

He somehow doubted that, but he crossed his arms, waiting for her to go on.

"In all my years, no one has given me a chance to choose my own purpose, and you are doing that," she supplied, this entire conversation clearly difficult for her. "Not only that, you've been patient with me and my shortcomings. I know I'm not a practical choice for this role, but you chose me anyway. I've been trying to figure out why. I still don't understand it."

By the Fates, that was the most she'd ever spoken at any given time.

She was looking anywhere but at him as she said, "Being a queen in title only feels pointless. The responsibility gives me purpose. You choosing me for this gives me a purpose, and it's something I've been seeking for a very long time."

He studied her, waiting for her to willingly meet his gaze again. When she finally did, he said, "I won't just give it to you, Kailia. Even if I change my mind down the road, there's still the council."

"I know." Then she gave him a small smile. "But I have to start somewhere."

She shrugged, clearly out of words to say, and even as he stared at her, he knew this wasn't the conclusion he should come to. He'd sat in the steaming tub and gone through every reason this was a terrible idea. Why it had been a terrible idea from the start.

But he still found himself saying, "Tomorrow night?"

Her smile grew a little more, one of the most genuine he'd ever seen from her. She nodded. "Tomorrow night."

This was a terrible fucking idea, but he'd claimed her as his. He wasn't about to let her go now. He wasn't sure he could, even if he wanted to.

-))☾·☼·☽((-

He wasn't surprised to find Tybalt there when he entered the dining room. He was, however, surprised to learn he'd sent Jarek and Fallon back to Aimonway, Wren returning with them.

Grabbing a bottle of ale from the icebox, he turned back to the male, bracing himself for wherever this conversation was about to go. Except his mind was already back on the female upstairs and the fact that tomorrow night, he'd be calling her wife. Something he'd fought so hard against for so long. Something that had been pushed on him for decades, only to be the one pushing it on someone else now. That was some twisted irony, but he supposed that was fitting given everything that had been happening this year.

"Where is Kailia?" Tybalt asked, seated at the table.

"Upstairs," Cethin answered, pulling out the chair at the head of the table, the wooden legs scraping along the rug.

"You are both healed?" Tybalt asked, watching him.

Cethin sighed, sitting back in his chair and steepling his forefinger along his temple. His eyes flickered to Razik, seated across from the Commander. His face was apathetic and unreadable as always.

"There is no need for pleasantries, Tybalt," Cethin said, picking up the ale and taking a drink.

"There's always time for pleasantries," Tybalt replied, settling back into his chair as well. "Sometimes I think we skip over them far too often. It's damaging in many ways. Like skipping straight to a meal without the alcohol."

Cethin huffed a small chuckle under his breath. "While I see your point, I think we can all agree the past several days have been intense."

"All the more reason for pleasantries," Tybalt said, lifting his glass of liquor in a cheers motion before taking a drink. Lowering the glass, his features morphed into something a little more serious. "Do you still plan on returning to Aimonway tomorrow?"

"Yes," Cethin answered tightly, his grip on the ale bottle flexing.

"I'm sure you're ready to leave," Tybalt said too casually. "When was the last time you were here?"

Cethin dragged his eyes back to the male. "That's not important."

"I think it might be."

Cethin's gaze flicked to Razik again, and even if he wanted to have this conversation, which he didn't, there was no way in fuck he was having it in front of that male.

"You don't think being here has had any impact on your decisions these last few days?" Tybalt questioned, with a knowing look on his face and both hands wrapped around his liquor glass.

"No," Cethin ground out. "I think being attacked numerous times in the last few months has impacted my decisions. I think being no closer to figuring out who or what is responsible for the Fae deaths these last decades has impacted my decisions."

Tybalt nodded, and Cethin hated the look on his face. The male was easier to deal with when he was the Commander and

Cethin was the king. The sympathy and understanding staring back at him now? This was not that. This was a male who'd known him his entire life. Who was family. Who had suffered as much as he had, just in different ways. But all he was doing was dragging up the past. Things no one could change. Things they needed to move on from, and the best way to move on was to accept change.

"I just think—"

"I just think you're trying to fill a role that you're not meant to," Cethin interjected harshly.

"Watch it, Sutara," Razik growled, smoke unfurling with his exhale and black sparks flickering at his fingertips.

Cethin sneered at the male. "Everyone at this table knows the reason you're still a part of any of this is because of your relations. That does not extend to you getting to interfere in anything else."

"Cethin," Tybalt tried. "Razik understands there have been mistakes made—"

"Mistakes?" Cethin snarled.

"Mistakes that *everyone* is guilty of," Tybalt continued. "The Cadre will be dealt with. I can assure you of that."

"And Razik? Who is no longer part of the Cadre?" Cethin pushed, bringing his eyes back to the male.

Razik was tense, every muscle rigid. A muscle feathered in his jaw as he held his godsdamn tongue for once.

"Razik is still the best option for Kailia's guard, especially considering the escalation of attacks," Tybalt said. "If you set aside the grudges and think like the king you are, you'd agree."

Cethin scoffed. "It's because of the grudges and the animosity between us that I believe he's *not* the best option," he countered. "How can that not affect his job when it requires us to be around each other constantly?"

"I can't do my job when you won't let me," Razik ground out. "How am I supposed to keep her protected when you keep her sequestered in your rooms at all times?"

"I've discussed the situation with him extensively," Tybalt cut in again. "He understands that some…adjustments need to be made on his end. If Kailia's safety is truly your primary concern, you'll do the same."

How was he supposed to argue that? When he was about to tell them she would be his wife tomorrow night? When his argument for that was all for her safety?

As much as he hated to admit it, and never would out loud, Tybalt was right. Razik was the best choice. His skill and wit were leagues above the others because of his bloodline. He put in just as much work as everyone else, trained just as hard, but his bloodline gave him an advantage. That was something Cethin could relate to all too well.

"Fine," Cethin conceded begrudgingly. "For Kailia."

Tybalt nodded, visibly relaxing some and taking another drink of his liquor. "When will you return tomorrow?"

"Midday," Cethin answered tightly, thinking he might grab another bottle of ale to take upstairs with him after this.

"And tomorrow night?" Tybalt pushed.

Cethin knew exactly what he was asking.

He met the male's eyes. "Tomorrow night I gain a wife." He slid his stare to Razik and added with a sardonic smirk. "Her choice."

"You sure about that?" Razik asked, arching a brow.

"Razik," Tybalt barked. Then he stood, bracing both his hands on the table and leaning in. Gone were the compassion and under-standing. This was the Commander. This was the male that had been his mother's guard and Hand of the Queen. "This is the prob-lem. It has nothing to do with training or responsibilities or being well-suited for a role. The problem is the two of you. Neither of you is going anywhere, so fix your godsdamn shit."

He straightened, rounding the table and heading for the door, but he stopped near Cethin. Holding his stare, he said, "You're making a mistake with this, but I know you're going to do it anyway. Sacrifices follow mistakes. Mistakes are the reason you hold that throne right now and can't stand to be in this house. Be prepared to face those sacrifices when the time comes."

Cethin took two bottles of ale and the liquor bottle back upstairs with him that night.

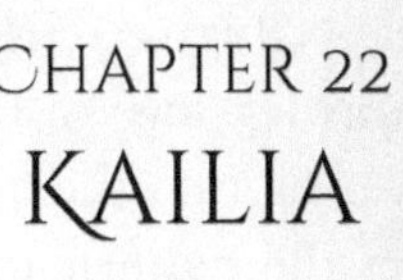
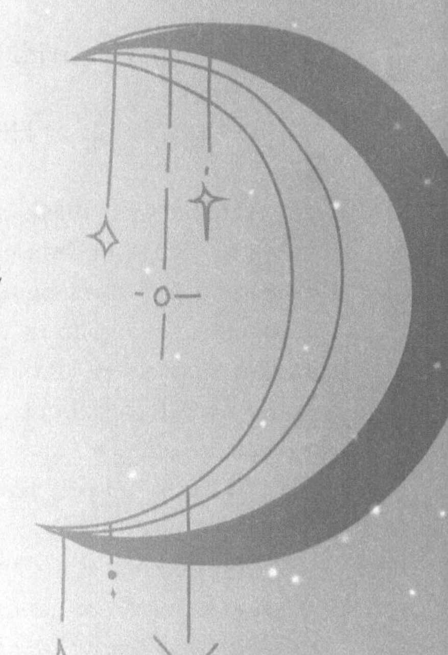

CHAPTER 22
KAILIA

"**A**re you ready?" Cethin asked, striding into the dressing room.

She'd heard him coming, of course. She'd been standing in front of the mirror for the last twenty minutes, studying herself in her black dress with the slit up the side. Cethin had said he liked them. Not that it had any bearing on why she chose this dress. He'd said to wear what she was comfortable in, and this was the closest thing to her usual attire. She'd thought about asking to retrieve her own clothing, but that would invite questions about where she'd been living before he'd brought her here. He already asked too many. Her plan had been to go collect them when she could sneak away, but with her magic still not working properly, who knew when that would be.

Turning to him, she was about to say something, but she froze. He was leaning against the doorjamb. Staring at her.

"Is this not appropriate?" she asked, looking down at the black dress. The bodice and the sleeves were black lace, with the front dipping between her breasts to her navel. While the black skirt draped to the floor, there was fine silver detailing all along the edging and the slit. With her shorter stature, it actually dragged a bit like a train.

She looked up at him again. "You said black. You're wearing black."

And he was. Black pants that were clearly tailored to fit him perfectly, hugging muscled thighs. His black jacket with silver threading and silver buttons was over a black shirt with small black buttons, a black pattern woven into the cloth. Without thinking, she took a step closer, finding the pattern to be celestial—moons and stars. Everything about him spoke to the king he was. Everything except the bare feet.

"Black is perfect, Kailia," he said, his voice sounding strange. "You look beautiful."

Her stomach did something at his words, and she didn't know what to do with her hands, so she held them stiffly at her side.

"Are you ready?" he asked again, extending a hand to her. His features were soft and coaxing, his silver eyes bright and his hair pulled back. She'd left her hair down, the black tresses flowing over her shoulders in loose waves.

"Where are we going?" she asked.

He smiled, something a little mischievous. "You'll see," he answered as she slipped her fingers into his waiting palm.

A moment later, her bare feet connected with hard earth, and she'd never been happier to feel the cool spring air swirl around her. There were towering pine trees and rocky cliffs looming. A lake spread out before them, the full moon reflecting on the surface, and the sound of rushing water greeted her ears.

Turning in place, she found a waterfall cascading down the cliffside, pouring into the lake. She'd seen a lot of places in this realm, but this would certainly be one of the most breathtaking if it weren't for the godsdamn cliffs.

An icy brush of power skated across her lower back, and she waited for his touch to follow, but it never did. Instead, she found herself turning to look for him.

He was standing a few feet away, his hands in his pockets, watching her with a small smile on his lips.

"Where are we?" she asked, tipping her head back. The cliffs were so tall she couldn't see where the waterfall even began. Even in the dark, the full moon illuminated everything with a soft white glow.

When he didn't answer right away, she turned back to him. His eyes flickered to the waterfall and back to her. "Lunae Falls," he finally answered. "A temple lies behind the falls, but the waters only flow under a full moon."

She whirled back to the waterfall, the spray like sparkling starlight under the luminous orb in the clear night sky. "You're serious? Are there people in the temple? Are they trapped there when the waters aren't flowing? Inside the cliffs?"

"Why would I lie about that?" he asked, coming to her side and glancing at her sidelong. "And no, Kailia. No one is trapped inside the cliffs or the temple. We can come back tomorrow and see if you'd like. I know the circumstances around all of this are unconventional. Despite that, I still wanted the night to be memorable."

"It would have been memorable either way. Practically speaking," she said, drifting closer to the water's edge and farther from the cliffs. "But this is…not what I imagined tonight would be like."

He huffed a laugh. "And what did you imagine, tiny fiend?"

She shrugged. "I'm not entirely sure. Just a standard union ceremony, I suppose."

"About that," he replied, shifting to face her. "Things are different in Avonleya in many ways, and one of those ways is our union ceremonies. Some choose…something different."

She stared back at him. "All of this is already very different from what I've observed in other places, I assure you," she replied flatly.

"Different traditions for different cultures, I suppose," he said. "But you will need to choose where your Mark goes."

"I mean, the hand is common, is it not?" she asked, perplexed.

"If that is what you choose," he answered. "We do things our own way."

"Our own way," she echoed, her dreams chasing her memories.

He nodded as a figure appeared from the trees, a glass bowl in her hands. Her dark skin glowed in the moonlight, and her hair was piled atop her head, while a silver circlet adorned her brow. Her bare feet were soundless on the ground, and she came to a stop before them, placing the bowl at her feet.

"Thank you for coming, Niara," Cethin said with a smile.

The Witch returned it, clasping her hands in front of her. "There are few I would do this for. You are one of them," she replied. Then she turned to Kailia. "You are doing well?"

She nodded, unsure why the Healer was here. "I am."

"While Niara is our primary Healer, she is also the High Witch of Avonleya," Cethin explained, but Niara rolled her eyes, the moonlight making the brown color look almost violet. "A title she does not like to flaunt," he added with a wink. "She rarely performs these rites."

"But exceptions are made for some," Niara finished. "Are you both ready?"

Cethin glanced at Kailia, and she nodded, briefly wondering what he would do if she said no. If she suddenly changed her mind. He'd made it clear he wasn't about to let her go any time soon. Or ever, considering he'd reminded her multiple times that the union was binding.

"Step into the water," Niara instructed, and Kailia suddenly realized why Cethin was barefoot.

He stepped into the lake first, deep enough for the water to meet his ankles, the water lapping at the hem of his pants. Then he reached for her hand, keeping her steady as she did the same, the train of her dress floating atop the surface like a night sky with its silver detailing. The icy waters distracted her from the burn of his touch. The burn she'd been mentally preparing herself for all day.

Niara stood on the shore, stooping down to pull a braided cord of silvers, fiery orange, and blacks from the water.

"Place your palms together," she said.

Confused, Kailia looked at Cethin. Unions required merging blood by slicing their palms with ceremonial daggers. But Cethin was holding his hands up, palms facing out and towards her. He nodded in encouragement, and tentatively, she did the same. Bringing her hands up, she pressed them against his, so much larger than her own.

"A rope representing your bloodlines, bathed in water enchanted by the moon," Niara intoned, beginning to wind the braided cord around their wrists in an intricate fashion. "As the rope binds your hands, your souls also bind."

Her bloodline? She didn't know what her bloodline was, but something in her soul warmed. Not the burning of a physical touch, but something...more.

"The gods," Cethin said softly. "The colors represent the gods our magic comes from. I had it made the day you agreed to the bargain."

He had?

"Call your power," Niara ordered.

Inky dark tendrils appeared, winding and tangling with the cord on their wrists, and after studying what he was doing, Kailia called forth her smoke and ashes. Sucking in a breath, her muscles tensed as she worked to hold herself steady. Because that something in her soul was more than warm now. Intensifying into something hot and heady.

"As your magic merges into one, your souls also merge," Niara recited, and Kailia could swear the waters around them had stilled. As if even the lake was holding its breath to observe...whatever this was.

The Witch turned to Cethin. "If your intention is binding, speak the words."

Silver eyes held hers with an intensity she was unsure what to do with, but his words were strong and steady, not an ounce of trepidation.

"Beneath the moon and stars, I claim you in the night and shadows. A bond that is eternal, and a union that marks my soul and makes it yours. Your heartbeat in my soul, this night I bind myself to you."

When he finished, Niara stepped forward, the glass bowl of

enchanted moon water in hand. She poured the water over one set of the linked hands. It shimmered there, but before Kailia could ask, Niara turned to her.

"If your intention is binding, speak the words."

Kailia swallowed, her throat going dry because this was all so much more intimate than she'd imagined it would be. She now understood why the union ceremonies took place privately rather than in front of others. She couldn't imagine the emotions if they had actually cared for one another.

Swallowing again, her words weren't nearly as steady as she recalled what Cethin had said a moment ago. "Beneath the moon and stars, I claim you in the night and shadows. A bond that is eternal, and a union that marks my soul and makes it yours. Your heartbeat in my soul, this night I bind myself to you."

Niara did the same thing, dumping the rest of the water on their other hands. "As the moon illuminates the dark, she marks you as each other's."

"Breathe, Kailia," Cethin whispered, and she didn't understand what he meant.

But then the cord around their wrists erupted in bright light, bathing them in a white glow. That warm and heady thing in her soul erupted too. She could feel it everywhere—from her toes to the crown of her head. But on her left palm, there was a stinging sensation, sharp and biting, as if tiny shards of glass were being pressed into her flesh. She tried to yank her hands back, but the cords at her wrists held them there. More than that, Cethin interlocked their fingers, keeping their palms joined tightly together. She couldn't see anything, all of it too bright and blinding, but she could feel the icy touch of his power wrapping around her as if to comfort her. There was a pulsing in her soul. An erratic heartbeat thrumming in her ears that drowned out everything else.

She didn't know how long they stood there, but everything slowly faded. The light. The stinging on her palm. She was trembling, suddenly feeling the iciness of the lake as the sound of the waterfall rushed over her again, the pulsing sound waning. Niara was gone, and the cord that had wound around their wrists was now in the water, floating between them.

"Breathe, Kailia," Cethin said again, a soft order. "Look at me and breathe."

She lifted her gaze, finding Cethin's eyes glowing as bright as the stars. The warmth in her soul stirred, her racing heartbeat slowing and her breathing evening out as seconds ticked by.

"What was that?" she finally asked.

Cethin didn't answer, but he did release her hands. He bent to retrieve the cord from the water, looping it around his neck. When he stood again, he reached for her hand, turning the left one face up. A Mark was there. Not black like union Marks, but silvery-white. Pale as moonlight.

She immediately looked at her other hand, finding it bare. Studying the new Mark, she asked, "This is a union Mark?"

"It is a Moon Mark," he replied. "They are only visible at night."

Moon Marks? She'd never heard of such a thing.

"I've seen plenty of people in the kingdom with Union Marks," she said, her trembling intensifying as the adrenaline of what she'd done waned.

"I mentioned some choose something different," he went on, gesturing to the shore. He didn't touch her, but she felt his hand hovering along her lower back as she moved. The long dress had become heavy, laden down with the lake water. "By some, I meant those I descend from."

"I don't understand," she said, her teeth beginning to chatter.

"I'll explain at home…wife," he replied, holding out his hand once more. His *bare* hand. There was no Mark adorning his palm.

"Where is your Mark then?"

"At home. I'll explain at home," he said again, worry flickering in his eyes. "When you're warm."

She looked from Cethin to the waterfall to the full moon, feeling like she'd just participated in something far bigger than a simple marriage.

Feeling as if once again, she'd thought she was the cat in this game they were playing when she was really the mouse.

-ᗡ·☉·Ƈᕤ-

Sliding her arms into the plush robe, she cinched the sash. She was freezing, so it was rather ridiculous that she'd put on one of the silk nightdresses that Cethin procured for her. They were just so godsdamn comfortable and easy to move in. Actually, they'd be great for hunting in if they had a little more support in the chest. Or any support, really.

Wandering down the hall to the sitting room, she went still at the fire in the hearth on the other side of the room. Cethin was standing before it, his back to her with one hand in his pocket. He'd lost his jacket, the garment tossed over a nearby armchair, and he'd pulled the band from his hair, letting the strands brush his shoulders. He'd rolled back the sleeves of his tunic, the material tight around his biceps. She wasn't sure where the cord for the union went.

Clearing her throat lightly, she took a few more steps into the room, and he turned, smiling softly. Plucking up wineglasses from a nearby side table, he crossed the space, passing one to her.

"Come warm up by the fire," he said, already halfway back across the room.

"I'm warming up already," she replied, keeping her distance. Instead of going to the sofa in front of the hearth, she lowered into an armchair farther back, tucking her feet beneath her.

He studied her, clearly trying to decide why she'd refuse such a thing, but she didn't offer any explanations. Instead, she said, "Tell me what I just committed to. Why do I bear a Mark and you do not?"

"I do. And you committed to a marriage," Cethin answered, abandoning the hearth and moving to the chair across from her. With his legs spread wide, he propped his temple on his fist while his wineglass dangled from the fingers of his other hand. He'd undone several buttons at the top of the tunic, revealing the pale skin of his chest. "That is what the Bargain was."

"Yes, but I assumed that meant a standard union with a standard Union Mark," she countered, taking a sip of her wine. The sweet and crisp notes danced across her tongue.

He shrugged. "It was not specified when the Bargain was made."

"How convenient," she deadpanned.

He smirked, bringing his glass to his lips and holding her stare while he took a drink.

"Since this wasn't a standard union, what did I commit to?" Kailia pushed. "You said it was something your family chooses. What does that mean? And where is your Mark?"

He reached for his shirt, pulling it open wider to show her the left side of his chest. Sure enough, a pale silvery-white Mark was there, glimmering like moonlight, but his sat atop another Mark, this one black.

"Why is yours there? And why does it look different?" she demanded.

He smirked, letting his shirt fall back along his skin. "Because that is where I decided I wanted my Mark to go. You chose your hand."

"I didn't—" But she snapped her mouth shut when he arched a brow. "You could have told me…"

But he had. He'd said she needed to pick the place. She'd assumed he'd pick his hand so it was visible to everyone. A public claiming. She hadn't expected him to put his Mark in a place few would see unless he was shirtless, even if they'd only be visible at night. It made her feel as if she were some kind of secret. Something he didn't want to claim in public, and it made no sense. She didn't care, but he'd sure made it seem like *he'd* cared these last few months. Instead, he'd opted to place his Mark directly atop another one, as if it didn't matter to him at all. As if she wasn't deserving of her own place on his flesh.

Something in her chest made a weird twisting motion at the

thought, and she took another healthy drink of her wine before she said, "How is this different from any other union ceremony?"

Something like concern flickered across his features, gone in the next breath. "My bloodline has traditions of its own. Celestial Rites are one of them. Many of them have been adopted by Avonleya. Our Farewells and unions taking place on full moons, for example. But a Lunar Bond is a sacred rite that is kept closer. More private. Not all choose it, but some do."

Kailia turned her hand over, studying the shimmering Mark on her palm. "It will just…disappear during the day."

He nodded.

"Why would someone choose a Union Mark over this? If it is so much more sacred?" she asked.

"Union Marks are similar to mortal marriages. Simple and beautiful in their own right. But a Lunar Marriage is something more, and it can only be invoked by certain lineages."

"Let me guess," she all but drawled. "The royal ones?"

"Not always," he answered with a small smirk.

She hummed, running the pads of her fingers along the Mark. "So, in essence, it's simply a shinier version of a Union Mark."

"No," Cethin growled, and she straightened at the tone. At the utter fury simmering in that one syllable.

"Still your favorite word, I see," she murmured, draining her wine.

"Union Marks can be dissolved," he said tightly. "A Lunar Marriage cannot. It is eternal."

"So you've said."

She was still bothered by…all of it. He'd used this as a means to tie her to himself, but he didn't want that claim visible. If this rite was so much more than a union, if he was one of the few who could invoke it, why keep it hidden? The logical explanation was that it was because of her.

"Refill?"

She startled in the chair at finding him standing before her. Then she realized she hadn't heard him move. She always knew where everyone in the room was at all times. She was always observing and anticipating, but this male was…

She was becoming far too comfortable. Too lost in errant thoughts and notions that didn't matter. None of this mattered. She was a means to an end for him, and he was the same for her.

"No, thank you," she replied, moving to set the glass aside, but he took it from her before she could get too far.

Setting everything on a nearby table, he returned, slipping his hand into his pocket and pulling out something small and onyx.

Her arrowhead.

He held it out, the thing seeming almost small in his large palm. *Bare* large palm, but whatever.

"I am a male of my word," he said with another smirk.

"You're a male forced by a Bargain," she retorted, staring at the arrowhead and longing to take it. Instead, she looked up at him and said, "I don't want it back simply because of this Bargain."

His brows crashed together. "What do you mean? You've been fighting me for this from the very beginning."

"Yes, and you've been very annoying in all of it," she replied.

"I don't understand what has changed."

"A lot has changed in a short amount of time, and that is unsettling. A lot has changed and nothing at all."

He shoved a hand through his hair, pushing out a harsh breath. "Is this what it's like inside that head of yours all the time?"

"Yes."

He nodded, staring over the top of her for a moment before bringing his gaze back to hers. "While I think I understand your intention here, I would like to make sure. You feel as if you shouldn't have this back because you need to…earn it. To prove your loyalty?"

"Maybe?"

He rolled his lips in clear irritation before releasing another breath. Pinching the arrowhead in his fingers, he held it up between them. "The whole purpose of this was for you to help me protect the people of this kingdom. We need your weapons and your skill.

We need *you*, Kailia. And you need this back to help. What better way to prove that loyalty?"

She dropped her gaze to her lap, smoothing the soft material of her robe with her fingers. "I don't want everyone to know that this is how it started. That I was… I don't want these people I'm supposed to help rule over to think I once was going to walk away and leave them to their curses."

Cethin lowered to a crouch before her, one of his hands resting on the armrest. "Our story is just that, Kailia. It's ours. No one needs to know. Our secrets can stay in the shadows between us for the rest of time if we wish."

She found herself leaning closer, her heart thumping to an odd beat in her chest. "And what of the secrets we keep from each other?"

His smile was as dark as his magic, and he leaned in a fraction closer too. Close enough, she could feel his words dance across her lips. Her mind was screaming that he was too close, but every other part of her… She'd never wanted to pull someone nearer and shove them away at the same time. She didn't understand any of it.

"It will be my greatest pleasure to uncover every single one, wife. Even the ones you don't know you carry," he said, his cadence low, and the words seemed to skitter along her skin, pebbled flesh left in their wake.

Then he stood, dropping the arrowhead in her lap before he grabbed his jacket off the chair and headed down the hall to the bedchamber.

She loosed a shaky breath, feeling the Bargain Mark on her skin lift as the Bargain was completed. A marriage, and, in exchange, her arrow and protection.

A means to an end for both of them. Nothing more.

Picking up the arrowhead, she twisted it between her fingers. The weight of it was comfortable. Familiar. Everything that this situation wasn't.

Closing her fist tightly around it, she squeezed, feeling the edges slice her flesh and the blood well. This had never been about the arrowhead. She didn't need it to create more weapons. That had been a lie. She lost them all the time, and it had never been an issue. Which meant having it back now would not fix whatever was wrong with her power. It wasn't going to resolve why she couldn't move through the smoke and ashes that called to her.

No, this had never been about the arrow. Not entirely anyway.

Opening her hand, she looked down, shifting the arrowhead to the side. The moon Mark shimmered among the red, as if anointed by a blood moon rather than pale moonlight.

Maybe that would have been more fitting in the end.

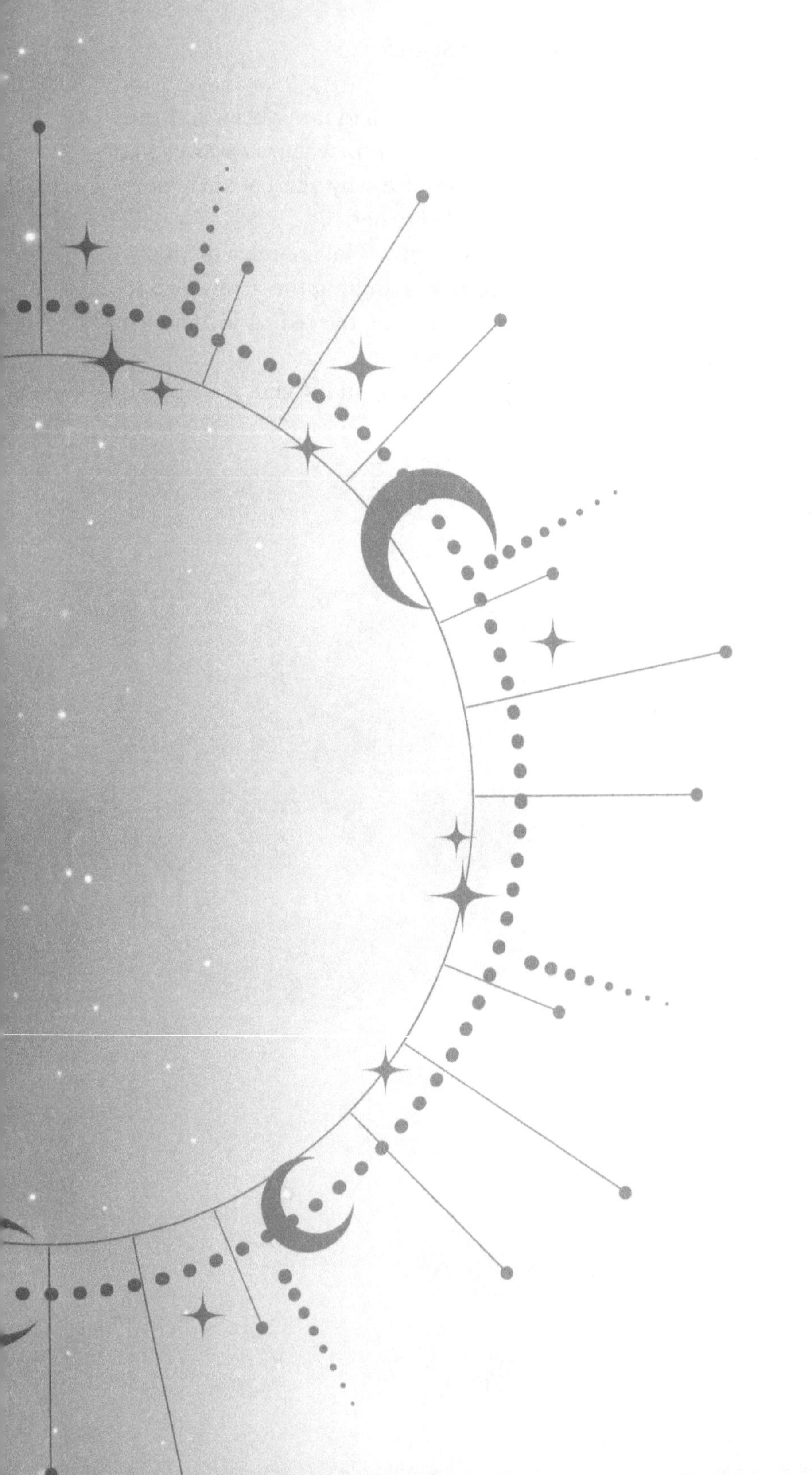

PART TWO
OF KINGS AND CURSES

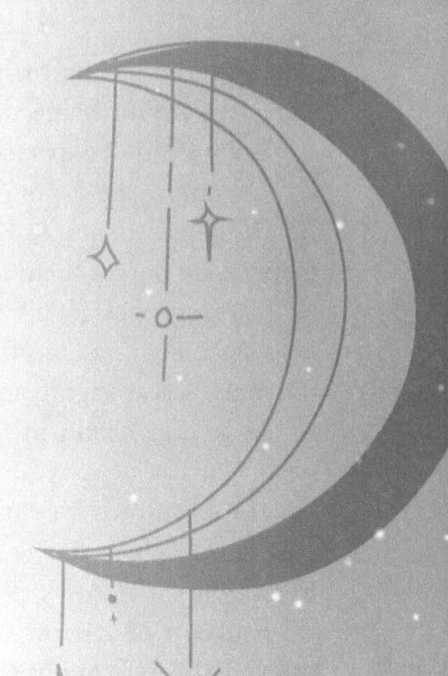

CHAPTER 23

RAZIK

"**A** Lunar Marriage?" Tybalt demanded, the doors to Cethin's study scarcely closed.

Cethin rounded his desk, taking a seat, while Kailia stood stiffly next to Razik, clearly unsure of what she should do or say.

The pair had come down for breakfast, all the Cadre already there along with Razik. Everyone was on edge, waiting for Tybalt's wrath over the events of the hunt. Tybalt had entered, already looking like someone had stolen an intricately woven pillow from him. Razik had never been more grateful he was Kailia's guard than in that moment, but another part of him felt guilty that he wouldn't be there when the Cadre was put through the wringer for the failures on the hunt.

Tybalt's eyes had swept the room, his pupils already glowing a faint red. Then they stilled when he reached Cethin and Kailia, gaze fixed on the backs of their hands. The male's voice had been nothing but a pure growl when he asked if he could speak to them privately. Razik had followed because Kailia was his charge, and he wasn't about to give his uncle a single reason to think he wasn't serious about handling this properly. More than that, he didn't understand what had triggered such a visceral response. If something was wrong, he needed to know to guard Kailia effectively.

But he hadn't expected his uncle to say those words.

Of course he'd noticed there were no Union Marks on their hands. He'd assumed Kailia had changed her mind. Not that Cethin had bound them together in a godsdamn Lunar Marriage.

Leaning back in his chair, Cethin was more than casual as he held Tybalt's stare, and for all his arrogance, Razik had to give it to the male. It was slightly impressive. A little. A minute amount of gall to act so nonchalant in the presence of a dragon clearly riding an edge.

"I told you we were moving the union up," Cethin said. Looking past the Commander, he added, "You can take a seat, wife. No need to stand in the doorway."

Kailia's eyes narrowed, her mouth pressing into a thin line as she went to the side opposite the hearth, perching on the edge of the velvet settee. Her fingers curled around the cushion as she looked between Cethin and Tybalt.

"You said you were moving the union up," Tybalt retorted. "You failed to mention you were initiating a Lunar Marriage. Who anointed it?"

Cethin remained silent, drumming his fingers on the desk.

"Of course she did," Tybalt spat, and Razik hated that he didn't understand what was going on. "She's the only one who would have possibly known how, but not without your help. How did you convince her?"

Cethin arched a brow. "Are you implying that I coerced Niara into doing something she didn't want to do? Kailia, did Niara appear to have apprehension about our night?"

"She did not," Kailia answered factually. "In truth, it was the most pleasant interaction I've had with her, but I assumed that was because there were no injuries to tend to this time."

Tybalt turned to her then, and Razik instinctively stepped closer to her. Not that he thought his uncle would do anything. His control was impeccable, but he *was* a dragon. A very irate dragon at the moment, and she was his charge. Cethin was halfway out of his chair too, but he'd paused when Razik had moved, slowly lowering back to his seat.

"Did Cethin explain what this marriage was before it was anointed, Kailia?" Tybalt asked, the words tight with restraint.

"I knew what I was getting myself into," Kailia replied, lifting her chin.

Tybalt shook his head, turning back to Cethin. "Your mother—"

"Is not here," Cethin interjected, a pointed look on his face. "Neither of my parents is here, and that is not something I can dwell on. I have a kingdom to protect, responsibilities to adhere to, and promises to keep. That is what I have done."

"You are going to have to face all of this some day, Cethin."

"And today is not that day," he replied, straightening and reaching for a stack of papers on his desk. "If there's nothing else, I have things to get caught up on."

Tybalt sighed, dropping into the chair on the opposite side of the desk, and Razik watched as the male shifted from concerned family friend to the Commander of the Forces. "I have the official report from Ariadne."

Cethin paused, setting down a piece of paper and sitting back in his chair. "And?"

"And they were Avonleyan."

"We assumed as much," Cethin replied, glancing over at Razik and Kailia. Razik was listening intently, but he was also watching the new queen. She hadn't shown any emotion at the mention of the attack. Nothing of the utter panic and mania she'd been in when they'd found her in that clearing, bodies at her feet and blood everywhere.

"We have reason to believe they were part of the Elder Clan," Tybalt added solemnly.

"Shit," Cethin muttered, rubbing at his brow with his thumb and forefinger.

"What is that? What does that mean?" Kailia asked.

Cethin glanced at Razik and jerked his chin. Surprised at being allowed to godsdamn speak at all, he didn't show it. Instead, he said,

"The Elder Clan are exactly what they sound like. They're a group of beings centuries old. Some are believed to have been here when this realm was created. That's never been substantiated, but if not them, then their descendants. They keep old traditions and records, and they are tasked with keeping the sacred places in the kingdom protected."

"Like the temple at Lunae Falls?" Kailia asked.

"No, that is a Witch temple," Cethin answered absentmindedly, obviously deep in thought. "These are sacred places from when the world was created. There are creatures there that the Elder Clan keeps at bay, and in return, we let them be. They are highly respected and knowledgeable, but they have a fault in relying too much on ancient ways and prophecies. It's a balance to keep the peace with them."

"And if they are the ones who attacked you, it could be a problem," Tybalt supplied. Shifting his attention back to the king, he added, "A big problem, Cethin."

"One I've handled before," the king replied.

"With Tethys at your side."

Darkness drifted off the king in faint wisps. "I'm more than capable."

"Yes, but at what cost?" Tybalt countered with a pointed look at the new queen.

"I have it handled," Cethin gritted out.

"That doesn't mean it won't bite you in the ass in the end," Tybalt replied, getting to his feet. "If I learn anything more, I'll let you know, but I wanted you to be aware." Turning to Razik, he added, "She goes nowhere alone."

Razik nodded, his arms crossed where he still stood next to Kailia. At least she waited until Tybalt was gone before she said, "He does not like me."

Cethin sighed, slumping back in his chair. "It's not you, Kailia. It's the situation."

"I don't think that's true."

"You're right. He doesn't," Razik said plainly, taking a seat in the chair his uncle had vacated.

"Razik, can you not?" Cethin muttered, rubbing at his brow again.

He shrugged. "I'm not going to try to convince her of something that's more than obvious. It's not like it matters. She's not going anywhere. You made sure of that."

"Yeah," Cethin murmured. Then he sighed, looking at the stacks of papers on his desk. It clearly pained him to ask, "Can you escort Kailia around today? I have…this to do." He picked up a stack of papers and dropped them unceremoniously back onto his desk, a few fluttering to the floor.

"Anything in particular we need to handle?" Razik asked.

"Don't let her stab anyone," he muttered.

"That's only you," she retorted, getting to her feet.

"Tell that to those you left bleeding out in Shira Forest, tiny fiend," Cethin replied. He didn't smile, but he winked at her.

With a huff, she crossed the room, Razik following.

"Greybane," Cethin called after him.

But Razik didn't slow. He just threw a wave over his shoulder. He knew he was just going to reiterate the underlying meaning of his previous words. Don't let her stab anyone, but also make sure there's no reason for her to stab anyone.

"Where to, your Majesty?" Razik asked once they were outside the study, two of Cethin's guards glancing at each other at the title.

"My rooms, I suppose?" she answered.

"Is that where you plan to spend your days? Because I'm not standing outside those doors all the fucking time."

She looked up at him, eyeing him warily. Her gaze darted to the guards too before she said, "It's probably best."

Razik shrugged and, with an exaggerated flourish, motioned for her to lead the way. But once they rounded a corner and entered a stairwell, he said, "We're away from prying ears now, Lia. Where would you like to go?"

She stilled, one foot on a stair. She wouldn't even look at him when she said, "I don't know what you mean."

"You don't?" he asked, and his disbelieving tone had her turning to him.

"No, *Raz*, I don't. Enlighten me," she retorted.

"Considering you seemed as though you were actually enjoying yourself on the hunt, I assume that means you don't enjoy being cooped up in the same rooms day in and day out," Razik replied. "More than that, Cethin talked you into a union that made you a queen."

"In title only," she interrupted.

"Still a queen. Still going to be known throughout the kingdom. You're going to get bored, and you're going to get bored quickly. Since you're not afraid to stab the godsdamn king multiple times when you're *not* bored, I can only imagine what will happen when you are," he said.

She eyed him, lowering her foot back off the step. "You are…"

"Correct," he deadpanned.

"I was going to say a dick," she said with an apathetic shrug that rivaled his own.

"Still astounded by your observational talents," Razik said. "But if there's nothing *you* want to do today, the least you can do is accompany me on an errand."

"How is that my job?"

"It's not. I just don't want to stand outside your door all day. Again."

"You can come inside. I'll deal with Cethin."

He smirked. "I'm sure you will."

Her brow furrowed. "I don't know what that means."

"Because you avoid people and social interactions," he said. "Give me your hand." When she eyed his outstretched hand, he added, "I could help with this, you know."

Her gaze snapped to his. "Help with what?"

He gave her a knowing look. "All of it. Help you work up to social engagements. Get used to small touches. Learning what you should know to be the queen of this kingdom. I'm a walking, talking resource, Kailia. Use me to your advantage rather than trying to gather all your information by eavesdropping. It makes you a busybody."

"Why does everyone keep calling me that? I am not a busy-body," she muttered.

"Yes, you are. We all are, but it's more useful if you can apply the things you see and hear to things you already know."

She stared back at him for a long moment before she said, "Fine," and slipped her fingers into his still-waiting palm.

A moment later, they stood on the docks by the Edria Sea. Kailia immediately wrapped her arms around herself as she looked around, and Razik cursed internally. He was so used to having the dragon fire in his veins to keep him warm, he never worried about the weather. It wasn't overly cold today, but the docks were always cooler due to the sea breeze, and she was in a lightweight dark green dress with short sleeves and a fitted bodice.

Plucking a cloak from a swirl of black flames, he handed it over to her.

"Thank you," Kailia murmured, quickly draping it over her shoulders and clasping the brass hooks.

"I keep it for Wren," he replied, because he often forgot the same thing with her, despite trying to be better about it.

She nodded. "Where is she today?"

He shrugged. "Not outdoors," he answered. After the hunt, she'd likely spend the next week inside.

"You and Wren are very different," Kailia replied, falling into step beside him as he made his way down the boardwalk.

"There's those observational skills again," he replied dryly. Then he huffed a laugh when she lifted her hand and flipped him her middle finger. "Very unqueenly, Lia."

She rolled her eyes. "I meant it is an unlikely pairing considering how different you two are."

"Yep," he said, climbing some wooden steps.

"So you just…see each other when you need your power refilled or want a fuck?" she asked, genuine curiosity in her tone.

"So crass," he chided as they came to an unmarked door.

"Sometimes the facts are," she replied, looking up at the nonde-script building. "This is where your errand is?"

"Yes. When we go inside, I need you to not ask questions," he said.

"Why?"

"That's a question, Lia."

"We're not inside, Raz."

"If I'm a dick, you're a smartass," he retorted.

"For stating a fact?"

He swiped a hand down his face. "Just no questions. And pull your hood up."

Her eyes narrowed, but she did as he said, pulling the hood of the cloak up and hiding her features. "Anything else?" she drawled.

"Are you like this with Cethin too?" he asked, reaching for the door handle.

"Like what?"

"Annoyingly mouthy."

"Fuck off, Raz," she muttered, pushing past him and shoving the door open.

They stepped inside, the room becoming so dim it was hard to see anything when the door closed behind them. He shifted his eyes to see better, scanning the room of wooden tables.

"It's a tavern," Kailia murmured. "You brought me to a tavern for an errand? What is it? Finding someone else for your bed tonight?"

He looked down at her, not minding this side of her personality coming out when she wasn't on her best behavior inside a castle. "What kind of taverns do you frequent that you think that's what taverns are for?"

"It's just an observation," she replied, staying close but keeping enough distance between them that they didn't touch.

"I think you're confusing taverns with brothels."

She scoffed. "I am not. Brothels are where people go openly looking for a partner. Taverns are where they go when they're trying to hide the fact that that's what they're looking for." She paused, then added, "Or where one goes to take advantage of the unsuspecting."

"You have spent too much time in your smoke and ashes, Lia," he muttered, making his way through the room while also making sure she remained at his side.

They reached a booth in the back, and he nodded to the group sitting there. Three males and a female, all of them from the ships that sailed along the continent transferring goods from one side of the Olwen Mountains to the other. There were cards and coin on the table, the group of them in the middle of a hand.

"Greybane," one of the males greeted. His pale blue eyes skipped to Kailia, taking her in. "You've never brought a companion with you. Who's this?"

"That's not your concern, MacMillan," Razik replied, shifting to hide her a little more from view. "Did you get what I asked for?"

The male shook his head, laying his cards face down on the table. Pulling a sack from the space beside him, he passed it over.

Razik looked over the contents for a solid minute before nodding and pulling a small pouch of coin from a swirl of black flames, tossing it on the table. The male swiped it up, not bothering to count it. He knew he was good for it.

"Pleasure as always, Greybane," he said with a smarmy grin. His gaze skipped back to Kailia. Gesturing to the cards, he added, "Sure you and the female don't want in? It's quite the competition right now."

"A competition?" Kailia asked, peeking around Razik.

"No," he said sternly, taking a step back and reaching to bring Kailia with him.

Except the male on the other side of the booth also reached for her, grabbing her arm and pulling her down to his lap. Or attempting to as he said, "Aw, she can stay. Can't you, pretty thing?"

Before anyone could so much as move, Kailia had spun, pulling a dagger from the gods-knew-where. The blade was pressed along his throat, and Razik didn't understand why he was bellowing in pain.

Then he noticed the small knife protruding from his hand, pinning it to the table.

Shit.

Fucking shit.

"What the fuck?" MacMillan barked, on his feet and a dagger of his own in hand. "Who the fuck is this, Greybane?"

"Still none of your concern," Razik answered. "Let's go," he ground out to Kailia.

"She stabbed Jenkins. I think she made it our concern," crooned the female, climbing atop the table like a lithe cat, a knife in hand.

"Come here," MacMallin snarled, reaching for Kailia himself.

"I wouldn't—" Razik started, but it was too late.

Kailia had twisted away from his grasp, her dagger flying and embedding itself in the male's shoulder as another knife flew at the female.

"Gods-fucking-dammit," Razik growled, pandemonium erupting around them.

Because when Kailia had thrown her dagger, the other female had leapt to avoid the knife, sending a mug of ale flying from their table directly onto those in the next booth. Sticky mead spilled onto the patrons and their table. That guy had reached over the booth, smashing a bottle atop the head of the card game's third male. Another had rounded the table, going for Jenkins, whose hand was still stuck to the table while MacMallin was going for Kailia yet again. And she—

"Where do you keep getting these fucking blades?" Razik growled, looping an arm around her waist, more than prepared for the fit that was about to happen. He'd already summoned his black flames, using them to combat the ashes she was trying to rake down his body. He Traveled them out of the tavern a moment before another male was hit so hard, he stumbled back directly to where they'd been standing.

As soon as they appeared in his study at Tybalt's home, he released Kailia, dropping her onto the rug. She was on her knees, gasping. Her eyes were wild and frantic as she took in the space. He lowered to a crouch before her, catching her wrist when she tried to strike out with her dagger.

"Lia, it's me," he growled, releasing her when she yanked her arm back.

Her ashes swirled around her, but she didn't try to move in them from what he could tell. She did, however, cock her arm back again.

"Do not throw that at me," he warned in a low growl.

But of course she fucking did.

His hand snapped up, catching it by the hilt. Flipping it, he threw it right back at her, aiming just to the left. She lurched to the side, not that she would have needed to, and then she spun back to him.

"You threw my own dagger at me," she snapped, those ashes still vibrating around her in a frenzy, but there was a glimmer of clarity in her eyes.

"You threw it at me first," he retorted, grabbing the sack beside him and getting back to his feet. "For the record, it wasn't going to hit you because my aim is *that* good," he added, echoing her words from the hunt.

She went quiet, and he let her be as he moved to his desk. Pulling open a drawer, he retrieved a thick ledger, flipping it open until he found the page he wanted. For several minutes, there was quiet while he let her collect herself. He put some books away that he'd been using for research while gathering some other ones, feeling her eyes on him the entire time.

Eventually, he said, "There's water on the cart over there."

She nodded, slowly getting to her feet and heading in the direction he'd indicated. Pouring herself a glass, she drank half of it before setting it aside.

"Do you want to talk about it?" he asked, not looking up from the book he was searching through.

"Talk about what?" she asked.

That had him meeting her stare with a frankness. "You started a brawl in a tavern, Lia."

"Which we won."

"Which we… How in the fuck do you figure that?"

"Neither of us was hit, neither of us is bleeding, and we are no longer in the tavern," she said matter-of-factly.

"Kailia," the name flat and monotone.

"What?"

Flipping the book closed, he rested his hand atop it. "You can't stab someone anytime they touch you."

"I can if it's not invited."

"Admittedly, today's situation is not the best example," he sighed.

"You took me to the tavern," she accused, coming closer to the desk.

"Are you seriously trying to tell me all of this was my fault?" he asked, pointing at his chest.

"You are the one who needed to get— What's even in that?" she asked, reaching for the sack.

But before her fingers closed on the fabric, he'd snatched it up. "It's mine."

She blinked at him. "I wasn't going to steal it."

He scoffed. "As if you could steal something from me."

"I could," she protested.

"It wasn't a challenge, Lia," he deadpanned.

She hummed. "Well, what was so important we got into a brawl for it?"

"*We* didn't— Nevermind," he growled, handing her the sack.

She opened it, looked inside, and then back at him. "It's a bowl."

"Yep," he said, swiping the sack back and placing it in a drawer. He'd deal with it later.

"Why did we go to a tavern to collect a bowl?"

"Don't tell Cethin I took you to the tavern," he answered, grabbing the book from the desk and handing it to her before heading towards the spiral staircase that would take them down to his chambers.

"But you're fine if I tell him you threw a dagger at me?" she asked, following him.

Razik shrugged, glancing at her to see her eyes darting around the space, cataloguing everything as she moved.

"What is this?" she asked.

"A book," he answered as she held up the thing.

Her lips pursed. "Why did you give it to me?"

"I didn't. I'm letting you borrow it. Basic Avonleyan history, geography, notable places and people. You know, things you should be aware of as the queen."

As they reached the staircase, he stepped to the side, gesturing for her to go first, but she hesitated, looking up at him.

"Don't tell Cethin I started a brawl," she said. Then added thoughtfully as she undid the clasps of the cloak she still wore, the book tucked under her arm, "I don't think a queen is supposed to do that."

He waited until she was handing him the garment before he said, "If Cethin knew another male had laid a finger on you, a knife through the hand would be a blessing compared to what he would do to them. Remember that, Kailia."

Her features seemed to sharpen as the smoke in her eyes swirled a little faster. "I know exactly what the king is capable of."

"Do you?" Razik asked. "Because as far as I'm aware, you two hardly know each other. You've been on your best behavior around each other, minus the whole stabbing him four times thing."

Her eyes narrowed, but he moved around her. As he descended the stairs, he called over his shoulder, "You're his wife, Kailia. He'll do anything to protect you."

"I don't need his protection," she retorted, following him down the stairs.

"Until you can think through your panic and don't blindly react, you absolutely do."

"You didn't do anything to step in today," she argued.

"Why would I deny you the right to defend yourself?" he asked, leading her through the space. "I didn't interfere until I had to."

"You didn't have to," she insisted.

"I did, because if it's discovered the new queen is starting brawls by the docks, it'll be both our asses," he grumbled. "But more so mine, even though you started the whole debacle."

"I think you started it by going there for a bowl," she mused.

He said nothing more, done with the conversation. But he'd

cracked some kind of code today. Taking her out. Doing random things. Letting her get into a godsdamn brawl. He needed her comfortable around him if he was going to figure out her motives, and if brawls in a tavern were what it was going to take, he needed to get her a different cloak that would hide her face better.

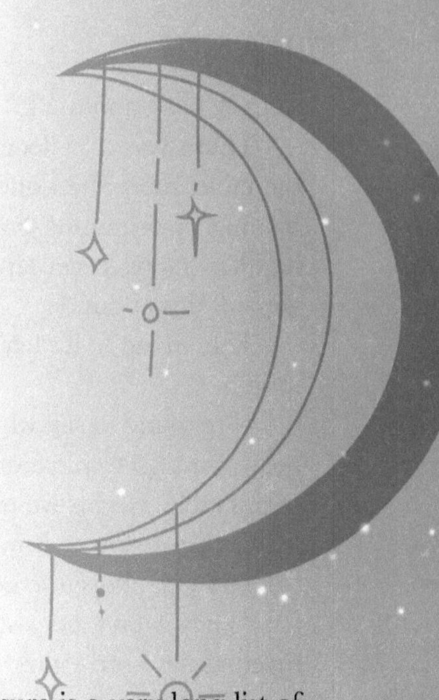

CHAPTER 24

CETHIN

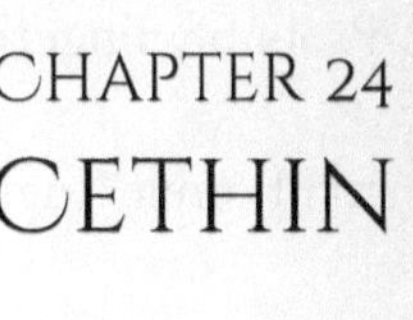

"Before we get started with what I'm sure is a very long list of topics to go over today," Cethin said from the head of the table, "we need to discuss the upcoming Union Celebration."

All eyes went to Kailia, who was seated to his right. He'd asked her to attend today's advisory council meeting, at least for this part of it. He'd never wish these meetings on anyone, and he'd told Kailia she could leave after this initial matter was handled if she wanted to.

"As the Union itself will take place on the night of the full moon," Lady Mariel was saying, "I think we all assumed the Union Celebration would take place a few days later. Give the two of you time to…celebrate on your own."

Gods, he fucking wished.

As it stood, he couldn't even touch Kailia without warning her first, or he risked being stabbed. Again.

He could feel Tybalt's eyes on him to his left, and he internally sighed. Guess he'd get this over with. It wasn't like anyone could do anything about it anyway. What was done was done.

Keeping his features impassive and casual, he said, "The Union

321

Celebration can happen on the full moon. The Union itself has already been anointed."

There was a collective gasp and jolts of surprise from around the table, more than one pair of eyes darting to his left hand where his fingers drummed on the table. A few looked at Kailia, but she had her hands in her lap. Probably fingering the dagger at her thigh with all this attention.

The thought had a small smile tugging at the corner of his mouth.

"I'm going to say what we're all thinking," Lord Harlan said, not nearly enough trepidation in his tone after the last time Kailia had sat at this table. His brown eyes narrowed. "There is no Union Mark?"

Cethin made a show of looking out the window, where the sun was still well above the horizon.

"They won't be visible for quite a few hours," he answered, meeting the Lord's gaze once more.

The entire room went still, and he waited to see who was going to be the one to question him. He hadn't expected it to be his personal Hand.

"Are you saying you… It's a Lunar Marriage?" Zayan asked.

Cethin turned to the male, finding his face pale and eyes wide.

"I am," Cethin answered. "The Rite was performed beneath the full moon at Lunae Falls a week ago. Which means we are free to hold the celebration on the next full moon."

"You're serious?" Lady Mariel asked, trying to blink away her surprise. "After everything…"

"You didn't think this was something to discuss with this council?" Lord Harlin asked, a hard edge to his voice.

"I think you are growing a little too bold in your position, Lord Harlin," Cethin said coldly, waiting until the male lowered his gaze before he went on. "For decades, this council has pushed me towards a union. This last year, that push became a shove. Now that I have done what was asked, you are upset. I'm wondering if there is any pleasing you at this point."

"We have a right to be taken aback by this development," Lady

Carlin interjected. "I don't think any of us expected you to enter into a Lunar Marriage after everything."

"I agreed to the marriage you all demanded of me. How that union took place was still my prerogative," Cethin replied tightly. "Contrary to what this council seems to think, you don't get a say in every facet of my personal life."

"I don't think that's what anyone is trying to imply," Lord Tovan tried diplomatically. "We are all just a little shocked and need a minute to process the…new developments."

"The only thing that needs to be processed is the Union Celebration," Cethin retorted. "Contract the necessary merchants and businesses to ensure it happens on the next full moon."

"Since this all happened so suddenly, I think it would be wise for our new queen to say a few words. So we can all get to know her better," Tybalt said suddenly, his usually warm brown eyes dark and hard as he stared at Kailia.

Razik shifted from where he stood behind her at the wall. He'd been leaning against it with his arms crossed, but he straightened now, gaze darting from his uncle to Kailia.

"What would you like to know?" Cethin asked, glancing at his wife sidelong. She hadn't moved, and he wondered if she was even breathing at this point.

"We know she's from Shadowfen, but tell us more," the Commander said. "What are your parents' occupations?"

She stared straight at the dragon as she said simply, "I'm not sure what occupations are available in the After."

Tybalt blinked at the statement, and Cethin was both proud of her for calling the Commander out on the bullshit he was attempting to pull while also feeling like a jackass for never asking her that question. But in his defense, she answered everything like that. Direct yet obscure simultaneously. He was trying, but she didn't simply share things. It was taking time and patience. The time he had loads of. The patience was…exhausting. He wasn't a stranger to the notion, but he'd never experienced it with people and relationships. Action had always been his preference, even when his parents had opted to wait and move with caution. He'd dove right in, not content to wait.

This was forcing him to wait. *She* was forcing him to go slowly and move with caution. At any moment he felt like he'd go backwards ten steps for the few he'd managed to gain. The only way he'd successfully learned anything about her was by watching her every move and listening to what she was saying beyond the words spoken.

She'd also become a distraction. That much was evident from the piles of reports and neglected meetings on his schedule.

"My apologies, your Majesty," Tybalt said, the words tight. "My inquiry was insensitive."

Kailia shrugged. "Relations are common conversation topics. I simply don't have the answer to that particular question. Perhaps another?"

Cethin was pressing his thumb to the corner of his mouth to hide his smirk. He was fairly certain she wasn't purposely goading Tybalt, but the Commander was working to hide his irritation.

"How long have you been in Aimonway?" Lord Tovan tried.

She turned to him, and Cethin could swear he flinched back. It was minuscule, but it was definitely there.

"I visited several times before relocating to the castle after the Esbat Festival," she answered.

"And your...occupation?" Lady Mariel asked.

"Queen."

The Lady winced. "Before that, I mean."

At that, ashes fluttered around her. "I hunt things."

And *that* answer had Cethin fighting to keep his features devoid of emotion. He shouldn't be surprised. Ash Riders were commonly hired for their stealth and skill, but now he wanted to know *who*. Who had she worked for in the past? What had she hunted down? Did that have something to do with why she couldn't stand to be touched?

After an extended awkward silence, Cethin said, "Any other questions at this time?" He took his time, looking each person at the table in the eye. Then he faltered as he realized he'd neglected to introduce Kailia to the newest member of the council.

"Lord Astor," he said. The male straightened at the address. "My apologies for not offering you a formal introduction. My wife, Kailia. Kailia, Corveth Astor, the newest member of the advisory council."

"It's a pleasure to meet you," she replied with ease, head tilting as she studied him.

To his credit, the male didn't fidget or wince like the other members had today. He held Kailia's stare as he said, "The pleasure is all mine, your Majesty."

"What territory do you represent?" Kailia asked

"Everfall, your Majesty."

She hummed. "I hear the city is beautiful."

"It is. We would love to host you both the next time you visit."

"I would like that as well," she replied. "Is there a time of year you suggest?"

"Summer is best. Autumn is beautiful, but the weather takes a turn rather quickly, and the winter can be dreadful at times."

His smile was kind as he spoke, his onyx hair a little unruly. His clothing wasn't as formal and proper as the others at the table. In fact, his clothing was rather worn. He'd come in work boots, covered with dust and grime, rather than polished shoes or boots, and he was conversing with Kailia as if she were just another person. He was being respectful, yes, but Kailia was visibly more comfortable in her conversation.

Cethin also had a feeling that a trip to Everfall was in their near future. This was the first time Kailia had shown any interest in Avonleya in general.

She didn't stay for the rest of the advisory council meeting, and Cethin couldn't blame her. He wouldn't have stayed if he didn't have to. She left shortly after her brief conversation with Corveth, Razik with her, before the conversations turned to the attacks, four more Fae that were found dead south of Aimonway, the Elder Clan treaties, and more.

It was well into the night when they finally adjourned, tabling issues while coming to terms on others. But the matter of the new Fae deaths had him making his way to his study when the moon was already starting to fade from the sky. The options were this or going back to his rooms, where despite his best efforts, his movements would wake Kailia. She didn't sleep through anything, and he suddenly wondered if her revelation about hunting things today had anything to do with that.

As it turned out, it didn't matter whether or not he went to their rooms. Less than an hour later, there was a soft tap on the door before Kailia was drifting into the study. Her midnight hair was flowing around her, faint ashes floating amidst the strands, and her eyes swirled languidly, as if her magic had stirred awake as well. She was clutching a book to her chest, each step into the study soundless.

Shifting back in his chair, he propped an elbow on the armrest while steepling a finger along his temple.

"Glad to see you made the wise decision to wear a robe while wandering the castle halls. The night watch will be grateful," he mused when she paused to study a map on the wall.

But at his words, she twisted to face him, her expression pensive. "Why would the night watch be grateful I wore a robe?"

"Had any of them seen you in the nightclothes I'm sure you're wearing beneath it, I'd have been compelled to relieve them of their duties." He paused before adding casually, "And possibly their eyesight."

"That's absurd," she scoffed, shuffling a few steps closer.

"You've stabbed me for less, tiny fiend," he deadpanned. "What brings you down here at this hour? Can't sleep?"

"I slept a bit," she replied, now at the side of his desk. She ran her fingers along the smooth surface.

"But?"

"Do you sleep?" she asked instead. "I've yet to see it."

He smiled softly. "Yes, I sleep."

But he didn't tell her he only slept when he'd pushed himself to the point of exhaustion. He didn't tell her he only slept if his power became so depleted, it forced him into a semi-conscious state.

He didn't tell her that he understood the dangers of dreaming.

She was still exploring his desk, and he wondered if she'd realized she'd rounded the corner as she leaned in to study a glass container, the contents swirling and twisting but never merging into one.

"What are you reading?" he asked after a few minutes of watching her.

She straightened, as if just realizing how odd this entire situation might be. Then she looked down at the book she'd tucked under her arm. Turning to face him, she leaned back against the desk, holding it out to him. "Razik let me borrow it."

"Did he now?" Cethin asked, taking the book. "And where is your guard who's not supposed to let you go anywhere alone?"

She shrugged. "He told me once I'm in our rooms for the night, he's off duty until breakfast unless summoned. I didn't summon him."

"Sneaking out then," he commented, thumbing through the pages.

She tsked. "I'm not a child. I didn't sneak out anywhere. I'm told this is my home now."

"It is," Cethin said flatly, glancing up from the book.

"Then I presume I am free to move about my *home* without an escort."

"I was attacked in this castle shortly before the Esbat Festival, Kailia."

"Where I understand you used my arrow to defend yourself."

"I did."

"You're welcome."

His brows shot up. "For the arrow? That you've been going on about for weeks?"

"For the protection I was providing even before we'd formally met," she replied, and gods. She said it so simply, he wasn't sure if she was being a smart ass or simply stating something she thought to be true.

He shook his head, hiding his smile as he returned to the book. It was entirely about Avonleya. The major cities. How territories were divided. Various landmarks. There was history and policy, laws and notable leaders both past and present.

"You've been reading this?" he asked.

"Mhmm," she hummed, toying with a reed pen he'd been using to sign off on some requests from various cities.

"Why?"

She paused mid-twirl of the pen in her fingers. "Why have I been reading about the kingdom I suddenly find myself queen of?"

He nodded, setting the book aside and shifting closer in his chair. She moved back, but with nowhere to go, she ended up perching on the edge of the desk, crossing her ankles, her bare feet now off the floor.

"I suppose because if this is to be my life, I should know the kingdom and people I'm serving," she answered, leaning back on her hands as she tilted her head, watching him. Resuming this game they'd been playing of observing each other to try to gain the upper hand.

"Can I ask you another question?" he asked, watching the robe slip down one of her shoulders and confirming his suspicion of what kind of nightclothes she was wearing.

"I cannot stop you," she replied. "Doesn't mean I'll answer it."

Fair enough.

Dragging his gaze from that thin strap at her shoulder back to her bright eyes, he asked, "Why don't you like to be touched?"

She clearly hadn't expected the question to be *that*. Not with the way her eyes went wide, swirling a little faster. Not with the way her lips pursed and she swallowed thickly. Not with the way her other hand drifted to her thigh, where he was certain a dagger was hidden beneath the robe. Not as a full-body shiver shuddered through her form like even the mere thought of being touched was too much.

When she didn't answer, he settled back in his chair, putting a little more space between them. Her shoulders relaxed some, inching down from her ears.

At least until he said, "If it wasn't clear when I made you my wife, I'm not going anywhere, and neither are you. I'll figure you out with or without your help."

Because this was what he did. He dug deep and pushed limits, picking at details and unraveling threads. He was willing to do uncomfortable things to get what he wanted, and he'd drag others right along with him if required. Of course, he preferred to keep his sins hidden in the shadows, but that meant pulling others into the dark with him sometimes. He'd done it for his kingdom to give them the lives and freedoms they deserve—was still willing to make the sacrifices for them—and this was no different. *She* was no different.

Her features hardened at his words, and she pushed off her hands, leaning forward. Unfortunately for him, that made the other side of her robe slip down her shoulder, the garment now caught in the bend of her elbows, and it left a whole lot of cleavage on display.

"I truly didn't think you cared about the touching, seeing as you don't even sleep in the same bed," she said sharply.

He propped his head on a fist. "You are upset I'm not sharing your bed?"

"That is *not* what I said."

"That's what it sounded like to me."

"Then your education was lacking if that's what you think those words strung together indicated."

He smirked. "I assure you my academics were rigorous, but my studies also included learning to read people and all the things they *weren't* saying."

Her features scrunched up in a way that told him she thought that was the most inane thing she'd ever heard. "That's not a thing."

"It absolutely is, tiny fiend," he replied.

"Is that so?" she demanded.

"It is."

"I would just say what I'm thinking."

"I want to believe that, but…"

She sat up straighter, the move pushing out her chest, and fuck him, because that nightdress was cut far too low and the sheerness left little to the imagination. Contrary to her belief, he hadn't picked out her wardrobe. He'd simply put in an order for all the clothing a queen would require, and whoever had been given the task had included these items that tortured him daily.

"But what?" Kailia asked, and Cethin wasn't sure if she was offended or if it was a genuine question.

"But I believe that watching from the smoke and ashes may have affected your own education in that area," he answered. "You can read people, sure, but you find it difficult to interact with them or use that knowledge to your advantage."

She blinked at him, her features turning a faint shade of red that wasn't from embarrassment. That was anger.

"You know nothing of my past, *husband*."

"I'm aware, *wife*. That was why I asked a question. I assume your past has everything to do with why you fear touch."

"I don't fear touch," she retorted. "I just don't like it."

"Then you've never been touched properly," he replied, the words simple in the same way she often spoke. As if it were merely a fact.

Her eyes narrowed. "And I suppose *you* are the one who could change all that? You are the one who could touch me *properly?*"

He said nothing, remaining motionless in the same way she often did. Watching and waiting.

"Tell me, king, what is the proper way to touch someone? To get what you want with soft touches? To maintain control with punishing ones? To manipulate with caresses? To claim ownership with ones that leave bruises behind? If that is the case, I've been touched properly so many times, they linger like phantoms. Living and breathing, with memories of their own. I do not need more," she finished, her small frame heaving slightly with emotion he only saw from her when she was lost to her panic.

Long, silent moments passed. Him watching her. Her perched on the desk, once more emotionless as she regained her composure. He gave her that time. They were in no hurry. He needed the respite to get his own emotions under control because his power was straining and writhing beneath his skin. He'd assumed she'd experienced something traumatic. No one was that averse to touch who hadn't, but to hear it said aloud made him want to let that power loose. Let the death in his veins feast.

Finally, each word tight and controlled, he said, "None of those are the proper way to touch someone, Kailia. I'd love to meet the people who taught you they were."

"Too bad you're locked behind your Wards," she sneered.

"For now," he agreed.

"What does that mean?"

"Another conversation for another time. Back to you not liking touch—"

"There's nothing more to say."

"That's where you're wrong," he replied. "There is absolutely a proper way to touch someone. Soft touches to give you what *you* want. Caresses to bring pleasure. Possessive ones that don't leave bruises but security, knowing you are cared for."

"And to maintain control?" she countered, lifting her chin.

"If I wanted control, I'd take it, and I wouldn't need to touch you," he replied. "Touch can be all those things you've experienced, but touch can also be safety and pleasure and desire."

"And I suppose you want to show me that?" she asked, eyeing him with derision.

"I wouldn't say no," he said with a mocking smirk.

"I'm sure not," she scoffed, leaning back on her hands once more. "Looks like you'll have to bestow security, pleasure, and desire another way, husband."

His brow arched at that. "Is that so?"

She paused, a glimpse of hesitation sparking. A curiosity he was more than willing to assuage after this heavy conversation.

"I could, you know," he replied, sitting straighter in his desk chair, hands resting loosely on the armrests where she could see them. Where they'd stay. He didn't miss her eyes darting warily to them.

"I'd tell you to untie the sash at your waist. Tell you to pull up that godsdamn nightdress that taunts me every fucking night, spread your legs wide, and show me the cunt you won't let me touch," he continued conversationally.

"That…is crass," she said, the words a little breathy.

"Yes, but because I am well educated in reading the words people won't say, I noticed how your nostrils flared and how your pupils dilated. I noticed the slight bob of your throat and how you leaned imperceptibly closer." He paused, pointedly dropping his gaze before bringing it back to hers. "I noticed you uncrossed your ankles, your legs opening the barest amount. That would be the desire part because while crass, it also made you *want.*"

Her jaw clenched. "Even if that were true, how does that offer security or pleasure?"

"I'm not done," he said, keeping his hands in place as he leaned towards her. "The security part comes when I tell you I'll let you return to our rooms alone tonight."

"How is that security?" she asked in confusion.

"So that when you're lying in that bed you wish I'd share with you—"

"I never said that," she interjected.

"When you're in that bed," he continued, "you'll have security in the knowledge I won't interrupt you when you eventually give in and drag your own fingers between your breasts, across your stomach, and down lower."

"That's my own touch bringing me pleasure, not you," she retorted.

"But you'll be thinking of me," he countered. "You'll be wondering if I'm right. Wondering what it would feel like to have my fingers inside you rather than your own." He stood then, shoving his hands into his pockets as he leaned in close, his next words fanning across her lips. "And those thoughts are what will push you over the edge of pleasure, wife."

Picking up the book, he handed it back to her before he left her still perched on his desk. He had to because he was seconds away from throwing caution to the wind and taking a chance on touching her. Of showing her what touch could do. What it *should* do.

But doing so would ruin all the progress he'd made, and tonight was a big step forward. Her composure had slipped, and she'd revealed another part of herself. Another puzzle piece clicking into place.

So he made his way down to the castle catacombs where his preferred workspace was. Because it was either that or go back on his word and see if she really was finding her own pleasure. Or he could go somewhere to find his own release, but as tempting as that was, he'd been doing enough of that on his own lately.

More sins in the shadows would have to suffice for now.

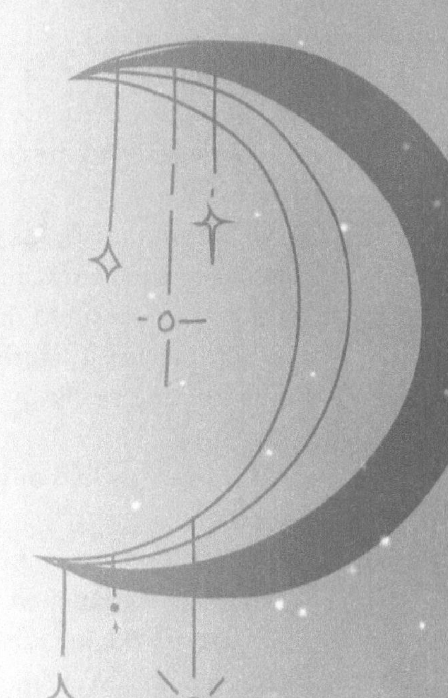

CHAPTER 25

KAILIA

"**M**other of Temural!" Kailia cried, her bow in hand and an arrow nocked and aimed before she registered the figure standing inside the sitting room of the royal chambers.

But then she did realize who it was, and she still debated letting that arrow fly. If anything because the way he was looking at her—with that arrogant smirk and heated silver stare—made her think of last night. The words he'd said. The confident way he'd told her what she'd do because of them. How he'd been fucking right. How, despite her conviction to *not* let it happen, she'd found herself with her hand sliding down her torso, over her navel, and lower.

But he'd also been wrong. Because the thought of anyone else touching her made even her own touch turn into something burning and torturous. All the need and lust coiling in her core had vanished at the thought, and instead, she'd found herself in an ice-cold bath to erase the burning on her flesh.

"Serafina?" Cethin asked, that knowing look still on his face despite an obvious attempt to be nonchalant. "You know, most of the people in this realm don't dare utter the names of the death god, his wife, or their children."

"Perhaps among the mortals and even the Fae Courts across the sea, but I know there are worse things to fear in this world than gods and goddesses who are far too busy among other realms to interfere here," she replied.

Cethin hummed, his gaze raking over her. "Have we graduated from daggers to arrows in your attempts to harm me?"

Slowly she lowered the bow, still holding the arrow to the string with her fingers. "I figured since this deal included your protection, there's nothing really to stop me at this point. What are you even doing here?"

His brows arched at the sudden change of subject. "I live here, tiny fiend."

"But you're never actually *here*."

His features flattened. "I promised to give you space."

"That still doesn't answer why you're here now."

She could swear that arrogance faltered a fraction, as if he suddenly wasn't sure of himself. But it was gone in the next blink, his casual control back in place.

"I thought we'd have breakfast together here today," he answered. "Just the two of us."

"Why?"

He studied her, and she didn't understand how that was a complicated question.

"I suppose for appearance's sake, wife," he finally answered. "I just need to bathe and dress. What are your plans for the day?"

"I'm sure the same as every other day," she retorted while he brushed past her and headed down the hall.

"Which is?" he called back over his shoulder, pushing through the bedchamber door.

"Nothing," she said, following him. "A queen in title only gives me little to do other than read history."

"That seems important for a queen wanting more than a title."

"It is, but— What are you doing?"

He was pulling his tunic over his head, and that was all sorts of pale bare skin on display with dips and indents that did things to her. She'd seen plenty of naked bodies, but her reaction to Cethin was always different. Always something she didn't know what to do with. This conflict in her soul she didn't understand.

"I told you I needed to bathe and change," Cethin answered, thumbing the button on his pants.

That was a valid point. He *had* said that.

But then he'd drawn her into conversation and distracted her. That was her own fault though, right?

"Husbands and wives have conversations, Kailia," he said, as if he knew the internal struggle she was having in trying to sort this all out.

"Surely not while half dressed," she blurted.

At least he'd paused the undressing, even if his pants were now merely hanging on his hips with the flap open.

His smile was pure amusement when he said, "Of course not. There's often no clothing involved. Whispered conversations while heads rest on pillows after other activities." When she only blinked at him, he added, "It's things like this that make me question your claims of fucking experience, wife."

Kailia pursed her lips. This male was one of the few people who could rile her up enough to forget herself and what she should be focusing on. How was he so godsdamn distracting all the fucking time with just his words? Then again, she shouldn't be surprised. It was how he appeared to get everything he wanted, and she needed to remember that.

He said nothing else, leaving her with the echoes of his dark chuckle as he went to the bathing chamber. Leaving the door open. The sound of shifting fabric and the tub filling had her turning on her heel and making her way back to the sitting room.

Only to find herself cursing again.

"Fucking Temural!" she cried, her bow raised once more. Then, "What are you doing here?"

"I've told you multiple times I'm not standing in the hall all day, Lia," Razik said from the chair he was occupying. "Why do you have your bow in hand?"

"Why do males constantly question a female with a weapon?" she grumbled, sending the bow and arrow away in a swirl of ashes.

"I don't care if you're armed," Razik replied flatly. "Just curious why you feel the need to be so in your own rooms? But if the answer is Cethin, I understand. Just want to caution you that repeatedly stabbing him will raise questions."

"By the gods," she grumbled, throwing her hands in the air as she turned to go to the dining room.

It was smaller and far more intimate than the main dining hall they usually ate in. With a balcony that faced east, it housed a table for eight, but only two places were set at one end. Thankfully, staff had already been here because there was a small breakfast spread on the table.

She filled a plate, taking three of those rolls with cinnamon and some fruit. She heard Razik enter the room behind her, but she didn't say anything, trying to get her defenses back up before Cethin returned.

Taking a bite of her roll, she tracked Razik as he filled the other plate before taking a seat, letting the silence linger. He seemed to enjoy the quiet as much as she did, but sometimes he forced her into conversation. Thankfully, today was not one of those days.

At least not until Cethin entered the room.

He came to a sudden halt, eyes narrowing on Razik, who had seemed surprised to see him here. But the shock was gone in the next blink, replaced with his usual apathy.

"What are you doing here?" Cethin asked, scanning the table. His lips thinned at finding Razik in his seat with his plate.

Razik took his time taking a drink of pomegranate juice before he answered with a lazy drawl and a pointed look at her. "My job."

"There is no need to be in here," Cethin said with all the command of the king he was.

But once again, Razik clearly didn't appear to give two fucks. He remained seated, sprawled casually in his chair and eating one of the cinnamon rolls.

"Kailia and I have an agreement," Razik said after a moment. "She doesn't like being left alone on this entire floor, and I don't like standing in the hall for hours on end. As the queen, she allows me to be in these rooms to do my job."

Well, that wasn't entirely true, Kailia thought to herself. She very much preferred solitude, but she had told him he could come into the rooms instead of standing in the hallway all day.

Cethin turned to her, the look on his face the portrait of frustrated annoyance, and for the life of her, she could not figure out the animosity between these two. If Cethin was questioning her experience with fucking, then she was questioning their aggressive denial of ever having been lovers.

"Kailia?" Cethin asked.

"What?" she replied, cutting off another piece of her roll with her fork.

"Is that true?"

"Why would he lie about that?" When Cethin only stared back at her, she added, "I find it odd you would assign a guard to me that you do not fully trust."

"I don't—" Cethin sighed, pinching the bridge of his nose, and she could swear her own heartbeat was increasing at his stress. Which was strange and not at all logical. "We were planning a private breakfast this morning."

"I was not part of that planning. Just informed of it," she said. "That didn't give me much time to give Razik notice." She could swear Razik snickered under his breath, but she paid him no mind. "I also still don't understand why."

"Just…forget it," Cethin sighed, reaching to slide some sausage to another platter before he filled the former plate with food. "You could have at least saved me a roll," he muttered after a minute.

"As she already said, I wasn't made aware you'd be joining us," Razik said.

"*You* joined *us*," Cethin ground out between clenched teeth, taking the seat next to Kailia.

Razik shrugged. "Looks like you need to work on communication."

Before Cethin could reply, Kailia said, "I would like to go to Shadowfen."

Both males went silent, turning to stare at her.

"Why would you want to go there?" Razik asked after a long moment of silence.

"Because that is where I'm supposed to be from. I think it would be helpful if I'd actually been there," she answered, pushing her plate back.

"She's not wrong," Razik said, glancing at Cethin.

"I know she's not wrong," he snapped. With an elbow planted on his armrest, he rubbed at his brow with his forefinger. "The problem is, few know of this…arrangement. We'd have to go alone. To Shadowfen."

"I'm sure Razik can come with us," Kailia said in confusion. "Or Tybalt. But he doesn't like me, so I'd definitely prefer Razik."

Cethin's features pinched, as if those words pained him to hear. "My schedule is packed for the next few weeks."

"I can take her," Razik said simply. "It's not like we have anything else to do."

"I am amenable to that," Kailia agreed. "Shall we go today?"

"No," Cethin interjected, and Kailia found him glaring at Razik. "I'll take her. I just need to clear my schedule." Meeting her gaze, he asked, "Can you wait a few days?"

"You really don't have to accompany me," she offered. "We can go and be back within a day or two."

He ran a hand down his face in obvious exasperation that she didn't understand. Wouldn't it be easier and more convenient for him if Razik simply Traveled her there?

"Give me a few hours to talk to Zayan," Cethin said. "Can you at least wait that long?"

She could feel Razik's gaze on her, and she shifted, sparing him a glance. More expressions she couldn't decipher, despite decades of studying behavior and trying to make sense of it all. But the male almost looked confused as his sapphire eyes flickered from her to Cethin and back.

"We can wait," Kailia answered. "But rearranging your schedule still seems unnecessary."

Cethin was already pushing to his feet, his plate of food

untouched. "I'll be back in a few hours. Greybane, don't take her there without me."

Then he was striding from the room with purpose, and she watched him go. Straight. Regal. The king she'd watched from the ashes for months.

"He's trying to figure you out," Razik said after they heard the main doors close.

She shifted to face him more. "What do you mean?"

"You've become this…infatuation of his," Razik said. "Something he's trying to work out. I've seen the way he watches you. It's the same way you observe everything and everyone around you trying to understand." Then he added, "You also frustrate him. It's enjoyable to witness."

"*You* frustrate him," she countered. "Although I believe you antagonize him on purpose."

"There's that astuteness again."

She sat back in her chair, glaring at the male. "Then again, you appear to purposely antagonize everyone."

Silence fell again, and for the first time in a long time, her thoughts became too loud. So incessant and all-consuming that she found herself saying, "Can I ask you something?"

"I'm not going to stop a queen," Razik replied, looking up from the book he'd summoned and laid on the table.

"I… This Union Celebration. It will involve…" She trailed off, shaking her hands out before smoothing them over her dress.

"Being on display. A feast. Visiting with those of the kingdom. Dancing," Razik supplied when she didn't continue.

"Dancing," she repeated, internally flinching.

Or externally, because Razik clearly saw it based on the way he tilted his head in question. "Not a great dancer, Lia?"

She felt her cheeks grow hot, and that made him sit up straighter. But it wasn't from embarrassment. Her whole body was going flush because dancing involved closeness and touching.

"I can't help if you don't tell me why that made you somehow go pale and flush all at once," Razik said, and his tone wasn't exactly kind, but it wasn't his usual asshole facade either.

"So astute," she muttered, trying to regulate her breathing.

"Lia."

Her name was a flat tone of impatience.

She sighed. "As I'm sure you are aware, dancing involves touching, which I don't do well with."

"And yet you made some sort of deal with Cethin," the male admonished. "Did you not think touch would be required of a queen? Of a wife?"

"Of course I knew that," she snapped.

"Did you make agreements regarding such things with Cethin?"

"Not exactly."

His lip curled. "Not exactly? Do I even want to know what that means?"

"It means— I don't know, Raz," she said, exasperation and panic clawing at her. "It means everyone is going to know exactly how unqualified I am for this. I have a lot to prove here."

Razik studied her for another long moment before flipping his book closed and settling back in his chair. "Cethin is an arrogant dick who's used to getting his way."

"I've gathered that," she murmured.

"But he's also intuitive and cunning," Razik went on. "He wouldn't have made you his queen if he didn't think you could handle it. He wouldn't do that to his people. His loyalty to this kingdom is the only admirable thing about him."

"Some would consider it a curse," she mused.

Razik shrugged. "My point is, despite this seeming impulsive and reckless, the fucker always has a reason. He clearly believes you can handle the pressures of being a queen."

"Obviously not considering it's in title only," she said. "Either way, prolonged touching is going to prove how wrong he is."

"So you start preparing yourself now," he countered. "Start small. I've seen him touch you. Start there."

As if she hadn't tried that in the past. But she wasn't about to bring that up and open herself up for more questions.

"And stop stabbing him. That will help too," Razik added as an afterthought.

She flipped the male her middle finger as she stood, fingering the dagger beneath her dress with her other hand. Maybe she'd start stabbing *him* instead.

–⟩⟩ ☉ ⟨⟨–

Taking a few steps down the cobbled street, she paused and turned, taking in the dark stone buildings. Fog and mist drifted along the ground, making everything appear darker. Even the shadows felt thicker here. Granted, the sun had dipped below the horizon, but Kailia had the impression the town of Shadowfen had this eerie feel to it even when the sun was high in the sky. It felt like there were eyes on her. She was used to doing the watching. Being the hunter, not the prey, and she definitely felt like prey right now.

"This is Shadowfen?" she asked, drifting closer to a shop. The heavy wooden door was shut tight with a single candle in the window.

"It is," Cethin answered, keeping a few paces between them. "The fog and mist roll in off the inlet."

She nodded, turning again and venturing deeper into the town. She understood why everyone was so surprised when she'd announced that this was where she was from. Which begged the question—

"Why did you have me tell people I was from here?" she asked Cethin, looking up to find dark windows. She hadn't seen a single person since they'd entered the town twenty minutes ago.

"Shadowfen is known for its dark places and secrets," Cethin explained. "If an Ash Rider was going to hide anywhere, this was the most likely place."

"So now I was hiding too?"

"I assume you know your kind is highly sought after. It makes perfect sense if you had been trying to go unnoticed. Which you were," he added pointedly.

She could see the logic in that.

They were nearing the town center where a well stood atop a small dais. Mist flowed up and over the top of the sides, and she'd just placed her foot on the first step when fingers wrapped around her arm.

She spun, a dagger in hand, but Cethin had already released her.

"I'm sorry I didn't get a chance to warn you," he said, his hand still outstretched and preparing to block her. "But going near the well can summon things."

Kailia looked over her shoulder, then back at him. "What kinds of things?"

"Things that will need more than arrows to kill," he replied, motioning for her to come away from the steps.

"They've never met my arrows," she countered, curiosity warring inside her along with the thrill of a challenging hunt.

"Let's save fighting creatures of old for tomorrow," Razik said from where he stood a few feet away, arms crossed and watching them. "You know, *start small.*"

Right.

Start small.

Taking a deep breath, she took a step closer to Cethin. Then another. He'd stilled, watching her carefully. She was fairly certain he'd stopped breathing. She stopped right beside him, her breaths already shallow. Her heart was doing this weird thing in her chest she'd never experienced before, and this couldn't possibly be what Razik meant.

"By Sargon, this is the most awkward thing I've ever witnessed," Razik said tonelessly.

"Shut up, Greybane," Cethin snapped.

Kailia had to agree with the sentiment.

"I'm going to see about sleeping arrangements. Leave you two to…figure out whatever this is," he said, waving a hand at them before turning and stalking off.

She wanted to call after him because, for some reason, she found a weird sense of comfort in his presence. Nothing sensuous. She didn't linger on him like she did Cethin, but she supposed she'd become accustomed to his presence after spending the last weeks with him every day.

Cethin had shifted on his feet, standing before her now, and she had to tip her head back to look up into his face.

"As much as I wish I did, I don't know what's going on in that head of yours, tiny fiend," he said, slowly reaching for a lock of her hair.

"Razik suggested that I…practice getting used to touching you. For the Union Celebration," she added hastily.

His eyes widened at the admission. "Why would he do that?"

Her brows crashed together. "Why would he offer a suggestion when I expressed trepidation over the event?"

Cethin's features fell. "Why would you talk to him about that instead of me?"

"Because you are always off doing…king things."

Despite stating simple facts, he clearly wasn't impressed with them. "What, exactly, did Greybane suggest?"

"Starting with small touches," she answered, smoothing her hands over her dress. Cethin had suggested a cloak before they left, and she was grateful for that now. The breeze from the inlet was cool, not to mention the dense fog. Everything felt damp and musty. But she much preferred cooler, even freezing, temperatures over stifling hot and humid ones.

"I've already been doing that," Cethin replied. "Or trying to. Things seem to have…intensified since you were attacked in Shira Forest, so I've stopped."

She nodded, averting her gaze because he wasn't wrong. She was well aware of her shortcomings. She was also well aware of how those shortcomings could be manipulated.

"Maybe if you shared more detail as to why you have such an aversion to touch, we could address that and—"

"That's not necessary," she interjected.

He nodded, that piercing silver gaze never leaving her. Finally, the hand fingering her hair pushed the locks back over her shoulder before pulling up the hood of her cloak. It was almost tender. Or it was tender? She didn't know.

"Are there some places that are worse than others for touch?"

She hated this. Hated admitting to a weakness. Hated being so vulnerable. Especially with a male who she knew would take advantage of them to gain what he wanted.

Swallowing thickly, she admitted, "My stomach, but really it's more…the prospect of being restrained. Held down."

He nodded again, darkness flickering in those silver depths. "Not being able to defend or free yourself."

She nodded, averting her gaze to where she spotted Razik coming out of a building. He whistled, waving them over, and Cethin gestured for her to go first, falling into step beside her. But he didn't touch her, and shouldn't he be? If that was what she'd said they needed to work on?

Razik pulled the door open when they reached him, and they stepped into a dimly lit room. Sconces held dripping candles that cast shadows across the stone floor. There were tables scattered throughout, with a bar running along one end. Far across the room, someone with a hood pulled up over their head was huddled over a table, a tankard between his gloved hands. Male, if she had to guess based on the build she could make out. If there were others here, they were hidden in the dark corners.

Razik led them to a corner booth on the opposite side of the room, the shadows here seeming to writhe. They weren't the heavy inkiness of Cethin's power. They felt more graceful and lithe, less chaotic.

Kailia slid in first, Cethin sliding in on her left.

"Ale good for everyone?" Razik asked, looking at her.

She nodded. It wasn't her favorite, but from the looks of this place, she wasn't sure there were many other options. She wasn't sure they should be drinking *anything* from here.

Razik returned with mugs, placing them down on the table. He slid one to her, then to Cethin, putting more force behind his, liquid sloshing over the side. Then he slipped into the booth on her right.

"Did you find sleeping accommodations?" Cethin asked, his voice low.

"I figured we'd go to Tenebrae Halls. I think they'll make room for their king," Razik said before taking a drink.

"Yeah," Cethin said, fingers clenched around the handle of his mug. "I just prefer to give more than a few hours' notice of my plans."

"They're going to have room. It's not as if people are clamoring to visit Shadowfen."

The fingers of Cethin's other hand drummed on the tabletop, the sound jarring in the otherwise silent tavern.

"Does anyone actually live in this town?" Kailia asked, her hands in her lap. Closer to her daggers.

"It's not a large population," Cethin answered. "But yes, there are people who live here."

"It's barely past sundown. This is when Avonleya is most active, and yet there wasn't a soul on the streets."

"They were out there," Razik said. "They just stay hidden. You should know all about that."

That would explain the constant unease and feeling of people watching her.

Cethin took a drink of his ale before he said, "Now that you've seen the lie of your origin, care to share where you're really from, wife?"

Razik paused, his mug halfway to his mouth, suspended in the air. His sapphire stare was pinned on her. If she'd learned anything about the male these past weeks, it was that he loved knowledge of any kind. Hoarded it like he hoarded his books.

She needed to offer them something. She was supposed to be trying here, and sharing personal information helped build trust. At least that was what she'd been told.

"You already know I came from across the Edria Sea," she said, eyeing the mug before her she had yet to touch.

"Only a handful of ships have made it through the Wards," Cethin mused. "Something I'd love to discuss more with you, but not right now. Where across the Edria are you from?"

"Various places," she answered. "I moved around a lot."

"That's not surprising considering your gifts," Cethin said with a small, encouraging smile.

She didn't return it.

"Did you prefer one place over another?" he asked after a moment.

"The farther north, the better," she answered. "I spent some time in Pyry with the Shifters there for a while."

"And then?"

"And then I went somewhere else."

"Any other continents besides Pyry?" Razik asked, both of them entirely focused on her now.

"The main continent," she answered, watching a drop of condensation slide down the mug.

"Novum?"

She nodded. "No one calls it that though."

"Were you raised in the Fae Courts then?" Cethin asked.

She pursed her lips, fingering one of the dagger hilts at her thigh. "No."

His brows crashed together, but it was Razik who said, "Surely not the mortal lands? I thought magic wasn't accessible in those lands? Were you with the Shifters in Novum before going to Pyry?"

"No," she answered tightly.

"The Witches?" Razik pushed.

"No," she ground out, suddenly finding the room too stuffy. Too hot. Too enclosed. "Can we go? I'd like to see more of the town."

Her hood was still in place, shrouding her features, but she still felt like they could see her clear as day. Cethin was watching her too intently, and even Razik's mask of boredom had slipped at this topic.

"Kailia—" Cethin started, but she didn't let him finish.

"Please," she pushed, feeling beads of sweat at her nape.

"Of course," he said, sliding across the seat, his mug still half full.

She moved fast, pushing past him and making her way to the door. Shoving it open, she stumbled into the dark night, sucking in a deep breath. But the air stalled in her lungs at what was lingering on the streets. Not the people hiding in the shadows, but translucent beings hovering off the ground.

"Fuck," Razik muttered, already summoning his dragon fire when he came to a stop at her side.

She could feel Cethin at her back, taking everything in. Gold swords raised in unison. There weren't many of them though. Sweeping her gaze over them again, she counted ten as she summoned her bow and three arrows. Then she made the first move, releasing the arrows and taking out three. The remaining phantoms scattered, trying to surround them. Razik had pivoted, his dragon fire incinerating one to ashes that got too close.

Kailia released two more arrows at the one nearest her, its keening wail filling the night. That left five, and if she could—

Ashes fluttered around her, trying to take her with them. She was trying. Trying to move among them. To let them carry her like they had nearly her entire existence. If she could, then she'd be able to end this in moments. She could move faster. Be quicker. Find her targets before they could even see her.

Instead, she shuddered as she stayed put. Her essence almost flickering as her power tried and she tried.

And failed.

With a growl of frustration, she summoned more arrows, shoving them at Cethin before she turned and released another. A second later, another wail of despair joined the first until a chorus was filling the night as they took out the last of them.

Her chest was heaving when she turned to face the males. Not from the fight. No, that had been exhilarating in the best way. She'd needed that outlet, but not being able to access her full power was slowly draining something inside her. Something primal and necessary. A piece of her she needed to survive.

A fine layer of ash covered the males from the beings Razik had incinerated, neither of them bothering to brush it off. Instead, they both left her standing there while they moved, bending down to gather things on the ground.

Her arrowheads.

It wasn't necessary, but she couldn't exactly tell them that. Not when they believed she needed them to create more weapons.

Dropping them into her palms, she closed her fist, feeling the skin break and blood seep.

"Tenebrae?" Razik asked after a long moment.

Cethin nodded.

No one said anything while they walked, Razik leading the way, and Cethin at her side. Too lost to her thoughts, she hardly noticed the buildings or the mist or the flickering candles in windows. She could still feel eyes on her, but she didn't care.

She needed to figure out what was wrong with her power. None of it made any sense. She could summon weapons, create them from her gifts. It made no sense that *this* part of her power had suddenly stopped working.

But she was running out of time. If she didn't figure things out, all of this was for nothing.

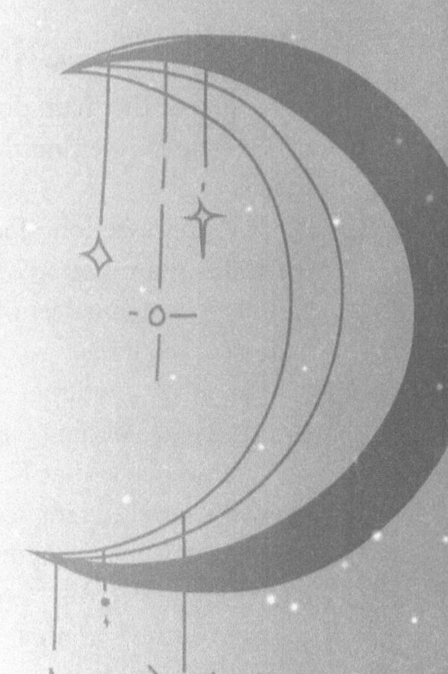

CHAPTER 26
CETHIN

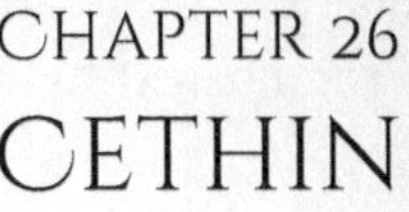

"While I'm sure I know the answer to this, I'm going to ask you anyway," Cethin said as they approached Tenebrae Halls. "Are you certain you don't want to simply Travel back to Aimonway? We can come back to Shadowfen tomorrow."

Kailia looked up at him, and he knew she wasn't being a smart ass when she asked, "Why would we do that?"

Trying to appeal to logic, since that was what it seemed like she responded to best, he said, "You don't like waking in unfamiliar places."

She appeared to consider that for a moment before she said, "I'd like to see Shadowfen in the sunlight. Here is fine."

Of course it was.

He held in his sigh as Razik pushed open the iron gates, the metal creaking and echoing in the now still night.

Tenebrae Halls was a large manor house that could have been classified as a miniature castle. Larger than any of the estate homes in Aimonway, it was sprawling. Stretching to both the left and right from the main doors, the towering west and east wings were manor homes in and of themselves. There was also a tower stretching to the sky in the middle. Their boots echoed on the stone floors when they entered the main doors. A set of curving stairs ran up each side of the grand foyer, marble statues and dark paintings adorning the space.

It didn't take long for someone to greet them, and the male led them down a maze of halls until they came to the west wing. Razik was given a smaller set of rooms next to the suite that he and Kailia were ushered into.

"Is there anything else I can bring you, your Majesties?" the escort asked, standing just inside the door.

Cethin glanced at Kailia, finding her taking in the space, but he knew she was listening to everything being said as well.

"Do you need anything, Kailia? Food? Wine? Hot water for a bath?"

She paused at that last one, looking back over her shoulder. "There are no pipes to carry the water here?"

He shook his head. "Tenebrae Halls is one of the oldest buildings in Avonleya. Some say it's as old as the kingdom itself. They haven't wanted to alter the original structure."

"I do not need anything," she replied, turning back to inspecting the room, no doubt counting exits and planning escape routes.

"Warm water to wash up in the basin if it's not too much trouble," Cethin answered, turning back to the male. He held out a few coin as well, which the male swiped up with a small bow of his head before leaving them alone.

"Is this where I would have lived if I'd truly been from here?" Kailia asked, draping her cloak over the back of a winged armchair.

"Perhaps," Cethin said, removing his own cloak. Ashes from the fight fluttered to the ground. "With your skill set, more than likely."

"What does that mean?"

She'd drifted to a window, pulling back the curtain to peer out into the darkness. There wasn't much by way of moonlight tonight, and certainly not in Shadowfen. The clouds in the sky were as dense as the fog along the ground. Even so, a small stream of moonlight trickled in, illuminating her warm features. Combined with the flickering of the sconces, she looked like an ethereal huntress with her bow still looped across her chest.

"You've been quiet since the fight," he ventured, avoiding her question and taking a seat in the armchair to unbuckle his boots. More white ashes drifted off him. The sight of them made him realize he definitely should have requested bathing water, and he lifted a hand, a swirl of darkness carrying his request to the staff asking for more water and some wine.

Kailia let the curtains fall closed, drifting to another window and pulling back the drapes.

"Something you want to talk about?" Cethin tried again.

"No," she answered without looking at him.

"It might help."

That had her turning, her brow pinched in a way that told him she was truly confused. "How would talking help?"

"Sometimes just saying things out loud helps ease the burden of carrying them," he replied, moving his boots to the side of the armchair before settling back to watch her.

She moved closer with that predatory grace she possessed before lowering into the armchair opposite him. "What would you like to talk about?"

Cethin shrugged. "Whatever you'd like. It doesn't have to be anything important. It can be casual conversation if you prefer."

"That seems pointless."

He huffed a laugh. "I'm sure it does, tiny fiend, but casual conversation can be as revealing as watching from the smoke and ashes. Speaking of which…"

He trailed off with a knowing look, wondering if she'd pick up on what he was insinuating.

"This doesn't seem like casual conversation," she said with a small frown, apparently understanding just fine. "This feels like a pointed and direct one."

"Fair enough," he conceded. "Tell me your favorite color."

Her brows flew up to her hairline. "What?"

"Casual conversation, wife," he reminded her.

"Having a favorite color also seems pointless."

"So I can have white and pink and yellow garments procured for you, and you'd be fine with that?"

Her features twisted into something that could only be described as abject distaste. "You can, but I will not wear them."

"Then you have color preferences," he said with a smirk.

She studied him, and by the Fates, he wished he knew what she was thinking. Because he hadn't been speaking like a fool when he'd said casual conversation can be as revealing as watching. You could only learn so much by observing from afar. More than that, he was incredibly adept at reading people.

Aside from her.

"I suppose I prefer the darker colors that Avonleya favors," she finally said.

"That seems beneficial for the queen."

"Agreed."

"Do you prefer cakes or pies?" he asked.

A laugh escaped her. An honest and genuine bark of amusement.

"That is an absurd question," she said, fighting a smile.

"But an important one, nonetheless," he countered.

She'd propped her head in her hand, black strands framing her face. "Sweets were an unnecessary indulgence growing up."

Cethin had to work to keep his shock from showing at her willingly divulging something of her past. But the shock was quickly replaced with an excitement at having chipped away at her defensive walls a little.

Treading carefully, he asked, "Because your family did not have the funds for such things?"

"I was...raised with others. In a communal colony, I guess one could call it," she answered, watching him as carefully as he was watching her.

He paused, praying to the Fates this wasn't about to shut her down. "Like an orphanage?"

Her answering smile was sharp and joyless. "I think an orphanage would have been paradise in comparison. We weren't left wanting by any means. We had food and beds and clothing, but..."

She trailed off with a shrug. "I suppose one can never really say which is better without having lived both experiences."

Cethin nodded, contemplating the best way to ask another sensitive question when they were interrupted by a knock.

Cursing internally, he answered the door, finding the male staff member and a few others with large buckets of steaming water. Another held a bottle of wine and two glasses, along with a plate of cheese, crackers, and nuts. After they'd hauled everything in and left, each with a handful of coin for their trouble, he turned back to Kailia, where she was still sitting in the armchair, head propped in her hand and clearly lost to memories or thoughts or both.

"As much as I'm enjoying our conversation, I will feel terrible if I have to summon someone with Anala's gifts to reheat our water," he said, her amber gaze sliding to him.

"I'm sure they wouldn't object considering you are their king," she replied.

"King or not, it would still be an avoidable inconvenience for everyone," he answered while pulling the cork from the wine bottle. He poured two glasses as he asked, "Would you like to bathe first?"

"That's not necessary," she answered quickly.

"I didn't say it was," he answered, crossing the room and extending a glass to her. "But if you would enjoy a hot bath after the events of the day and evening, I'm going to insist you indulge a little, tiny fiend."

She reached for the glass, her fingers brushing along his. She paused, as if surprised she'd done such a thing, and he fought a shiver. Because somehow, all it took for him to find himself aroused and wanting was a godsdamn brush of her fingers.

Taking the glass, he heard her murmur to herself, "Start small." Then she stood so abruptly, he didn't have time to take steps back to give her the space he normally did. She barely came to his shoulders, and she tipped her head back to peer up at him, her teeth sinking into her lower lip as she clearly warred with herself to stay this close to him.

Moving slowly, he let a wisp of his darkness brush along her lips before he ran his thumb along her lower one, pulling it from her teeth. He heard the quiet, gasped inhale, and he could feel her heart racing. For the briefest of moments, he could swear her mask slipped. He thought she was going to ask for more, but then she cleared her throat, stepping to the side and out of reach.

"Are you sure you don't mind me bathing first?" she asked, backing towards the bathing chamber.

"I insist," he answered with a tight smile before taking a drink of his wine.

"Thank you," she said softly before turning. He heard the bathing room door shut, and he sank into the armchair with an audible groan.

Taking another healthy drink of wine, he tipped his head back and closed his eyes, reminding himself this was progress. She'd shared her arrows with him tonight. That had to account for something. Fuck, that might even mean more to her than letting him touch her.

—⟩⟩·☽·⟨⟨—

"Blood of death."

He jolted awake at the hissing voice, his power bursting forth in a bid to protect him. Stumbling to his feet, the wineglass in his fingers slipped to the ground, shattering. He'd clearly fallen asleep, aided by the wine. Foolish to drink when he knew his physical body was being pushed to the point of exhaustion. It couldn't have been more than fifteen minutes since Kailia had gone to the bathing room.

Unless she'd returned to find him sleeping and had let him be.

Something to figure out later because at the moment he was alone with one of the phantoms, and this time, he didn't have an arrow to use or a stolen arrowhead.

"Who sent you?" Cethin asked.

"You shall see when you meet him, blood of the traitorous

ones," the creature purred in that eerie way of theirs. The same answer the last one had given him months ago in the castle.

"What do you want?" Cethin attempted, trying to remember all the questions he'd posed before.

The phantom's bloodless lips pulled up in a poisonous smile, its unseeing eyes seeming to glow brighter when it answered simply, "You."

"Why?" Cethin demanded, sidestepping as the being drifted closer.

"Your mother. Your uncle. Your grandparents. Any blood of those who betrayed him," the creature replied.

"That didn't answer the question," Cethin gritted out, putting a sofa between them.

"But it did," the phantom hissed.

Cethin couldn't decide if the things were sentient or not. Their answers were uniform, all of them responding the same as though they shared a collective mind. But they could also hold a conversation, albeit a stilted and frustrating one.

Kind of like conversing with Kailia.

"How did you get here?" Cethin asked, edging closer to the bedchamber to see if Kailia was sleeping. He could send a message to Razik, but the movement might cause the thing to attack. It had long been proven that his own magic was defenseless against them. No, his options were the wife who begrudgingly tolerated him or the dragon who despised him. A part of him debated if taking his chances with the phantom was perhaps the best option after all.

"I go where I am summoned. Where the traitors dwell," the creature answered, pulling a gold dagger from a swirl of white mist.

"Right, right," Cethin grumbled, having heard that answer before. "But how did you get here? To this realm?"

The phantom's head tipped too far to the side, its ear nearly touching its shoulder. If it had eyes, Cethin was certain it'd be studying him.

"The cursed king sent a call into the voids," the phantom recited. "Foolish when anything can answer." Then it straightened, head snapping to the side. "You're too late this time."

Distracted, Cethin turned to see who the phantom was speaking to, only to turn directly into the path of an arrow. The thing embedded in his chest, below his collarbone on the left side, and curses flew from his lips as another whizzed past him.

"Get down!" Kailia cried, and by the Fates, at what point had it become normal that he couldn't godsdamn protect himself?

But he dropped to his knee a second before a gold dagger flew through the air right where he'd been standing. The blade hit the wood mantel above the fireplace, sinking in deep, while that keening wail filled the room.

The door to the space burst open, and Kailia let two more arrows fly.

"Fucking Fates!" Razik barked, lurching to the side to avoid a fate similar to Cethin's current predicament.

Or to avoid the phantom that drifted into the room behind him.

"Two?" Cethin growled, grabbing the arrow shaft and yanking it from his shoulder.

"Glad to see those basic arithmetic lessons stuck," Razik growled, summoning black flames. It was just precautionary though. Kailia had already taken care of the being, another wail echoing the first.

"Make sure there aren't more of them," he told the male. Razik nodded, muttering under his breath as he left the room, and Cethin turned back to Kailia.

A very naked Kailia.

Warm brown skin on full display. Wet midnight hair hanging over her shoulders and covering her breasts. Droplets of water running down her flesh, clearly having come straight from the bath. Her bow still in hand with another arrow nocked and ready.

Just...

Fuck me, was all he could think as he swiped a hand down his face. Razik had seen her. The phantoms had seen her. Those things were dead, but Razik—

A sound rumbled in his chest as he sent his darkness to her, wrapping it around her and hiding...everything.

Kailia slowly lifted her arm, studying his magic clinging to her.

Ashes fluttered as she sent her bow to what he assumed was a pocket realm, but by Arius. Feeling her magic alongside his only heightened the possessive and primal turmoil in his soul right now. Between their conversation in his study the night prior, the talk of touching in the town square, and now this? He needed her to give somewhere. He'd settle for being able to press his lips to her cheek at this point.

She was clearly being affected too. He could see her chest moving a little faster, and he knew that wasn't adrenaline from the second fight of the night. Not with the way her lips were slightly parted and the way she was looking at his magic.

The door opening again is what finally broke whatever spell they were under, and Cethin whirled around to find Razik back. Cethin was across the room in a few long strides, blocking Kailia from view.

"Relax, Sutara," Razik drawled, dropping into the same armchair Cethin had been sitting in. "I already saw, and Lia is well aware I'm not interested."

"You've discussed it?" Cethin demanded. Who had instigated that conversation? Was *she* interested?

"She asks a lot of questions," he said with a shrug, toeing at the broken shards of glass on the floor.

That had a muscle ticking in Cethin's jaw as he ground his molars. Kailia rarely asked him questions. He had to coax any information from her.

Ignoring the comment, he turned to face Kailia. Before he could say anything though, she was stepping closer, eliminating space between them. She reached up, fingers hovering over the arrow wound. Her head tilted to the side, hair shifting, and he found himself internally cursing Razik's presence yet again. If he weren't here, he wouldn't let his power hide anything.

"You didn't die," she murmured. Then her gaze flicked to his hand. "And you have my arrow."

"Gods forbid this all becomes about an arrow again," he retorted, rolling his eyes and extending the thing to her.

She snatched it from his hand, bringing the point close to her face as she studied it intensely. Confused, Cethin glanced over his shoulder at Razik, but the male just shrugged, taking a drink directly from the wine bottle he'd found next to the chair.

"Something wrong with your arrow?" he finally asked, returning his attention to his wife.

"Yes. You didn't die," she answered.

He heard Razik's snort of amusement, but he ignored the male as he usually did.

"Guess you'll have to try harder next time," he said, and her gaze snapped to his.

"If I were trying, you'd be dead," she retorted.

"These 'accidental' stabbings are becoming a little too coincidental, tiny fiend," he mused, watching her amber eyes swirl faster in her irritation.

"It is hardly my fault you keep getting in the way of my blades," she admonished. "Especially not when I was protecting you. Again."

He hummed in response. Something that only made her bristle more.

"Perhaps you should put some clothes on. Then we can discuss what to do from here," he suggested.

"I thought we were staying until morning?"

He blinked at her incredulously. "That was before I was impaled with an arrow. I need to see Niara."

"You do. Razik and I can stay," she argued.

"No," he ground out.

"It'd probably be better if you go anyway," she continued thoughtfully. "Those things only show up when you're in the company."

"That's not—" But he stopped speaking as he thought about her words. That couldn't be true. Could it? Yes, they always focused on him in the fights, but were they only showing up where when he was present?

Then again, when he'd asked that phantom what it wanted, the answer had been crystal clear.

You.

Kailia said nothing else before she turned and went into the bedchamber, and Cethin made his way back to the armchairs, taking the one across from Razik.

"Is she right?" Cethin asked idly. Not really speaking to Razik, just speaking out loud.

"The only time you weren't there from the beginning was the first time we saw them," Razik replied, rubbing at his jaw. "But as soon as you showed up, you were all they cared about. It's been that way ever since."

"But all the Fae deaths these last decades," Cethin argued, trying to make the connection.

"Maybe…" Razik released a heavy sigh before he said, "Maybe they're not related at all."

And Cethin couldn't stomach the thought of that. If that were true, then they were dealing with two separate threats. He'd garnered this arrangement with Kailia under the belief that these beings were the threat to the Fae. Having her weapons to fight against them was to protect the Fae and his people. If it were true they were fighting two separate enemies, it would appear as if he forced her to his side simply to protect him.

"Do you really need Niara for that?" Razik asked, jerking his chin at the wound.

Blood had soaked into the fabric around it, and he was still filthy from the first fight. Maybe he could take a bath and clean it well…

"Tell her we'll come back in a few days," Razik suggested when Cethin didn't answer.

"Zayan had a fit when I rescheduled these two days. I can't imagine if I blow off the next several," Cethin muttered.

"That's odd," Razik said.

Cethin glanced at the male. "What is?"

"Thought you were the king."

Cethin sent him a bland look. "If you understood anything about responsibility, you'd understand why my duty has to be put first."

Razik's answering smile was razor sharp. "I understand responsibility just fine. I'm the one who spends my days with your wife while you're fulfilling your so-called duties."

"Only because you wormed your way into the position using your relationship with Tybalt," Cethin bit back.

Razik shrugged a shoulder in that apathetic way of his. "Better than forcing a marriage using the power of my title."

"Fuck off, Greybane," Cethin snapped, more of his darkness appearing and drifting across the floor like the fog outside.

Razik smirked, black flames appearing at his feet.

"My jilted lovers theory stands," Kailia announced, garnering both of their attention.

She wore a robe, the sash cinched tight at her waist, and her wet hair was braided over her shoulder. Cethin stood, crossing the room to her.

Guilt churned in his gut, but he refused to leave her here alone with Razik. The phantoms were one thing. The other creatures that prowled around Shadowfen were something else completely. More than that, this wound wasn't even beginning to heal. He could still feel a steady flow of blood, which meant he definitely needed Niara. And sleep apparently.

"I'm sorry, tiny fiend," he said with a sigh. "We need to go back to Aimonway."

The disappointment was evident, her features falling and lips pursing. But she nodded, saying simply, "Fine."

They quickly paid an extra fee to Tenebrae for the mess and inconvenience before Traveling back to the castle. Razik immediately went his own way once Kailia was settled in their rooms, and Cethin found Niara. He'd been right. The wound needed extra care, much like when he'd been stabbed by Kailia's dagger. He'd been feeling groggy, and his vision had even blurred some. He'd assumed that was his body demanding rest, but now he wondered if it had more to do with her weapons. The arrowhead was smaller than the dagger, and that would explain why it'd taken longer to affect him.

When he finally pushed through the doors to their rooms an hour later, he wasn't surprised to find the sitting room empty. He was surprised to find her still awake though, sitting against the headboard with that book propped against her knees.

She looked up, gaze lingering on his bare torso before sliding to the wound and finally his face.

"Still not dead," he said with a wink.

"Those are different pants," she replied.

He huffed a laugh. "Niara insisted I bathe before she treated the wound. Said it'd be pointless otherwise."

Kailia nodded, eyeing him warily. "And now you will disappear to wherever it is you go in the nights?"

"Are you missing me, wife?" he asked wryly as he removed his shoes.

When he turned back, she was watching him, hands smoothing over the furs on the bed. "I...enjoyed the time in Shadowfen. The fighting, yes, but also the... I enjoyed the time. Would you have slept there?"

His brow furrowed. "What do you mean?"

"You never sleep," she said in exasperation. "Would you have slept if we'd stayed there tonight?"

Perplexed by where this conversation was going, he said carefully, "I sleep, Kailia. Not often, but I do. I need to sleep, actually, and I was planning to do so in another room."

She nodded again, hands still moving over the furs.

"Unless you want me to sleep here?" he ventured, bracing himself for whatever innocent snark was about to come from her.

But instead, she nodded to herself before she said, "I think sleeping in the same bed would be a small start."

He blinked in surprise. "Kailia... Are you sure? People move around when they sleep."

"I know that."

"Okay, and if you wake up pressed against me or my arm is around you, am I going to be stabbed?"

"Possibly," she affirmed.

He stared at her for another long moment before he silently made his way to the bed. Pulling back the covers, he blew out the candles on the bedside table before he slipped between the sheets, relaxing into the pillow. Truth be told, he had rarely slept here even before Kailia had become a part of this. He'd actually forgotten how comfortable this bed was.

His eyelids were already heavy, and he felt her shift next to him.

"Relax, Kailia," he said into the dark room. "I can feel your heart racing."

"You cannot," she scoffed, but her tone was breathy. Anxious.

Cethin reached for one of the extra pillows, placing it between them like a barrier. He couldn't promise it would keep them from finding one another in their sleep. If anything, their magic was going to seek each other out. But the point wasn't to prevent anything, only to give her a semblance of comfort.

This was a small start, and as he finally gave in to the sleep that called to him, all he could think was that maybe the stabbing would be worth it.

KAILIA

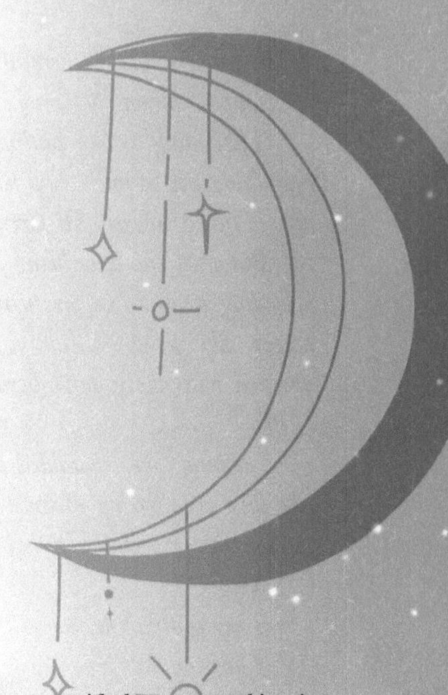

S napping up straight, she turned to the right to see if there was a king in the bed beside her.

Instead, she found a sanded stone wall.

Her gaze falling to her lap, she smoothed her hand over the scratchy wool blanket. The air was musty and humid. She was in a small bed scarcely large enough for a grown male.

In a panic, she tugged at her sleeve, a breath of relief escaping her when she saw the Mark, stark against her skin.

Dream.

Dream, dream, dream.

She was dreaming.

But she knew how this dream went.

Someone was going to come through that door soon. It didn't matter who. They were all nightmares. Still, it had been awhile since she'd found herself here. She could count on one hand how many times her dreams had brought her to this place since she'd found herself with the title of wife and queen.

Throwing the blanket back, she swung her legs over the side of the bed. Her bare feet touched the cool floor, her long black dress pooling around her ankles. She summoned her bow, looping it across her chest, and because she had to know if *her power was broken here too, she took a deep breath, closed her eyes, and tried to disappear among her smoke and ashes.*

They sang to her, pulling her into their embrace. Weightless. Nothing and everything all at once. She felt the tears burning at the back of her eyes. She'd missed this—missed this piece of herself—so very much.

But then she was being jostled and jerked, pulled in a direction she wasn't intending to go. The joy turned to panic as she once again lost control of her power. She fought, straining to go where she wanted, until finally she was dumped onto the ground beside the stream that ran through the middle of the Cliffs.

Gasping, she scrambled to her feet. It was dangerous to be out in the open like this, even in her dreams. They'd find her. They'd find her and drag her to those rooms, especially if they knew she'd lost control of her power.

No.

They couldn't know.

They couldn't—

She went still when she spotted him, his back to her and hands in his pockets. His silver hair was loose, reaching his shoulders, and his posture was almost relaxed. Like the rare times he actually spent some of the night with her. Black pants. Black tunic.

It made sense that he was here. They'd been spending more time together. Ever since that day in Shadowfen, he even slept in the same bed as her. Sometimes. Not every night. Okay, twice. She was still as confused about that development as she was when she'd asked him to come sleep beside her.

But none of that mattered right now. She was being foolish to let herself get distracted here. They would find her, and then they'd both be fucked. She really hoped this was one of the dreams where he interacted with her. Sometimes he didn't. Sometimes he seemed to be observing, and other times he spoke to her. She wasn't one to question dreams and what they were trying to show her, but this time, out here, she really needed it to be the latter.

"We need to go," she said, her voice thankfully firm and unwavering.

He turned at the sound, silver eyes piercing as they took her in, but he said nothing.

"Cethin? We can't stay here," she insisted, looking around nervously.

"Where does this stream lead?" he asked instead.

She glanced at the water. She knew exactly where it led. Out to the beach and beyond.

She also knew what it was used for.

"Not now," she hissed, feeling sweat beading at her nape. Tugging at her sleeve again, she saw the Mark, but it did nothing to reassure her now.

"Tell me of that," Cethin said, the words dark and commanding.

She looked back up to see his gaze on her arm too, a fury dancing in his eyes that she didn't understand.

"There really isn't time," she said, nerves and adrenaline making her heart pound at an erratic rhythm.

Cethin looked around. "There's no one here, Kailia."

"They're here," she said, each word a hurried breath of syllables. "They're coming."

"Maybe I want to see."

"No," she said brusquely, and without thinking, her hand snapped out, latching on to his and tugging. "Please, Cethin."

His eyes dropped, transfixed on the place where their hands met, and something again passed over his features she couldn't comprehend.

Slowly, his eyes lifted to hers. He shifted their palms, interlocking their fingers, as he said, "Lead the way. Show me."

They couldn't risk leaving. Not right now. They'd wasted too much time here.

So they slipped into a stairwell, climbing flights of stairs as quickly as they could. She was marked here. They wouldn't be able to hide for long, but there was one place she'd found where it took them longer to track her down. At least in her dreams it did.

Her ashes fluttered along the door, the only way she'd figured out how to get in. It swung open, and she slipped inside, pulling Cethin in with her and quickly shutting the door behind him. Dropping his hand, she leaned against it, her bow digging into her back. Her eyes fell closed as she listened. As she sent her ashes beneath the door to search. To feel for them coming.

"Kailia?"

Her eyes snapped open, finding his once again pinned on her.

It was dark in here. She could barely make him out, but she knew he stepped closer. So close, that if she moved an inch, they'd brush against each other.

"What do you fear here?" Cethin asked, his voice low and rough.

Everything.

Her eyes dropped to the ground. The answer was on the tip of her tongue, waiting to fall from her lips. But that would be admitting yet another weakness to the male. Even in her dreams, she couldn't do that.

But in her dreams, she was stronger. Able to overcome the weaknesses easier. She'd fought her demons here. Spilled blood in vengeance, so she knew exactly how to do it outside of the dream planes.

What if…

She slowly dragged her eyes from his boots up his tall frame to his face. Sharp features mixed with shadows, whether from the dark room or his own power, she didn't know. But they made him more foreboding. The male she knew he truly was.

But here, she was in control. Here…

Here, she could take and test. She could start small here, in a place that was her own.

She pushed off the door, bringing her shaking hand up and placing her fingertips on his chest. He went preternaturally still in that way only the immortals could.

Until he brought his own hand up, wisps of his dark power dancing along her fingers before he placed his hand atop hers and pressed her palm flat along his tunic.

Atop his heart, beating at the same frenetic rhythm hers was.

She paused there, letting herself get used to just…feeling. Of touching someone else without feeling the need to recoil. Of letting the coolness of his magic soothe the burn of physical contact.

Fingers still trembling, she tentatively slid her palm up. Across his collarbone, over a shoulder, pausing at his neck. Her thumb swiped, and she felt his throat bob when he swallowed. The only part of him that moved.

If anyone knew…

But no one knew what happened in dreams. Secrets stayed locked here.

Her eyes were fixed on his lips, and he clearly noticed because his tongue slid across the bottom one. Pushing onto her tiptoes, she slid her hand up farther, cupping his jaw so she could swipe her thumb along the same path his tongue had traveled.

She felt his whole body shudder beneath her hand.

Marveled at the feel of it.

She knew touch was as controlling as their power could be. Her power with touch had been from withholding it. Choosing not to give that to anyone. But this...

This was a different kind of power.

His breaths were uneven against the pad of her thumb where it still hovered along his lip.

"Can I tell you a secret?" she whispered, the words sounding harsh in the quiet of the room.

"I would sit at your feet for days to hear them all, wife. Then I'd take them all to the grave with me, guarding them even in the After," he answered, and gods. Something deep in her belly clenched at the words.

"You're right," she said simply, thumbing his bottom lip once more, delighting in the way his breath hitched at the motion. "My experience with fucking is limited. I have experience, but only once. It was—" She paused, rolling her lips at the memory. "But that was just the act of fucking as I understand it. It wasn't..." Her thumb swiped again.

His eyes were darting between hers, and she could see the desperate bid to try to understand what she was telling him.

"There were no gentle touches," she said in a hushed rush. "No slow explorations. No letting me...do this," she continued, brushing her thumb across his lip again. "There was no kiss—"

She went rigid, yanking her hand back and spinning to the door. Her ashes had felt them, warning her. Lifting her bow over her head, an arrow appeared in her other hand.

A reminder that while secrets stayed locked in her dreams, so did her nightmares.

But he *was the nightmare when she awoke. She knew the truth, even if he kept it hidden from everyone else.*

-)) ⊙ ((-

She lurched up, turning to the right. Again, there was no king in the bed, but she wasn't in the Cliffs either. Shoving back the blankets, she checked her forearm, finding it bare.

Back in the castle.

Back in Avonleya.

She flopped down on the bed, pushing stray hair from her face.

Of course he wasn't here. It'd been over a week since they'd visited Shadowfen. He'd slept beside her twice. The first night, he'd slept so deeply, she'd woken before him the next morning. The pillow was still between them, but he'd rolled into it, and her arm was stretched across it, her fingertips barely brushing his forearm.

Lying there, listening to his steady breathing, it would have been so easy to slip from the bed and explore if it weren't for her power not working right. Even in her dreams, it had still taken control. Taking her somewhere she hadn't intended to go.

The second night he'd slept in the bed with her, he'd been gone when she'd woken, so she had no idea if they'd woken in the same position or another.

Glancing at the small clock on the mantel across the room, she figured she'd better get up. Razik became grumpier than usual if they stayed in the rooms too long. She didn't mind leaving, so she let the male escort her around the castle and Aimonway. It was good for her to get to know the halls and local markets, but even Razik didn't take her from the city, despite his obvious contempt for Cethin. Anything involving leaving Aimonway seemed to take at least a day's worth of planning, if not a week.

It'd become routine to wander through all the rooms on their floor, making sure no one else was here. Then she made her way to the main bathing chamber, leaving the door open so she could hear if anyone entered.

She pulled her nightdress off, rinsed her mouth, and piled her hair atop her head before climbing into the filling tub of hot water. According to Cethin, those with fire magic heated the tanks of water that were pumped throughout the castle. In the mortal king-doms across the sea, only the wealthy had such a luxury, and their tanks weren't heated by magic since magic couldn't be found in the mortal lands. But in Avonleya, at least in Aimonway, it seemed fairly standard. It was why she'd been surprised to learn Tenebrae Halls didn't have the ability.

Choosing from the array of oils and salts along the ledge, she dumped something in that smelled faintly like juniper berries and lavender before tipping her head back. Her hand glided through the water, playing with the small bubbles that took over the surface, while the other hand toyed with the crystal that still hung around her neck. It had started out as a symbol of her control against Cethin, something to irritate him, but it had since become a comfort in a way. Like the Mark on her arm in her dreams, she supposed.

She'd been here for weeks now. The Union Celebration was approaching quickly, and she was no closer to figuring out the mess with her power. There was so much of it *not* working. Yes, not being able to move through her smoke and ashes was an issue. A big fucking problem.

But also…

Cethin had been stabbed with her dagger and pierced with her arrow and had survived both encounters. No one else had ever survived when struck with those weapons. Her other daggers, sure. The arrows not woven with her magic, yes. But Cethin had survived both of her weapons that were created from her magic.

How?

And why couldn't she move through her smoke and ashes?

For the briefest of moments in that dream, she'd felt like herself again. Whole. Complete despite her physical body being nothing but ashes. It was something that had always been hers. The one freedom no one could take from her, and now it was eluding her. As if she'd somehow failed her magic, and now it was punishing her for it. It was messing with her on every level. She was getting too distracted. She was missing things that should be obvious, feeling too out of sorts. As if every step was on uneven ground and she couldn't find her footing.

They'd told her. Warned her that something like this could happen. They'd told her it was why they pushed her to have absolute control over her magic. Maybe they'd been right all along.

Maybe all that agony and torture had been necessary. But others learned to control their magic without such extreme measures. Then again, there weren't many like her.

They'd warned her about that too.

How she'd be hunted for her abilities.

So she'd vowed to become the hunter.

She had people to protect just as much as Cethin did. Despite what he thought, she did understand the responsibility of protecting people. She knew he thought her selfish and cold for withholding her weapons, but she wondered if he'd ever considered why. Or did he truly think that was who she was? That couldn't be true, or he wouldn't have made her his queen. Then again, he would clearly do whatever it took to get what he wanted.

She sank deeper into the tub, water lapping at her chin as her dream flitted through her mind. The feel of his heartbeat beneath her palm. The stubble along his jaw. His breath on the pad of her thumb. She'd marveled at it, and it had all made her so…curious. It almost made her understand the allure of physical contact. But she'd been the one doing the touching, not the other way around.

Her eyes had fallen closed as the relaxing scents wafted around her. If it weren't for the ache in her stomach, she'd sit in here for hours. But she'd become accustomed to regular meals since coming here. Hunger used to be something she could easily ignore, but not when eating properly replaced the habit of eating once every other day.

The sound of the door and heavy footsteps had her opening her eyes and staring at the doorway. Razik usually called out for her, only venturing back to the bedchamber if she didn't answer, but these footfalls were getting nearer. Sure enough, Cethin came through the door, and it took him far longer than it should have for him to notice her in the tub. His head was down, hand running through his hair before he pulled his tunic over his head.

When he turned to presumably start the water for a bath, he came to an abrupt halt at seeing her in the tub. He blinked several times, eyes scanning the receding bubbles before he finally managed to drag his gaze to her face. He looked…tired. Exhausted.

Her head canted to the side a little as she said, "You didn't sleep."

He swallowed thickly, and she remembered the feel of that action beneath her fingers. Would it feel different outside her dreams?

"Sleep is often a luxury," he replied, his voice husky and gruff.

"You're the king," she said simply.

"I don't know why everyone seems to think I need reminding of that lately," he grumbled petulantly, turning to a sink to rinse his mouth and clean his teeth.

When he did so, she saw the dried blood on his arm, and her eyes narrowed. "Did someone else stab you?"

"What?" he asked, still focused on his tasks. She could swear there was a slight tremor in his hand. But then he seemed to realize what she was referring to, rubbing at the dried smear of red. His sigh was heavy. "No, Kailia. That is something reserved just for you."

For whatever reason, the words made her feel something warm in her chest. She may not be adept at social interactions, but even she knew she didn't want to examine the reason for that feeling too closely.

He turned off the sink faucet, using a hand towel to wipe his mouth as he turned back to her. Leaning against the sink counter and bracing his hands behind him, he said, "I apologize for bursting in on you. I didn't think you'd still be here at this time."

"I believe I've been in the bath longer than I thought," she replied. "I think I lost track of time."

He hummed, still watching her.

"Where do you go?" she asked, swiping her fingers through the water. "When the rest of the kingdom sleeps," she clarified.

"To my study," he answered.

"Not every night," she countered.

His brows arched, and his lips tilted up in that cocky grin. Or they tried to. He was clearly too exhausted to muster much. "Have you gone looking for me, tiny fiend?"

"At times," she replied. "Only once have I found you there."

"How often?"

She shrugged, the water rippling with the movement. "Enough to know that's not where you go most nights."

"And then?"

"Then what?" she asked in confusion.

"When you don't find me, do you simply come back to bed and sleep?"

She shifted, maneuvering so she could rest her arms on the edge of the tub and face him more. His eyes never left her, and she rested her chin atop her arms when she said, "The first few times, I searched some, but when it became clear you did not wish to be found, yes. I returned to these rooms."

Never mind the fact that if she could use her magic, that wouldn't have been the case. She would have flitted through the castle until she'd found wherever he hid in the nights.

Cethin nodded, and even though he was looking at her, she could swear he wasn't looking *at* her. As if he were seeing through her, too lost in his thoughts. Despite his obvious exhaustion, there was a buzz of energy around him. A charge of restlessness and something more she didn't know how to place. His fingers flexed where they gripped the counter, and he kept pushing his other hand through his tangled hair. Hair that looked like he'd been doing that same action all night. He'd lost his shoes somewhere else, his bare feet crossed at the ankles.

"You should simply move your rooms to wherever you disappear to," she said. "Seems as though it would be more convenient."

Those words pulled him from whatever trance he was in, but instead of the arrogant retort she'd come to expect, he said, "I've thought about it, but it would raise too many questions. It wouldn't matter anyway. The ghosts of our past haunt us no matter where we are."

She lifted her head because there was a tortured agony she recognized in his tone. Never once in all of this had she expected the Avonleyan King to be a mirror of her own tortured soul, but that was what this was. It was the first time she'd ever felt like he was showing her something real.

And she didn't know what to do with that in the slightest. It made things entirely too complicated.

That charged energy in the room seemed to intensify, and she watched as Cethin pushed off the sink, padding forward as though unbidden. He stopped directly beside the tub, staring down at her with a look she so desperately wanted to understand. No one had ever looked at her like that before, and how was she supposed to build defenses against something she couldn't understand?

She'd had to tip her head back to hold his stare, and she felt a few strands of hair slip free with the new angle, fluttering against her cheek. She saw one of his hands flex in her periphery, her body tensing at the movement. Of course he noticed.

His lips thinned, and he rubbed his fingertips together before he slowly lowered to a crouch before her. "Kailia…" He trailed off, a hand raking through his hair yet again. "Can I touch you? Just your arm," he added quickly.

"Why?" she asked in genuine curiosity.

"Because… I just—" Silver eyes searched hers, and they weren't as bright as normal. As if his dark magic was hiding him as much as he hid away in the night. "I can't help but wonder if you'd keep the ghosts away in the same way you keep the spirit creatures at bay."

"Are you asking me to protect you yet again, king?"

"Desperately, wife."

She felt his magic brush along her arm before his hand followed. He turned her arm over, as if looking for something, before gently returning it to its original position and cupping her elbow. His thumb swiped along her skin in small circles, over and over. His shoulders sagged, a low sound rumbling from his chest and his thumb never ceasing its movement. True to his word, his hand never moved, only touching her arm.

When she shifted to free her other arm, his thumb stilled. His lips parted to say something, but he quickly swallowed the words when he saw her reaching for him. He stayed so still, as still as he had in her dream. Her fingertips slid along his jaw, the stubble as scratchy and coarse as it had been then too. So slowly, she pressed her palm to his cheek, and his eyes fell closed as he leaned into the touch, nuzzling against her hand. He shifted from a crouch to his knees, his thumb resuming the circles along her flesh, while his other hand curled over the lip of the tub.

What an odd feeling to have a king on his knees before her.

Because while she avoided physical touch, he clearly craved it. Just another thing working against her in all of this.

Apparently touch was his weakness too.

CHAPTER 28

RAZIK

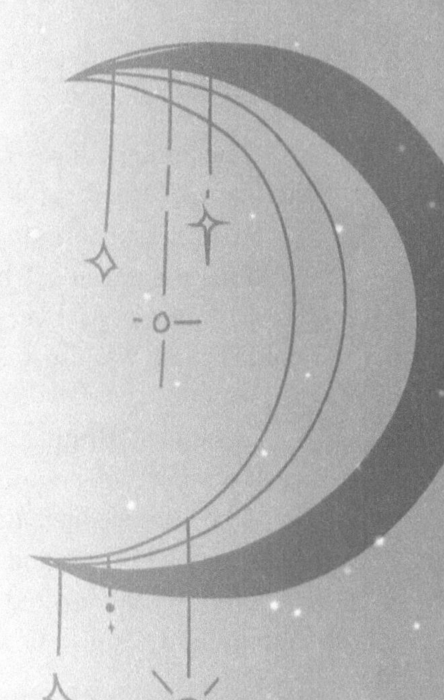

"Fucking Fates, Greybane. You need a fuck or a fight. Or both," Bram grumbled, setting his chair upright after dodging a burst of black flames. "Now my breakfast is burnt, you prick."

Wren was silent beside Razik, but she stood, grabbing another plate and beginning to pile food on it. Once finished, she passed it down to Bram before sitting once more and pointedly ignoring him.

Great.

He cared about the feelings of exactly two people, and one of them was now pissed at him.

But Bram knew exactly what he was doing when he ran his mouth yet again about Wren. The male spent the rest of breakfast sulking, while the Cadre discussed the training plans for the day. Until his uncle strode in, features grim.

Everyone fell silent, straightening, and their food forgotten.

"More Fae were found dead this morning. Six of them," Tybalt said. "Jarek, Fallon, and Draven, head to the docks and see what you can find out."

"They were found here? In Aimonway?" Razik demanded.

Tybalt's gaze slid to him. "That would be why I'm sending them there."

"The attacks have never been on this side of the Nightmist Mountains," Razik replied.

"Are you truly arguing with me about this right now?"

"I'm not arguing," he retorted, but he kept his comments to himself after that. Everyone thought he was the broody ass, but when Tybalt was in a sour mood, even he steered clear of the dragon.

Turning to Bram and Ariadne, the Commander said, "There are also reports of creatures stirring southwest of Shira Forest."

"The ones we have no defenses against?" Ariadne asked, already checking the buckles and weapons on her leathers.

"No," Tybalt gritted out. "If reports are accurate, we'll need Cethin, but I want to be sure before we bring it to him."

Shit.

If they needed Cethin, then the reports involved the creatures of old. It would be the first time they'd have to deal with them without his parents.

Just…fuck.

The Cadre filed out, and he met his uncle's gaze again. "Do you need me to do anything?"

"Just keep watching her," Tybalt bit out. "The creatures of old have been under control for over a century. She shows up and suddenly there are issues with them and the Elder Clans? It's not a coincidence."

Razik wanted to argue with him. No, not argue. He wanted to talk out what he'd been thinking about the phantoms, Kailia, and all the fuckery. But with his uncle's mood, it looked like that would have to wait a little longer.

Tybalt left as quickly as he'd arrived, no doubt to oversee training since the Cadre were now otherwise occupied. Finishing off his juice, Razik stood as he set his glass down, already annoyed that Cethin and Kailia hadn't come down for breakfast today. That meant that when he got up to their floor, Cethin would likely be there.

As he started to leave, the sound of another chair scraping echoed, and he turned to find Wren following him.

"Did you need something?" he asked flatly.

"Yes. I need to talk to you," she bit back.

"I don't have time right now."

"Then make the fucking time, Razik."

He stopped, turning to face her fully. That was definitely fury shining in her navy blue eyes, her hands on her hips. Looks like it was the day for everyone to be in pissy moods then.

Grabbing her hand, he Traveled them to his rooms in the castle. She immediately yanked her hand from his, and he crossed his arms, waiting.

"What you did to Bram this morning was unnecessary," she spat.

"He knew exactly what he was doing, Wren," he replied, his voice monotone.

"Don't do that," she bit out, waving a hand dismissively at him. "Don't take on your bored indifference with me. I don't appreciate it."

"You are the one who asked me to make it clear you were off limits to the Cadre. Now you're berating me for it?" he demanded.

"Fucking Anahita, Razik! He offered to help me at the markets today. That was it!" she cried.

"There are plenty of others to help with that."

"Like you?" she countered, mirroring him and crossing her arms.

"Yes, like—" He stopped, eyeing her as he realized the trap he'd stepped directly into.

"You've been busy, Razik," she said, her tone softening a fraction. "And it's fine. It's your job. We don't spend as much time together, and I've had to fill that time somehow. I'm not like you. I can't sit around for days with only books for company." When Razik didn't say anything, she asked, "Was he right? Do you need to release some tension? Because I've hardly seen you other than to refill your power after the last attack in Shadowfen."

Yes. No. Not now, obviously. He had to get to Kailia before she disappeared, forcing him to spend his day tracking her down.

He sighed. "Are you with him, Wren? Because if you are, that's no longer an option. We both agreed if someone came along, the casual fucking would stop."

"You think I wouldn't have already told you if we were? I'd like to think you know me better than that," she said with a small smile that told him her anger was abating.

"Meet me here tonight?" he asked.

She nodded. "Right after my date with Bram."

"Not funny," he deadpanned, his lip curling in a slight sneer.

"A little funny," Wren tossed back.

He shook his head in dry amusement, Traveling to the king's floor. Knocking twice, he pushed through the doors, finding Lia in the sitting room. Her legs were tucked beneath her, and the book he'd given her was open on her lap, a cup of tea steaming on the side table next to her.

"How many times are you going to read that?" he asked, trying to determine if Cethin was here or not as he made his way to a chair.

"How many times am I supposed to?" she asked. There was something different about her today, but he couldn't put his finger on it.

"I suppose as many as you'd like, but I can get you others," he answered, stretching out his legs and crossing his ankles.

"In that case, that would be appreciated," she replied, smoothing her hand over a page. "You are later than usual today."

"Is Cethin here?"

"Should he be?"

"Are you going to do this all day?"

Her brows pinched. "Do what?"

"Answer my questions with a question."

Slowly closing the book, she said, "That is irritating to you."

At least that was an accurate observation instead of another question.

"Yes," he said, picking at a stray thread on the chair.

"But most things irritate you. Why is this any different?"

Fair fucking point there.

"I don't know, Lia," he half grumbled, half drawled. "According to some people, it's because I need a good fuck."

"And you don't think that would help?"

"Of course it would fucking help."

"Then… I really don't understand why you are irritated with me. You already know I can be of no assistance in that matter," she replied, reaching for her tea.

"I wasn't asking—" He swallowed his growl of annoyance.

"Are you irritated with me because I am his wife now?"

His head snapped up. "What?"

"Cethin," she answered, as if that clarified anything.

"What does Cethin have to do with any of this?" he demanded.

She eyed him over her teacup, as if she were waiting for him to realize something. It took far longer than it should have for him to figure out what she was insinuating.

Standing from the chair, he stalked across the room, taking the teacup from her hand and setting it aside. Honestly, it was a miracle he didn't throw the damn thing across the room. He wasn't surprised when she lurched to her feet, standing on the sofa with a dagger in hand.

A dagger poised at his throat.

If he weren't so godsdamn pissed off, he'd admire how skilled and trained she actually was. Too bad he was that pissed off.

Leaning forward a fraction, he felt the edge of the blade prick his flesh, and he leaned imperceptibly closer.

"Lia, I am only going to say this one more time, and if you ever bring it up again, I will haul your ass into the sky and drop you in the coldest stream I can find. Then I'll steal every single one of your arrows and daggers and hide them where you'll never find them. *Then* you and I will have a brawl ourselves," he ground out. "Cethin and I have never been and never will be lovers. We will never be friends. We will never be godsdamn acquaintances. We suffer each other's company because we have to. Is that clear?"

Her amber eyes were bright, swirling erratically with smoke. She leaned in closer, that blade sinking in a little more, and he felt a trickle of blood run down his neck.

"Let me make myself clear, *Raz*," she said, and her tone was so dark and predatory, the dragon in his soul immediately raised its head. A warning growl rumbled from his chest, and she fucking *smiled*. "If you ever threaten me again, we'll see if you're as talented as the king you hate so much in surviving one of my blades. Is *that* clear?"

His answering smile was all teeth when he said, "It appears we've come to an understanding."

"It appears we have."

They eyed each other a moment longer before Kailia pulled her dagger away at the same time he took a step back. She dropped gracefully back down on the sofa, her feet tucked under her, while he swiped at the blood on his neck. His magic was already working to heal the small cut.

"Is there a reason you didn't come down to breakfast today?" he asked.

"No," she answered, the word more of a murmur as she studied the cover of the book in her lap far too hard.

"Did you eat then? Or do you need food?"

"Cethin and I ate a small breakfast here."

"Great, then let's go," he said, crossing the room to grab her cloak from the hooks near the door.

He needed to get out of the castle. Get some air. He'd go flying if he could. Two arguments with two different females was more than enough for one day, even if his own actions were the reasons for both of them.

"Do I need to put it on, or just bring it with me today?" she asked, plucking the cloak from his outstretched hand, careful not to touch him.

"That's your choice, but we're going to my study at Tybalt's for more books," he answered.

She nodded, the other book tucked under her arm. When she tossed the cloak over her shoulder, he held out his hand again, and she swallowed thickly before placing her fingers in his.

"So starting small isn't going well?" he asked.

Her eyes went wide. "Why would you say that? Did Cethin say something?"

He paused, tilting his head. "Should he have said something to me? Is there something I should be aware of?"

"No," she answered in a rush. "Can we go please?"

He nodded, eyeing her as he Traveled them to the Greybane Estate, directly into his study. Taking the book from beneath her arm, he returned it to its proper place on the shelves before scanning for another volume that would be helpful to her. The problem was, she was so godsdamn quiet on her feet, he couldn't hear where she was in the room. Which meant she could be touching anything.

"Lia," he called out, her name bordering on a growl.

"What?" she answered from somewhere to his right.

"What are you doing?"

"Looking for a book."

"You don't need to. I'm finding what you need."

"I'm looking for a different book."

"Tell me what book, and I'll find it."

"I don't know *exactly* which book."

A growl of frustration rumbled from his chest, and he abandoned his own search to track her down.

She was at the far end of the study, fingers trailing along spines. His eyes narrowed, warding off a twitch in his left eye.

"How are you looking for a book if you don't know which book you're looking for?" he asked, trying to keep his voice even. The last thing he wanted was another argument with her today, especially when she was more of the stab first, communicate reasonably later, type.

She paused, hand dropping to her side. "I don't know," she admitted. "I was hoping the titles would be of assistance, but many of these are in languages I do not know."

"This is the part where you tell me what it is you're looking for, and then I find the book for you," he said in annoyance.

Kailia nodded, shaking her hands out as she worried her bottom lip.

"Did something happen this morning?" he finally asked. "You are different today."

Her eyes snapped back to his. "No," she said in a rush. "I need…"

"Spit it out, Lia."

"I need your help," she said, the words sounding agonized. As if asking him for help with whatever this was physically pained her.

"That is part of my job, you know," he said flatly.

Her lips pursed. "Which is why I don't want to tell you," she snapped. "Because I'm just a job to you, and this is— Well, it's something you won't understand."

He frowned when she turned back to the bookcase. For whatever reason, those words made him…uncomfortable. Something he was definitely not accustomed to feeling.

"I helped with Cethin, didn't I?" he argued for some unknown reason. "Is that what this is about?"

"No," she answered, sounding irritated. "This has nothing to do with Cethin. Not directly anyway."

"Who are you going to ask for help then if not me? Who else do you have, Lia?"

He realized how much of an asshole thing that was to say as soon as the words left his mouth. And yeah, he was a dick in general, but he was never intentionally cruel for no reason.

She had gone utterly still, her back to him and fingertips lingering on the spine of a book. Slowly, she turned back to him, her eyes swirling violently while the rest of her body was too still. Too calm.

"I know I'm not well-versed in social cues," she said, each word calm and deliberate, "but I do believe it is things like this that make me 'just a job' to you. You are the very type that makes me believe it is easier to do things on my own. Manipulating me by making me believe I have no other options? That I have no one else? I learned long ago that the one person I can ever truly depend on is myself, Razik Greybane. I have no use for you or anyone else."

He winced, her words hitting dark places she didn't even realize, but he absolutely fucking deserved it.

"I'd like to return to the castle," she added.

He nodded, extending his hand and wishing this day were already over.

-)) ⊙ ((-

"Did you get them?" he asked, sliding on his tunic as Wren entered his rooms.

It was the next morning, and thank the Fates. Yesterday had been miserable. Kailia hadn't spoken to him for the rest of the day. In fact, she'd godsdamn dismissed him. He'd held his ground on not standing outside in the hall, but she'd stayed in the bedchamber and he'd sat in the sitting room. For hours, he'd contemplated what she could need help with. He didn't think it was the touching. She'd already confided in him about that, so it wouldn't have been a big deal. This was clearly something very personal. He'd certainly fucked up the trust he'd been carefully building day after day.

The only good thing about yesterday had been losing himself in Wren for a few hours. Not that sex fixed everything, but it definitely fucking helped. The flying helped too. So did the *serena sabre* up in the mountains. The one thing that would have helped even more was a good round of sparring.

Wren flashed him a smile, setting down the paper sack on the side table. She'd offered to run this errand for him before getting ready for the day. While she'd smoothed down her hair and tied it back, it still had that just-fucked look to it, along with that satisfied glow in her blue eyes and golden skin.

"You're lucky I actually like you. I'm one of maybe three people," she said, crossing the room and pulling her tunic over her head as she made her way to the bathing chamber.

"I'm aware," he muttered after her.

Her light laughter echoed before running water sounded.

"Need anything before I go?" he called out to her.

"You gave me plenty last night, Razik," she answered, her tone teasing.

He shook his head, but a smirk tugged at his lips. Slipping on his boots, he grabbed the paper sack and made his way to the king's floor. He'd waited long enough this morning that Cethin should be gone, and if the pair did go downstairs for breakfast, she should be back up here by now.

Nodding to the guard that was on duty on their floor, he pushed through the doors. Kailia was standing near the window, fiddling with that crystal necklace she always wore. At his entrance, she glanced at the door before turning back to the window.

"Ready to go?" he asked, dropping the bag onto the low table before the sofa.

"I'm not going anywhere today," she replied simply.

"Come now," he scoffed. "You're going to let your anger with me keep you locked inside all day? Didn't know I had so much control over you."

"You don't," she spat.

"Mhmm," he hummed. Then he flicked the paper bag with his fingers. "I brought you something."

"I don't want it."

"Lia," he growled, swiping a hand down his face. He pushed out a harsh breath. "About what I said yesterday."

She scoffed. "I'm sure I just 'took it the wrong way,' right? Because I don't understand common interactions?"

He let those words hang in the air, understanding that such an explanation had likely been used against her in the past.

"It doesn't matter what I meant. What matters is how you perceived it," he replied.

She finally peered over her shoulder at him. "What?"

"It doesn't matter how I said something or my intention behind it," he repeated. "What matters is how *you* heard it and how you interpreted it." When she only stared at him, he pushed, "I know what it's like to be alone. To feel like your singular purpose is to be used by others. I didn't mean to imply that you are just a job. I was..." He let out another long breath, not used to having to explain himself. Not used to *caring* enough to explain himself. "I was trying to tell you that you *aren't* alone. That I'm here to help you. Not because it's my job but because I understand loneliness. I understand how we come to find peace in solitude because we are forced to spend so much time there. Because others don't understand us, despite some trying. Eventually they—"

"Stop trying," she cut in, taking a few steps closer. "And they start trying to figure out how they can use you."

Razik nodded once, his jaw taut. "Or force you into doing what they want."

Her head canted to the side, a tentative curiosity in her eyes. "I can't imagine anyone forcing you to do anything."

His answering smile was devoid of anything kind or cheerful. "I could say the same for you, yet somehow, here you are."

Anger flared once more. "Are you saying this whole arrangement is my fault?"

"Of course not," he said dismissively. "You're far too clever to fall for such a thing."

She hummed, coming closer, but she was still a few feet away when she pushed onto her tiptoes, trying to peer into the bag.

"It's not going to bite," he said, rolling his eyes and shoving it closer to her.

She snatched it up, pulling a handle on each side to open it wider. Reaching inside, she pulled out a roll with cinnamon and frosting, still lukewarm from the freshest batch.

"These are Cethin's favorites," she said dubiously.

"I think they're also yours," Razik retorted dryly.

"Perhaps," she said, sinking her teeth into the pastry.

He debated asking how she'd gone three centuries without having such a thing, but he'd dug his way out of one hole. He wasn't about to jump into another.

When she'd finished two of the four rolls and had set the rest aside for later, he asked, "Any place in particular you'd like to go today? Into Aimonway?"

She was quiet in that unnerving way she had. She never shifted or fidgeted while she debated things, making it increasingly hard to read her. It was ironic, really. She may be challenged in understanding social interactions, but in turn, she was a challenge to understand herself.

Finally, she said, "If you're still willing, I would like new books to read regarding Avonleya."

"Of course," he answered.

She hesitated before adding, "And anything you might have regarding Ash Riders."

He couldn't have hidden his surprise if he'd wanted to, but he nodded once, reaching for her hand.

Once they were in his study at Tybalt's, he leaned against his desk, crossing his arms. "Anything in particular regarding Ash Riders?" he asked while Kailia did her usual scan of the place. That was more than warrior training. She moved with the stealth of spies and the lethal grace of mercenaries. Her mannerisms only supported his suspicions.

After a moment, she met his gaze, and there was something almost…tormented there.

"Maybe it doesn't even need to be about Ash Riders," she said thoughtfully.

"I'd love to weigh in on that if only I knew what you were trying to learn," he retorted dryly.

She sent him an equally dry look as she lifted a hand, ashes fluttering around it. "My power is broken."

"Power can't be broken."

"I don't know how else to describe it," she said, frustration seeping into her tone. "I can't move through my magic like I've been able to for centuries. It's been weeks—months—since I've been able to. Anytime I try, it takes control and takes me someplace else. Somewhere I'm not trying to go. It's unsettling."

"I thought once Cethin gave you back that arrowhead, your magic was supposed to work properly again?" he asked, already sorting through books in his mind he could research in. Some were here, but those that would likely be most useful were somewhere else.

"Well, it's not," she answered simply.

"Why haven't you said anything? Does Cethin know?" he demanded.

Lia shook her head, her fingers flexing slightly at her sides. "I'm not naïve. I know why he bound me in a union. What purpose will I serve if I can't even use my magic properly for his kingdom?"

She wasn't entirely wrong, which is why he weighed his words a bit before replying. Cethin *had* bound her to the kingdom as his queen to use her for her weapons. And yes, having an Ash Rider was certainly an advantage with how rare they were. But he'd also watched the king with her for weeks now. It may have started out that way, but his obsession with her went far beyond that now. So once again, he found himself defending Cethin to her.

"He'd want to know," he said. "Not only for those reasons, but because he understands a power that is difficult to control."

"He seems to control his magic fine," she replied.

"You've seen a fraction of his power, Kailia," Razik said darkly. "You'd do well to remember that."

"I'm well aware of what he's capable of," she retorted, wandering towards a bookshelf.

"Not that one," he said, going in the opposite direction and leading her to an area off to the left. Calling over his shoulder, he added, "It'd be useful to know your lineage. That would help with this."

"I'm sure it would," she replied, a few paces behind him.

"You don't know it? Or you're not offering up the information?"

"I know as much as anyone else about Ash Riders," she answered.

"Do you know if both your parents were Ash Riders?"

"No."

His irritation already spiking, he asked evenly, "Let's try this, Lia: rather than me attempting to drag information out of you, you share what you know."

"I already said I don't know my lineage," she replied, stepping around him to peruse the books.

"Do you have theories?" he gritted out.

She glanced up at him. "That would be helpful?"

"Yes, Lia, that would be helpful."

She straightened. "Why? It's not factual."

"How do you think things are discovered to eventually become fact? Theories are followed and investigated to be proven true or false." She nodded, clearly mulling that over. "If anything, it will give us a place to start," he added.

After a long moment, she said, "I don't know if both my parents were Ash Riders, but I believe my mother was."

"Any theories about your father?"

She came closer as he pulled a book from a shelf, holding it out to her before looking for another.

"I don't think he was Fae. My magic is too…"

"You're too powerful," he finished for her.

"It's not that per se," she said, opening the book and skimming pages. "The only other Ash Riders I know of are males, and their powers are slightly different."

That had him turning to face her completely because he'd never heard of such a thing. Ash Riders were so rare that information on them was scarce to begin with, but the theory that their gifts varied by their gender was one he'd never come across.

"Slightly different how?" he asked.

She didn't even look up from the pages when she answered, "The males can't create weapons from their power like I can."

"And why do you believe your mother was an Ash Rider but possibly not your father?"

Her entire body tensed at the question. It was slight, but he saw it. Saw the minute tremor in her fingers as she ran them down the page, clearly trying to collect herself.

Which is why he didn't understand when her answer was simply, "I heard rumors that my mother could do the same."

Leaving that statement to unpack for another day, he asked, "Do Ash Rider males possess a gift that you do not? That you are aware of, I mean."

Her answering smile was a terrifying thing, pointed and full of a wicked delight. "They can turn their hands into ashes and pull out your insides while you still breathe."

Logically, he should balk at that, but his bloodline and his dragon had him understanding the delight in her smile now. "Is that a theory or a fact?"

She tipped her head from side to side, considering. "Based on my limited knowledge, I'd say fact."

"And you've met other female Ash Riders? To know they can't do this too?"

"No," she answered. "I knew of other males, but not females."

He stopped with the questions then, his mind working to sort through everything she'd shared and the knowledge he'd collected over the decades. He needed other books to make sure he was recalling things correctly, but now that she'd said it, he didn't remember ever reading about a female Ash Rider. Only males.

Ash Riders weren't Fae. To have the gifts, they had to descend from Anala, making them Avonleyan. Other realms called them Legacy.

But what if…

What if she was neither? What if she was something else entirely?

CHAPTER 29
CETHIN

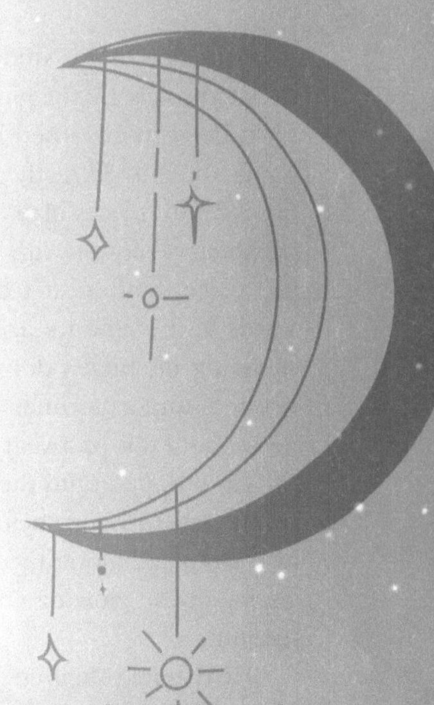

Was she searching for him tonight?

He tossed the thin stick of charcoal onto the work-table at the thought, watching it roll along the surface before going over the edge and dropping to the floor with a soft ping. Sitting back in his chair, he rubbed at his eyes before shoving a hand through his hair. Only then did he remember the slice on his arm wasn't fully healed, and he'd now smeared blood all over the side of his face.

With a sigh, he stood, making his way to a basin he kept down here for this very reason. Dipping a cloth in the water, he quickly wiped his face, then his arm, pressing the fabric to the cut. As he applied pressure, he wandered over to the slate hanging on the wall. Sconces and candelabras lit up this side of the room, allowing him to see. Notes, symbols, and Marks written with chalk covered nearly every inch.

Studying the boards, he grabbed a piece of felt, erasing a few things before picking up a piece of chalk. Tossing the cloth aside, Cethin made a few notes based on what he'd learned tonight before swiping up the leather journal from the worktable and crossing to the other side of the room.

This side of his study beneath the castle was much darker, illuminated solely by the glowing embers in the white marble fireplace. He'd been so absorbed in his work, he'd forgotten to keep the fire going tonight. Directly in front of the fireplace was a low table littered with pieces of parchment, an unlit lantern, and a half-empty decanter of liquor with an empty glass beside it. No one knew of this place. Staff didn't clean it. He'd spent years making sure the wards and glamours around it were sufficient before he'd started spending his nights down here decades ago. Even then, it was for research and experiments. He didn't start sleeping down here most nights until this past year.

He dropped onto the high-back settee behind the table, pouring two fingers of liquor before settling back in his seat. With his healing arm stretched along the back of the settee, he sipped at the liquid, staring at the glowing embers and going over what he'd worked on tonight.

He'd finally figured out where he'd been going wrong with a Mark, and he felt confident in actually using it now. It had never looked quite right before. He might be taking risks down here night after night messing around with blood magic, but even he wasn't reckless enough to *use* the Marks until he was sure they were drawn correctly. Intricate and in another language entirely, drawing one thing wrong altered the entire purpose of the Mark, let alone the cost. Because all magic had a cost. For the Fae, the cost was physical. They needed more food and sleep to refuel their magic. For Avonleyans, the cost was time since they could no longer drink the blood of the Fae without the risk of triggering a curse. But Marks? Blood magic? The costs for those were far harder to navigate. Some costs were simple, but sometimes the cost was steep and not known until it was too late.

Until regret was the bitter aftertaste.

Or until those left behind were forced to bear the burden of costs that lingered like ghosts and spirits.

Tybalt had told him of the newly murdered Fae found a few days ago, and it was then he'd realized how distracted he'd become with Kailia. Which was why his thoughts constantly wandering back to her was irritating tonight. More than that, he'd gone through all of this to have her help this kingdom—help protect the Fae—and she wasn't even the godsdamn solution he'd thought she was.

He hurled his glass of liquor into the fireplace, flames exploding when alcohol met heat and glass shards flew outward. He thought he'd done it. Thought he'd figured this all out when the ship had finally made it through the Wards. But it had been months since a new ship had arrived. There had been four in total, and for the life of him, he couldn't figure out why the Blood Marks he was invoking worked sometimes and not others. He'd charted moon phases and star patterns, monitored seasons and the tides of the sea. None of it seemed to matter, but of course it mattered. Everything fucking mattered when it came to blood magic. That was why it was forbidden except under very specific circumstances, and it was why his parents had refused to utilize it to fix the myriad of problems afflicting their kingdom.

He rubbed at his eyes again, the never-ending exhaustion taking hold. Normally he could go days—weeks—without sleep as long as he wasn't using his power much, but blood magic drained his physical energy far faster, requiring him to sleep more often. The exhaustion also led to lowered defenses, especially around Kailia. It was dangerous, and yet all he could think about right now was going to her. Seeing if he could get her to touch him like she had that day in the bathing chamber. How he'd savored that touch like a neglected pup.

Affection wasn't something he was used to. Yes, he fucked. Had partners in his bed. Shared intimate touches. But affection was something else entirely. His mother hadn't been particularly affectionate, and his father, while more attentive than his mother, was still the king. Not that he didn't try. They'd spent quality time together when schedules allowed, but that was rare, making those quiet moments on the water or at the country estate that much more sacred.

He wasn't naïve enough to think Kailia's touches were out of affection either. He was a curiosity to her as much as she was to him. Except she was becoming something more. Something that had started out as a means to an end, even if it was coupled with intrigue. And sure, maybe a bit of lust because that was nature. But that curiosity had turned into obsession, and now it was...

Something he couldn't dwell on.

He had work to do and a kingdom to protect, no matter the cost. So he pushed off the settee and went back to work. Dragging a knife along his flesh once more, he dipped his finger in his blood and began to draw.

⟶⟩ ☉ ⟨⟵

"Your grace," Zayan gritted out.

Cethin slid his gaze to him, completely unaware of what he'd said but picking up on his frustration. "Yes?"

Zayan set down the quill he was using, sighing and rubbing dramatically at his temples. "If I may speak boldly, this is becoming a problem."

"What is?" Cethin asked, looking down at the parchment before him. At the long list of items Zayan wanted to cover today.

"Things that used to take us an hour to discuss are now taking a full day," he answered. "Ever since—"

He cut himself off, pressing his lips into a thin line, but Cethin didn't need him to finish the thought.

"Correct me if I'm wrong, Zayan," he said, too exhausted to care that his darkness was a shimmering mist around his drumming fingers on the tabletop. "But were you not one of the main advocates for me taking a wife?"

"I was," Zayan replied.

"Was it not assumed that when I took a partner, my attention would become divided in some respects? Or was I to take one, bed her, and leave her to her own devices while hopefully growing a babe, all in an effort to satisfy the Advisory Council?"

The male's eyes went wide at the bluntness. "Of course not, your grace."

"Then I'm going to need you to be more specific about what the problem is. I'm not in the mood to dance around topics. Speak your concerns plainly or get over them," he snapped, the darkness in his soul a writhing thing that was becoming too intense. Too restless. Too chaotic.

"She's not Fae," Zayan blurted, immediately dropping his eyes to the papers spread out before him.

Cethin blinked because *that* was the fucking problem?

"That did not clear up the issue," Cethin said too calmly, using every bit of his remaining energy to keep his power in check.

Zayan took a deep breath while clearly gathering his courage. When he met Cethin's gaze once more, there was a renewed resolve and hardness in the male's dark eyes. "We all thought you would choose a Fae as your partner," Zayan said, his words steadier. "It is the custom of Avonleya, and it is why it was suggested you seek a partner at the Esbat Festival when all the Fae were gathered. Instead, you chose something else, more Fae are turning up dead, and the people are talking."

"My mother wasn't Fae," Cethin countered.

"Yes, but she had proven herself long before Tethys took her as his wife. This female—"

"She has a fucking name, but you can call her 'her Majesty,'" Cethin interjected with a steely command.

"No one knows anything about her. They see her every once in a while out with Razik, but never with you. Rumors are growing, and restlessness is being sown. Even the Elder Clans are unhappy," Zayan continued, growing far too bold as he continued his rant.

"What do the Elder Clans have to do with this?"

"Rumors eventually become truths if never proven false, your Majesty," the Hand said with a sad smile. "There are rumors she has repeatedly harmed you, and then there are rumors the Elder Clans attacked her. The people see it as a sign from the Fates."

Cethin swallowed his huff of disbelief. He had given and given and given to this kingdom. It was his highest priority and where all his loyalty lay. He'd proven himself time and time again, and still it wasn't enough. For his mother. His father. For Zayan or Tybalt. For the council, the clans, the people. For her.

"They don't trust her," Zayan said, beginning to gather his things, smartly sensing that Cethin would not be finishing their agenda today. "And because of that, they begin to question you. I am simply the messenger, your grace."

Then he was gone, leaving Cethin alone in his study.

It had been a mistake to make her queen in title only. He'd done it to protect his kingdom, but it had sown seeds of doubt. The people needed to see them. See her with him. He'd hoped the Union Celebration would help, but that was still nearly two weeks away.

With a sigh, he got to his feet. Apparently, her time to acclimate was up. A royal title would always do what it did best: force a person into roles and duties they never asked for.

Then again, he supposed *he'd* done that to her.

He took his time climbing to their floor, finding their space empty. After sending a note to Razik, he made some tea, hoping it would help wake him up. Stepping out onto the balcony, he braced his elbows on the railing, holding the teacup between his hands. Only then did he acknowledge the panther sitting in the corner to the right. Black fur glistening in the daylight, her tail switched behind her, and her silver eyes were pinned on him.

Shirina, the spirit animal bonded to the goddess of night and shadows.

"I have nothing to say to her," he said without looking at the panther.

The panther didn't move. Her tail only continued to swish along the marble floor.

"But you can tell Altaria I await his return," he added, referring to another of the spirit animals, before bringing his tea to his lips.

With that, the panther stood, stretching her front legs out and back arching. Then, with a flash of faint silver light, she was gone.

Moments later, he heard the doors open, the voices of Razik and Kailia carrying to him.

"Cethin?" Kailia called out, appearing in the balcony doorway a moment later.

It had been cool this morning, but this late in the day, the sun had warmed the air. Spring had finally taken over, and the summer season was well on its way. Despite that, she'd only removed her shoes, her cloak still around her shoulders and clasped at her throat, that blue crystal laying below the silver clip.

"Sorry to interrupt your day," Cethin said, shifting so he leaned back against the rail. Her dress was shorter in the front, stopping at her knees, while the back graced her heels. It was lightweight, which he supposed is why she still wore the cloak, and he could see the outlines of the daggers at her thighs. "You look beautiful, by the way."

She paused, amber eyes looking him up and down. "You look fatigued."

His answering smile was likely as tired as he felt and, apparently, looked. "Where were you off to today?"

Kailia glanced over her shoulder at Razik before she answered. "We were at Razik's study. He was finding me more books to read to understand the kingdom better."

Cethin bristled at the idea of her spending time in his private space at the Greybane Estate. "Do you go there often?"

"The last few days, yes," she answered. "But before that, no. Are you well?"

"Why would you think I wasn't?"

"Because you bid us to return in the middle of the day. You are usually otherwise occupied at this time." She paused before adding, "I suppose you are busy all the time. But I usually see you at breakfast and dinner, and it is neither of those times."

"Right," he muttered, setting his empty teacup on the balcony ledge. He cleared his throat. "I was looking to see if you'd like to spend the day in the city with me."

"Why?" she asked in clear confusion.

"To spend time together."

"We cannot do that here?"

"We could, but this is part of that 'need to be convincing' thing, wife," he replied. "I'm told the people are having doubts because you are not seen enough."

"Razik and I go into Aimonway quite often," she argued.

"Yes. With Razik. Not me."

She took a step towards him, her eyes narrowing. "To be sure I am understanding correctly: you are upset I am not seen enough with you when you don't even spend your nights here? Or any of your days? I cannot do much convincing when my husband is a phantom, Cethin."

His gaze flicked to Razik, who was leaning along the doorjamb with his arms crossed and a small smirk on his lips. The male only arched a brow at Cethin's attention. He hated that they were having this discussion in front of him.

"Your presence is not needed," he snapped at the male.

"I'm her guard, not yours," Razik replied apathetically.

"There is nothing to guard her from right now."

"There is if you're going to Aimonway."

"For the love of——" He stopped, grinding his teeth before returning his focus to Kailia. "That's a fair statement, and something I would like to discuss more with you. Perhaps somewhere in the city? If you're willing?"

"My willingness has not been taken into account in any of this. I don't know why you'd start now," she replied simply as she turned on her heel and went back inside.

Cethin held in a sigh, dragging a hand down his face before swiping up the teacup and following her. He changed into slightly more casual attire, and moments later they Traveled to the city center. If Razik was going to be with them, there was no need for additional guards, and Cethin knew there was no way Razik was staying behind. He should be grateful the male was taking his role so seriously, but considering who it was, it only irritated him more.

It took less than a minute before the whispers and stares began as people noticed them standing in the middle of the city. Letting his magic go first, his hand followed, dropping to the small of Kailia's back. She was naturally still, but she tensed for the briefest of moments before stepping closer to him.

"Start small," he murmured. "And breathe, tiny fiend."

She nodded, taking in a shaky inhale.

"Let's go somewhere and get a drink," Razik said, his voice low. "Everyone can relax some, but the two of you can still be seen together."

Cethin nodded. "Astra?"

Razik's answering look was incredulous. "No. We're not taking her to Astra right now."

"It's not like we can just go sit down in a tavern," he bit back.

Razik stared at him, but it was Kailia who said, "A tavern would be nice."

Cethin pulled at the back of his neck. The king and queen in a godsdamn tavern. Fucking Fates.

Pushing out a long breath, he said, "I suppose we could go to The Dark Star. Are you okay with walking? It's not terribly far."

She nodded, and the three of them set off, stepping into the tavern some twenty minutes later. It wasn't as dark and unkempt as some places, but it was still a tavern. Dimly lit, at least the floor wasn't sticky with spilled ale and other liquids as they were immediately led to a private space upstairs.

The room overlooked the main floor below, and their stools had backs at their high-top table, unlike those below.

"This is a fancy tavern," Kailia said, leaning over him to peer down below.

Until her shoulder pressed into his arm, and she went still. Locks of her black hair brushed along the back of his hand.

Gently winding those strands around his finger, he said, "It is one of the…more proper establishments of its kind."

Her brow furrowed. "I don't understand how sitting up here is going to convince anyone of anything. They can't even see us."

"She has a point," Razik muttered. "It also takes twice as long to get our ale."

"At least they have more than ale," she said, sitting back in her chair and resting her chin in her hand. "Do you suppose they have card games here?"

"No, Lia," Razik said, immediately accompanied by a pointed look.

Not understanding the exchange, Cethin asked, "Do you play cards, Kailia?"

"I would," she replied.

"Your wife likes anything that involves competition," Razik said, his gaze still pinned on her. "And she is overly competitive."

"I don't think someone can be *overly* competitive. The purpose behind any sort of competition is to win. It's in the definition," she bit back.

"A game of cards is not necessarily a competition," Razik retorted.

"Then why did they call it that?"

"Wait," Cethin cut in at the same time Razik muttered, "Fuck."

Cethin shifted to face Kailia fully. "Where were you when you played cards?"

"I didn't play cards," she answered.

The conversation paused when the server approached, two mugs of ale and a glass of wine balanced on her tray. But the moment she was down the stairs, Cethin turned back to Kailia.

"Where were you that you witnessed a card game recently?"

She took a drink of her wine before she said, "A tavern."

His head whipped to Razik. "You took her to a tavern?"

The male shrugged. "She stabbed someone. More than one, actually."

"Razik!" she hissed, eyes wide with betrayal.

He leaned forward, pointing a finger at her from across the table. "We had an agreement. You broke it first by telling him we went there."

"You took her to a godsdamn tavern?" Cethin cut in, so much rage coursing through him. His magic was pressing at him so insistently his veins were taking on a faint grey hue.

Razik noticed, straightening as he recognized the potential threat. His eyes shifted, glowing softly. "Get yourself under control, Sutara."

"Which tavern?" Cethin demanded instead. But when Razik didn't answer, he turned back to his wife. "Kailia?"

She shrugged, taking another drink of wine. "Somewhere by the docks. This wine is really good. Do we have this kind at the castle?"

"The godsdamn docks?" It took everything in him not to bellow the words. Actually, it took everything in him not to go across the table and hit the male in the face. "What were you thinking, Greybane?"

"I'm thinking this is probably not the place for this conversation," he said in a pointed low growl.

"Agreed," Kailia offered. "You look like you're about to start a brawl, and I don't believe that would be very convincing of us, husband. But I wouldn't be opposed to another brawl."

He blinked at her, his vision blurred with fury. Coupled with his existing exhaustion, he knew the male was right because he was seconds away from starting that brawl Kailia mentioned.

"Another brawl?" he asked, his tone dangerously low and quiet.

"By Sargon, Lia," Razik glowered. "The majority of the time we can't get you to give us straight answers, but with this, you won't stop running your mouth."

"By stating I wouldn't be opposed to a brawl? How is that a problem?" she asked in confusion.

"Finish your godsdamn drinks," Cethin snarled. "We can't simply leave, but as soon as we're done, we're going somewhere to discuss this."

The next fifteen minutes seemed to drag on forever, and he knew Razik was taking his time just to be a dick. There was absolutely no reason for him to take fifteen minutes to finish half a mug of ale. He'd been to taverns with him. He knew the male could take down a full mug in less time than it took to fill it.

The moment they were back in their rooms, Cethin rounded on Razik. Darkness swirled as thick tendrils coiled in the male's direction.

"Why in the fuck would you take her to a godsdamn tavern? And by the docks? When was this?" Cethin demanded.

"Relax, Sutara. It was before she was even announced as your betrothed. And I made sure her face was hidden. Well, until the brawl. Then her hood slipped back, but no one knew who she was yet," Razik said, far too casually for the way this conversation was about to go.

"It doesn't fucking matter, Greybane!" Cethin yelled. "Why would you even put her in that position?"

"What position? Getting her out of this fucking castle? Letting her get to know all sides of the capital city? She's the godsdamn queen, and you want her to simply stay locked away," Razik spat, his eyes glowing brighter than they had before and smoke furling with each exhale. "And in case you haven't figured it out yet, she's perfectly capable of protecting herself. Fuck, she protects *you* half the godsdamn time."

"You're done, Greybane," Cethin snarled. "I'm demanding Tybalt remove you as her guard."

"No!" Kailia interjected, speaking for the first time since they'd returned.

She pushed her tiny frame between them, wincing at the physical touch but shoving at them both anyway. In the next blink, she held a dagger in each hand, one pointed at each of them.

"Razik, can you leave, so I can speak with my husband?" she asked, every bit of her amber glare directed at Cethin.

"Sure thing," he all but drawled. Then he added while smirking at Cethin, "See you in the morning, Lia."

Before Cethin could respond, Kailia was pressing the point of her dagger to his chest, and she held it there until they heard the door close behind Razik.

"I do not want another guard, Cethin," she said, the words steady and firm.

"Too bad, wife. He's proven time and again that he can't be trusted with your safety."

"My safety?" she repeated. "Cethin, it was one of my first days here. He got me out of the castle and took me with him on an errand, and I'm grateful he did. The only reason I get out of these walls is because of him. You are always tending to your duties, and

I'm left to… I get restless," she finished, as if that explained everything.

"You got in the middle of a godsdamn brawl, Kailia," Cethin gritted out. "That was irresponsible of him to—"

"Someone grabbed me," she interjected. "He grabbed me and tried to pull me onto his lap. I panicked and shoved a dagger through his hand. His companions were not happy with my actions."

"Someone grabbed you?" he asked, the words low and dark for an entirely different reason now.

"It wasn't intentional. The stabbing, I mean. I think the grabbing was definitely intentional."

He pinched the bridge of his nose, trying to clear his mind enough to converse with her properly, but between the exhaustion and now the thought of someone grabbing her. Touching her. He couldn't see past it.

He'd have to deal with that later. "I still think another personal guard is in order, Kailia."

"No," she repeated, a thread of panic in her tone as she pressed the dagger point a bit more firmly to his chest. "It takes me ages to become comfortable around someone. I find it incredibly difficult, but the thought of starting that process all over again is overwhelming."

Godsdammit.

He stepped back before turning and heading to the bedchamber.

"Where are you going?"

"To change," he muttered, not stopping until he was in the dressing closet. He quickly slipped into looser, lightweight pants. He left his shirt off, contemplating a hot bath, but he needed to have a conversation with Kailia first. One he wished he were far more rested for, but fate was rarely on his side.

"That is not dinner attire," Kailia said when he emerged into the bedchamber.

"We will not be at dinner tonight," he answered, leaning against the doorjamb. "We need to figure all this out."

Surprise flitted across her features. "You are staying here for the rest of the day."

"I am," he affirmed.

"With me?"

A small smile tugged at his lips. "If that is amenable to you."

"It is, but you are always…gone," she finished.

"I have responsibilities, yes, but I also know this was a transition for you. I was trying to give you space to adjust, but it's causing some tension throughout the kingdom. Not to mention inside the castle and these rooms," he added.

"I don't know how there can be tension in these rooms when you're never here," she scoffed.

He pushed off the doorway, not stopping until he was right in front of her. Her head tipped back, exposing her slender throat, and his finger itched to slide along it. Feel her soft skin. That pulse fluttering beneath his touch.

"You keep saying things like that. I'm starting to think you miss me, tiny fiend," he said, his tone low and a touch raspy.

"No."

"No?" he asked, letting his magic out to trace the path he desperately wanted to. He heard the gasp she tried to swallow. This was a dangerous game to be playing when he was too exhausted to properly control his power.

"I simply don't like not knowing my role. I need a purpose. Something to focus on," she replied, the words a little breathy. "Ever since you brought me here, I feel as if I do not have one. I told you this when we discussed my role being in title only."

"And what additional roles would you like?"

"Considering you never allow me with you, I don't know the options," she retorted. "But surely there are things I could handle so you can sleep more than once a moon cycle."

"I sleep more than that," he said defensively, rearing back some.

"You are a liar, king," she replied, crossing her arms, then uncrossing them and shaking out her hands.

"You tell me a truth, and I'll tell you one," he proposed.

She eyed him, his darkness still lingering, and she slowly lifted a hand. He thought she was going to touch him, and he leaned a little closer, anticipating it. Craving it. But instead, she drew a single finger through his magic.

"Tell me a truth about these shadows," she said.

"They're not shadows," he answered.

"What?"

"That was a truth," he replied. "Your turn. Tell me a truth about your past."

She paused, her head tilting a fraction while she continued to toy with his magic. "I didn't see the sun for the first time until I was nearly twenty years."

He recoiled fully, staring at her. "What?"

Surprised, she went still, her brows pinching together. "You asked for a truth."

"I did, but…" He fell silent, unsure of what to even say to any of this. He wanted to pull her into his chest and hold her. Protect her from whatever had kept her locked away for twenty godsdamn years. If he'd been curious about her past before, he was desperate for it now. That seemed to be what she elicited from him the most: desperate need.

For information.

For understanding.

For her.

And therein lay the entire godsdamn problem.

But…

"Another truth exchange?" he asked.

She eyed him for a moment, but then slowly nodded.

"How long have you been in Avonleya?"

"Less than a year," she answered.

He nodded. He'd suspected as much. Not on the first ship, but on one of the two after. "How'd you know your ship would get through the Wards?"

"I didn't," she said. "It wasn't the first time I'd tried. I was a stowaway on the ships anyway. When they didn't make it, I used my power to return to the continent."

"How many times did you try? And why were you so determined?

She smiled, a small thing that told him she was enjoying this little game. "I believe it's your turn to give me a truth," she said.

"Fair enough," he acquiesced.

"Where do you go at night?"

"I already told you. I have another study."

"But *where* is it? And what do you do there?"

He slid his hands into his pockets, debating. He could tell her, and she'd still never find it without him. There were too many glamours and Wards around it.

"Beneath the castle," he answered. "There is a network of catacombs. I have a study there. And what I do down there is work."

"On what?"

"I think that's enough truths for today," he said. "But I would enjoy your company on the balcony. Beneath the sun."

"Only if you tell me that Razik will still be my guard," she said, lifting her chin.

He was too exhausted to argue about the male right now, but even if that weren't the case, it wouldn't have mattered. "Just…no more tavern brawls, please."

She was fighting a small smile when he extended a hand to her, and she slowly slipped the tips of her fingers into his palm. "I make no promises, husband."

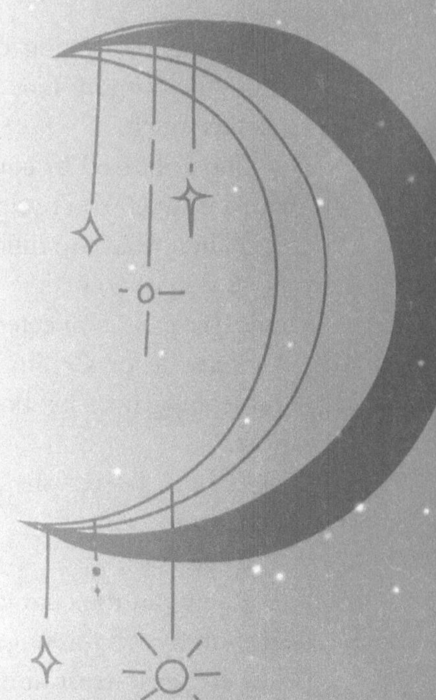

CHAPTER 30
RAZIK

"Where did you put your bowl?"

Razik glanced up from the book he was paging through. He sat at his desk, while Kailia was across the room in another area of his study. Barefoot, her knees were bent, and a book of her own was propped against them.

"That is very random," Razik said, returning his attention to the book. It was written in the Celestial language, which was a pain in the ass to translate.

"Sort of," she admitted. "But after the conversation about the tavern brawl with Cethin—"

"The one you weren't supposed to mention," he interrupted, half listening to her as he worked on translating a word.

"Yes, that one," she continued. "It reminded me you went there for a bowl, and I haven't seen it since. I've been in this study a lot recently, which leads me to believe you keep it elsewhere."

"I like you a lot more when you're quietly observing and trying to go unnoticed," he muttered, making a note on a piece of parchment.

"It wasn't small. I think I'd have seen it if it were here," she mused. "Is it in your rooms downstairs?"

417

He sighed, setting down his charcoal and leaning back in his chair. "By Sargon, Lia. You're especially annoying today. You never talk this much."

She appeared to contemplate that for a minute before she said with a frown, "You're right. I don't."

"Then what's so different today?"

"I don't know," she murmured, almost more to herself than to him. Her gaze connected with his once more. "It is strange."

"Save it for Cethin," Razik grumbled, picking up his charcoal and leaning over his book once more. "He'd love to hear you talk more."

"I have been," she replied. "Talking to him, I mean. Or he's been around more?"

By the Fates.

Razik put the charcoal back down and rubbed at his brow with his thumb and forefinger as he reminded himself he needed this. Needed her to trust him. That her wanting to casually converse was a good thing. That this was exactly what Tybalt had put him in this position for.

"Why does your face look like that?" Kailia asked when he lifted his head to meet her stare once more.

He sighed. "That's a rude question, Lia."

She frowned. "Oh." Then she added, "You excel at being rude."

"Yes, but it's not a good look for a queen."

"No one else is here."

He inhaled deeply, swallowing his growing impatience. "I'm glad to see Cethin has finally figured out you are getting lonely."

Those words had her straightening, the book falling closed and forgotten. With a frown, she said, "I prefer solitude."

"Me too, yet here we are," he muttered.

She sent him a bland look.

"Despite that, even those of us who prefer solitude tend to have one or two people we don't entirely hate being around," he went on, ignoring her displeasure. "You constantly tell Cethin he's never around."

"Because he's not."

"And that bothers you."

"No, it doesn't."

It was his turn to send her a frank look. "It does, or you wouldn't bring it up all the time. I'm not saying I understand it, but I'm calling it like I see it."

"Well, you're wrong."

"Rarely," he muttered.

"And as arrogant as he is," she tacked on.

That had him grinding his molars, and they both fell silent, the tension in the room thick. He wasn't about to be the one to break it, so he went back to the book. The book wasn't about Ash Riders, but about curses and enchantments. He was hoping to find something regarding stifling a certain part of one's power. It made no sense that only one piece of her magic was being affected. Why not all of it?

"When's the last time you tried to move through your ashes?" he asked after a good solid hour had ticked by of both of them studiously ignoring the other.

Kailia lifted her head, a weird look of suspicion on her face. "Why?"

"Maybe it was a fluke," he said with a shrug. "If you haven't tried in a while—"

"It wasn't a fluke, Raz," she interrupted, her jaw tight and tone harsh. "If you couldn't shift into your beast form, you'd know in your soul something was wrong."

Fair point.

He rubbed at his jaw. "Recently then?"

"The last time I attempted it was in my dreams, and even there, it failed."

His hand dropped to the desk. "Even in your dreams your power isn't working?"

She nodded. "I haven't tried outside my dreams since the attack in Shira Forest. I don't know where I will be pulled to. Or if I will be able to get back…" She trailed off, before adding, "Do you know what it is like not to be able to trust yourself? When you're the only one you've been able to rely on for so long?"

There was a faint tremble in her voice, and shit. This was an emotion he'd yet to see from her. And that was the thing. He actually understood *why* she was becoming more conversational around him. She was becoming comfortable. Wren had been the same. Quiet for a long time until she became comfortable enough around him to be a pain in his ass. It was what he needed from Kailia, yes, but he hadn't planned on adding to the number of people he cared about because that was exactly what was happening.

He hadn't been lying to appease her when he said she was more than a job; he just hadn't wanted to admit as much to himself. Sure, he was a broody dick, but he actually liked that about himself. It kept others at arm's length, and yet somehow, this tiny, stabby thing was here. In his study. Talking.

"Lia," he sighed, closing the book and pushing it aside. "I need more than a few days, but as much as I hate to say this, I think we should loop Cethin in on—"

"No," she interjected. "He can't know."

"Okay. What about Tybalt?" he ventured.

"The Commander does not like me."

"Even if that's valid, you are still his queen. He takes his duties seriously," Razik replied, unable to hide the hint of bitterness.

She was quiet for a few seconds before she said, "I would prefer no one else know."

He knew it was a terrible idea, but he also knew that insisting on this would only end with her putting her defenses back in place.

"Fine," he said flatly.

"That upsets you," she noted, and he could feel her watching him. Because that's what she did. Watched and observed and analyzed.

"It's fine. You're the queen, but beyond that, I'm not going to make you do anything."

She nodded, setting her book aside. Twisting so her feet were now on the floor, she smoothed her hands along her thighs to her knees. Once. Twice. Three times.

"What is it, Lia?" he asked

"The Union Celebration is a week away."

"I know."

"And there will be dancing."

"I know that as well."

"And I don't…"

Understanding dawning, he said, "You don't know how to dance."

"I assume I will be expected to. Dance, I mean."

"With Cethin for sure," Razik affirmed. "But also with others." She visibly winced. "You need to have a conversation with Cethin about that."

"I'll do it. It's part of my role now."

"That role also includes not stabbing random people," he deadpanned.

"Right," she murmured, hands smoothing along her thighs again.

Pushing away from his desk, he stood, sending a message off in a swirl of black flames. "Let's go."

She stood too, looking perplexed. "Go where?"

He didn't answer though. He only reached for her, letting her place her hand in his, before Traveling them out of the study.

⤜)) ⊙ ((⤐

He'd taken them to a place in the city where the younglings came for dance instruction. Fortunately, they were currently at their academic lessons, and the rehearsals for the adult performers took place earlier in the day, leaving the small studio open. He'd offered the madam a good amount of coin to let them use the place privately until her next class in three hours. Then, he'd offered her even more to stay and play the piano for them as well as to buy her silence. It was Cethin's funds anyway, so he wasn't out anything.

It took a while for Wren to meet them, but she was here now, giving Kailia a warm smile and hello. Unfortunately, Bram was with her.

"Can I talk to you, Greybane?" the male asked.

"What?" Razik asked, stepping into his line of sight when his gaze lingered on Wren.

Bram refocused, squaring his shoulders. "Ariadne and I have been monitoring the southwest near Shira Forest. The rumors are true about the creatures of old waking."

"Have there been sightings?"

"Not yet, but all the signs are there. That and…" He swiped a hand over his short black hair. "There are whisperings the same is starting near Shadowfen and Everfall."

"Fuck," Razik muttered. "The Commander knows?"

"Of course," Bram said. "But he's holding off on telling the king. I don't know. Just feels like this is something Cethin should be aware of."

"So you're skirting around command?" Razik asked, arching a brow.

The warrior paled slightly, knowing that if his insubordination was reported to Tybalt, it was grounds for punishment, perhaps even dismissal from the Cadre all together. But the male lifted his chin, voice firm with conviction when he said, "My loyalty is to the king, not the Commander."

"Then why are you coming to me?" Razik asked.

Bram's brows knitted together. "Because you see Cethin every day, and it will be easier for you to find a moment to speak privately than it will be for me."

Razik said nothing, but he finally gave the male a sharp nod. It wasn't a promise he'd do anything with the information—that wasn't his place—but it was an acknowledgement nonetheless.

Bram nodded in return, but then he hesitated. "About Wren—"

"Leave," Razik snarled.

The male rolled his eyes, but he turned and left, and Razik returned his attention to the females.

Kailia was listening intently as the dance madam explained the steps of the first dance she'd be expected to perform with Cethin. Razik knew it, of course. Tybalt had ensured that he knew the dances and ways of nobility as much as he'd ensured he knew how to swing a sword and shift into his dragon form mid-step. Most Avonleyans knew the traditional dances though, whether Legacy descendants, Fae, or other.

Kailia was still, her usual stoicism and unreadable mask in place. Her gaze flickered to Razik at his approach, and he saw the glimmer of panic there.

"It's not that bad," he said, his hand falling to Wren's lower back. "We'll show you, and then you can practice."

Lia nodded, and as the madam made her way to the piano, he saw Lia brush her fingers over the hilt of the dagger at her thigh. Not to stab the female, but something he'd come to realize was a self-soothing action for her.

Guiding Wren to the dance floor, he turned to face her. Sliding his hand to her hip, he took her other hand in his, and when the first notes sounded, they both moved. There was no concentration needed. He'd attended hundreds of balls and ceremonies over the centuries, and so had Wren.

"I never thought I'd see the day Razik Greybane let another person beneath his scaly skin," Wren mused.

"I haven't," he muttered, twirling her out before pulling her back in.

"You are currently in a madam's studio so she can learn how to dance, Razik," Wren said with a knowing look.

"I'm her guard."

"This goes beyond your job, and you know it."

He glanced at Lia, who was observing them with rapt attention.

"I don't want to give Tybalt a reason to doubt me," he said as they continued to move through the steps.

Wren's brows drew together. "Why would he doubt you?"

"That's not the point," he said instead. "She has no one else, and—"

"And you see a kindred soul," Wren said in understanding. She spun under his arm, and when she was pressed back against him, she added, "Careful, Razik. You keep collecting us, and you'll have a whole family pretty soon. You can keep us with all your other treasure."

He rolled his eyes at her teasing tone. "And who, exactly, am I collecting?"

"Anyone who has been abandoned," she answered, her voice soft.

He slid his gaze to hers, navy blue eyes full of a warmth he'd come to know all too well. Which is why he didn't want to tell her what he already knew. Bram was sniffing around for more than a friendship or a fuck. The fact that the male hadn't given up after these last months was proof enough. Anyone else would have found a quick fuck not worth the trouble.

And he didn't know how to let it happen. Because when he claimed something as his, there was no turning back. She was his to guard and protect. It was in his nature as a dragon and in his blood with his lineage. But he knew that soon enough, Bram was going to go around him the same way he'd gone around Tybalt tonight.

The song finished, and he dipped Wren back, her long hair grazing the floor. She laughed, caught off guard, and when he pulled her back up, her hand came to his chest.

"It's okay to let someone else in," she whispered.

"I don't need anyone else. You and Tybalt are plenty," he muttered.

Wren only hummed, patting his chest a few times before sauntering over to Kailia. Kailia asked her some questions, Wren explaining a few steps and some timing, before Kailia was making her way to where he stood waiting. She worried her bottom lip, and he could see her visibly trembling.

"I can summon Cethin for this," Razik said, watching her carefully. "If you call for him, he will come."

She shook her head. "He's seen enough of my weaknesses," she murmured, wiping her palms along her dress.

Then she stepped forward, placing a hand on his shoulder and the other into his waiting palm. He gave her a moment before he brought his hand to her waist. Her entire body was tense, arms rigid.

"Lia, you can't dance when you're as stiff as a day-old dead animal," he said flatly.

"Why would you compare it to that?" she asked, eyes on her feet.

"Because it was a metaphor you'd understand without question, yet you asked a question anyway."

She looked up, gauging his facial expression, before she rolled her eyes. "Stop speaking and let me concentrate."

He nodded to the madam, and they started to move. Attempting to guide her as best he could, her eyes never left their feet.

It was terrible.

He was fairly certain he'd never seen a youngling as awful as she was at this. For as gracefully as she moved when stalking people and prey, her steps were forced and clumsy here.

"Lia, you have to relax," Razik said when they had to start over for the fifth time in three minutes.

"I'm trying. I just…" She stepped back, yanking out the leather band from the end of her braid and shaking out the plait. Her agitation was clear as she moved, ashes fluttering to the floor around her. Lifting her head, she met his gaze, and her eyes voiced the question he was thinking.

How in the realms was she going to dance with others if she couldn't even do so with him? A male she spent most of her days with? A male she clearly trusted to some extent?

"Let's try again," he said, motioning her back to him.

"Maybe I should watch you and Wren again," she said, taking a step back.

"That's not the issue, and you know it."

"That is not the way to teach her this," came a dark voice, cool and icy.

They all turned, Wren and the madam clamoring to their feet at finding Cethin in the doorway of the studio. How he'd known they were here, Razik didn't know, but pissed off didn't even begin to describe the king.

Darkness writhed around him, silver eyes glowing. They'd be a lot brighter if it weren't for the inky swirls in them. His boots echoed on the polished floor as he strode across it, stopping a few feet away from them.

Kailia was watching him, and Razik wasn't sure if she was about to go to him or stab him. He was never sure what she was about to do, and that was half the problem. He wasn't sure *she* was entirely sure she knew what she was going to do all the time. It made it entirely too difficult to get a feel for her.

"Your Majesty," Razik said, working to keep the drawl out of his tone. Since the three of them weren't alone, he bowed his head and went through the expected formalities.

"Cethin, what are you doing here?" Kailia asked, looking up at him with a puzzled expression.

"I was in the city on business and ran into Bram," Cethin gritted out, his stare locked on Razik. "He mentioned he'd escorted Wren to the two of you a bit ago."

"And you are upset he did that?" Kailia asked.

Razik had to work extra hard to keep his lips from turning up in amusement as a muscle in Cethin's jaw ticked.

"No, Kailia, I am not upset by that. I'm upset because—"

"Wren, can you get everyone some water?" Razik interrupted, and Cethin's head snapped to the other two females. Razik had assumed the male had forgotten they were even here, and he'd been right because Cethin's features softened a fraction as he forced some of the tension to leave his limbs.

"Yes, that would be much appreciated, Wren. Thank you," Cethin said with a tight smile. "And Madam Vera, thank you as well for generously allowing the queen to practice here. I trust you've been compensated, but I will add more to whatever has already been paid."

The madam's cheeks turned a faint shade of pink as she curtsied to Cethin, murmuring something about that not being necessary.

"Would you mind playing the song again?" he asked, and she skittered over to the piano, taking a seat on the bench. "Just give us a moment."

Razik made to step back, but Cethin said with a low snarl, "Stay there."

More than irritated with the command but unable to do anything about it in a public place, Razik's feet stayed planted while

Cethin's attention returned to Kailia. He motioned her forward with a crook of his finger, and she slowly approached.

"You need to get the steps down. Then work on the touching," he said, his tone a shade calmer with his wife before him. "Think of the dance like a hunt," he coached, motioning for her hands. But he didn't touch her. His hands stayed at his sides while one of hers went to his shoulder. Her other arm was raised in the air, and whether it was the lack of touch or simply his presence, her limbs weren't as rigid.

Cethin nodded to the madam, and she began playing. Kailia stumbled through the first few steps, but Cethin didn't falter. Instead of guiding her with his hands, his magic was there. Dark tendrils and wisps nudging her this way and that. Even the twirls were shrouded in the inky swirls, and his gaze never once left hers. Razik would never admit it out loud, but it was something to witness. A dark and haunting beauty to it all. The knowledge of *why* the king was teaching her this only added to the moment.

When the last notes echoed in the studio, the quiet was heavy. Wren had returned at some point, a tray of water still in her hands as she'd stilled to watch the two.

And him?

Razik had this odd sense of uncertainty. Maybe Tybalt was wrong. Maybe Kailia didn't have any ulterior motives in any of this. Maybe *he'd* been wrong because the way she was looking at the king in this moment showed no trace of a female who'd been forced into a marriage. If the goal was to be convincing, this was all they needed to do to show everyone at the Union Celebration.

Cethin was the first to step back, Kailia's hands lowering back to her sides. Looking from her to Razik and back again, Cethin said in a low tone, "All either of you needed to do was ask."

"I didn't want to burden you with this," Kailia said. "Razik was only helping at my request."

"You don't need to defend me to him, Lia," Razik said in his usual bored tone.

Cethin ignored him, saying to Kailia, "I'll see you for dinner."

He bid farewell to Wren and Madam Vera, and then he was gone as quickly as he'd appeared.

"He is upset," Kailia said, staring at the doorway.

"With me, not you," Razik said, gesturing her closer.

"How is it your fault?" she asked, positioning her hands. "I asked for your help."

"If the choices for a direction for his anger are you or me, it's going to be me every time," he said, moving as the music started. He actually had to concentrate on this. How had Cethin moved through this dance with his hands at his sides the entire time? He'd made it look effortless, and it was…not.

But that was how the next hour went, and by the end of it, Kailia was moving with the same grace she did everything else with. Of course, she couldn't very well dance like this at the Union Celebration. That would be something to tackle another day.

They left before the younglings started showing up for their lessons, the madam's coin purse much fuller now. Bram was waiting for Wren, and Razik said nothing as he lightly touched Kailia's arm to Travel them back to the castle.

Her rooms were empty, and wanting to leave before Cethin returned, he headed for the doors.

"Raz?"

Turning back to Kailia, he found her watching him curiously. "What?"

"The animosity between you and him? If you're not jilted lovers, then…why?"

Why?

As if there were a simple answer to that question.

As if there were a simple way to explain he was left behind in a realm he wasn't born in to be forced into a position without a choice.

As if Cethin weren't at the center of all of that.

No, there wasn't enough time to answer that, and she may be more comfortable with him, but Wren was wrong. He didn't need another person to care about.

So he said simply, "Ask your husband," and he left.

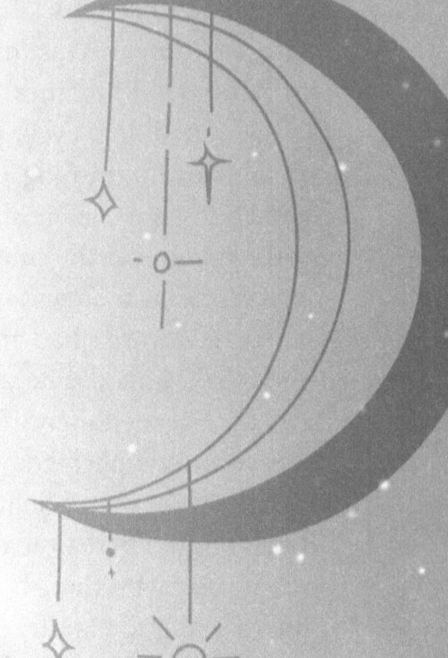

CHAPTER 31
KAILIA

S he was never one for pacing.

It involved too much movement. Gave away too many things. Exposed too many weaknesses. No, instead she'd been trained to stand still. So still, even her ashes had no reason to drift or flutter. No movement drew no attention. It was easier to observe. To blend in. To disappear into the shadows and smoke when the time came. No one missed what they never noticed to begin with.

Even when she heard the door open, she didn't move from her post near the window in their bedchamber. Still able to see the sky, despite the moon being hidden behind clouds tonight, she'd been waiting in here on purpose. It gave her time to gauge his current mood, even if it was only for a few seconds.

She'd come to differentiate their footsteps now. Knew this was Cethin and not Razik returning for some reason or another. And she could tell Cethin was still upset from earlier today. His footfalls were harsher, more pronounced than usual. Those were the types of footfalls she'd feared as a child.

Those types of footfalls signaled unacceptable failure.

But she was no longer a child, and now those types of footballs had her descending into a place of focused calm. The world quieted. All her senses honed in on the approach, waiting to see if this was a threat. Was this prey coming to her? She much preferred the hunt, but sometimes, they came straight to her anyway.

Cethin didn't even pause when he entered the room, going straight to the dressing closet. She knew he'd seen her. He always seemed to know where she was. That much was evident today when he'd found her at the small dance studio with Razik.

I'm glad to see Cethin has finally figured out you are getting lonely.

Razik's words had rolled around in her mind these last hours while she'd waited. She wasn't lonely. Was she?

No. She definitely preferred solitude and being alone. People were too…complicated.

Like right now. She needed to learn to dance appropriately, and Razik had offered to teach her. She didn't understand why Cethin was so upset by that. It was a solution to a problem and one less thing for him to handle.

He emerged from the dressing room some time later, having changed into a soft grey tunic and fresh black pants for dinner. His silver hair was pulled back, half of it tied up, and this time, those silver irises glanced over at her. Briefly. As if simply scanning the room.

As if she were that easy to dismiss.

Most of the time, that was what she wanted. She wanted to be the one that blended in so seamlessly, it wasn't noticed whether she was there or gone.

But for some reason, she didn't like being dismissed by *him*.

When Cethin started to leave the bedchamber, she found herself calling out, "That's it?"

He paused, not even looking back at her when he asked, "What?"

"You're going to say nothing to me?" she asked, still unmoving.

This time, he did look back over his shoulder when he said, "No, Kailia. I have nothing to say to you right now."

She frowned. "I do not understand why you are angry."

"I know," he answered, turning away and attempting to leave once more.

He knew?

But if he knew, then he was intentionally leaving her confused, and that was…a cruelty she'd always known he possessed. A cruelness that was only the beginning of what he was capable of, despite how well he kept it hidden from his people. Even she was questioning herself, which is why these little reminders weren't a bad thing.

"Let's go to dinner," he said after a moment, and he sounded beyond weary. He sounded as if he hadn't slept in weeks, and maybe he hadn't. She wouldn't know outside of the two nights he slept in the same bed as her.

"No," she replied, working to keep that one word controlled rather than a shout of defiance.

He'd made it a few more steps before he stilled once more. When he turned to face her, he was rubbing at his brow, stray silver strands framing his face, dancing across his sharp cheekbones and brushing his jaw.

"Kailia, I cannot do this with you right now," he said, still not looking at her.

"But I wish to discuss this now."

"No."

"You and that godsdamn word," she growled, unable to keep her irritation from her tone any longer. She'd taken two steps towards him before realizing it, her fingers inching toward the dagger.

But he…

He had taken two steps back.

"If you won't discuss this now, then I won't go to dinner tonight," she said plainly, trying to figure out what kind of game he was playing this time. He never backed away from her. If anything, he crowded her while somehow also giving her space. It was a perplexing contradiction she'd spent far too much time contemplating as of late.

"Then you won't be upholding your end of the bargain," he said just as simply. "You know. The convincing part."

"So you are allowed to come and go as you please, but I am

required to attend whatever you demand?" she asked. "Is that how your parents portrayed the thrones as well?"

"My parents are not part of this discussion."

"I have no one to model the desired actions, Cethin," she said, her ashes vibrating. Her *soul* vibrating with confusion and anger and a helplessness she hadn't felt in a very long time. A helplessness she'd vowed never to feel again, and yet since coming here, that very emotion had been slowly winding around her. Tightening. Strangling.

"This is something we can discuss later," he said, again turning away from her.

"Then I will see you after dinner. Or tomorrow, I suppose. Since spending time with me in these rooms is as appealing to you as sleeping in the stables with the horses," she snapped.

He turned back, that exasperation turning into something a little darker. A simmering fury at what she could only assume was her pushing back. A king was used to being obeyed without question, but he was the one who'd made her his queen. If anyone was at fault for any of this, it was him. He was at fault for all of it.

"I find the stables quite comforting actually," he answered, and she felt her mouth drop open. What kind of answer was that?

It took her a moment before she said, "That sounded like you'd prefer to sleep with the equine rather than spend any amount of time with me." When he only stared back at her, she added, "If that is the case, then I truly do not understand why you care if I'm dancing with Razik, spending time outside these walls, or if I were to find my way to another's bed because—"

Darkness rippled, a wave of inky fog undulating along the floor until she was standing in a knee-deep flood of magic. The iciness of it had her gasping, sharp pricks of bitter cold against her flesh that had her whole body shuddering. Not from the cold but because it wasn't fire.

He was a few steps away from her now, and she wasn't entirely sure when he'd moved. But that darkness drifted in his eyes, making them look like swirling silver orbs.

"Do not ever suggest sharing another's bed, wife. The day you took that Mark, you became only mine," he snarled, his magic pulsing with each word.

She lifted her hand, flipping it over to look at the Mark on her palm. She could swear it had a pulse of its own, beating at an erratic rhythm. Bright as the hidden moonlight, she'd spent a good portion of her nights these last weeks wondering if it had been a mistake. If she should have found another way. But spending too much time on the what-ifs distracted from the things she could control. The pieces she could move and the outcomes she could guide.

"You have nothing to say to that?" he demanded, his hands fisted as he shoved them into his pockets.

"So now we are discussing things?" she asked. "Minutes ago, you said you didn't wish to discuss anything. If that's no longer the case, explain your reaction at the dance studio."

"Kailia!" he barked. "You can't..." He trailed off, pulling his hands from his pockets. One went to his hair, remembering too late that it was tied back. His fingers got caught in the strands, more of them falling free.

"If you can't, then I can," she retorted, taking one step, the space between them fraught with tension but something more. Something she couldn't name, but something that made her want more of it. "You do not get to throw a fit when I am simply trying to do what is required of me. The Union Celebration is next week. I understand there will be dancing required. I am trying to prepare for what will be expected of me."

"Then ask me," he snapped, his breaths shallow and sharp, as if he was wrestling with some kind of unseen threat.

"When?" she cried. "When am I supposed to ask you? When you're absent during the nights? When you're gone all day? Between conversations when I'm on display at meals? You shoved me into an arena and told me to fight with no training. Which is fine. I'm used to such things, but you certainly don't get to question how I teach myself to fight and survive when you can't even be bothered enough to ensure I have proper weapons."

"Because I do not trust myself around you right now!" he snarled, taking two steps towards her, and it was too close.

She stumbled back, but he was having none of it. For every step back she took, he closed the distance until she was backed against a wall.

With his fists shoved into his pockets once more, she could feel him. Feel him vibrating in the same way she was—with fury and desperation and helplessness—but what could he possibly feel helpless about? The king of the continent that had once ruled the realm. A king who could have anything and anyone laid at his feet. A king who would do anything to get what he wanted, no matter the costs.

This close, she could see the light stubble along his jaw. The glowing flecks of molten silver in his eyes. The faint grey shade of his veins as his magic continued to pulse and seek and writhe.

Until there was a muttered, "Fuck it," and he was pitching forward. His mouth crashed onto hers, and *oh.*

This was nothing like what she had imagined a kiss would be.

Even though she was rigid and stiff, her lips were not. His were soft and plush against hers, and in the back of her mind she knew she should be stabbing him because she suddenly felt like the prey. But she wasn't stabbing him. No, she was too caught up in the hot mouth pulling a hard and sucking kiss from her lips. She'd always imagined a kiss to be gentle and kind and intimate. That was what she'd observed anyway.

This was not gentle nor kind. This was intimate in a desperate way. As if she were something he'd been craving for days and months and years. This somehow sent her thoughts scattering, but also had her entirely focused on where their mouths met. This was a different kind of hunter and prey, and she wasn't sure which one she wanted to be. The huntress. The hunted. Or both.

It was only their mouths touching, a brush of their noses here and there. No hands or fingers. Hers were still pressed to her sides, too frozen to do anything, but that was the strange thing. Usually an unexpected touch had her soul screaming and her body reacting on instinct.

His tongue brushed against the seam of her lips, and without thought, she parted them. Then, his tongue was inside her mouth. He was groaning, a deep and guttural sound that she was swallowing down as she tentatively licked against his tongue. The groan became a growl, and a strangled sound of her own crawled up her throat.

If this was kissing—this struggle and fighting and chasing—then she thought she might like this very much. Because fighting and hunting and seeking was something she understood, unlike all the other things she'd been navigating lately.

He shifted, and she felt rather than heard his hands come up, bracing himself against the wall on either side of her head. So careful not to touch her.

But his magic did.

His magic brushed along her skin while he pressed his mouth to hers even harder. More earnest. While his tongue danced against hers, she marveled at how this touch—the press of mouths and lips, tongues and teeth—was so, so different from bruising fingers and harsh fists, from burning palms and unyielding holds.

This kind of touch was intoxicating and exciting and—

Dangerous.

The thought coursed through her like the flames and embers that used to torture her, and before she realized what she was doing, her dagger was out and at Cethin's throat. Her husband blinked back at her, lust and desire still clouding his gaze as he clearly tried to form coherent thoughts.

"Are you all right?" he asked, his voice so low and gravelly it made her thighs clench, and wasn't that an odd reaction to a voice? "I didn't mean to—"

"Kiss me?" she demanded.

"No, I definitely meant to do that," he answered, not a flicker of apology or regret on his elegant features. "But I didn't intend to lose that much control. Not right away. Not with it being your—"

He pressed his lips together, searching her face.

"My what?" she asked, trying to control the small tremor in her hand that held the dagger. Her shield. Her reminder to herself that she was in control, not him.

But he noticed the tremor too, and when he took a measured step back, he moved as if it physically pained him to do so. It pained her too, and she didn't... None of this made sense. How could one crave closeness and want to shove someone as far away as possible at the same time? How could one person make her feel so many emotions in the same moment? And why did she want to stab him but also kiss him again?

He ran his thumb along his bottom lip as he watched her. "That was foolish," he said. "That was why I was trying to keep my distance. You...distract me."

"How can I possibly distract you when we are never around each other?" she asked, her arm now at her side, but her dagger still clenched tightly in her fist.

"Your mere existence distracts me," he answered, agony and wonder merging in those few words. "Knowing you're out there at any given time. Wondering what you are doing. Who you're with. Life was easier when I didn't know you existed."

In an odd way, she understood exactly what he meant.

Silver eyes met hers once more, desperate and wanting and defeated. "You are a distraction I cannot afford, but one I am finding myself so utterly obsessed with, I keep forgetting why it's a terrible thing."

And she understood that too.

-)) ⊙ ((-

Dinner was a tense performance that kept her on edge. Every time Cethin moved, she had to remind herself to relax. Whenever he leaned in to speak softly to her, playing the perfect doting husband like he did every single night, all she could think about was his lips on hers. Her eyes would dip to his mouth, and his lips would curl up the smallest amount at the corners. She was sure to everyone else it appeared they were sharing an inside secret—and in a sense they were—but she was left wondering if everything from their rooms had been an act too. Which parts of him were real?

Now, she was watching him move silently about the sitting room, gathering various items. She had no doubt he was about to slip away to his study in the catacombs. But the Union Celebration was next week, and she needed…direction? Reassurance?

Answers.

She needed answers.

There was too much happening outside of her control in this moment, and she needed to turn the tables back in her favor.

"Can we speak now?" she asked, stepping from the dark corner she'd been watching from.

He didn't even jump, just confirming to her he always seemed to know where she was.

"Were you going to attempt to follow me tonight, tiny fiend?" he asked, straightening and slipping a hand into his pocket. The other rubbed along his jaw as his eyes ran over her, and there was no mistaking he was thinking about earlier.

And now so was she.

Dammit.

"Stop that," she said, coming closer. Each step was careful, making sure she kept her defenses up. Forcing herself to concentrate and remember her training. "You Travel wherever it is you go," she continued. "How could I possibly follow you?"

"I believe you'd find it easier than you think," he answered, his other hand going into his pocket now. He rocked back on his heels, watching her as much as she was watching him. "What would you like to speak about?"

"What would I…" She trailed off incredulously. "Cethin, what do you think I want to speak about?"

"There are a number of topics with you, wife," he replied conversationally. "But I'm hoping you want to discuss the way my lips felt on yours, because then I would want to discuss how you tasted with your tongue in my mouth."

"I…" She felt her cheeks warm, and she hated it. Clearing her throat, she said, "I do not wish to discuss that."

"That's disappointing," he said, and her eyes narrowed as she watched him fight a smile.

"Cethin," she deadpanned.

He sighed, all mirth leaving his face. "I'm not going to apologize for earlier today, Kailia."

"Which part?"

His brows knitted, and it took a long minute before he said, "After going over all my interactions with you today, I find there are none I feel the need to apologize for."

She scoffed. "Why were you upset about the dance studio?"

"Why was I upset that you went to learn something that involved a male—whom I cannot stand—touching you? You need clarification about that?"

"No, I need clarification on what I should have done differently since I cannot ask you for these things."

"I'm the only one you should be asking for anything you need."

"Then in that case, I need clarification on how I am to do that when you are never around."

They stared at each other, back in this place they so often found themselves. An impasse of wills and stubbornness. A place of push and pull and a struggle for dominance that each of them was trying to pretend didn't exist.

"Maybe we should stop pretending," she blurted.

His head tipped to the side. "And what are we pretending, wife?"

"I don't know," she admitted. "Perhaps that this is ever going to work? You should stop pretending I was the right choice for this, and I should stop pretending I can be what you need."

"You know very little of what I need," he said in the same voice that had rumbled from him after the kiss.

"I'm not disagreeing with you."

He'd drifted closer at some point. Not close enough to touch, but close enough that she could see the fine threading details on his tunic.

"And what do you feel you need to make this work?" Cethin asked,

"I need you to help me know what I should be doing, and to do that, you need to spend more than mealtimes with me," she answered, tensing as he moved closer still.

"Are you going to admit you miss me yet?"

"It has nothing to do with that."

He hummed, slowly lifting a hand. His magic came first, as it always did, brushing along her jaw before his fingertip followed. That single point of contact an icy balm to her heated skin. It skated down until it slipped under her chin, tipping her face up even more.

"I need you to stop going places and doing things with a male who is my rival in every way," he said.

"He's my guard, Cethin."

"I don't give a fuck."

Her eyes widened in understanding. "You are jealous." His lips pressed into a thin line, and for once, it was all she needed for confirmation. "I thought it was clear you are my husband, not him."

"By Arius, Kailia, that doesn't always stop someone, and I wouldn't put it past Razik to… He knows what he's doing," he said, removing his touch and moving to the sofa.

Kailia followed, making the conscious choice to sit closer rather than at the other end.

Start small.

"I asked Razik about the animosity between the two of you. He said to ask you," she ventured.

She knew what it took to get two people to this place. For two people to hate each other so greatly, something unforgivable and traumatic had to have happened. She'd tracked down the people who'd done unforgivable things to her, vowing to rip vengeance from their blood. Someday, she'd have extracted her vengeance from every single one of them. But Razik and Cethin had to live with each other every day, and *that* was something she couldn't understand.

Unless it wasn't by choice?

In which case, she understood not having a choice very well.

"Razik believes I am the reason he was abandoned to this realm," Cethin said, the wariness returning to his tone.

"Are you?" she asked.

"Yes."

"Then…?"

"There are things at play. Ancient traditions," Cethin said. "Many have tried to coerce him into compliance over the centuries, and each time he resisted— Well, it's not hard to see how we became what we are."

"And this tradition involves what? What could be so terrible that it would cause such a rivalry?"

Cethin eyed her as he said, "It involves a bond that would force him to protect me and give his life for me if required."

"Oh," Kailia whispered. Her feet were tucked under her, and she ran a palm over her thigh. "Then I suppose I understand the animosity on his end, but are you simply upset he will not agree to this?"

"It's more complicated than that," he answered. "At this point, I don't want it either, but he still blames me. For all of it. My mother was very insistent. She went to some extremes in attempts to get him to agree to the bond."

She was quiet for a long moment. Cethin had never voluntarily discussed his mother. Or his father, for that matter.

King Tethys had been dead for over a year before she'd found her way to these lands, and Queen Selinya was rarely spoken of. When she was mentioned though, it was usually in reverence.

But beyond all of that, none of Cethin's explanations gave her any insight as to why the Oracle would have appeared as Razik when she visited all those years ago. She'd been hoping there was a common thread buried in the reason for his hatred.

But perhaps there was.

She had been forced into a marriage, while Razik had possessed the strength to resist a bond being forced on him.

Now she needed to get him to talk about it with her.

But then another thought struck her.

"Why would that responsibility be placed on Razik and not Tybalt? Wouldn't his father be better suited?"

Cethin shook his head. "Tybalt is his uncle, and that is a story for him to tell. As for why Tybalt didn't take on the role, it is because one can only be bonded to one person in such a way."

"And he already is?"

Cethin nodded. "To my mother."

"That is why you know so much about the bond. Because Tybalt was bonded to your mother," she said, sorting through all the information. "Do you blame Razik for not wanting the same?"

He sighed, pulling the band from his hair, the strands falling around his face, and there was something intimate in it. Not like the kissing, but intimate in a different way. He looked disheveled and casual, and he had never once allowed himself to appear this way outside these rooms.

"In a way, yes, but not in the way he thinks," Cethin answered. "I think we—"

A knock on the door interrupted them, followed by a gruff, "Cethin?"

"Speaking of Tybalt," Cethin muttered, getting to his feet and going to answer the door.

The Commander slipped inside, immediately scanning the room and his features tightening when they skimmed over her. "There has been activity in the area we've been monitoring. We can't wait any longer to make a statement."

"You're sure?" Cethin asked, his entire demeanor changing.

Gone was the tired and contemplative male from a minute ago, replaced by a king who looked ready to go to war.

"I wouldn't have come here if I weren't," Tybalt replied.

"Yeah. All right," Cethin said, his magic converging around him as he spoke. It thickened, becoming so dense it obscured him, until it didn't. Until it receded, leaving Cethin in thick leathers while his dark power clung to him like a second skin. He looked...

Well, he looked like the king that was only whispered about across the sea in the same way the death god, his wife, and their children were only whispered of in most of the realm.

"Razik is on his way to stay with the queen," Tybalt was saying.

But she was on her feet at that. "I want to go. I can help."

"I think that would be unwise," Tybalt replied, scarcely glancing at her before giving Cethin a pointed look.

"If she wants to go, then she comes with us," Cethin said simply.

She was unprepared for what those words did to her. No hesitation. No debating or arguing or second-guessing. A simple acceptance of her and her capabilities.

"Cethin—" Tybalt started.

"Are you ready, Kailia?" Cethin asked, turning to her and ignoring the Commander's protest.

"Yes," she answered, summoning her bow as she approached the king.

He glanced down, noting her bare feet, but he said nothing. He only extended his hand, and when she placed her fingers in his waiting palm, he tugged her a little closer. Smirking at her gasp.

But that second of playfulness was gone a moment later when they stepped onto too-soft grass. She immediately recognized the Shira Forest behind her. If she was correct, they were on the opposite side of the forest from where the hunt had taken place. South, based on the warmer temperatures for the middle of the night and the stretch of river running off to the right.

Razik appeared, stepping from the air seconds behind them, and Wren was with him. She looked nervous, but relief flashed in her eyes when she saw the river. It made sense considering her affinity for water. Kailia could only assume she was here because Razik anticipated needing to draw power from her.

"Where is the threat?" she asked Cethin.

"They're watching. Give them a minute," he answered, squeezing her fingers.

It was then she realized they were still holding hands.

She hadn't pulled away from his touch the moment they got here.

That was when the earth beneath their feet shook, sending a violent tremor through the ground. She stumbled right into Cethin, his arm looping around her and keeping her on her feet. Razik had done the same for Wren, the female nestled into his side like they'd done this before.

"Where do you think it'll surface?" Razik growled, his eyes glowing and scanning the night.

"No idea," Tybalt answered, his eyes glowing too. "Ariadne and Bram are monitoring farther north. This was the area with the most activity."

"Cethin, I need direction here," she muttered, for the first time in a long time feeling out of her element in a fight.

"Just stay close, wife," he said, his fingers flexing where they still held her to him.

She was about to protest, to shove him off, but the ground shook again, jostling all of them, before things went silent and still, as if even the winds were holding their breath.

Then, a streak of bright light burst from the ground, shooting into the sky.

No. Not light.

A giant winged serpent.

It twisted in the air above them, bright multicolored wings flapping and keeping its glowing body airborne while it elicited a bone-rattling hiss, fangs bared. Its massive body coiled more, preparing to strike, and she had three arrows nocked and aimed.

But she didn't need to.

Cethin's magic was growing, twisting and swirling like a cyclone of darkness. He'd released her when she'd pulled her arrows, but now he was solely focused on his magic. More than his eyes were glowing. In the trickling moonlight and the light of the sky serpent, she could see the faint outline of his veins.

The serpent hissed again before it struck, diving straight for them, but Cethin met it with his power. Dark and light collided, exploding outward.

Kailia was yanked to the ground, Razik covering her and Wren with a shield of black flames, but she wanted to see.

"Lia!" Razik growled as she pulled free of him.

If she could just get past the flames…

Without thinking, she tried to step into her ashes. Felt her body go weightless, floating among the smoke of Razik's flames.

Then she was being tossed around once more, her body flickering in and out of existence, before she was dumped back on the ground. Having gone nowhere once again, Cethin was a few feet away.

Scrambling to find her bow, she looked up as another bone-shaking hiss rent through the night.

But Cethin was…

She could do nothing but watch, her mouth hanging open. Cethin's magic was coiling around the sky serpent like inky vines. Cethin himself was off the ground, his power beneath him like a moving platform of sand dunes. It rose and fell, lifting into the sky and avoiding the strikes of the serpent.

Then all those cords of black yanked simultaneously, dragging the serpent back to the ground. The shudder when it hit the earth had her losing her balance again, even on her knees, and her chin hit the ground, teeth sinking into her lip. She tasted blood, but hardly noticed as she managed to get her feet under her.

Only for an arm to loop around her waist.

She shrieked, her bow still on the ground a few feet away, and she couldn't grab her daggers because her arms were pinned to her sides.

"The creatures of old wake. It is a sign from the Fates," a female voice crooned into her ear. "We cannot let this be."

Kailia kicked and thrashed, hearing the female grunt when her bare foot connected with her knee, but she didn't release Kailia. Instead, she dragged her backwards a few more feet before shoving her at another. Someone bigger. Someone stronger. Someone with fire gifts because his touch burned and the smell of charred flesh reached her nostrils. Pain flared along her middle. Bile filled her throat, but there was a hand clamped over her mouth, so there was nowhere for it to go as she gagged on her own vomit. The palm keeping her quiet was burning as torturously as the one keeping her still.

Desperately, she slipped into her smoke and ashes, hoping to at least be released from their hold. She was pulled this way and that, her body twisting and tumbling, and then she was being dumped on the ground again, her stomach convulsing as she pushed onto her knees and retched.

Someone touched her hair, and Kailia jerked to the side, crawling away. Eyes wide, they fell on Wren, who was staring at her, palms up placatingly.

"Don't touch her," Razik said, crouching beside the female. "Cethin will handle it once he's done."

Once he's done.

She twisted around, finding the king with a hand raised and fist clenched, the two figures on the ground several feet away. They were clutching at their chests, muffled, agonized moans sounding.

"Leave one alive for questioning, Cethin!" Tybalt barked from where he stood at his side.

"We'll find another," Cethin responded, his tone nothing but icy death as the two figures continued to writhe in torment.

Razik had pulled Wren into his chest, her face buried there, but Kailia watched. Watched as the king tortured and took and drug out their deaths that she was certain could have been over in seconds.

Finally, the moans fell silent. Kailia had wrapped her arms around herself, feeling the tender flesh at her middle. The charred skin on her face where a hand had covered her mouth. There was a dagger in her hand, and she had no idea when she'd grabbed that from the sheath at her side. Thank the gods she hadn't stabbed Wren.

Cethin lowered to a crouch before her, a muscle ticking in his jaw as he noted the puddle of vomit before his still glowing eyes slid over her.

"Razik will bring your bow. We're going home," he said, a hard edge to his tone. "I have to touch you, but you can keep that dagger in your hand while I do. Okay?"

She only nodded, and seconds later, they were in the same positions on the floor of their bedchambers.

"What happened to the serpent?" she asked.

Cethin's eyes were raking over her again as he answered, "It slumbers once more."

"What's all over you?"

And how had she missed the splatters of gold all over his clothes, his hands, his face?

"The serpent's blood," he answered, reaching for her.

Instinctively, she raised the dagger, keeping it between them. He paused for only a moment, giving her a small, tight smile before he continued his movement, fingers brushing across her brow and pushing back stray hair.

"You have burns," he ground out.

Her eyes dropped to her lap, spying small splatters of bile on her dress. That was…just great.

"Yes," she whispered. "I can move through smoke and ashes, but fire still…"

He nodded. "I'll have Niara send up a salve."

"That's not necessary. They'll heal quickly enough," she answered, struggling to her feet.

Cethin followed, staying close. "I'll still send for it."

"Great," she muttered. "I'm going to clean up."

Avoiding a bath because of the burns, she used a cloth to wash herself as best she could. She rinsed her mouth and cleaned her teeth, feeling the phantom touches the entire time.

When she emerged, Cethin did the same, leaving her in the bedchamber. She found a glass jar of balm, along with a note from Niara with instructions, and she sighed, applying it to her stomach and her cheeks where the male's fingers had dug in.

She was nestled under the covers when Cethin returned in those loose linen pants and sans shirt, his moon Mark visible on his chest atop the other Mark.

Rounding the bed, he pulled back the blankets.

She didn't have it in her to lift her head as she murmured, "What are you doing?"

"Monitoring my wife," he answered.

"I have questions."

"I'm sure you do," he said with another grim smile. "But we'll save them for tomorrow."

That was fine with her. She was more than ready to escape to the safety of her dreams.

As sleep came for her, she could swear she felt the barest brush of fingers along her brow and down her hair.

And it didn't burn.

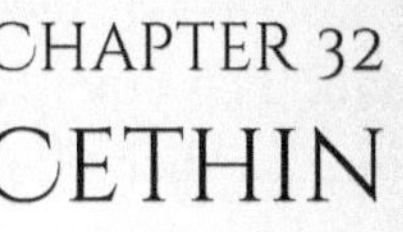

CHAPTER 32
CETHIN

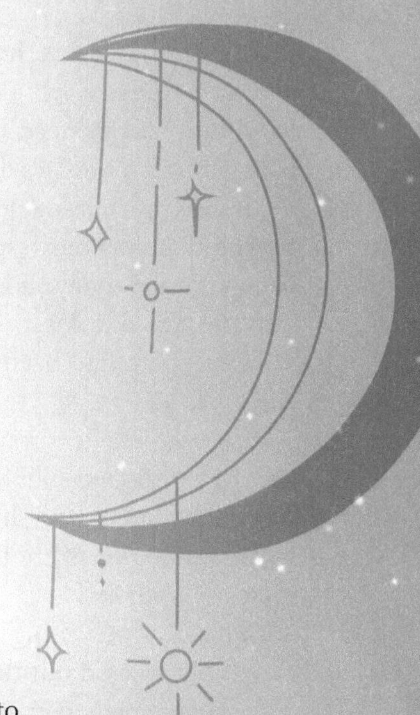

He didn't sleep.

He should have. He needed to.

After expending so much magic on the *nagasky* and then drawing out the draining of the two who had touched Kailia, his magic was down to the dregs. It'd been reckless to let it get so low. Razik or Tybalt could have handled the two Elder Clan members, but that hadn't been an option. From the moment he turned to see Kailia thrashing, saw the panic and agony clear on her face as she twisted and kicked and fought, he'd claimed those deaths. He'd enjoyed every second as he'd squeezed their life forces, feeling their hearts stuttering as if he held them in his fist. He'd debated drawing closer. Touching them so his darkness could seep into their blood and let death circulate until it touched every part of their souls and marked them for Arius when they crossed the Veil.

Then he'd seen Kailia huddled on the ground at his feet, a puddle of vomit to the side and her tiny frame trembling. The burn marks on her face. The still present panic as she rocked herself back and forth, certain she didn't realize she was doing so.

He'd ended them far sooner than they'd deserved, but she was more important than their deaths.

He'd brought her home. They'd both cleaned up. She'd slept, and he'd watched her do so. Watched as the imprint of another's hand that had silenced her slowly faded from a blistering red until only her warm brown skin remained.

It was fascinating to him she was so still even in her sleep. Maybe that was the response to whatever she'd experienced while being touched today though. The other two times he'd shared a bed with her, she'd at least rolled to her side or stretched her arm out. Tonight, there had been nothing but the steady rise and fall of her chest.

He was seated, propped against the headboard as he watched her. Her unbound hair was fanned across the pillow, and her long eyelashes fluttered as she dreamed. He wished he knew what she was dreaming of. Were they peaceful and calm, or were they nightmares of tonight?

The sun was rising when she stirred earlier than he'd anticipated. She peered out through bleary eyes until she saw him. Then her eyes snapped open, and she lurched upright.

"You are still here?" she rasped, sleep clinging to her voice and making it a little huskier in a way that sent a shiver down his spine.

"Avonleya still sleeps," he answered. "The sun has barely breached the horizon."

"I know, but you never stay," she said, toying with the ends of her hair. "I assumed you would have left once I fell asleep."

"Do you wish I had?"

"No. I mean…" Her hands dropped to her lap. "I'm surprised is all. I'm used to waking alone."

He nodded, bending a knee and propping his arm atop it.

"You didn't sleep," she observed, peering at him a little closer. "You should have slept. You used a lot of power."

"I'm aware," he murmured.

"Then why didn't you sleep?"

He shrugged before he said, "The burns on your face are gone, but I didn't check the others…"

Cethin trailed off as she shoved the blankets back to examine her torso. She hadn't worn one of the nightdresses last night, instead opting for loose pants and a short top that left her middle exposed. He assumed it was to not irritate the burns.

Her hands slid across her skin, and he followed their path with his gaze. A breath of relief came from her when she found her torso as healed as her cheeks.

"I'm sorry I didn't prevent that from happening," he said gruffly, gaze fixed on her middle where her fingers lingered. She may have healed, but the image of those burns was imprinted on his mind.

"Why are you apologizing for that? You didn't burn me," she said, shifting so she sat against the headboard now too.

"I should have anticipated members of the Elder Clan being there."

"You were fighting a serpent in the sky," she deadpanned. "I think we were all a little distracted."

"That's not an excuse," he retorted, the words sharper than he'd intended.

She studied him before she said, "You are upset?"

"With myself," he affirmed.

She nodded, pulling her hair over her shoulder. "Can you tell me of the sky serpent?"

"The *nagasky* are some of the creatures of old. They are believed to have been here since the realm was created," he answered. "For the most part they slumber, guarding sacred places from when the realm was born. It is part of our accords with the Elder Clans that they monitor the creatures of old and help keep them under control, and in return, we leave them be. It's a tenuous arrangement, and it has gotten more so in the last century."

"Why?"

"The Elder Clans keep traditions of old. Traditions from before the Sutara bloodline took the throne. The creatures of old fought in wars more ancient than this realm, and the Elder Clans fought alongside Avonleya in the Great War."

"If the creatures of old have been here since the realm was created, why aren't there any on the other continents?" Kailia asked.

She'd shifted closer as he spoke, and he was certain she hadn't realized it yet. There was no pillow barrier between them this time, and he could feel her. So could his magic. And despite him having nothing left, it stirred, as if trying to seek her out. It only added to his restlessness at not having any magic reserves. A gnawing in his soul that he knew would become unbearable soon enough.

"At one point in time, the entire realm was ruled under one. Avonleya was the central continent, and a High Queen resided here," he answered.

"In Elshira? The original capital?" Kailia asked.

Cethin shook his head. "No, the original capital was not Elshira. When the realm was created, there was another city. They say it was built into the sides of the mountains. We don't know where it is. Some believe it never existed at all and is a myth of old."

"And you?" she asked, facing him fully now.

"I've spent many decades searching for the Runic Lands and have never found them," he admitted. "But the creatures of old guard sacred sites, and I've seen them, so I'm inclined to believe the Runic Lands exist as well."

"You believe these creatures remain in Avonleya out of duty then? Not because the Wards trap them here?" she asked, absentmindedly braiding her hair, then unbraiding it before repeating the action.

"Not much is known about the creatures of old," he admitted. "Only that they are powerful. For a long time, only the Elder Clans could contain them. It is why the accords were struck."

"What changed?"

"I was born."

She stilled, her hair partially braided and fingers wound among the strands.

"They were stirring before then," he clarified. "My parents had kept them subdued, but when I was born, they woke. It has been a struggle to keep them contained since then. While it takes an entire faction of the Elder Clan to contain a creature of old, I am able to do so with my power alone."

"The Elder Clans feel threatened," Kailia said in understanding.

"Yes," he answered. "They have been trying to have more say in policies, and I've been attempting to include them. But they rely heavily on signs and prophecy, and basing all decisions on those things alone is not in the best interest for anyone."

She nodded, unwinding her hair again before shaking out her hands.

"But enough history for one morning. It's far too early. How are you feeling?" he asked.

"Well," she answered. Then she gave him a dubious look. "I slept."

"Physically well, yes," he replied, stretching his leg back out and ignoring her pointed words. "But external wounds heal differently than internal ones."

"That is true," she murmured, looking away from him.

"Did you learn the dances, then?"

Her eyes snapped back to his. "What?"

"The dances. Did you learn them for the Union Ceremony?"

"They weren't overly complicated," she admitted. "But the dances aren't the real issue."

"The touching," he supplied, already knowing the answer. It was why he'd gone to the dance studio after running into Bram. He would have gone anyway, of course, but at least he'd had a valid excuse for stalking her around Aimonway.

"I don't want to react unfavorably during the Union Celebration," Kailia said. "I don't think stabbing people at the event would bode well for me."

He huffed a laugh. "I prefer you save your stabbings for me anyway, tiny fiend."

She blinked at him. "That was the plan."

Another huff of laughter rumbled from his chest, and he slowly reached over to tuck her hair behind her ear. "I wish you had come to me first."

"We already discussed why I didn't," she said, sitting perfectly still until he withdrew his hand.

"Yes, but if you had, I would have told you I already had plans in place regarding you and dancing."

Her head tilted, the hair he'd tucked back slipping free again. "You do?"

He nodded, settling back against the headboard and stacking his hands on his abdomen. "We will have to dance. More than once. As for others, we can limit that."

"We can?" she asked, a hopefulness ringing in her tone.

"We are the king and queen, Kailia. More than that, it is well known there is a possessiveness associated with partners. No one will be surprised if I'm...particular about who touches you," he answered.

Her own huff of laughter sounded. "Surely I'll be expected to dance with more than you. Won't you be dancing with others?"

"Not if you don't wish me to."

She studied him, clearly unsure whether he was jesting or not. "How are these things usually handled?"

"That doesn't matter. We can handle them however we wish," he answered simply.

"I really don't need to give people more of a reason not to trust me. Won't refusing to dance with others make me appear...pretentious?" she asked, worrying her bottom lip.

"Again, I do not care what others think, but if it worries you, how many people do you think you could dance with before it becomes too much?"

She smoothed her hands over the blankets. Once. Twice. "If I know who it is beforehand, it might be better."

"People you are familiar with then? Not those you meet that night or have only met in passing?" he clarified.

Amber eyes met his, relief flickering in them. "Yes."

"Make a list then, wife," he said, dragging himself from the bed.

"Wait," she called after him, and he paused at the foot of the bed.

"Yes?"

"I... Thank you," she said softly, always watching him.

"I promised you protection at the start of all this. I never forget my promises," he said with a tight smile. "I'm going to get something to eat. Can I get you anything?"

Her face fell, eyes darting to the side, but a minute later, her features smoothed out, becoming that unreadable mask. "No, thank you."

"I'm coming back, Kailia," he said. "I'll be right back."

She only nodded, clearly not believing him.

Cethin grabbed a shirt and slipped on shoes before he Traveled. Not to the kitchens, but to the Greybane Estate, directly into Tybalt's study. The male was seated behind his desk, bent over a map, but he looked up at Cethin's appearance.

Sitting back in his chair, Tybalt's keen gaze swept over him before he said, "The area is secure. The Cadre is monitoring all the known sites for the foreseeable future."

Cethin nodded. "And the *nagasky*?"

"Was returned to its place of slumber. The Elder Clan members were also collected by their brethren. They were not happy, Cethin," Tybalt answered.

"That makes two of us," Cethin retorted, stepping between the chairs before the desk to peer at the map. Jarek, Fallon, and Draven were monitoring the western half of the kingdom, while Ariadne, Bram, and Tybalt were taking the eastern half. "Have there been any other stirrings?"

"Not from the creatures of old, but the Elder Clans requested a meeting," Tybalt replied. "This isn't good, Cethin. Things with them have been tense since your mother."

"My mother is the cause of many things," Cethin muttered. "But we can discuss this later. I came here because I need blood, Tybalt."

The male straightened. "And I'm going to tell you that's not a wise idea."

"We have rations stored for emergencies. This is one," Cethin replied. "I'm drained. It makes me…restless and irritable. Next week is the Union Celebration, and with the way things have been going lately, I'd prefer my reserves be full for that occasion."

Tybalt rubbed his temple, the hesitation clear.

"Unless you have other news I need to be made aware of, it's the only option," Cethin added. "Have you heard from her?"

Tybalt shook his head. "You know the cost of this?"

"It's been years since I've consumed rations," Cethin countered.

"It doesn't matter. Time doesn't erase the damage already done."

"It's not a request, Tybalt," he said. "The Elder Clan is restless. These phantoms are unpredictable. The creatures of old are stirring—"

"Ever since Kailia showed up," Tybalt cut in. "Surely you realize that? You've put the correlation together?"

"Kailia is not what we're discussing right now," Cethin snapped. "You and I both know what happens if my reserves are completely drained. We can't afford for me to go into the kind of slumber that will be required to fill my power even a fraction."

"And the amount of Fae blood it will require to fill your powers is large enough to push you over a different edge, Cethin. I cannot permit it," Tybalt said, shaking his head in refusal.

"Then what do you propose? I do not have a Source. I do not have a Guardian. My only options are blood or time. One of those I have. One I do not," Cethin retorted.

"This is why a Fae as a partner would have been a wiser choice," Tybalt sighed, rubbing at his temple again.

"Do not give me your opinion on that matter again," he replied, his tone low and dark.

"She's part of something bigger, and you refuse to see it," Tybalt growled.

"She'll be the salvation of this kingdom."

"That may be true," Tybalt agreed, pushing to his feet. "But she'll be *your* downfall in the process."

He moved to the wall behind his desk, pressing his palm flush against it. Magic rippled, black flames skittering across the surface before the wall dissolved, revealing a large icebox. Cethin came to his side, pressing his palm beside Tybalt's, the last of his magic appearing, faint and weak, alongside another burst of dragon fire.

The door to the icebox opened, revealing several dozen bottles of Fae blood. Reaching in, he grabbed two, downing the first one entirely. He hadn't been lying. It had been decades since he'd tasted Fae blood, but the rush of power through his veins was nearly as divine as being between a female's legs. There was a high and a peace and the feeling of never wanting to leave this state of mind.

The sharp snick of the icebox closing drew him back to reality, and he glared at the Commander. He could have let him enjoy the moment a little longer. At least he still had another bottle.

"Be careful, Cethin," Tybalt warned. "I say this not as the Commander of your forces, but as a male who watched you grow into who you are today. Be careful."

"Two bottles won't bring the curse upon me," he retorted, stepping back and preparing to leave.

"The blood isn't what I'm referring to," he answered, concern and apprehension shining in his warm brown eyes.

"I have it under control," Cethin answered, and then he was gone, back in his rooms.

He placed the bottle of blood at the back of the icebox in their small kitchenette, planning to drink it later today. Returning to the bedchamber, Kailia had nestled back down in the covers, but she was awake.

Swirling amber eyes tracked his every movement as he removed his shoes and pulled his tunic over his head, tossing it aside. Then he rounded the bed, climbing back in. She shifted, rolling to her side.

"You came back," she said softly.

"Always," he answered, propping a hand behind his head.

"Why?"

But he didn't answer, and eventually she rolled back over, a comfortable silence lulling them both to slumber.

He might not have answered her, but he knew the reason. It was fucked up and unsettling, yet here he was. He wasn't worried about the blood. He'd drink that bottle, his power would be restored, and he'd be fine to carry on. Everyone worried about the addiction Fae blood held for Avonleyans, and they weren't wrong to be concerned.

He was just learning there were much stronger addictions out there, and he was tired of trying to resist them.

—)) ☉ ((—

"Kailia? Are you ready?" he asked after knocking twice on the door.

People had been filing in for the last two hours in preparation for the Union Ceremony, members of their forces performing security duties. The smell of the various food delicacies being prepared had permeated the whole of the castle all day, and he was more than ready to eat. Throughout the next two weeks, more food would be prepared and delivered to various territories for those who weren't in attendance tonight, with smaller celebrations taking place throughout the kingdom.

But right now, they were due to officially start the celebration in the next twenty minutes.

He knocked again. "Kailia?"

"Come in," she called, and he pushed the door open to the lounge.

It was a small room off the great hall that was reserved for the king and queen. A door on the opposite side would lead out to a balcony that overlooked the hall with a set of stairs leading down into the room itself.

Kailia stood off to one side, Wren stepping back from smoothing down a spot on Kailia's dress.

"This seems excessive," Kailia murmured, lifting her hands and letting them fall back to her sides.

It was anything but excessive.

The black corset contained intricate detailing, while a combination of silk and lace draped down from her hips. A slit up the right side reached to the top of her thigh, and when she moved, he could see the small knife strapped there. The top of the corset was as sheer as the tights, running along her chest, collarbone, and over her shoulders, while the sleeves were the same silk and lace as the skirt. More sheer fabric layered over the skirts, flowing to the ground like a train, with a veil of the same pinned to her hair in the back. Small silver beads and black pearls were sewn strategically into the dress, giving the illusion of falling stars.

Or fluttering ashes.

Excessive was the last word on his mind as he stared at her.

"Why isn't he saying anything?" Kailia asked Wren, looking down at herself and smoothing her hands along the corset that hugged her slim waist.

"It's a good thing, Kailia," Wren said with a knowing smile.

"Can you all give us a moment?" Cethin asked.

Wren adjusted another layer of the train before she left with Razik. Cethin had been so focused on Kailia, he hadn't even noticed the male was in here.

When the door clicked shut, Kailia looked up at him, worrying her bottom lip. "They insisted that this is what I was to wear."

"You look ethereal, wife," he replied, still unable to move. Eyes still raking over her, trying to commit every bit of this moment to memory.

"It feels excessive," she repeated.

"You're a queen. There's nothing excessive. In fact, you're missing something," he said, finally moving from where he'd been rooted in place the last several minutes.

She frowned, turning to the mirror that had been brought in. "What could possibly be missing?"

He came up behind her, and she met his gaze in the glass reflection. Her hair was loose, free and flowing around her shoulders. That blue crystal still hung around her neck, and black slippers peeked out from under the hem of her dress. There was nothing else. No bracelets or rings. Just her and a natural beauty that could never be replicated.

Being careful not to touch her, he brought his arms around her, holding his palms face up. His magic swirled, darkness twisting and writhing, and when it receded, a circlet sat in his hands. Black pearls and sparkling diamonds adorned it, making it simple and elegant and perfect for her.

He lifted it, carefully setting it atop her head. The onyx metal came to a point in the center of her brow, and she was no longer holding his stare but staring at her reflection. He couldn't read her expression.

"What are you thinking?" he asked after a moment.

"I thought I'd feel different in this moment," she said, her head canting to the side as she studied herself.

"How so?"

"This moment is a culmination of so much, and yet I question if it's something I should have at all," she murmured, and he wasn't sure if she was talking to herself or to him.

"A ruler who feels deserving of their crown has become too comfortable on a throne," Cethin said.

She twisted to face him, and he stepped back to give her space.

"You do not feel deserving of your crown?" she asked.

He shook his head. "I sit on a throne because of the blood that flows in my veins, so I spend my days trying to prove to the kingdom I am there to serve them."

She nodded as another knock sounded. The door opened, Razik, Wren, Zayan, and Tybalt slipping in.

"Sorry to interrupt, but it's time," Tybalt said. "You are both ready?"

Cethin nodded, taking the crown Zayan held out to him. Silver and rubies, the contrast was stark compared to Kailia's circlet. He would prefer something simpler, but tradition and all that.

He unceremoniously set it atop his head, then adjusted the sleeves of his jacket as the others filed out the door on the opposite side of the room.

"Breathe, Kailia," he said softly as she slipped her arm through his.

She nodded, her fingers flexing on the crook of his arm.

"I need you to trust me tonight, wife," he coaxed. "Can you do that?"

"Just for tonight," she breathed.

"I'll take just for tonight for now," he replied, bending to brush his lips across her temple. It was scarcely a touch, but he couldn't help himself. He'd expected her to tense even more than she already was, but she relaxed a fraction. Her shoulders dropped some, and she inched closer to him.

He led her through the door, the black marble floor gleaming beneath their feet. Banners of black with silver moons and stars hung from the ceiling. Zayan was off to the right of the balcony overlooking the hall. Tybalt, Razik, and Wren were already down the stairs and waiting at the bottom.

Zayan smiled brightly. Even if Cethin could tell it was a little forced, no one else could from below. Extending an arm in their direction as they reached the top of the stairs, the Hand announced, his voice filling the entire hall, "Welcome his Majesty, King Cethin, and his wife and our new queen, Kailia."

As one, the entire room dropped to a knee. There were easily a thousand people in attendance, likely more.

Bending down, he felt the shudder that went through her when he whispered into her ear, "I know the list of people you are comfortable dancing with. The others have been informed as well. If at any point the touching becomes too much or you need a moment, you find me. No one else. Understood?"

She turned to look at him, the move placing her lips a breath away from his, and it took everything in him not to steal a kiss. "At what point did you think you could give your queen orders?"

The unexpected retort had the corner of his mouth curling up in a smirk. "I think you'd find you like my orders, wife."

She huffed a laugh, soft and delicate. "Somehow I doubt that."

"You'd realize that touch is something to crave rather than avoid. I'd prove it to you."

An unmistakable curiosity flickered across her features, but before she could reply, the sound of a throat softly clearing reminded them both they weren't alone. That a room full of people were still on a knee for them.

Shit.

He led Kailia forward, and the moment they stepped onto the first stair, the entire room rose. Excited chatter broke out as they watched them descend the staircase, a path left open down the center of the room that led to the dance floor.

Once in the center, Kailia turned to him, and as they got into position for the first dance, he said, "Back to the topic at hand."

She was looking at her feet, and she glanced at him before looking back down. "What topic?"

"Of me showing you touch can be more than torture."

Her gaze flew back to his. "You want to discuss this now?"

He shrugged, taking her hand in his and sliding his arm around her waist. His magic lingered beneath his palms, dark tendrils winding between their fingers. "Seems as good a time as any."

The music started, and he urged her into the first steps as she replied, "This hardly seems like a good time to discuss *that.*"

He hummed, twirling her out and pulling her back to him, tucking her in a little closer this time. "I stand by my comment."

"What comment?" she demanded, her gaze locked on his and her amber eyes blazing.

"That you would like my orders."

"Perhaps you would like mine," she retorted.

"Oh, wife, you have no idea," he said, his voice dropping an entire octave.

She scoffed, but there was a tentative spark of intrigue that danced in her eyes. "As if you'd let me give you orders."

He twirled her again, her steps perfect.

All of this so effortless.

When he pulled her back this time, her front was flush against his. His voice was low, his words feathering across her lips when he said, "You want me on my knees, I'm at your feet. You want me crawling to you, tell me how far. You want me to prove touch can be ecstasy, done. Tell me how to make you feel good, and I'll obey every word down to the letter. As long as it's my name on your lips when you fall into pleasure, I'll take any orders you want to give me, wife."

She was staring up at him, her hand clasped in his against his chest and a flush creeping along her cheeks. "You act like you've been thinking about this," she murmured.

"I absolutely have been," he answered.

He'd spent every night beside her in bed since the *nagasky*, and as he'd known it would, every night became an increasingly difficult exercise in self-control. Of forcing himself to keep his hands to himself. He'd had moments of weakness though. Like when he was sure she was in a deep enough sleep, he'd gently brush a knuckle along her cheek or run his fingers through her silky strands. If he were lucky, she'd roll over in her sleep, and her fingers would graze his arm or her leg would nudge against his. He absolutely understood how utterly pathetic it was. That he would hold his breath in those moments and hope that would be the night she'd seek him out in her sleep.

So yes, despite knowing it was a terrible idea, he'd been thinking about all the ways he could convince her to let him touch her. To prove that touch could be as pleasurable as it could be painful. To prove that she would only ever find the former at his hand and never the latter.

"Cethin I—" she started, but the song ended then, the crowd applauding. Her eyes widened as she stared up at him. "You were distracting me."

He smirked. "Yes, but every word was true."

He stepped back, wishing he didn't have to, but this was still a celebration. People came from everywhere to see them. So he took her hand and twirled her under his arm, her train flaring around her, and she laughed, caught off guard by the action. The crowd clapped more, some whistles sounding, and when he pulled her back to him, he pressed a kiss to the place just below her ear. He felt her stumble into him, felt her heart stutter. The musicians were starting their next number, and they were swept into another dance as others joined them.

Cethin managed to keep Kailia to himself for three more songs before others approached. The guards were under strict instruction as to who could be allowed near Kailia, while he was more than comfortable dancing with whomever asked. He'd been attending such events since he was born, raised to play the role of Crown Prince and then king from his first breath.

But after every dance with another, she came back to him without fail, relief flashing in her eyes as she took his hand and his arm went around her waist, pulling her close.

Maybe he was proving something after all.

CHAPTER 33

KAILIA

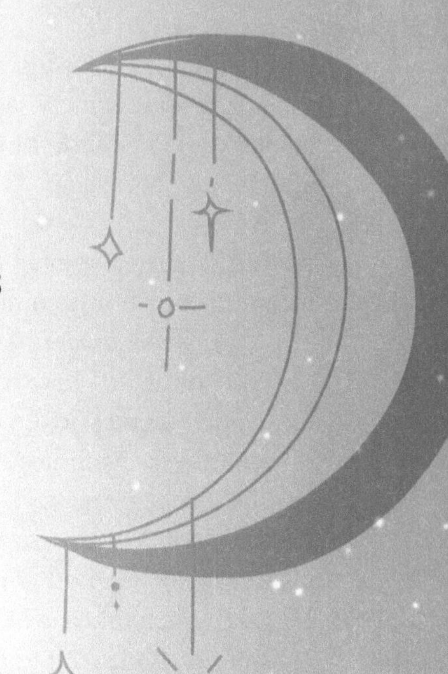

This night had been exactly what she'd expected it to be but also everything she hadn't.

The great hall was loud with people talking over one another, laughter, and music. More than once she found herself wishing she could escape in the smoke drifting from the sconces, but only when dancing with someone other than Cethin.

She'd danced with Tybalt, the Commander stiff but kind as he guided her around the dance floor. She'd also danced with Jarek, Zayan, and one of the advisory lords, but after each one, she'd found her way back to Cethin, his dark and icy magic erasing the burns left behind from the touch of others. Thankfully, food had been announced, and now she sat at the head table with Cethin at her side.

Using her fork, she cut off a slice of cake, dragging it through the raspberry drizzle she couldn't get enough of. It was almost as good as the rolls with cinnamon. And the spiced cakes they often had at dinner. And the peach cobbler with dollops of thick cream.

Cethin shifted beside her, his hand on the table right next to her plate. He was speaking to someone on his other side, but she was acutely aware of his every movement. She was also acutely aware he hadn't touched her since they'd sat at the table to eat. More than that, she was acutely aware that it bothered her, and *that* she couldn't understand. She couldn't understand how she'd started anticipating his touch.

No.

She'd started anticipating the brush of his magic because that meant his touch was coming.

A touch she *wanted*.

Not once in her nearly three centuries of life could she remember *wanting* to be touched. She tolerated touches. Suffered through them. At times, she lashed out when they were unexpected, but she'd never *wanted*.

She hadn't wanted to believe him—that he could make touch pleasurable—but here she was, wondering what else he could do. He used touch to tease her. Entice her. Irritate her.

But he also used it to distract her. Coax her. Help her.

And sometimes, she could swear he couldn't help it. As if he'd go mad if he didn't wrap her hair around his finger or brush his arm against hers.

It was all so…confusing.

"You are quiet, wife."

The soft words in her ear made stray hair flutter, and she jolted a little. Then she frowned. She was never taken by surprise. Ever. She always calculated every move. Tracked all the bodies. Knew the powers in the room. The quickest exits.

Her face must have betrayed her displeasure—which was another issue in and of itself—because Cethin had a look of concern when he asked, "What's wrong?"

She cleared her throat, getting herself back under control. "Nothing is wrong," she replied, setting down her fork and moving her hands to her lap.

"You look upset," he pushed.

"This is simply…a lot," she replied, deciding that was the simplest way to answer.

"I know it is," he said, his smile soft. "But you're doing so well."

Something inside her went molten at those words, and gods.

That was yet another thing she didn't understand or want to look at too closely. None of this had been part of the plan when she'd come here. Agreed to all this.

"Did you get enough to eat?" he asked, the words still low and quiet, meant just for her. To those looking on, this simply appeared to be an intimate conversation between a new husband and wife. Because they needed to be convincing. That was all this was. A show for his people.

The idea both comforted her and made her shift in her ornate chair. Who needed a chair this ostentatious?

"Kailia?" Cethin asked, the crease in his brow deepening. "Are you sure you are all right? Did something happen?"

"No," she replied, forcing a smile. "Nothing happened."

"Then what—"

"Ready for that dance, Lia?"

She looked up, finding Razik standing in front of them. Cethin was trying to tamper down his glare. It took a few seconds, but he managed to get his features twisted into something almost pleasant.

"We're having a private conversation," Cethin replied tightly.

"I'm aware. I've been watching. My job and all," Razik replied blandly. "But Lord Tovan is about to come over here and interrupt for a dance, and he's not on the approved list. I figured I'd save everyone from that awkward moment."

Cethin glanced over, and Kailia followed his gaze, where the lord was indeed watching them, clearly waiting for an opening.

"I can dance," Kailia said, stacking her mental defenses and reminding herself not to stab anyone. It was why she'd opted for the smaller knife rather than her dagger. If she did stab anyone, it wouldn't be as bad. In theory.

She stood, and Cethin did the same, pulling her chair back for her. Getting out from behind the table with the train and layers of dress was a feat. The dress had been better than she'd expected though. It left her room to move and access her knife.

Facing Razik, she took his hand, resting her other on his shoulder. All the time at the dance studio in the last week had made her comfortable enough to touch him. Not like Cethin, but in a way that she wasn't questioning his intentions. They'd both made it clear where they stood on things, and that was refreshing. Clear and simple terms. Guard and queen. Maybe something bordering on friends? He didn't coddle her and wasn't afraid to say things bluntly, and she appreciated that.

"Are you doing okay?" Razik asked, guiding her through the steps like he'd done countless times these last days. In the end, it had been more about getting her used to being touched than practicing the actual dance steps.

"Fine enough," she answered, reminding herself to smile.

"These aren't my favorite things either," he said. "They just come with the position."

"You are always in attendance at events like this?"

"Usually on duty, but yes. Since I was a child. My father was close with Cethin's parents, so I was forced to spend time with them and him," he answered, twirling her out and pulling her back.

"I asked Cethin. About the two of you. Like you told me to," she said, watching his features carefully, but in true fashion, he gave away nothing.

"Great," he replied. "Then you can stop bothering me about it."

She frowned slightly. "He told me Tybalt is your uncle."

That had his jaw clenching. "He's my father in every way that means anything."

"But do you know your parents?"

"This is not the place, Lia," he gritted out. "And even if it were, I wouldn't discuss it."

"I'm prying."

"Yes, you are," he said, his fingers flexing on her waist.

"I apologize."

He sighed. "You don't need to. It is simply not something I discuss or dwell on."

"You definitely dwell on it, but I can understand not wishing to discuss it."

"I do not dwell on it," he grumbled. She shrugged, and that seemed to irritate him more. "I don't dwell on it," he growled again.

"You certainly let it have control over you."

"Enough, Lia," he snarled.

"Sorry," she murmured. They danced for another few moments in silence, before she said, "Can I ask you something?"

"The gods know I can't stop you."

She sent him a bland look, but before she could ask her question, the song ended, and Razik was releasing her.

"I'll help you get back to Cethin," he said, stepping closer while keeping others back.

They'd made it a handful of steps when someone intercepted them.

"Your Majesty," the male greeted, bowing deeply.

It took a minute before she recognized him. The pitch black hair and grey eyes. Warm skin like her own. The new lord, Corveth Astor. She wasn't used to seeing him in such formal clothing.

"Congratulations again on your union," he said as he straightened.

"Thank you, Lord Astor," she replied with a small smile. "Are you enjoying the evening?"

"Very much so," he answered, his hands clasped behind his back. "It has been wonderful to see the two of you together. I hear that is rare."

"Cethin is rather busy, and I'm still learning," she admitted. "So we cherish the quiet moments."

The lord's smile was a knowing one. "I can't say I blame you. It's important to nurture that relationship."

"Speaking of," Razik interrupted. "I was in the process of escorting her Majesty back to her husband."

"Of course," the lord said. "I wasn't looking for a dance or to take any of your time. Only to offer congratulations on your union and new title. As a new lord myself, I understand still trying to get your feet under you. I apologize if I overstepped."

"Not at all," Kailia said. "I look forward to more conversations in the future, Lord Astor."

"Please call me Corveth," he said with another bow of his head while Razik urged her forward.

"He seems pleasant," she mused, Razik ensuring the crowd gave her ample room.

"They all do at events like this," he replied gruffly. "Pay more attention to how they act behind closed doors than in the public."

That seemed like sound advice.

"Where is Wren?" she asked, feeling the disadvantage of her height. Normally she was watching these events in the air, drifting among smoke and ashes. Down here, she felt as though she were being swallowed by the crowd despite Razik's efforts.

"She was dancing with Bram the last I saw," he replied tightly.

"How does that work? If she's with him, and you two are—"

"She's not with him," Razik interjected.

"Are you sure? Because it seems as though—"

That was when the first scream rang out.

A female scream that had them all whirling to the sound. Murmurs and panic immediately set off in the crowd as everyone tried to figure out what was happening.

Razik was already close, but somehow Jarek and Fallon materialized by her too.

"Who is stupid enough to pull something during the king's Union Celebration?" Jarek growled, keen gaze scanning the room.

But that was not the question Kailia was asking. She was wondering if it was a who or a what, because the answer to that was going to make all the difference.

"Everyone is going to need to move, Raz," she said, already having summoned her bow.

"Wait until we know what we're dealing with," he retorted.

"Raz?" Jarek asked, glancing over his shoulder.

"Shut up, and do your job," Razik snarled.

Gods, if only she could use her magic. She'd already know what they were dealing with. She couldn't see shit down here, not without—

"Lia!" Razik hissed sharply, but she was already moving.

Her bow slung across her chest, she crawled along the floor, between legs and dresses and shiny boots.

"I swear to Sargon, Lia," he was snarling, and she heard the grunts of people she could only assume Razik was shoving out of the way. But there were too many of them, and she was faster, even with her bow smacking into shins.

Finally, there was a decent opening, and she popped up.

"Fucking fuck! Where did you come from?"

She turned to find Bram, Wren tucked into his side. This was actually a fairly convenient place to have ended up when she really thought about it.

"Do you know what's going on?" she asked, unhooking her bow.

"Not ye—"

Another scream sounded. Then another and another.

And she didn't need to wonder anymore. Not as phantom after phantom drifted into view.

"Blood of death," they all hissed in unison, the hairs on the back of her neck standing on end at their eerie tone.

That was when mayhem let loose.

Everyone was screaming and running and trying to escape. She had arrows nocked, but without being able to move through her ashes, she couldn't be sure of her targets. There were too many innocent people in the way. Too many innocent people meeting gold blades as the phantoms drifted forward.

Shit.

Shit, shit, shit.

Ripping the three arrows from the string, she shoved them at Bram.

"Wait! You can't—" Bram started.

But she was moving again, trying her best not to brush up against people.

Razik appeared at her side, pupils shifted, smoke furling, and black flames wreathing his arms. "Kailia, you can't—"

Ashes swirled, her smoke mixing with his, and she shoved an armful of arrows at him. "Hand these out."

"No. We need to get you out of here," he snarled.

More screams. People everywhere. It was becoming too much, and she couldn't fight. She couldn't do anything with everyone in her way. People were going to die. So many people, and she was helpless—

"Everyone get down!"

The commanding voice echoed in the hall, everyone going still.

Because that was the voice of a king.

"On the floor! Now!" Cethin bellowed, and as everyone dropped to the ground—the floor becoming a sea of luxurious fabrics, terrified people, and those who'd already crossed the Veil—she saw him.

Tall and terrifying with his dark magic clinging to him. Silver eyes glowing. A black blade in his hand and waves of his inky power spilling across the room, hovering above the people.

The phantoms were still there, but all their targets were beneath them now. Of course, his magic didn't do much, but a cascade of dragon fire from Razik did. It spread atop the darkness, Cethin's magic keeping everyone from the heat while Razik's magic kept golden blades from claiming life while also keeping the phantoms from coming any closer. For beings that didn't touch the ground, they also didn't appear to be able to get airborne.

She met Cethin's gaze across the room, and he gave her a nod.

It was all she needed to be let loose here.

Summoning more arrows, the dying wails of the phantoms became a symphony only she could dance to. Tybalt couldn't fully shift. Razik was keeping the people protected along with Cethin, and she was free to do what she did best.

Of course, it would have been faster and easier and far more fun if she could use *all* of her magic, but this would do.

More arrows appeared on her string the moment she released the first three. She focused on those closest to Cethin first, and then it was all instinct and skill as she released arrow after arrow, turning in a circle, until there was one left.

Kailia stilled, two arrows nocked and the string pulled back. The phantom's features were twisted into rage, pupil-less eyes bright white.

"You are becoming tiresome," it hissed, gold sword pointed

directly at her. "Next time, this will end differently. We will have what we hunt."

Then it was gone, sinking into the floor as if the ground itself had swallowed it whole.

The flames and darkness vanished, and Razik doubled over, hands braced on his knees.

"Razik!" Wren cried, scrambling up from the ground and climbing over people, Bram right behind her.

When she reached him, she took his shoulders, urging him to sit, but he shook his head. "Not here," he muttered.

"Razik, don't be stupid. If they come back, we'll need you. We'll all need you," Wren insisted, gaze darting around. "I need a knife or a dagger or—"

Bram handed her one, but Razik pulled away. "I said not now."

"They won't come back," Kailia offered, her bow still in hand at her side. "At least, that has been our experience in the past. They won't attack again the same day." She paused, thinking it over. "Then again, I wasn't here the last time they attacked at the castle, so I guess—"

"That is not helpful right now, Lia," Razik growled, straightening. Or trying to.

"You look pitiful," she said, looking him up and down.

"Bram," Tybalt growled, coming up beside his nephew. "Help the others escort guests out or to their rooms. Everyone gets searched before they leave or retire for the night."

"Yes, Commander," the male replied. He turned to go, but not before asking Wren, "You are fine?"

"Yes, yes. Go on," she said, waving him off without even looking at him.

"Your Majesty," Tybalt said, face solemn. "Cethin asked me to bring you to him."

"But Razik—"

"Go with Tybalt, Lia," Razik said, Wren still fretting and trying to get him to let her refill his powers here. "He'll watch over you for now."

"She's sorted. Can we please go now?" Wren pleaded, worry written all over her face.

"Yes, go," Tybalt ordered.

"Thank you," Wren said, gripping Razik's arm, and the two of them disappearing in the next breath.

"This way, your Majesty," Tybalt said, motioning with his arm.

He stayed by her side, and while Razik had needed to keep people back, everyone seemed to naturally part for the Commander. They reached Cethin in a matter of minutes. He was speaking with Zayan, but the moment she was within reach, he turned away from his Hand.

He looked her over from head to toe before he took her hand and gently tugged her forward.

"Are you hurt?" he asked, voice low.

"Why would I be hurt?" she asked, watching the guests being led from the room. Tear-stained faces and haunted gazes. Seeing those that wouldn't get up and watching various members of the forces attempt to discreetly remove the bodies or cover them. There was no doing that unobtrusively with hundreds of people in the room.

"Now that I've retrieved her, will the king and queen please go to their quarters until we can secure the castle?" Tybalt asked, sounding more than a little annoyed.

"I think if the creatures wanted to enter our quarters, there wouldn't be any stopping them," Kailia replied, noticing the quick glances at her as people passed.

"That is not the point," Tybalt replied tightly with a pointed look at Cethin.

"It's for appearances' sake," Cethin said, leaning in to speak into her ear. "People want to know their king and queen are protected."

"Wouldn't they rather know we care by seeing us down here? You know, doing the caring?" she asked.

"By the Fates, there's two of you now," Tybalt muttered. "Just until we can secure the area and see if we can find any information about how any of this happened."

"Just for a bit, tiny fiend," Cethin coaxed, her hand still in his.

She nodded, but she didn't want to go to their quarters. She was restless, and the moment they were in their rooms, she made her way to the balcony, hoping the fresh air would help.

It didn't.

She was overstimulated from all the touching. The fight had adrenaline coursing through her. Beneath it all was an exhaustion from the evening. From being on display. And the people. And all the touching.

Her dress suddenly felt too constrictive, and she was clawing at the corset, the layers of lace and silk suddenly too much against her skin.

"Kailia, stop," Cethin said, his tone soft but the command firm. When she turned to him, he added, "Come with me."

She followed, her magic as restless as she was because she couldn't fucking use it. She could access a fraction of her well of power because it was broken. *She* was broken, and why did she think she could do any of this?

"I need you to breathe, wife," Cethin said softly, and she had no idea when they'd entered the bedchamber. She looked back at the doorway, seeing her own ashy footprints.

Fingers brushed along her arm, and she lurched back. Too much. Somehow—being away from everyone and everything— somehow that had made the little things overwhelming. A single touch. The sound of the crackling hearth. The brush of silk.

"I'll untie your dress. That is all," Cethin said, each word smooth and steady. "Okay?"

She nodded, turning so he could work the ties and clasps of the corset. When he was done, she moved to the dressing closet. Everything was too fitted or silky or scratchy.

Running her fingers along the rows of garments, she stopped when she came to something exceedingly soft. Shoving aside hangers, she studied the garment, rubbing her fingers along the fabric. She'd never felt something so soft. It was like butter in her fingers.

Pulling it from the hanger, she didn't care that it was Cethin's. She slipped it over her head, the hem falling to her knees. It was roomy, didn't cling to her, and she could still get to her knife with ease.

She frowned, lifting a hand. A swirl of ashes left a dagger in her palm, and she switched out the knife for the blade. Much better.

Tossing the knife onto the dresser, she went back out to the bedchamber. Cethin had lost his jacket and boots and was working the buttons of his shirt when he went utterly still.

"This is your shirt," she said, plucking at the tunic.

He nodded, gaze dragging down her body in a way that somehow made her feel like he was peeling the garment off her.

"I'm aware of that, wife," he said, his voice harsh and raspy.

"Do you not want me wearing it?"

"I definitely want you wearing it."

"Then why are you looking at me like that?"

He abandoned the buttons, prowling towards her, but he stilled once more when she took several steps back, the backs of her knees bumping into the bed. His hands curled into fists, but he didn't come any closer.

"How am I looking at you?"

"I don't know," she admitted, studying him. Something feral and needy on his features. Something hungry and wanting glimmering in his eyes, but there was no dark magic in them. Only bright silver irises. "You used a lot of power tonight."

"Not what I want to talk about right now," he said, the words laced with a growl.

"I don't want to talk either," she admitted, trying to keep from bouncing on her toes. Her heart was beating at a weird rhythm. "We should go for a walk. Or a hunt."

He blinked at her, some of that hunger flickering into confusion. "You want to go on a hunt? Right now?"

"Yes," she affirmed.

"You're not dressed for a hunt."

She looked down, forgetting she'd changed clothes. It suddenly seemed like a lot of work to change yet again, but she couldn't sit in here all night.

"Then let's go help downstairs," she finally said.

"Again, not dressed for that occasion," Cethin replied.

"Cethin, I need to do something," she said in frustration, shaking out her hands. "Just…*something*."

"You're restless," he said, understanding filling his features. "You're high off the fight."

"Yes. No. I think… I think it's everything. The entire night," she said, wanting to pace or move but forcing her feet to stay planted.

"I understand," he said, finishing undoing his shirt buttons while he kept his eyes on her. "I can help. If you'll let me."

"How?"

"I've felt the same after high stakes battles. Your body is still on edge from the stress of fighting. Your nerves are heightened, and you need to release the pent up energy," he said, sliding his shirt down his arms.

"Yes, all of that," she murmured, watching the muscles in his arms bunch and flex with the movements.

He nodded. "And in the past, you've…done what?"

She didn't answer, because how was she supposed to tell him she'd lose herself to her magic for hours, letting herself drift among ashes as the wind carried her wherever it willed until she felt like herself again? If she did that, she'd have to explain why that wasn't an option.

"What have *you* done in the past that worked?" she asked instead, watching deft fingers work his belt free and slide it from his waist.

He tossed it aside with the shirt. "There were several options. Sparring in the training arena with one of the Cadre. Finding a liquor bottle." The heat was back in his eyes when he added, "Bringing someone to my bed."

She tsked. "Fucking won't help."

"Another statement that has me questioning your experience with such things," he said knowingly. "That kind of release absolutely helps."

"I'll opt for the liquor bottle rather than roaming hands," she retorted.

"I wouldn't even need my hands. I wouldn't have to touch you at all."

"What?" she asked before she could stop herself, because surely not...

His lips lifted, curling into something full of dark promises. "Curious, wife?"

"Yes," she replied in genuine perplexity.

He barked a laugh, but his eyes darkened a shade. "You have to do exactly as I say," he said, the words somehow both a command and a warning.

The idea of giving up that control, of someone else having control over her, had her shaking her head, her heart racing even more.

"You can stop at any time, Kailia," he said, concern flickering among the heat and desire in his eyes. "I'm— I'll stay over here the entire time. I swear it."

Worrying her bottom lip, his gaze shot to the movement. His tongue darted out, and he shifted in place, but his feet stayed rooted to the spot. She shook out her hands again, feeling like she was going to do something incredibly brash any minute. Something that would undo everything she'd been carefully building. She was desperate, and *he* looked desperate. Desperate to help her or desperate for her, she didn't know. Because the only experience she had with fucking was because she'd been curious what all the fuss was about. It was never something she'd ever had any desire to do again, but if he wasn't going to touch her then... And what if this was like the kiss? Something unexpectedly wanted?

"You're thinking too hard, tiny fiend," he said. "Do you need a vow? A bargain? Let me show you. Let me— Just let me."

Again, she had this odd feeling. The same feeling she'd had when he'd been on his knees and she'd been in a tub. Only this time a king was begging, not to touch her or for her to touch him, but to...what?

"You'll stay over there?" she asked, shaking her hands out again before fisting the soft fabric draped around her.

"I won't come any closer. I swear it. And if you want to stop, we stop," he coaxed.

A few seconds passed, the air heavy with tension and anticipation. Finally, she nodded, and there was a flash of relief in Cethin's eyes before it flickered back to something darker and sinful and eager. Because suddenly the restless wild thing she was feeling inside? He was displaying it on the outside with dilated pupils and a vibrating energy that had him constantly shifting in place.

"Climb onto the bed, wife."

She frowned. She needed to move, not sit. "How is that going to—"

"Kailia." Her name was a growl that she felt all the way down to her toes.

Already backed up to the bed, she pushed onto her toes until she could slide up onto it. Then she stared at him, still not convinced this was going to do anything.

"What now?"

"I'm conflicted because seeing you in my shirt is making me feel all sorts of ways, but I also need you to take it off," he answered.

"What?" she asked, looking down at the tunic and smoothing her hands over it.

"Take it off, Kailia," he repeated, his tongue running across his lower lip again. "Unless we're stopping?"

"No," she answered, because she was more than curious and him watching her was making something warm in her belly.

Reaching for the hem, she pulled it over her head, leaving herself bare before him. Nudity was nudity. This didn't bother her. But hearing the rumble that sounded from the male across the room, it affected him. His teeth raked over his lip this time, and his head tilted as he shifted on his feet again.

"Fuck. This was simultaneously the best idea I've ever had and the worst," Cethin muttered, swiping a hand over his mouth. His eyes darted from her chest to her face and back to her breasts, his hands fisting at his sides now, and how could he make her feel... whatever this was just from him looking at her?

"That is a confusing statement," she murmured, her voice breathy.

"Well aware."

"What next?" she asked.

Somehow this was working. Somehow, he was distracting her from the anxious thing that needed out in the same way he'd distracted her during their initial dance tonight.

"I want to kiss you," he breathed, his hands fisted at his sides so tightly his knuckles were white even against his pale skin.

But his words made her remember the feel of his mouth on hers, soft and hungry. Unconsciously, she brought her fingers to her lips. "I think I want that too," she replied softly.

The sound that came from Cethin sounded *pained*, but he said, "I know you do, but I swore to stay over here. I keep my promises, wife."

"Okay," she whispered, finding herself disappointed in that answer.

"I can't touch you, so I need you to do it," he continued.

"What?"

"You heard me," he said, the agony gone, replaced with that icy darkness. "Start at your throat and drag your fingers down."

This felt like too much. Awkward and exposed, but he was watching her, eager and needy. There was a power here that she hadn't expected. The same power she'd recognized that day in the tub, and she liked control. He might be telling her what to do, but the knowledge that she was in control had her bringing her fingers to her neck. Brushing them along her throat. Dragging them along her collarbone. Holding his stare.

The restlessness in her soul was shifting. Gooseflesh popped up under the touch, her nerve endings hyperaware to every sense right now.

"Don't touch your breasts. Go between them," he ordered when she started dragging her fingers down her chest.

The idea of anyone giving her orders like this should irritate her, but it didn't. Instead, she was dragging her fingers through the valley of her breasts, watching him watching her.

"Keep going," he growled as she made her way down to her navel. But when she paused above the apex of her thighs, he said, "More."

One word.

One word that she felt in her soul, her core clenching, and *gods*. How?

"Kailia, don't make me say it again. Move your fingers," he said with a snarl. His feet were still planted, but he was leaning forward, straining to see. The position had the muscles in his abdomen tensed and flexing.

Slowly, she moved her fingers again. Lower and lower until she could press them between her legs. Her hips lifted, and a surprised gasp came from her. How was she this sensitive from nothing but the brush of her own fingers? What would it feel like if they were his? Would his hands be like his lips?

"Stay with me, Kailia," he said, pulling her back to the moment.

Her attention snapped back to him, forcing away thoughts of what she couldn't have. What she'd never be able to handle.

"There she is," Cethin purred. "Keep your eyes right here with me. Yes?"

She nodded, not trusting herself to speak. This was all wildly confusing, but also wildly intoxicating in a way she'd never experienced.

"Good. Now spread your legs so I can see and do that again," he ordered, sliding his fists into his pockets.

By Temural, his mouth was...

His gaze entirely trained on her hand, she placed it flat on her belly, and she spread her legs wider, too wound up to care what she looked like or what he was thinking. Her fingers strummed that spot that made pleasure dart up her spine.

"Yeah, just like that," he murmured. She wasn't entirely sure if he was speaking to her or more to himself, but she also didn't care.

She'd done this before. Many times she'd brought herself to climax, but never like this. Never after a battle. Never with someone watching her so desperately, like the thought of not being able to witness this would make him perish.

Her fingers moved, pressing and circling and rubbing. Soft gasps and small sounds came from her, and the entire time, she couldn't stop watching him. Watching him shift from foot to foot. Watching him pull his hands from his pockets. Swipe a hand down his face. Push a hand through his hair. Press a palm to the front of his pants.

And he kept speaking. Soft words of praise and filthy words that had her keening inside.

"Like that, wife," and, "so good," and "you know what you like," and "now sink a finger in. Let me see it. Fuck me. I bet you taste so good."

He shifted again, hands at the flap of his pants. "I'm going to move, Kailia, but I'm not coming closer. I'm going to sit, okay?"

She nodded, the movement erratic as she continued to bring herself closer to the edge of pleasure.

Until he undid the flap of his pants and dipped his hand in, pulling out his cock, throbbing and hard. He dropped into the armchair facing the bed, spreading his legs as wide as he could with his pants still on.

There was a different anticipation in her belly now. Her breathing had changed, each inhale sharp and shallow as she watched him slide his hand down his length. She was watching him, but his eyes were fixed on her hand that had stilled over her cunt, one finger inside herself.

"Add another finger," he growled, his hand making long strokes over himself.

Without conscious thought, she did, another finger sliding in with ease because seeing him touch himself did things to her she'd never experienced. Slippery and wet, she started moving her fingers again, adding to the sensation that watching him brought. The tensing of his jaw. The muscles flexing in his forearm as he moved his hand.

"Gods, someday you're going to let me touch you, wife," he groaned when her legs fell open wider of their own accord. "It'll be my fingers in that warm cunt. My lips on your breasts. My cock being squeezed when you come." Each word was harsh and agonized, a different kind of torture she was beginning to understand. She shouldn't want any of that.

But she did.

He rolled his palm over the head of his cock, his strokes alternating now. Soft and hard, soft and hard. She found herself mimicking his movements, rolling that bundle of nerves with her thumb. Pressing and releasing. He didn't even need words at this point, but she was devouring every syllable and sound that came from him.

"Touch your breasts," he demanded, and again, she should have hated the command, but she was getting close.

Everything in her was tightening. At some point, she'd braced herself with her other hand, leaning back on it as she'd let him see everything. Her hand left her cunt, her palm running back up her torso, squeezing one breast and then the other, a jolt traveling straight between her legs. She rolled a nipple, then plucked at the other, spurred on by Cethin's spat curses.

"Fuck me, that's good, wife. You're doing so well."

By the gods. He'd been right. She was thoroughly distracted, a release glimmering and coiling inside her, tightening with every touch as she brought her hand back to her center, massaging her clit once more. Every flick and rub, every press and stroke mirrored his as his movements grew more erratic. Her breaths were nothing but sharp gasps, her toes curling around the bedframe where her feet rested.

And she took him in.

The veins on his forearms. Narrow hips. The bunching muscles of his abdomen. The dusting of fine hair that led to where his hand was shuttling up and down his cock, squeezing the tip every third pass. Tense thighs. Tight jaw. Disheveled hair. Blazing eyes.

All of it for her.

"Let it go, wife," he gritted out. "I want to see. I want to see all of you. Let go. Give it to me."

She wrestled with listening to a command again, but her body listened, as if it knew what she needed. As if it knew this was the way to get it. As if *he* was the only way to get it. Pleasure cascaded through her, waves and waves of warmth spreading from her fingers to her toes and dragging her into something blissful and calm, that restlessness from earlier completely gone and replaced with the exhaustion that had been buried beneath all the sensations.

And as if that was what he'd been waiting for, Cethin grunted, "Fuck, yes. Just like that. So good, wife. Look at you," as he came, his release spilling over his fist and pooling on his taut stomach.

Then it was just the sound of their heavy breathing as they stared at each other from across the room. He was more relaxed than she'd ever seen him. He still looked tired, weighed down by his responsibilities, but he was loose. Unguarded. The same way he'd been in the bathing chamber that day but different. There he'd looked tortured and desperate; here he looked tired but sated.

It was then she realized that this whole affair had been for him as much as it'd been for her, but he'd let her be in control the entire time. Not once did he push for more. She'd practically invited him to come over and kiss her, and he'd still held to their original rules.

They took turns cleaning up in the bathing chamber, and when she climbed into the bed, so did he. He'd stopped putting the pillows between them since the *nagasky*. Neither of them spoke because what was there to say? She felt like she should thank him, but that also felt silly. How does one thank someone for an orgasm? Even if that release had calmed her soul in a way she'd only ever found by getting lost in her power?

She rolled over to face him, one hand tucked beneath her cheek. His breathing was slow and even, but she didn't think he was asleep yet. Despite that, she slowly slid her other hand over until her fingers brushed along his abdomen, settling her palm there. Skin to skin. Touch and sensation that she was in control of.

His muscles went taut beneath her touch, but he said nothing. He didn't move. Each breath becoming measured and controlled.

And for the first time in her life, she fell asleep while touching another.

CHAPTER 34

RAZIK

"**A**re you almost ready?" Wren called out.

He ignored her, searching the shelves for a specific volume he knew was in this room. He didn't get to come here nearly as often as he liked, so he figured he might as well grab some books while he could. The whole idea of Kailia's power not working in her dreams had given him a few new theories, but they were ones he definitely could not throw out unless he was sure.

"Razik, seriously," Wren said, appearing in the room. "I know this is where you'd prefer to spend your days, but most of us do not like spending our time in caves."

"What's wrong with my cave?" he asked, finally finding the book tucked away on a bottom shelf.

"There's nothing wrong with it for *you*," she said. "And I know why you came here. I'm just ready to go back."

He didn't say anything in response, grabbing the other two books he'd already collected. He didn't know what she was complaining about. For centuries he'd been working to make this place his own. It wasn't a simple godsdamn hole in the side of a mountain. Few people knew about it, and he liked it that way.

People were busybodies, and nobody could touch the things he kept here.

This is also where he came when his power was too low, and after the events of the Union Ceremony two nights ago, it had been pretty fucking low. Primal instincts took over when his power was that depleted, and it had taken everything not to draw from Wren right then and there. But he hated doing so in front of people. Source bonds were rare in Avonleya these days. It made him feel like he was on display somehow. More than that, he hated that it put Wren on display. She'd dealt with enough shit in her life.

Feeling more than a little vulnerable with his magic reserves so depleted, he'd Traveled them to his cave where they wouldn't be disturbed. It was the one place he felt like he could truly let his guard down because no one knew where it was. Tybalt knew the location. Wren knew of it, having been here, but even she wouldn't be able to tell anyone exactly where in the Nightmist Mountains his cave was hidden. Beyond that, he had so many wards around the thing, no one could ever simply stumble onto it either.

It was completely hidden. Completely secure. Completely his.

But they'd been here nearly two days now, and Wren didn't like staying holed up for long, even if they weren't in a cave. She was a social thing and needed interaction beyond him. He couldn't exactly blame her, given how little he cared for conversation and how he'd rather be reading.

"Did you rest enough?" he asked, slipping the books into a leather bag.

"Yes, Razik," she said with a roll of her eyes.

"I took a lot from you. There is no way your reserves are refilled because mine aren't even full," he replied.

"And I can't do anything about that for a few more days," she retorted.

"Which is why I'd rather you stay here. Where it's safe," he argued.

"Razik, I'll be fine," she insisted. "Please don't make me stay here."

"I'm not going to make you do anything," he said flatly. "Will you at least stay at the castle for the next few days? Don't leave?"

She patted his chest as he slipped an arm around her waist. "Sure, Razik."

"You're placating me," he grumbled.

"I would never," she said with a wink as he Traveled them back to the castle.

She went to pull away, but he caught her hand. Looking back over her shoulder, she waited for him to speak.

"I know you hate it, but it is my responsibility to keep you safe. It's part of the exchange here," he said, searching her eyes.

"I know, Razik."

"And I know I can be an ass, but if something happened to you because you were vulnerable after I took too much power from you…"

Her smile was soft, full of understanding. She moved back to him, pushing onto her toes to press a chaste kiss to his cheek. "I know, Razik."

"So you'll be back here tonight?" he asked when she pulled away once more.

"Yes, and I'll stay on the castle grounds all day," she added, walking backwards towards the door. "Let's go."

He sighed, following her out and down to the dining room. It was much later than usual, and he was relieved to only find Kailia. Although he didn't miss the flash of disappointment on Wren's features.

"Good morning," Kailia greeted, setting down her teacup. "I was questioning if you were going to be here today."

"Where else would I be?" he asked, letting Wren fill her plate before he did.

"You weren't here yesterday," she pointed out.

"I can't spend every day with you, Lia."

She frowned. "But you do."

"And every once in a while, I need a day off. What did you do?"

"I stayed in my rooms. With Cethin."

He arched a brow, setting the bag of books aside and picking up a plate. "Then it sounds like you were in good hands. I'm sure security was doubled in the hall after the events of the Union Celebration."

"Yeah," she murmured.

They ate in silence. Or he did while Kailia drank her tea. Wren chattered about this and that, and he could tell she was more than ready to find other company when she finished her breakfast and excused herself.

"Anything I need to know about?" he asked Kailia after a few minutes of comfortable silence.

"What would you need to know about?" she asked, fiddling with her teacup.

He looked up from his nearly empty plate. "I don't know. That's why I asked you."

"Oh."

She set her teacup aside, looking anywhere but at him.

Setting his silverware down, he sat back in his chair. "What is wrong with you today?"

That had her eyes snapping to his. "What is wrong with *you* today?"

"Lia," he said with a growl, studying her.

There was something different about her, but he couldn't put his finger on it. Cethin's scent was clinging to her. More than sleeping beside him but not strong enough to indicate they'd fucked. But something had definitely happened between the two.

"If you don't want to talk about it, fine. Let's go," he said, forgoing the rest of his breakfast and getting to his feet.

"There's nothing to talk about," she retorted, standing as well.

"Right. That's why you smell like Cethin," he volleyed back, picking up the bag of books.

"We share living quarters. That only makes sense," she reasoned. "You smell like Wren."

"Because I siphoned power from her, then stayed close to her while she slept to replenish what I took," he said flatly. "*You* didn't siphon power from our esteemed king, but you definitely took something from him."

"I don't know what that means," she snapped.

"Apparently you didn't take enough because you're easily irritated today," he bit back, extending a hand to her. When she slipped her fingers into his, he squeezed them as he leaned in and added, "And by that I mean—"

"I know what you mean," she interjected.

He smirked, Traveling them to his study. It didn't go unnoticed that she didn't immediately yank her hand away like she usually did. It was a slow pull back, almost like an afterthought as she peered around him to the bag in his other hand.

"What's that?"

"Books I collected while I was replenishing my magic," he answered, rounding his desk and taking a seat. Pulling out the books, he stacked them in a neat pile before taking the first one and opening it.

She'd wandered to her usual perch on the sofa across the room, all the books he'd pulled for her tidily arranged, but she didn't pick one up. Instead, she tucked her feet under herself, and before she even opened her mouth, he sighed.

So much for a quiet day of researching.

"Are you able to fully refill your reserves from Wren?" she asked.

"My Source bond with Wren is not up for discussion," he answered, pointedly keeping his eyes fixed on the book, hoping she'd take the hint.

"I'm not asking about your bond with her per se. Just the Source bond in general."

"That depends on how powerful each participant is. Ideally, Source and dependent are equally matched."

"But you're more powerful than Wren."

He nodded.

"So...you can't fully refill your reserves? That's why you still look so tired?"

By the Fates.

"Is that why Cethin always looks so exhausted?"

"Cethin doesn't have a Source," Razik replied.

"I know that, but— After the incident with the *nagasky*, he was to the point of passing out from exhaustion. He never sleeps, but his power never seems to lessen. And he used a lot of power that night. How would he refill his reserves so quickly?" she asked, as if suddenly realizing all of this.

He had a few ideas about how Cethin was keeping his reserves full, and if he was right, the king was being just plain stupid.

"That sounds like something you should ask him, not me," Razik answered. "Do the two of you ever talk?"

She sent him a glare. "Yes, we speak. Quite a bit as of late, actually."

"Then write this down to talk to him about later. Better yet, all these random things you ask me? Add those to that list too."

Kailia scowled at him. "Why are you being such an ass today? More so than usual, I mean. Is it the whole needing a fuck thing again?"

"No," he grumbled.

"Are you upset?"

"No."

"Then…?"

Razik rubbed his brow. "Sometimes we just have days, Lia. Days where there's nothing in particular wrong or shitty, you just…" He shrugged, not sure how else to explain this mood.

She studied him in that too-observant way of hers before she said simply, "Okay."

"Okay?" he repeated.

She nodded, picking up one of her books and getting comfortable on the sofa.

Okay.

Simple and accepting. As if she was willing to simply sit here with him, foul mood and all. No prying. No arguing or hurt feelings.

A simple acceptance of who he was.

Something he'd never once experienced in all his centuries.

⁃⊃⋅⊙⋅⊂⁃

"We have an errand to run," Razik said when Kailia finally emerged from her bedchamber. "What took you so long today?"

"I don't owe you any explanations," she retorted, brushing past him to go to the dining room.

He followed, eyes narrowed as he tried to figure out what had her in a mood today. It couldn't be her cycle because he'd scent that blood. More than that, Cethin would likely be hovering more than usual and extra protective. But...

"When was your last cycle?" he asked as she piled pastries and cinnamon rolls onto a plate.

She went still, her eyes swirling almost violently when she slowly dragged them up to him. "Who asks that?"

"It's a reasonable question."

"From a partner. Or a Healer. Not... Why are you asking that?"

"I thought maybe it was responsible for the delightful mood I get to enjoy today—"

"Because you are so full of joy every day," she interrupted blandly.

"But I realized I'd scent that," he went on, ignoring her commentary. "Then I realized it might give us insight into your bloodline. Fae get their cycles every season. Avonleyans vary depending on which god or goddess they descend from, and it gets really fucked when bloodlines merge."

Kailia was staring at him, holding her plate with two hands. "It is odd to me that you know any and all of that."

"It's basic anatomy and is a natural part of life for roughly half the realm's population. Why wouldn't I know that?"

She sat with that for a minute, taking a bite of pastry. "I suppose that makes sense. Plus, you have Wren." She shrugged again. "What errand do we have to run?"

"That didn't answer my question."

"I'm not going to answer it," she said simply.

"So I have to deal with this mood all day without an explanation?"

"I deal with you every day, don't I?"

A small growl rumbled from his chest in annoyance. "Let's go."

"I'm going to finish my breakfast first," she replied flatly, lowering pointedly into a chair with her plate of food.

"What have you been doing all morning?" he grumbled, crossing his arms.

Her lips thinned as she focused on her plate. Normally, he wouldn't care. Normally, he'd let someone sit in their foul mood because that was what he preferred. He hated people prying and digging and pushing. But she was different somehow. She didn't irritate him as much as most did, and despite her odd mannerisms and misunderstood social cues, he somehow understood her. Was drawn to her. Not in any sort of romantic way, but still a pull to her. He'd attribute it to spending every day with her, but he'd been around long enough to know when there was more at play. Forces and fate and things he'd been pushing back against his entire life. Things he was supposed to embrace that he viewed as curses, and it made this whole relationship with Kailia complicated. He needed her to be comfortable with him, but he hated that this was also fulfilling something designed by the Fates he loathed so much.

She didn't answer him, and he was too lost to his internal debating to push her anymore, but by the gods did she take her time eating those godsdamn pastries.

"We're late now," he griped when she finally stood.

"You didn't tell me time was of the essence," she replied.

He shook his head while she did whatever else she needed to do before they left. She'd become far more comfortable as of late. It'd been three weeks since the Union Celebration. With each outing, she interacted with others more and more, but beyond that, the Avonleyan people were becoming more comfortable with *her*. He was sure the fact that she took down those spirit creatures and saved as many as she could at the celebration had a large hand in that. Silver lining or whatever that shit saying was. Shit, because who wanted a silver lining when you could have gold?

Some time later, he Traveled them to the docks, and she looked up at him with a frown. "The docks? Are we going to another tavern?"

"Not another. The same one," he answered, leading the way. "Pull your hood up."

She had to run a little to keep up with his long strides, and he should care about that, but he was annoyed with how long she'd taken to get going today.

"A hood isn't going to do anything, Raz," she argued. "I'm well-known now."

"So am I."

"You don't wear a hood."

"Then don't wear one, Lia."

He heard her noise of irritation, but she didn't pull up the hood of her lightweight cloak. Neither of them spoke the rest of the way to the tavern, but as soon as they stepped inside, she made her way to a table off to the side and took a seat.

"What are you doing?" Razik growled, glancing to the booth in the back where his contacts were waiting.

"I'm sitting while you do whatever it is you're here to do," she replied, speaking as if he was stupid for even asking that question.

"By Sargon, what is up your ass today, Lia?"

But he didn't give her a chance to answer. Let her sit there if that was what she wanted to do. He turned and headed over to the booth, the exchange of coin for product going much smoother without an impulsive queen with a blade. When he returned to her, he arched a brow at the mug of ale before her.

Half gone.

Setting the cloth sack on the bench, he slid into the booth across from her. "If you were worried about your image as queen, drinking in this tavern is not the thing you should be doing," he said dryly.

She shrugged.

"Kailia," he said in a low warning.

"How did you meet Wren?" she asked.

"What does that have to do with anything?" he retorted, thrown off by the sudden change in subject.

"Nothing," she said. "It's just something I've been wondering."

Razik shifted, getting more comfortable, and he signaled the server for a mug of ale of his own.

"You're very protective of her," Kailia added.

"She's my Source. Of course I'm protective of her," he said, sliding some coin to the server as he placed a mug on the table.

"But…how do you have a Source and Cethin doesn't?"

He stiffened at the question. A question that had plagued him since it had become known that he had a Source. They'd kept it a secret for nearly a year after it had happened, but once word spread, there had certainly been a fallout that went back to Cethin. Everything always led back to Cethin.

"The Fae deaths aren't a recent development," he said, indulging Kailia in this rather than having to deal with her abysmal mood the rest of the day. "It's only been in the last hundred years or so that they started happening. But even before then, with the Wards going up and separating Avonleya from the rest of the realm, there was worry about the Fae becoming scarce. Most worried because they're decent people who care about more than themselves, but some worried because of a resource that would be lost."

She nodded, drinking her ale and making a face that made him wonder why she was putting herself through this.

"When the Fae deaths started to become more common, some found lucrative opportunities with the Fae by pandering to those who were becoming more and more anxious about losing the Fae for their own personal needs," Razik continued.

"And Cethin did nothing to stop this?" she asked.

"Cethin wasn't the king yet, but regardless, it was addressed, yes. There were already laws in place, but King Tethys imposed harsher consequences. But laws and potential consequences aren't enough to deter some, especially if they've been running black market operations far longer than anyone realized," Razik explained.

"Was it ever discovered who had started it or how it went undiscovered for so long?" she asked, signaling for another mug of ale.

Razik eyed her, but he said nothing about the alcohol. "No," he answered. "It's something that is still being investigated as far as I know, but efforts have shifted to figuring out what's killing off the Fae. Anyway, Wren was part of that black market ring. Her parents had sold her off in exchange for their own freedom. She was discovered during a raid."

"By you?"

He nodded. "We'd been given a tip on a holding house, and the Cadre was sent to look into it. We ended up having to infiltrate an entire auction. The Fae were being put up to purchase for Source purposes. I had to bid on her to keep up appearances until we had adequate proof of everything. When all was said and done, we rescued thirteen Fae that day. Everyone else had someone. Either with their family or at least a sibling or cousin, but she—" He cleared his throat, taking a drink of his ale.

"She had no one," Kailia finished.

He nodded. "I offered her the money I'd used to bid on her. She refused, too shaken by the whole thing, so instead, I offered her protection. I didn't want her pressured to be a Source for anyone else, and I think she would have been. Being alone is dangerous for a Fae. I proposed the Source bond solely as a means to free her from that danger. It wasn't supposed to be anything more. I never intended to ever draw from her, but if she had the title, others would leave her alone. Long story short, we ended up in a battle another night nearly a year later with the same black market ring. I had to use a lot of magic and was wounded. She insisted I draw from her, and that was how it was discovered."

"How were you wounded? You can shift into a dragon, and you have dragon fire. There are few powers stronger than dragon fire," she mused, and he didn't miss the way her words rolled into one another as she drained her second mug of ale. He also didn't miss when she ordered another.

"Maybe we should go back to the castle," Razik ventured.

She waved him off. "Cethin's busy anyway."

"No one enjoys pissing off Cethin more than I do, but the queen getting drunk in a tavern by the docks isn't good for anyone, Lia."

"I'm not drunk," she admonished with a glare. "Besides, if he wanted a say in how I spend my days, he should try spending some of them with me."

"I should have guessed your pissy mood stemmed from Cethin. Mine usually do too," he said, drinking the last of his ale.

He waved off the server when he approached holding Kailia's third mug. He didn't need more ale if the queen was determined to drink her weight today. She was impulsive enough without alcohol. When she said nothing in response, he figured he could at least try to reason with her.

"There's a lot going on right now, especially with more Fae discovered dead last week so close to Aimonway," Razik offered.

"I'm aware," she ground out, picking up her mug.

"And you think he should forgo those responsibilities to spend time with you?" he asked flatly.

"I'm not a child, Razik," she retorted. "I understand his duties and responsibilities, but if he bothered to see my usefulness beyond my arrows, I could help."

"I doubt he's intentionally excluding you, Lia. He's protecting you." When she scoffed, he added, "And you are queen in title only. Why would he put such a burden on you? You are usually far more logical than this."

"I know," she muttered. "I'm just...frustrated about several things. Anyway, you never answered how you were wounded if dragon fire is all but unstoppable."

"You answered your own question. It's powerful and nearly unbeatable, but it's not invincible."

She leaned forward, peering at him. The smoke in her eyes was slower, languid. The alcohol impacting her magic as much as it was affecting her physical body. "Cethin's magic isn't affected."

"I'm aware," he deadpanned.

"He's stronger than you."

"In terms of magic, yes."

She nodded. "Is he the only thing stronger than you in Avonleya?"

He narrowed his eyes. "That's a very specific question, Lia."

"Do you think if one of those phantom things stabbed you with their sword, it would affect you?"

Her words were definitely slurring together now.

"I don't think I want to find out, but considering dragon fire kills them, I'm going to guess it wouldn't kill me," he answered.

She hummed. "That's plausible. So…just Cethin then?"

He sighed. "The creatures of old are formidable opponents for dragons."

She hummed again. "That makes sense. Cethin said they were difficult to control until he was born. That would mean your uncle wouldn't have been able to do so." She took a drink before she added, "Cethin said they've been quieter lately."

"They have been. It's why Tybalt has called a few of the Cadre back to Aimonway to help with the Fae deaths," Razik replied, shaking his head when the server made his round. She did not need another drink, but this was probably the best tavern for her to do this in when he really thought about it. People came here because they wanted to go unnoticed. No one was going to draw attention to themselves by bringing attention to the queen.

"Right," she murmured. Elbows planted on the table, she rested her chin in her palms. "Do you miss it? The Cadre, I mean."

"Sometimes," he answered. "I still train in the mornings, but it's not the same."

"Yeah," she mused. "I miss it sometimes too."

"Miss what? Training?"

She nodded. "Among other things."

"You can train whenever you want. You know that right?" he asked.

"Maybe," she hummed. "But it'd probably give away too many secrets."

He huffed in amusement as he stood, extending a hand for her. "Let's get you back before Cethin comes looking and discovers you here."

"He did try to make me promise there would be no more tavern brawls," she said, slipping her fingers into his hand without so much as a flinch.

"And you said…?" Razik asked, keeping her steady as she got to her feet.

"I don't make promises I can't keep," she answered. "Just like him."

Razik wasn't entirely sure what that meant, but he'd leave that between them. He Traveled them back to the castle, where Kailia promptly fell asleep on the sofa. There had to be more to her mood and demeanor today than simply Cethin. Then again, maybe not. Cethin could put him in a foul mood and make him want to drink simply by speaking.

He settled into an armchair, pulling a book from a pocket realm to research more and try to figure out her power. There was something he was missing in all of this, and it was driving him mad because he knew once he figured it out, it was going to be obvious.

An hour later, there was a burst of magic, and Razik plucked a note from it. He skimmed it once before incinerating it with black flames.

Bram wanted to talk to him about Wren.

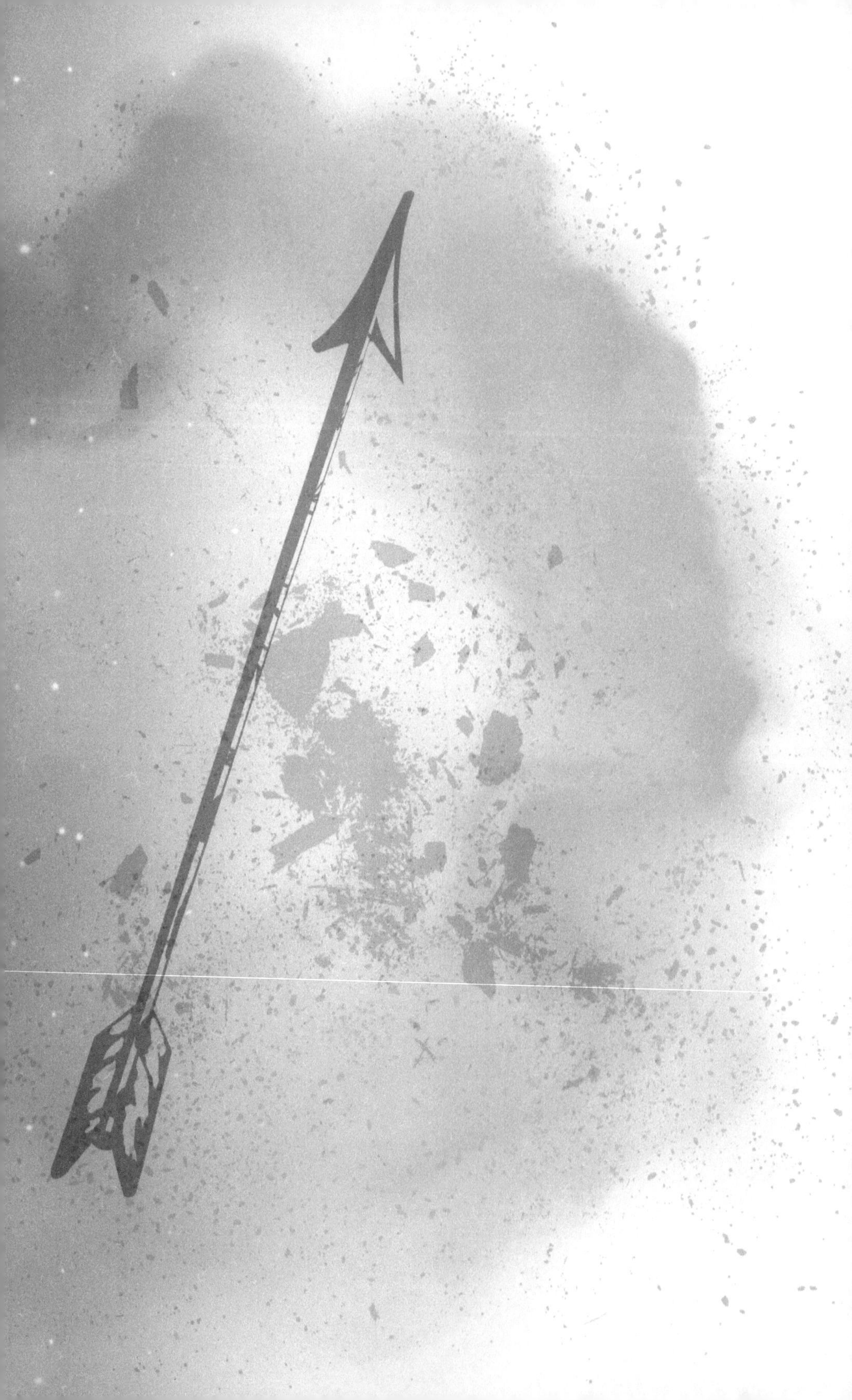

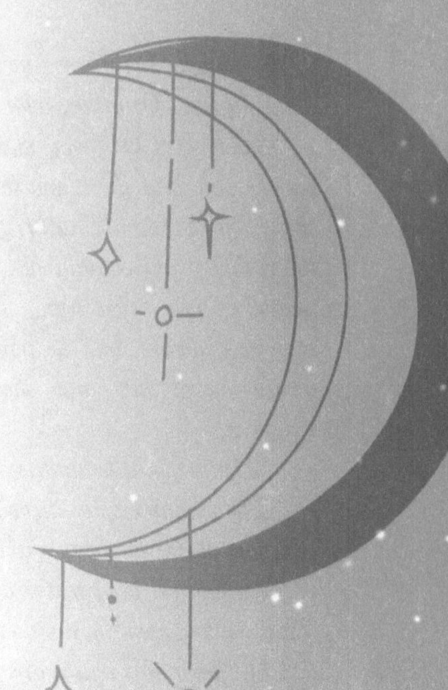

CHAPTER 35
KAILIA

The heavy footfalls roused her, and she blinked sleep from her eyes.

Rocky walls. Thin mattress. Small room.

The footfalls were getting nearer, and she scrambled to shove back the thin blanket. The Mark on her arm was there, telling her this was a dream, but she'd woken too late. She didn't have enough time to prepare for what was about to happen.

She tried though. Gods, did she try when the two males barged into the room. Tall and muscled, she was no match for them as they each took an arm and dragged her from her room, her heels slicing open as she tried to dig them in. She twisted and thrashed, hoping for the tiniest loosening of their hold that she could work with, but their grips were solid and firm.

They passed others in the halls, but they kept their eyes down. No one intervened. She didn't blame them. She wouldn't have intervened either. Not back then anyway. Now it was different, but this was a dream.

Dream.

Dream, dream, dream.

She repeated it over and over as she was marched upstairs to the upper levels. It was a dream. None of it was real. She simply needed to figure out how to wake herself up. That was all. She could survive that long.

A door was pushed open, and she was shoved through. She kept her balance

507

easily enough. Even here, she'd already been trained in stealth and silence, given what she was. Or rather, what they wanted her to be.

She took in the room, knowing exactly where they were with the metal table on one side and the manacles bolted to the wall on the other. The table was shirastone that would nullify a Fae's powers, but the manacles were more. Something that could contain her. Even knowing that this wasn't real, she started trembling. Her entire being shook with the knowledge of what was coming. It may be a dream, but the pain would be very real until she woke up. Then it would haunt her, and she'd made so much progress with Cethin and Razik and—

"Hello, my little huntress."

The feminine voice turned her blood cold. Every other thought left her mind. The knowledge the female was dead. That she was free and not in these Cliffs. That it had all been truths woven with lies so she didn't know what was true. That she had seen the sun and knew what the stars looked like.

She forgot this was a dream as she stood so very still.

The female's footsteps were light and graceful while she slowly circled Kailia. Olive skin. Black hair with streaks of red in it. The same red dress she always wore that reached her ankles. Red painted nails and dark, depthless eyes.

The Baroness of the Cliffs.

She'd been taught the Baroness kept them safe from the rest of the world. The leader of the colony housed inside the enchanted cliffs, they'd been told it was for their own safety. That if others discovered what kind of power they had, they would want it for themselves.

That hadn't been entirely a lie, but the truth had still been manipulated and used against everyone who had resided there. Either way, that perceived protection came with a cost, and if the Baroness was here, Kailia had failed to fulfill her end of the payment.

The Baroness reached out, her fingers trailing across Kailia's midsection as she moved, a pensive look on her face that would almost be convincing if it weren't for the something 'other' that lingered in her eyes. Something Kailia could never quite decipher, but she attributed that to not easily understanding body language and facial reactions.

"I am told you are making poor choices," the Baroness said, a small pout forming on red lips.

Kailia said nothing, having learned long ago to wait and learn what she did wrong before apologizing and potentially revealing something else entirely. She'd learned such a tactic from the Baroness after all.

Fingers grazed up her arm until a single nail was running along her jaw and tipping her chin up. "What have you been taught about control, Kailia?"

"That without control, I have nothing but the blood in my veins," she answered.

"And would you say you have control right now?"

It was no use lying. She already knew. The Baroness always knew everything going on in the Cliffs.

The Baroness's mock pout deepened, and she took a step back, nodding her chin to the males who stood on either side of the door. Each one gripped her biceps, pulling her towards the manacles.

"Wait!" she cried, twisting in their hold, once again trying to dig in her heels.

"Something to show me?" the Baroness asked, arching a perfect brow.

"I can create the weapons you want," she answered, her voice trembling. "I can make them. I can—"

"While the weapons will prove useful, how will you be useful if you cannot move among your magic?" the Baroness posed. "Move across the room, Kailia. Prove your worth more than the blood you carry."

But she couldn't.

Because her magic was broken. Cracked and fractured somehow. No matter what she did, she couldn't repair it. If she tried to move among her ashes now, she didn't know where she'd end up. Where her power would drag her. It would only make things so much worse when she was eventually found and brought back here. They always found her. Always brought her back.

When she didn't answer, when she did nothing, the Baroness shook her head. "I'm so disappointed in your choice, my little huntress."

As if this was her choice. As if she was choosing to not have control over her magic.

The chains rattled with the force of her trembling as the manacles were snapped into place around her wrists and ankles.

The Baroness stepped in front of her once more, gripping her jaw sharply, nails digging in. "If you cannot contribute to this colony with your magic, then perhaps it is finally time for you to visit the producing rooms."

She didn't entirely know what happened in the producing rooms, but the males and females assigned to those rooms always looked haunted. Vacant eyes. Faces always down, and eventually, they just…disappeared.

Releasing her face, the Baroness said, "Something I will be considering, but in the meantime…" She turned, her frown lifting into a smile. "Cain?"

Kailia hadn't seen him standing in the dark corner. Too consumed with the Baroness, she had no idea when he'd arrived. But he stepped forward now, the fire at his fingertips illuminating the dark spaces.

"Use this time to think about your choice, my little huntress," the Baroness said, not looking back as she left the room.

The two escorts stayed, one standing on either side of the door.

And Cain?

Kailia screamed as he pressed a palm of flames to her navel.

Her power thrashed in her veins, unable to save her because of the manacles. The metal nullified most magic, including hers. The scent of charred flesh filled the room as Cain slowly dragged his hand along her torso.

She couldn't think. She couldn't get air down.

Not as that hand trailed up her arm. Clasped her throat. The fire never lessening.

There was only the pain and her screams.

There was only the cost of failure.

—⁑⊙⁑—

Someone was holding her down by the shoulders. She was being jostled. They were touching her, and she was burning, and—

That wasn't flames. It was an icy brush of something dark and cold that chilled her bones but also pulled her out of the thrall of her nightmares.

She lurched to the side, tumbling to the floor as she retched.

"Fucking Fates," she heard a male mutter. "Lia, are you—"

"Do not ask if she's all right when you took her out and let her get so drunk—"

"I don't let her do anything, Sutara. She's the queen. If she wants to drink her weight in ale every once in a while, I'm not going to stop her."

Right.

The awful ale she'd consumed three large mugs of. That was what she was vomiting up right now.

She could still smell the scent of burning flesh, and her entire body still felt like it was being tortured with flames, even if the cold magic had lessened the intensity. When someone crouched beside her, she scrambled to the side, her stomach still convulsing.

"It's me, Kailia," Cethin coaxed. "I'm going to hold your hair back. Okay?"

It probably didn't make much difference now. Strands were matted to her sweaty brow and neck while locks hung limply over her shoulders, grazing the same floor she'd vomited on.

She let him carefully gather the strands anyway, flinching whenever he accidentally grazed her skin. Her muscles ached as if she'd been in those shackles for days, arching in pain as Cain reminded her she may be descended from Anala, but fire was still a weakness.

The minutes passed, the vomiting turning to dry heaving as her stomach continued to convulse, cramping and making her curl in on herself. Razik had retrieved a rubbish bin so at least she wasn't retching onto the floor anymore.

"Can I help you back to the sofa?" Cethin asked softly when she'd finally stilled, panting from everything.

"I can do it," she rasped, her throat raw.

"But I can—"

"I said I'll do it," she interjected, pushing up with shaking arms.

Cethin released her hair as she staggered the few steps to the sofa and collapsed back onto it. She pulled her legs to her chest, wrapping her arms around them and pressing her brow to her knees, willing her heart rate to slow and her breathing to even out.

"Drink some water, Lia," Razik said, and she lifted her head, finding him extending a glass to her.

She took a small sip to get the taste of bile out of her mouth. Anything more would have come right back up. Razik took a step back while Cethin took a step closer, worry etched across his elegant features.

"What do you need, Kailia?" Cethin asked.

A bath.

To be left alone.

Time to get back into the right state of mind.

Cethin started to lower onto the sofa beside her, and she stiffened, her aching muscles screaming as they tensed again. He paused, and she saw the two males exchange a look. Oddly, all she could think about was that it only took her nightmares to make the two be civil with one another, even if it was fleeting.

Taking a seat on the sofa, Cethin left extra room between them. She watched his fingers drum on his thigh as he studied her. She let her brow fall back to her knees, willing the small spots in her vision to disappear.

"You know nothing?" Razik asked, his tone tight.

"Why would I know anything?" Cethin retorted.

When Razik didn't answer, she peeked out at them again, catching another exchange of knowing looks.

"If you had summoned me sooner, I may have been able to help more," Cethin finally answered, returning his attention to her. Everything about him softened when his eyes found hers, and he leaned a little closer. "Tell us how we can help."

"There's nothing to be done," she answered, forcing herself to uncoil. "I think I'll take a bath."

Cethin scrambled to his feet as well. "You don't want to talk about what happened?"

"Why would I do that?"

"I can't help if I don't know what we're dealing with."

"There's nothing to help with," she replied, each step unsteady as she made her way to the hall.

It took far longer than it should have to get into the tub. Probably because of the icy water she'd filled it with to cool her heated skin. Then she was freezing when she got out. Slipping on her usual dress, she grabbed a fur blanket from the bed, wrapping it around her shoulders.

She shouldn't have been surprised to find both males waiting for her in the sitting room when she reappeared. The mess had been cleaned from the floor, and there was a small spread of food—breads, crackers, soup. Cethin had changed at some point, but Razik was still in his clothing from the day. It was dark, but not past midnight yet, and she sank back onto the sofa utterly exhausted, her wet braid making her dress damp where it draped over her shoulder.

"How are you feeling?" Cethin ventured, setting aside the glass of liquor he'd been nursing.

"I'll be fine," she replied.

"Can we talk about what happened?"

"There's nothing to discuss."

"There's plenty to discuss," he countered. "The tavern today. The dream. Why I suddenly can't get near you without you flinching away."

"We are trying to help," Razik offered, and she glanced at him, thrown off by the unusual display of blatant concern.

"I already told you there's nothing to help with," she sighed, pulling the blanket tighter around herself.

"You were screaming, Kailia," Cethin replied, the words sounding almost haunted. "You were screaming, and I— You were screaming like your soul was being tortured."

"You can't possibly know that," she retorted weakly.

"I can," he countered. "Because your screams of agony were the same as those I end slowly with my power. When I am..."

He trailed off, but she didn't need him to finish.

When *he* was the one doing the torturing.

But she recognized they weren't going to let this go. That she needed to give them something so they would stop pushing for more.

"I was raised and trained to be in complete control of myself and my power at all times," she said, both of the males going still and quiet. "When I couldn't do that, I was punished."

"How?" Cethin asked, his voice a low growl that rivaled Razik's.

She wouldn't look at him, focusing instead on the soft fur of the blanket on her skin. "Usually chained to a wall with metal that suppressed my magic while a fire wielder used their gifts." There were simultaneous low rumbles from the males, but neither moved. "It was the same way they got my magic to manifest when I was a child," she offered. "Without the manacles, obviously."

"I need you to clarify that you were a *child*, and to get your magic to manifest, they *burned* you until it did so?" Razik asked in a tone so dark and cold, her every instinct went on high alert.

Kailia glanced at him, his pupils having shifted and his body vibrating. Her brow furrowed, recognizing the struggle. "Are you fighting a full shift?"

"Yes," he ground out.

"Why?"

"Why? Because you were— You were a godsdamn child, Kailia," Razik snarled.

"I know, but you didn't know me then. And why are you talking to me like it was my fault I was raised there?"

"He's not. Not intentionally," Cethin cut in. "We're just processing. That was your dream? You were reliving…that."

She nodded. "Usually in my dreams, I have more warning, but with the alcohol… It was my fault, really."

"Absolutely not," Cethin snarled. He reached for her, stopping right before he made contact, and pulled his hand back with a frustrated sound. "None of what you endured was your fault."

"Others experienced the same. Many worse than what I was subjected to," she replied. It was how she'd survived. Constantly telling herself it could be worse. That she'd witnessed others experiencing worse, both inside those cliffs and outside them.

Cethin blinked at her, and this time he didn't stop when he reached for her. There was no brush of his magic. Only skin-to-skin contact as he gently cupped her chin and tipped her face up to his.

"Someone else experiencing trauma doesn't negate yours and the things you face because of it, Kailia. Do you understand?" he asked, searching her eyes.

It took her a minute to mull that over. Who was she to deserve sympathy and comfort when it could have been worse? When it *was* worse for so many others?

"You can have sympathy for others and what they went through, but it doesn't lessen what you went through," Cethin pushed. "It doesn't invalidate what you felt and how it has affected you since."

That made a little more sense, and she nodded, seeing the potential truth in his words.

"Tell us more about where you were raised, Lia," Razik said, and she twisted to face him.

He'd taken a seat in the armchair across from them, perched on the edge.

"There are islands to the south of the main continent," she said.

"The Southern Islands," Razik supplied.

Kailia nodded. "One of them... There are enchanted cliffs there. They housed a large colony of people. Powerful people. Fae. Shifters. Witches. Other beings... Everyone was expected to contribute to the colony, and your power determined where and how you did that. We were told the cliffs kept us hidden from people who wanted to use us."

She stole a glance at Cethin, his silver gaze pinned on her, but there was no other reaction to her words. Only an intensity as he gave her his undivided attention.

"Those of us with rare gifts were trained for other things, while those with powerful common gifts were expected to help supply even more powerful beings to the colony," she went on, watching the king. "After I found myself free of the cliffs, I learned that the Baroness, who ran the cliffs, was trying to create powerful beings using powerful bloodlines."

"Are you saying the colony in those cliffs was used for essentially breeding experiments? With power?" Razik demanded.

She nodded. "I suppose that's the most direct way to explain it. There were other nuances, but yes."

"And you were forced to..." Cethin trailed off, a too-calm fury in his words, but the darkness in his irises betrayed him.

Her head canted to the side. "That would make you upset?"

He jolted back as if she'd struck him. "Of course it would. Only a monster wouldn't be upset by that."

She nodded. "I've found there are more monsters in the realm than not. They are just incredibly skilled at remaining hidden. Some are even beloved, with their true natures hidden beneath benevolent actions and perceived kindness."

"How did you get out?" Razik asked, pulling her attention back to him.

She adjusted her blanket, pursing her lips as she stared out the window at the dark night sky. "There was one who had escaped well before my time. Or that's the story I was told. He'd gone head-to-head with the Baroness and had gained his freedom decades before my time. He was this enigma. A whispered legend among the people of the cliffs. There were rumors he would come back, leaving a blood trail in his wake of the guards and those who enforced the laws of the colony. I didn't know whether or not he was real. Not until he showed up on the night I was sent to— Not until he showed up one night and gave me a way out."

"And you don't know who it was?" Cethin asked.

She twisted back to him, watching his features carefully. "The only name I've ever known him by is the Reaper. He eventually returned to the Cliffs, decades after I had left. I'm told he killed the Baroness and anyone who sided with her. There are rumors he bound himself to the Cliffs themselves. That he knows if anyone tries to return to them, and he shows up to end them."

"You've never met him again?" Cethin asked. "Or know where he is?"

"Why would you want to know that?"

"I'd like to thank the male who saved my wife," he said, each word tight and filled with violence.

"You sound like you want to harm him," she said skeptically.

"The violence isn't for him, Lia. It's the entire situation. All of it," Razik supplied. "Where did you go after you got out?"

"As far north as I could," she answered, still studying Cethin.

"That's when you went to Pyry," Razik reasoned, and she nodded. "And then?"

She reached for a cracker, her empty stomach making her nauseated all over again. "I stayed with the Shifters in Pyry for quite some time. Until some of their allies came to visit. I was offered a position, and in exchange I was given a place to stay and additional training."

"And how did you come to Avonleya?"

"On a ship."

Razik rolled his eyes. "Obviously, Lia. Why? What made you decide to do so?"

"I vowed to hunt down everyone who had a hand in what was done to me in those Cliffs. I was told some had found their way here," she answered. "So I followed."

"And did you find them? End them?" Cethin demanded.

"Not yet, but I will," she replied simply, selecting a piece of bread this time.

"We'll help."

"Not needed," she answered.

"Kailia, you can't expect us to sit back and do nothing when you tell us there are people responsible for everything you experienced in our own godsdamn kingdom," he seethed.

"That is a concern, but… If it's true that some of these people made their way here, what if they know who you are?" Razik posed.

She paused her chewing. "What do you mean?"

"Exactly what I said. You've been hunting them, but what if they've been hunting you too? And they're trying to get to you?"

"You think this is somehow connected to the attacks from the Elder Clans?" Cethin asked, his body rigid with tension.

"I don't believe in coincidences," Razik answered. "But I do believe someone knows who you are and where you came from, Lia."

"But…why?" she asked. "What would they want with me now?"

"The same thing they wanted centuries ago. The same thing Ash Riders are coveted for across the realm. Your power and your bloodline," Razik answered.

As if she didn't know that was where her value lay. In what she could offer others. Hadn't that been proven time and time again? In the Cliffs. Once she'd gotten out. In Pyry. In the mortal lands. Even here. She was bound to Cethin because of her arrows. Nothing more.

"When you first came to Avonleya, where did you stay? Where did you go?" Razik asked, leaning forward with his arms braced on his knees.

"I didn't stay in one place much," she murmured.

"But you had to have gone somewhere," Razik pushed. "We might be able to—"

"That's enough for now," Cethin cut in, and she glanced over at him, finding his attention still fixed on her. "She has relived enough for now," he repeated. "I'll stay the rest of the night."

"Cethin, if I'm right and someone is hunting her, she needs to be watched at all times," Razik warned.

"Are you telling me you're not able to do your job well enough?"

Razik bristled, getting to his feet. "No, you dick. I'm telling you to stop leaving your wife unattended when I'm off duty so she doesn't feel the need to drink her weight in ale."

He was gone before Cethin could answer, the heavy doors to their rooms slamming shut behind him.

Kailia could feel Cethin's gaze boring into her, and she fixated on the piece of bread in her hand.

"Is what he said true? That's why you went to the tavern today?" Cethin asked, each word measured and stilted.

"We went to the tavern because he needed to collect something," she replied.

"And the ale?" When she didn't answer, he pushed, "You can speak plainly, Kailia."

"I understand your responsibilities," she said, setting the bread aside before she made a bigger mess with the crumbs. "But I don't entirely understand what has happened. For a while, you were here when I woke in the mornings, but these last few days it has gone back to how it was. I woke up this morning to find you gone and was...confused by it all. Trying to figure out what I'm doing right and wrong."

"You're doing nothing wrong, wife," he answered. "With more Fae deaths last week, the pressures have increased."

"And instead of letting me help, you leave me behind. I know my position is in title only, but I could help," she insisted. "If you'd let me."

"You understand the mixed messages you're sending when I couldn't convince you to help in the beginning without coercing you into a marriage, yet now you are upset because I'm not asking for your help?" Cethin asked, and her gaze snapped to him.

He'd propped his elbow on the back of the sofa, temple against his fist as he watched her.

"I can see how that could be perplexing," she replied.

"But I can include you more if that is truly what you want," he added.

"I think I would like that."

"It'd likely help everyone accept you more as well. To see you interacting. Although saving everyone at the Union Ceremony certainly helped in that respect."

"Right," she murmured. Because safety and security was what she could offer them. That's where her value lies.

"Kailia?"

"Hmm?"

"Were you forced to— In those Cliffs. Is that where your experience with sex came from?"

She lifted her gaze to his once more, finding a mixture of anger and dread on his features.

"I was tortured with fire and fists," she said, knowing what he was asking. "The one and only time I was sent to the rooms where there was forced sex was the night the Reaper freed me. I was never touched in that way, but only because my magic was useful to the Baroness in other ways. Until it wasn't."

He leaned in, catching the end of her braid and tugging lightly to pull her closer too. "I'll help you hunt them down, Kailia. Every last one. They'll pay for their part in this."

"I know," she said softly. "I'm going to ensure it costs them everything."

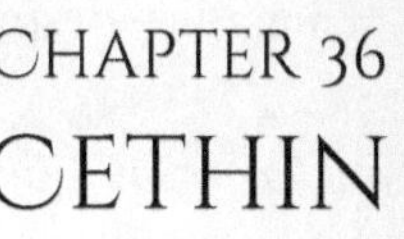

CHAPTER 36
CETHIN

"Come in," Cethin called from his desk, glancing up from the endless reports and paperwork.

Kailia looked up too. He'd given her a small pile of mundane things. Why she wanted to spend her days here doing this was beyond him, but ever since the night she'd told them some of her past, she'd spent her days in this study whenever he was here. There hadn't been any advisory meetings, and he didn't let her sit in on daily updates from Zayan. He wasn't about to hand over his kingdom to her, but ever since the night of their union, she'd insisted this is what she'd wanted. He thought she'd been trying to appease him in some way, but nearly three months later, she was just as relentless.

Tybalt came through the door, and Razik stood at his uncle's entrance. If Kailia was here, that meant Razik was here. Which was fine, Cethin supposed. Annoying, but fine. Annoying because the male was proving useful, and more than once, when Kailia had posed a question about this matter or that, Razik had offered sound counsel and insights. Almost as if he was her Hand of the Queen in a way.

"Your Majesties," Tybalt said with a bow of his head. He looked from Cethin to Kailia and back before he said, "I have a sensitive matter to discuss, Cethin."

"Of what nature?"

"One that I'd rather discuss with you alone."

He studied the Commander. His grim features and the tight line of his jaw. The faintly glowing eyes, despite not having shifted. And he knew.

"You can speak in front of your queen, Commander," Cethin said, sitting back in his chair and rubbing his temple.

"Cethin, I don't think—"

"More Fae were discovered dead?" he interrupted.

Tybalt paused, his lips pressing into a thin line. "Yes."

"How many?"

He hesitated, glancing at Kailia again. Razik had moved closer, standing beside her, and she had set her work aside, listening intently.

"Twenty-five," Tybalt finally answered. "Near Everfall."

"Everfall?" Kailia asked. "Haven't the recent attacks been here? Near Aimonway?"

"Yes," Tybalt answered. "We thought there had been a tactic. A pattern we'd been seeing, but this breaks any of those patterns."

"We can't consider it a one-off either," Cethin said, shoving a hand through his hair. "Not when it claimed the lives of twenty-five Fae. That's more than the last three attacks combined."

"Agreed," Tybalt said.

"And there are no clues as to why this keeps happening? Nothing that links them all together?" Kailia asked.

"The victims are always Fae. That's it," Cethin answered.

"There has to be something," she argued.

"Nothing we've discovered after years of investigation," Tybalt replied. "But something has caused the increase in deaths."

"So much for bringing the Fae to Aimonway to keep them safe," Cethin muttered.

"But they didn't all come to Aimonway if these were found near Everfall. Isn't that on the other side of the continent?" Kailia asked.

"Not quite," Razik answered. "It's on the east side of the Olwen Mountains in the Korra Forest."

"Why wouldn't they come to Aimonway?"

"We can't force them to uproot their lives," Cethin said. "We offered protection, and some chose to take it. Not that it has done any good."

"We'd hoped with so many Fae in one area, it might draw the threats closer. Make them easier to identify," Tybalt said.

"You were using the Fae as bait?" Kailia asked.

"In a sense, I guess you could call it that," Tybalt answered. "With the intention of intervening before there were any more deaths."

"That did not work," Kailia said, her words tight.

"Obviously," Tybalt retorted.

"Enough," Cethin said, getting to his feet. "I'll go to Everfall. Send word to Lord Astor. I want to see for myself."

"I can send the Cadre," Tybalt argued. "I think that would be the wiser option."

"I'm going," Cethin said, his tone leaving no room for argument. "I'm done sitting here going through reports when this is still going on and escalating. Someone is trying to get our attention, and they need to know they fucking have it."

"And if the phantom creatures show up and make things worse?" Tybalt demanded.

Cethin turned, his gaze landing on his wife. "Then it's a good thing the queen will be with me."

─❯❯ � ❮❮─

"Your Majesties," the newest lord greeted. "Welcome to Everfall." He bowed at the waist before straightening again. "My apologies for not being more prepared," he added, looking down at his attire with a slightly sheepish smile.

His black hair had been trimmed since the last advisory session, and his grey eyes seemed darker in a way. Brown pants and a black tunic were apparently his favored attire. Cethin had never paid much attention to his power, especially in a room full of people with strong bloodlines, but with fewer people around, it was easier to distinguish, feeling familiar yet different and as powerful as any of the others advisors if not more so.

"I apologize for the short notice," Cethin said with a warm smile. "I also apologize for taking so long to come visit. I try to visit newly appointed lords and ladies closer to their acceptance."

"No need to apologize, your grace. You've had far more important things to tend to with the Fae and your new wife," he replied, switching his attention to Kailia. "It is lovely to see you out and about though, your grace."

"It's good to see you again, Lord Astor," she replied with a smile of her own.

The lord clicked his tongue. "I told you before, you can call me Corveth."

"Yes," she mused. "You did say that when we discussed how we were both getting used to our new titles and roles."

"And you are doing well?"

"I am, thank you."

Cethin glanced at Razik. This was the most casual exchange he'd witnessed with Kailia, outside of speaking to him or Razik. Had they visited Everfall? No, because while Razik pushed boundaries, even he wouldn't take the queen from Aimonway without notice.

"Well, don't let me keep you standing out here in the town square for people to stare at," Corveth said, clapping his hands together. "I was helping some folks on the edge of town with some sheep shearing, but I can escort you to the Everfall Manor before I head back out there."

"Actually, if we could go to the site of the attack, that would be preferable right now," Cethin said, stepping closer to Kailia.

"Yes, of course," Corveth said in a rush. "Right this way."

"You don't want to Travel there?" Razik asked as the lord started down the road.

"I know this is important, but I'd like to see more of the town if we can," Kailia said, looking up at him. "I rarely get to leave Aimonway."

Razik shrugged, checking in with Cethin. "Doesn't matter to me."

While he would have preferred to simply get to the site and start searching, he'd also been making an effort to include Kailia more. He'd been meaning to bring her to Everfall for weeks, and they weren't in any real hurry. It wasn't as if their presence would bring back the dead.

"We can walk," he said, letting his darkness brush along her arm before he pressed his palm to the small of her back.

She offered him a tentative smile, and he took it as a win. Since her nightmare, he'd felt like they'd started over with the touching thing. She was making efforts though, and that was all he could ask of her. Well, that and for more details about her past, but he wasn't about to push her on that right now.

They made their way down the stone streets, and as they did, Kailia drifted farther and farther to Corveth's side, engrossed in conversation as he pointed out various parts of the town. The city itself was at the base of the Olwen Mountains, crawling up the mountainside to the north and going deeper into the forest to the south.

Most of the homes and buildings were two stories high, constructed from the same stone as the streets. Wood shutters adorned windows, while greenery climbed the sides. As the city crawled up the side of the mountain, the roads becoming steeper, one could find the Everfall Manor at the north end, overlooking the city.

But as they went south, the houses and buildings became farther apart. Small animal farms, gardens, and crops were spread out, and beyond that lay Korra Forest, with evergreen and fir trees dominating over the ash and birch trees. It was a few miles into the forest that they came to a clearing.

Where they found nothing.

There was no dried blood. No signs of struggle or a fight. No ripped pieces of fabric, lost weapons, or paths that would indicate a body being dragged here.

There was absolutely nothing to show twenty-five Fae had been found dead here this morning except for the spots of crushed foliage.

"How were they discovered?" Cethin asked, watching as Razik prowled around the perimeter.

"Sheep farmer," Corveth answered grimly. "The one I'm helping today. Some of his sheep got loose. We tracked them down and found them here."

Kailia turned. "*You* found the Fae?"

The male nodded, his thumbs hooked in his pockets. "I sent word to the castle straight away. Commander Greybane was here within minutes, some others with him."

"Jarek and Fallon," Razik supplied, rubbing his jaw. "There's nothing, Cethin. Nothing here that could indicate what happened."

"I'm sorry to be a bother, but I did leave Henrik and Rania in a pinch," Corveth said, wincing when all eyes fell on him. "If you have no further need for me, would it be all right if I return to finish helping them?"

"We can find our own way back," Cethin said. "But you'll join us for dinner?"

"Of course, your Majesty," Corveth said with a bow. "Thank you for understanding."

The male turned, heading back the way they'd come. If the farm was the one Cethin was thinking of, it was only a mile back along the path.

Kailia had wandered away from him, not inspecting the perimeter like Razik was, but walking through the clearing. She'd removed her boots, those now discarded on the ground beside Cethin. Her bare feet were soundless as she moved, and she lifted a hand, letting her ashes flow and snake along the ground as if they were searching as well.

"Aren't there creatures of old nearby here?" she asked as she continued on a path known only to her.

Cethin nodded. "The *stryx* slumber in the Olwen Mountains."

"The creatures have been stirring. Could they be doing this?"

"The Fae were being targeted before the creatures of old began stirring. More than that, some Fae have been found far from the resting places. There aren't any creatures of old near Aimonway," Cethin explained.

"Only those who can shift and those who hide in the shadows then?"

Cethin glanced at Razik, who was watching her as closely as he was.

"I don't think I'd classify myself as a creature of old, Lia," Razik deadpanned.

"I didn't say *you* were a creature of old, Raz," she replied. "But I do believe the dragons you descend from are likely as old as the creatures who slumber here, no?"

"That's valid logic," he grumbled.

"Logical, sure," Cethin interjected. "But either way, it has nothing to do with who or what is targeting the Fae."

"Maybe they're not being targeted," Kailia said simply, still wandering around the clearing. She looked over her shoulder, peering at him when she added, "Maybe they are the unfortunate cost of something bigger."

"I'd thought that at one point," Cethin said. "That they were being used to get to me, but that was when I thought the deaths were related to the phantom attacks."

"And now?" she asked, turning to face them from across the clearing.

"And now we're back to not having any ideas or theories," he answered. "The phantom creatures only seem to come for me."

Her head tilted in thought. "Do you think they are creatures of old as well?"

"If they are, I've never come across them in books I've read," Razik answered.

"And they only showed up in the last few months," Cethin added. "There's no way they've been here for centuries like the creatures of old."

There wasn't much to say after that. They searched the clearing for another hour, but there was nothing to find and nothing to see. Kailia wanted to explore more of Everfall, so they Traveled back to the town center, then walked to Everfall Manor. They were shown to rooms where they could change and clean up before meeting Corveth for dinner when the moon was high in the sky.

The lord wasn't in a relationship with anyone, but there were some members of Everfall present who helped govern the town. Cethin sat at the head of the table, Kailia to his right with Razik at her side. Corveth was to his left, having changed into slightly more formal attire. They were well into their third course of the evening, the conversation light and easy.

"I'm sorry we weren't able to be of more help today," Corveth offered with an apologetic smile.

"Nothing to apologize for," Cethin answered, despite his disappointment that they'd found nothing. "At this point, we can't leave any stone unturned."

"Understandable," the lord replied, leaning back for his plate to be cleared before dessert was served. "What a time to become queen. In the midst of so much turmoil," he continued, turning his attention back to Kailia.

It hadn't escaped Cethin that the lord made sure to include her in every conversation. She clearly felt at ease around him, and he was patient with her. Never making her feel uncomfortable with his questions. It likely did help that they were both unexpectedly shoved into their positions.

"How are you adjusting to the castle?" the lord continued. "So different from where you grew up."

"Very different, yes," she answered as a dish of some kind of pudding was placed before her. "But there are some similarities."

"Oh?" Corveth asked. "That provides some comfort, then?"

"Not really," she said, picking up her spoon.

The lord chuckled, but Cethin frowned. What about her life in Aimonway could be similar to where she grew up?

The thought bothered him the rest of the dinner, and when they retired for the night, he waited until they'd changed into nightclothes before asking her about it.

He stood outside the bathing chamber, and when she emerged, she jolted.

"By Temural, Cethin," she said irritably, her hand at her thigh where a weapon was usually hidden. "Why are you standing right here?"

"In what ways is Aimonway similar to where you were raised?" he asked instead.

She blinked at him in surprise, carefully stepping around him. "It was merely conversation."

"Bullshit," he challenged. "Even in casual conversation you are blunt and specific."

"You don't need to point out my flaws," she said flatly. "I'm well aware of them."

"That was not my intention, but it is a fact, nevertheless. If you said Aimonway is similar to where you grew up, then you meant it. I want to know how."

"Why? What purpose does that serve?" she asked, and he knew it was a genuine question. But knowing that frustrated him more. That she was putting this life into the same sphere as her childhood after what he'd learned about how and where she grew up didn't sit right with him.

"What purpose does it serve? Kailia, you were tortured to the point that you avoid physical contact at all costs. You saying Aimonway is in any way like that is my concern," he answered tightly.

"But why do you care?" she asked. "You have what you want. What does it matter now?"

He stared at her, unsure how to answer that. "You think I have everything I want?"

She shrugged, turning away from him to pull back the blankets on the bed, but the dismissal made something in him snap.

He was across the room in seconds. She spun, eyes wide, when she found he was already standing over her. Stumbling back, she lost her balance, but he was there, an arm around her waist keeping her from falling onto the bed. He heard her gasp, and he caught her wrist as she went for her thigh, despite no weapon being there.

Slowly, she dragged her eyes to his. Her magic swirled frantically. Fury stared back at him, but there was more there too. Something he didn't quite understand.

"If I had everything I wanted, my people would be safe. We wouldn't be finding dead Fae every other week. The Wards would be gone, and we'd be free to move about the realm as we once were able to. If I had everything I wanted, my parents wouldn't be gone. I wouldn't be chained to a fucking throne because of the blood that runs in my veins. I sure as fuck wouldn't be risking—"

He cut himself off, the words sitting on the tip of his tongue. Words that would damn him and reveal far too much. She was staring up at him, listening intently. That unreadable face devoid of any emotion, leaving him once again wondering what she'd thought of his little tirade.

Clearing his throat, he straightened, making sure she was steady before he released her and took a step back. He didn't apologize, and he wasn't going to. For the first time since she'd come into his life, he wished she hadn't. He wished he were free to go find someone to get lost in. Someone who wouldn't flinch at a touch. Someone who would touch him back, even if it was just a show.

Yet the mere thought of touching someone else had him internally disgusted.

No. Instead of being able to get lost in a good fuck or even have someone in his life who *wanted* to be with him, he was with someone who would rather stab him than let him prove touch could be something to crave. Instead, he was going to extreme measures to convince her of...what, exactly? He wasn't sure he even knew anymore.

All he knew was that each day he was becoming more desperate. More obsessed. Needing her to give just a godsdamn inch. She wasn't going anywhere, and neither was he.

"I wasn't able to leave the Cliffs," Kailia said into the silence. "I didn't have a lot of freedom, and sometimes, it feels the same. I was ignored unless I was needed, and after my power manifested, I was only needed for what I could offer. I was only useful if I could control my power and provide weapons."

"And you believe that is all I want from you?" he asked, shoving down all the arguments he wanted to make. He wasn't about to debate her feelings with her. People did that to him all the time, as if his feelings were wrong and invalid.

"I think you want more. I think you want things from me you don't even realize yet," she answered. "Things you don't even realize I could give you."

"And what do you want?" he asked, searching her face for something. Anything.

She hesitated, the first time she'd ever shown any real uncertainty, as she bit her lower lip and looked at the floor beside him. He wanted to step closer. Tilt her face up to his and pull the answer from her, but he didn't want to interfere either. She was this never-ending conundrum of perplexities and secrets that simultaneously drove him mad and kept him intrigued to no end.

"I don't think I know anymore," she finally admitted, still staring at a spot on the floor. "I don't know, and I find that unsettling."

"Why?"

"Because there was a plan and then…" She trailed off.

"We have centuries left if the Fates allow it," he said. "And every single one of those years will be spent with me. That means you don't have to figure it out on your own."

She finally looked at him again. "You make me want things I can't have."

"What makes you think there is anything you can't have? Anything I wouldn't give you?" he asked.

"I want to believe that. I truly do."

The words were nothing but a whisper. The pained agony of a tortured soul, and for reasons he'd never be able to explain, they had him surging forward. Her eyes went wide, but she didn't flinch back. Not this time. No, this time she was leaning in as he brought his mouth to hers, tilting her face just right, and by the Fates, when did he suddenly not know what to do with himself when kissing someone?

He was debating what to do with his hands. Would she push him away if he touched her any more than he already was? If he cupped her jaw or slid his hand into her hair? Would she tense if he pressed his body against hers just to godsdamn *feel* her?

It was hard to think about any of that when her mouth was so warm. He tried to be so careful as he tentatively licked along the seam of her lips, hoping he wasn't pushing her too far or asking for too much. He didn't know with her. He never knew, and he both loved and hated it. Loved that she was a constant enigma that kept him always wondering what she'd do next, and hated that he couldn't read her. Couldn't figure her out. Never knew where he stood with her. Knew that wasn't entirely her fault but also resented her a little for it.

She pulled back, and he froze, waiting to see what she'd do next. Her breaths were fast as she stood so godsdamn still.

Until she pushed up onto her toes, capturing his lips again before he could do anything more than suck in a breath. This kiss was aggressive and almost violent, so much like her, and still he fisted his hands at his sides, not willing to be the reason she stopped any of this. It had to be her. She had to initiate all of it from here on out, because he knew if he let his control slip even a little, it would shatter completely.

With every tentative movement of her lips, he let himself get lost in her a little more. Every sense narrowed in on how soft her lips were against his. How slick her tongue was as it explored and fought with his. The soft sounds that came from her when he pressed back with his mouth.

He might not have touched her with his hands, but he'd told her he didn't need them to make her feel. Pulling back, the soft moan of disappointment turned into a sharp gasp of surprise when he dropped his lips to her neck. She tipped her head back, and he worked his way up, pressing hard, wet, open-mouthed kisses as he went, marking his pathway to her ear.

That was when it happened.

Her hands landed on his chest. Touching him. Tentatively sliding along his flesh. By the gods, he was going to come just from her fingers on his skin.

Then the bells sounded.

The warning echoed through the night air, the sound more than a little jarring with their open windows.

Kailia jerked back, eyes wide as she scrambled to the window. He followed, trying to think through the lust and sudden burst of adrenaline. But as soon as he saw what was drifting along the streets, any thoughts of kissing and touching and where it could lead were gone.

"We need—" Kailia started, but he'd already grabbed her elbow, tugging her from the room. Gods, he wished they could Travel, but they were too close in proximity to them. Just like they couldn't Travel away from them in battles, they couldn't Travel in too close either.

They ran, racing down the stairs and halls as fast as they could. At some point, Razik appeared, running alongside them. They burst through the doors of Everfall Manor, continuing down the paths and streets until they found the phantoms.

Kailia had summoned her bow, arrows already nocked, and he once again stood by, helpless. He'd lost count of how many times this had happened now. How many times he'd been useless while she'd defended him and their towns and their people.

"They have fucking arrows now?" Razik growled, more in annoyance than anything.

Cethin was inclined to agree. Every time they met these things in battle, the creatures seemed to have gained a new skill. The phantoms drifted along with bows of their own. They weren't as fast as Kailia, but she still couldn't take them all down at once.

"You need to get out of here," Razik snarled, dragon fire flaring as he caught an arrow and incinerated it while Kailia took out the phantom who'd shot it.

The sound of footsteps had him turning to find Corveth and several guards running down the street. The phantoms saw them too. Or sensed them? Considering he wasn't sure if they could actually see with their pupil-less eyes. A few of them diverted their attention to the newcomers, but the majority stayed fixated on Cethin.

"Shit," Razik muttered, starting to turn.

A wave of darkness rose between the innocents and the phantoms. Cethin knew it wouldn't do much, knew it couldn't stop the phantoms, but if they couldn't see them, maybe it'd buy them some time.

In the end, it didn't matter. Every attack, every arrow, every onslaught was directed at them.

At him.

Hisses of frustration and curses of "blood of death" filled the air as Razik and Kailia worked to combat each and every one. The most Cethin could do was catch an arrow as Kailia spun out of the way, killing the phantom. The three of them watched as it crackled, turning to ash while light flared from the cracks before it dissolved into nothing. Until silence was all that remained while they watched errant ashes from Razik's kills drift slowly to the ground.

Kailia dropped to a crouch, her breathing fast and heavy, and the action had Cethin dropping to his knees beside her and Razik lowering to a crouch too. Carefully, Cethin reached out, tipping her chin up. His eyes went wide as he found tears glimmering in amber depths, the smoke in them swirling slow and sluggish.

"Are you hurt?" Cethin demanded, gaze darting over her, looking for blood, cuts, bruises.

She shook her head, but instead of answering him, her eyes slid to Razik. "I can't do this much longer," she whispered, the words bordering on an anguished sob.

"What is she talking about?" Cethin demanded, anger slithering along his spine at Razik knowing something about her he didn't.

"Not here," Razik retorted grimly, gaze flickering to him then back to Kailia. "Let's get inside."

She nodded, and Cethin reached for her arm as she stood. She still held her bow, and he still held the arrow he'd caught, the gold arrowhead glinting in the faint moonlight. Razik took her other arm, and Cethin Traveled them all back to their room.

Setting the arrow on a side table, he grabbed a blanket, returning to wrap it around Kailia's shoulders. She was still in her nightdress, her bow disappearing among a swirl of ashes, and he remained shirtless in loose pants.

"What is this about?" Cethin demanded as she lowered to a chair, pulling her knees to her chest.

But before anyone could answer him, there was a knock on the door and Lord Astor was calling, "Your Majesties? Are you all right? Do you need anything?"

Cethin jerked his chin at Razik to go handle the lord, and while he did that, Cethin crouched before Kailia. His hands on either side of her, he looked up into her face.

"Tell me what's going on, Kailia. Tell me how I can help?" he urged softly, slowly reaching to brush hair off her brow.

"Has it ever occurred to you that you might be the one putting these people in danger? These creatures attack wherever you are," she said, her voice cracking a fraction.

That hadn't been what he'd expected her to say, and he swallowed thickly, because of course that had occurred to him. It was why he spent most nights in his study. It was why he risked using blood magic. It was why he was doing everything he could to figure this out.

"Yes," he answered her, the word raw and vulnerable.

She nodded, the tears that glimmered minutes ago now gone, but an unmistakable agony still shimmered in her eyes.

"If it's true, what will you do to stop the attacks? What would you give up?" she pushed.

"Anything," he answered immediately.

"Me?"

His breath caught, lungs seizing at the very idea.

"Tell me what's going on, Kailia," he urged again, not willing to answer her question.

But she closed her eyes and tipped her head back, going quiet.

That was fine.

He'd figure it out his own way, like he had with everything else, and in the meantime, he'd prove to her she was more to him than the arrows and what she had to offer.

What would he give up?

Everything.

But never her.

CHAPTER 37
KAILIA

"I need you to attend the Advisory Council meeting today," Cethin said

Kailia looked up from the book she'd taken from Razik's study yesterday, glaring at her husband as he adjusted the sleeves of his fine jacket. Actually, why was he wearing that? He'd been in the routine meeting with his advisors the last two days, and he'd never dressed this formally. In the months since she'd been here to see him attend these meetings, he'd never dressed like this. Wore his crown? Yes. Dressed like this? No.

But instead of addressing any of that, she went back to her book as she said dismissively, "I have plans today."

"You'll have to change them," he said simply.

She pursed her lips, and when she tried to sneak a glance at him, she found him watching her with a faint smile on his mouth. It made a slow anger burn in her belly.

They'd been back from Everfall for nearly two weeks, and up until the convening of the Advisory Council, he'd been including her in most of his duties, introducing her to more and more people, and discussing some simple things related to the kingdom over meals. She'd even been allowed to sit in on a planning meeting with the Cadre, despite Commander Greybane's obvious disapproval, but even the Commander couldn't argue against it when she was the only one who could supply the arrows that could kill the phantoms.

But the last two days she'd been left to her own devices. Razik was with her, of course, but she'd been left to overthink and overanalyze everything. Had she said something wrong? Inadvertently offended someone? What had she done that had made Cethin suddenly not want her involved in certain aspects of the kingdom? He was confusing, including her so thoroughly one minute and telling her she couldn't come with him another. The lack of clear direction and sudden shifts in his decisions put her on edge. Every time she thought she had figured out what she needed to be doing, something changed. She liked routine. Not constant upheaval of what she knew.

"I'd suggest changing your attire as well," he said casually, striding from the bedchamber.

She looked down at herself, still in her nightclothes, because what did it matter if she was being relegated to the side once more? She knew she was being petty and intentionally difficult, but Cethin was letting her have her moments. Almost as if he knew she'd never been allowed to express such emotions before. Always doing what she thought would prove her worth, making sure her value was irreplaceable. Such pettiness would mark her as difficult, and she was already walking a thin line with her trouble interacting with others.

She frowned as she ruminated on all of this. At some point, she'd come to feel…safe with Cethin. At least safe enough to be in a foul mood and not care if he knew it.

Now she faced the conundrum of digging in her heels because of said foul mood in a bid to make a point, or giving in and following his suggestion without a fight because her curiosity about suddenly being invited to the council meeting was winning out.

With a huff, she set the book aside and threw off the blanket she had wrapped around her shoulders. She bathed quickly, piling her hair atop her head to keep it from getting wet. Uncertain of what this was all about, she followed Cethin's lead and dressed in something more formal and elegant. Long-sleeved and black with silver embellishments, the dress clung to her chest and torso before draping at her hips. She debated the lightweight cloak, but it was nearly the Summer Solstice. The days were already warm, and she was wearing long sleeves. But more layers provided more places to keep weapons hidden, and that always outweighed any discomfort.

Reaching out, she fingered the fabric of the cloak. It had never been a question she'd entertained, yet here she was, once again wondering when she'd felt comfortable enough to debate such things. Especially here. With him. The king whispered about in hushed voices and dark shadows across the sea. That was who she'd been prepared to face when she'd stepped off that boat all those months ago.

"Razik is here, and you should eat something before the meeting," Cethin said, pulling her from her thoughts.

She turned to find him in the doorway, hands clasped behind his back, but when she met his gaze, he strode forward into the dressing room. Stopping a foot in front of her, he lifted a hand, and her stomach dipped as she anticipated his touch. Not out of dread, but out of want. Another thing that had flipped in the months that she'd been here.

Which is why she shoved down the disappointment when, instead of touching her, he asked, "May I?" as he reached above her head.

Unsure of what he was asking, she nodded slowly, tensing to retreat, but then she went still as he carefully extracted the pins keeping her hair piled atop her head. With a care she didn't understand, he let down the strands, gently draping them over her shoulders and down her back.

"You'll leave it down today? Out of a braid?" he asked, his voice laced with a touch of gravel.

"That was my plan, but is there a specific reason?" she replied, his fingers lingering in the black locks.

"I like it down. Reminds me of the first time I saw you," he replied, finally pulling his hand back as if it was the last thing he wanted to do.

For some reason, it was the last thing she wanted him to do too.

Although she was starting to understand it all a little better, and that thought was unnerving. Because she'd never *wanted* a touch until he'd slowly and patiently shown her it could be different. She couldn't trust him, but somehow, with this, she did. Somehow, despite the forced bargains and marriage and all she knew about him, she trusted his hands and his touch.

"Kailia?" he asked, his brow pinched, and she realized she'd been standing here staring at him.

"Sorry," she said quickly, shaking out her hands before smoothing them down her dress.

His gaze dipped to the movement, brows pinching a bit before smoothing back out. "I didn't mean to make you nervous about this meeting."

"I'm not nervous about that."

"Then…?" His head tilted, studying her as he waited for a response.

"It's nothing," she said dismissively, knowing full well Cethin didn't believe her, but he didn't try to stop her as she moved past him and made her way to the dining room.

Razik was seated there, a plate full of food, and he glared at her. "About time."

"I wasn't aware I had plans today," she retorted, snagging the last two cinnamon rolls along with some fruit and sausage.

Razik's eyes flicked to Cethin and back. "I was also only made aware of those plans this morning. Something else we need to be prepared for, Sutara?"

"In time," he answered airily, taking a seat next to her. "You never leave any of these for me, tiny fiend."

He was reaching for a roll, but he jerked his hand back a moment before her fork would have connected with it. Instead, the tines hit the tabletop with a sharp clink.

Cethin blinked at her before reaching for a cheese pastry. "A fork is a stabbing method we haven't explored yet."

She sent him a flat look. "Try to take food off my plate again, and I won't miss next time."

"Then you admit you missed this time?"

"No. I didn't think showing up at the council meeting with your hand bleeding would serve either of us well," she replied, taking a bite of the roll. "Maybe you should simply order more," she added as she chewed.

"I have been," he retorted. "It doesn't seem to matter."

She shrugged, swallowing her bite. "Perhaps if you were present at more breakfasts, that would help."

She heard Razik's muffled snicker, but Cethin didn't even glare at the male. The king simply hummed, indulging in his own food.

The rest of the meal was quiet, and soon enough, she was being escorted by Razik and Cethin to the formal meeting room. Cethin had placed her circlet on her head before they left, the metal cool against her brow.

When they reached the doors, he wasted no time. Interlacing their fingers, they strode into the room side-by-side, with Razik a step behind them.

All the advisors stood, bowing at their entrance, and Cethin pulled out her chair for her before taking his seat at the head of the table to her left. There was even a chair to her right for Razik. After they were seated, the others sat once more, and she found Zayan directly across from her with the Commander next to him. The Hand of the King appeared nervous, fidgeting and mindlessly stacking papers, while the Commander's formidable mask was in place.

She snuck a peek at Razik to find him studying his uncle, and she finally believed he didn't know what this was about either. She'd thought he might have been pretending not to know, but she was fairly certain he was as perplexed about all this as she was.

"Thank you all for extending your stay an extra day," Cethin started, sitting back in his chair. He was all casual, arrogant grace with one hand on the table.

Everyone around the table murmured pleasantries, some studying her and others avoiding her gaze. Except for Corveth. He was looking at her with a warm expression, almost as though he was pleased with something. As if he knew something she didn't.

Apparently he did, because the next words Cethin spoke had her nearly falling out of her chair.

"As required, Kailia is present for the vote required to instate her fully as Queen of Avonleya," Cethin said. "We've discussed this extensively for the last two days. I've addressed concerns, but if any new ones have come to light since we adjourned yesterday, now is the time to voice them."

She glanced at Razik to find his gaze still locked on his uncle, something she didn't understand passing between them. Then she turned her head to look at Cethin. He wasn't looking at her; instead, his eyes were sliding slowly around the table, giving each person a chance to speak. He looked intimidating, but somehow open to their commentary. As though he'd be willing to discuss it, but no one was changing his mind.

And here she was, once again wondering what had changed. What had happened that he was suddenly willing to allow her this position fully? Not in title only, but as his equal. His partner.

Sole ruler if something happened to him.

No one spoke until he got to Corveth, the young lord lacing his fingers and placing them on the table before him. "As I've said from the start of this conversation, I've witnessed her risk herself for others in my very own city. There was no hesitation. Only action and selflessness. If that doesn't speak to what a queen should be, then I don't know what does. I am honored to vote yes on this matter."

Kailia felt her cheeks heat, gaze dropping to the table before she remembered to keep her chin up. Shoulders back. Spine straight.

One by one, the other advisors agreed until the last one to vote was Commander Greybane. She could swear Razik wasn't even breathing next to her, and she couldn't work out why. It also wasn't her main focus as she met the Commander's gaze.

As it always was when he interacted with her, everything about him was harsh and cold. A muscle in his jaw ticked, and he ground his molars.

"Razik spends his days with her," the Commander finally said. "If he is in agreement to this, then his vote will count as mine."

Razik wouldn't look at her as he replied, "I haven't been present for the previous discussions. Without that knowledge, I think it would be wise for you to cast your own vote, Commander."

"Again, you spend your days with her, Razik," Tybalt answered. "If you feel she is ready for this responsibility and doesn't pose a risk to our kingdom and everything that has been built over the centuries, then cast your vote on my behalf."

This was cruel. Even she recognized that. To put his nephew in such a position. But was that why he'd been appointed her guard to begin with? To spy on her and report back to his uncle?

It shouldn't surprise her, really. In fact, she'd suspected as much in the beginning. It was smart, especially considering how reckless Cethin had been with all of this. Just like she'd become comfortable with Cethin, the same had happened with Razik, and maybe she'd forgotten they each had roles to play in all this.

"Razik," Cethin said after seconds of tense silence ticked by. "Do you have any concerns, or are you prepared to vote?"

For the first time since she'd known him, the male faltered. He glanced at his uncle again, clearly unsure what he was supposed to do. Was this a test for him? More than that, if he was hesitating, why? What had she done to give him pause?

Razik cleared his throat, shifting in his chair. "I will trust any concerns were already thoroughly discussed and alleviated, and as such, I'll trust the opinions of this council who have all unanimously voted yes and cast my vote the same."

She couldn't gauge the look on the Commander's face as his eyes slid from his nephew to her, but she held his stare until he looked away first. Cethin said some other things that she really should have been paying attention to, but all she could think was that she'd done it. She was queen in more than title. The very thing she'd wanted, and yet something in her stomach twisted uncomfortably.

Bringing her eyes to Cethin, she found him already looking at her. Faint wisps of his power flitted in his silver eyes, and he reached for her hand, lifting it to press his lips to her knuckles.

The crowns. The finer clothing. The formalities.

All of it for her.
Did he even realize he'd laid his kingdom at her feet?

-⟩⟩ ⊙ ⟨⟨-

A sigh of relief escaped her when she made it to the beach without being seen.

It was hot. Muggy and humid. The moment she stepped from the enchanted Cliff's entrance, her dress was clinging to her. Plucking at it, all she could think about was how she'd prefer the never-ending cold of Pyry over this.

The brand beneath her skin was glowing softly, and she checked her forearm again to make sure the Mark was still there. A reassurance she still needed after all this time.

Even if this was a dream though, she still needed to get moving. They'd still find her, but if she made it to the trees, she could pick them off one by one with her arrows.

She started walking, bare feet sinking into the sand, but then she paused when she saw him. Moonlight glinting off silver hair. Hands in his pockets as he stared out at the sea. He was finding her in her dreams more and more as of late.

She hesitated another moment before she changed course and headed towards him instead of the trees. She told herself it was to bring him with her, like she had that time inside the Cliffs, but she knew better. Knew it was more. These moments were almost sacred, her dreams a place to explore and share secrets she could never reveal otherwise.

He must have heard her coming, but he didn't show it. Didn't move or shift as she approached. Not until she lifted a hand and tentatively ran it down his broad back, the muscles flexing beneath her fingers as he turned. Her breath seized and her belly dipped at the way he looked at her. As if these moments were cherished, but she was what he treasured. No one had ever looked at her like that. This wasn't because of her magic or her abilities. He looked at her as if he understood her down to her core, which was impossible in reality, but here…

Here she could pretend. Here she could act on desires, and no one had to know.

She frowned when she realized she was disappointed at the thought.

"*You're beautiful, wife,*" Cethin said, hands still in his pockets.

"*We need to get off the beach,*" she replied, glancing over her shoulder at the Cliffs.

"*You fear them still?*" he asked, following her gaze. "*Despite being free of them?*"

Pulling her bow over her head, she tightened her fingers around the grip. The feel of it in her hand a comfort she'd come to rely on.

"*I don't know if I'll ever be free of them if they still haunt my dreams,*" she admitted.

"*If you could return to have vengeance, would you?*"

"*This is not the time for pointless conversations, Cethin,*" she answered. "*We need to get into the cover of the trees.*"

But he turned back to the water instead. "*I've always preferred the waves. Something I got from my father.*"

"*The waves cannot hide you,*" she insisted, itching to grab his arm and tug him to the dense foliage behind them.

"*Oh, but they can if you know how to listen to them,*" he answered, something mournful and melancholy lingering in his tone.

Finally resigning herself to the fact she wasn't going to convince him to leave the shore, she repositioned so she could see the Cliffs, nocking an arrow just in case.

Cethin noted the movement, a scowl forming on his perfect lips. "*I hate that your past still haunts you.*"

"*I find the past to be as determined as the phantoms that hunt you,*" she replied. "*It haunts every chance it gets.*"

"*That it does,*" he murmured, and to her chagrin, he lowered to the sand. "*Sit, wife.*"

She bristled. "*That isn't wise here.*"

"*We can hide from the rest of the world. Just for a moment,*" he countered, resting his arms atop his bent knees.

"*I don't like the beach. Or the sand. Or the heat,*" she blurted, feeling the grains of sand between her toes.

"*Understandably so,*" he replied. "*I prefer to be out on the water.*"

She shifted again before finally lowering to her knees and sitting back on her heels, still able to see the Cliffs.

Cethin was quiet, and for some reason, she found herself saying, "You made me a queen today."

The words were quiet, barely audible over the sound of the rolling waves.

He turned his head to look at her. "Did I?"

"I don't know why."

"You're my wife. Why wouldn't I make you queen?"

"You said you wouldn't," she answered. "And why would you when you don't even know me?"

"Perhaps I know you better than you think."

"I don't think—"

But she was cut off as a blade protruded through his chest. His eyes went wide, mouth gaping and blood dripping from the corner.

"Cethin!" she cried, scrambling to her feet. Her arrow was aimed in the next breath as she met grey eyes swirling with ashes and smoke.

"Do not fail us now, sister."

-⟩⟩ ☉ ⟨⟨-

"Kailia. Kailia, wake up."

She jolted upright, her heart racing and hands trembling as she shoved at the blankets to see her forearm. No Mark. Not a dream. Real, real, real.

Her gaze snapped to Cethin. The room was dark, but she could still make out his figure. He'd been leaning over her, but he'd shifted back when she'd woken. His chest was bare, and his hands were at his sides as he searched her face.

Swiping at stray pieces of hair with her fingers, she took him in. No blade in his chest. No blood at his mouth. Breathing. Looking at her the same way he'd done in her dream.

Real, real, real.

"Kailia," he said, her name so godsdamn gentle and tender that it had tears burning at the backs of her eyes. He shouldn't be looking at her like that. Shouldn't be saying her name like that. Not outside her dreams, where her secrets were still shrouded in smoke and ashes.

"It was nothing," she said, her voice surprisingly steady for how erratically her heart was still beating. "Just a nightmare."

"Tell me about it," he urged, leaning closer.

"I… It was only my past determined to haunt me."

"I wish I could change your past," he admitted, his fingers curling into the blankets in an obvious effort not to reach for her. "Even if it did make you who you are today, I wish things were different."

She nodded, wishing the same. Wishing she'd found her way to Avonleya whole and at peace instead of a tortured soul with fractured power and an aversion to touch.

"But we don't have to let the past haunt our future," he added. "Tell me the worst of it, Kailia. Tell me, and I'll fix it."

The bark of laughter that came from her was harsh and loud in their quiet rooms. "You can't fix it, Cethin. You can't fix me. That's not how things work."

"I didn't say it'd be immediate. And you're perfect. I'm not looking to fix *you*; I'm looking to help. Believe it or not, we're the same, tiny fiend. Too persistent to give up and too stubborn to break. I need to know what we are facing."

We.

As if he was part of this. As if her weaknesses were his too.

"You know about the touching," she said, feeling entirely too vulnerable and exposed.

"I do."

"And you know why," she added.

For the most part anyway.

"What else?" he pushed. "What were you referring to when you told Razik you didn't know if you could do this anymore?"

Dammit.

She thought he'd forgotten about that, but she should have known better. He didn't simply forget anything.

But he'd given her something today. Something he didn't have to. Something she still didn't fully understand.

"My power is broken," she whispered. "And it's slowly killing me. Not literally," she added in a rush. "But I feel like I'm slowly dying inside, unable to move through my ashes. It's...driving me a little mad. I don't feel like myself, and I feel...a little lost. Like a piece of me is missing."

He nodded, taking in her words. Then he reached out, wrapping a hand around the crystal at her throat. He gave the necklace a light tug that had her leaning closer to him, his lips hovering over hers. "I have an idea, wife. Something to discuss later, but tonight..."

He trailed off, his eyes dipping to her mouth, and gods, she wanted the same thing. Wanted to press her lips to his. Wanted to touch him. Wanted him to touch her.

But as soon as she thought it, she was pulling back, the cord of the necklace digging into her flesh.

"You would have to trust me," he urged, fist still wrapped around the crystal and not letting her get too far.

"I do. I mean, I'm trying, but Cethin, I..." She shook her head, unsure of how to explain any of this.

"Let me help," he urged. "You'll be in control the entire time. Like when I stayed across the room."

"But I hadn't wanted you to stay across the room in the end," she protested.

He smirked. "I know, which is why I'm proposing something different now. Small steps, remember."

She tried to smile, but knew it was more of a terrified grimace as her throat bobbed with a swallow. "It will be rather pointless."

"Is it something you want?"

Kailia stared back at him—at her husband—still able to see the blade and blood. Her own scream echoing in her mind at seeing him like that. She knew in that moment she wouldn't have reacted like that for anyone else. Maybe Razik, but that was different. That wasn't—

"Yes," she said in a harsh breath, willing to admit that rather than finish that thought.

With another pull of the necklace, he brought her back to him, his lips brushing over hers in a kiss so featherlight, she wondered if it could even be called a kiss. Then he released her, stretching out on his side facing her. He pulled the blankets back, patting the space in front of him.

"Lie down, back to me," he said.

She stared at him, her body frozen at the idea but also burning at the thought of touching him.

"You're in control," he said again. "Trust me, Kailia. Lie down and lean against me."

Trying to hide her trembling, she moved, nestling down onto the bed and slowly sliding back against him. His bare chest had that icy coolness to it, and she found herself melting into it. Her arms and back were bare, with only the thin straps of her nightdress keeping it up. Only her back and his chest were touching, and she exhaled a shuddering breath. She could do this if it was all he asked of her.

He gave her a long moment before he moved, her body instantly tensing. Moving an arm over her, he held it there, his hand hovering above her torso. "Relax, wife," he coaxed, his voice rough. "You're in control. Move my hand where you want it."

"What?" she asked in confusion, but her body was already responding at the thought. Her skin was tingling, and she was suddenly warm, despite the coolness of Cethin at her back.

"You heard me. You control where my hand goes. You know what you like, tiny fiend. You already showed me that."

Seconds passed, the offer hanging in the air between them, until she finally raised a hand, placing her palm to the back of his hand. Turning his hand over, she studied it for another moment. The calluses that told the story he was more than a pampered prince. He'd trained and trained hard. The white skin was so stark against her own, and when she interlaced their fingers, she watched his flex slightly.

Cethin was unmoving other than the rise and fall of his chest behind her. She could swear his heartbeat was as irregular as her own when she began moving his hand, placing it at her hip. She paused, relishing in the touch.

No, relishing in not feeling the need to lash out at being touched.

Guiding his hand, she moved it down her outer thigh, only the silk of the nightdress separating their flesh. Even then, she could feel the roughness of his calluses through the material.

Again and again she brought his hand to her hip and moved it down her thigh as far as she could comfortably reach before doing it again. There wasn't any panic. There wasn't any madness. There was only a faint fire in her belly that was growing, wanting more.

On the next pass, she didn't lift his hand back to her hip. Instead, she dragged it back up, the nightdress going with it and sliding up her leg. Only then did she lift her hand and place his palm on her flesh, dragging it up and up and, *oh gods.* Who'd have thought touch could be intoxicating?

"You're doing so well, wife," he murmured in her ear, a raggedness to his tone now. "We can stop if you—"

"No," she interjected, squeezing her small hand around his large one. "This—Just let me…"

Instead of finishing her thought, she moved his hand up and down her leg, waiting for the irrational part of her to lift its head and shove him away.

But it didn't.

Her breathing matched his, and she felt the sharp inhale behind her when she guided his hand inward a little, feeling his fingers on her inner thigh. *By the gods.*

Cethin shifted behind her, and she felt his length press against her. He didn't apologize, and she didn't want him to. There was a different kind of power and control in knowing she was doing this to him, but she was also fighting the urge to writhe back against him.

Trying to take her mind off that, she changed how she was guiding his hand. Instead of stopping at her hip, she took it higher, gliding his palm over her stomach, skating his fingers below her breasts. He didn't push. Didn't try to guide her anywhere else. He was frozen and still behind her, and before she could think about it too much, she guided his hand higher, stilling as his large palm covered her left breast.

Then she squeezed his hand, his fingers flexing in return.

She couldn't stop the small moan that came from her throat, but it mingled perfectly with the low groan that sounded behind her. Doing it again, she arched back into him because this time, he swiped the pad of his finger over her nipple. One small action of his own that had her wanting more.

She'd touched herself multiple times. She'd been touched by another. She'd been tortured and burned and so much more, but never *this*. Never something that made her crave more of it as though she would die without it.

This kind of touch was new, and now, all she could think about was getting more of it.

Her hand still on his, she guided it up. Over the swell of her breasts, across her collarbone, up to her neck. Using his fingers, she traced her throat, feeling her own pulse. Cethin shifted, somehow pressing closer to her, and then she felt the soft press of lips below her ear.

"Are you all right?" he asked.

She nodded, but then found words she'd never intended to say spilling from her mouth. "I want more. I don't know what that is, but I want— I just *want*."

"Say the word and we stop," he said, his entire body once more still behind her. Still, but vibrating with an intensity she could feel pouring off him.

She nodded again, the movement sharp and jerky. "Yes," she gasped.

That confirmation was all he needed. His other arm snaked beneath her, banding around her middle and tugging her back into him even more while the hand she'd been guiding went back to her breast. Squeezing. Massaging. Plucking at her nipple through the silk.

"It's been a special kind of torture to sleep beside you these nights and not be able to touch you," he rasped, the words bordering on a groan.

She felt that touch and those words to her core, the sensation making her grow warm and wet. Without thought, she pressed her hips back, feeling his hard cock grind against her.

His mouth skated down her jaw, then beneath it to her neck, all the while exploring with his other hand. She was mindlessly pushing back against him now, too lost to the sensation of being touched without having to fear the cost. This was so much better than being drunk on ale in a godsdamn tavern.

But it wasn't enough, and she was suddenly desperate for more.

Reaching for his hand, he went utterly still when she pressed her palm to the back of his hand again.

"Enough for tonight?" he asked, each word a ragged breath.

"No," she replied, her own voice as husky as his. She didn't elaborate. She simply guided his hand back down. Over her stomach, her navel, lower and lower until she was grinding it against her needy cunt.

"Fuck me," Cethin breathed, and he shifted again. If she cared to look over her shoulder at him, she'd find his head tipped back and eyes closed, working to keep his restraint.

But she didn't care.

All she cared about was how his hand felt on her center. The coolness and friction the perfect mix. Frantically, she pulled at her nightdress, bunching the fabric at her waist, and then there was nothing between them. Only his rough hand against her soft flesh as she bucked against him.

Then she pulled her hand away.

He went still once more, each breath a panted burst of air from his chest until he finally said, "This isn't what I intended tonight."

"I don't care," she replied, rocking against his hand again.

"Kailia—"

"Cethin, *please*. I believe you. I trust you. Just— *Please*."

He moved fast then, propping himself onto an elbow while rolling her onto her back. His gaze moved down her, from her neck to her still-covered breasts to the place his hand was cupping her bare cunt.

The first brush of his fingers against that bundle of nerves pulled a moan from her that should have been embarrassing. Instead, she bucked into his hand more. Cethin took the hint, that brush of fingertips becoming a firm press as he massaged her clit. His eyes darted from his hand to her face, watching her squirm beneath him.

"Look at you," he crooned, the words full of dark lust. "Finally letting me touch you. Letting me prove to you— Gods, you look fucking divine beneath my hand, wife."

The sound that came from her could only be described as a whimper, and his chuckle was dark. He inched his hand lower, hesitating as he dragged a finger along her folds.

"Yes," she rasped, her hips bucking again.

But he tsked at her. "I've waited a long time for this, wife."

The touches that followed were both excruciating and exhilarating. A juxtaposition of feelings and sensations she'd never experienced before as he moved his fingers slowly against her. Mapping out every place his fingers touched as if getting to know the feel of her until he finally dipped the tip of his finger inside her.

The noises that came from her weren't intelligible as she tried to sink onto that digit even more. Needing more. Wanting it with everything she was. This was taking back something that had been stolen from her. Decades and decades of fearing touch when it could have been pleasure and safety and tenderness all this time.

Cethin took his time, despite her hips and words begging for more.

"Shh. Let me show you. Let me make you feel good," he soothed, moving that finger in and out, deep and slow. With each pass, he pressed his palm to her bundle of nerves, making her writhe against the plush mattress. She didn't register the movement of his hips next to her, mindless movements of his own as he focused on his task.

That single finger drove her to a pleasurable madness, so different from the irrational terror that drove her to react on instinct. Instead, her instincts were rocking her hips as she rode his finger. Her hands fisting the fabric of her nightdress, the sheets, whatever she could grab. It was unintelligible sounds and cries until he was expertly pressing his hand hard against her clit with his finger deep inside her.

The orgasm rolled through her, all of her limbs shaking as she fell apart. His hand kept moving, guiding her through it all. Her eyes fell closed in utter bliss, but she heard his words, low and rough.

"So godsdamn perfect, wife. You take it so well. Someday it'll be more. I'll do whatever you want, tiny fiend."

She sighed as the last of her pleasure abated, acutely attuned to all the sensations around her. The silk against her skin. The plush bedding. The rough fingertip pulling from her and gliding along the crease of her thigh. The male body so near.

He let her take her time, not making a sound as she lay with her eyes closed. Slowly, she let it sink in that she could have this. Cethin would give this to her anytime she asked. It wasn't just about the release. It was the trust and the safety. The patience and gentleness.

Her eyes fluttered open, and she found him still propped on an elbow, watching her. An almost smile played on his lips, and he moved to brush her hair off her brow, the movement measured and slow.

She shifted, feeling her nightdress slip back down her legs as she rolled onto her side to face him. "Can I touch you?" she whispered. "Not like *that,*" she clarified quickly.

"You can touch me however you like, wife," he replied, rolling onto his back and bracing his hands behind his head.

It was her turn to prop up on an elbow before lifting a hand. She traced the muscles on his abdomen, still a little mesmerized at the feel of bare flesh beneath her fingers. For a long time, it was just this. Him letting her explore at her own pace in the quiet. Muscles flexing beneath her touch and sharp inhales of restraint.

"Why did you make me queen?" she asked, breaking the comfortable silence as she mapped out the veins on his forearm.

There was no hesitation in his answer when he said, "Because you're so much more than arrows."

She nodded, no more words exchanged between them as she

brushed her fingertips along his temple, his lips, down his chest, and through the fine hair below his navel. She couldn't do more, not now, and he didn't ask for it.

But when she gingerly lay down with her head on his chest and her palm on his stomach, the way his arm curled around her and held her there told her she'd given him more than enough tonight.

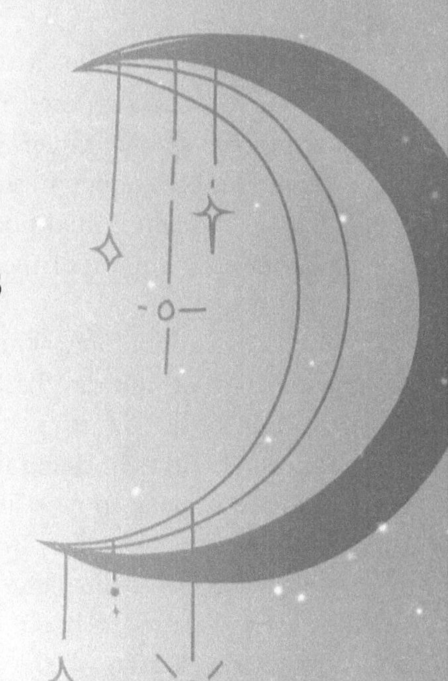

CHAPTER 38

RAZIK

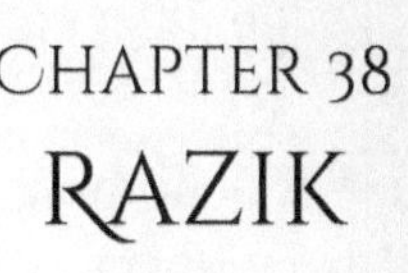

The smell of ale and too many bodies assaulted him as soon as he pulled open the door to the tavern by the docks. While he'd brought Kailia here when he had items to procure, she didn't know this was the main tavern the Cadre frequented. They were always watched and scrutinized. But here, in a tavern off the beaten path by the docks, it was easier to go about unnoticed, which made it easier to actually unwind. They had to be mindful of their surroundings, but when everyone in the room was trying to be overlooked, it helped. It was also the best place to hear rumors and gossip first. More than once they'd discovered leads simply by listening to the chatter in taverns like this one.

Of course, when he brought Lia here, it was at the beginning of the day, not the end of the day, when even Avonleyans were finding their way to their beds.

It had been a long day with Kailia suddenly queen in ever regard. He hadn't had a chance to talk to his uncle about putting him in the middle of things by making him cast a vote. A head's up on the matter would have been nice from either his uncle or Cethin. Instead, he'd been as blindsided as Kailia had been. If they'd been discussing the matter for two godsdamn days, either of the males could have told him. Mostly, though, he was upset with his uncle. What was he supposed to do? Bring up his concerns in front of everyone at the table? Not that he had concerns. Maybe not concerns big enough to stop what had happened today, but his uncle hadn't thought it might be a good idea to ask him *before* putting him on the spot in front of the king and all his advisors?

Whatever.

It was done now. There was nothing he could do to change it. The rest of the day had been spent with Kailia as usual, which meant he'd had to sit through the remainder of the advisory meeting and then spend time in Cethin's presence. He could tell the king was trying to ease her into her new responsibilities, and Razik was more than a little ready to be done with the day when they retired early for the night.

Except now he had this fucking meet up with Bram.

A quick scan of the room found the male wasn't here yet, so Razik ordered a mug of ale and found a table in the back. The ale was nearly gone when Bram finally showed up.

"Sorry about that. The streets are busy tonight," the male said, signaling a server for two more mugs.

Razik didn't reply. Small and mundane talk was not something he ever partook in.

"Right. Guess, I'll get to the point," Bram muttered after the ales were delivered. He slid one across the table to Razik. "I bought a small estate."

Razik gripped the handle of his mug. "If you had me meet you here to celebrate that, we're going to have a problem."

"I didn't ask you to meet me here to celebrate that, you dick," Bram retorted, taking a drink. "I'm telling you that because I need you to know I no longer reside in the Cadre barracks when I tell you I'm going to ask Wren to live at my place with me."

Even knowing the conversation was going to be about Wren, the dragon in his soul still lifted its head with a snarl. Or the snarl was his because Bram leaned away, watching him with a dubious look.

"Males usually retire from the Cadre when they're ready for a family," Razik said tightly.

"I'm not looking to retire. I worked too hard to earn my spot on the Cadre to retire from it a handful of years later," Bram replied.

"Then you don't need to be sniffing around Wren."

The look morphed into a glare, his light green eyes seeming to darken. He leaned forward, the sleeves of his tunic pulling up to reveal pieces of the ink that ran along his arms as he pointed a finger at Razik. "Fuck you, Greybane. I've been nothing but respectful to Wren, and I sure as fuck have been around more than you lately."

"You were stationed beyond the Nightmist Mountains a few weeks ago," Razik retorted.

"And you were in Everfall for a few days, leaving her behind."

"I still fail to see your point in asking me here," Razik gritted out.

"I already told you: I'm going to ask Wren to live with me," Bram said, eyeing him as though he was looking for a hidden catch.

"What does that have to do with me?"

The male sat back in his chair, clearly exasperated. "Fuck, Greybane. What doesn't it have to do with you? She's your Source. She stays with you often enough, and you're more than a little protective of her. For a while there, if I even looked at her, I had to worry about your godsdamn dragon fire."

"She's a grown-ass female. She can do what she wants," Razik said, bringing his mug to his mouth and taking a long drink.

"But she'll do what *you* want," Bram shot back.

"And?"

"And I'm hoping when she comes to you about it, after I ask her, you'll put her before your own judgments and interests," the male said, far too pointedly.

"She has rooms at the castle," Razik said tightly after a few moments.

"I know," Bram said. "But I want more for her and us. This isn't a fling or casual fucking."

"You've only really been interacting with her for a few months."

"I've been watching her for far longer."

Razik eyed him, asking the question that could potentially

decide the whole matter for them. "Do you think she's your twin flame?"

"As much as I wish that were true, no," Bram answered.

At least he was honest. Razik wouldn't have believed him if he'd said yes. The pull of a twin flame bond was said to be strong, especially for males in the beginning. If it had been that, he would have expected Bram to become more agitated and irritable, not to mention territorial, long before this conversation.

"And if one comes along one day, you'll just drop her?" Razik pushed.

"The odds of ever meeting my twin flame are considerable," Bram argued. "Especially with the Wards and the Fae population dwindling here."

"That doesn't answer my question."

"By the Fates," Bram growled, running a hand over his short black hair. "Won't I be in the same predicament if she finds a twin flame? No. Wait. That's not the point." The male leaned forward again, his agitation growing. "We live for centuries. No one bases their life around what ifs. So many things can change over the decades."

Razik knew that. Knew he was asking something ridiculous of the male, but he'd also made a promise to protect Wren. She'd already been abandoned, and he'd found the best way to keep that from happening again was to avoid situations like this.

"What's she supposed to do when you're gone on missions?" Razik asked.

"She's one of the few people who understands what this life entails. She'd know what she's getting into from the start because she's already been living this life with you. I see her more than I would otherwise because of who she is to you. To be honest, I tried to get her out of my system, but she's always around, and..." He pushed out a long breath before taking another drink of ale. "I don't want her out of my system anymore, Greybane. I want *her*."

Godsdammit.

What was he supposed to say to that?

"I see her as much as you do, if not more, these days," Bram repeated, as if he felt he needed to keep defending himself or make a case.

"I already said she's a grown-ass female," Razik said flatly. "She can make her own decisions, and I won't stand in her way. We always knew something like this could happen, and we have a standing agreement."

Bram's eyes narrowed, as though he was looking for a catch. "So...if she says yes and we start something, you'll stop being a godsdamn prick?"

"No," Razik shrugged, his chair scraping on the stone floor as he stood.

Bram sighed, but he said nothing else as Razik made his way across the crowded tavern and out into the night. He was a prick to everyone; he certainly wasn't going to change because of this.

-⫯)⊙(⫯-

"Different clothes," Razik said when he pushed through the doors to the king's floor and found Kailia in her usual dress, sitting on a sofa.

She looked down at her attire. The black dress with slits on either side, bare arms, dagger at her thigh, and bare feet. Bringing her gaze back to his, she asked, "What's wrong with what I am wearing?"

"We're going to the training arenas," Razik said brusquely, not in the mood to explain himself or his reasoning today. Of course, he was going to have to because Kailia was who she was.

But to his surprise, she perked up, getting to her feet. "The training arenas? To train?"

"What else would one do there?" he asked dryly.

Taking a minute to think about that, she said, "I'm not sure. I've never been to them here. Sometimes the training areas I've been in were used for demonstrations or punishments."

He should talk to her about that. Try to get information about where she trained and who trained her and how long she'd been training, but he was too on edge. He'd already sent a message asking Jarek and Fallon to meet him at the arenas because he really needed to get out some aggression.

So instead of doing any of that, he simply said, "Go change."

"I train in this," she answered with a shrug.

She trained in a dress?

Nevermind. He wasn't about to stand here and argue with her. If she wanted to train in a godsdamn dress, then so be it.

Extending his hand, she took it without a flinch or wince. It hadn't escaped him how comfortable she'd become around him these last months. He should feel some sort of way about that. A sense of accomplishment. She trusted him, at least to some extent, and that had always been his goal.

The issue was now convoluted by this mess with Wren. They should be two separate things, completely independent of each other, but they weren't. Somehow, he'd come to *care* for the queen in the same way he cared about Wren. At some point, she'd become his as much as Wren was, and now Wren would be leaving him alone. Moving on to someone else.

Not that she'd talked to him about it yet.

His meeting with Bram had been nearly a week ago, and as far as he knew, the male hadn't approached Wren yet. If Razik had to guess, he was waiting until the Summer Solstice Festival in two days. It was cliche and stupid and exactly what Wren deserved.

The rational side of him knew change was inevitable. They were immortal. Things couldn't stay the same for hundreds of years. But the irrational side of him didn't want to admit that he hated it. So instead of dealing with any of that bullshit, he was going to spar with Jarek and Fallon, seeking a different kind of pain and adrenaline to kill the sense of inadequacy and abandonment trying to climb up from the depths of his soul where he kept those useless emotions buried.

The sun was high, the air hot even in the mountains when they appeared in the stone training arena. It was circular with a dirt floor, large enough for a hundred warriors to easily train without it being too tight, and there were several dozen here. Some training on their own, others new warriors being led through drills.

He immediately recognized Fallon's laugh, following the sound to find her bouncing around on her toes and evading Jarek's strikes. She ducked, swiping out with her foot as she did, but Jarek jumped, reaching to grab her ankle. His fingers grazed her boot, but he didn't catch her in time. The males of the Cadre may have the bulk, but the females were far faster with less body mass.

"I would like to join them," Kailia said matter-of-factly from his side.

He glanced down at her, her eyes swirling so fast that the grey was almost eclipsing the amber color. She was excited about this, he realized. She was a stabby, sadistic little thing. He shouldn't be surprised, but he felt a twinge of guilt at not realizing this would have secured her trust a lot faster.

No.

Not guilt.

Annoyance.

And guilt, he supposed. Annoyance because it would have made things a whole lot easier, and guilt because she likely needed to expend her own pent-up aggression, especially with not being able to move through her magic. Something he still hadn't figured out. The new theory he'd come up with was her proximity to something —like not being able to Travel when the phantoms were present— but he had yet to come up with what the trigger could be for her magic. There wasn't a common presence when she'd tried to move in her magic. Fuck, she couldn't even do so in her dreams.

"Fuck, Greybane," Jarek jeered, pulling Razik from his thoughts. "You look like you want to hit something. Or someone."

"I do," Razik replied, pulling his tunic over his head and tossing it aside. Stretching his neck to the left, then to the right, he added, "The queen would also like to spar."

"We're not sparring with the queen," Jarek said immediately.

"I don't object," Kailia protested, eyeing the warrior.

"With all due respect, your Majesty, if I lay a hand on you, I will face your husband."

Kailia's lips pursed, fingers flexing at her sides. "I will handle Cethin if it comes to that."

"Nope. I refuse," Jarek said, crossing his arms in emphasis.

"You refuse an order from your queen?" she asked, and while Razik knew it was pure curiosity and not an affront, it had the desired effect of making the male hesitate.

"If you're going to be insistent, spar with Fallon," Jarek offered, gaze flicking to the female.

"Way to throw me to the wolves," she drawled, fixing her braid that had come loose.

Jarek winked at her. "We all know Cethin will handle the wolves."

She rolled her eyes before refocusing on Kailia. "You are sure? I won't go easy on you."

"Why would you?" Kailia asked, brow furrowing.

"Because you're royalty, Lia," Razik said, ready to be done standing around. "Ready, Ophanim?"

"You're really okay with this?" the male asked doubtfully, still eyeing Kailia.

"You're welcome to try to stop her, but I'm not responsible when you're bleeding," Razik said flatly.

"Fucking Fates, whatever is usually up your ass seems to have crawled up there even higher today," Jarek grumbled, moving away from the females so they'd have more room.

Razik hardly gave him a chance to get situated before he was making the first move, lunging and landing a blow to Jarek's side. The male grunted, letting out a sharp curse, but his counterattack was swift, and Razik took a hit to the jaw.

For the next hour, he let himself fall into the muscle memory of practiced movements, too focused on his opponent to think about anything else. He'd flown in the sky for hours over the last several days. He'd done *serena sabre* in the mountains. He'd tried to get lost in books and research, but none of that kept his focus. His mind constantly wandered back to things he didn't want to think about. Sparring though? If your mind wandered in a sparring ring, you paid in pain, pride, and blood.

The males were both panting messes of sweat and bruises when they called a truce to get water. They'd both gotten in decent hits, both of them knocked to their backs at various times. There'd been taunts and curses, helping each other up just to knock the other back onto their ass.

He nodded in thanks, catching the waterskin Jarek tossed to him as they both turned to watch the females, and Razik couldn't hide his smirk. Fallon had been worried about sparring, but there clearly hadn't been a need. If Fallon was fast, Kailia was a blur as she moved. Razik could only imagine the damage she would do if she could actually move through her smoke and ashes. Every movement and hit was as intentional as she was. She missed nothing, and that was saying something because Fallon was as formidable as any of the Cadre.

Fallon smiled tightly as she got back to her feet, Kailia standing still and watching her a few paces away. Fallon had clearly gotten a few hits in. There was a bruise on Kailia's cheek, and there was blood on her arm from somewhere. But mostly there were ashes scattered all over the ground, some in the shape of her footprints and others that had been at one point.

Kailia tilted her head, those ashes stirring, and as Razik studied her, he realized she was feeling the vibrations of the ground through them. It was godsdamn brilliant and explained why she always wanted to be barefoot. When Fallon lunged, Kailia was already moving, having felt the momentum and energy from Fallon before she'd fully moved. Fallon's strike hit nothing but air while Kailia appeared behind her, landing a clean kick to the female's lower back.

"Fucking Arius," Jarek breathed, just as entranced.

In fact, many around the arena had stopped to watch, and Razik was internally cursing himself yet again, but this information would have been fantastic to have months ago. All he'd had to do was bring her to the godsdamn training arena.

Kailia moved, striking out with a fist. Fallon blocked it, immediately following up with a counterstrike. The two broke apart, Fallon bouncing on her toes while Kailia watched, remaining still.

"Take a break," Razik called out, striding into their space and coming between them.

He heard Fallon mutter something, but she was smiling as she took the waterskin from Jarek. The female had enjoyed this as much as Kailia had, even if she had gotten her ass handed to her.

Offering his waterskin to Kailia, she took a long drink.

"I would enjoy doing this more often," she mused.

"I'm sure you would," Razik said flatly.

"With weapons," she added thoughtfully.

"Fuck no. Hand-to-hand combat is one thing. You with sharp objects is another."

She frowned in contemplation. "Training with weapons is as important as training without them."

He couldn't exactly argue that, but that kind of training would need to be coordinated with Cethin. Because, again, Kailia with blades was completely different from what they'd done today.

Taking another drink, she handed the waterskin back to him before gathering her hair. It had been down this entire time, some strands sticking to her forehead. Separating the thick locks into three sections, she began braiding it, and that was when he saw it.

The single tendril of inky darkness.

It was as dark as her hair, blending in perfectly. She would have never seen it. The magic was tucked in with the hair at the back of her head. The only reason he was seeing it now was because she'd gathered her hair a certain way and some strands had slipped free.

All the aggression he'd just worked off flooded back through him in waves.

He said nothing to Jarek and Fallon as he gripped Kailia's elbow and Traveled them. Not back to her rooms, but to his.

The moment they were there, she jerked her arm free, glaring at him. "That was rude," she snapped, crossing her arms.

He should have known. He should have godsdamn known the moment she'd said she couldn't use her magic in her dreams.

"Has Cethin ever been in your dreams?" he demanded, knowing his eyes were glowing brightly as he fought a full shift.

Kailia clearly sensed the same because she was eyeing him

warily when she answered, "I don't see how that is any of your business."

"Answer the question, Lia."

"What does it matter if he has?" she countered.

He swore viciously. "I told you his dark magic was a fraction of his power. I told you you'd do well to remember that."

"I know that. I saw what he did to those members of the Elder Clan without touching them."

He huffed a derisive sound. "Not touching them was a mercy. Do you understand that? And that's still not even— Kailia, Cethin can dream-walk. He can do more than that. I thought he would have told you. I thought— Fuck!"

She was not the one who should be on the receiving end of his anger.

No, that was the arrogant king who was used to getting his way. Who'd manipulated her and coerced her into a marriage she didn't fully understand.

And now she was looking at him, perplexed and uncertain, clearly trying to work things out. But she couldn't. Because she was too literal and didn't conform to normal social interactions, and Cethin had fully taken advantage of that.

"What is that? Dream-walking. What does that mean?" she asked.

Too calm.

Too still.

Too unpredictable.

He was torn. Stay here and explain everything, or track down Cethin and make him face what he'd done. Make him answer all her godsdamn questions, but then be left wondering what he'd omitted. All of this was Cethin's fucking mess. It always was. Everything always led back to him and his lineage. Always the priority. Always the one everyone else was expected to sacrifice for.

Not this time.

"Stay here, Lia. All right? Stay here, and I'll be back—"

She shook her head, ashes spilling off her. "I'm asking you to explain this to me, Raz."

"I'm not the one who owes you an explanation," he snarled.

"Razik—"

"Stay here," he ordered again.

Then he was Traveling.

He went to Cethin's study first. When he found it empty, he sent a message with his dragon fire before Traveling to the council room where he often met with Zayan. Receiving a message back from Cethin immediately, he Traveled to their rooms where the king was waiting for him.

"Where is she? What happened?" Cethin demanded.

It took everything Razik had not to drive his fist into the male's face.

"*You* happened," Razik snarled, keeping space between them so he *didn't* follow through on that desire.

"What are you talking about? You said something happened with Kailia. Where is she, Greybane?" Cethin snapped, that inky darkness that matched the tendril in Kailia's hair creeping along the floor.

That was all he needed to dream-walk. He needed a connection to the person. A physical connection was best, but at some point, he'd let a minute piece of his magic latch on to her.

"How long have you been lying to her?" Razik demanded.

Cethin blinked, a flicker of confusion cutting through the increasing concern. "What are you talking about?"

"I thought you would have at least told her what she was getting into with you," Razik went on, each word a barbed sneer. "But as usual, you did whatever it took to get what you wanted, not caring about the cost or who suffered for it."

He hadn't been expecting it, but he should have been. Cethin's power was expansive. Razik knew he struggled daily to control it. Knew his parents had made him work tirelessly to master it, and despite that, all these centuries later, the power was a second away from overtaking him. He could be as unpredictable as Kailia, which is how he suddenly found himself flung into the wall. Razik's head snapped back against the stone, small spots appearing in his vision, and his wings ripped free at the assault.

"I will not ask you again," Cethin said, his voice dark and deadly. "Where is my wife?"

It took another second for his vision to clear, but when it did, he found Cethin with his hand raised, death glinting in glowing silver eyes.

"Don't you fucking dare," Razik growled, pushing off the wall. His wings flaring wide, dragon fire coiled up his legs and arms, but Cethin did it anyway. He closed his fist, and as he did, Razik felt the agony in his chest. As if his heart was being squeezed by the male's fingers. He snarled a curse as he sank to his knees, seconds away from losing control and shifting fully when Cethin let up.

He glared up at the male, his words too raspy as he pushed back to his feet. "You did all of this. When were you going to tell your *wife* you can dream-walk?"

The male paused, every part of him going still. "She knows?"

"She does now," Razik snapped, taking a step towards him. "Tell me why I was the one who had to tell her after I found your magic clinging to her? What else doesn't she know? Does she even understand what a Lunar Marriage is? Fully? Or did you keep that from her too?"

"Where is she, Razik?" Cethin asked again, a barely restrained panic in his tone.

"You're no better than your fucking mother," Razik spat, shoving at the male's chest. "In fact, I think you're worse. At least I knew what she was trying to force me into. Who she was attempting to force me to tie my life to. But Kailia has no idea. You forced her into so much that she doesn't understand."

He was thrown back again, twisting in time to avoid his wings being crushed against the wall. Which meant his face met the stone. He felt his nose break, blood instantly cascading down his face.

And he laughed.

Turning to face Cethin, he wiped at the blood with his arm. "She's here for something. Tybalt knows it. It's why he assigned me as her guard. You've lied to her, but I pray to the Fates, she's played you for the fool. I hope she gets exactly what she wants, and you're left in godsdamn ruin, Sutara." Cethin opened his mouth, but before he could ask the same godsdamn question yet again, he added, "She's waiting in my rooms for you. I hope she has a dagger ready to shove into your chest."

The king didn't wait, Traveling before Razik had even finished speaking. He followed, but his rooms were empty.

"You said she was here," Cethin snarled, rounding on him. More and more of his darkness was appearing, the floor now an ankle-deep layer of dark fog.

"I told her to wait here," Razik answered, tipping his head back while he went to grab something for his face. The first thing he found was a tunic, and he pressed it to his nose. It'd heal before tomorrow, but he'd probably go see Niara to have it healed even faster. "Although I don't blame her if she left. Hopefully she finds her way back across the Edria before you track her down."

"She'll come to me," Cethin retorted, looking around the room as if he expected her to simply appear.

Razik snorted a derisive laugh, then cursed. That shit hurt with a broken nose. It took longer than it should have for Cethin's words to register.

He lowered the tunic, staring at the king.

At the male he'd loathed for centuries.

The arrogant ass who was catered to and given everything he wanted.

The one everyone was expected to bow to, sacrifice for, and trust in.

"You're the reason her power isn't working," Razik said, disbelief coursing through him. Cethin merely stared back at him, and it was all the answer he needed.

He should have seen it from the very beginning, but for a reason he'd never be able to explain, he'd thought even *this* male couldn't be that cruel. Watching her slowly go mad day after day, trying to figure out why her magic wasn't doing what it should. Leaving her on her own. Letting her struggle.

Razik's bark of laughter was utter vitriol. "I hope she fucking destroys you for this."

CHAPTER 39

CETHIN

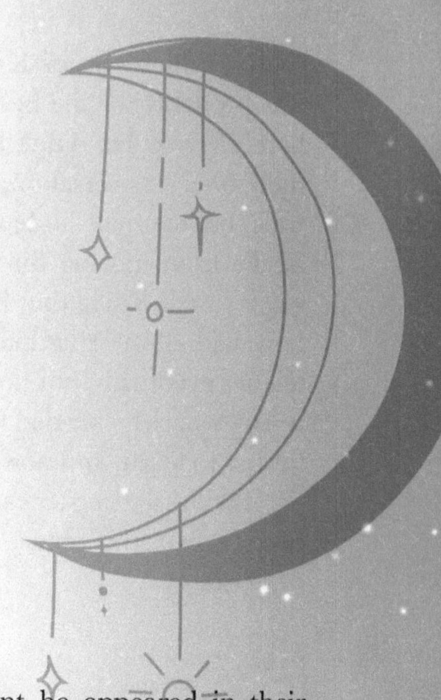

"Kailia?" he called out the moment he appeared in their rooms having Traveled from Razik's quarters. "Kailia, are you here?"

Moving systematically through the space, he checked each room, but he knew she wasn't here. He couldn't sense her power, and unless she'd suddenly expended all she had, he'd sense her magic.

His darkness trailed after him, straining and reaching. He was too worried about finding her to even try to rein it back in fully. He still had some measure of control, but there was no subduing it fully. Not when he was furious with Razik. The male had no business telling her anything about him. Then again, the male didn't understand sacrificing for something or someone other than himself. He wouldn't expect him to understand why he'd done things the way he had, which is why he hadn't bothered offering an explanation. If he hadn't been concerned with tracking down Kailia, he would have gone straight to Tybalt and ordered Razik away from Kailia and out of Avonleya for good.

That would come, but she was more important right now.

Despite it being pointless, he did one more sweep of all their rooms, calling out for Kailia again. Of course, she didn't answer. It was probably for the best. He didn't want to have this conversation here anyway. He didn't know how much Razik had told her. From their brief conversation, it was strictly about his ability to dreamwalk, but the male had just figured out that Cethin had been keeping Kailia from moving through her magic. He had no doubt he'd be eager to tell Kailia that information as well. The fucker may as well have laid all the kingdom's secrets before her. Things he planned to tell her eventually, but nothing that should have been shared yet. She wasn't where he needed her to be yet. This information was too soon for her to learn, and now everything was likely fucked.

Taking a deep breath that did absolutely nothing, he sent a message with his magic. It was simple and direct. Something she'd understand.

Wife—

Come to me. Your ashes know the way. I'll be waiting.

Traveling once more, he slipped his shoes off and slipped his hands into his pockets while he waited. Not even the gentle roll of the waves meeting the shore was enough to bring him the peace they usually provided. Instead, his darkness twisted and rolled around him, a dense fog slowly taking over the beach while he stared out at the sea. The sea he used to stare at for hours and hours, willing a single ship to appear.

The water was warming up, but it was still a shock of cold as it rolled over his toes. It did nothing to assuage the chaos pulling at his soul. Wanting to strike out, wound, destroy. Wanting to take and feast, waiting for Kailia to show up as anxiously as he was.

The Summer Solstice Festival was in two days, daylight stretching on longer than the night. His people anticipated the Winter Solstice far more. He huffed a humorless laugh to himself. How fitting that all his secrets seemed to be coming to light as the longest day of the year neared.

In the end, it took her longer than he'd expected for her to answer his summons. He'd known she wouldn't come right away. She was trying to process what she'd learned, and she'd prefer to do that on her own. Get her feelings sorted and emotions under control before she sought him out.

He was debating using other methods to track her down when he felt her.

Felt the surge of power flicker in and out until a swirl of smoke and ashes deposited her on the beach next to him. The sun was nearing the horizon, pinks and oranges overtaking the sky as the night slowly crept in to claim its territory once more.

Cethin turned, hands still in his pockets as he looked down at her. She'd pushed herself onto her knees, the surf breaking around her and soaking her dress. Her face was down, staring at the sand where he stood a foot or so away. Her black hair was a mess of knots and tangles, hanging limply around her shoulders, and her hands were flat on her thighs, fingers of her left hand on the hilt of her dagger.

She didn't move, and for a long moment neither did he. Not until he said, "Look at me, tiny fiend."

When she didn't, he took a step closer, lowering to a crouch before her. He didn't warn her with his magic. Not as he reached out and placed a fingertip beneath her chin, forcing her head up, but she didn't pull back from his touch like he'd expected. Smoke and ashes swirled violently in amber eyes. Eyes he still couldn't read, her face a mask of the same disposition. It was because of this he'd had to resort to stalking her dreams. How else was he to learn about her when she kept herself so closed off?

Ashes and smoke drifted around her, and his own magic chased it, trying to swirl and wind among her power. Wanting to coax it and lull it and subdue it. Cethin couldn't tell if she was affected by any of it.

"Kailia?" he ventured, her name sharper than he'd intended. "What did Razik tell you?"

"What is dream-walking?" she asked, her voice too calm.

He ground his molars, wanting an answer to his own question rather than the give and take this was obviously going to be.

"I can enter people's dreams. Not control them, but be present. Interact if I choose," he answered, watching her carefully for any hint of a reaction as he pulled his hand back.

"You can do this to anyone?"

"It's easier if I have a connection of some sort. A point of contact. Be touching someone, for example."

Something hardened in her eyes. The first hint of any emotion. "You were in my dreams while I slept alone. You weren't touching me then."

"The day I proposed my bargain and escorted you through the gardens, I ran my fingers along your hair and let a thread of my magic cling to it. A single point of contact is all I need," he said again.

"To make sure I understand, you've been watching me in my dreams?" she asked.

"Yes."

"This entire time."

"Since that day in the gardens."

She nodded. Her next words were quiet and soft, murmuring more to herself than to him. She turned her arm over, running her fingers along her bare forearm as she studied it. "Dreams are supposed to be safe. I'm supposed to be safe there. That was the whole point…"

"You are safe, Kailia. I made a promise to protect you. That's what I was doing," he tried, attempting to pull his magic back to himself.

Her head snapped up, fury clear as the darkening sky. There was no need to guess her emotions this time.

"Keeping me safe? Protecting me? That's what you were doing?" she demanded.

"Yes," he insisted.

"How long have you known my magic hasn't been working properly? How long have you known it would bring me to you?"

The words had a dangerous edge to them. An edge he hadn't

heard from her in weeks as he'd painstakingly worked to break down her walls. This was the same hard female who'd demanded an arrow back at the Esbat Festival.

"How long, *husband?*" she hissed, and some twisted part of him relished this. This wasn't the careful mask she always kept in place. This was an uncontrolled emotion. Raw and real, even if it was anger directed at him.

"Since you left the gardens after lying to me about needing the arrow back for your power to work properly," he finally answered.

Her eyes narrowed. "How did you know I was lying? No. Wait." She shook her head as if trying to clear her thoughts of so many questions so she could stay focused on one. "How did you know my power wasn't working right? Do you…" She'd been sitting back on her heels, and she pushed up onto her knees now. For a split second, it looked like she was going to reach for him. He wished she would have. Instead, she shook out her hands and asked, "Do you know what's wrong with my power?"

"Yes," he answered, holding her stare.

Her features brightened, a tentative hope shining through. "Then you can help me——" The hope was fleeting, and she frowned. "Why would my ashes bring me to you unless you had something to do with…" It wasn't a realization so much as a confirmation of something she'd suspected. He expected nothing less after he'd sent that message to her, and he watched more emotions play across her face than he'd ever seen from her. Dread and fury, betrayal and hurt. "How?" she whispered.

Her smoke was swirling around her, the ashes she commanded trembling. His own magic could feel it all as it continued to drift and slink around them.

Cethin reached out, Kailia going utterly still as he picked up the crystal at her throat. "Blue kyanite is a useful crystal for my abilities," he mused, twisting it gently between his thumb and forefinger. "It's known to help you channel your self-worth, but it also opens your mind to more lucid dreams."

"What does that have to do with my magic?"

"I placed an enchantment on this particular crystal, ensuring that you would always come back to me."

That whenever she tried to move through her power in his presence, she never went anywhere. That in her dreams, her ashes brought her directly to him.

In the next breath, he was cursing as she lunged at him. She was so godsdamn unpredictable, he hadn't expected her to move so fast. His back hit the sand, some of the air forced from his lungs at the surprisingly hard impact. The waves kept rolling in, soaking his tunic, pants, and hair, and Kailia was atop him, straddling his waist with a dagger to his throat.

"You did this to me?" she demanded. "For months, I have been going mad. For months, I've spent hours searching for answers. Filled with worry that I would never be the same, and you—"

"You never asked me," he interrupted calmly, trying desperately not to focus on the fact she had her thighs on either side of him. Battling that and trying to control his magic was…not easy, especially when he *wanted* to focus on how she felt atop him. "Never once did you ask me for help."

"As if you would have told me any of this," she sneered, leaning closer. Her hair dragged along his chest, and he could feel her breath on his lips with each snarled word.

"I would have helped," he countered, digging his fingers into the sand so he didn't reach up and grip her hips.

Her features twisted into a furious disgust. "Helped? You would have painted yourself the hero, all while fixing the very problem *you* created." The dagger still at his throat, she reached up and tugged at the crystal, trying to yank it free. "You acted as if you didn't know where this necklace came from. Feigned jealousy about it."

"You cannot remove it yourself," he said conversationally.

"Then take it off," she demanded. "Now."

"I can't do that, tiny fiend. The entire purpose of the necklace is to ensure you always come back to me."

A growl of frustration came from her, and the dagger pressed a little sharper against his throat. "I don't understand. I was given this necklace by the merchant."

"That I Traveled to after you left the castle," he said. "I paid for the necklace and paid even more for them to ensure you received it. I also asked Wren to ensure you put it on. Don't be angry with her, though. She thought it a sweet gesture when I asked her not to tell you it was from me."

"So you used her too?" Kailia snarled.

"If you want to call it that."

"How'd you even know about that necklace?"

"I saw you looking at it the night before."

Her brows knitted. "You saw me… You were watching me?"

He pushed onto his elbows, feeling the blade of the dagger break skin, the shallow cut welling with blood. "For nearly as long as you've been watching me, tiny fiend."

Then she was the one cursing as he rolled, her now underneath him. With one hand, he pinned her arm above her head, the dagger gripped in her fist. His other hand gripped her hip, keeping her from trying to buck him off, mainly because he knew she didn't realize what kind of friction that would create. Then again, maybe he should let her try to find out because there was no way she couldn't feel his cock pressing against her.

"How do you know I was watching you?" she ground out.

"I didn't always know it was you," he admitted, aware that she was too still and likely planning to distract him with questions until she could gain the upper hand once more. "I can sense others' power. The strength of it. I can tell if someone's power levels are low or full because of that gift. For months, I felt a strong power, but it was fleeting. Flickering in and out. The day you showed up at the battle with the phantoms was the day I realized it had been you the entire time."

"So you trapped me? Forced me into a bargain, and then chained me to you with a necklace? Knowing it would cut me off from some of my power? Knowing what that does to a person to not have access to a part of themselves?"

There was a crack in her last words, a tortured and unbearable agony ringing in them.

"I did what I had to," he said simply. "I told you to believe the rumors, Kailia. I told you all of them were true."

She stared up at him, her gaze bouncing around his face as if searching for something. Whatever it was, she wouldn't find it. He had no regrets about what he'd done.

Finally, she said, "So none of it was real? You told me it had to be real, and none of it was? It was all simply a means to an end?"

"Why would you think this isn't real? I told you this marriage was for life, wife," he replied, tugging on his soaking tunic to show her the moon Mark on his chest just beginning to appear with the setting sun. "A Lunar Marriage binds us together in this life and all the ones after."

Her words were bitter, that hardness back in her gaze when she said, "Then it shall be my mission to hunt you down in every life and make you regret ever binding yourself to me."

Releasing her hip, he fingered the crystal at her throat again. "It shouldn't be too hard to find me, tiny fiend. No hunting necessary."

A cry of frustrated fury escaped her, and while he'd been prepared for her to try to maneuver out from under him, he hadn't been prepared for her to use her power. For her smoke to gather in his face, making his eyes and lungs burn as something solid, but somehow not at the same time, hit him square in the chest.

He managed to keep a hold of her wrist, keeping that dagger far from sinking into his flesh once again as they rolled in the sand, but of course, she had another one. This one hadn't been strapped to her thigh but pulled from her ashes, and now it was embedded in his side.

Again.

Cethin hissed out a curse, still keeping his grip on her as he came to a stop on his back. "I understand why you feel I deserve this," he ground out, pulling the dagger free with his other hand. "But perhaps you need to get a little more creative rather than simply stabbing me."

"I will ensure the next time I impale you with a sharp object, it will be your end," she retorted, trying to yank her arm free where she lay on the beach next to him.

He smirked, turning his head to look at her. "It's another normal day then? Are there any secrets you need to share with me?"

"You've been in my dreams. You should know them all by now," she retorted. "I'd like my dagger back."

He couldn't help his bark of laughter. "The dagger you just stabbed me with?"

"I'm already in possession of the other one," she said, again trying to free her arm from his grasp. "What other dagger would I be referring to?"

"Forgive me for not finding it in my best interest to return the blade you harmed me with."

She scoffed, twisting again as she sat up, and he followed. "You can let me go now. It's not as if I can go anywhere."

"That's true."

She looked pointedly at his hand wrapped around her arm. "Then release me."

His eyes narrowed, but he slowly lifted his fingers from her skin. "We have more to discuss."

Scooting back across the sand and putting space between them, she replied, "I don't think I want to speak with you any more today."

"Too bad. We need to discuss how we move forward from here. You are still my queen."

"I'm not *your* anything," she spat.

"Wrong, *wife.*"

She pursed her lips, her now wet hair sticking to her face and collarbone, and her sea-soaked dress clinging to her. Sand clung to her damp skin. The sun was nearly gone now, and she looked exquisite sitting among the surf in the twilight.

"Tell me what you are thinking, Kailia," he urged after two full minutes of silence ticked by.

"To what end?" she countered. "So you can use my words and thoughts to manipulate me even further? Not that it makes a difference. You will simply come for them when I'm asleep."

"If you're expecting me to apologize for what I did, I won't."

Her laugh was humorless. "The cursed don't feel guilt, king."

"If sitting on a beach, soaked to the bone with you is a curse, I'll ensure I do the same in every lifetime to relive this moment over and over."

"I hate you. I always have."

"But at least it's real," he countered. "More real than the lies you spun in the gardens or the facade you've tried so desperately to keep in place for months."

Her head canted to the side, the familiar curiosity shining in her eyes despite her obvious anger. "You told me we had to be convincing. How else was I supposed to do that? It is not as if I could openly despise you, *husband*."

"Is that what we're calling how you feel about me? Hatred and contempt?"

"I don't know why you'd think otherwise," she answered.

He hummed. "So many mixed messages, tiny fiend."

Pushing to his feet, he extended a hand to her. She merely blinked at it, pointedly standing on her own.

"We still have a kingdom to lead, Kailia," he said. "We can continue to discuss this, but we still need to move forward."

"I intend to," she replied.

He knew this wasn't the end of it. He'd watched her in her dreams as those who had wronged her came for her, and she'd cut them down to nothing. He'd seen her do the same when someone merely touched her. Truthfully, he'd expected more rage, but he shouldn't have when he really thought about it. She was cunning and contemplative. Unpredictable, yes, but rarely brash. No, he wasn't stupid enough to believe there wouldn't be consequences for this, but he also didn't regret it. No part of him did.

He'd long ago learned that sacrifices for his kingdom came at a cost, and he'd never apologize for paying it. He was the one who'd gotten ships past the Wards. He was the one who kept the creatures of old at bay. He was the one his parents called in when there were uprisings or the Elder Clans got too bold. And he would be the one to free his people of these godsforsaken Wards that kept them contained. Because his people trusted him. His kingdom looked to him for protection. He understood his responsibilities. His role and duty had been reiterated to him since he was born, a part of him as much as his magic was, even if he resented some of the things he was now forced to deal with daily.

But it hadn't been as monotonous as of late.

Not with Kailia in his study, or knowing he'd get to see her at dinner. Not with watching her sleep so many nights, when she was convinced he was gone. Not with seeing her in her dreams, watching her cleverness and skill, learning secrets she worked so hard to keep hidden.

No, there was no regret and no guilt, and if she hated him for this, he didn't care. He'd told her once that the veil between love and hate was thin, and that he'd be fine with either from her. Nothing had changed.

She could hate him, but she was still his. In this lifetime and all those to come.

Extending his hand to her once more, he said, "Let's go home."

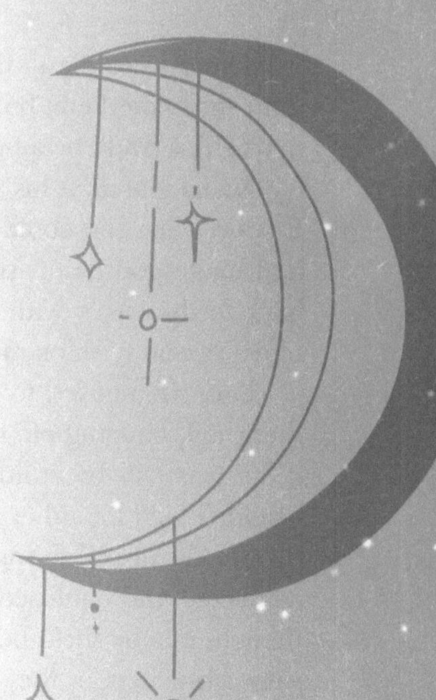

CHAPTER 40
KAILIA

She stared back at him. At the king she'd always known was capable of cruelty. The king who was willing to sacrifice anyone and anything for his own gain.

"Let's go home," Cethin said, extending a hand to her.

Home.

She'd never truly had one of those. First was the Cliffs, then Pyry. Admittedly, that was the continent she preferred, although having to wear so many layers in the frigid climate made it difficult to move quietly and conceal weapons. After Pyry, she spent decades in Baylorin, the capital city of one of the mortal kingdoms across the Edria. But after that, and in between those three places, she went wherever her ashes carried her. Enjoying the freedom. Taking in the sky. Sun, moon, stars, clouds. She didn't care. But never had she felt like she had a home. Places to live, yes, but the word home invoked a different feeling she was sure she'd never experienced. Home was supposed to be a place that was safe and accepting. Home was supposed to be free of expectations and demands. She'd always envisioned a home as a place where she wasn't used or exploited, but simply free to exist with others who cared for her because she existed, not because of her abilities.

There were many things she was sure she'd never experienced until she came here, but for the briefest of moments, she'd thought maybe this could be a home.

Kailia glared at his waiting hand, but she slid her fingers into it. It wasn't like she could get back to the castle on her own. Cethin had made godsdamn sure of that. She certainly didn't *want* to go back to the castle with him, but she'd come too far in this to give him a reason to think anything else.

Plus, she needed to bathe. Sand clung to her, and her dress was drenched, hanging off her body. At least Cethin was bleeding, even if he was still breathing. Apparently, this new dagger she'd tried wouldn't kill him either.

She'd stopped trying to figure out a way to end his life for a bit, conflicted and confused about her purpose. For a few weeks, she'd thought maybe she'd been wrong. Maybe the stories she'd been told were fabricated, or they had the wrong king.

But this? What she'd learned tonight?

"Do you need anything before I take my leave?" Cethin asked, pulling her from her thoughts. She hadn't realized he'd been moving around the bedchamber where he'd Traveled them. He'd already changed, apparently forgoing the bath, which made sense considering he was still bleeding. Shirtless, he wore his usual pants with a tunic in hand, and his moon Mark was bright atop the other Mark now. She could only assume he was going to see Niara and then go to his study. The sun may have set, but there were still hours left of daily activities in the kingdom that loved the night.

"You said we had more to discuss," she said, eyes narrowing as she clenched her fist in a bid to avoid seeing her own moon Mark.

"And you said you didn't want to speak to me any more tonight."

"Since when has what I wanted mattered?"

His lips thinned, his jaw tensing as he stepped into her personal space, forcing her to tip her head back to look up at him. "It's always mattered, Kailia."

Reaching up, she gripped the crystal at her throat. The fucking crystal she'd foolishly thought was a symbol of rebellion. Something to irritate Cethin, when he'd been playing her for a fool all along. Something she'd stupidly fallen for despite all her training. She should have put this together long ago.

She yanked on the crystal, the leather cord digging into the back of her neck. "If that's the truth, then remove this."

"In time, wife," he replied, reaching out to finger her wet strands of hair. "But I think tonight, it would be in my best interest to give you some space to process everything you've learned today. We can discuss more in the morning."

"I didn't realize there was anything else to discuss when it clearly does not matter what I say," she snapped, shoving his hand away from her.

He smiled down at her. A condescending thing. As if she were a child throwing some kind of tantrum. As if he hadn't seen her single-handedly kill people.

As if she didn't regularly save him from those phantoms.

Truth be told, she *had* saved him the first time, mainly because she wanted to be the one to end his life. But before she could do that, some other pieces of this hunt needed to be moved into place. Maybe he knew all that. She had no way of knowing how much he'd seen and learned in her dreams. This had drastically changed the game. If he'd learned her darkest plans, he hadn't let on, but she couldn't believe anything he said or did now.

Cethin took a step back, glancing down at the wound in his side. With a sigh, he said, "I have to go see Niara about this. I've asked Orson and Riggs to stand guard outside the rooms." Meeting her gaze once more, he added pointedly, "If you leave this floor, I will know, tiny fiend." She sent him a saccharine smile, and he smirked. "Glad to see we've finally dropped all pretenses."

When she didn't reply, he didn't bother saying anything else. He only reminded her again that he'd be notified if she left.

She waited until she heard the main doors close before she crossed to one of the many balconies, throwing the doors open wide. The marble floor was cool beneath her bare feet, the warmth of the sun already lost. Gripping the railing, she stared out at the mountains. Guards and doors shouldn't be an obstacle for her.

Under any other circumstances, she'd simply climb over the railing and jump, slipping into her ashes and letting them carry her to the ground.

But he'd stolen that from her.

Stolen so much more than that.

She'd faced betrayal before. It wasn't something new, but this time was different. Cethin had made her feel...

Well, he'd just made her *feel*.

She'd always found purpose, being paid for her services, but this had been different. For a reason she still hadn't worked out, he'd entrusted her with his kingdom. That had felt noble. So much bigger than killing for a wealthy merchant or stealing for a bitter partner. She'd never cared about their reasons; she'd cared that she was paid. Of course, when she'd crossed the Edria, she'd needed to spy, not draw attention to herself.

Then there was Razik.

A relationship of sorts had formed there. Friendship, but more. Nothing romantic or lust-filled, but a connection she'd found herself truly enjoying. She looked forward to her days with him, researching or exploring Aimonway. He didn't coddle her, and his apathetic broodiness worked in her favor because he was blunt and unbothered when she said something awkward or socially inept.

Cethin had still been more though. He'd been patient with her. Letting her slowly acclimate to his touch. Warning her with his magic before taking her hand or pressing a palm to her lower back. Showing her he didn't need to touch her to make her feel wanted or give her pleasure, but then when he *had* touched her, showing her touch didn't need to be torture or manipulation.

No, he'd saved all that for her dreams. She'd spilled secrets to him, telling him things she'd never say in reality. He'd known. He'd known the entire time. Every whispered confession and forbidden desire. Every careful exploration while she thought she'd been safe and alone.

Somehow this hurt more than the fire magic she was tortured with or the touches that maimed. This felt like *she* was the one who'd been stabbed. As if there was a blade in her chest, twisting and digging in deeper and deeper until each breath was a strangled gasp.

He was no different from every other person who'd learned what she was and tried to use her. Tried to cage her. Tried to force her to answer to their desires and dreams. Tried to manipulate her and capitalize on her misunderstandings of social cues.

Sucking in a shaky breath, her chest still tight, she pushed off the balcony railing. Each step back inside left an ashy footprint. She shucked off the wet dress as she moved, leaving it on the bedchamber floor. Undergarments followed. Reaching the bathing chamber, she turned the faucet on, letting the tub fill with hot water. She wanted no reminders of his cool touch right now.

As it filled, she turned to the mirror, bracing her hands on the countertop. The smoke in her eyes was writhing the same way her soul was. Her ashes fluttered around her, and her amber eyes seemed brighter than usual. A calm she hadn't felt in months settled over her. Everything in her going still and quiet, but her magic trembled with anticipation.

She'd vowed long ago to destroy every person who'd had a part in her being in those Cliffs. More than that, she'd vowed vengeance against anyone who tried to use her.

Cethin was both.

Lifting a hand, a swirl of ashes left an arrow between her fingers. So similar to her own, save for the gold airhead.

The phantom's arrow Cethin had caught and so foolishly left lying around their rooms. Or he was testing her. Either way, a mistake on his part.

Still holding it, she climbed into the bath. Sinking in up to her neck, she held the arrow above the water, twirling it between her fingers.

Another swirl of ashes carried a message for her.

Figure out how to get me to you. I'm ready.

She was always the huntress, never the prey.

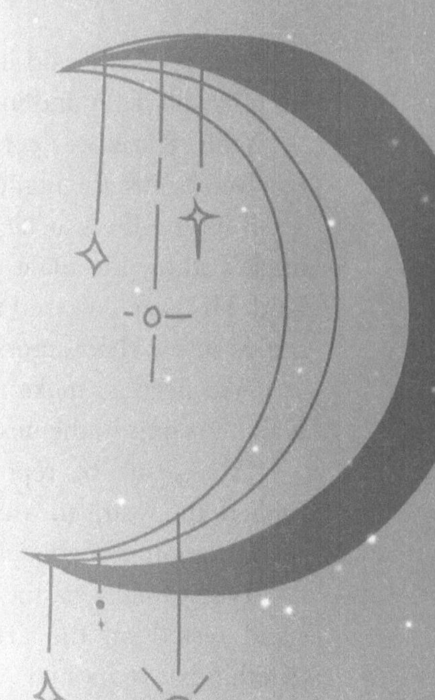

CHAPTER 41
RAZIK

"Good morning, Magdalena," Razik greeted, the words tight despite his effort to at least sound pleasant.

Magdalena, with her infinite patience and kind heart, wasn't even phased. "Razik, my dear! Are you here for breakfast?"

"Not this time."

"It's been a while," she replied with her ever-cheery disposition. "I'm beginning to think you've found pastries elsewhere."

"I would never, Magdalena," he answered, offering her a small smile. "I'll plan for breakfast here tomorrow."

"Lovely!" she exclaimed. "I'll be sure to have your favorites on hand."

Magdalena had been the head of Tybalt's household staff for as long as Razik had lived here. Even when he'd been a youngling, she'd been at least a century old. Several staff had come and gone, but never her. A constant he'd clung to over the centuries when he really thought about it.

"Looking forward to it," he answered. "But right now, I have to go see Tybalt."

"Ah, yes," she said in understanding. "He has been holed up in his office all night and into the morning. I'm certain he hasn't slept."

Yeah, Razik was certain of that too, considering the missive he received before the night was even half over.

Rapping his knuckles on the door twice, he let himself into his uncle's study, the male behind his desk studying a report of some kind. His gaze flickered to Razik, then back to the paper, and Razik settled into a chair across from him.

"We need to make this quick," Razik started. "I have to be at Kailia's rooms in the next twenty minutes."

"You won't be reporting to the queen's rooms today," Tybalt replied, the words measured.

Irritation immediately settled in. "And why is that?"

Tybalt finally set the report down and sat back in his chair. One hand rested on the armrest, while the other sat atop his desk. "Cethin has requested— No, Cethin has *ordered* me to remove you as her personal guard. Care to explain why?"

"Sure. Cethin is an arrogant prick who kept things from his wife and is blaming me for her finding out," Razik replied, and although he tried to sound casual about it, even he could hear the simmering anger in his words.

That fucking son of a bitch. He'd violated Kailia by going into her dreams without her knowledge, somehow kept her from using her power, and tricked her into a Lunar Marriage. Of course Cethin's solution is to blame him and have him removed from his post.

"Razik," Tybalt ground out, his patience clearly running thin. "For months, you have been gathering information on the queen. You've built a relationship with her, and now, when you are in a trusted position, you do *this?*"

Razik leaned forward, jamming a forefinger on the desk in emphasis as he said, "I built that relationship by being upfront with her. Why do you think she trusts me? When I learned Cethin was visiting her dreams, and she had no idea, yes, I told her. My loyalty is to her, not him."

"They are one and the same, Razik!" Tybalt bellowed. "I do not know how to make that any clearer to you. The day you voted to make her queen in more than title, you ensured they were on equal footing."

"That's on you," he retorted. "You are the one who threw me into the vote without notice. We should have discussed that beforehand, and you know it."

"Would it have changed anything? If I had come to you and told you I was going to have you vote, and that vote needed to be no. Would you have honored my request?"

Razik opened his mouth to answer, but the words wouldn't come. Would he have? With Kailia at his side and the eyes of the highest-ranking lords and ladies on him, would he have denied her something she had told him more than once she wanted?

"That's what I thought," Tybalt said when he remained silent.

"If you didn't want her in the position, then *you* should have voted yourself," Razik said. "You're not putting this on me, Tybalt."

"Tell me then, Razik. There's no one else here. Do you honestly believe she should be in the position? Have you learned enough about her to confidently say she should be the queen of Avonleya?" Tybalt asked, the question genuine despite the tension between them right now.

"I believe she could be good for Avonleya," he answered. "She's not from here, not that the people know that, and she brings perspectives from outside the Wards. In time, I think she could be a great queen."

"But right now? If something happens to Cethin, the crown now falls solely to her, even if they have children."

"I'm not a fucking Oracle," Razik bit out. "I can't predict that any more than you can."

"That's fair," Tybalt acquiesced. "Then let me ask you if you still believe she has other motives, or do you think her intentions are pure?"

Razik hesitated. He *did* still believe she had come to Avonleya for a reason. He'd just never figured out what it was. Not yet anyway.

"I think those two things can both be true," Razik answered. "I also think that since Cethin and Kailia have equal power here,

Kailia can decide for herself if she wants me removed as her personal guard."

"And she has," Tybalt said. "She agreed with Cethin."

"What?" Razik demanded, blinking back his shock. There was nothing else to say if that was true. More than that, it meant Cethin had spun yet another tale to convince her of this.

"Knowing that, do you care to revisit any of the things we've discussed this morning?" Tybalt asked.

"None of my answers and comments change. I don't say things simply to appease anyone," Razik snapped.

"I am well aware of that," Tybalt said, a bit of empathy breaking through the hardness of the Commander. "But you don't build the kind of relationship you have with Kailia and not become invested in some way yourself, Razik."

"It's not like that. She was my job, and I was hunting for information. If she doesn't want me anymore, that's fine."

He rubbed his brow the instant the words left his mouth. He'd never intended to say that last part aloud.

"Razik—" Tybalt started.

"I said it's fine," Razik growled, getting to his feet. "If there's nothing else, I'm going to take some days for myself. When I return, I'll be ready to report back to the Cadre."

Tybalt nodded, watching him closely. "I only request that you check in with me daily."

"No need," Razik called over his shoulder, making his way to the door.

"Not as your Commander, Razik, but as your family," he called back.

Razik waved him off, but he'd do it. He'd send a note every morning and night solely because Tybalt had asked.

He made his way down the various halls to his rooms, wanting to grab a few things from his study before he Traveled to his cave. But when he pushed the doors open to his rooms, he found Wren seated on the edge of a sofa, wringing her hands together in her lap. As soon as she saw him, she lurched to her feet, looking anxious.

"Wren," he said tightly, instinctively scanning her for any sign of injury. "What are you doing here?"

"Waiting for you," she answered. "I was told you'd come here this morning. I was hoping to speak with you before you start your day with Kailia."

"I'm actually heading to my cave for a few days," he said, moving around her to climb the spiral iron staircase to his study. "You can come with, if you want, but I'll be there for a bit."

"You know I go stir-crazy there," she replied, her steps light as she followed him. "But I do need to speak with you."

"We are speaking now."

Feminine fingers wrapped around his forearm, tugging. "Razik, please. Can you stop for a minute?"

With an audible sigh of irritation, he turned to face her, crossing his arms. "What?"

"Okay, well, you don't need to be a dick before I've even said anything," she snapped, her own irritation flaring. When he only stared back at her, waiting for her to get on with it, she said, "Fine. I need to discuss our current arrangement."

"What about it?"

"We both agreed that if a relationship came along with someone else, we would be transparent about it," she ventured, the irritation bleeding back into trepidation.

"And?"

"…and that's happened. I think?"

"You think?" he deadpanned. "If that were the case, you'd know, Wren."

"Fine, then it has," she said, throwing her hands up in frustration. "With Bram. And before you say anything, I know you don't like him, and you think I'm being foolish about all this."

"It's your life, Wren," he said, uncrossing his arms and turning away from her, even more ready to get the fuck out of here and retreat to his cave for a while.

"You don't…" He heard her footsteps as she chased after him. "Razik, I'm trying to talk to you. He bought an estate house and wants me to live there with him."

"You don't need my permission," he answered, picking up two books before rummaging through a desk drawer for a journal he'd been writing notes in.

"I know that, but you're still a big part of all this," she argued. "If you have strong feelings about this one way or another, I'd like to hear them."

Slamming the drawer, he leveled his gaze on her. "I don't care what you do, Wren. If you want to live with Bram, then do it."

"You…don't care?" she asked, her brows knitting together.

"No, I don't."

She nodded, at an obvious loss for words as she pressed her lips together. He turned away from her again, finding a leather bag to shove the books and journal into. He opened another drawer and pulled out the last sack he'd collected from the sailors.

"Anything else?" he asked, grabbing both bags in one hand.

"You're being cruel, and I don't understand why," Wren answered, lifting her chin in an effort to hide her hurt.

"I'm not being cruel. I'm being frank," he said. "Like I always am."

"Not with me," she countered. "And we need to discuss what this would mean for us if I do this."

"It would mean when I need you, I'll come find you. It would mean we stop fucking. Inconvenient for me, but I'm sure I can find others. It would mean you'd become his responsibility and no longer mine," he said apathetically. "You can let me know what you decide when I get back."

Try as she might, she couldn't hold back the two tears that slid down her face. "I don't deserve that, and you know it."

"We don't deserve a lot of things in life. The Fates don't give a fuck," he replied, turning away from her.

"I can tell you my decision right now," she bit out, the hurt and anger evident in the words. "Whenever you return, you can find me at Bram's."

"I expected nothing less," he answered with a sneer.

"Fuck you, Razik Greybane," she bit out. "Don't come to find me until I let you know I'm ready to see you again."

"I'm sure you'll be plenty busy," he retorted.

He forced himself to look back at her and see the hurt. If he was going to be a jackass, he was going to face the result of that. Let the guilt weigh on him. It was just another layer of inadequacy at this point.

So he took in her tear-stained face and hurt-filled eyes before he Traveled, leaving her in his study.

⤙ ☉ ⤚

A few days had turned into ten.

That was how long he'd been at his cave. Not the entire time. He'd ventured out at least once a day to fly. Sometimes during the day, but more often at night. Despite not being born in this realm, he'd still acclimated to the schedule of the kingdom, preferring moonlight over daylight.

He hadn't contacted Wren. He absolutely knew he should. He'd been an utter ass to her, but that was an apology he owed her in person. A simple note wouldn't do. She knew him, and an actual spoken apology would mean more than anything because he rarely apologized for anything.

As requested, he checked in with Tybalt twice a day, every day. Which is why he knew the creatures of old were stirring again. His uncle was far more gracious than he was, providing updates from his daily reports, as well as letting him know if Kailia left the castle. Razik never acknowledged that part of his reports, but he appreciated them. Despite the queen no longer wanting him around, some part of him was still satisfied to know what she was doing.

He hated that he cared at all.

Now he sat in one of the pools of hot springs that were housed in the network of passages off the main part of his cave. The steaming water lapped around him as he sat on a ledge beneath the water. It allowed him to be submerged nearly to his shoulders, and he rested his head back against the edge.

When he wasn't flying, he was buried in books. The books he'd brought with him had been useless, and he'd resorted to selecting random books off his shelves. Everything led to a dead-end, so it didn't seem to matter what book he looked in at this point. He'd hoped to stumble upon something useful. Then again, all knowledge was useful, but nothing for what he needed right now.

He was missing something. There was no way, after spending weeks and weeks with Kailia, he wouldn't have picked up on what her underlying motives were. She had to have slipped up at some point, even if it was something minor. Something that had seemed unimportant at the time but actually gave her away. These were the types of things she spent her time in her magic watching and listening for. When he looked at it that way, Cethin was probably smart in figuring out a way to keep her from doing so in the castle, especially in the beginning when she very clearly hadn't wanted to be there.

That had changed at some point. He'd watched it happen slowly over these last months. He'd like to say it was all his own doing, but Cethin had clearly had a bigger impact. Razik could always tell when something significant had transpired between them. She was quieter and more contemplative, likely processing the interaction and how it was affecting her.

It hadn't all been Cethin though. She'd fought to keep Razik as her personal guard at one point. She hadn't backed down, pushing back against the king, which made it all the harder to believe this was what she wanted. She didn't let Cethin push her around. He didn't know what the terms of their bargain were regarding their marriage, but he knew she would have had her own demands. The one thing he'd heard her repeatedly request, though, was to be queen in more than title.

He sat up straight at the thought.

It couldn't be that obvious, could it?

But it was.

It absolutely fucking was.

"Motherfucker," he growled, climbing out of the water and grabbing the nearby towel.

They'd missed it. They all had. She was awkward and a little odd, but she was also a godsdamn Ash Rider. She'd told them she'd been trained in stealth and spying. She'd told them she'd been trained as a mercenary too. Everything. Every bit of information she'd given them and the way she had delivered it had been on purpose. This entire time, she'd been doing the exact thing he had been. She'd been gathering information for her own purposes.

And they'd readily handed it over.

Every fucking conversation.

He could look back on them all and see it. How she asked him to help her get to know the kingdom. How he'd willingly offered to help her figure out her role as queen. The seemingly innocent questions about the markets and the intense studying of the other cities and the continent. All of it would be expected of her, but she'd played her role so godsdamn well. She'd bided her time, keeping her questions about the kingdom simple and superficial for a long while until they got more invasive. When she'd be visibly irritated that Cethin wouldn't tell her where he went during the latest hours of the night. The increasing desperation to figure out her power. Her asking what in Avonleya would be a threat to the dragons. He ignored every suspicion because after she got her answer, she'd move on to another topic, as if it were merely her curiosity and bid to understand and nothing more.

She'd used him and played them all. If he was right in this, she'd always wanted that crown. Always wanted the throne. That was why she'd agreed to this bargain with Cethin. Which meant—

None of the stabbings were an accident.

All of them had been on purpose, but Cethin had kept his secrets from her. Almost as if he'd known what she was doing. How much did he tell her the day Razik had handed Kailia that information on a silver fucking platter? So furious with Cethin because he thought he was taking advantage of Kailia, when it had been the other way around this entire time. Did she know what he was now? Did she know why none of her blades or arrows had ended his life? Because that was the only way she was going to have that throne all to herself.

It all fit. Every single memory and discussion that came back to him only furthered his theory.

But why?

What did she have to gain by ruling Avonleya?

Unless she wasn't working alone.

He uttered more curses as he frantically dressed and threw a few things into a leather bag before Traveling to Tybalt's estate.

"Tybalt?" he called out, bursting into his uncle's study.

But it was empty. He wasn't here.

He tried his office at the castle, finding that space empty too.

Who could she be working with? Someone who came with her on the ship? Or did she find someone when she got here? Had she had a contact here for decades, somehow finding a way to communicate? It could be done, although the cost to get around the Wards was great. That was proven time and time again, most recently with King Tethys's death.

He tried the offices near the warriors' barracks next, sending a message with his magic. Those offices were empty too.

Fuck.

Fuck, fuck, fuck.

The training arenas were next, many of the warriors cursing at his sudden appearance.

"Where is the Commander?" he growled at one of them as the male passed. He was young, and Razik's demeanor clearly scared the piss out of him because he stumbled back, falling onto his ass. He couldn't even speak. Just opened and closed his mouth like a gaping fish.

Useless.

He turned to find another, but a senior warrior was already making his way over.

"The Commander. Where is he?" Razik growled again.

The male frowned. "He's in Everfall with the king and queen. The Cadre went with them. Left this morning when the lord sent word of the creatures of old waking."

Razik said nothing else, Traveling to Everfall. He didn't know where they'd be exactly. The creatures of old in these parts tended to stay in the Olwen Mountains. He'd gone to the city center, hoping to pick up some gossip about the whereabouts of the royals.

The royals.

Equal footing and equal power.

Power that would—

His next realization made his overheated blood run cold.

Because they were bound by a Lunar Marriage. But it hadn't always been known as such a thing. It had once been called a Lunar Bonding. A few small details had been altered for marriage unions, but the original bond had been between other beings during one of the decades of the Everlasting War. It wasn't well-known, which is why Tybalt and the other advisors had the reactions they did when Cethin announced it. Many knew the term but not what it all entailed. Not even Selinya and Tethys had invoked a Lunar Marriage.

There were several components to the bonding, but the biggest one was their power. The beings who'd created the Lunar Bonding were losing the war, and in an effort to keep their power not only from being lost but also to keep it from the gods they were fighting, they'd created the bonding. If either party of the Lunar Bond died, their power was transferred to the other party. All of it. Every facet of their magic. The catch was that if one party killed the other, both powers were lost to the chaos between the stars.

Which meant if Kailia killed Cethin, she'd lose her power. But if she truly knew what the Lunar Marriage was and someone else killed Cethin, she gained all of his power. All of this hinged on exactly how much Kailia had learned, and Razik didn't know. She'd never seemed bothered by it, which had led him to believe she didn't fully understand what a Lunar Marriage encompassed, but if she did...

A screech echoed. A sound Razik hadn't heard in decades.

The *stryx* were awake.

He didn't have time to wait for Tybalt's response anymore.

Razik shifted as he leapt into the darkening night. He'd cover more ground faster this way, and he'd be able to spot them from the sky.

Kailia had used him. He'd fucked things up with Wren. Tybalt was losing faith in him. He wasn't about to lose his kingdom—the only home he'd ever known—too. He refused to look his uncle in the eyes in failure again.

Powerful black wings beat, pushing him hard and fast. He let loose a roar that answered the call of the *stryx* as he went to save his home.

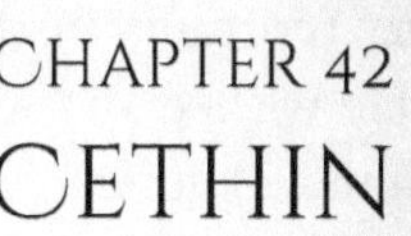

CHAPTER 42
CETHIN

The sound of a dragon's roar had him grinding his molars as they moved. The terrain was getting steeper as they went deeper into the Olwen Mountains. He turned, reaching for Kailia's hand to help her over a ledge as they climbed a steep embankment. Ariadne and Draven were with him, while Tybalt, Jarek, Fallon, and Bram had accompanied Corveth.

The lord had reported seeing at least three of the *stryx* when they arrived this morning after his request for immediate assistance. There had been no slow awakening like there had been with the *nagasky*. As far as they'd known, the creatures of old had gone back to slumber. Apparently, they'd all been wrong.

Unlike the *nagasky* in the southwest and the *nagasea* of Shadowfen, the *stryx* were solitary creatures. The other two creatures moved in groups, but the *stryx* always scattered, going out on their own. It made them harder to track down, which is why they'd split up. Cethin was hoping they'd found the first one, so he could take care of it. The others were tracking two more to keep them busy until Cethin could come to them.

He wasn't prepared for this though. Over the last week, he'd been spending his nights and morning hours in his study in the catacombs. Things were still tense between him and Kailia, and while they put on a good front when out and about together, things were very different when they were alone.

He understood her feelings of betrayal, and more than that, he understood she needed time to process everything. When the missive came from Lord Astor this morning, he'd known there was no way she was staying behind. He wished she would have, especially after what had happened when they'd gone to subdue the *nagasky*.

"Do you think we are close?" Kailia asked, wandering around the new area, her face to the sky and bow in hand.

"I hope so," he answered. "Although a *stryx* tends to find you, not the other way around."

She hummed, her only acknowledgement, and he jerked his chin at Ariadne to stay close to her. The female nodded, edging closer, as Cethin fell back to walk with Draven.

"Have you seen anything?" he asked, his voice low.

Draven shook his head, eyes continuously scanning their surroundings. "Nothing noted."

He wasn't focused on the sky like the rest of them. Cethin had instructed him to watch for any signs of the Elder Clan. The last thing he needed was for them to come for Kailia again, but considering they were the guardians of the creatures of old and this was the second time they'd woken in a matter of months, he had no doubts they were involved somehow.

"Keep watching," Cethin said, clapping him on the shoulder before moving back to walk with Kailia.

She scarcely glanced at him, and a muscle in his jaw ticked at the obvious dismissal. Yes, he deserved it, but she was still keeping plenty of secrets of her own. To continue to hold this against him was rather hypocritical of her.

"You said the *stryx* can fly, but they are not like the *nagasky?*" she asked, her usual dress swishing around her ankles as she moved.

He'd offered her a cloak before they'd set out on this hunt, but she'd refused, claiming she could hunt better this way. While he was in pants, boots, and a long-sleeved tunic and jacket, she was in her sleeveless dress with the high slits and bare feet. It was ridiculous, but telling her that with the urgency of the situation was a battle he'd chosen not to fight today. As soon as this was dealt with, they'd go home anyway.

"Yes," he answered. "The *nagasky* are winged serpents. The *stryx* are…"

"Horned owls with fangs," Ariadne offered grimly.

That was one way to describe them.

"Owls?" Kailia asked, turning to face him.

For the first time in over a week, she held his gaze, that old curiosity flickering in her eyes. It seemed for the moment, she was forgetting to be angry with him. He'd call that progress.

"Much larger than a standard owl," he clarified. "They are bigger than most land animals."

"The size of a dragon?" she asked.

"Not quite, but close. Their wingspan isn't quite as large, and Ariadne is correct. Their beaks are bigger and longer with fangs, and they have curved horns," Cethin explained.

"Didn't you or Razik tell me there were four different creatures of old?" she asked, turning back to the sky once more.

"The *felidae* are said to exist, but we have never seen them. Only heard rumors," he answered.

She looked back at him over her shoulder. "Like the Runic Lands."

He smiled softly. "Yes. It is said the *felidae* guard the Runic Lands."

Another screech sounded, this time closer.

"You don't think my arrows would work on them?" she asked, one appearing from her ashes. "Or the blades I can create?"

"Considering they are immune to dragon fire, I'm going to assume not," he answered.

"But we don't know," she countered. "Until you, I'd never met anyone or anything that could survive my arrows or blades."

He saw the look Draven and Ariadne exchanged at that, but wisely, neither of them said anything.

The next screech reached them, sounding much closer, a moment before the *stryx* appeared from behind some rocks overhead. It dove quickly, and he wrapped an arm around Kailia's waist to Travel them out of the way while Draven and Ariadne did the same. They ended up on opposite sides of the space, the *stryx* standing between them.

She was massive.

Her grey wings stretched out, the beast scratched the rocky earth with sharp talons. The sound reverberated through his bones, and Kailia clamped her hands over her ears, her bow clattering to the ground.

The *stryx* tilted her head too far to one side in that unnerving way standard owls could. Then she turned her head completely the other way, looking behind herself.

"By the gods," Kailia breathed, retrieving her bow with her eyes fixed on the creature. "And there are three of them?"

"That's what Lord Astor said," Cethin replied tightly as he pulled up more and more of his magic.

He didn't want to release it yet. The *stryx* were more agile than the *nagasky*. While he could go into direct combat with the other creatures of old, it was far easier to subdue a *stryx* by casting a net of power rather than using ropes of darkness. But keeping this much magic at the surface was nearly impossible. More than that, he needed to reserve some for the other creatures.

Right as he was about to release that net of dark power, cries of surprise rang out. The *stryx* turned, honing in on where Ariadne and Draven were. Cethin didn't know what was happening over there with the creature blocking his view, but he was out of time.

With a burst of energy, he cast his power outward, flinging it over the creature. She screeched, the sound deafening this close, and Cethin stumbled forward as the *stryx* tried to take flight. He yanked hard on his magic to keep the thing on the ground. They never wanted to kill the creatures, only send them back to slumber. Taking out such ancient creatures could upset a balance they didn't know about, and there were enough curses on his kingdom the way it was.

He pulled up more and more power as he wrestled with the creature, letting his darkness lift him off the ground to hover closer. Faintly, the sounds of weapons clashing reached him, but he couldn't focus on anything else. This was using too much of his power as it was. If he had enough to subdue another, it would take the last of it, and that would still leave a third to contend with.

Tightening the net, he forced the *stryx's* head to the ground, the giant creature on her belly as she tried to break through his magic. Striding forward, he placed his hand on her beak, a different kind of magic rippling out. Her frantic eyes glowed, flashing to silver for a brief moment before returning to their pale white color, until finally her eyes closed, settling into a deep sleep.

His chest heaving, he turned to check on Kailia, finding her standing with her bow, an arrow nocked and aimed. His magic lowering him back to the ground, he scanned her once before shifting back to look beyond the *stryx* to where Ariadne and Draven had been.

Only to find them still engaged in a battle with several Elder Clan members.

He'd known they would be close by, and the sight of them had him rushing back to Kailia and herding her back into the small overhang they'd been huddled in before the *stryx*.

"What are you doing?" she demanded in outrage, attempting to shove at him with her elbow as he jostled her.

"The Elder Clan is here. Ariadne and Draven are handling them. We just need to sit tight for a minute," he answered, maneuvering so he blocked her from view.

"They're here?" she asked, immediately trying to peer around him.

"Yes," he ground out. "Stay out of sight."

"If only I could disappear among something like smoke and ashes to do so," she deadpanned.

The sudden snark took him by surprise. A delighted surprise, but surprise nonetheless. Mainly because she was actually speaking to him.

He shifted to peer across the expanse again, still hearing the sounds of fighting.

"Did you know across the sea you are called the cursed king?" she asked suddenly.

He glanced back at her, then he turned to face her fully when he saw what she held. "Why do you have that here of all places? And where did you get it?"

Because in her hand was his crown, the silver and rubies almost dull in the fading sunlight.

"From our rooms, of course," she answered, coming closer and motioning for him to stoop down.

"Kailia, this really isn't the time—"

"Most call you that because of the Wards," she cut in. "It makes sense, but the Wards were in place long before you were called king. Even still, I think it's fitting all things considered."

"Because I am the king now?" he asked, wondering where she was going with this.

"One would certainly think you cursed with the way the phantoms come for you," she mused, toying with his crown. "I guess there are multiple reasons to call you the cursed king."

"Something to be discussed later," he said tightly, the sound of the battle waning. They must be close to having things under control. "Let's take her out of here and come back."

He'd taken a whole two steps when she said, "I think the biggest reason I'd call you the cursed king though is because you haven't figured out that you are the reason for all the Fae deaths."

For a moment, all thoughts of the battle and the creatures of old and their safety were gone, completely eclipsed by her words. He stilled, slowly turning to face her once more. "What are you talking about?"

She was staring back at him, features hard and cold. Something dark and wicked that he'd seen from her but a handful of times.

Moving with the grace of the predator she was, she brushed past him, ashy footprints left behind. Approaching the slumbering *stryx*, she paused beside it, taking the creature in.

"They truly are majestic creatures," she said thoughtfully. "And yet they are kept slumbering and caged, used for their abilities."

She lifted a hand as if to touch it, and that was what had him lurching forward and breaking him free of all the thoughts swirling as he tried to figure out what was happening here.

"Don't, Kailia," he warned, knowing if he had to struggle with the creature again, he'd have nothing left for the other two.

He knew more than he let on. He'd observed her in her dreams for months. Seen things she hadn't realized he knew yet. Or rather, she was likely questioning what all he knew, but didn't want to bring it up because she didn't know. Their battle for dominance hung in the balance, waiting for one of them to tip it. Despite the things he'd gleaned from her dreams, there were still details that evaded him. Things he couldn't figure out no matter how many times he slipped into her dreams or danced around topics in conversation.

She paused, her fingers inches from the creature's feathers. His crown was looped around her arm, her bow still in her other hand.

"We don't cage them," he continued, the words causing her gaze to slide back to him. "They are not domesticated creatures. They guard sacred sites. According to the Elder Clans, that's what they've always done. Long before my family assumed the throne, that was their purpose. According to history texts and knowledge from the Elder Clan, they came with those who created this world for that purpose. We don't know what disturbs them enough to wake them, but they are not the threat. We recognize that. It's why we do not kill them. We return them to their purpose. Let me show you."

Moving forward, he took her hand, then rested his other gently on the *stryx's* beak once more. Traveling them deep into the Olwen Mountains, they appeared inside a nest tucked into an overhang. It was bigger than the *stryx* was, and the creature immediately settled in, tucking her face beneath a wing.

Guiding Kailia out of the nest, they made their way down the steep embankment until they came to a relatively flat area. Keeping his voice low, he gently turned her to face another direction, pointing off into the distance. "See there?" he asked. "Another slumbers. There are several nests in the area, and they all guard this."

He guided her to face yet another direction, where two giant onyx doors were built into the mountainside. They were tucked so far into the shadows, they were nearly impossible to spot unless you knew they were there.

"What's behind them?" Kailia asked, stepping closer.

"Another time," he answered tightly. "But I wanted you to see that they are not caged or harmed. They are not forced into their positions. They guard these sites because they choose to, but they also do not differentiate between friend and foe."

"What would happen if they were simply given freedom?" she asked.

"While I'm glad you are once again speaking with me, tiny fiend, this is truly a conversation to be continued at home," he said, taking her hand once more. "We need to get back and get the other two creatures returned to their nests."

Before she could reply, he Traveled them to the same clearing, planning to meet up with Draven and Ariadne. He could get a report, then they could hopefully track down Tybalt and the others.

But the moment they appeared, Draven was rushing forward, stumbling over the terrain.

"Cethin! Thanks the Fates," Draven called. "Ariadne is hurt, but you need to know that—"

The male's eyes went wide as a swirl of smoke and ashes appeared in the air behind him. Cethin glanced to his side, where Kailia still stood, then back to the warrior.

"Draven?" he asked, taking a single step, but the male slumped to the ground in a heap.

Standing over him was a male with black hair and grey eyes. Eyes he'd never seen swirl with smoke until now. He was corporeal, but his hand was still ashes, and clutched between his fingers was…

A spinal cord.

As if he'd reached inside Draven's body and pulled the entire thing out of him.

His mind raced as he frantically tried to sort through what he was seeing. Lord Corveth Astor wasn't an Ash Rider, but the male standing before him fucking was and he looked exactly like the lord.

The male dropped the bones atop Draven's body, discs and vertebrae scattering at the lack of care as his hand reformed into flesh and bone. He wasn't wearing the dirty boots and work clothes Cethin was used to seeing him in. Instead, he straightened his sleeves and pulled at the lapels of his fine jacket. His polished boots had a few scuffs, but nothing like they would be from working on sheep farms or in shops.

He stretched his neck from side to side before settling his gaze on them once more. His lips curled into a wicked smirk as he beheld them, and Cethin stepped in front of Kailia, blocking her from his view.

"Explain yourself," Cethin demanded, rallying his power despite not having any to spare.

"I think my sister would explain things better than I ever could," he answered simply.

Sister.

Do not fail us now, sister.

Ever since the dream where he'd been stabbed, he'd been trying to place that voice. Kailia had been so distraught by that nightmare, the details had fallen by the wayside as he'd worked to soothe her. He'd never seen the face of the male who'd shoved a sword through his back, so he'd never been able to discern if he'd seen him in her dreams before. It had made it harder to place the voice, and now it was far too late.

Stepping to the side so he could keep both Kailia and Corveth in his line of vision, he slowly backed away.

"Now would be the time to explain yourself, wife," he said sharply with all the authority of his title and the crown that had fallen to her feet.

Her smile was a mirror of Corveth's as she watched him put distance between them. Her head canted to the side a little, long dark strands sliding over her shoulder. "A king has his secrets, and so does a queen," she said simply.

"Kailia, I don't know what's going on here, but—"

"That's the thing, *husband*," she interjected, casually twirling one of her arrows between her fingers. "You should know. You should know so much after all those late nights in your study. I don't need to know where it is to know what you do down there."

"For someone who prefers direct and blunt communication, you're certainly speaking in riddles right now, tiny fiend."

Her eyes narrowed. "Then allow me to be blunt, *king* You say you coerced me into this bargain because you needed my arrows to save your people, yet you could never make the connection the thing they needed saving from was *you.*"

"Don't speak to me about what I've sacrificed for my people, Kailia," he snarled. "You have no idea the things I've done to ensure they can live peaceful and comfortable lives."

"But I do know," she purred. "I know all the things you've done and the curses you've brought upon yourself, starting with the blood magic to bring ships across your Wards."

Words escaped him. She couldn't possibly— No one knew what he did in that study in the darkest hours of the night.

Corveth was still standing near Draven's body, hands in his pockets. He rocked back on his heels as though watching a form of entertainment play out in front of him.

"You know there is a cost for magic, but blood magic?" Kailia asked, faux pity in her voice. "Princes should not play with things they do not understand."

"I understand just fine the cost of power and blood magic," he spat, taking a step toward her, but she raised her bow, that arrow back on the string. He sent her a derisive smirk. "We both know that arrow won't do anything, wife. You've tried that weapon already."

"Then I suppose I'll have to try this one," she answered.

Tossing her arrow aside, a swirl of ashes left another in her hand. It was nearly identical to hers save for the gold arrowhead.

Fuck.

He didn't know if that arrow would affect him. He doubted it, but this wasn't the ideal time to find out.

She casually nocked the arrow while she continued speaking. "If you understood the cost of your magic, you'd realize that every time you successfully let something past the Wards, Fae are found dead the next morning."

"No," he said. "Only a handful of ships have made it past the

Wards and only in the last year. None in recent months, and there have been dozens of Fae found dead."

"I didn't say it was always ships," she replied calmly. "I said every time you successfully let something past the Wards. More than ships and those from across the sea answer your calls."

No.

That couldn't be true.

He shook his head, denial coursing through him. There had been a time, when he was young and his parents hadn't realized what he could do, that he'd let unwanted beings into the kingdom, but not now. His mother had put a stop to that the moment she'd figured it out.

She had to be wrong. None of that could be true, because if it was—

"No," he ground out, shaking his head as he desperately tried to explain any of this.

But Kailia's smile was knowing, a sinister thing he hadn't thought she was capable of. "Yes, Cethin. A cursed king who sacrifices his own people."

"You're wrong," he growled, unwilling to believe a word of it.

"Denial doesn't change the truth," she replied. "Corveth has been here for decades. He didn't arrive on a ship."

Cethin glanced at the male, still silent with a faint smile on his lips as he watched this all play out.

"He came looking for sanctuary, and instead he found the prince and the kingdom responsible for so much death and misery," Kailia snarled.

"How can you possibly believe that after these last months?" Cethin demanded, straining to keep his magic in check. He needed to be strategic about all of this. Two Ash Riders. Two creatures of old still out there. The Elder Clan still hovering. They'd said the creatures awakening was an omen. They hadn't wanted Kailia on the throne. Despite knowing so much of her plans, he'd thought he could sway her. He could have never prepared for any of *this* though.

"I'll admit these last few weeks, I second-guessed myself," she confessed. "Seeing the people. You including me on matters. How kind and gracious you are with those in your care. I thought maybe it wasn't a mask. Maybe everyone was wrong. Because how could you be the cruel and cursed prince? The king everyone speaks of across the sea?" Somehow her features darkened even more, twilight casting shadows across her face. "Then you showed me exactly how you do it. How you use and betray without care of who pays the cost."

Her last words were cold and filled with vitriol.

"Kailia, we can talk about all that. We can—"

But he was cut off by the roar of a dragon that had all three of them looking to the dark sky, the last rays of sunlight fading completely.

"You said you were handling the others," Kailia said sharply, her gaze cutting to Corveth.

"I did," Corveth answered, his words smooth and icy. "This shouldn't be possible."

But a black dragon was flying hard and fast for them, a dark spot against the stars. He half expected Kailia to release her arrow, but she didn't. There wasn't time to debate anything else as the dragon banked before landing behind Cethin. The ground shook beneath them, everyone stumbling at the impact, but when Cethin looked up, it wasn't glowing red eyes he found.

They were sapphire blue.

Razik.

He didn't know how or why the male was here, but this was the first time he'd ever been happy to see him.

His scales were black as night, and they seemed to absorb the moonlight. Two horns protruded from his diamond-shaped head, and a spiked tail curled around Cethin as a growl rumbled from his chest. Those glowing eyes were fixed on Kailia with a resentment Cethin had only ever seen directed at him.

"You're too late," she said simply, lifting her bow and taking aim.

Too many things happened at once.

Razik loosed a roar just as a *stryx* came diving in, as hard and fast as Razik had been flying. The creatures of old were impervious to dragon fire, and they were one of the few creatures that were a threat to the dragons. Razik didn't have a choice but to go airborne. Not only to keep himself out of harm's way, but it would also lead the thing away from Cethin and the others.

Cethin let his magic free, his darkness surrounding him in a vortex of protection.

The force of Razik's wings flapping sent a gust of air swirling around them all.

A gust of wind that should have blown an arrow off course.

But not the one Kailia had released.

Not the one with a gold arrowhead that sank deep into Cethin's chest.

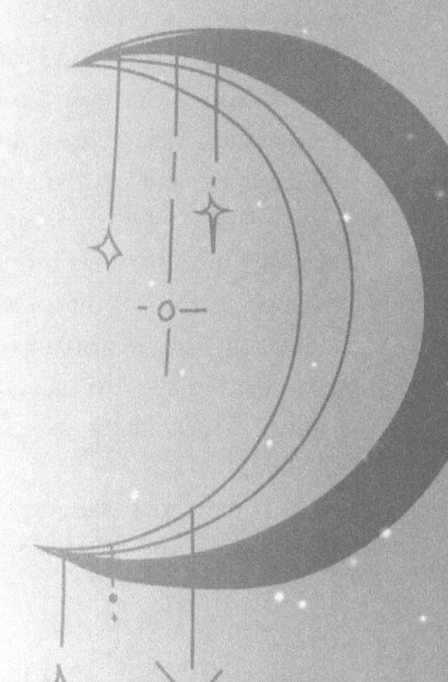

CHAPTER 43
KAILIA

Corveth had come through on his end, and thank Temural for that.

There was a reason they'd brought Cethin here. Of course, the *stryxes* had been for Tybalt since she thought she'd taken care of Razik by dismissing him as her personal guard and leaving him behind, but the male had shown up anyway. Surprising, considering his disdain for the king, but his uncle must have somehow gotten word to him. It was no matter, though. Razik had told her that the creatures of old were the single formidable threat to them in Avonleya, so Corveth had woken the *stryxes*.

Now she stared at her husband, the phantom's arrow protruding from the center of his chest. He'd grimaced at the impact, and he reached up, snapping the arrow in half with a grunt of pain. Smart to let Niara remove the rest, although she was hoping even the skilled Healer would be too late to save him this time.

She was already suspecting that she was right about the effects of the phantom's arrows. The moment the arrow had pierced Cethin's flesh, his darkness had dissipated. The same way it did with the gold swords or the swipe of the phantom's hand. It became nothing. A nuisance brushed away.

Corveth sauntered forward, giving her a wide berth. He may be her brother, but even he knew not to touch her. Especially not right now, with the thrill of the hunt and victory coursing through her. Fleetingly, she wished she'd have Cethin to go to at the end of this to release all the energy, but she knew that would never happen again and there would never be another. He'd betrayed her too deeply, proving that letting people get too close only led to a different kind of torture.

Cethin tried to back away from Corveth, but he stumbled, dropping to his knees, as if the task of standing was suddenly too difficult.

Her brother laughed. A dark chuckle that echoed in the mountains while the dragon and the *stryx* struggled with each other in the sky.

Kailia watched as Corveth crouched before the cursed king, pulling a dagger from his own ashes. Reaching for his arm, Cethin tried to pull it back, but Corveth easily snagged it, pinning his wrist to the ground.

"I've waited so very long to see one of his on their knees," Corveth said casually, sliding his dagger across Cethin's palm. Then Cethin barked a curse as Corveth dug the tip of the dagger in even deeper.

"Why?" Cethin asked, his voice a weak rasp as he lifted his head to meet her gaze.

He wasn't asking Corveth.

He was asking her.

"Centuries ago, when the Reaper gave me freedom from the Cliffs, I made a promise to myself," she answered, Corveth standing with his dagger in hand. Cethin's blood glistened on the blade. "I vowed I would hunt down every single person who tortured me within those Cliffs, but more than that, I'd find anyone who had a hand in locking us away there. The Reaper found some of them before I had the chance. Others I've hunted down and taken my own vengeance."

Corveth came to her side, sending her a questioning look. She nodded, and he reached for the crystal at her throat.

"I traveled across the continent trying to learn anything I could about the Cliffs, but no one knew of them. There were rumors, but nothing substantial. No one knew of the things happening on that island. No one knew of the colony hidden away, not for our own safety, but for the purposes of those in power," she continued as Corveth used the tip of his dagger, covered in Cethin's blood, to draw a Mark on the crystal.

It flared brightly when he finished, the leather cord at her throat snapping free. She caught the necklace as it slid from her neck. Summoning her ashes, they devoured, sinking into the crystal until it was nothing but the same in her palm. Opening her hand, she let the ashes float away, and then she moved.

Her soul sighed as she went weightless for the first time in months. Going where *she* directed, moving and twisting in a freedom she had thought she'd lost forever.

She reappeared behind Cethin, settling her hands on his upper arms as she rested her chin on his shoulder. "I learned little until I went to Baylorin, the capital city of Windonelle," she said, her voice low as she murmured in Cethin's ear. "And there? I found one who not only knew of the Cliffs, but knew so much more. I learned I had a brother who was trapped behind the Wards of your kingdom, but more than that, I learned that your beloved kingdom was the reason we were in the Cliffs to begin with. That a prince had been born, and *he* was the reason those Cliffs had been created. That he'd convinced his parents that in order to free themselves from their exile, they needed stronger, more powerful beings."

Cethin shook his head, the movement languid and slow. "That's not…true."

"No?" she asked, pushing back to her feet and moving around him. "Did you not tell me you would do *anything* for your people? Anything to free them of the Wards? Did you not force me into a bargain? Have you not been sacrificing your own people in your attempts to bring in ships that would carry those who survived the Cliffs? Luring in more Fae with promises of safety, only to present them with death?"

"Kailia, I didn't…" He shook his head as if trying to clear his thoughts. "My parents would— *I* would never condone such a thing."

"There's no need to lie to me anymore," she replied, striding to where his crown lay on the ground. She scooped it up, holding it between her hands. "I learned all of this, and then I learned there were those in Baylorin wanting to end the Avonleyan rule. A rule that had once been over the entire realm, but had slowly decreased to this continent. A plan was proposed to infiltrate the kingdom. We just needed a way in. Of course, it would be your carelessness that would provide an avenue. But while we waited and bided our time, I trained. Because like you, husband, I also keep my promises, particularly those I make to myself.

"It took time. So much godsdamn time. I couldn't appear too eager. Not with you. I studied you from the ashes. A simpering female falling at your feet would never work. All the females here tripped over themselves at the mere idea of becoming your queen," she scoffed. "You were bored and needed something more. Something to intrigue you. Something to obsess over. I may not have been educated in the art of reading people, but I could read *you* so easily."

Her ashes converged, winding around the king's crown. They twisted and encased, seeping in behind the rubies and bending the spires. They tangled and maimed, ripping apart and tearing, until that crown became nothing but ashes she let fall at her feet.

"I swore I would find my brother. I swore I would find the cursed king, and then? I would take everything from him to save his people from the same fate I'd endured. I'd free them from the one who used them for his own gain," she said, her smoke swirling and leaving her circlet on her brow. "You were the last one for me to find to complete my vengeance."

She moved through her ashes, appearing directly in front of him. A king on his knees at her feet. She lowered to a crouch before him once more, using the tip of her finger to tip his face up, his head lolling and eyes drooping as though he was fighting sleep.

"I did what I had to do to get close enough to end you," she whispered, cupping his jaw. "I told you you'd lost before we even began."

"I know," he rasped, and she could swear he was leaning into her touch. "I've known…since I learned…of you." He sucked in a rattling breath. "Remember…I've been watching you…nearly as long…as you've been watching me." The words were shallow. Breathy. "It was worth it," he managed, slumping down on his side.

"None of it was real," she retorted, needing him to know that before he crossed the Veil. But for some reason, she felt like she was trying to convince herself more than him.

"Treat them well…wife. They're your people now…"

His eyes closed at those words.

It was worth it.

He couldn't have meant that. He was confused as death came for him.

It didn't matter anyway.

She straightened, staring down at the king with the weight of her circlet on her brow. Feeling Corveth come to her side, she asked, "What now?"

"I'll take care of him," he answered. "But you need to prepare for what's to come. People will want answers, and those closest to him will fight against this with everything they have."

"They will fail," she replied simply, her bow appearing in her hand. She looped it across her chest, turning to face her brother. "From the ashes, something new will be reborn."

Corveth smiled. "You did well, Kailia."

She didn't return the smile. She didn't need his praise. Yes, she'd come for him, but more than that, she'd come for herself. Seeking vengeance to free her tortured soul.

A king at her feet.

A crown on her head.

Freedom in her ashes.

Smoke surrounded her, and she became weightless, letting her ashes carry her away.

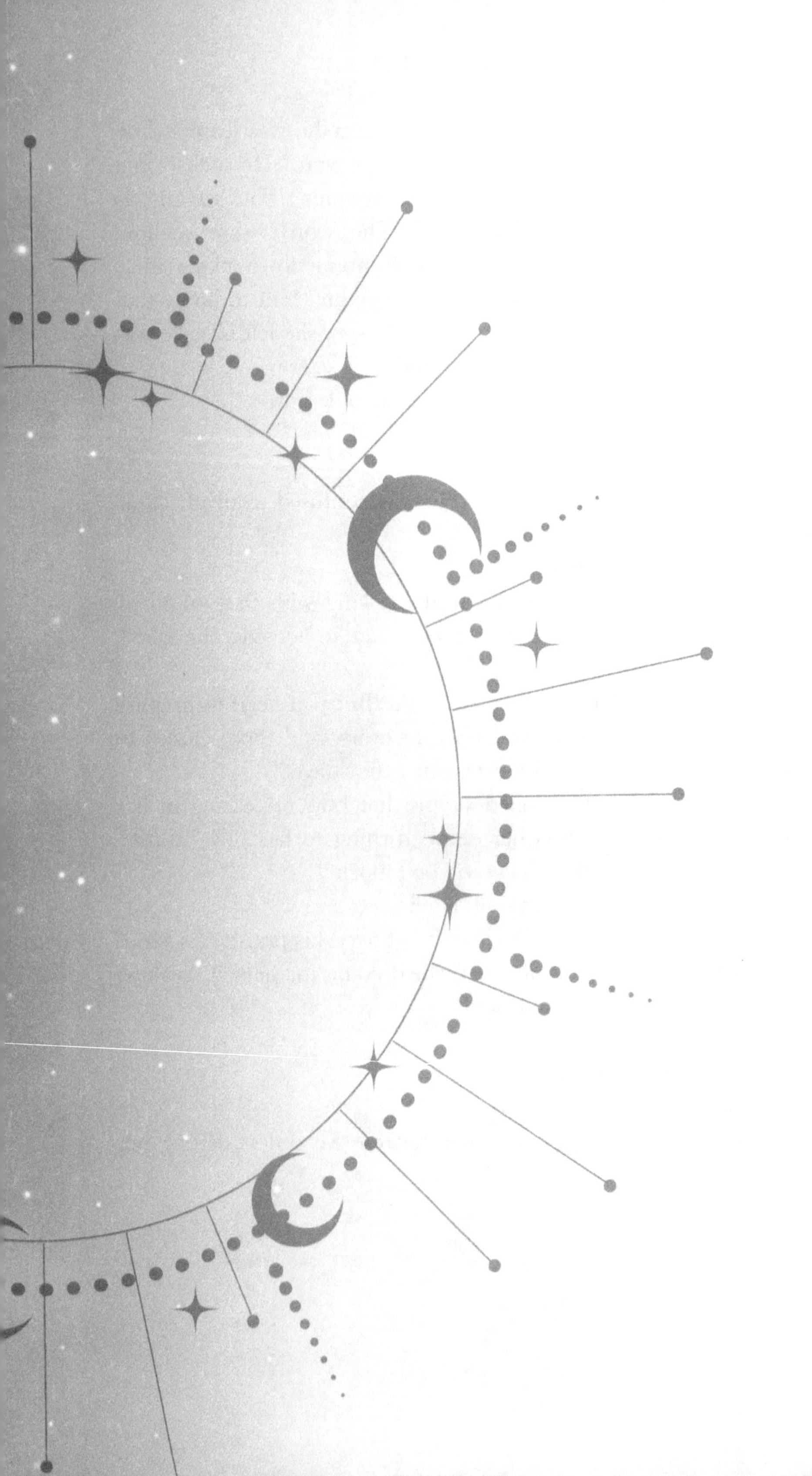

THE GODDESS OF NIGHT AND SHADOWS

She stood on the sand, watching the panther prowl closer.

She'd felt the spirit animal enter these lands, knew her bonded would find her.

Shirina came to a stop beside her, sitting and twisting to look up at her with glowing silver eyes.

She had so much to atone for, and yet the panther stood by her, a steadfast friend for centuries.

"You come with a message?" she asked.

The feline gave a low growl, the sound rumbling from her chest.

"I see," she replied, pursing her lips.

Her son had refused her yet again.

But then Shirina lifted a paw, dragging it along the sand. A moment later, a piece of parchment appeared. She bent to retrieve it, reading the quick scrawl she immediately recognized as that of her Guardian, and cold fury coursed through her at the words she read.

Clenching her fist, the parchment crumpled in her hand, shadows appearing and devouring it. Then she crouched before the panther, running her fingers through her soft fur.

"This is the last hour we will be bonded, my friend," she said, her voice as cold as the stars, and her silver strands flowing on the sea breeze. "I must release you to be bonded to another in the future. You will know when it is time."

Shirina leaned into her palm, and she smiled tightly at the feline.

Releasing her, she pulled a dagger and cut a thin line on her forearm. Dipping her finger into the stream of blood, she drew a Mark in the sand. "I trust you with those I cherish, Shirina. When the moon reaches its peak, our bond will be no more."

The panther bowed her head, and the female stood, shadows beginning to converge around her. Lifting a palm, another swirl of shadows left a vial of blood in her hand. Blood that would get her back across Wards. To her kingdom where she'd been known as Selinya.

To her son.

To those who were trying to deliver him to the After, and to those who should have prevented all of this.

Saylah stepped into her power, shadow-walking to deliver the wrath of a goddess.

A NOTE FROM MELISSA

This note is always one of the last things I write before I finalize a book, and right now is no different. The book is nearly done, and it's when I sit back and reflect on what I learned from writing this particular book. On this side of writing it, what did my soul need? What did the characters fight to have told? I get a little more transparent and real because my characters and stories teach me things along the way in the same way I hope they touch you.

And this book?

This is the book that almost did me in, friends.

Not because of dark themes or the subject matter. Not because of the characters or the length of it, but because of adapting to a new world and journey in my publishing career. (Much like a new queen trying to adapt to a new role.) I pushed my body physically, mentally, and emotionally, willing to do anything in my power to not disappoint my publishers, my team, and my readers.

Sometimes we have to push through those hard seasons, right? There's no way around it. There are contracts in place. People I employ and a family that depends on me. Readers who champion me and love on me so dang hard, and it is always my goal to give back as much as I can. To never disappoint you if I am able. Sometimes, we have hard seasons of surviving, and sometimes, we even thrive in those seasons. Seasons of giving everything we have (like a king desperate to ensure his people live good and peaceful lives).

That was the season I was in. If last year was about learning and experiencing the ins and outs of my new publishing journey, this year will be about restructuring so I can continue to thrive without feeling like I'm constantly kicking to keep my head above water. This year will be learning to manage my own neurodivergence and to better understand my own processing and functioning so I can keep doing all the things. Keep writing. Keep providing. Keep giving back.

Seasons of surviving are okay, friends. They are a part of life, but we're never meant to stay there. They're never meant to be a continuous state of being. We're not supposed to have a few moments of peace in our cave while living every other day with unyielding pressures. We're meant to learn from them. To continuously be growing and evolving rather than remaining stuck in patterns that may have served us once, but now suffocate us.

So that is what I will be doing in this next season. Learning and growing. Putting new systems in place to protect my health—physically, mentally, and emotionally. The conclusion of the Avonleya Series is coming. As soon as I have a release date to share, I'll shout it across all my platforms, but I'm going to take a moment to breathe. To look at my calendar full of events and commitments and ensure I can get you that next book without having to sacrifice my mental health, push through immense hand/wrist pain, or work while on family vacations.

There's still so many exciting things to come, and I want to be able to fully enjoy them. I have secrets I've been keeping, and soon, I get to share some of them with you all. From the bottom of my soul, thank you for continuing to come along for the chaos.

Keep Looking for the Stars-

Melissa

facebook.com/melissakroehrich

instagram.com/melissa_k_roehrich

tiktok.com/@authormelissakroehrich

threads.com/@melissa_k_roehrich

amazon.com/~/e/B09GGGTLTM

NEED MORE?

-)) :⊙: ((-

There's more for you to explore in the Chaosverse! Journey across the Edria Sea to read Scarlett's story! Available now on Kindle Unlimited, Amazon E-Book, Paperback, Hardcover, and Audiobook.

Turn the page for peek at the first chapter.

CHAPTER 1

SCARLETT

"You are sure he will be here tonight?" a cool female voice asked, bored from where its bearer perched on a low garden wall.

"I have tracked him for weeks," replied a voice of silk and honey. "He will be here."

"You said the same thing an hour ago," the first snarled, flipping a dagger in her hand.

"Then why did you ask me the same godsdamned question?"

"Kindly remember I get him first."

"You always do," the second voice crooned.

"Enough. Both of you." An icy, third, female voice cut in through the bickering.

If the moon were out at all that night, it would have illuminated the three figures who sat in the shadows on that garden wall, waiting. Completely in black, from the boots to the hoods up over their heads, there were weapons gleaming on every inch of them. Steel daggers and swords. Bows and arrows. Hatchets and whips. Three women who knew how to use every single one of the weapons that adorned them with lethal efficiency. Three women who knew how to use their bodies as weapons— in all the ways a woman could use her body. Three women who were far more clever than most and that was perhaps their

633

most valuable of weapons. Three women who had been raised together. Trained together. Three women feared by most. Nightmares come to life.

As it were, there was no moon out that night so the male, also dressed in black, did not see the women creeping along the wall as he passed them, despite constantly looking over his shoulder. The male did not hear the feet landing behind him softer than a cat. The male did not know he was not alone until a dagger was pressing into his back and that voice of silk and honey purred into his ear, "Hello, Dracon."

The male swore and reached for his own blade at his side. Before his hand touched the hilt, the voice clicked her tongue. "I wouldn't do that if I were you."

"I've been waiting for you for weeks, you bitch," the male sneered at her. "Ever since you let it be known that Death's Shadow had begun trailing me."

"Is that so?" she whispered softly.

"Yes, so let's have it out like the trained professionals we are instead of you cowardly shoving a dagger through my back."

"Hmm, as delightful as that does sound, I don't think that will happen on this night."

"Why not?"

The woman stepped back from him, releasing Dracon with a shove that had him stumbling a few steps. "Because tonight my sisters have joined me." Even in the darkness, the woman could still see the male's face drain of color.

"What?" he whispered.

A cruel smile spread across her face.

"One in particular has a score to settle with you." The woman's tone went dark and filled with wicked amusement as the other two women prowled from the shadows. She sniffed the air, her delicate nostrils flaring. "Why is it that you two make them piss themselves more than I do?"

"No." The male's breathing was ragged as he stumbled back from them. "No. I haven't done anything to warrant this. No!"

"Well, that just isn't true," one of the women said sweetly as she stepped towards him.

"It is true! I've only done paying jobs. Just like you." The male tripped over something as he backed away from them and fell to the stone ground. He continued to push himself away on his hands. "I've done nothing to warrant sending his Wraiths after me!"

The woman pulled a dagger from her side with a gloved hand, tapping the point against her fingertip. "He didn't send us. Sometimes we collect our own debts, and I've been looking for you for a very long time." Her voice was wildfire and snow and ice and shadows.

"Then clearly you lot aren't as good as the rumors claim," he sneered.

In less time than it took him to draw another breath, the dagger flew from her hand and went clear through his, pinning it to the ground beneath him.

He screamed in agony, reaching to pull out the dagger piercing him, but another boot came down on his other hand. He gasped around the pain.

"You're right," the woman who had thrown the dagger purred. "We're better."

The one he had called Death's Shadow stalked toward him and wrenched the dagger from his hand. She tossed it back to the thrower, who caught it with ease, scowled, and grumbled, "Gods, it smells like him now."

The other two women each hooked an arm under his shoulders and began dragging him along the path. The male was kicking his booted feet, twisting to and fro, trying any way to break their hold on him. They acted as if they were hauling a sack of potatoes. They'd been trained extensively on how to handle his kind.

And how to kill them.

"Where are you taking me? Where are we going?" he cried.

"Death's Maiden has questions for you," the third woman said as they threw him against the low garden wall. It was overgrown with thick ivy and thorns, and the male yelped as they cut into his palms, his skin, his face.

"No. Please, no," he begged. "I will take the third over her!"

Death's Maiden crouched before him, tilting his head back with her finger to peer into his eyes. "Oh, Death Incarnate shall have her turn…when I am done with you." There was nothing human in her eyes as she surveyed the male before her. "Seven years ago you were hired to kill my mother…and me."

At those words, the man began trembling. "You— You are the daughter. You are the one who— You've been missing for the last seven years."

"Apparently, I've been found."

She plunged a dagger up through the bottom of the man's foot, right through his boot. The tip came out the other side, slicing through the laces.

The male screamed again, sobbing. "It was a paying job. He tricked me. I didn't know."

"You didn't know who you were killing? That seems highly unlikely,"

Death's Maiden said with a laugh tinged with madness. She pulled another dagger from her boot as she remained crouching before him. "Who was with you that day?"

"I cannot say," he sobbed again.

"Well, that is a pity," she sighed. Then she brought that dagger down into the male's thigh.

"I cannot say," he cried, breathing through his teeth around the pain. "I am forbidden. I am bound by ancient blood magic. I cannot say."

"Foolery," the third, Death Incarnate, snapped. "There is no one here who can do such magic. Magic is not found here."

"There is," the male gasped. "I swear it!"

"He lies," she snarled, bringing her eyes to meet Death's Maiden's.

"Perhaps he does. I don't give a shit." She stood. "We have hours to discover if he is indeed feeding us lies." Dracon began thrashing again, writhing on the ground. "Tell me, Dracon, did you know that your Fae magic will not heal you here?"

Dracon was trembling violently now. "I didn't know your mother was who she was until it was too late. I swear it!"

Death's Maiden only smirked. "Do you remember exactly how you killed my mother? How you took her apart piece by piece? Because I do. I was hidden in a trash bin in that alley and saw the whole fucking thing."

Dracon began whimpering as the other two women came to her side. The three of them stood gazing down at him, cruelty on every line of their faces. They all drew daggers from their cloaks and advanced.

Dracon's screams began anew.

⁃ᐣᑒ ⊙ ᑕᐠ⁃

Scarlett Monrhoe woke to Dracon's screams still echoing in her mind. She rarely dreamt of that night anymore. This dream was actually a happy memory. She was usually jarred from the depths of slumber by nightmares that had her drenched in sweat and her throat raw from screaming. They were the reason she hadn't slept well in months, so she wasn't entirely surprised she'd fallen asleep in the middle of the day.

She sat draped over a chair with the early afternoon sun filtering into the parlor of the Tyndell Manor. The tea she'd been sipping on had long since grown cold beside her. The book she had been reading was still in her lap, open and waiting. It was a rather old leather-bound book she'd stumbled upon a few days ago. She'd been through the small Tyndell library numerous times and didn't know how she'd missed the book when searching the shelves for something new, but there it had been, sticking out like a sore thumb on the shelf.

It was not just about the fallen kingdom of Avonleya. That kingdom had been on a continent across the sea but had been defeated when they sought to overthrow King Deimas and Queen Esmeray. The king and queen gave their lives for the war by using their magic to not only defeat and lock away the Avonleyans but also to protect them from the Fae Courts to the north and south of their human lands. Their sacrifices had provided the humans protection from the Fae who desired to enslave the mortals that shared the continent. This book, however, went into more detail about the conquered kingdoms: things she hadn't been taught in her extensive studies, details about their strange magic, and the gods and long extinct bloodlines.

"Are you really going to just sit in here and read all day?" a young woman drawled from the doorway, her hip propped against the door frame. Her golden hair was braided and swept to the side. Scarlett smirked at Tava Tyndell, daughter of the Lord of the house. The two girls were very different. Scarlett was all confidence and swagger. Tava was entirely submissive and gentle on the outside, the way Ladies of nobility were trained to be from a young age, but she was clever enough and enjoyed getting into a little trouble with Scarlett every now and then. The fact that Scarlett wasn't raised in a noble household accounted for their stark differences, but the girls were friends nonetheless.

"Unless you have something better in mind, I'm quite content to lounge in the sun all day, thank you very much," Scarlett replied, her attention turning back to the book.

"She is waiting for you. Out in the training quarters," Tava whispered, fidgeting with her spirit amulet at her neck. Three interlocked circles, side-by-side— the symbol of Falein, the goddess of cleverness and wisdom.

Scarlett slowly dragged her eyes back to her. "How long has she been here?"

Tava's voice was hushed. "Only a few minutes. She nearly made my heart stop when she stepped from the shadows and sent me to you right away."

"Is she alone?" Scarlett asked.

"I do not know, but we do not have much time. Drake and the other men are out hunting, and they will return soon," Tava answered.

Scarlett uncoiled from the chair, tucking her book under her arm. "Lead the way."

The girls walked silently from the parlor, nodding to a couple of passing servants in the hallway. They slipped out the back terrace doors and crossed the grounds to the training quarters.

The Tyndell Manor resided on a sprawling estate, complete with its own stables, garden, training quarters, and archery grounds. The manor itself was two stories with a dozen suites, several studies, sitting rooms and the like. Lord Tyndell was the noble of the manor, residing there with his two children, Drake and Tava. His wife, she had been told, had passed from a wasting disease when the children were young.

While Scarlett currently resided with nobility, she was not noble by blood. Not this type of nobility anyway. She had plenty of wealth thanks to her mother, who had been a highly sought after healer in the capital city until her death when Scarlett was nine. She had never known her father. When her mother died, she was taken in by the Fellowship across the street from the Healer's Compound her mother had run. She had resided at the Fellowship until she had been sent to live with the Tyndells a year ago when she was eighteen.

Scarlett's long dress swished across the grass as they hurried the final few feet and pushed open the doors to the training barracks. The main room was empty, and Scarlett glanced at Tava. The girl shrugged her shoulders, biting her bottom lip nervously. Scarlett huffed a loud sigh, then snarled to the empty room, "While I certainly have all the time in the world these days, I don't particularly enjoy being summoned like a godsdamned dog."

"So temperamental lately. Although, I guess that is nothing new," a female voice drawled, flipping a dagger in her hand as she came into view from the darkest corner of the room. "For the love of Arius, did you take a stroll around the grounds before you came to see me?"

Scarlett rolled her eyes, throwing the woman a vulgar gesture as she meandered to the wall of weapons. Swords gleamed, their hilts varying from large and intricate to basic and dull. Hunting knives, bows and quivers full of arrows, daggers, and hatchets all adorned the wall.

"You've been living here nearly a year now, and you still haven't learned how to act like a Lady?" the woman asked, coming up beside her. Two scimitars hung at her waist while a sword was strapped to her back.

"It would appear not," Scarlett replied, picking up a basic sword. There was nothing special about it as she checked its balance. Deciding it would do for today, she turned to face the other. She was slightly taller than Scarlett and had pale skin with ashy blonde hair. Her eyes were the color of honey.

"Good," she replied, a feral smile spreading across her face. "I'd hate to have to break in a new partner. The guys at the Fellowship just aren't the same."

"You mean none of them are as pretty to look at?" Scarlett asked, leading the way to one of the training rings.

"I mean," the woman said, getting into a defensive sparring position, "that none of them are as wonderful as myself; and they bore me to no end, despite being plenty pretty to look at."

"The self-love in this room is truly astounding," Tava mused from her position by the building's entrance, keeping watch.

Scarlett and the woman both laughed as they entered into a dance of thrusts, side steps, twirls, and lunges. Their swords sang as they whipped through the air. They were blurs, moving so fast you couldn't tell where one stopped and the other began. Scarlett cursed as she realized a mistake too late, and the woman brought her sword down in a winning maneuver. The other woman snickered, lowering her sword. "You're out of practice."

"Unlike you, I don't live in a keep full of thieves and assassins who can spar with me at all hours of the day," Scarlett scowled.

"Now, now," she chided, "we could have you gone from here tonight. You know what is required of you."

"I have no desire to go from one prison to another," Scarlett scoffed.

"He wants you to come home," the woman said softly, closing the small distance between them so that Tava could not hear.

"That is no longer my home, Nuri."

"And this place is?" she asked, her brows rising.

"No, but for now I am protected here, I suppose. Until I figure out…something else. Until I can disappear."

"Please don't do anything stupid."

"You're one to talk," Scarlett replied with a pointed look.

"We're not talking about me," Nuri said with a dismissive wave of her hand. "Come home, Scarlett. You want to disappear? No one knew you were alive for years there."

"Yes, but again, I have a measure of protection here…from all of them."

"You would be just as protected there. He has said so more than once. You just need to give in on this one thing," Nuri insisted.

"I will not be shoved back into a cage of hiding," Scarlett snarled.

"You're in a cage now," Nuri bit back, readying herself in the training ring again.

"Because he shoved me into one," Scarlett replied, anger seeping into her tone.

"You shoved yourself into one and refuse to let yourself back out," Nuri snapped.

Scarlett lunged at Nuri, initiating their next sparring match, and nearly tripped on her long gown.

"You wouldn't have to wear such things at the Fellowship," Nuri said with a smirk. "Just saying."

"Tell me why you're here, Nuri," Scarlett ground out as she blocked Nuri's thrust.

"He has an assignment for you," she said, ducking to avoid Scarlett's next move. She swiped out with her foot, and Scarlett jumped her attempt to knock her to the ground.

"You cannot be serious?" Scarlett whirled and thrust out with her sword.

"I would not joke about something like this," Nuri replied as she shoved back against Scarlett's block. "And neither would he. In fact, he has sent the assignment with a very enticing payment when completed."

"I do not need any further funds from *him*," Scarlett seethed. "I need nothing from him, not anymore."

"He knows this. Which is why he offers something else," Nuri said. The girls were both breathing hard, equally skilled in almost every way. "Gods, it's been an age since I've sparred with anyone of worth." Nuri's grin was one of wicked delight as they moved around the ring in a dance of maneuvers that can only come from intense training and practice.

"Apparently, I'm not as out of practice as one thought then," Scarlett managed to get out between breaths.

"I mean, you're still not at your best, but your mediocre is still better than most of those at the Fellowship," Nuri said, somehow managing to shrug as she said it.

"Whatever," Scarlett muttered, landing a blow with her foot to the girl's stomach.

Nuri laughed as she held up her hands to stop the match. "A truce then, Sister. We do need to discuss this assignment."

"You can tell the Assassin Lord he can take his *assignment* and shove it up his—"

"You haven't even heard what he is offering you yet, Scarlett, and trust me. When you hear what he is offering for payment, I think you will change your mind."

"I highly doubt that."

Nuri closed the distance between them again and lowered her voice. "He has learned who hired Dracon."

"I know who hired Dracon. I know who ordered my mother killed. We discovered that shortly after we took out Dracon," Scarlett replied lethally.

"But he knows how to find him and will aid you in ending him."

Scarlett nearly dropped her sword to the dirt floor of the training building. "He is lying."

"He is not, Scarlett." Nuri's honey-colored eyes were fixed on her. "He knows, and he will tell you if you agree to and complete this assignment. He also said that if you agree to the assignment, you will be allowed back into the Syndicate to train and utilize our resources."

"Did he tell you?"

"He's not stupid," Nuri drawled. "He knows I would tell you even if he forbade it."

"Who is the assignment?"

"I am not to say anything unless you agree first."

"Why? Am I to kill you that I must agree to such terms?"

"Of course not," Nuri snapped. "Not that you could."

"We both know that's not true."

"I don't think we know that at all."

"Is this his target or the king's?"

"I don't know. I don't know who the target is," Nuri answered.

"How are you supposed to tell me the assignment then?"

"He will send it to you."

"He's always so fucking dramatic," Scarlett grumbled, rolling her eyes.

"The men have returned," Tava hissed from the doorway. "They just entered the stables."

"What am I to tell him?" Nuri asked, pulling the hood of her cloak up and sheathing her blade at her back.

"For fuck's sake, Nuri, of course I'm going to do it if he will aid me in this," Scarlett snapped as she hurried across the floor to put the sword back. She turned to face her, but she had already vanished into the shadows.

"Hurry, Scarlett," Tava whispered. "They are going to come out any time."

Scarlett joined Tava, and they hurried from the training quarters but not fast enough.

As they stepped out into the sunshine once more, two men came from the stables at the same moment.

"Shit," Tava muttered. The young Lady rarely swore, being of nobility and all. She turned to Scarlett and whispered, "Mikale is here."

"I know," Scarlett said with a smile that didn't reach her eyes. "It's fine. I can handle him."

The Lairwood Family had long been the Hands to the king, and Mikale Lairwood was in line to be the Hand to the Crown Prince, Prince Callan. Mikale had also set his sights on Scarlett and made his intentions clear about a year ago. The same time she had come to reside at Tyndell Manor. Despite having refused him on more than one occasion, he was persistent; and because Lord Tyndell was the leader of the king's armies, and Mikale was currently a Commander in said armies, she found herself in the young Lord's presence far more often than she wished. However, the fact remained that she had no noble blood in her veins, and there was no way Lord Lairwood would approve of a union to anyone without noble blood in the family.

Mikale, however, was also the reason she was now living at the Tyndell Manor.

"At least Drake is with him," Tava said tentatively.

"Yes," Scarlett whispered. Drake wouldn't do much though. She closed her eyes and willed the ice in her veins to calm, soothing the anger that threatened to spill from her mouth.

"Tava. Scarlett," Drake greeted them as he neared, eyeing them suspiciously. "What are you two doing down here?"

"Looking for you, of course," Tava replied to her brother.

"For?" he asked with a raised brow.

"I was hoping you were back so we could go riding," Scarlett cut in with a wink at Drake.

"Go riding in dresses?" Mikale drawled with a sneer. "How demure you have become, *Lady*."

"You'd be surprised at the things I can do in a dress," Scarlett replied coolly.

"I am sure I would be," he answered, his eyes sweeping over the lavender colored gown that was fitted across the bodice before flowing to the ground. "Care to enlighten me?" He took a step closer to her.

"Come any closer to me, and you'll find out exactly what I can do in a dress," Scarlett said with calm fury.

Mikale's lips twitched in amusement, and Scarlett saw red, her hands curling to fists at her sides.

"Take that next step, Mikale. We all know Scarlett would wipe the floor with your ass," a man said, coming up behind Mikale and Drake. "And we'd all love to see it."

Scarlett's heart stumbled, and she couldn't help the smile that filled her face as she breathed, "Cassius."

CONTENT INFORMATION

Below please find the potential triggers for the Avonleya Series as well as tropes and tags. Note this information is current as of January 2026. For the most up-to-date content information, please visit Melissa's website: www.melissakroehrich.com

Trigger Warnings

Depression, Sexual Scenes, References to Sexual Assault/Rape (not between the FMC/MMC, not on page), Death, Child Abandonment, Physical Abuse (on page and memories), PTSD, Murder, Attempted Murder, Blood, Gore, Profanity, Stalking, Violence, Grief, Torture

Tropes

Forced Proximity, Forced Marriage, Found Family, Slow Burn, Meddling Gods, Loads of Yearning, He Falls First, Full Cast is Centuries Old, Who's Hunting Who?, Touch Her and Die, All the Banter, Broody Dragon, King with Something to Prove, Stabby FMC, Kingdom Politics

Tags:

Neurodivergent FMC, Trauma Rep, Fae, Gods, Dragons, Shifters, Vampires, Witches, & More, Queer Normative, M/F Relationship (inc. main), Touch Aversion, Everything is Not as it Seems, Multi-POV, Third Person, Extensive World Building, Interconnected Universe, High Fantasy

Acknowledgments

I'd be remiss to not start with **you, the reader**. You continue to show up for my chaos, and that means more than I could ever express in words. I hope you understand the immense power you have simply by reading books and talking about them. You change lives, and you've changed mine. Thank you.

To my agent, **Katie Shea Boutillier** and the Donald Maass Literary Agency, thank you for all the endless emails and phone calls. I simply could not navigate all the new without you, and I am beyond grateful for your continued guidance and letting me talk things out on the phone with you.

To my Chaos Team: **Brit Irvin, Sara Abel, and Sarah Mori**, another book down. Thank you for sticking with me and handling all the things when I disappeared into the writing cave for months on end. Thank you for managing my chaos when I'm traveling. And honestly, when I'm just surviving. Thank you for being part of my life. I'm so honored you continue to choose to do so.

To my forever soulmate, **Miranda Lyn**: Your encouragement saved me. Sitting in zoom with you was a bright light in the trenches of writing. Thank you for simply sitting with me in the darkness.

To my colleagues and friends, **LJ Andrews, Frankie Diane Mallis, Penn Cole, and Amber V. Nicole,** thank you for the encouragement when we're fighting for our lives in the trenches. Some of us talk every day, and some of us every few months, but knowing you're there, in the hard and in the celebrations, means the world to me. It was something I didn't know I needed until I had it, and I don't take any of you for granted.

To my beta readers, **Ashley Nolan and Rachel Betancourt**, thank you for pushing through this one. I know our timeline got tight.

To my editors, **Megan Visger and Jasmine McKie**, you make me and my writing better. Thank you for all your effort and time with this one. I know the timelines were tight, and somehow we came out on the other side. There's no one else I'd rather scarcely survive with.

To my audiobook narrators, **Laura Horowitz and Gregory Salinas**, I will forever adore you. There's nothing you can do about it. I don't make the rules.

To my **ARC and Street Teams**, your love and enthusiasm are unmatched. I am so honored you continue to choose to be part of my little world. Thank you.

To the **Chaos Archives Patreon Members,** look at you, little chaos goblins hoarding as much chaos as you possibly can. I know the world is a mess right now, and I'm honored you choose to spend some of your resources by hanging out with me in Patreon. A very special thank you to the **Chaos Tier**— Alexia Nice, Alli MacManus, Allison Barnes, Alyssa Hollis, Amanda Escapetoerilea, Amelia Gage, Angela Hackett, Angela Miles, Annistyn Corbell, Aryana O'Connor, Ashley Van Durmen, Bobbie Wright, Bridget Meyer, Brittney Rodgers, Caitlin Juntti, Cara Barbardo, Charlee Umstead, Christina Smyth, Corina Clem, Domanyk Black, Heather Kerby, Helen, Jennifer Brisbois, Jordan Hamann, Kate Broderick, Katie Clark, Katie Mossell, Kelsey O'Brien, Komal Shah, Lauren Bollen, Lily Lapujade, Malika Meidinger, Melissa Foerster, Michelle Brucal, Missy VanDiepen, Misty Rourke, Niki Nelson, Olivia Klinkhammer, Rachael Rubio, Rachel Hatley, Rashu, Rebekah Rivera, Reem Santrisi, Rita Olander, Sammie Szeto, Sierra Berge, Stephanie Morgan, Stuti Shah, Tara Perdomo, Taylor Jones, Teresa Van Athen, Tinsley Phelps, Tricia L. Pelc, and Tyla Smart.

To **my boys**— You keep getting bigger, and our conversations have starting shifting from video games and superheroes to deeper things like beliefs and values. I am so proud of who you are all becoming. I promise to not work the next time we're on a ship.

To **my husband**— Thank you for managing everything else while I was writing this one. I know it was intense, and I'm so grateful you are always the brightest star in my sky. I love you.

ABOUT THE AUTHOR

Melissa K. Roehrich is a dark fantasy romance author living her best life in the Middle-of-Nowhere, North Dakota. She resides on a hobby farm where she homeschools her three boys with her husband. They have four dogs, several barn cats, and chickens. When she's not writing or reading, she's probably watching reruns of *How I Met Your Mother* or *Gilmore Girls* while trying to convince her husband they need to add goats to the farm. She loves coffee and traveling and dreams of owning a dragon someday.

Scan the QR code for links to social media and other ways to stay connected!

www.ingramcontent.com/pod-product-compliance
Lightning Source LLC
Chambersburg PA
CBHW022007300726
48970CB00003B/784